DRAW
Manga Action

TECHNIQUES FOR CREATING DYNAMIC MOVEMENT IN YOUR ART

DAVID FÜLEKI

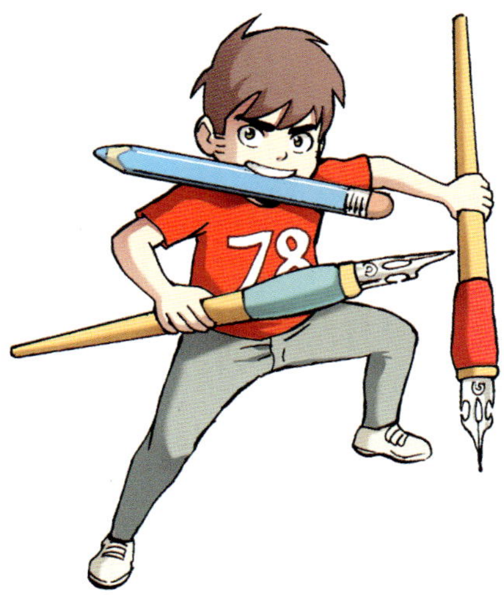

DAVID & CHARLES
— PUBLISHING —

www.davidandcharles.com

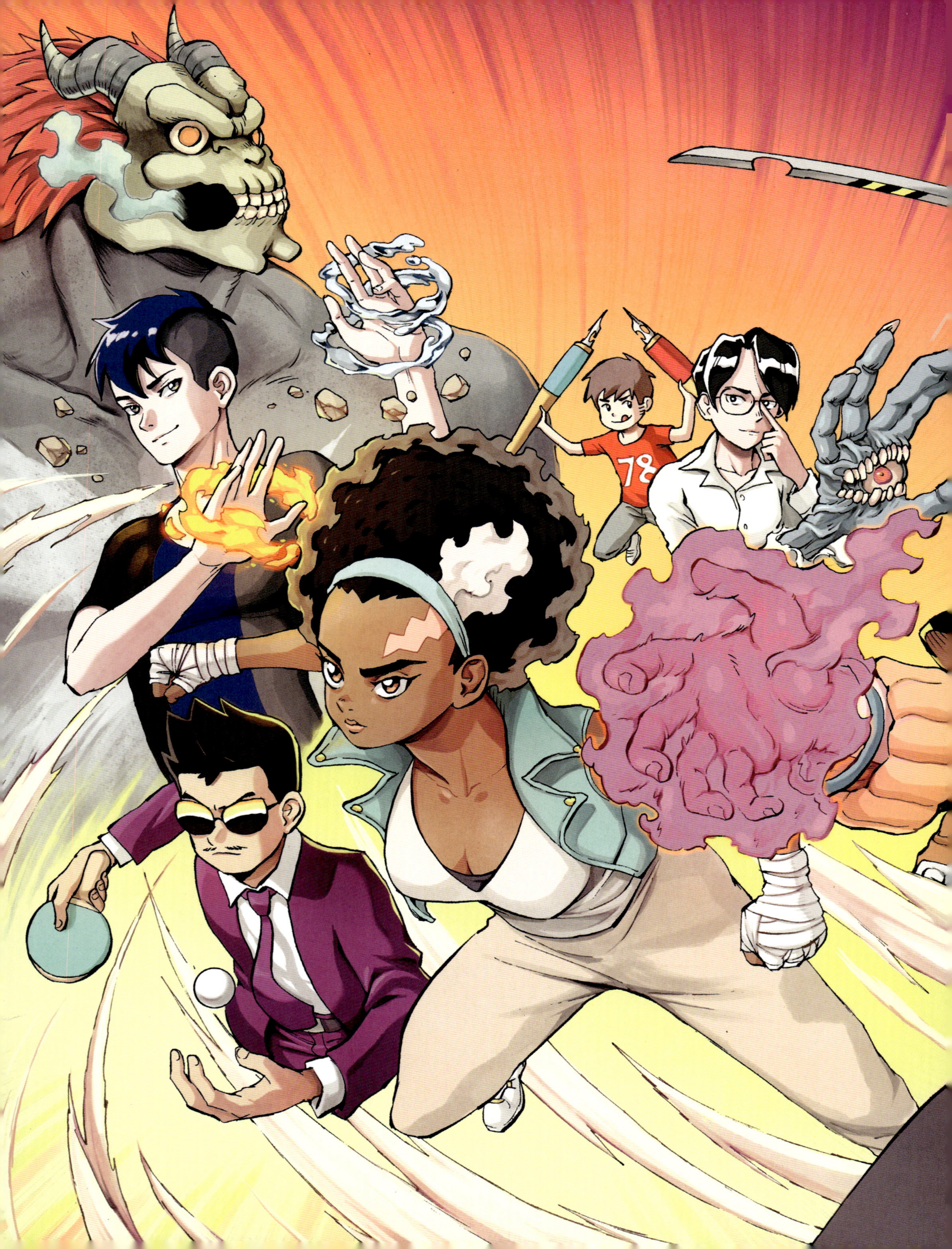

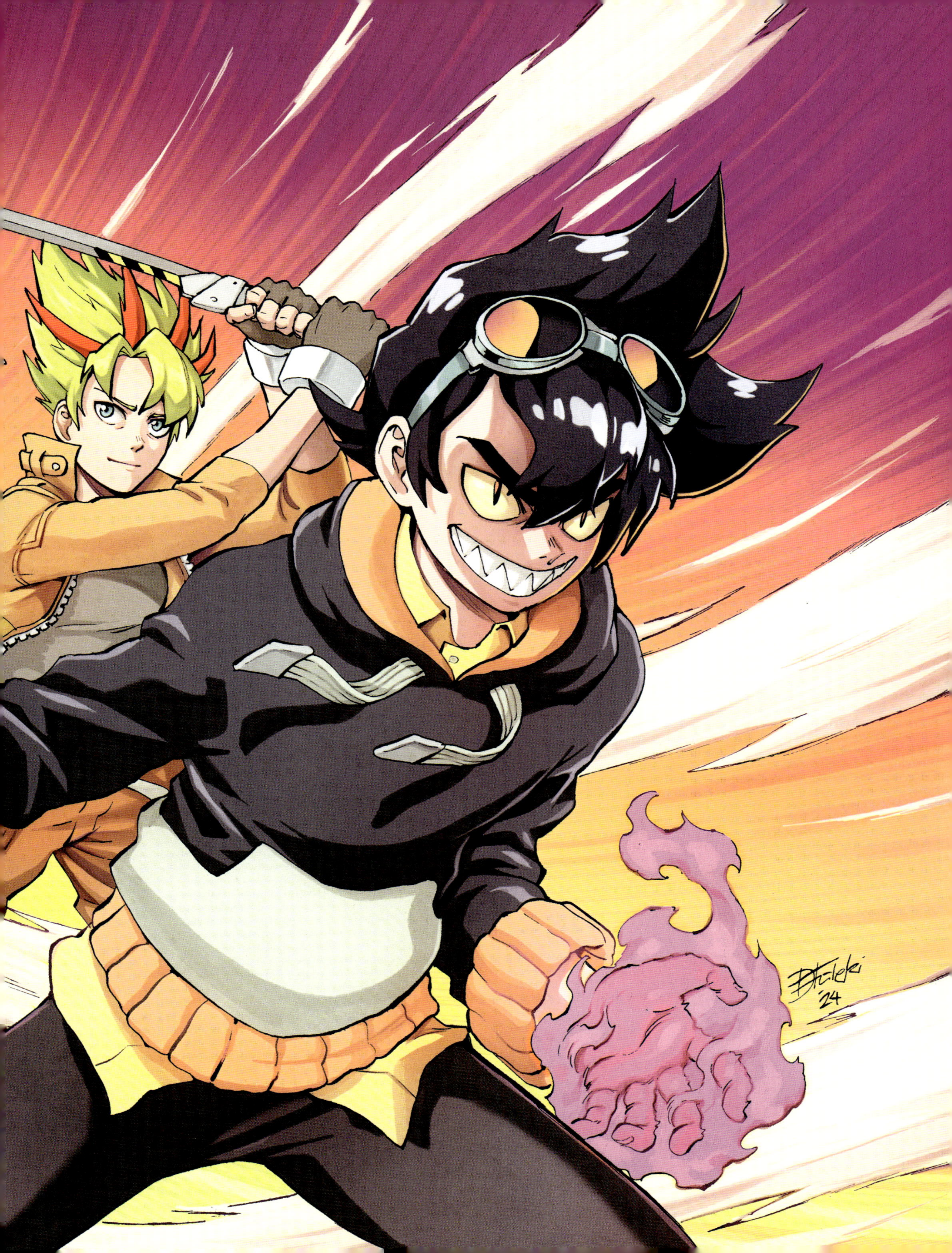

CONTENTS

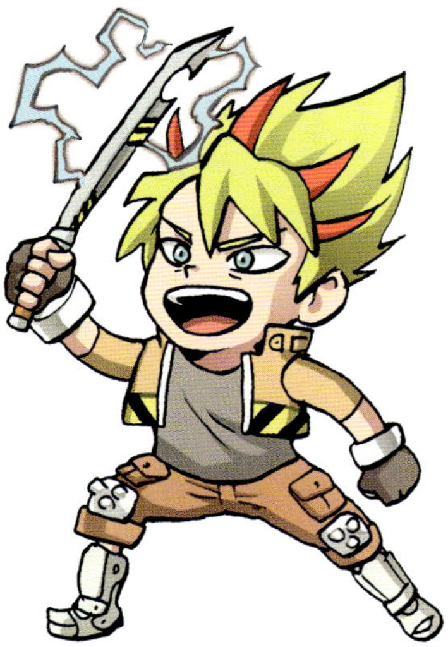

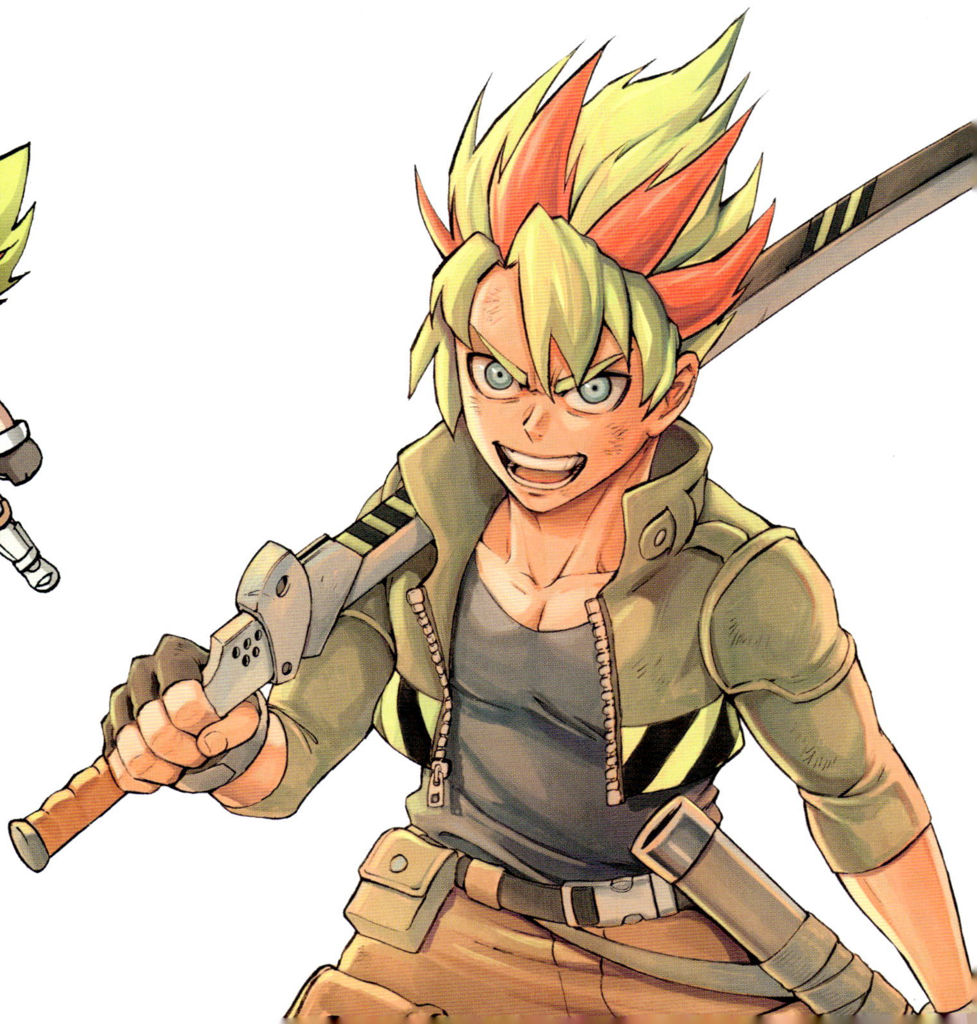

FOREWORD

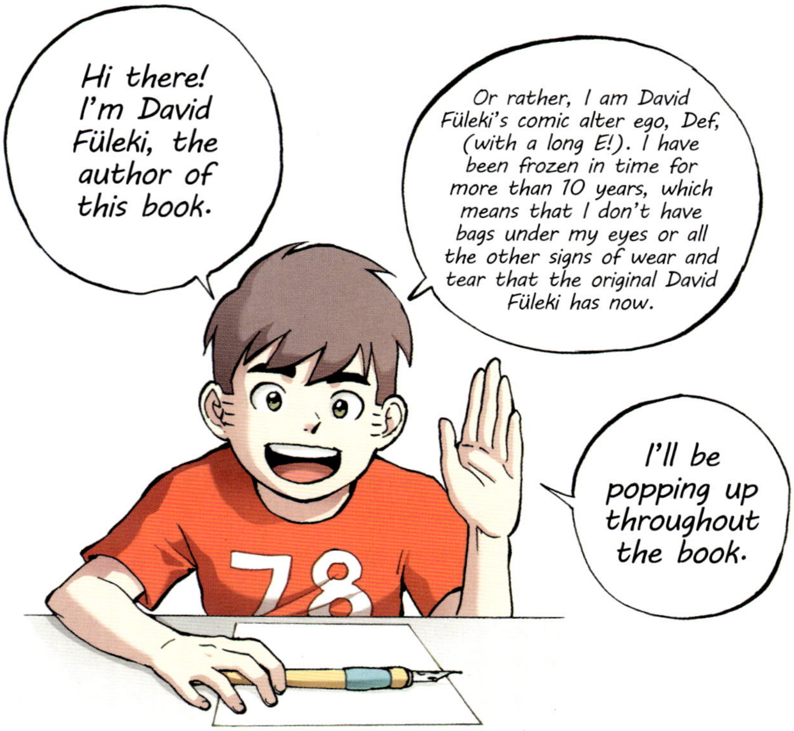

Whether as a standalone genre or a stylistic device, manga goes hand in hand with action. Action features most prominently in *shōnen* and *seinen* manga – titles primarily aimed at boys and young men. Battle manga – the ultimate action genre – thrives on intense, over-the-top combat. It provides the perfect basis for a potentially long-running, mega-successful series (such as *Dragon Ball*, *One Piece*, or *Naruto*).

With dozens of extravagant characters and endless possible fight combinations, battle manga can fill pages upon pages with action. This tempting setup attracts many aspiring mangaka worldwide – all too often, however, they rush straight into the fights. That's not how it works! It doesn't matter how cool the action is, how exotic the characters, or how flashy their abilities and attacks are – without proper buildup, the reader won't feel any real emotion. You need to slow down and start with the basics!

In this book, we'll cover the key fundamentals you need for drawing manga, always with a focus on action. Well-developed and believable protagonists, antagonists, and sidekicks constitute the backbone of any great story. Along the way, we'll create a sample concept for an action manga, complete with its heroes and its own world, to help illustrate many of the lessons in a practical way.

Before we dive in, however, a few words about myself. My qualifications for writing a tutorial book on the action genre, and on manga in general, come from my bachelor's and master's degrees in Media Studies at TU Chemnitz, and more than 20-years' experience as a mangaka. Since my first publication in the legendary *shōnen* manga magazine *BANZAI!* in 2001, thousands more followed – many of them award-winning, and recently even a few bestsellers.

I've explored a wide range of genres, including comedy, fantasy, horror, drama, autobiographical, and even educational comics, and some rather bold erotica, and action always plays a central role.

MY WORKSPACE

There are two work desks in our living room – much to the dismay of my wife, Susan, who has to put up with the chaos. Right now, she's standing at the height-adjustable desk, which is used for digital work. At the moment, she's helping me color a picture book about a journey to the moon, preparing the base colors that I'll later refine.

Tech setup: two scanners (for different formats; one is also better for color scans, the other for black-and-white), two monitors (one in a graphics tablet), a printer, and a desk lamp.

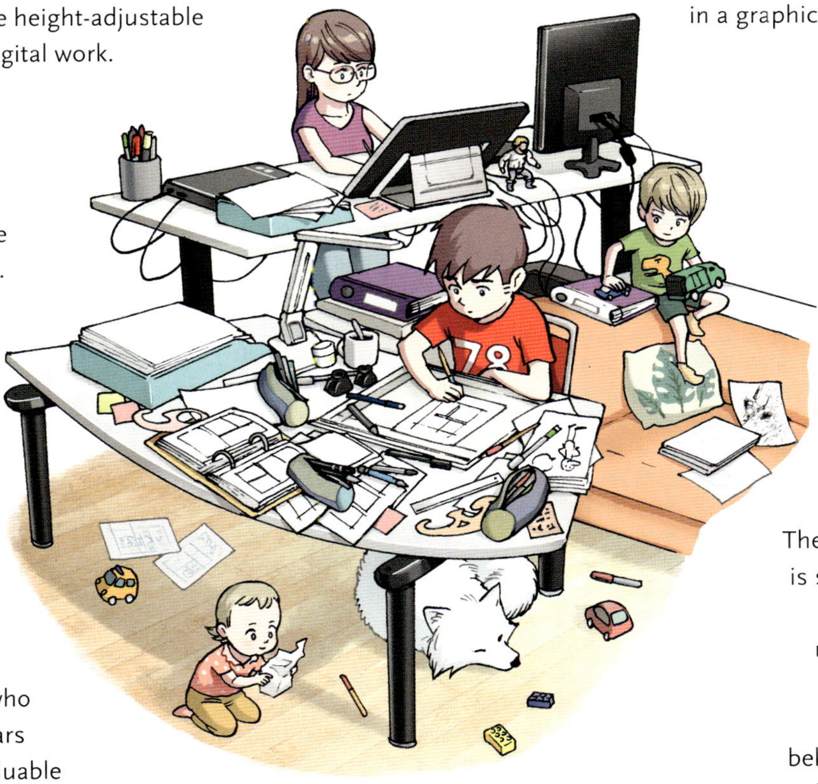

My son, Vincent (three) uses my folders and drawing materials as streets and ramps for his toy cars.

Despite being adjustable, the desk always stays at standing height – it's better for the back.

The analog work desk is slightly curved and has storage space under the desktop. The piles of paper and folders on it belong to around five different projects at any given time.

My daughter, Vivienne (who has just turned one), clears the desk and destroys valuable original pages. Her brother did exactly the same at her age.

Under the desk: my 11-year-old dog, Anne, who warms my feet; and lots of toys, which are bad for my feet.

DRAWING MATERIALS

In manga, as with every art form, every style and every working material is allowed. You can roughly divide materials into two types: traditional materials, analog materials, and digital. On the next pages, we'll get an overview and I will introduce you to my tools.

CLASSIC MANGA STYLE

Classic manga is drawn in black-and-white. In the early days of manga production, cheap reproduction methods meant that pages could only be printed in black ink on white paper. Even gray areas posed a challenge in printing. This is why manga are typically not in color and have distinctive screentone areas (which appear gray from a distance but are actually made up of black-and-white patterns or tiny ink dots). This visual style still shapes the worldwide perception of what a "typical" manga looks like. However, higher-quality reproduction options and the rise of full-color webmanga have increased the possibilities for expression.

DIP PEN

Since I belong more to the traditional camp, I'll start by showing you my most essential tools: two Tachikawa dip pens fitted with G-pen nibs from Zebra. They sit comfortably in the hand, something that is crucial for my drawing sessions, which can sometimes last up to 16 hours. G-pen nibs create dynamic strokes with strong line variation – perfect for dynamic scenes.

Why two dip pens? I use the one with the blue grip for new nibs, which produce finer lines. The red-grip one I use with older nibs that have held up well and don't scratch the paper (how long they last is pure luck!). Since their tips are no longer as sharp, they create thicker lines – which is often useful when inking outlines, for example. Character outlines should ideally be a bit thicker to help separate them from the other elements in the picture.

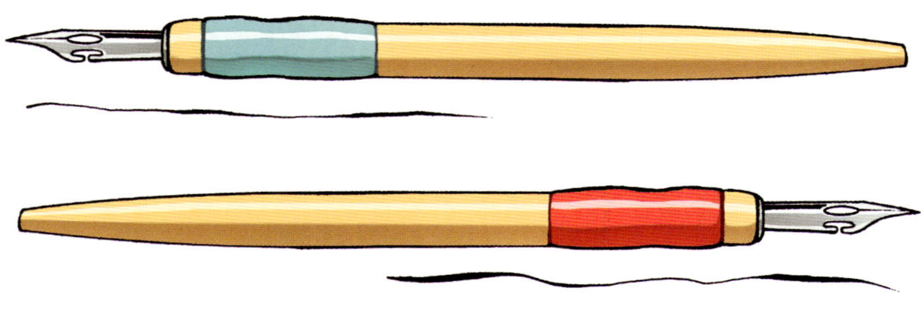

I will draw some strokes for some of the tools presented (as here on the left), to demonstrate the line variance.

During the course of this materials overview, I will also mention brands or models of pens, or show them in drawings. However, this is not to say that other drawing tools do not fulfil the same purpose. I myself switch back and forth a lot between suppliers and like to try new things out.

TIPS FOR WORKING WITH A NIB AND INK

Tip 1: "My G-Pen isn't drawing properly. What am I doing wrong?" This is one of the most common questions I see on my Instagram channel (@davidfuleki, if you don't follow me yet!). The issue is usually a thin layer of oil or wax on the nib. This coating protects against quick wear and rust, but it also reduces the amount of ink the nib can take on. That's why you should remove this protective layer. Acetone works well for this. Personally, I burn it off with fire – but be careful! Firstly, don't do this near paper or any other flammable material. Secondly, it can ruin the nib. Once it starts turning rainbow-colored in the flame, you should stop.

Tip 2: clean your nib with water after every use. It's best to use a heavy, shallow bowl with a small capacity, so that the mess isn't too bad if it tips over. If your nib is properly prepped, you should be able to draw for several minutes at a time. When the ink runs out, dip the nib briefly in water, dry it with a handkerchief or tissue kept handy, then dip it again briefly in water before loading it with ink.

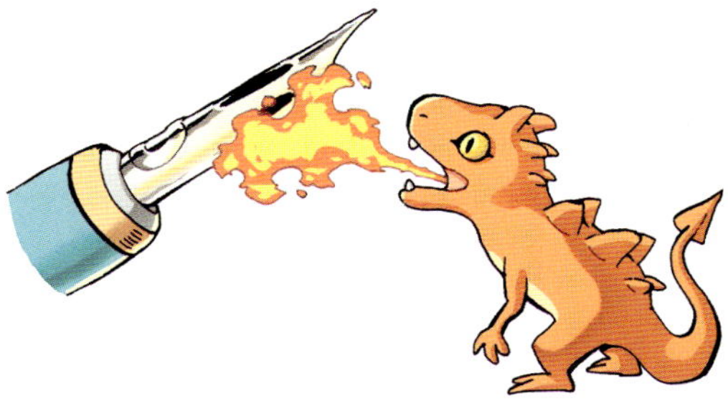

Tip 3: experiment with different inks and paper. Personally, I like using Pilot drawing ink and 68lb/letter size (100gsm A4) copier paper. I can work quickly and efficiently with this combination. However, because of different stylistic approaches and your own individual workflow, you might find a completely different pen/nib/ink/paper combination works better for you.

WORKING WITH FOUNTAIN PENS

I enjoy working with various Lamy models. In fact, I have already drawn several manga books almost completely on paper using a combination of these fountain pens with fine, medium, and thick strokes.

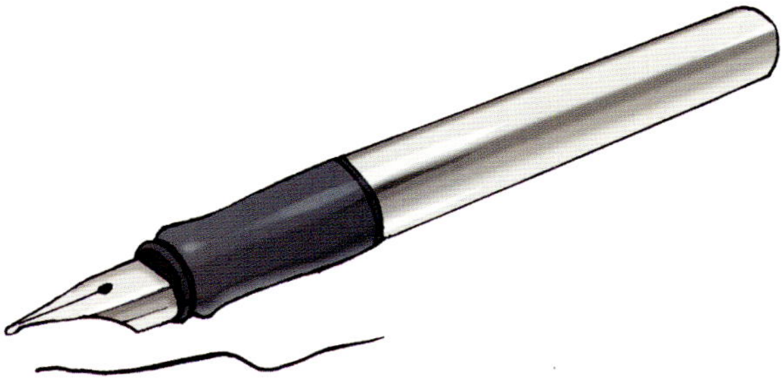

One advantage is that ink cartridges (use black ink!) allow you to draw for long interrupted stretches. One downside is the reduction in line variation compared with a dip pen.

However, sometimes you need a consistent, more controlled line, and that's where a fountain pen can be the perfect complementary tool.

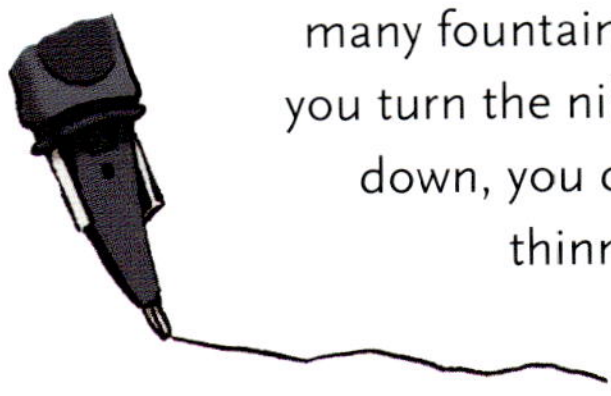

This trick works with many fountain pens: if you turn the nib upside down, you can draw thinner lines.

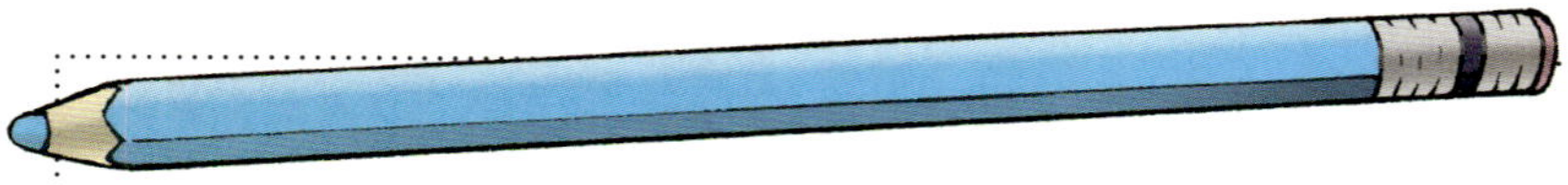

For preliminary sketches, I almost exclusively use a blue-colored pencil. Most of the time, I work with a Prismacolor Col-Erase pencil in Light Blue, while for finer details, I use a mechanical pencil with a light blue lead. The advantage of this method is that once a drawing or page has been inked, you can scan it in, including the sketch lines. With a few clicks in the graphics program, the blue lines can easily be made invisible, saving a lot of time on erasing. Erasers also slightly damage the inked lines. The downside is that normal graphite pencils are a little more precise, and their lines are easier to erase than colored pencil lines.

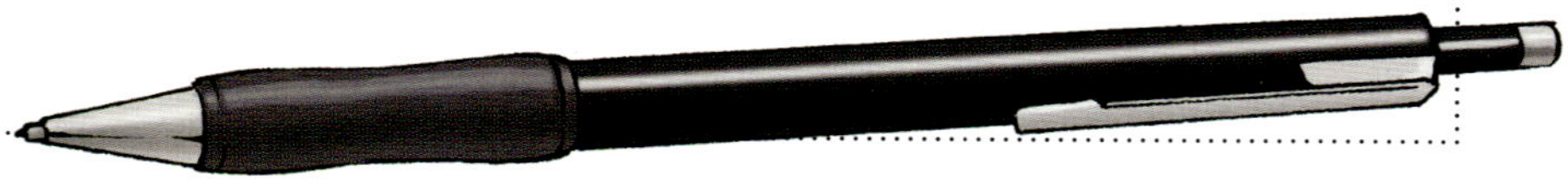

I use fineliners of various brands and nib sizes. To list all the models I use would take up a large part of this book. The most important thing here is that the pens have to be very precise, as they are used for the finest details, such as drawing backgrounds.

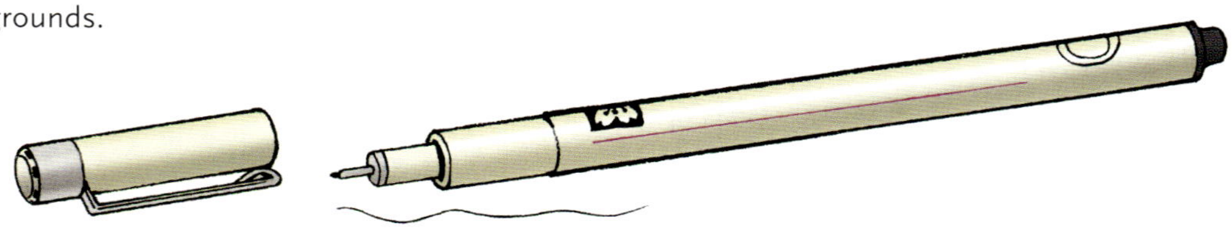

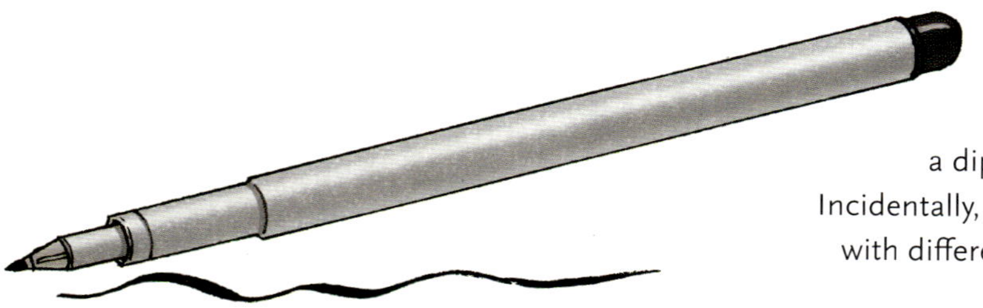

Brush pens are versatile tools that also offer a good introduction to working with dynamic strokes. So, if you are still not used to using a dip pen or an ink brush, then try out these pens. Incidentally, I mainly use models from Zebra and Tombow with different degrees of hardness for varying line styles.

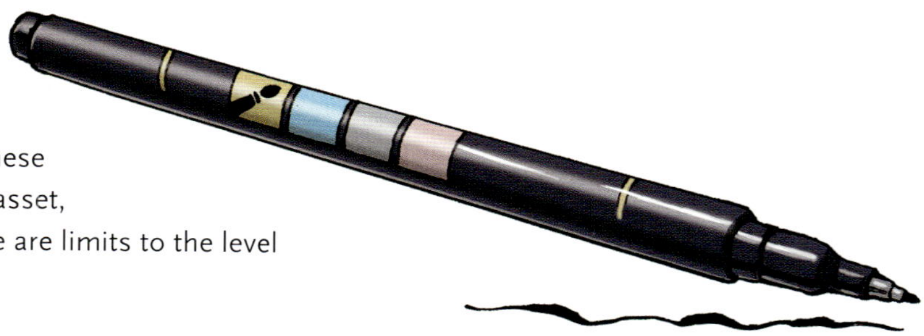

In the past, I've drawn entire manga using these pens. Their dynamic line variation is a great asset, especially in the action genre. However, there are limits to the level of detail they can achieve.

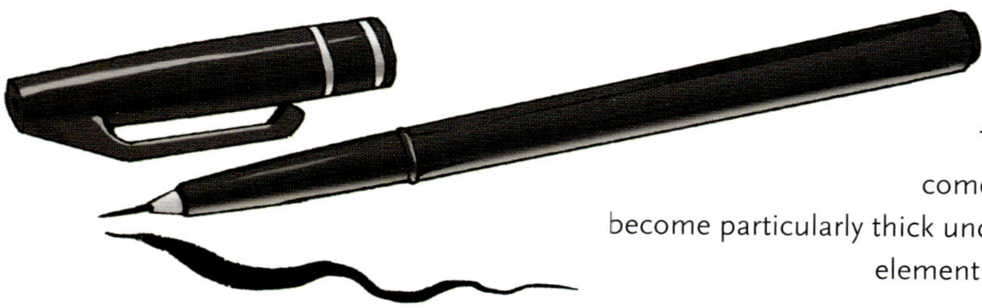

This Pentel brush pen has a bristle tip that comes close to a traditional brush. The strokes become particularly thick under pressure. I like to use tools like this for elements such as sound effects or blood splatters.

Thick black markers are especially useful for filling in black areas. However, I increasingly fill in digitally. In my drawings, I mark areas to be filled with a small cross and later fill them quickly with a single click in my graphics software.

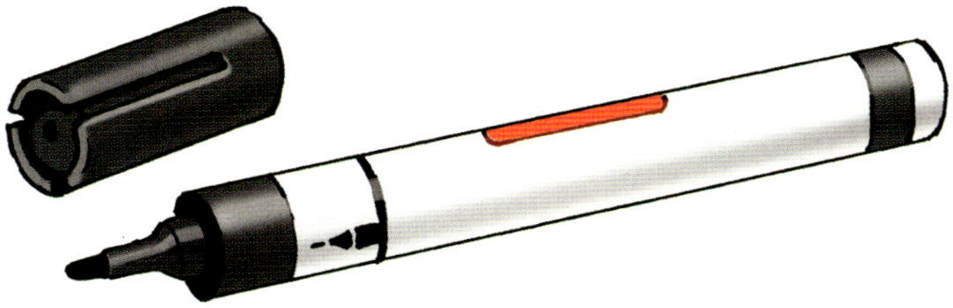

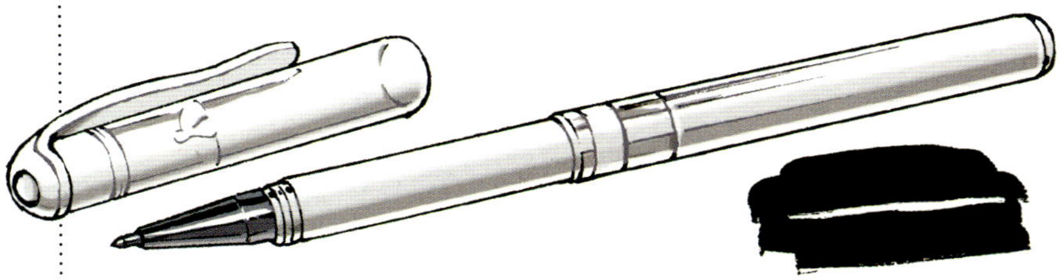

For corrections: a white gel pen is very precise, but it runs out quickly. Traditional opaque white is cheaper but frustrating to work with. That's why most of my corrections are now done digitally.

I also use a variety of rulers (including curved and circle rulers), compasses, sharpeners, erasers, and so on.

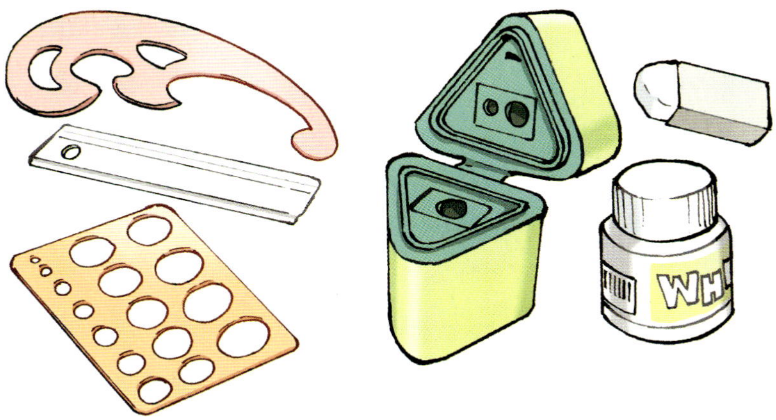

And then, of course, there's the graphics tablet. As previously mentioned, I consider myself more of a traditional, analog artist, but working on the computer and the tablet using a stylus and a graphics program now takes up roughly half of my total editing time. And that's fine – it streamlines a lot of processes and helps avoid a lot of frustration. I tend to switch between different tablets, and so far, they've all been great!

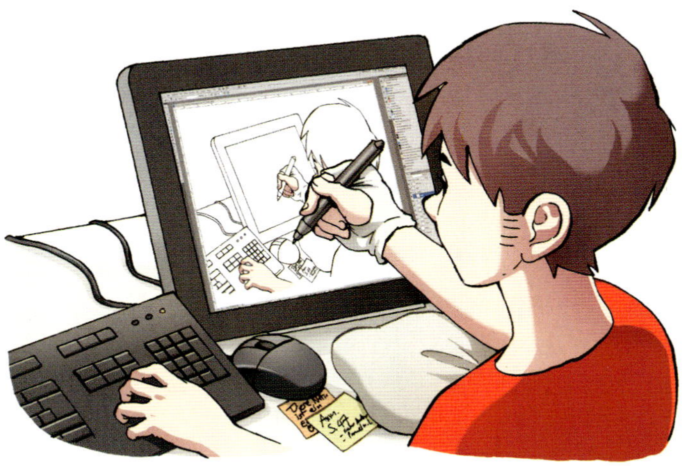

Software, on the other hand, is trickier – I don't particularly enjoy diving into complex new programs, but I've been using Adobe Photoshop for two decades now and can do just about anything with it. I also use Clip Studio occasionally.

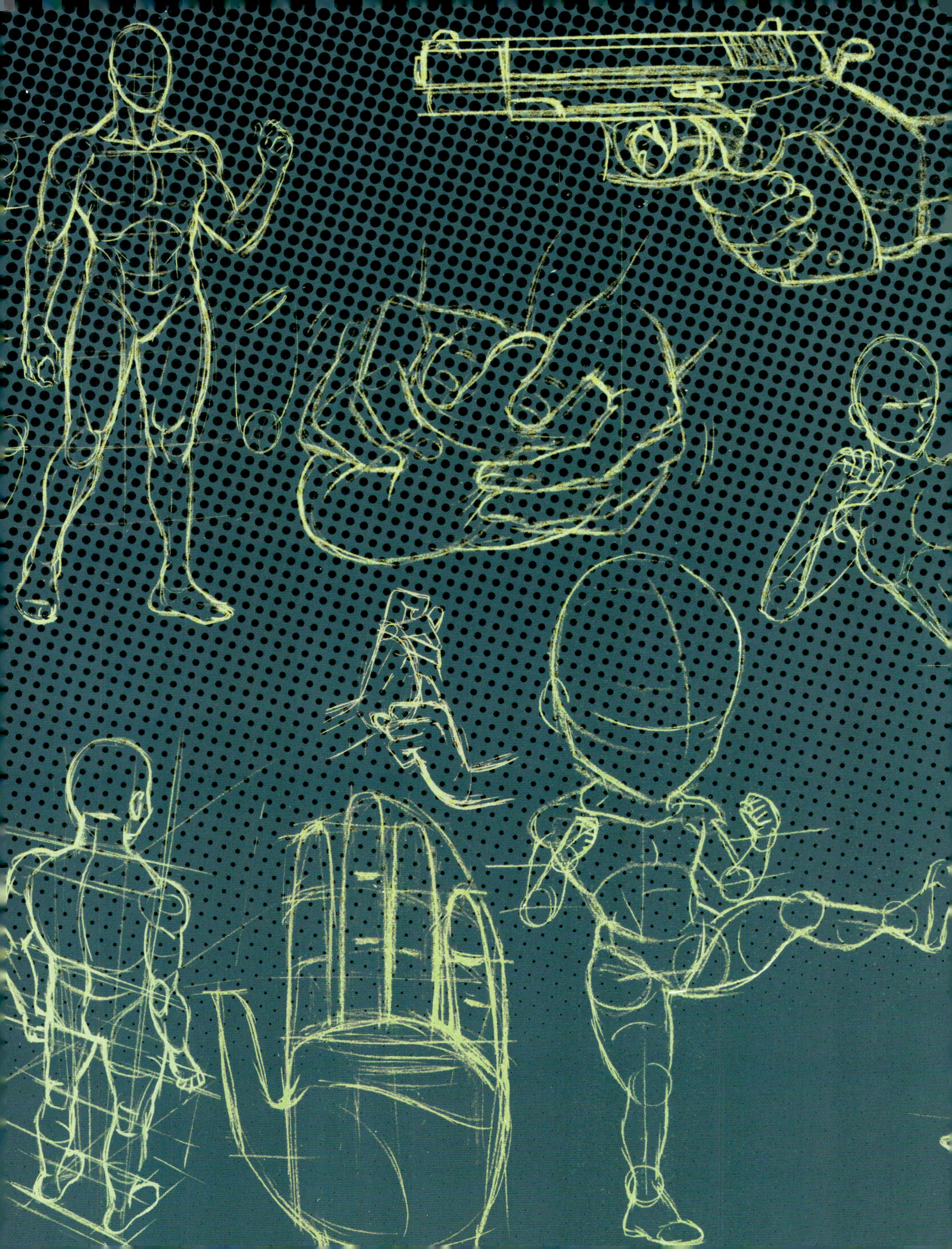

1. ANATOMY AND DRAWING BASICS

In the following lessons, we'll look at various models and instructions that will give you a good basic knowledge – body part by body part. We'll mostly stick to realistic proportions. Once you have sufficiently mastered these, you'll be able to make them exaggerated or abstract and develop your own style.

BASIC ANATOMY

Let's start by looking at the body as a whole in a neutral standing pose from three different angles. In the sketches, key reference points are highlighted.

The ribcage and hips are marked in orange. These serve as a solid foundation for aligning the rest of the body. The joints are highlighted in red. By keeping an eye on how they relate to the body parts that they connect, you should be able to produce a well-balanced anatomy.

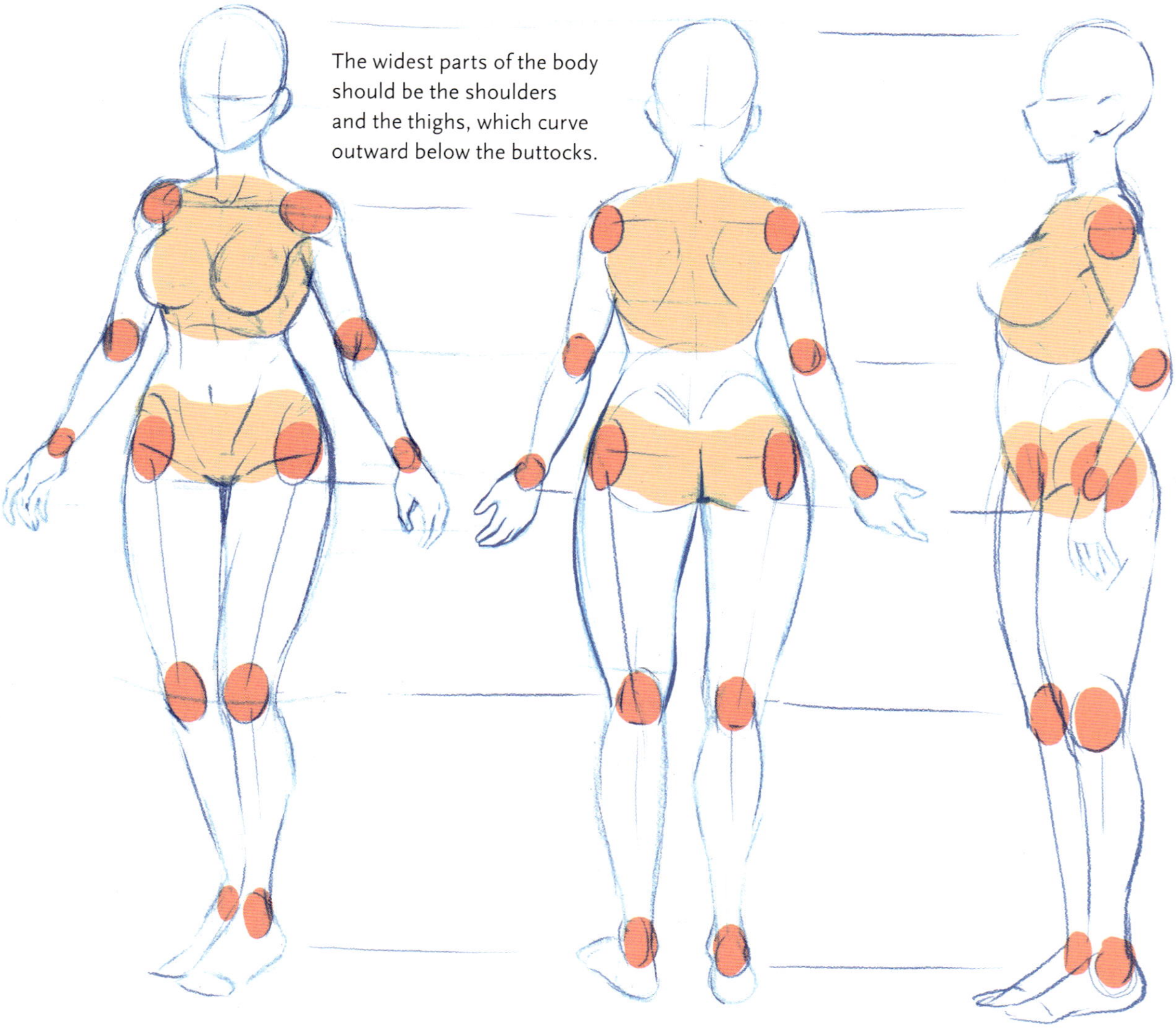

The widest parts of the body should be the shoulders and the thighs, which curve outward below the buttocks.

You can also see the horizontal reference lines running across the three body views. These serve two purposes: firstly, they help in aligning the heights of corresponding body parts across all three sketches, ensuring consistent proportions. Secondly, they divide the body into sections, providing additional proportional reference points. The knees are positioned at one-quarter height, while the hips sit at the halfway point. The upper half can be divided into thirds: one third covers the buttocks and abdomen, the next covers the ribcage up to the shoulders, and the final third contains the head.

Some people find it helpful to start with something even simpler, like the stick figures you can see on the right. Even experienced professionals like to come back to these models to avoid any risk with proportions, especially in complex pictures with many characters. This is because there's nothing more frustrating than having sketched or drawn a character far along only to realize it just doesn't fit into the composition. It's better to do a few extra sketches in the beginning than to have to erase everything later in frustration.

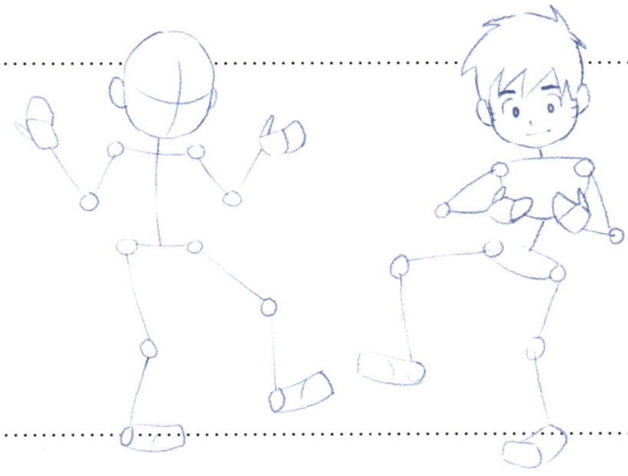

And this is what the sketches on the left look like once inked. Don't be scared. In the following lessons, you'll encounter these mannequins more often. When practicing, feel free to add details as you like, or go straight into character design mode and add faces, hairstyles, and clothing.

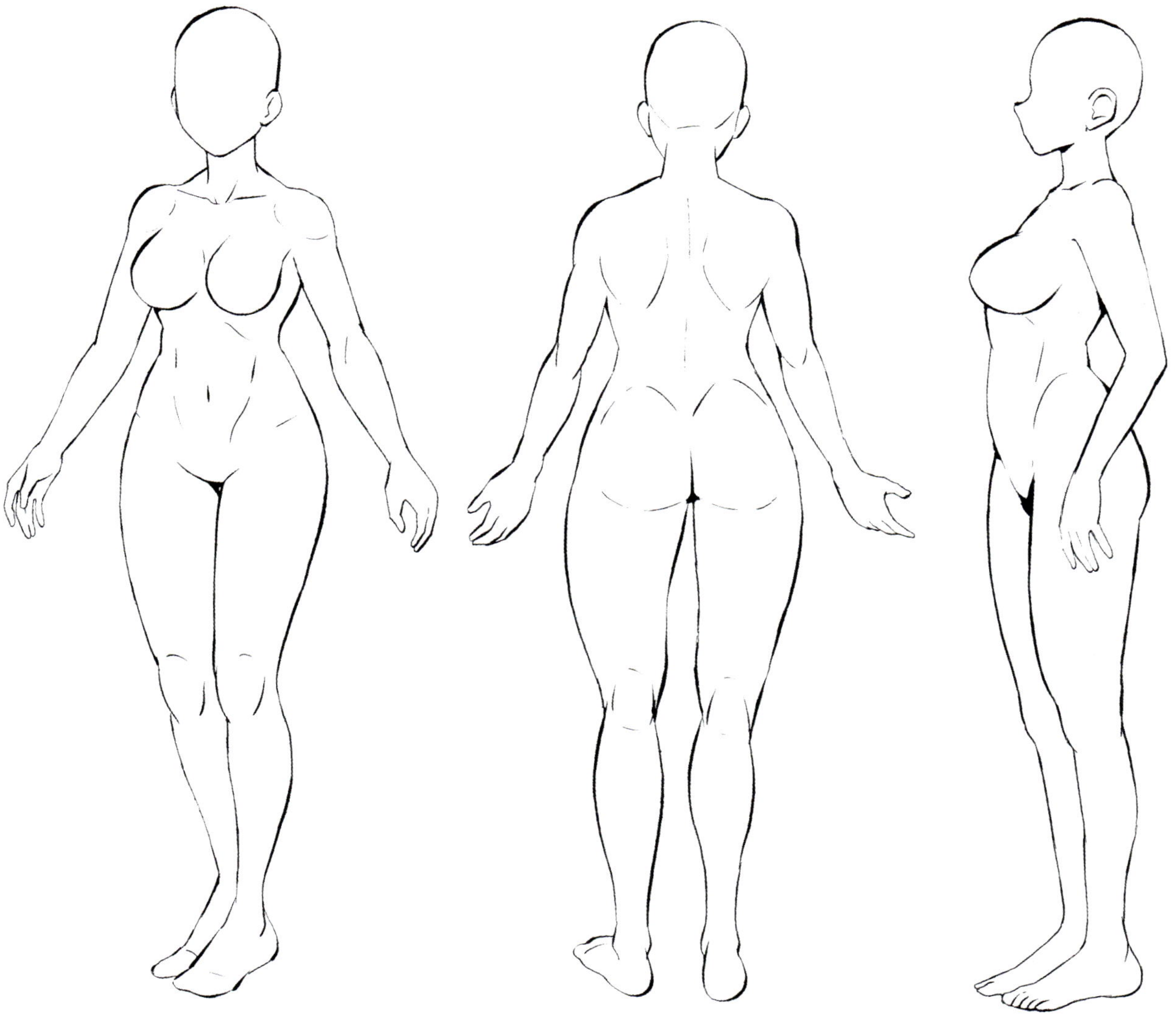

MUSCLES

One can hardly avoid depicting muscles – especially in stories that focus on fighting. Even with a strong graphic stylization, at least a rough understanding of the interplay of different muscles is essential. However, most action manga features very realistic and well-defined musculature. You can work your way up to a sufficient understanding of the muscles step-by-step.

On this double page, you can see two anatomy models in a frontal view with highlighted muscle groups. Since front views appear much more often than side or back views, it's worth practicing and drawing some of the muscle areas that are color-coded here. Even this slight change in posture makes some of the muscles clearer in their three-dimensionality, particularly in the arm area in this example.

The sketches next to the anatomy models show the adjacent body parts in a simplified form to emphasize their plasticity and the position of the joints. Even when drawing complex muscles, it is advisable to start with rough models like these first and then work your way up – muscle by muscle.

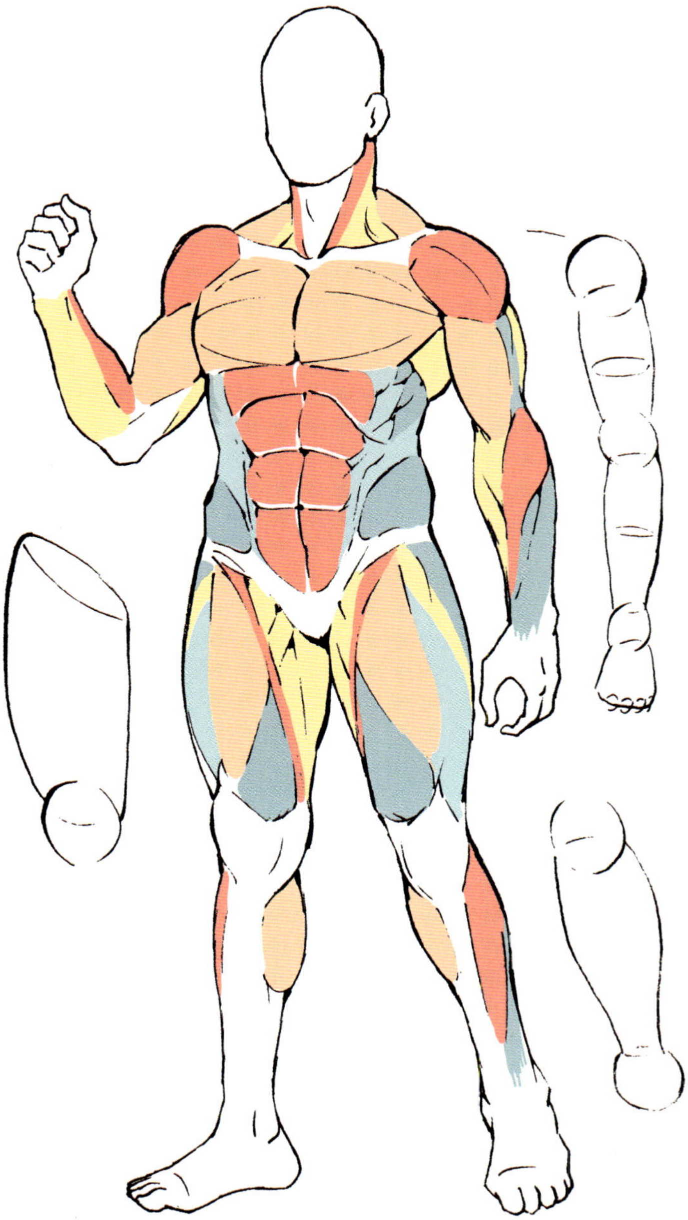

Highly detailed muscles, like those in the example below, usually make sense only when depicting male characters. However, the fundamental principles of anatomy apply across all genders. In fact, as you gradually develop a deeper understanding of anatomy, you'll start to notice how similar the muscles of other creatures are to those of humans. Even in quadrupeds, the same basic structures exist – even if the muscles are developed differently according to the different stresses. With this basic knowledge, it also becomes easier to design entirely new beings, such as fantasy creatures or monsters. Give it a try!

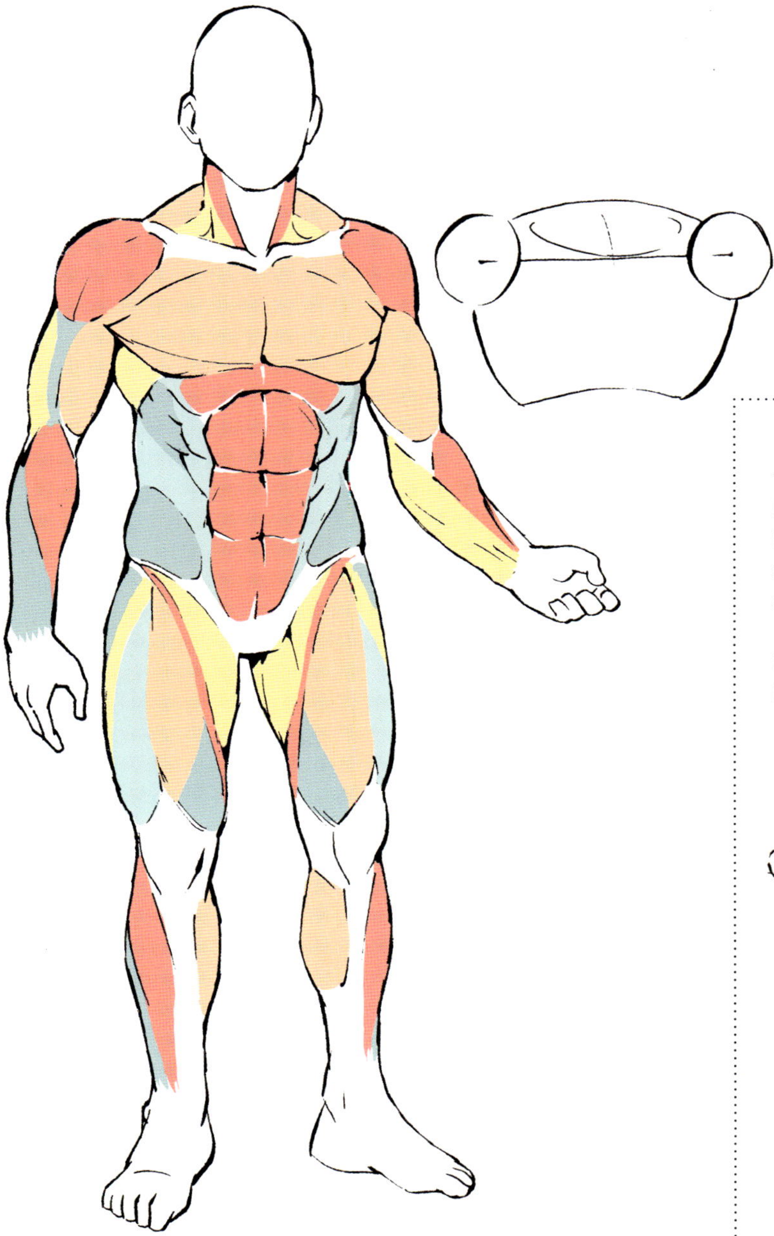

Here's a comparison of the upper body and foreleg/arm musculature of a deer and a human. The biggest differences can be seen in the development of the shoulder muscles and the neck area. Many animals even have a well-developed brachiocephalic muscle (highlighted in light green here), whereas in humans, it exists only in a rudimentary, barely noticeable form.

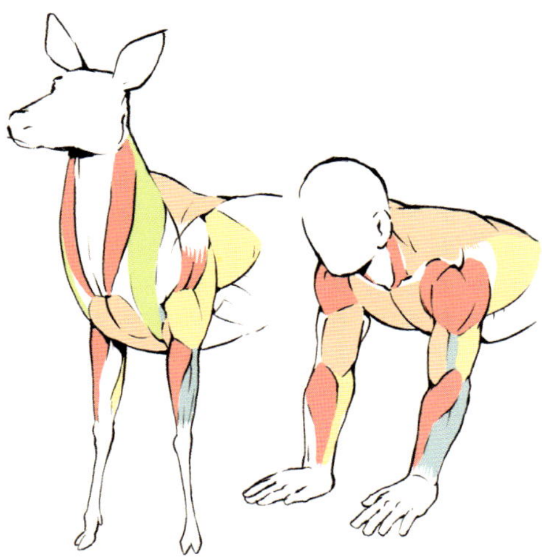

BACK VIEW

Since the back muscles are seen far less frequently than the front, this area is initially more difficult to grasp.

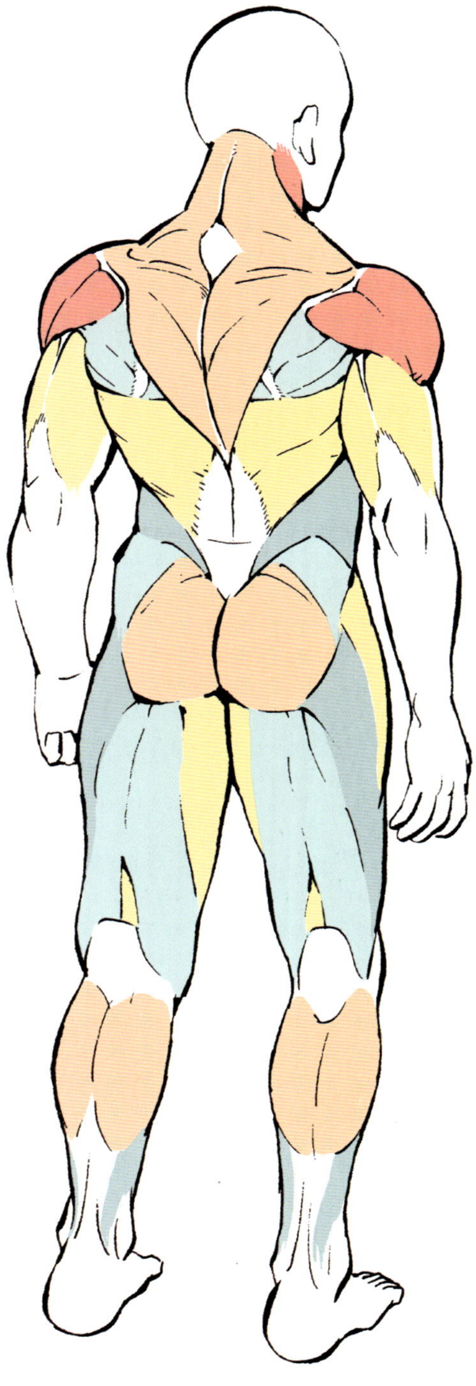

SIDE VIEW

Together with the front view from the previous pages, you can now form a rough 360-degree model of the muscular system.

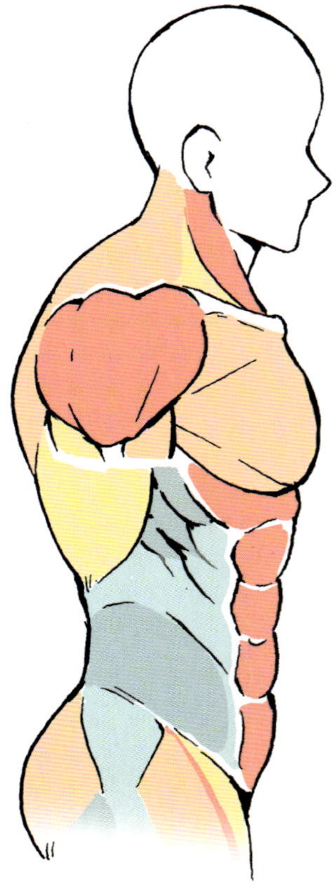

Impressive as it is, the flexibility of the muscles can also be challenging for artists. Here, we're working with simple standing poses, but when any movement occurs, muscles shift and slide, making it tricky to track them all.

If you want to master the finer interactions between muscle groups, thorough study is key. Life drawing courses, for example, are incredibly helpful. However, if you only need certain repeated complex poses for your manga project, it's best to focus on mastering those first, and the rest will follow over time.

ARMS

In action manga, arm muscles play a particularly important role, so we're going to take a closer look at them here. You'll notice right away: the more you dive into the details, the more muscle structure turns into a real labyrinth.

Even if you don't plan on drawing heavily defined arms, try sketching a few of the examples below. This will improve your understanding of musculature and help you draw simplified arms more effectively.

On the right, you'll find a highly simplified version of the arm muscles, highlighting the ones most relevant for most drawings.

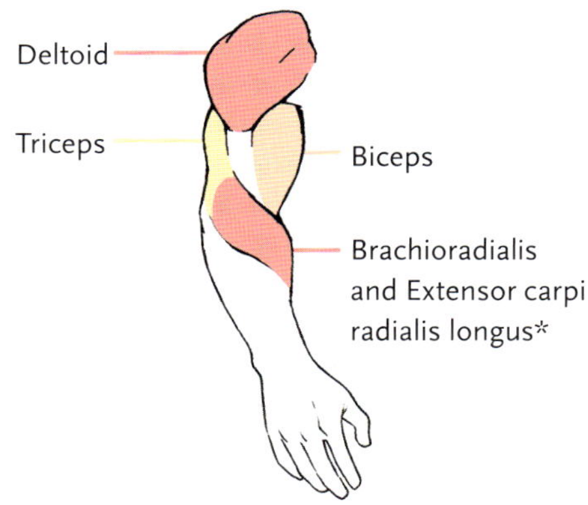

* Don't worry, there won't be a quiz on this!

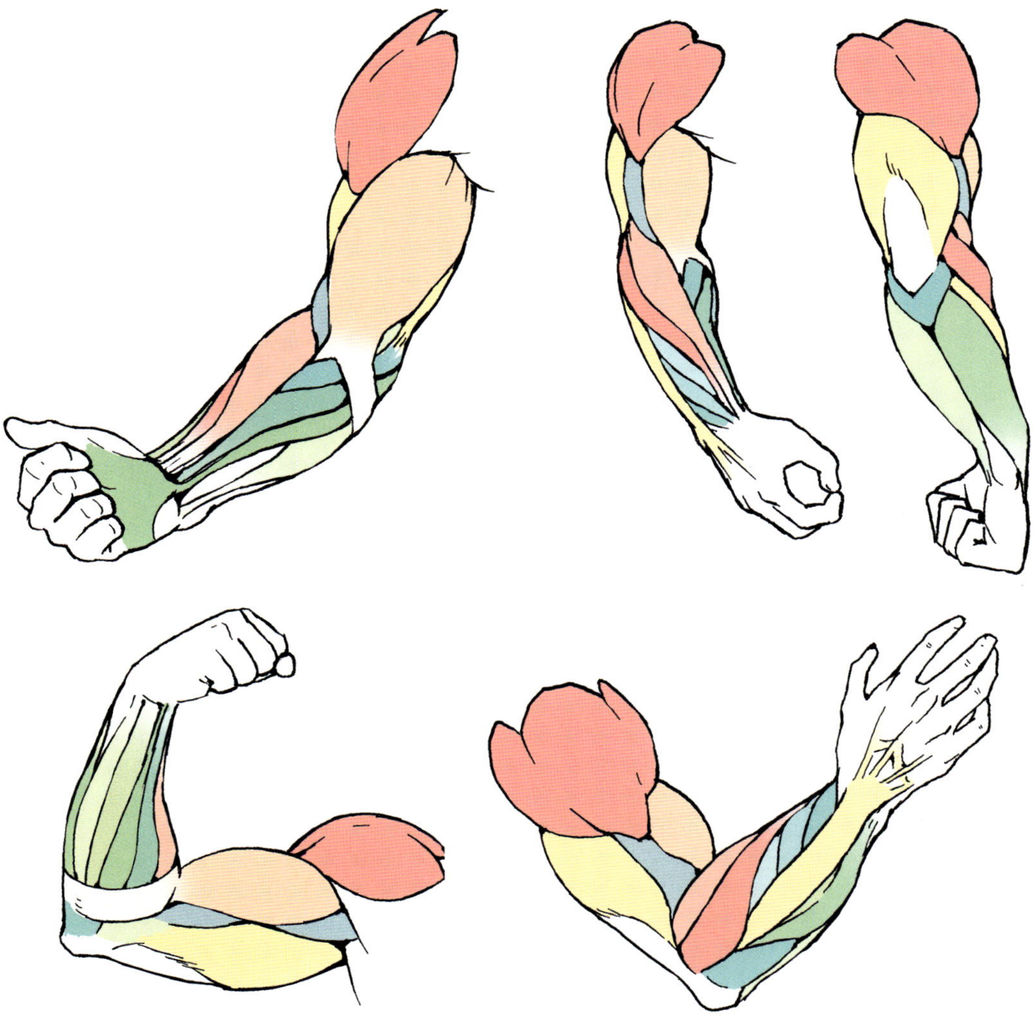

BODY TYPES

Nothing is more boring than a manga filled with identical characters, each one barely distinguishable from the next. It sounds obvious, yet comics around the world keep making this mistake. This often results in comics overpopulated with attractive, athletic young people. In the worst cases, they all have similar hairstyles, faces, dress sense, and so on. One way to create visual variety is through different body types. This is especially important in action manga, where different physiques can and should be used creatively, as they directly affect fights, chases, and other dynamic scenes. We'll look at some options over the next few pages.

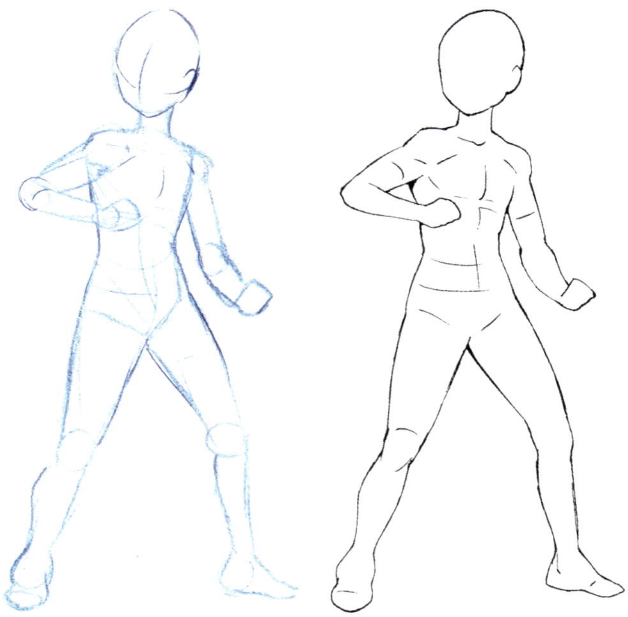

STANDARD

The typical action manga hero has the following features: teenager, fairly athletic, minimal body fat, and well-proportioned for a normal range of hand-to-hand combat moves. Unfortunately, it's a rather generic but tried-and-tested formula, calculated to maximize reader-identification. However, placing this standard character in a world full of highly exaggerated bodies can make them feel unique by contrast.

All the designs on these two pages are not gendered and can be adapted as needed. Again, the preliminary sketches help break down the drawing process.

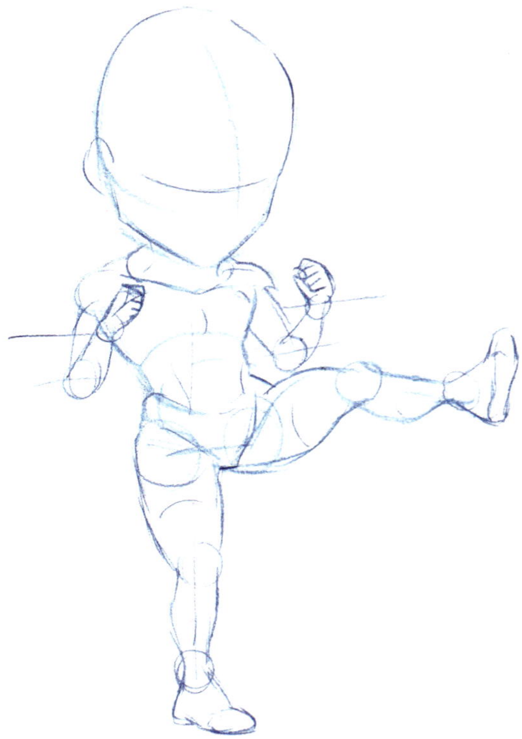

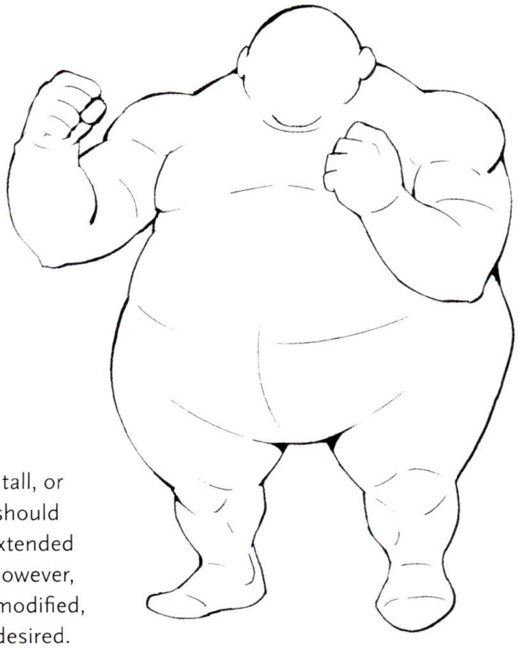

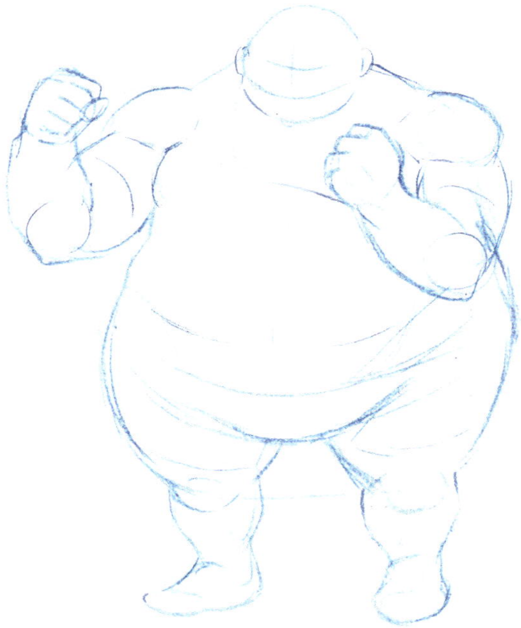

Heavy, slight, tall, or short bodies should become the extended foundation. However, these can be modified, of course, as desired. In manga, there are no limitations to body types. They do not have to look realistic. Also try to significantly modify individual body parts. This will create exciting silhouettes and increase the recognition effect.

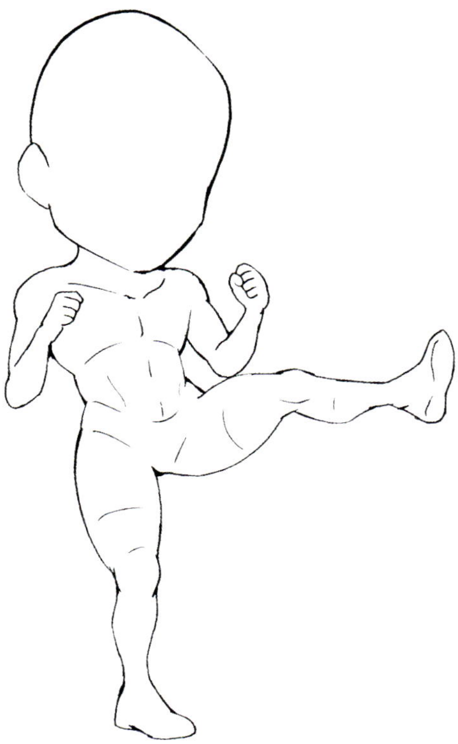

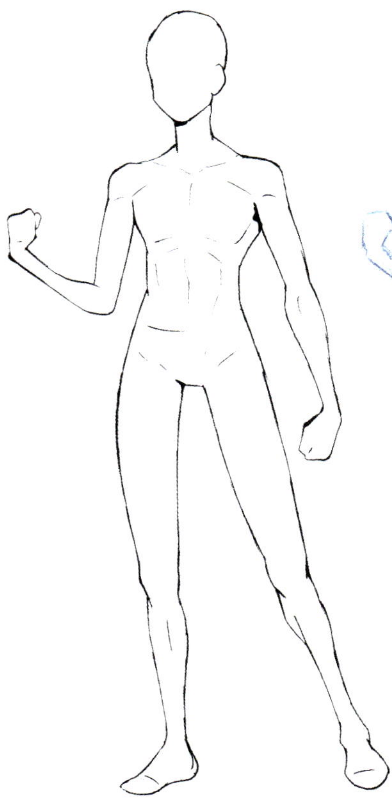

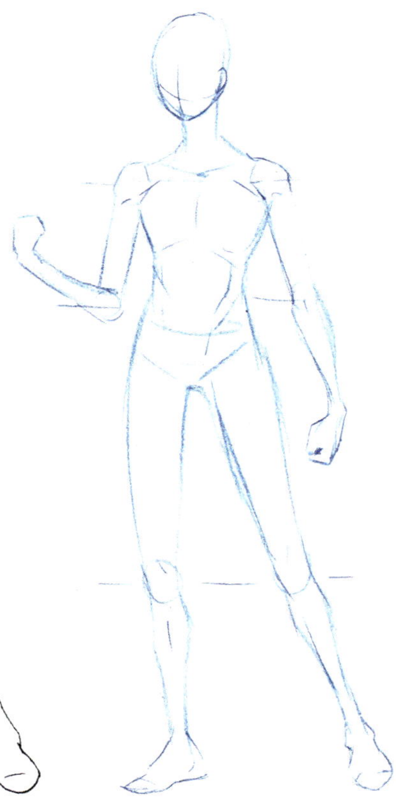

ATHLETE

We already know the guy below from the "Muscles" section. He has the standard body seen in many American superhero comics: defined down to the hindmost muscles, a broad chest, biceps like thighs, thighs like small cars.

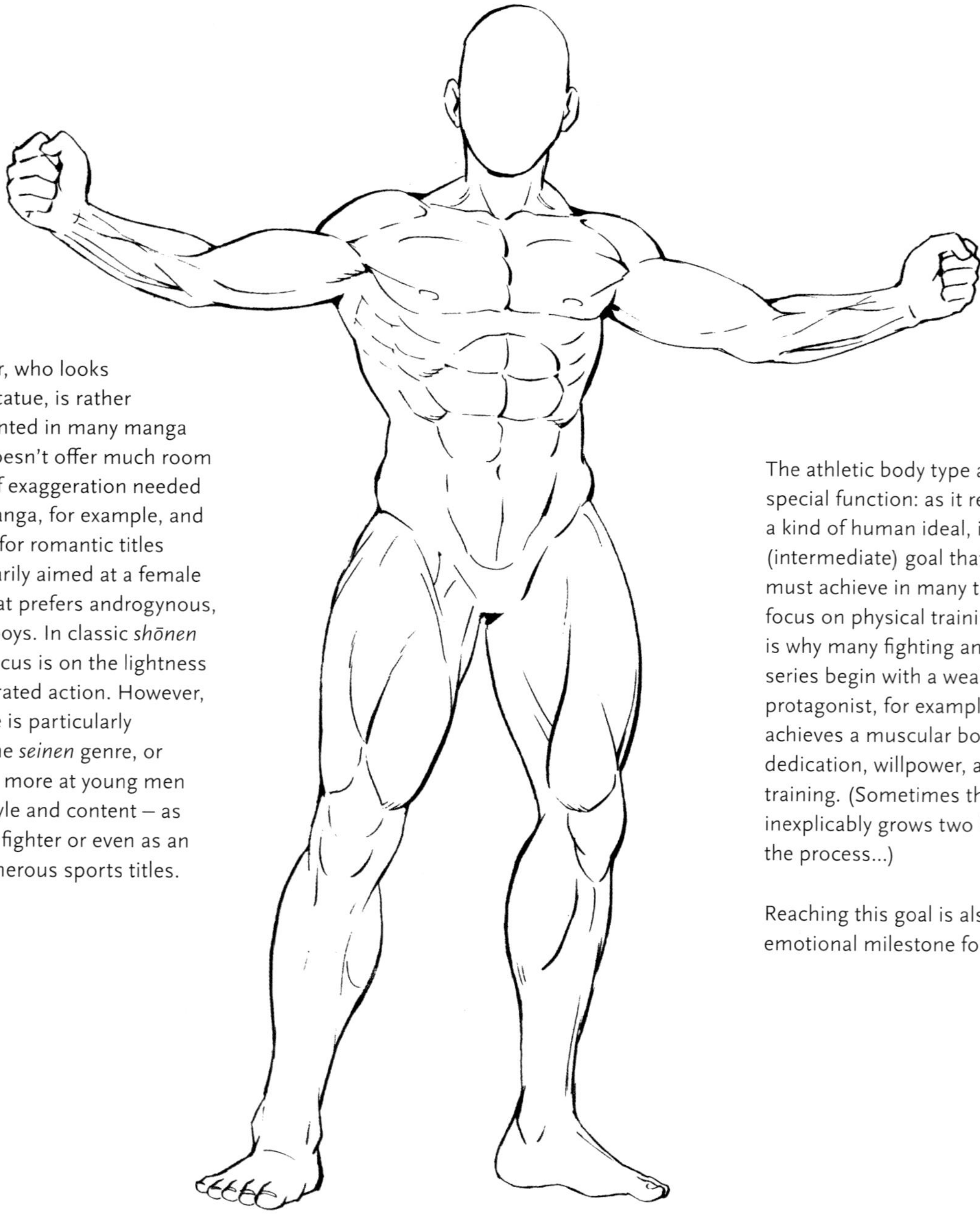

This character, who looks like a Greek statue, is rather underrepresented in many manga genres. He doesn't offer much room for the kind of exaggeration needed in comedy manga, for example, and is too macho for romantic titles that are primarily aimed at a female readership that prefers androgynous, long-limbed boys. In classic *shōnen* manga, the focus is on the lightness of the exaggerated action. However, this body type is particularly common in the *seinen* genre, or manga aimed more at young men in terms of style and content – as a well-trained fighter or even as an athlete in numerous sports titles.

The athletic body type also has a special function: as it represents a kind of human ideal, it is an (intermediate) goal that the hero must achieve in many titles that focus on physical training. This is why many fighting and sports series begin with a weak or obese protagonist, for example, who achieves a muscular body through dedication, willpower, and hard training. (Sometimes the hero even inexplicably grows two heads taller in the process...)

Reaching this goal is also an emotional milestone for the reader.

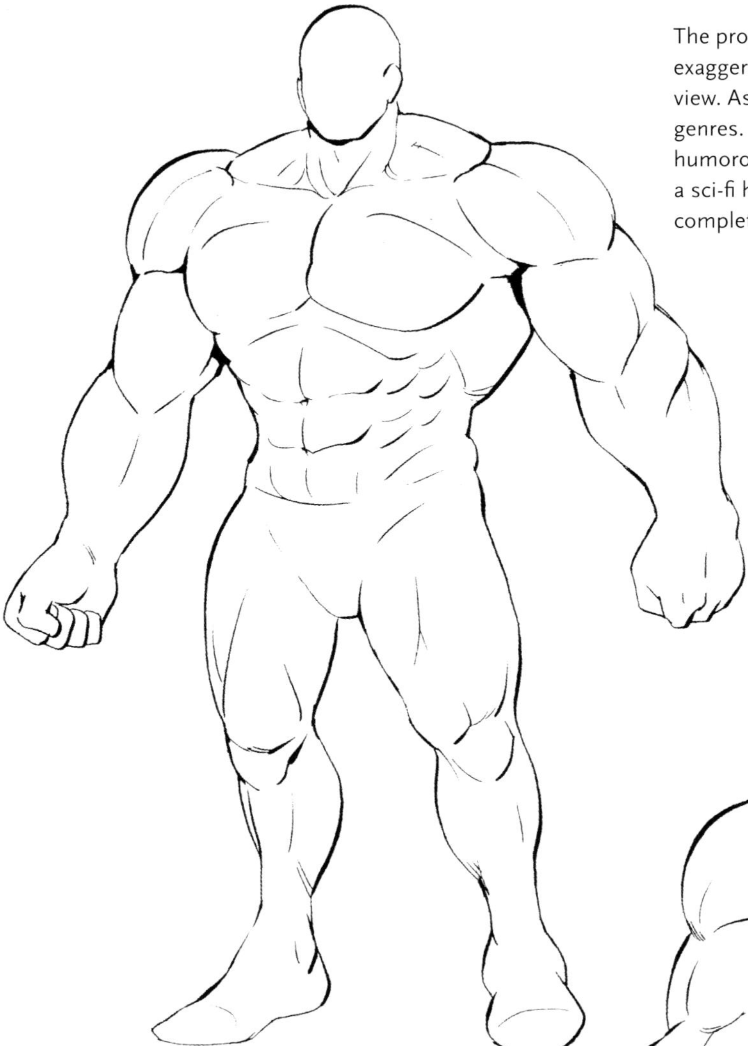

The proportions are also deliberately amplified, with the exaggeratedly broad back or the shortened legs in the rear view. As a result, this body type fits into a wide range of genres. It would make a good pumped-up superhero in a humorous context, for example, but also a super mutant in a sci-fi horror shocker. Or, depending on the character, in a completely different role.

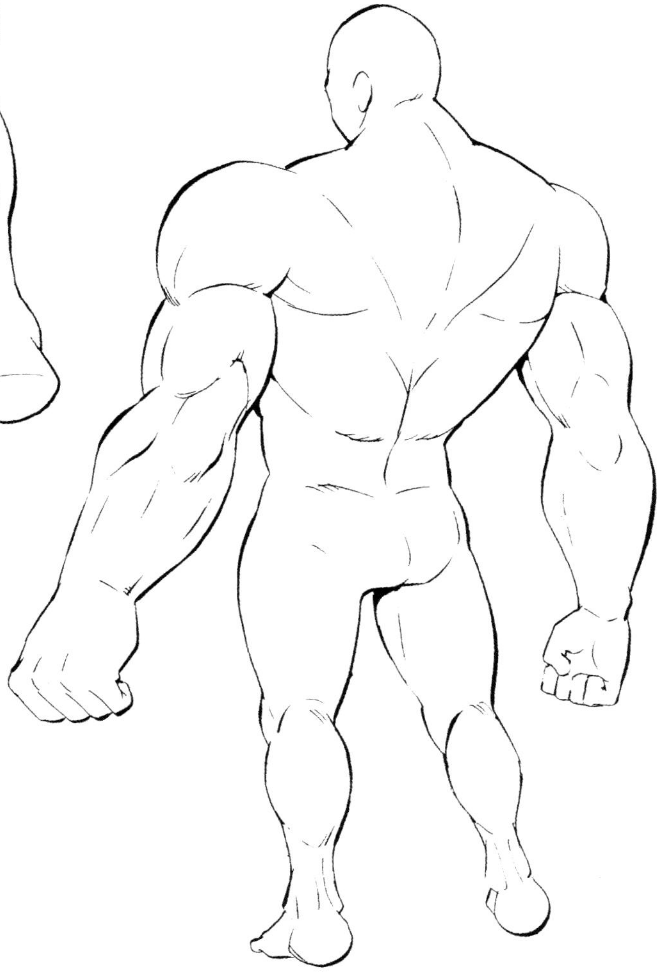

As mentioned on the previous double page, don't be afraid to exaggerate even more. Have a go at increasing the contrast between the arms and legs of the model on the right: spindly legs, with massive hands like excavator shovels dragging along the ground. Anything goes, as long as it's interesting!

COLOSSUS

Another body type we want to focus on is the colossus – a big, heavy, muscle-bound guy who is particularly at home in the action genre. Characters with this build are often portrayed as rather dim and have simple roles: they're usually cast as the bodyguard of an evil mastermind or a hatchet man. These figures are a kind of "middle boss" that the hero must overcome to reach the real boss.

Even if women aren't genetically predisposed to this body type, in manga you can make it happen! And a colossus character doesn't have to be dim-witted, just because that is the stereotype. Make your colossus super-intelligent, subvert their expected role, or even elevate them from the bodyguard to the final boss role. Whatever direction you take, here are some body views for inspiration and practice.

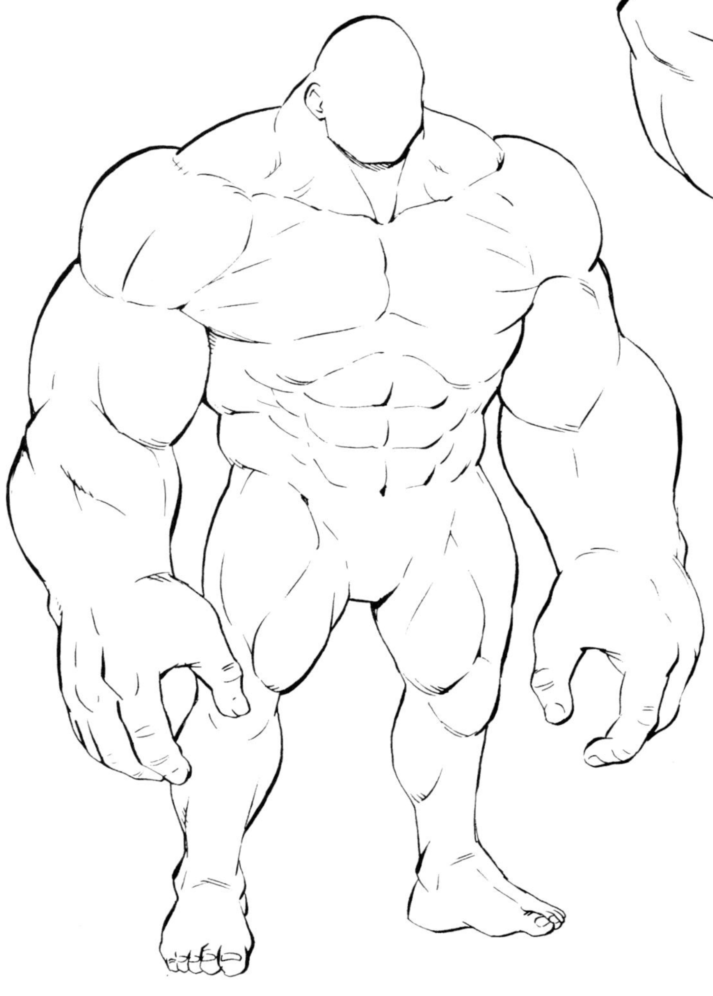

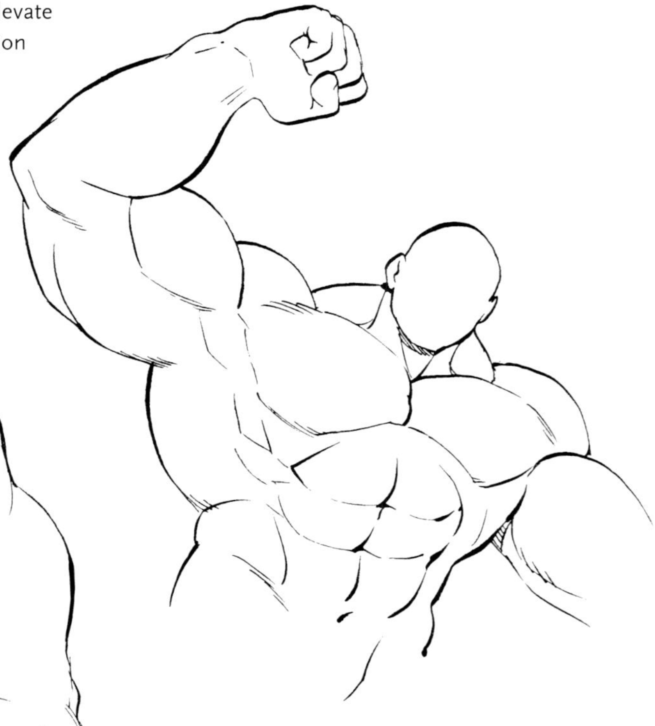

If you compare the individual body parts, you should recognize the muscles we focused on a few pages earlier – just in a more exaggerated form. One key decision you'll need to make for the design is the level of body fat. Lower body fat makes the muscle fibers stand out more, meaning you'll have to draw more lines to indicate where one muscle meets another. Higher body fat softens these lines, making everything rounder. Both extremes – and everything in between – can be imposing and intimidating in their own way.

This figure is still fairly realistic. A hardcore bodybuilder could get pumped like this with countless workouts and protein shakes. But by tweaking certain details – like making the head (much) smaller – you can instantly create a more monstrous appearance. You can amplify the effect further by broadening the shoulders and thickening the neck.

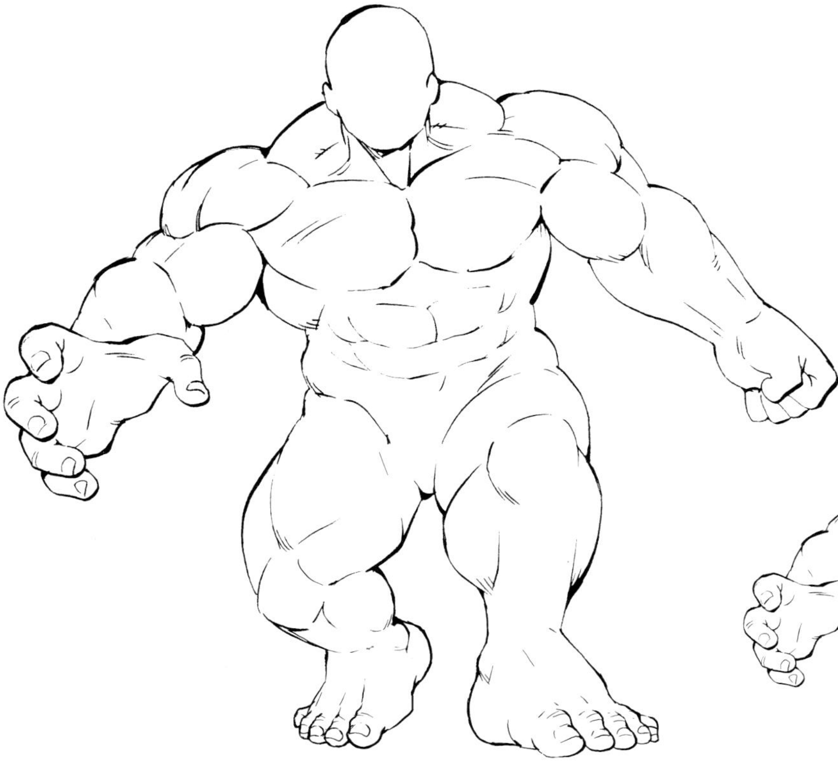

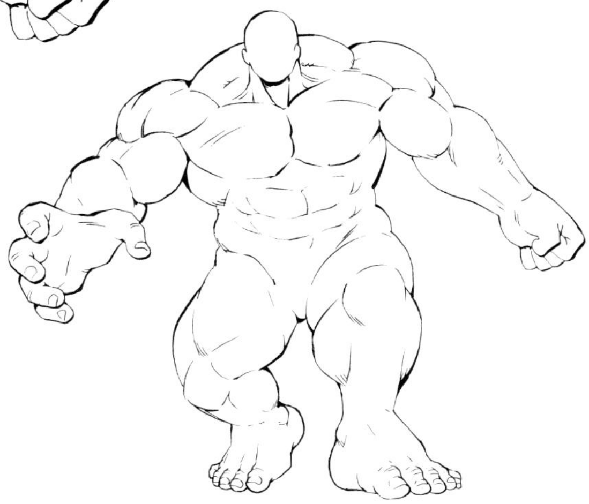

Don't be afraid to push exaggeration even further. Double the mass of the arm muscles, or let the character skip leg-training so that their lower body withers away. That shifts the focus to the area you choose. Or create an asymmetrical design, with only one arm pumped while the other remains skinny.

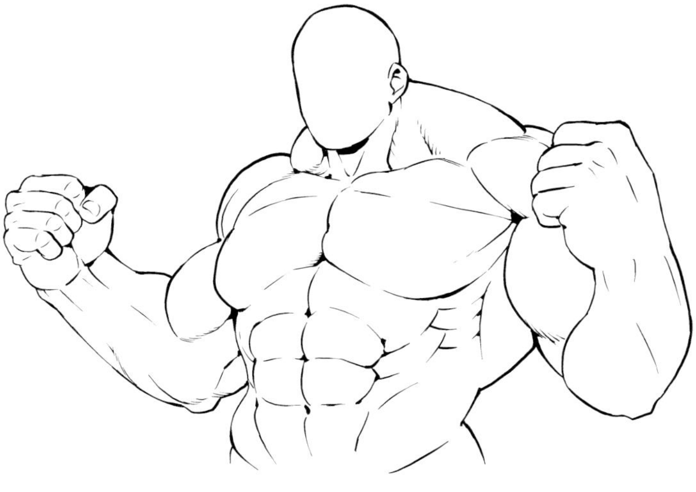

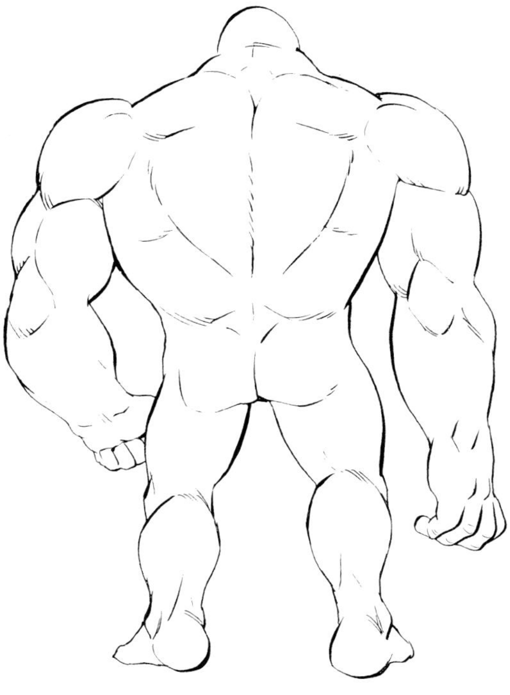

ANATOMY WITH REFERENCE PHOTOS

When you hit a wall you should use reference material. This is especially true when depicting complex movements, which constantly occur in dynamic action scenes. Even with a strong grasp of anatomy and a solid understanding of muscle interaction, you'll still come across barriers that you can only overcome by looking for the required information on specific postures – in photos, for example.

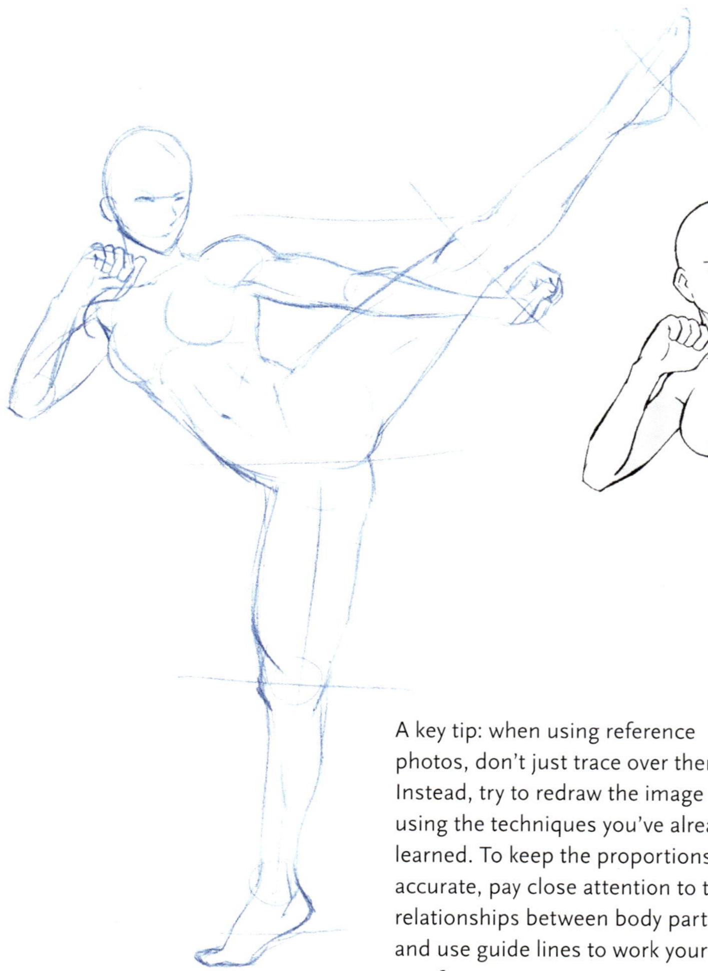

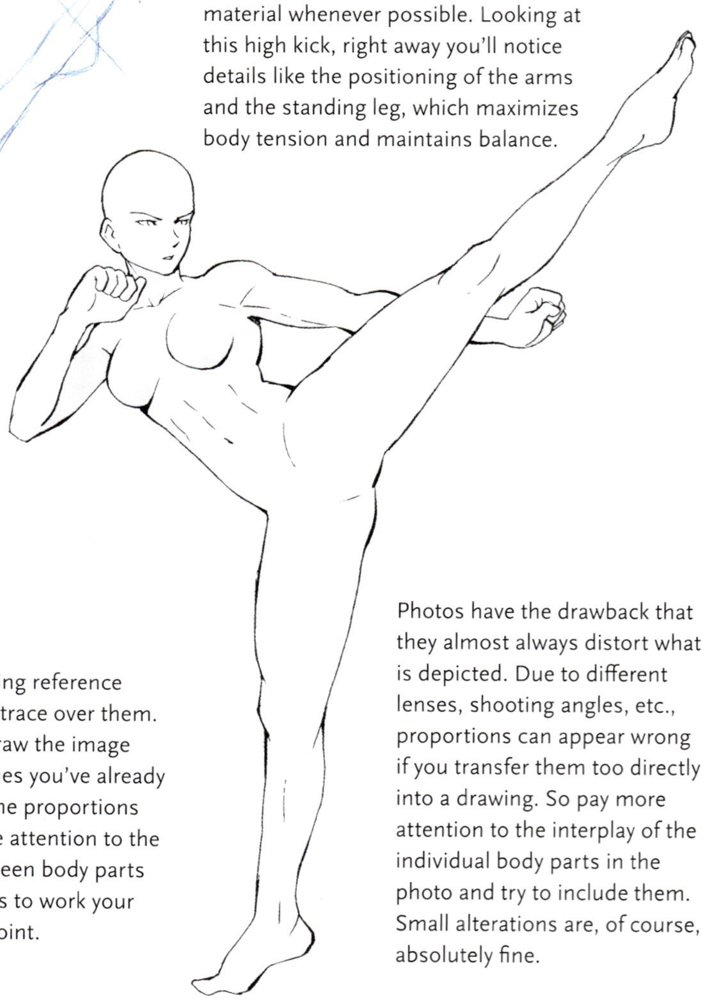

Martial arts techniques should always be cross-checked with reference material whenever possible. Looking at this high kick, right away you'll notice details like the positioning of the arms and the standing leg, which maximizes body tension and maintains balance.

A key tip: when using reference photos, don't just trace over them. Instead, try to redraw the image using the techniques you've already learned. To keep the proportions accurate, pay close attention to the relationships between body parts and use guide lines to work your way from joint to joint.

Photos have the drawback that they almost always distort what is depicted. Due to different lenses, shooting angles, etc., proportions can appear wrong if you transfer them too directly into a drawing. So pay more attention to the interplay of the individual body parts in the photo and try to include them. Small alterations are, of course, absolutely fine.

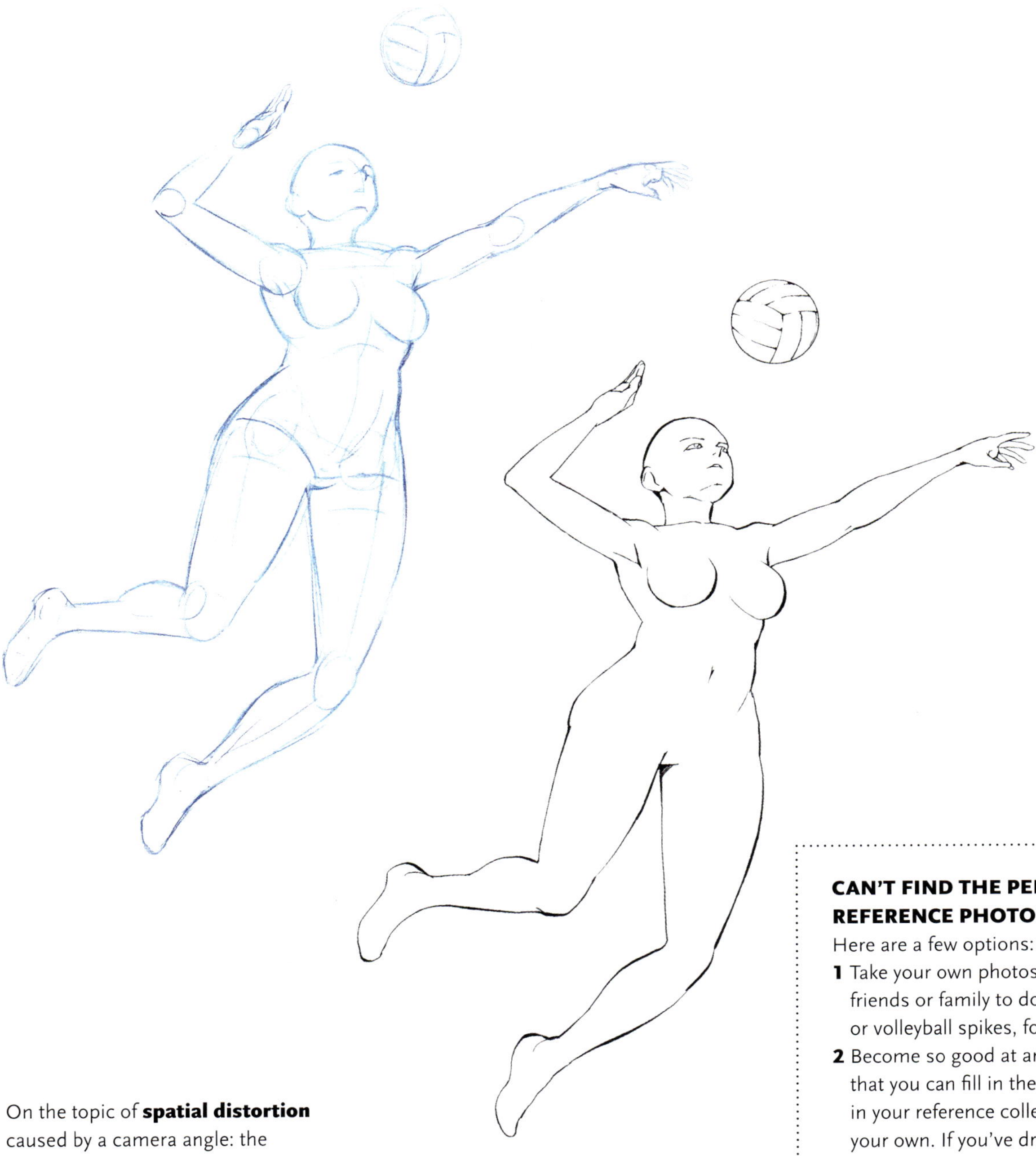

On the topic of **spatial distortion** caused by a camera angle: the volleyball player shown here was drawn using a reference photo taken from a slightly low angle. So we're looking up at her, but you can only tell from small details, like the curve of the collarbone.

CAN'T FIND THE PERFECT REFERENCE PHOTO?

Here are a few options:

1 Take your own photos. Ask friends or family to do high kicks or volleyball spikes, for example.
2 Become so good at anatomy that you can fill in the gaps in your reference collection on your own. If you've drawn a lot of martial arts or a specific sport for example, you'll start to develop an instinct for how those movements work.
3 If it isn't working with a particular reference photo, try using others with similar poses.
4 Multiple video stills can also be really useful, like a flip book to help you comprehend a punch in a boxing match, for example.

WORKING WITH MANNEQUINS

In art schools and in many artistic adult education courses, you can study anatomy with a live model. However, if that's not an option, mannequins are more practical and easily available. These figures are a great help when drawing bodies and anatomy.

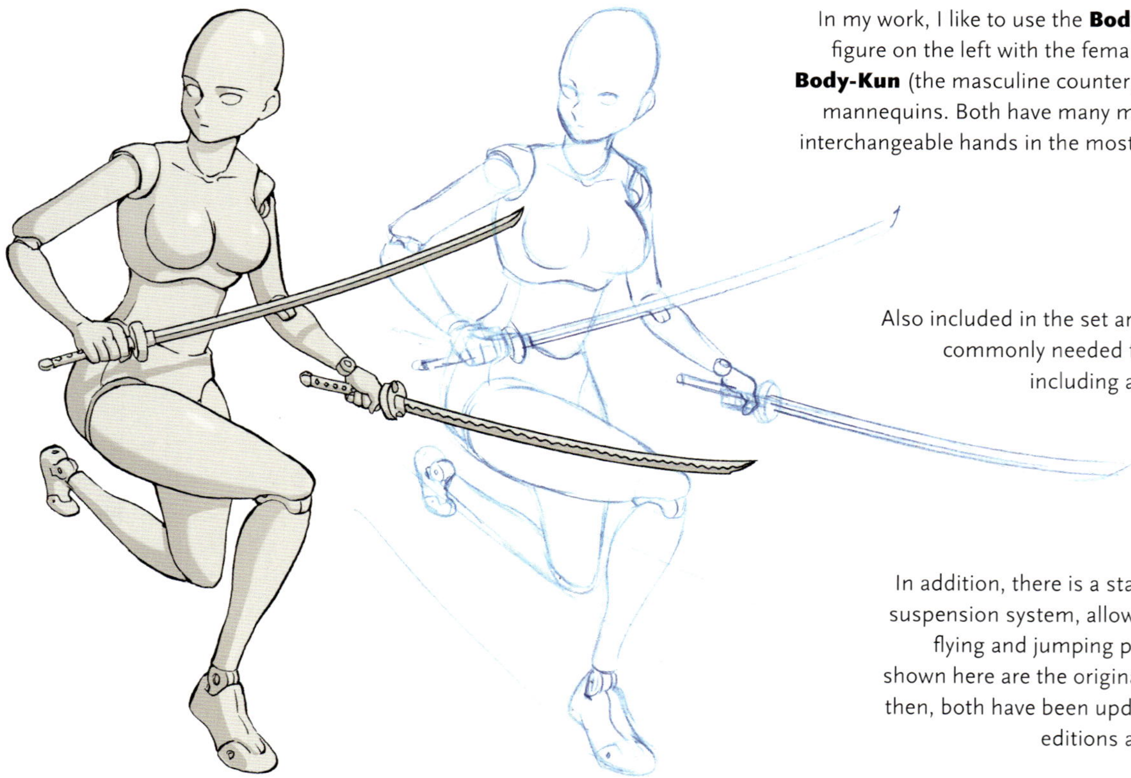

In my work, I like to use the **Body-Chan** (the gray figure on the left with the female body type) and **Body-Kun** (the masculine counterpart on the right) mannequins. Both have many movable parts and interchangeable hands in the most common poses.

Also included in the set are various objects commonly needed for manga poses, including a *katana* for each.

In addition, there is a stand with a kind of suspension system, allowing you to create flying and jumping poses. The figures shown here are the original versions. Since then, both have been updated, and special editions are now available.

Next to (or below) the two mannequins, you can see a preliminary sketch for each. This illustrates the process of working with mannequins: position all the limbs, choose the pose you need, and then draw it.

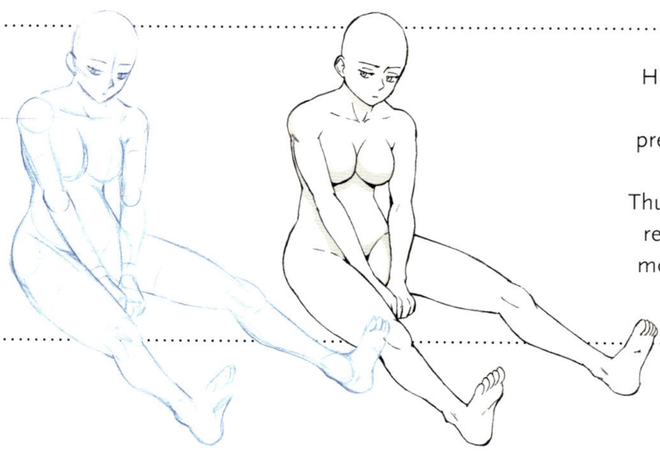

Here you can see the many extra lines I add to the preliminary sketch to better capture the proportions. Thus, the mannequins don't replace the other reference models – they complement them.

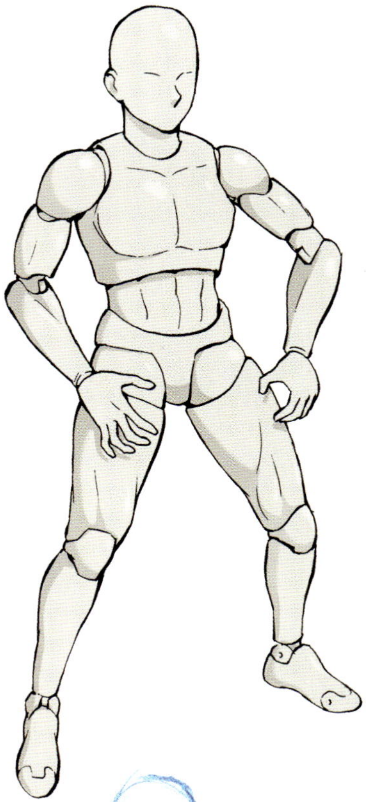

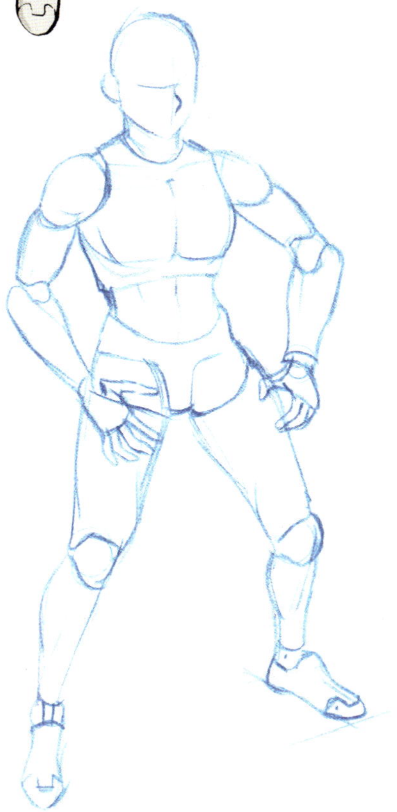

Later on, we'll take a closer look at the topic of perspective, which is extremely important in manga. Drawing figures with spatial distortion is extremely tricky, and we need every tool available. Mannequins can be really useful here too, especially when combined with a camera. If you happen to have a lens that captures distortions better than the human eye, all the better. Pose the mannequin, take a photo from exactly the angle you want to use in your manga, and then draw from this photo.

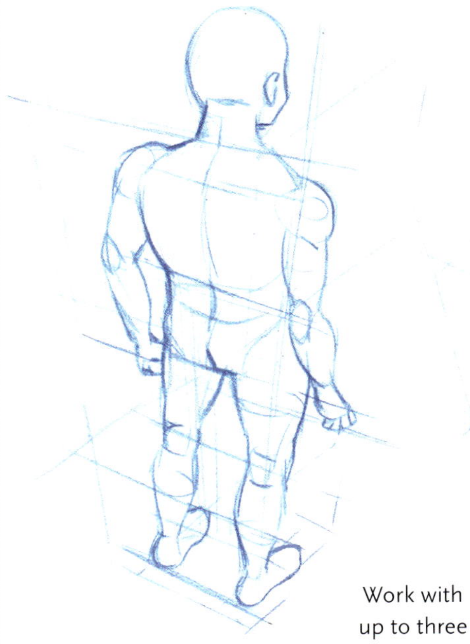

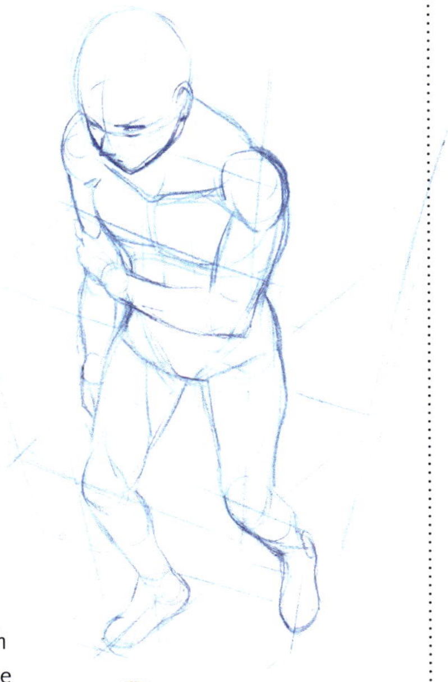

Work with up to three vanishing points. Lots of guide lines are needed to properly capture the three-dimensional space.

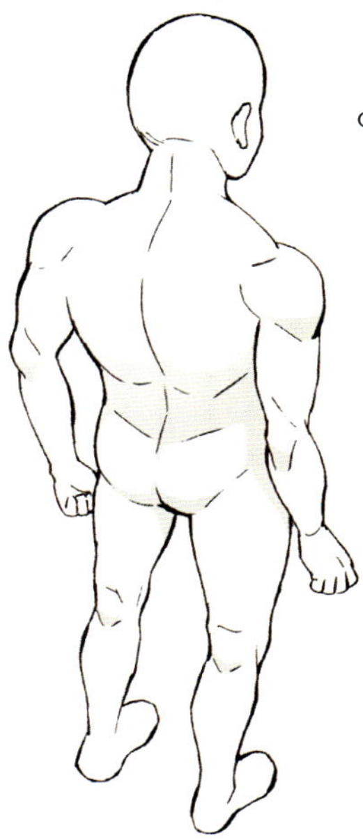

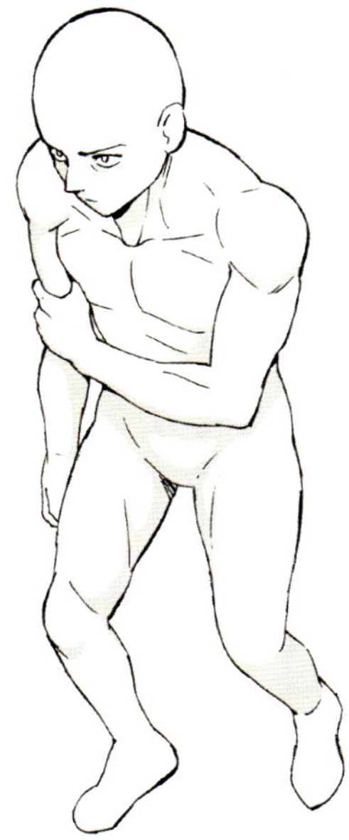

FACIAL EXPRESSIONS

Let's take a look at some expressions regularly needed for manga. Depending on the context, facial expressions can be interpreted in different ways. For action manga in particular, highly expressive faces are essential – extreme euphoria, screams of pain, determined battle cries, and much more.

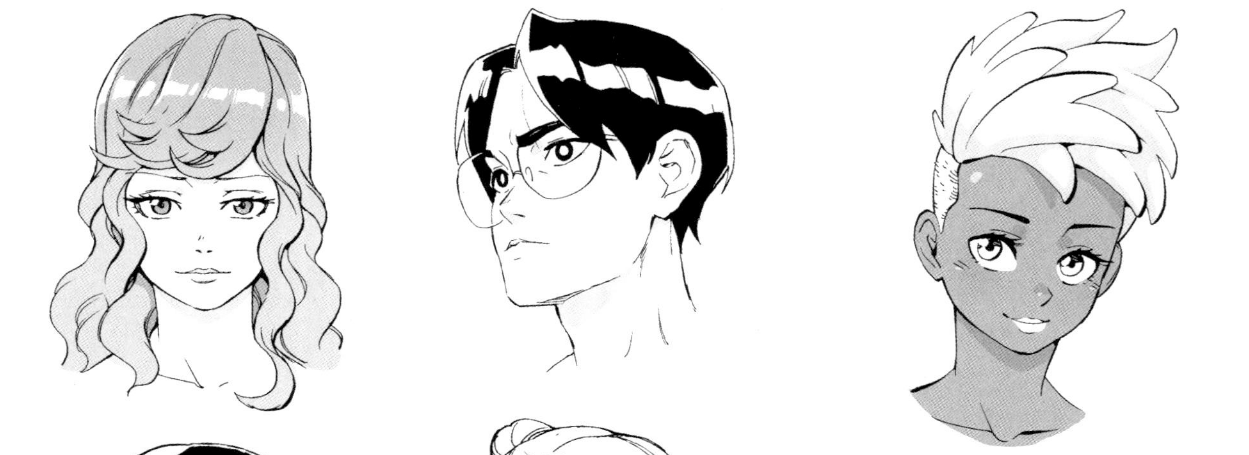

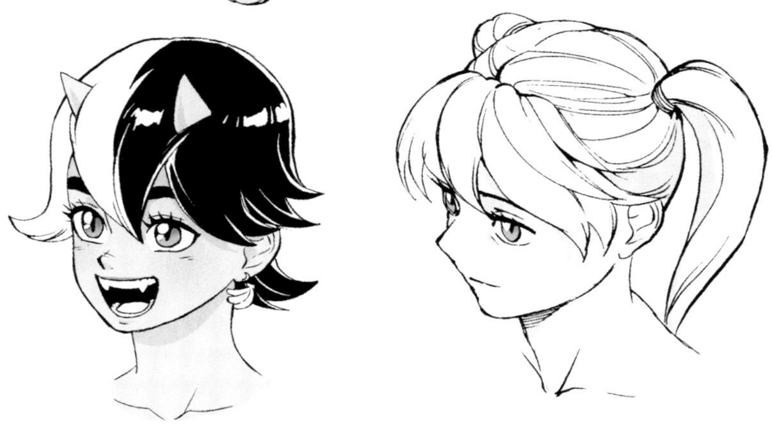

Is it just a gentle smile, or a slightly crazed look? Seriousness, or a blank, murderous stare? Cheerful glee, or a villain's wicked laugh? The context of a scene can cast even seemingly innocent expressions in a much darker light.

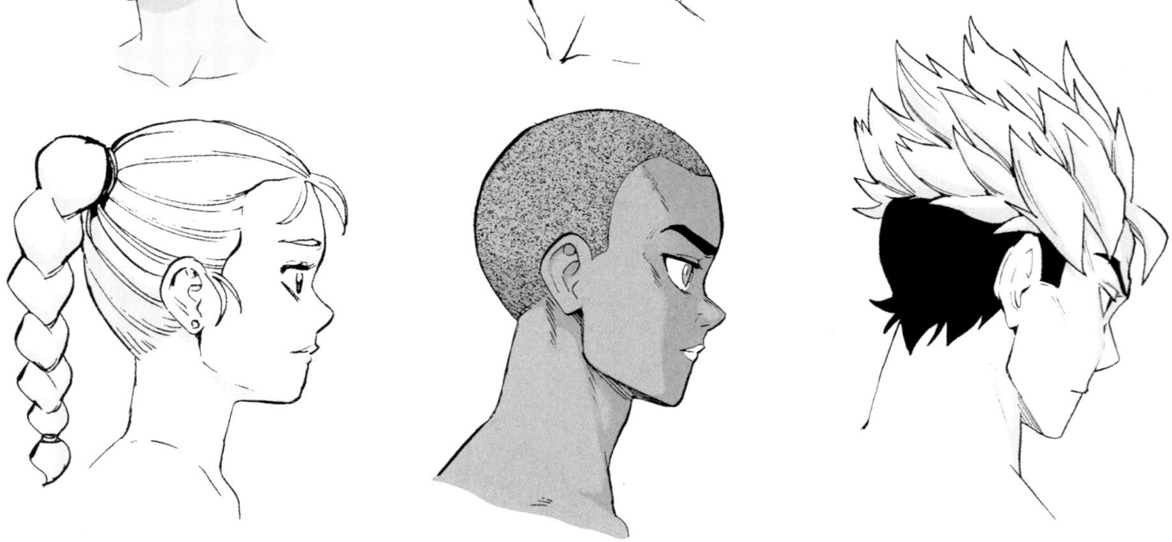

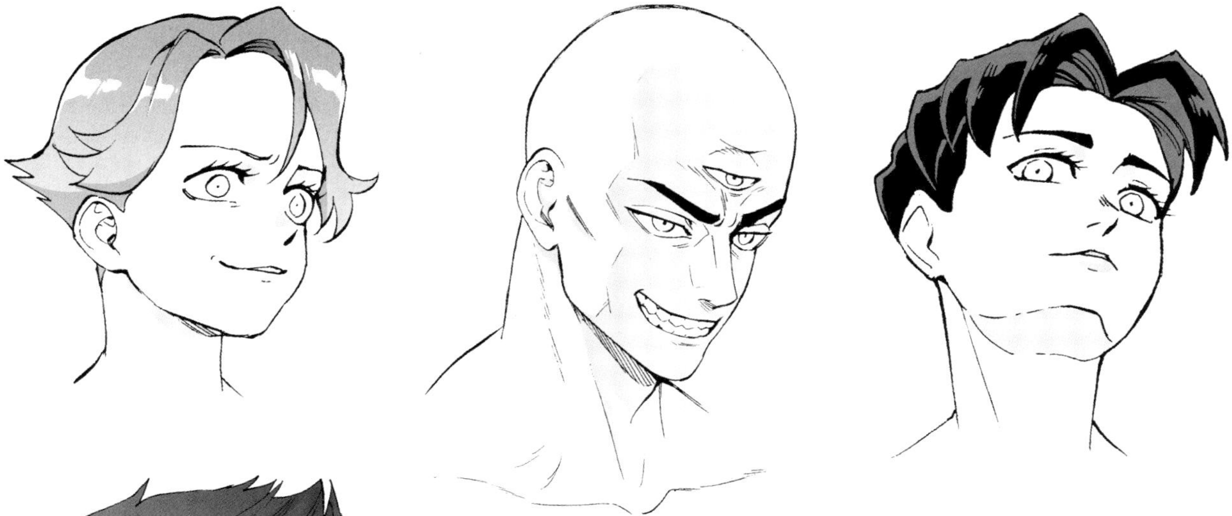

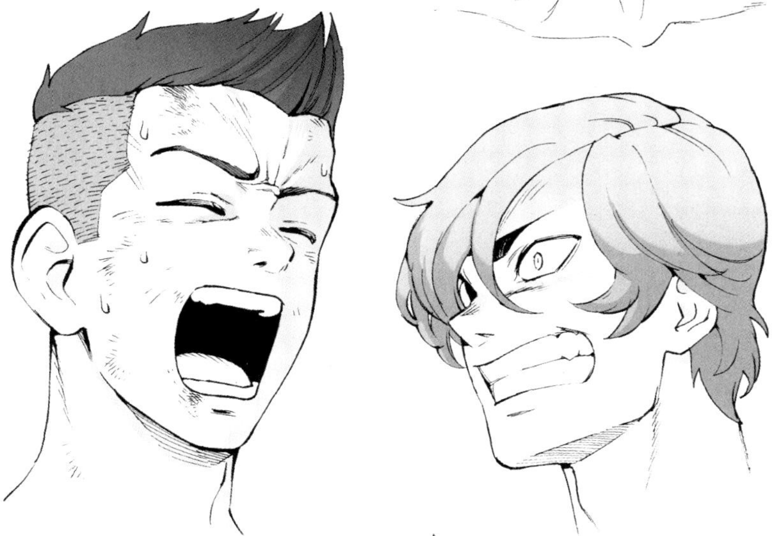

Here's a collection of aversive facial expressions, that is, expressions that convey negative emotions. On the top row, we meet arrogance; in one face, we're practically being looked down on. In the middle: pain and rage. At the bottom: three levels of determination as it emerges in the face of an enemy, from calm to defiant. These intense emotions are especially effective at drawing readers in.

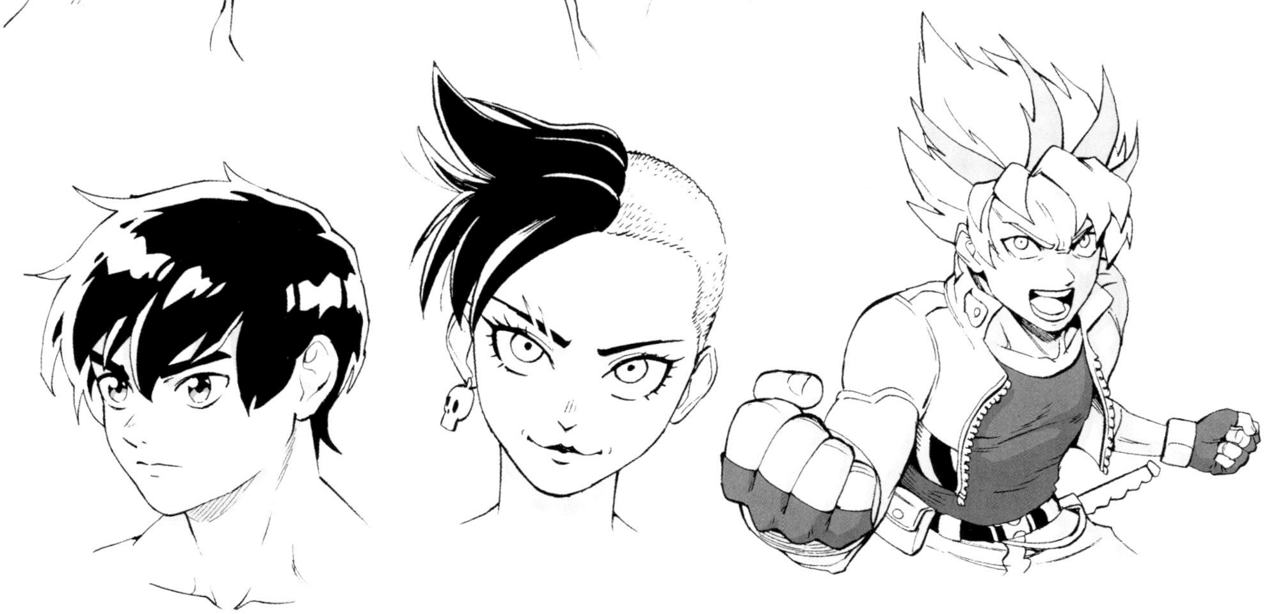

HANDS

Hands are extremely important in comics. Gesticulating amplifies emotions, and if you have your characters constantly doing something with their hands, you can make otherwise bland dialogue scenes more engaging. On the following pages, we'll also explore more dynamic ways to use them. But first, the basics! Let's ease into it with a few tips and tricks.

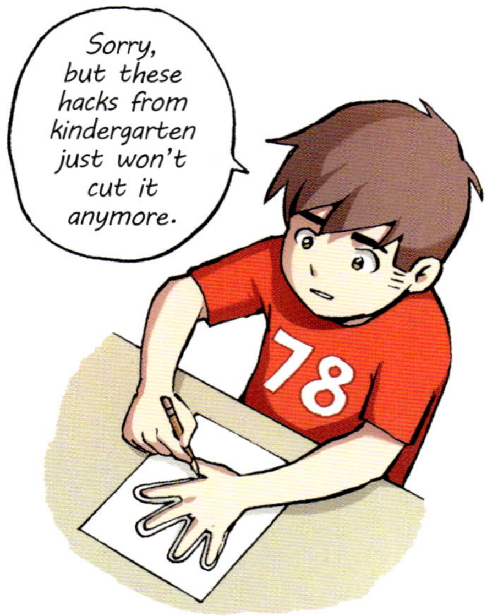

Getting anatomy right – and that includes the hands, of course – has a lot to do with how well you can portray the relationships between all the little parts. Even with something as simple as an open hand, there are lots of tricks. You'll find a few of them here, plus, as usual, some rough sketches with helpful guide lines.

BACK OF THE HAND

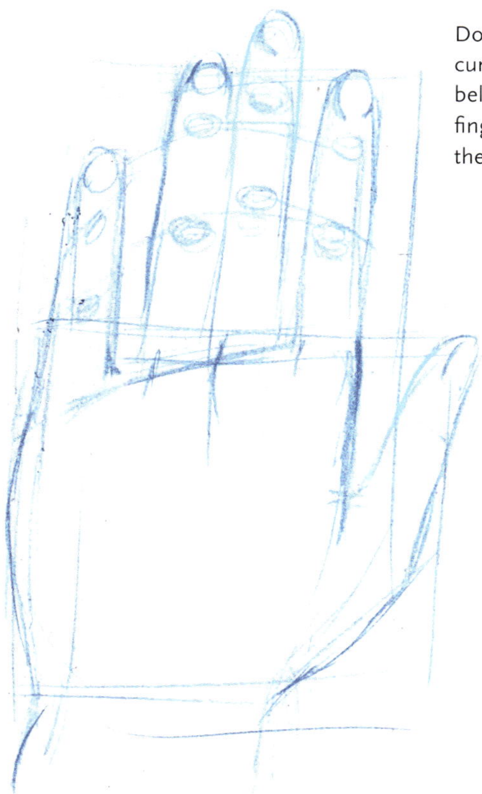

The gap between the little finger and the ring finger is wider than the one between the forefinger and middle finger.

Don't forget the curve at the wrist below the middle finger. This is called the ulnar head.

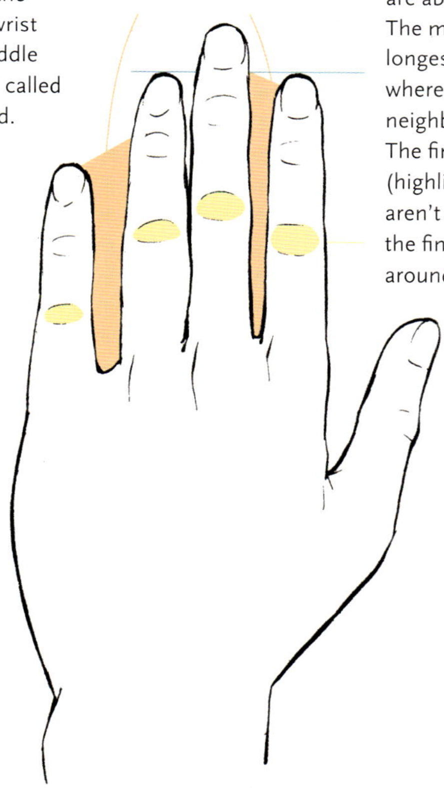

The forefinger and ring fingers are about the same length. The middle finger is the longest. Its nail starts about where the nails of the two neighboring fingers end. The fingers' middle knuckles (highlighted in yellow here) aren't exactly halfway along the finger length, but rather at around 40 percent.

The thumb is clearly angled outward in relation to the other four fingers. It ends roughly at the height of the middle knuckle of the little finger.

PALM OF THE HAND

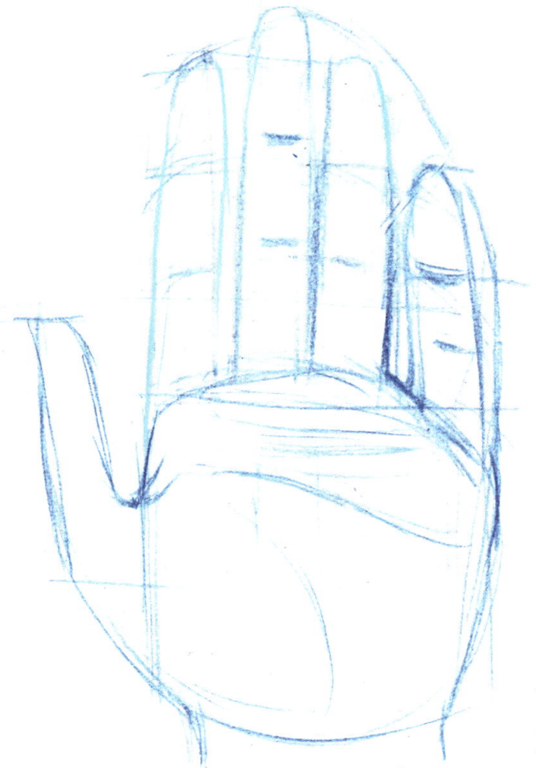

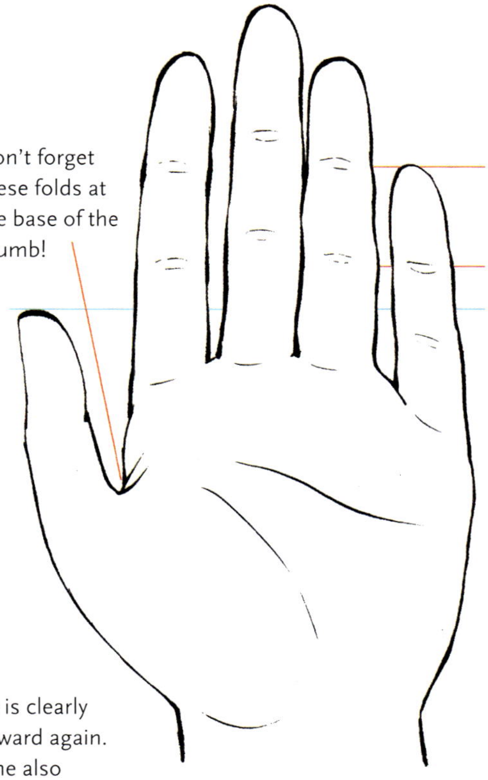

Don't forget these folds at the base of the thumb!

The last phalanx of the little finger is at the same height as the middle knuckle of the forefinger and ring finger.

The thumb is clearly angled outward again. The blue line also indicates the height at which it ends.

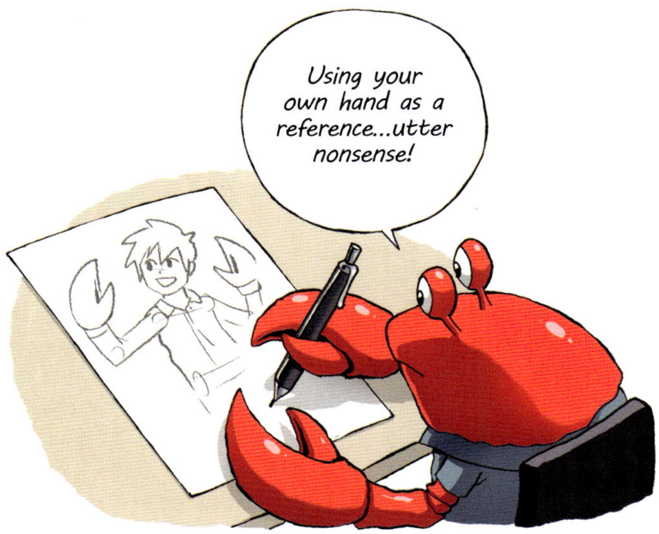

You could fill an entire book with instructions on how to draw hands – many already have – and there would still be a model that you urgently need for your manga missing from it. Fortunately, you usually have two reference guides at the end of your arms. It's best to take a hand selfie from the exact angle you need and draw from it. Easier said than done, of course, but with more tips and models in the following pages, it should get much easier.

STRUCTURE OF THE HAND

Don't be alarmed! Wanting to simplify things a bit, we suddenly find ourselves faced with the complicated hand skeleton. Unless you're working on a project that features the "walking skinless undead" or something similar, you don't need to master this level of anatomy just yet, but it doesn't hurt to have at least seen the bones of the hand and fingers.

The middle phalanx (marked in yellow) is absent in the thumb.

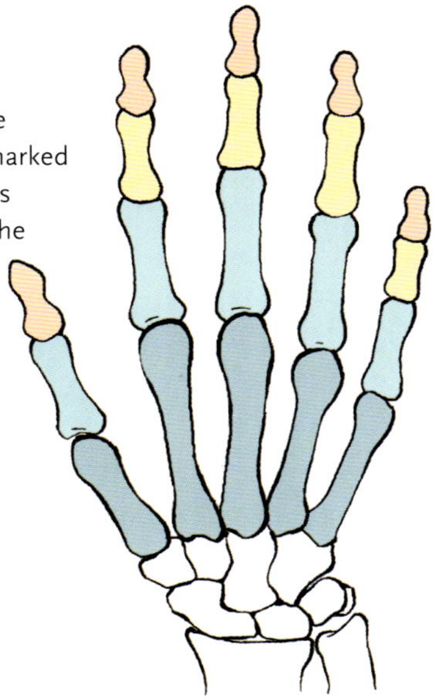

Now, we reduce the hand to its simplest basic shapes. The metacarpus and carpus (these are the many smaller bones in the wrist) are simplified into a shape like a pentagon. The highest point is at the base of the middle finger.

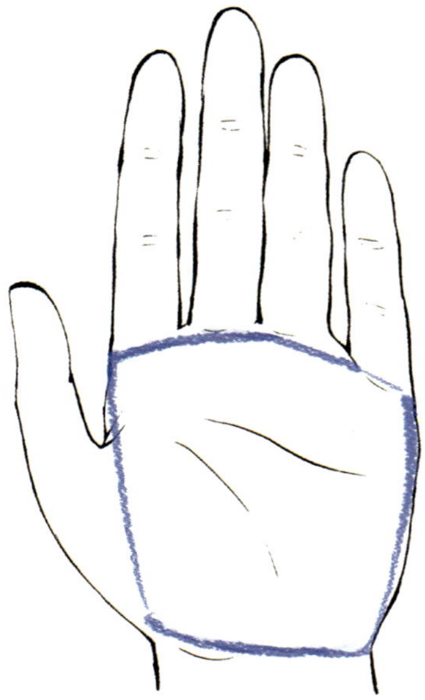

Next come the individual phalanges. For the metacarpal bone of the thumb, we add a sort of triangle. Look at a real hand to see how flexible this area at the base of the thumb is.

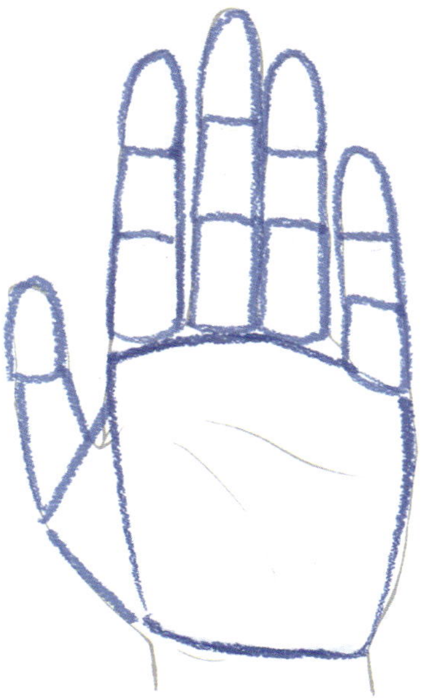

The marked points are the finger joints. The red ones are hinge joints, which only move back and forth in one direction. The purple ones are ball joints and are much more flexible. The most flexible joint is the orange saddle joint at the base of the thumb, which has already been mentioned.

The purple points are called the metacarpophalangeal joints.

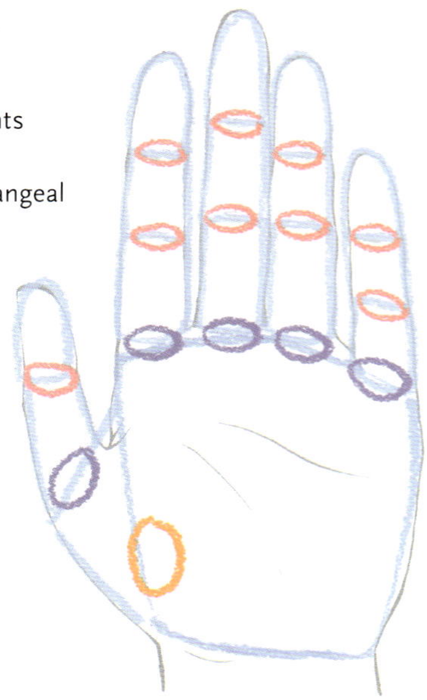

Next, we will look at the simplified hand model, divided into shapes, and transfer each element into a three-dimensional form. Start with the palm/back of the hand pentagon, keeping in mind that it is slightly curved. Then, mark the ball joints of the metacarpophalangeal joints and work your way, phalanx by phalanx, toward the fingertips.

However, this model doesn't replace the reference hand! Instead, it serves as a complement. With the geometric shapes in the sketches, you'll soon find it easier to bring the reference images over into drawings.

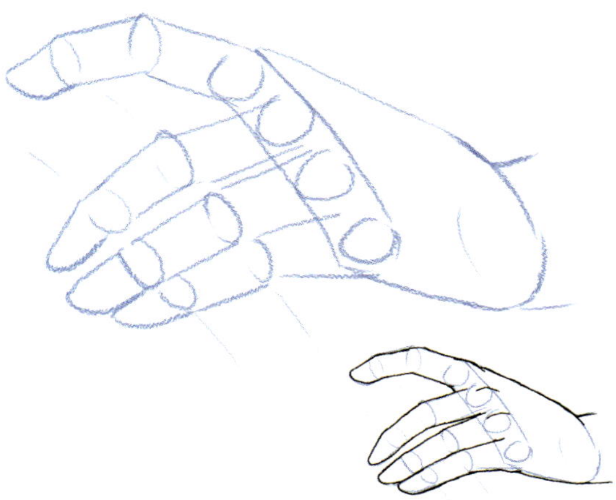

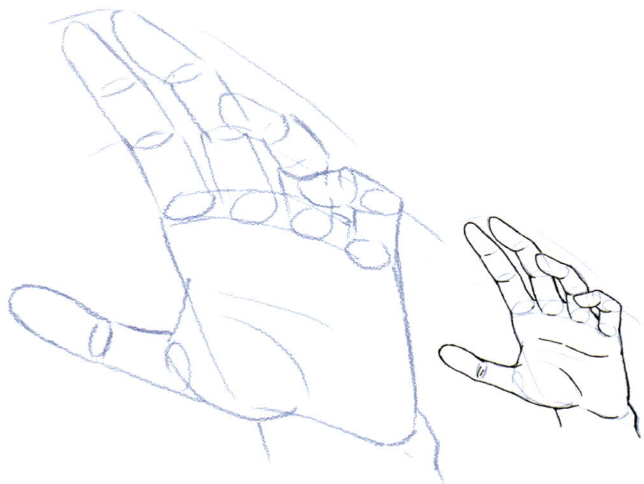

It's best to use a variety of reference images and copy the model to them to get a better feel for it. Gradually, you'll notice that you'll be able to draw simpler hand positions without references.

Complex hand positions – and there are countless ones – are difficult for most people to draw entirely without references. And that's perfectly fine!

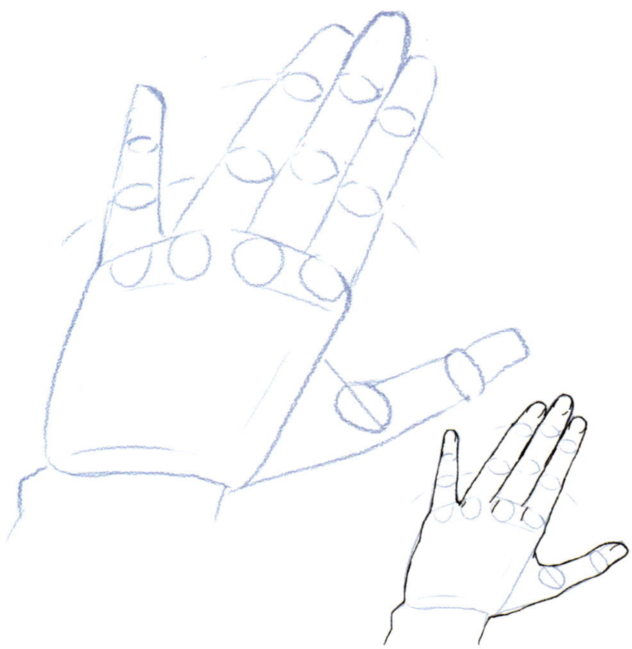

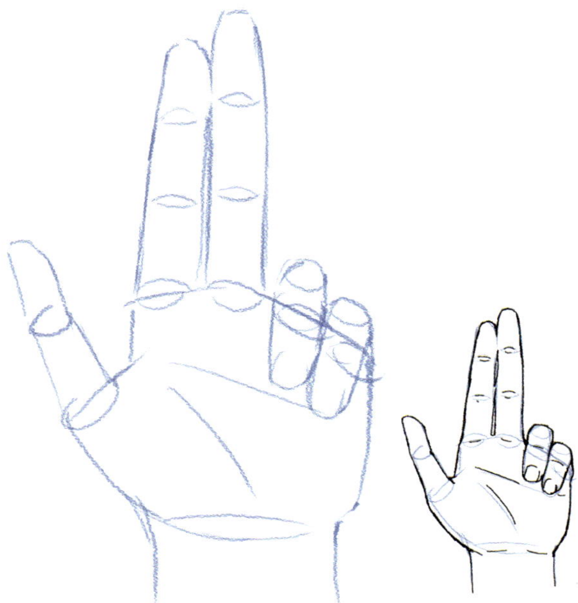

HANDS IN ACTION

A fundamental strength of manga is its ability to bring action and dynamism even to seemingly mundane activities. It highlights the emotions and intensity with which our heroes pursue their passion. Here are a few examples:

Placing a go piece

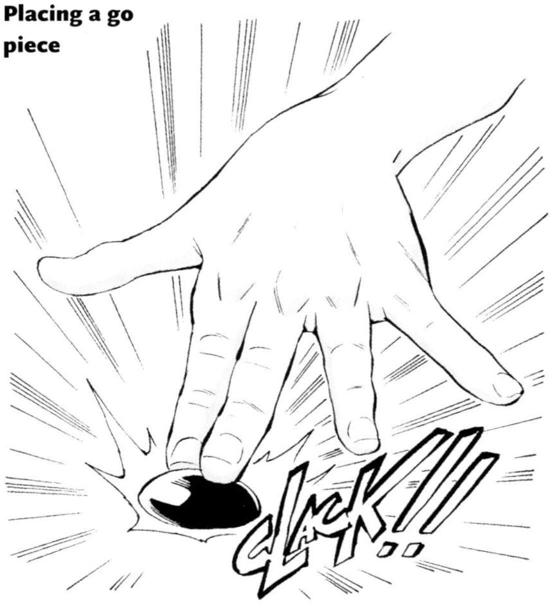

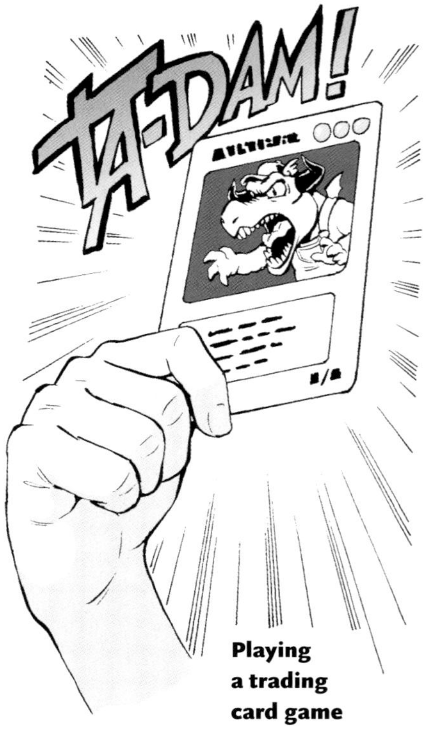

Playing a trading card game

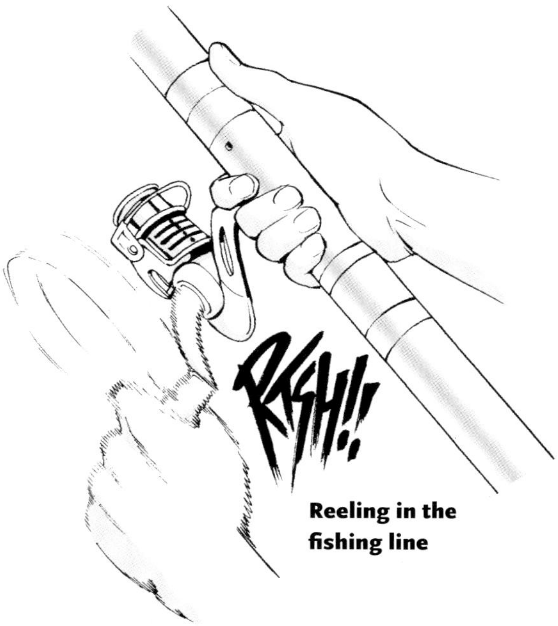

Reeling in the fishing line

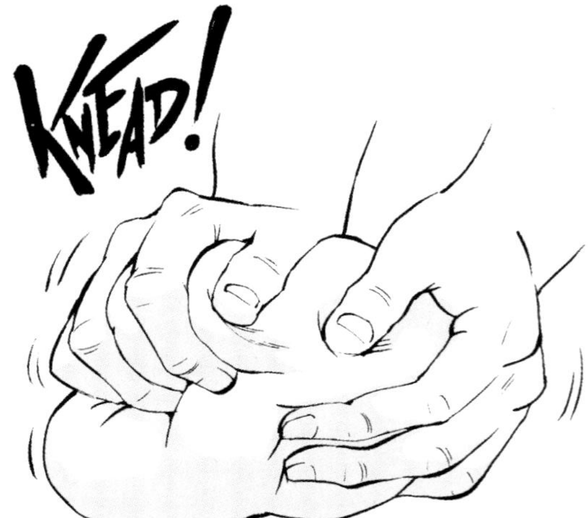

Kneading dough

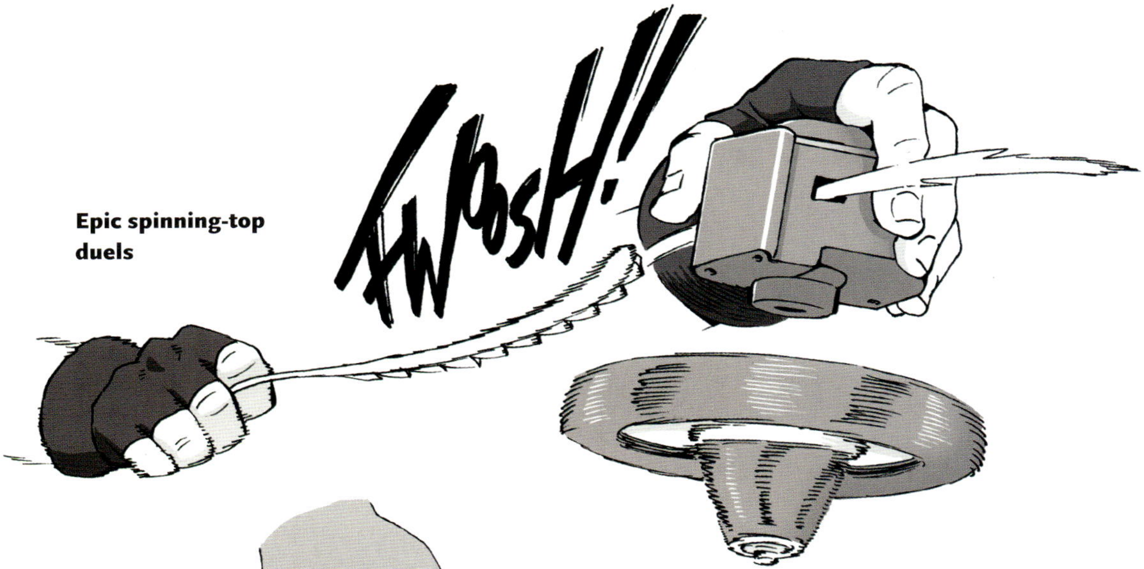

Epic spinning-top duels

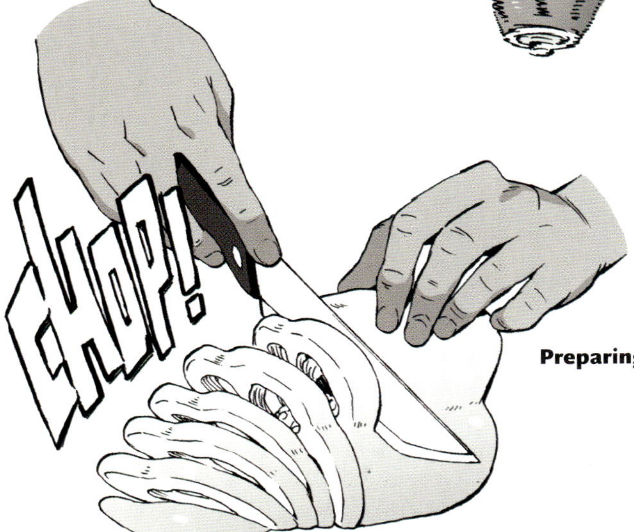

Preparing food

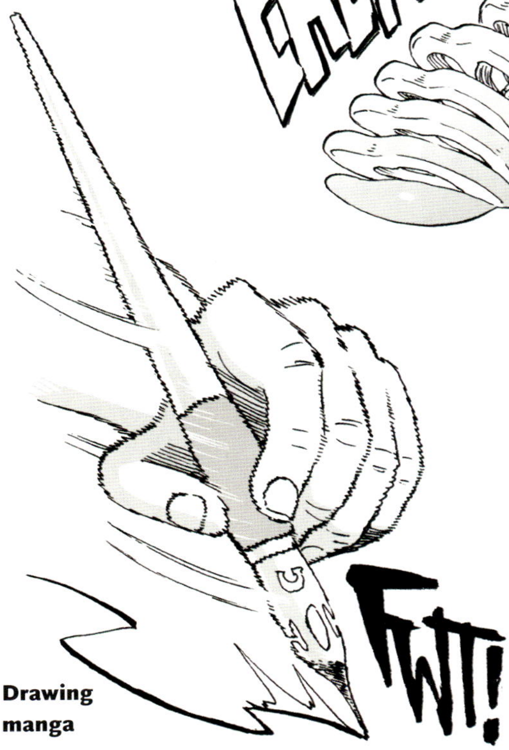

Drawing manga

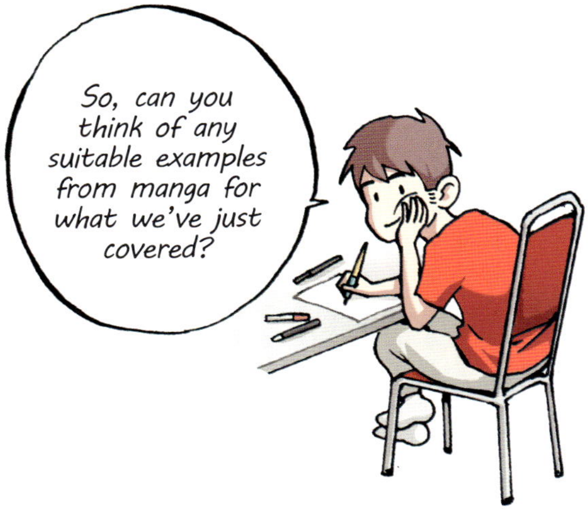

HANDS HOLDING WEAPONS

Weapons naturally play an important role in the action genre, and each weapon requires a particular way of being handled and held. Do your research, especially for more exotic weapons, to understand how they are wielded, and consult reference material. Here are some examples of a basic weapons arsenal.

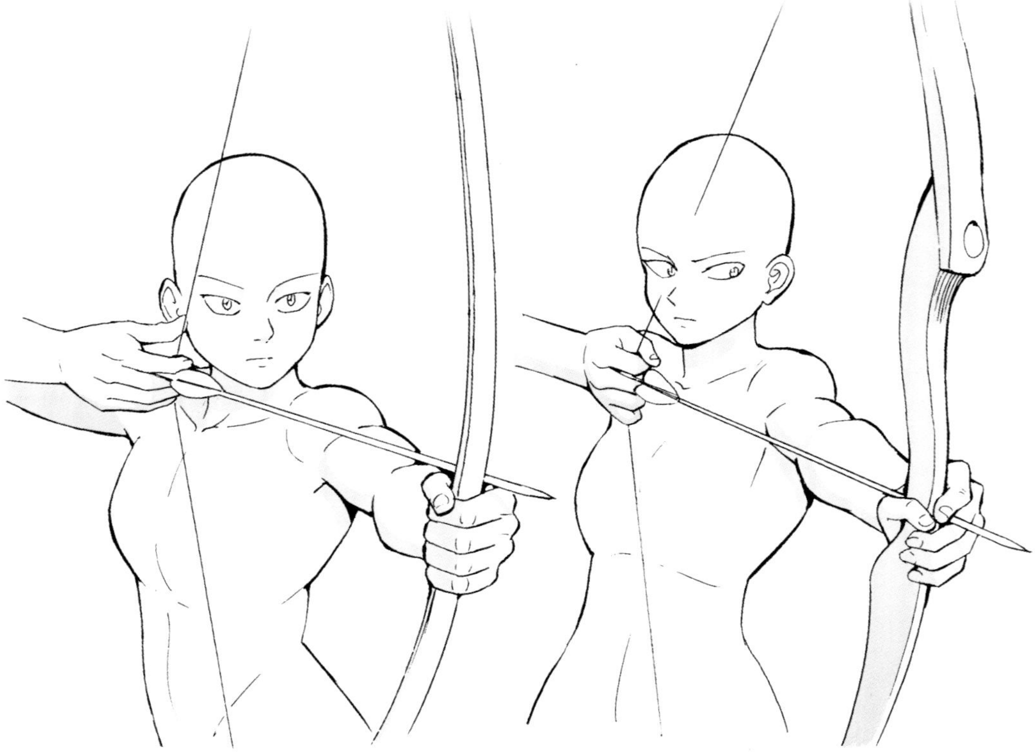

The examples with the bow and arrow and pistol, show that a weapon may be handled in many different ways (an astonishing variety of different ways in some cases).

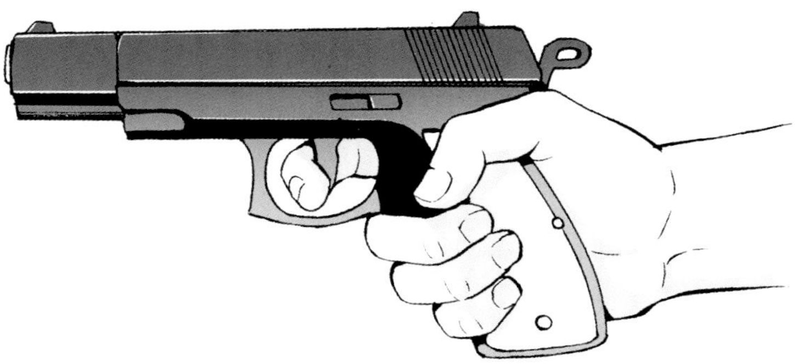

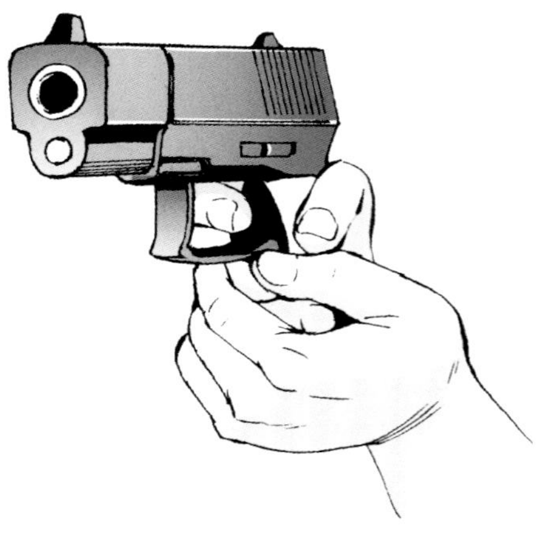

Some weapons – like this heavy hammer – are rather cumbersome. As a result, the body must also form a stable counterweight. This slows down the dynamism of the weapon wielder. If you want your characters to remain agile, give them sleeker weapons.

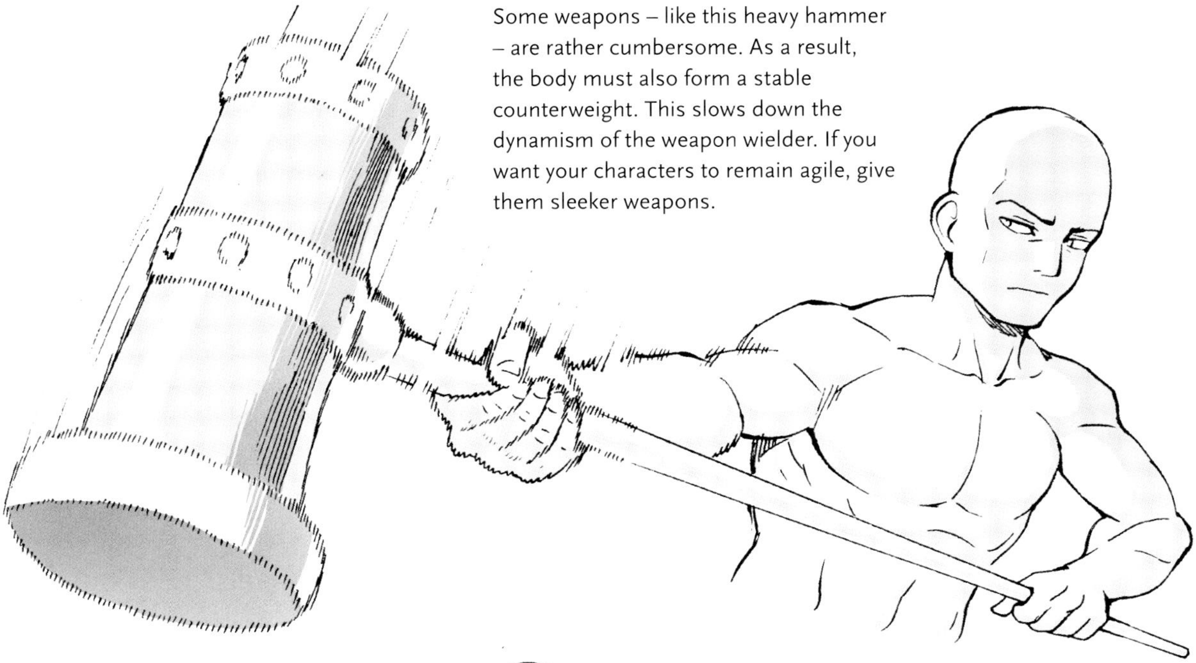

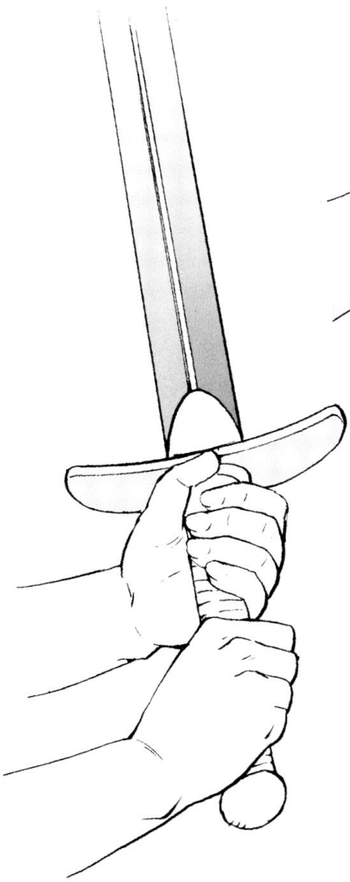

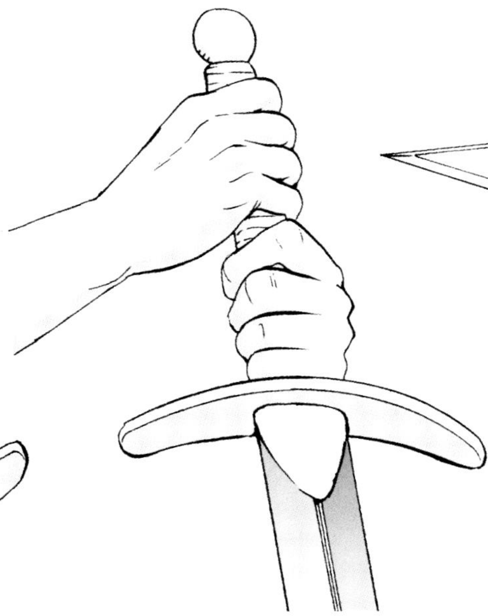

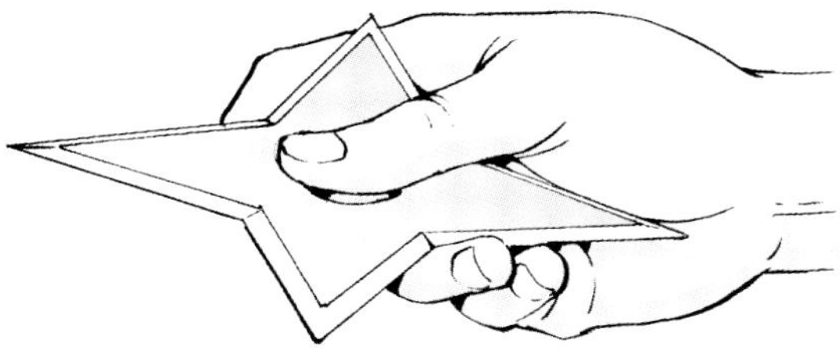

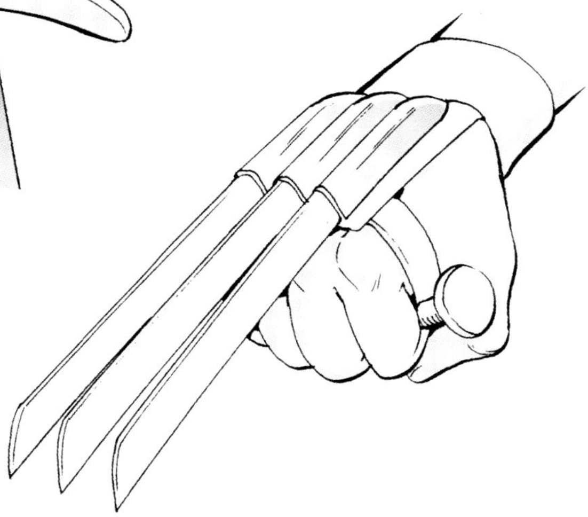

HANDS IN SPORT

Are you planning to draw an action-packed sports manga? Then delve deeply into the different hand positions associated with the sport of your choice. Each bat has its specific grip variations, and every ball game has its own throwing techniques. You can see some examples here. Of course, even within the sports represented, there's a great deal more variety. The different throwing techniques in basketball, the reception techniques in volleyball, ways of handling a table tennis racket, and so on. But at least this gives you a sense of how hands are used in various ways in sports.

BALL SPORTS WITH A BAT

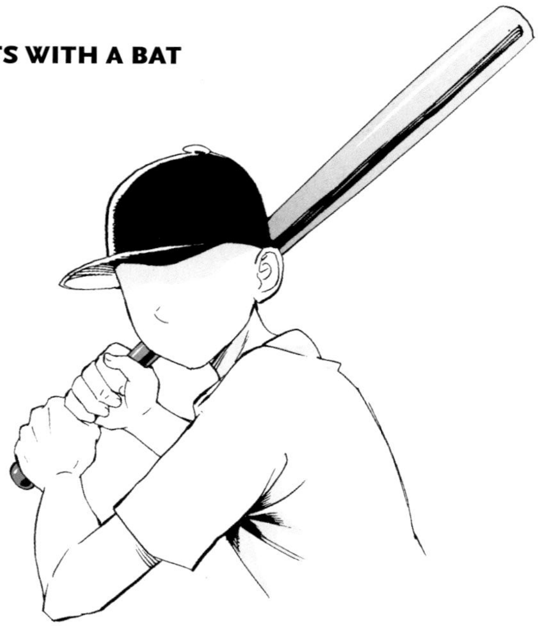

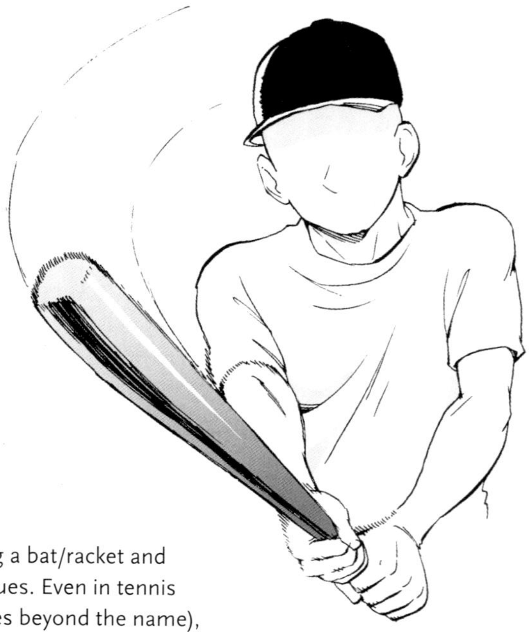

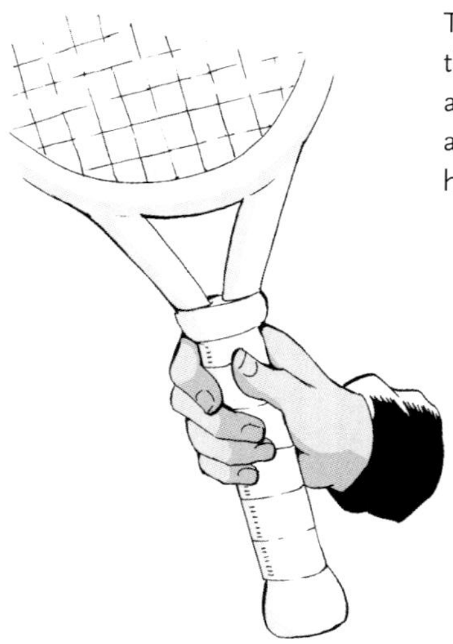

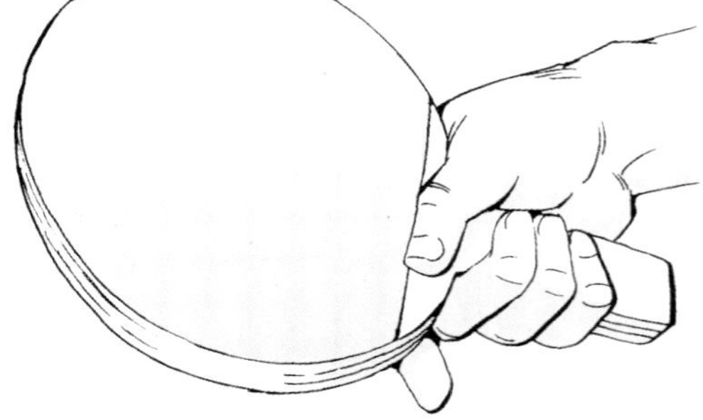

Three ball sports, each involving a bat/racket and three very different grip techniques. Even in tennis and table tennis (the affinity goes beyond the name), an outstretched forefinger, for instance, can make a huge difference.

BALL SPORTS WITH HANDS

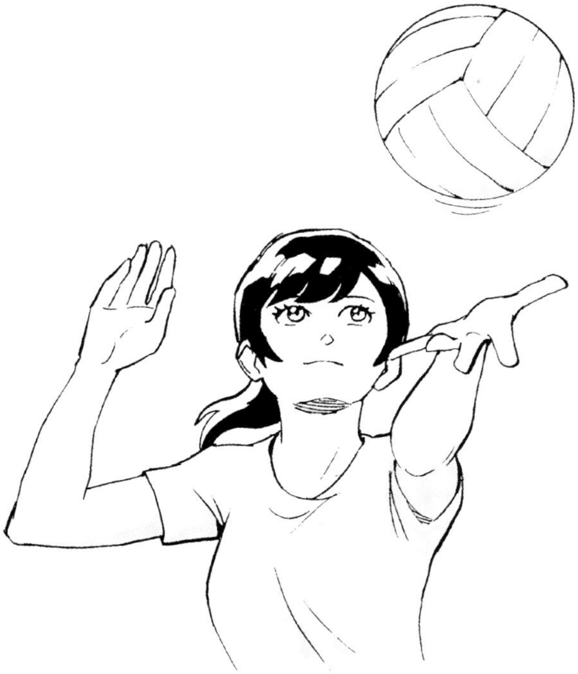

Keep your eye on the ball! While this primarily applies to the hands, make sure that the athletes focus on their equipment in ball sport scenes.

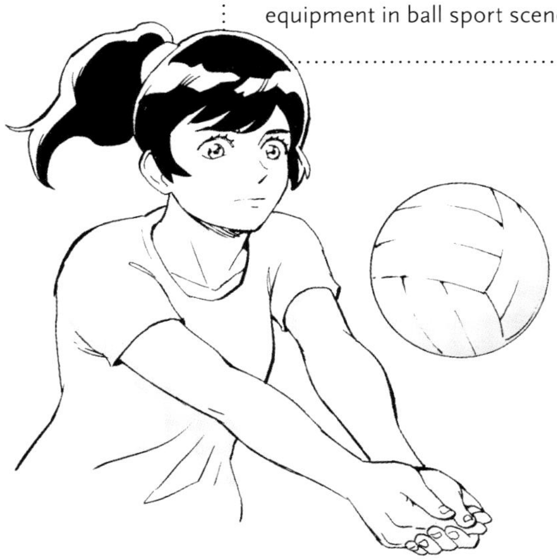

Three ball sports in which the hands touch the ball directly – three very different ball contact philosophies. In volleyball, the ball is only touched briefly; in bowling, the fingers actually penetrate the ball; and in basketball, it is dribbled and thrown.

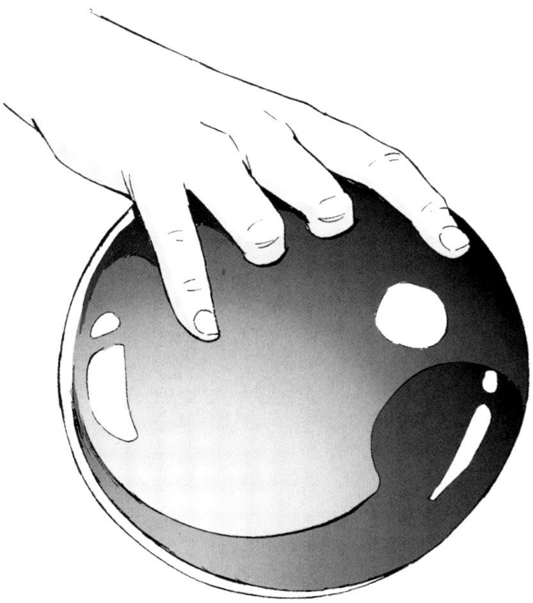

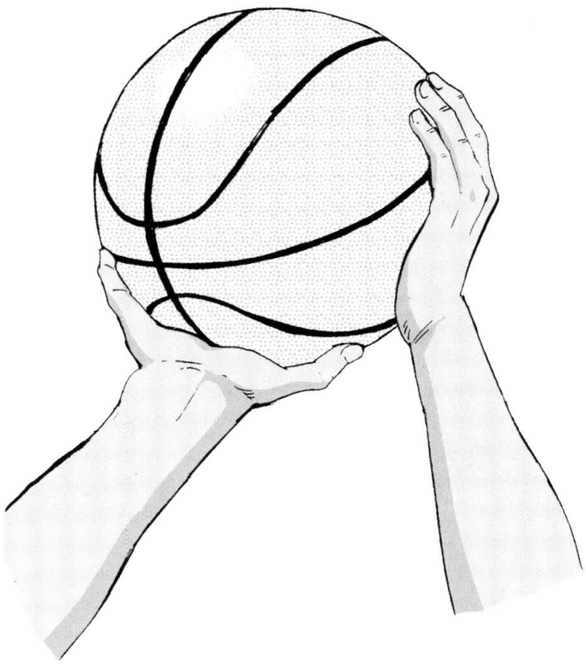

HAND GESTURES IN COMBAT

Let's take a look at some sample images of hand gestures associated with iconic roles, especially in manga. Stories with supernatural elements, especially, feature specific gestures used to initiate energy attacks or cast magic. If you want to incorporate these elements into your story, try experimenting with a few tensed finger positions using one or both hands, and see what looks cool when combined with effects.

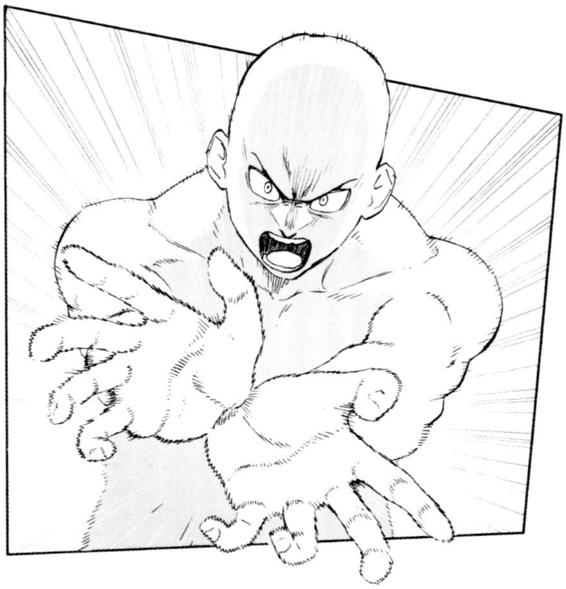

This gesture – the palms extended forward, and the fingers spread apart – should be familiar to every manga/anime fan. Many naturally think first of the famous Kamehameha technique from *Dragon Ball*, but other well-known techniques from Japanese pop culture also result in this striking pose. Sometimes the gesture is used to push the opponent away through pure physical contact, and other times, the hands fire a projectile made of pure *ki*, energy, or magic.

Also, pay attention to how zoom lines in the image are aligned to converge at the vanishing point at the point of contact between the hands. This helps to focus attention on the attack.

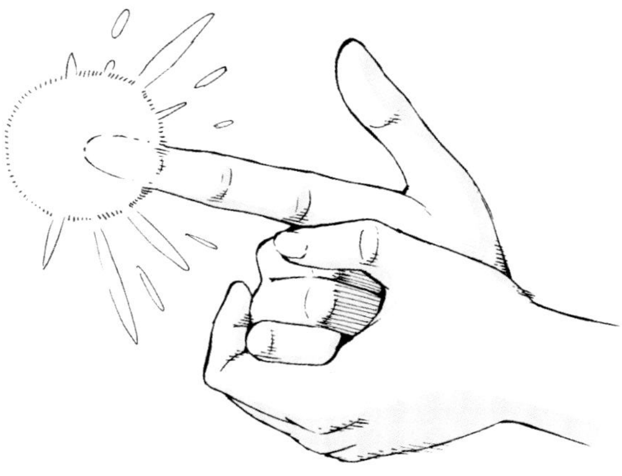

This pistol gesture also appears in a *shōnen* classic. Simple, but iconic! After all, every child has "fired" a finger gun at some point.

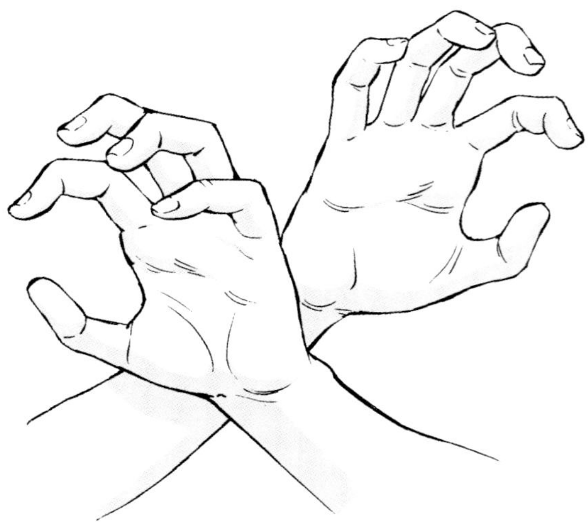

This crossed-hands gesture screams "defensive technique with immediate counterattack".

NINJA HAND SIGNS

You're probably familiar with these from the *shōnen* hit *Naruto*: the sometimes labyrinthine finger knots that, in combination with incantations, are performed in sequence to unleash special techniques. However, *kuji-in* (as they are technically known) actually have their origins in historical Asia and were really used as part of Taoist practices.

Some combinations are said to enhance perception, others supposedly accelerate wound healing, and so on. This is not scientific from today's perspective, but the effect of the practice is comparable to that of meditation. However, their use in *Naruto* shows how traditional practices can be reinterpreted and turned into a pillar of modern pop culture.

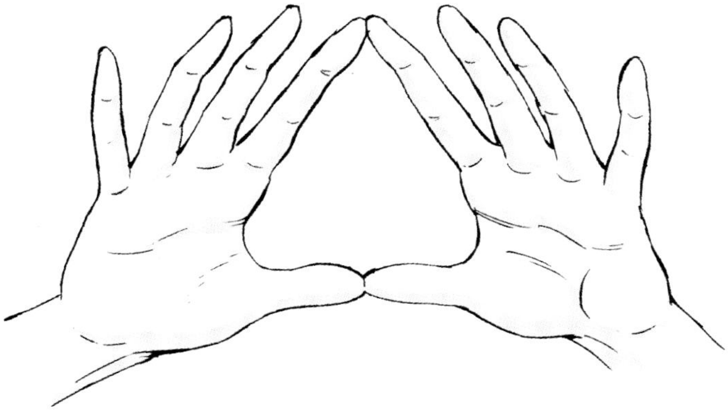

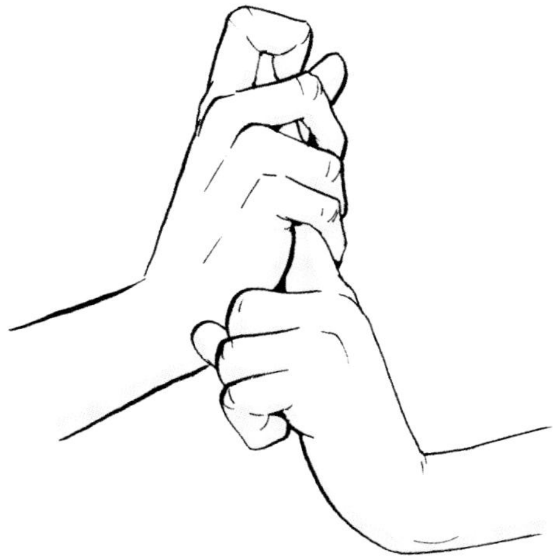

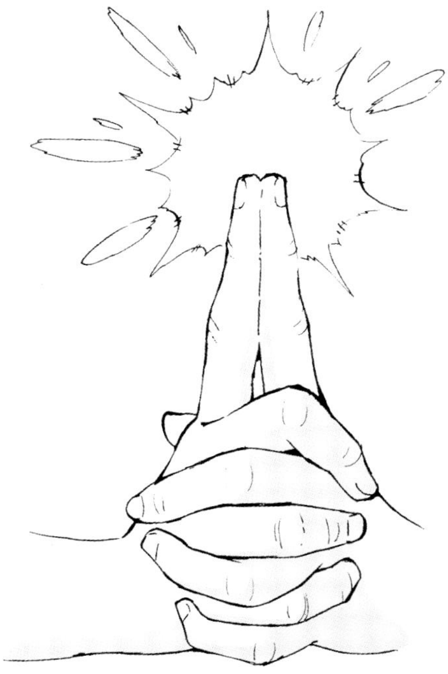

Since fiction isn't based on real science anyway, energy can be released from all parts of the body: eyes, mouth, and sometimes even the feet – or, in the case of demons or aliens, from horns and antennae. Even so, nothing beats the hands! Depending on how they're positioned, they can be deployed in many different ways and are easy to read. Examples: big attacks are generated with both hands and outstretched fingers. A focused energy beam comes from an outstretched forefinger. It immediately makes sense and is therefore especially popular in the action genre.

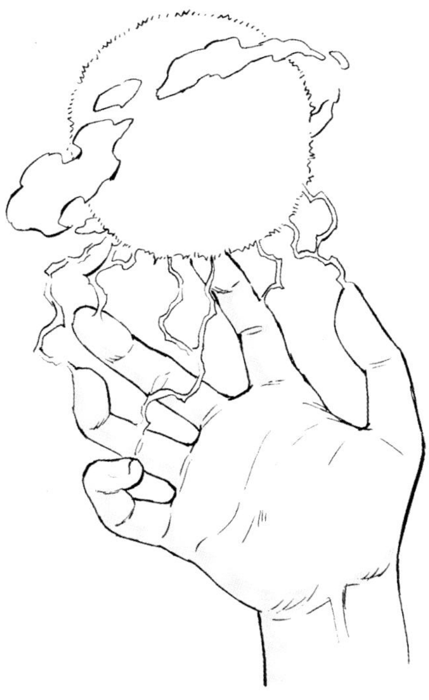

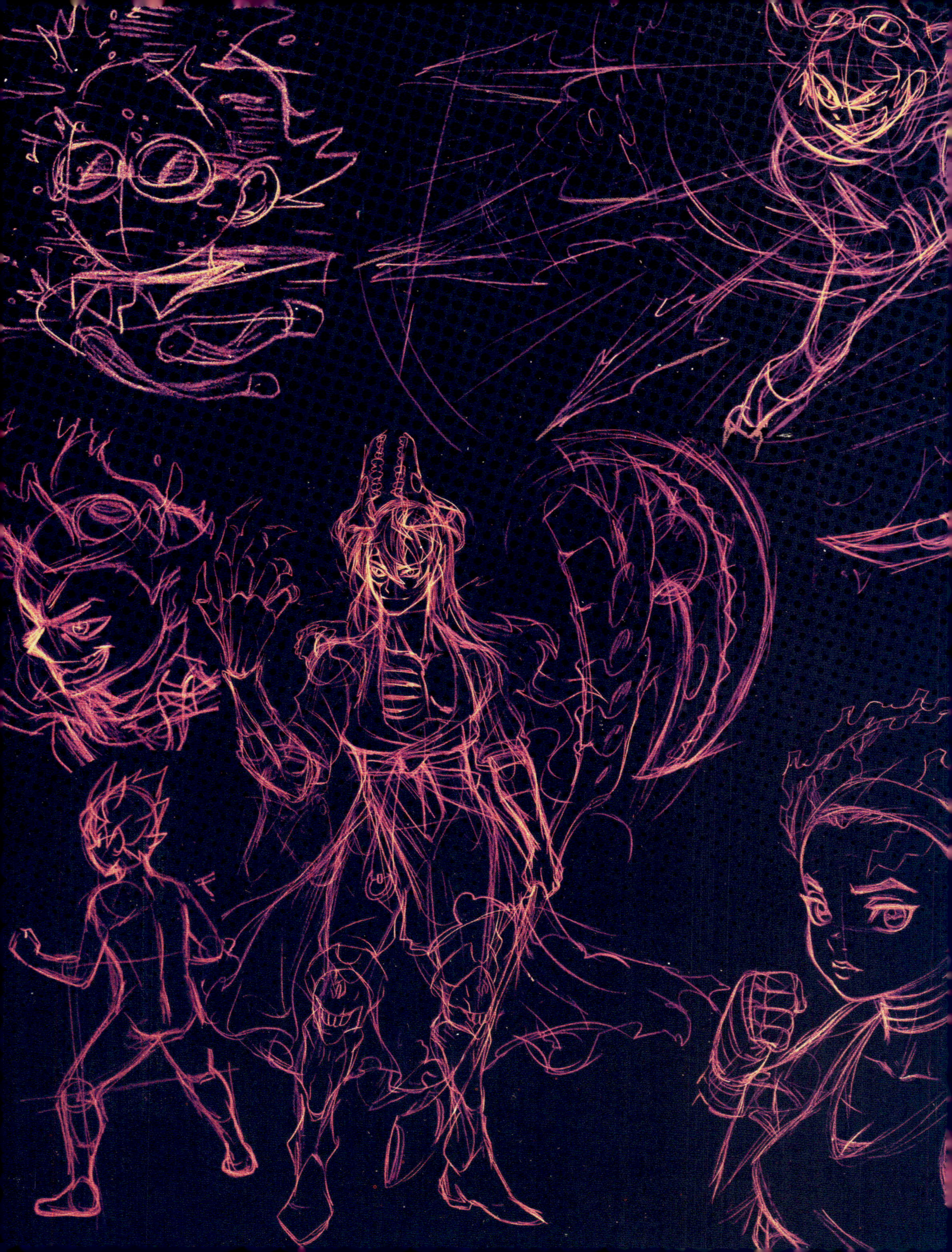

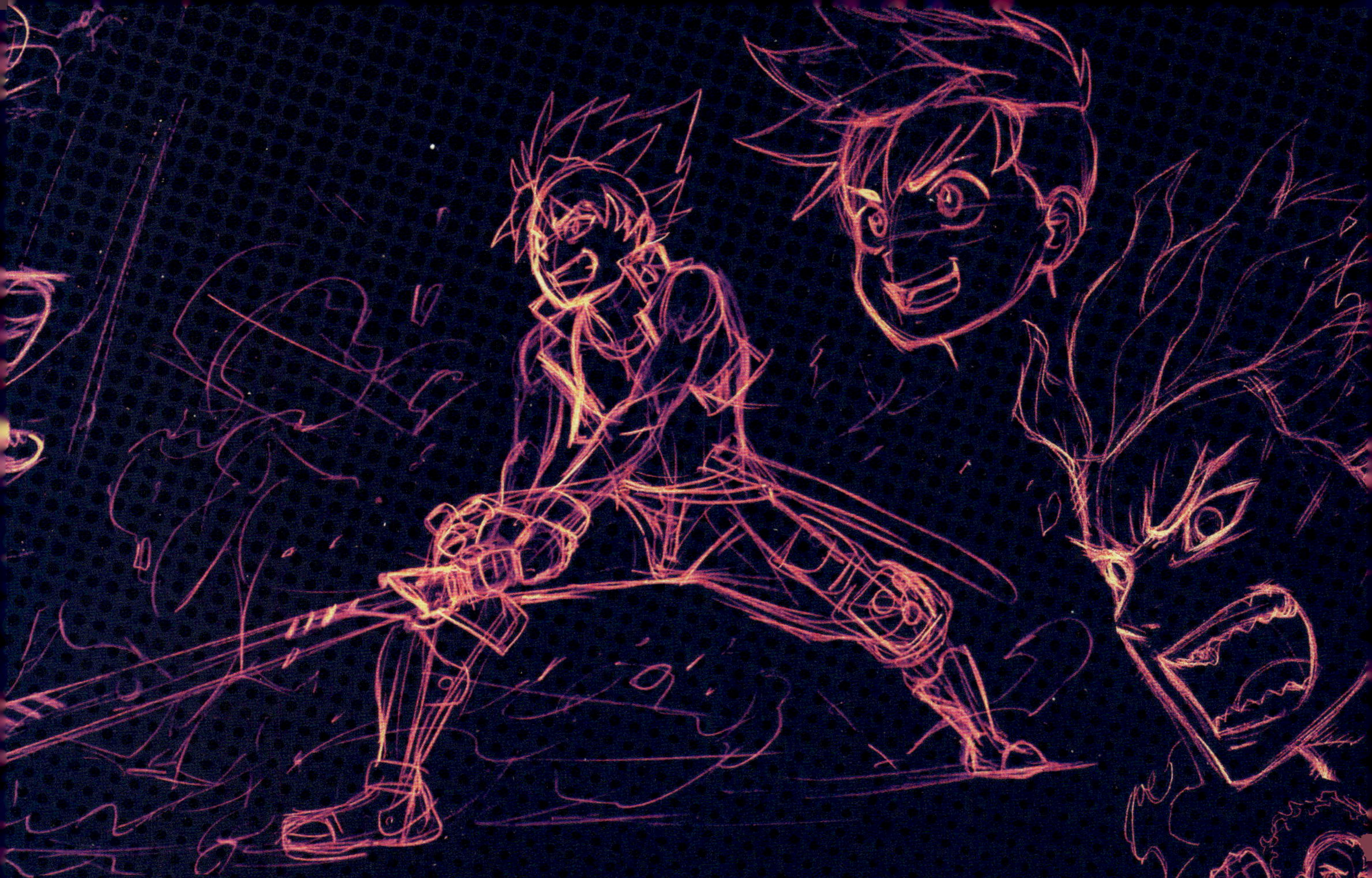

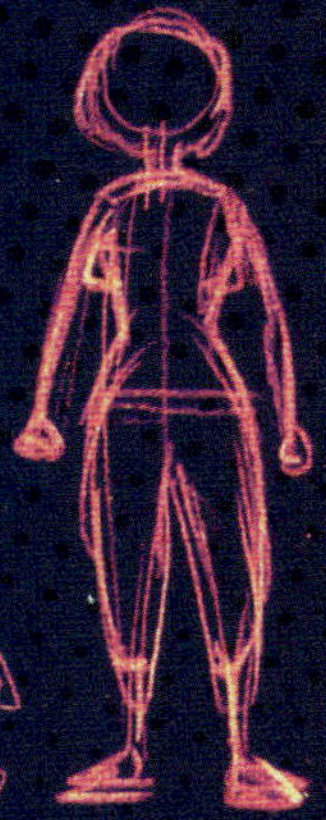

2. CHARACTER DESIGN

Action is entertaining in itself, and the medium of manga gives us complete creative freedom. As mangaka, we don't have to worry about budgets like filmmakers, but what is the point of the most intense battle, the fiercest fight, or the most athletic sports match, if the characters are soulless and simply uninteresting? That's why, in this chapter, we want to look at the basic features of the topic of character design. The aim: to develop vivid characters who earn the readers' empathy.

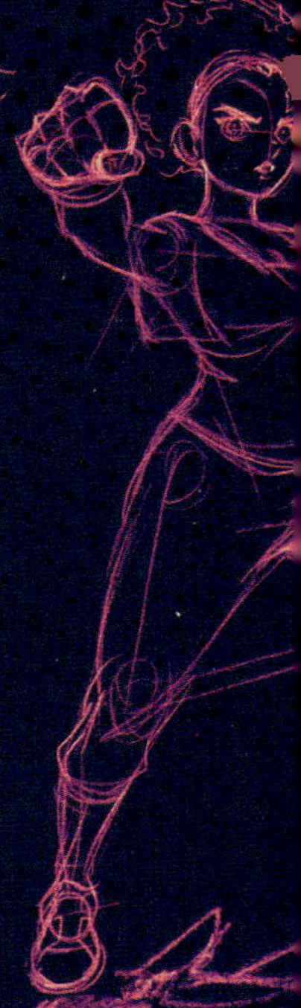

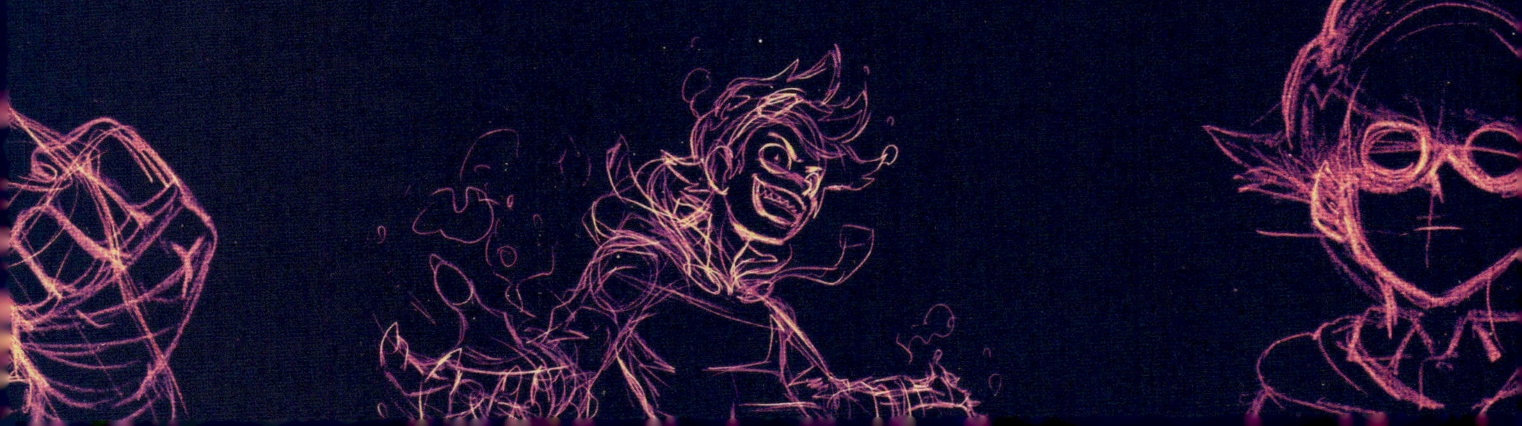

DEVELOPING CHARACTERS

When it comes to developing a completely new story, there are two possible approaches: you can either start with a rough plot and then add in the characters, or begin by developing the characters and then spin the story around them. For our purposes, we'll go with the latter, because well-developed characters interacting with each other leads to dynamic exchanges, and that's where the action is, in the concept.

FIRST DRAFTS

Let's start with the heroes of our project. Teenage boys with a striking hairstyle are classic for the genre, so I start by sketching out a few ideas for possible protagonists.

Here, you can see a first draft in both front view and profile. The character comes across as an upbeat adventurer who is fleet of foot, but he still lacks depth so I'm not quite satisfied yet.

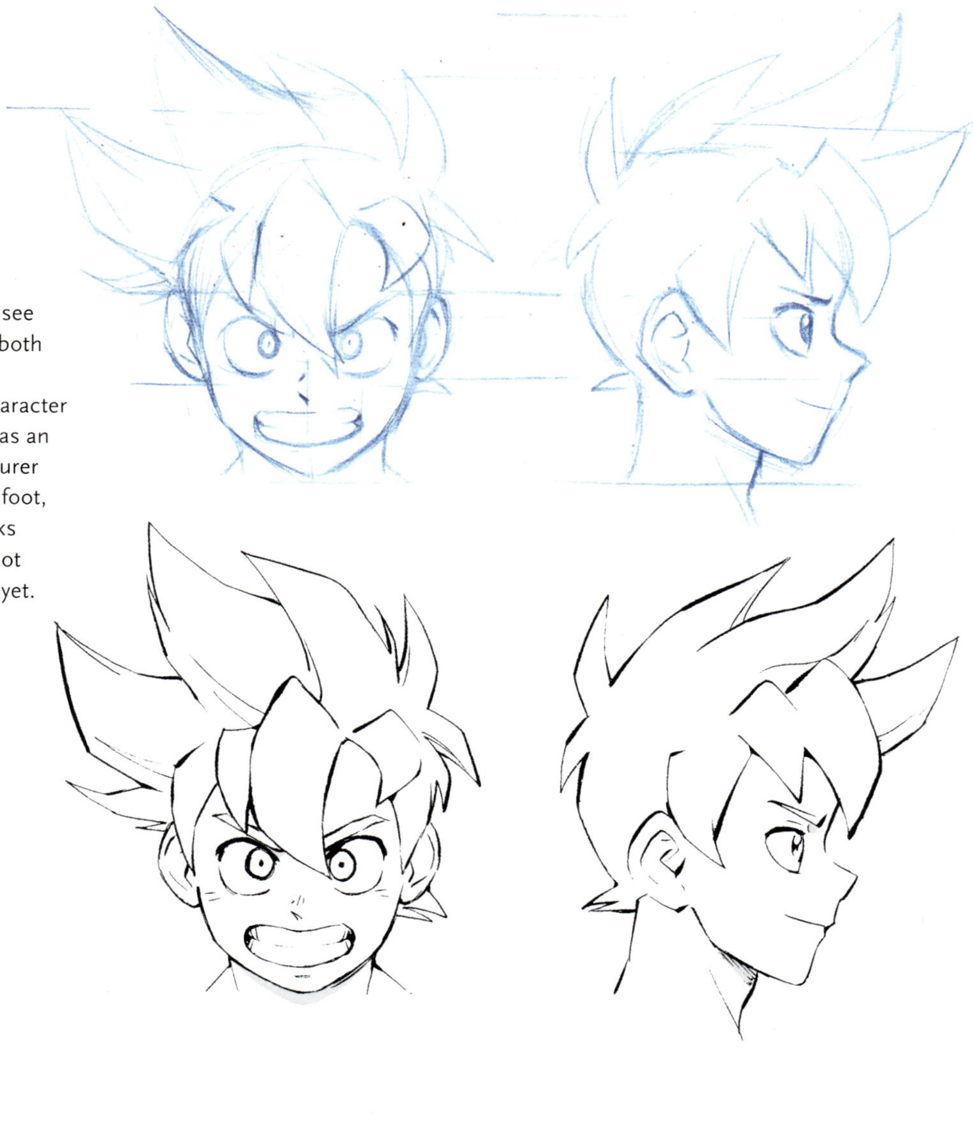

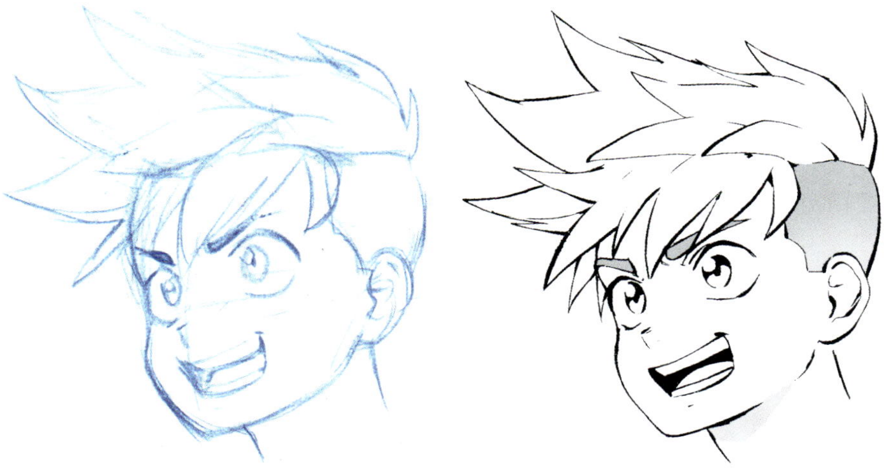

It's heading in the right direction, but I'm still not completely convinced. By the way, even something like the hair color can make a huge difference in a case like this, but I'm not quite sold on the dark-haired version either.

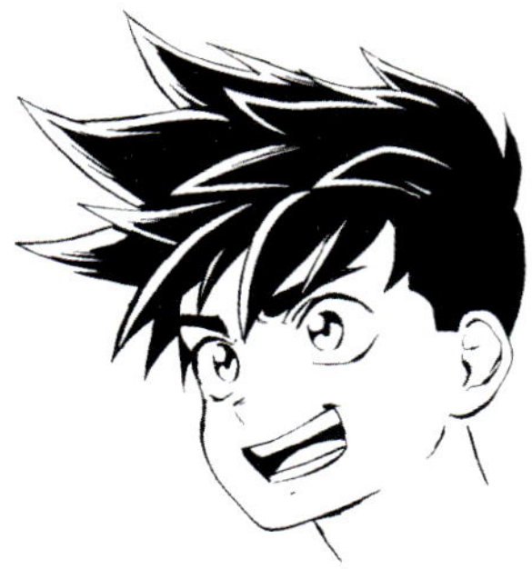

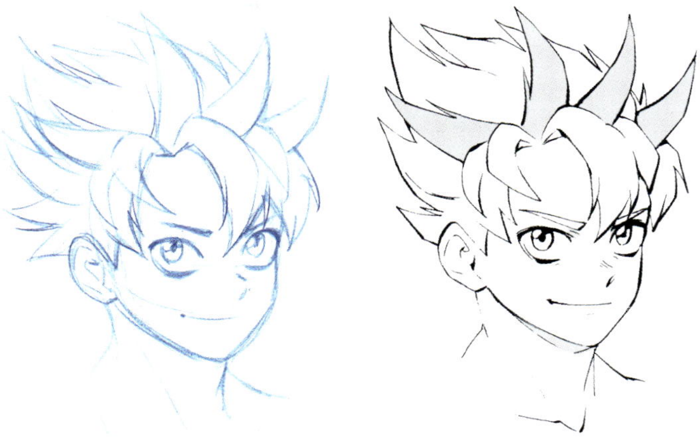

This design works for me! The odd two-tone hairstyle, a determined gaze that already hints at a bit more depth, and the beginnings of dark circles under the eyes – this character has potential!

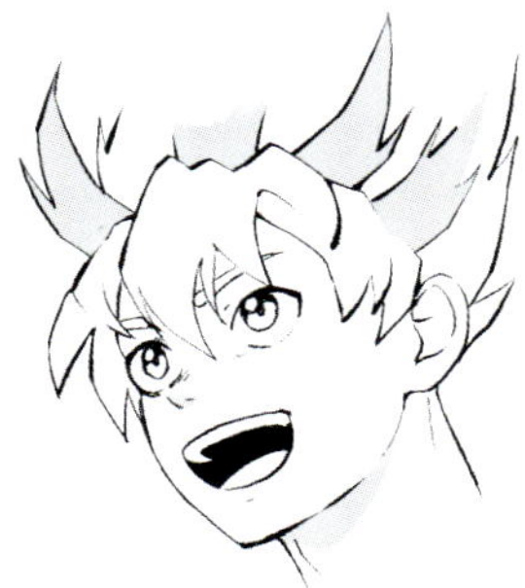

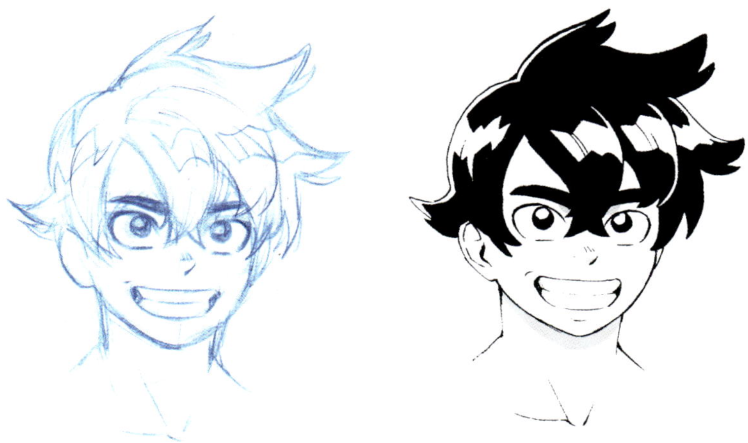

For our concept, we're going with two protagonists, so I draw up another character with a classic messy mop of dark hair. You might already notice that even though they're roughly the same age, there are already some clear contrasts. Quite literally in the different black areas, but also in smaller details like the eyes or how softly the hair falls. On the next double page, we'll develop those contrasts even further.

WHOLE BODY VIEWS

At this point, we are defining body types and outfits that might stay with us throughout an entire manga, so this is an issue worthy of extra thought. After all, you'll be drawing every single detail over and over again. If your story involves a lot of action – and especially fight scenes – then the clothing should suit that. It's also a good idea to include elements that enhance the dynamism of action sequences. Hairstyles, accessories like scarves fluttering in the wind, or belts and ribbons are all simple ways of doing this.

Hero A gets a warrior-inspired look, like a cyber samurai. His appearance is aggressive, underlined through his strong postures as well as the warning stripes on his vest.

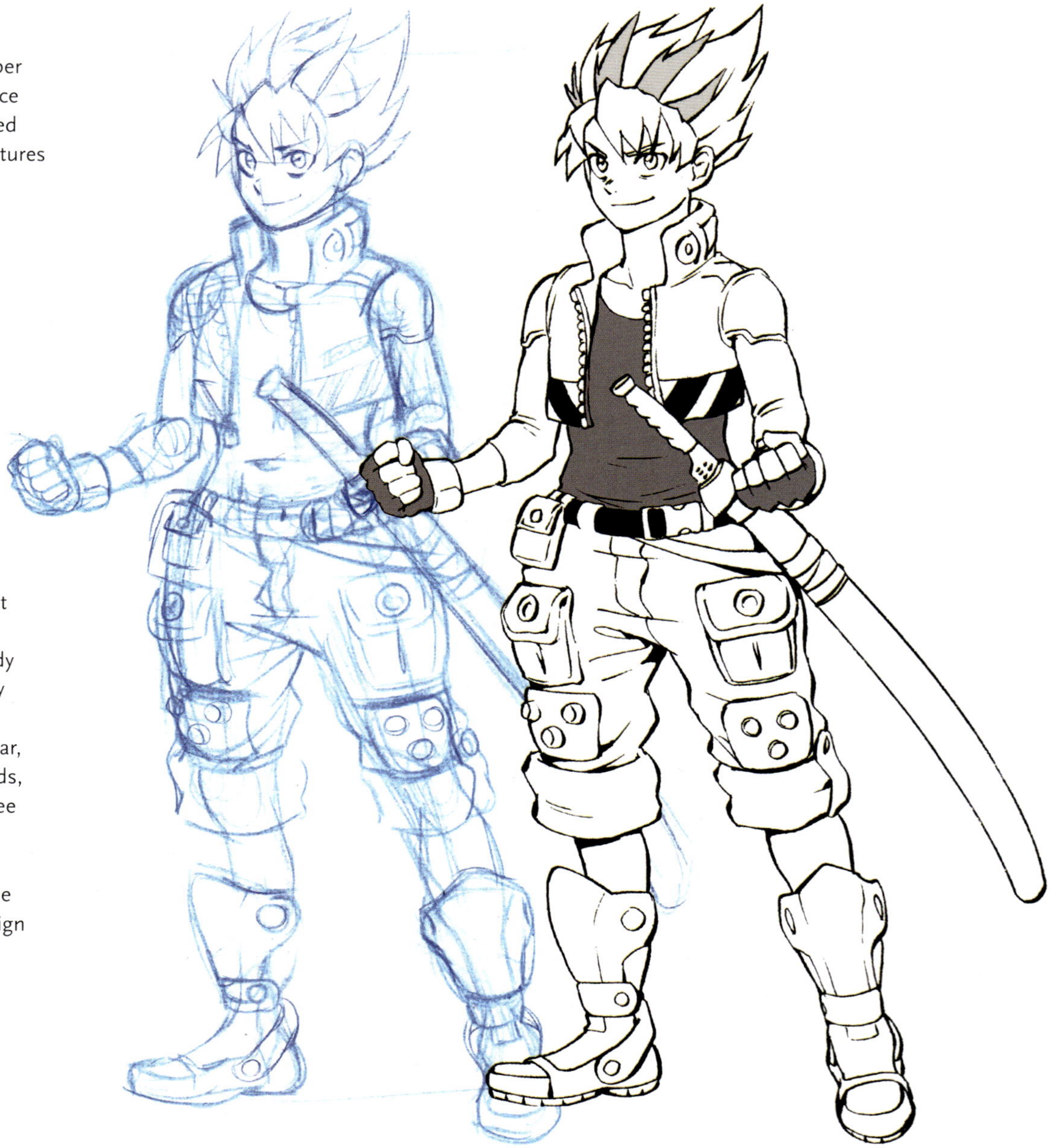

However, his outfit isn't just for intimidation – it's also functional. Body parts that are especially vulnerable are better protected: the high collar, the light shoulder guards, gloves, wrist wraps, knee pads, reinforced boots. First and foremost, the clothes should of course look cool, but their design also tells us a lot about where this character comes from and what they've been through.

Hero B looks more normal (in his default state; later his design will become less ordinary): modern, more comfortable clothes, and a more relaxed posture than Hero A. Here, the contrasts from the previous double page are further enhanced. Hero A has light hair and clothing, while Hero B has a darker look with black areas. Aggressive and battle-ready vs. relaxed and casual. Tall vs. a head shorter. Armed vs. (seemingly) unarmed. Look closely at the silhouettes on the right. There are several clear distinguishing features, easily identifying the two even from a distance.

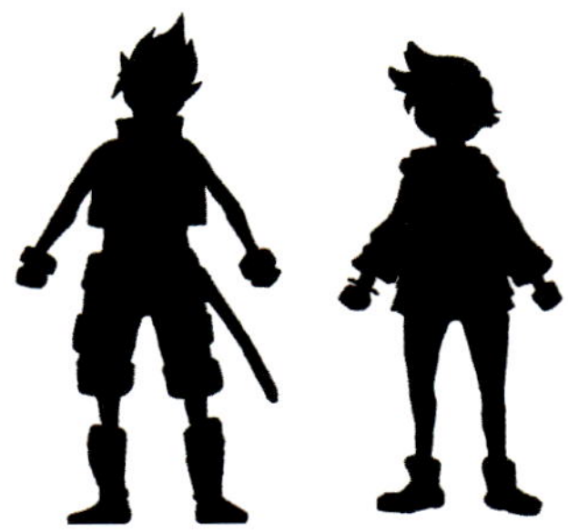

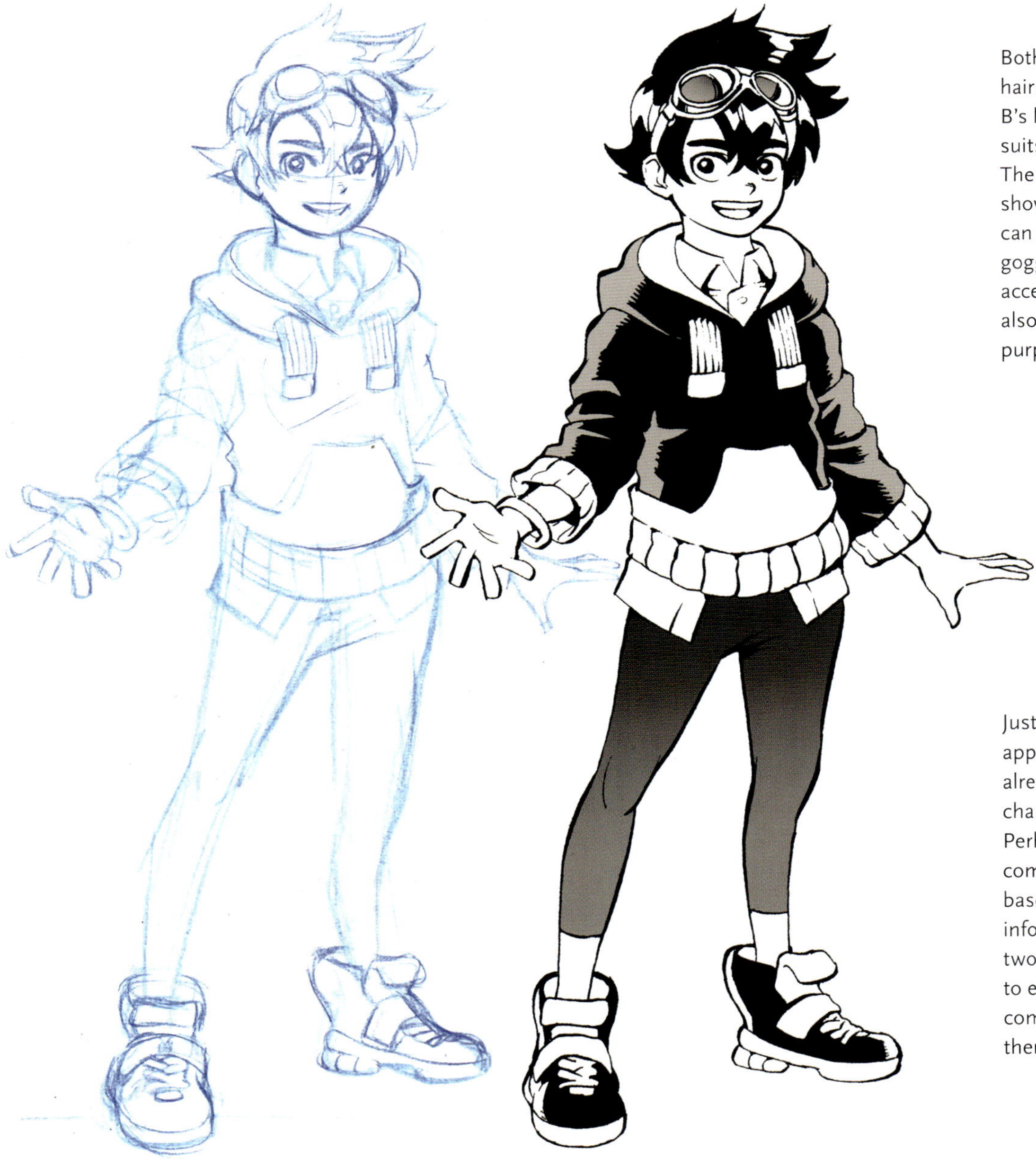

Both heroes have messy hairstyles. However, Hero B's hair is looser, which suits his overall appearance. The following pages will show how this element can be played with. The goggles are a classic manga accessory, but here they'll also serve a practical purpose. More on that later.

Just by looking at their appearances, you can already get a sense of their character and other traits. Perhaps you've already come up with some ideas, based purely on the visual information, about how the two of them might relate to each other, where they come from, what motivates them, and so on.

THE CHARACTER DIAMOND

When it comes to creating characters, there are countless approaches and models that can help. One that focuses primarily on the core aspects of a character will be the subject of the next few pages: the **Freeman Character Diamond**.

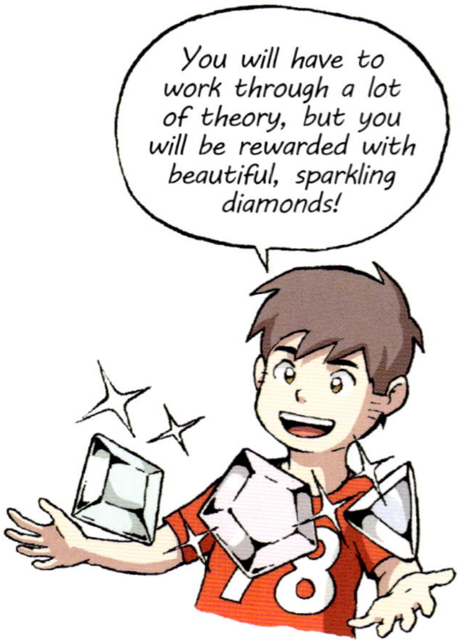

Screenwriter and novelist David Freeman developed this simple yet effective model as a tool for other writers to create strong characters who stand out through a few distinctive character traits, or their unique combination. The diamond or polygon shape is used for illustration; each corner represents one of the core traits. The more corners there are, the more complex the character becomes.

1 **NUMBER OF CORNERS**
Background or secondary characters with brief appearances typically only require one or two traits. For readers, it is enough to know, for example, what profession the character has (conveying a core skill). In an action scene where the hero faces off against a small army of many uniformed enemies, it is sufficient to know that the enemies, for instance, belong to a gang.

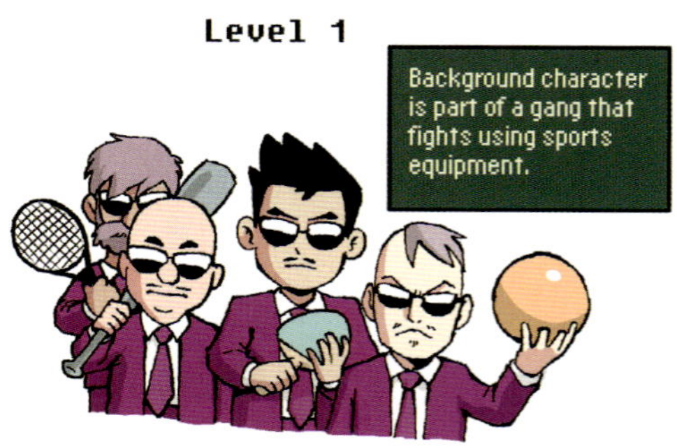

2 This function or character trait is tied to further pieces of information, for example: that the character is just a henchman and not a boss or general, that the enemies are battle-hardened due to their training, their moral principles, and so on.

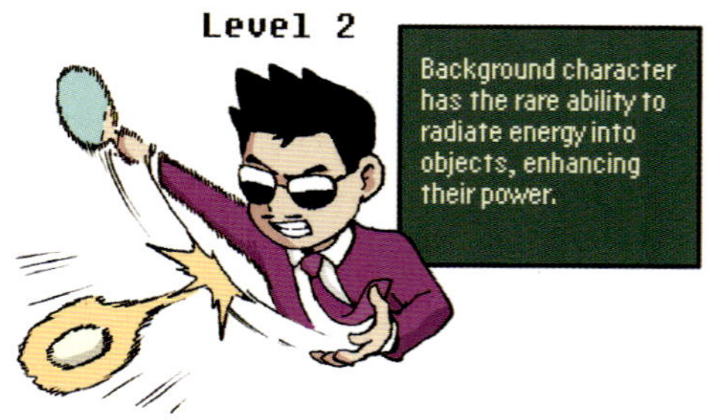

3

Three "corners" work well for supporting characters who appear more frequently or for longer in the story. Even with just three, you can already create some pretty interesting combinations. Many manga protagonists actually don't go beyond three character traits (unfortunately), which isn't exactly a great sign, and something we want to avoid.

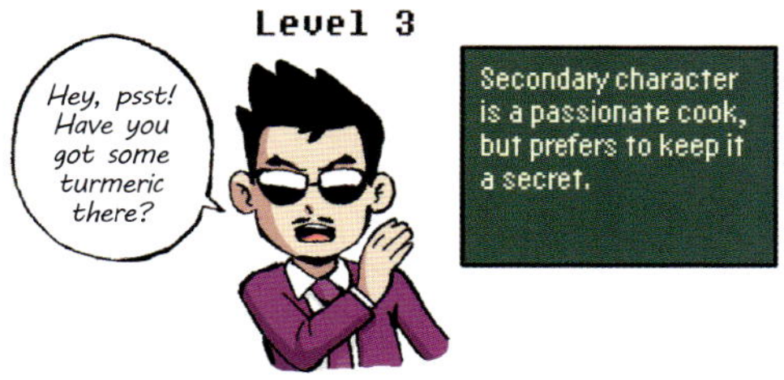

4

Four corners are a solid benchmark and will be enough for most characters who play bigger roles in a story. It's a good balance to make a character interesting, but not overly complex.

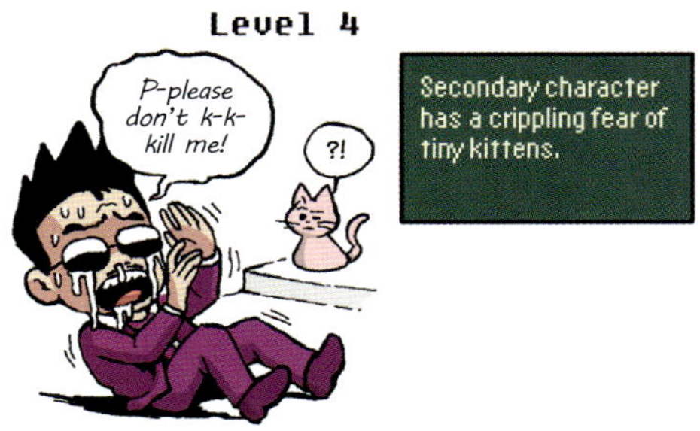

5

Five corners are ideal for all main characters. A mix of five character traits which are not all completely conventional almost guarantees a unique character design. That's why we also want to take a closer look at this diamond later.

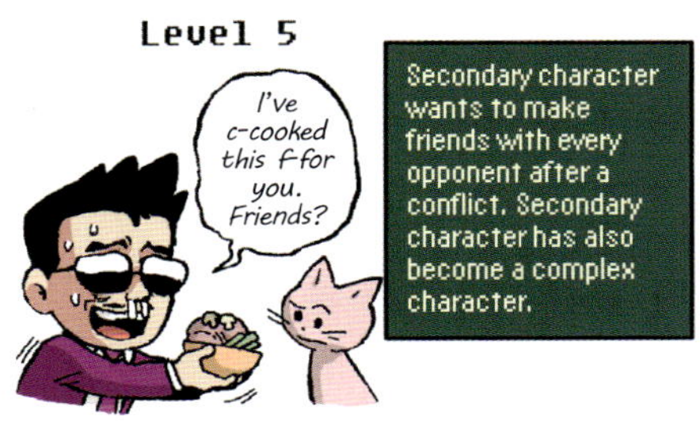

6

In special cases, you can also use more than five corners. This usually happens in long-running series, where an important character might gain a new defining trait long after their introduction. The main character suddenly turns out to be an alien or a reincarnated god, or gains a twist through some backstory element that flips everything on its head. This is totally legitimate and can bring fresh impetus to the story. However, a **sixth corner** has to be earned, because it instantly makes everything more complex; and if the sixth corner is something with a big impact, you need to think carefully before going ahead, because it can also put readers off by making them suddenly feel like they don't really know their beloved hero anymore.

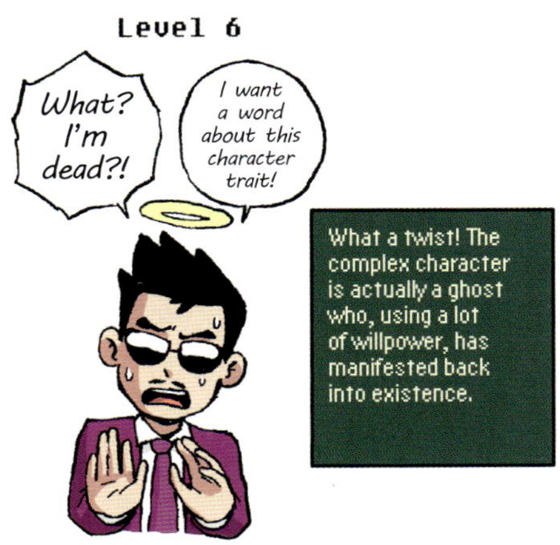

CHARACTER TRAITS

So what exactly is a character trait, or a defining quality? When using this model, a few common mistakes tend to pop up. Let's take a quick look at the most common ones.

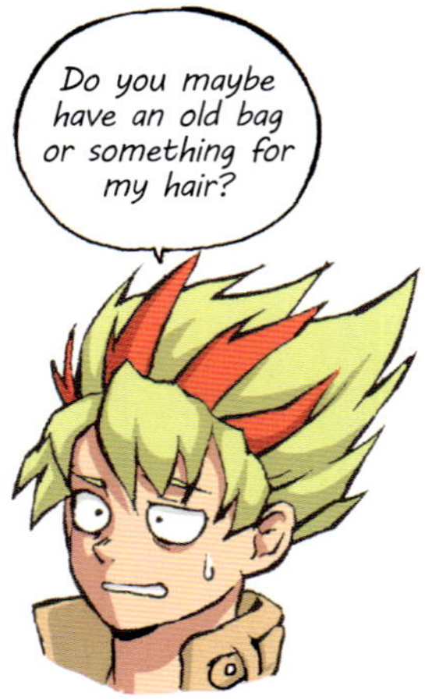

1 A physical feature is not a character trait!

Green hair, tall stature, or silver, sparkling eyes are not in themselves defining corners of a character diamond. But they *can* become part of one: in a world of tiny creatures, the tall one clearly stands out, and that quality takes on a defining role. Green hair might reflect a punk attitude. In that case, the character trait would be "punk", and the hairstyle would simply be a visual expression of it. Silver eyes could be the mark of a nearly extinct race which the character belongs to. Then, the ancestry or ethnicity would be the character trait, and the eyes a supporting detail.

2 Are your traits really different?

Sometimes it feels like you've filled all the corners of your diamond, until you take a closer look and realize that one trait is just a corollary of another. In the worst case, you've actually got three traits that are really just one. For example: "intelligent", "collects rare books", and "good with computers". These can all be rolled into one character trait: "inquisitive" and the other characteristics are secondary to this one.

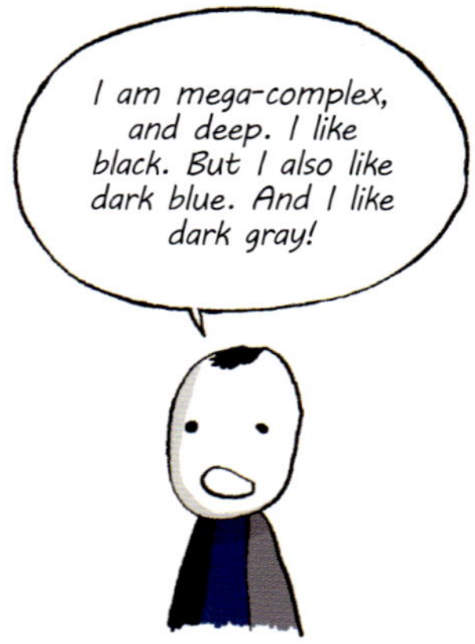

3 Does the trait really define the character?

Not every preference, obsession, quirk, phobia, and so on, is worth having its own corner on the diamond. For each trait, ask yourself whether it has a fundamental influence on how the character sees the world.

ASSIGNMENT

Now you know: a main character should have five defining traits. In addition, they also have many other traits, preferences, hobbies, and so on, but these don't fundamentally shape them. Take a few central characters from manga, anime, but also from films, novels, and other narrative media, and try to break them down into their five central character traits. It's possible that two people might analyze the same character and come up with slightly different results. That's okay, because sometimes it also depends on the individual perspective you have as a reader or viewer. What's important is that with this exercise, you can practice recognizing which qualities truly stand out and which can be bundled together into a character trait.

I am also taking on the assignment and creating the diamonds for three well-known heroes. You can find the answers on the next page.

Motivation: wants to be the strongest.

Carries within him the power of a giant were-ape ("Ōzaru").
- Has a monkey tail, which is initially his greatest weakness.
- Transforms into the giant ape during a full moon and goes berserk.

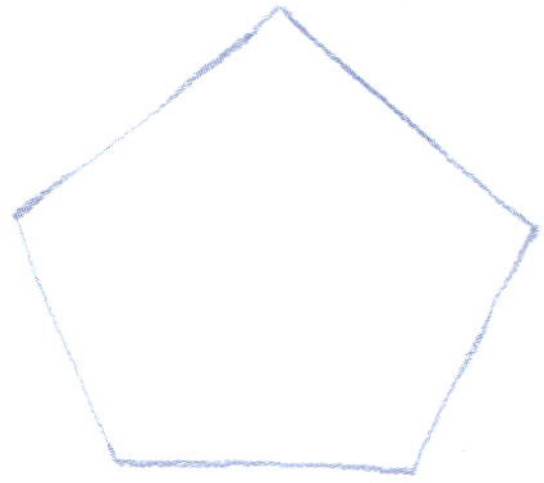

Gullible.
- Optimist.
- Loyal to his comrades in arms.
- Very stupid.

Strong fighter.
- Trains a lot and under extreme conditions.
- Can use supernatural techniques.
- Combat genius who comes up with creative solutions.

Extremely greedy.
- Devours inhuman amounts of food and is strongly influenced by food.

Motivation: wants to be King of the Pirates.

Ate Gum-Gum Fruit.
- Gained Devil Powers (superpowers) as a result. Body is made of rubber with the corresponding qualities.
- As a result, can no longer swim.

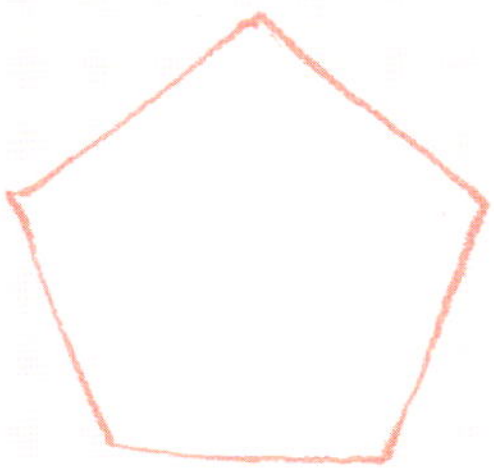

Gullible.
- Optimist.
- Loyal.
- Quite stupid.
- Makes many friends and allies.

Strong fighter.
- Trains a lot and under extreme conditions.
- Has access to various supernatural abilities.
- Combat genius who comes up with creative solutions.

Extremely greedy.

Motivation: wants to become Hokage (the mayor of his village, which essentially means he wants to become the strongest).

Carries a huge fox monster inside him.
- Has access to special power (superpowers) as a result.
- Has conversations with the fox – conflict!
- People are afraid of him – he is an outsider because of that.

Gullible.
- Optimist.
- Loyal.
- Not the brightest.
- Believes in the goodness of people.
- Wants lots of friends.

Is a ninja.
- Trains a lot and under extreme conditions.
- Has access to various supernatural abilities.
- Combat genius who comes up with creative solutions.

Likes to eat noodle soup.

SOLUTION

So, did you recognize them? Of course you did! The three most popular manga heroes that the classic *shōnen* battle manga has produced: Son Goku from *Dragon Ball*, Monkey D. Luffy from *One Piece*, and Naruto Uzumaki from *Naruto* are the characters behind these three pentagons.

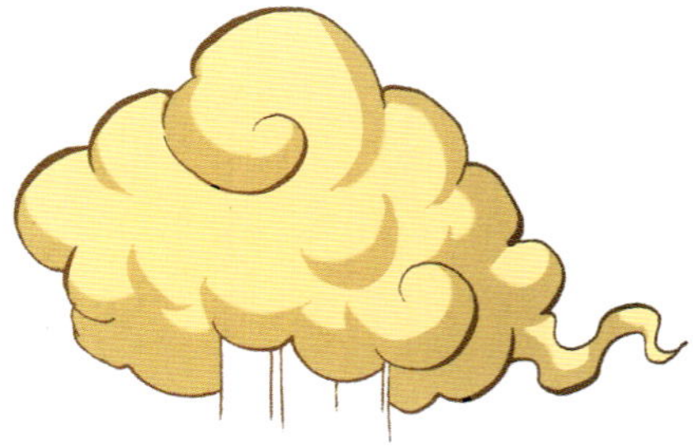

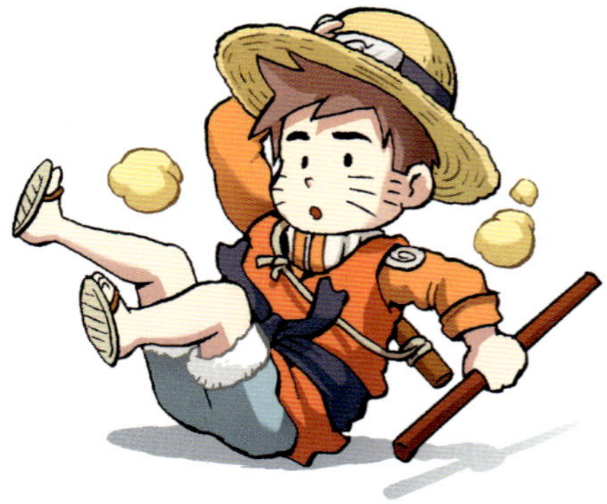

You will have noticed the following:

- These three characters are very similar in many respects. Some of their characteristics are basically identical. All three are somewhat defined by food, for example. Favorite foods are not normally legitimate character traits for the diamond, but in all these three cases they are, because two of them are absolute gluttons and Naruto's visits to his favorite ramen restaurant are essential for him, for social reasons alone.
- All three have supernatural powers, fueled by several sources. Different masters, different forces of nature made docile, mysterious powers that are already anchored in their genes, etc.
- All three have glaring weaknesses or other disadvantages that are directly linked to their enormous powers.
- All three have a relatively low IQ as a further weakness, but they make up for it with their engaging social behavior.
- All three are strong fighters and want to be the strongest. Who or what exactly is the strongest in each world is defined differently. But the basic drive is the same for all of them.

Despite all these similarities, they're still easy to tell apart, because each pentagon is ultimately unique in the world of pop culture, and each one brings its own interesting **potential for conflict** – both within the character and in the world around them. That means tension between different character traits (for example: the hero wants friends, but people avoid him because of the power inside him), but also between the protagonist's goals and the world he lives in (e.g, the hero wants to live as a pirate, but that makes him an outlaw who's constantly being hunted).

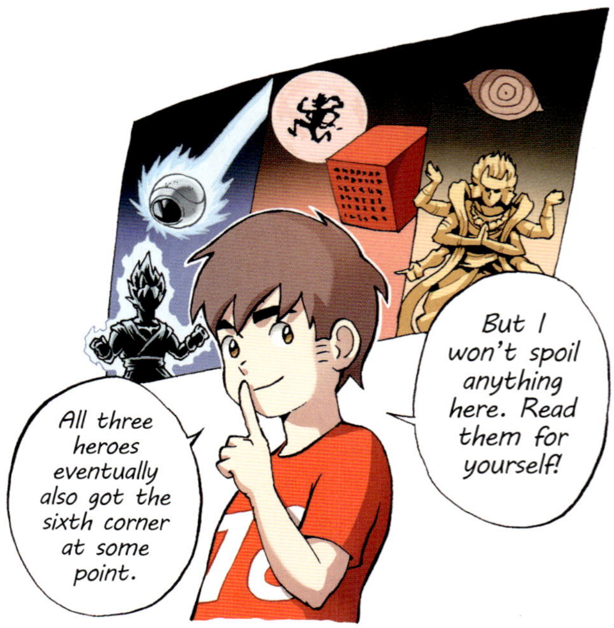

SPEAKING OF CONFLICT POTENTIAL:
Think about who the rivals – the figures they have to measure themselves against – are for these three heroes. Not just the villains, but also the friends they're in constant competition with (Vegeta for Son Goku, Trafalgar Law for Luffy, Sasuke for Naruto, and so on). You'll notice that among the opponents, there are many similarities (often more similarities than differences), but there's always one or two key differences that are enough to create a socio-dynamic tension between the characters, which can easily carry an entire series for dozens of volumes.

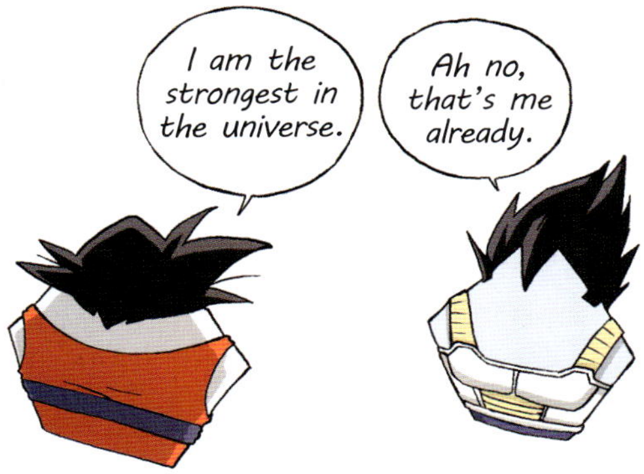

AVOID MARY SUES AND GARY STUS!

The most boring character type you can create is one without weaknesses. Even worse is a character who is exceptionally good at everything. For female protagonists who fit this description, there's the derogatory term "Mary Sue", and for the male counterpart, "Gary Stu".

There have always been characters who are far too versatile and succeed at everything. However, the Mary Sue phenomenon emerged in modern pop culture when fan fiction gained importance. These are stories written by fans that take place in an already established fictional universe, and introduce a new character who immediately shows the established characters how good they are at everything. The result is a plot that lacks tension, where every looming problem is nipped in the bud because Mary Sue and Gary Stu always have the solution, leaving the other heroes in awe.

So think about the weaknesses of your character! Throw them at the other characters in your story to chew on, instead of making them universally liked. Even if it's your alter ego, be honest with yourself and maybe even exaggerate a minor flaw.

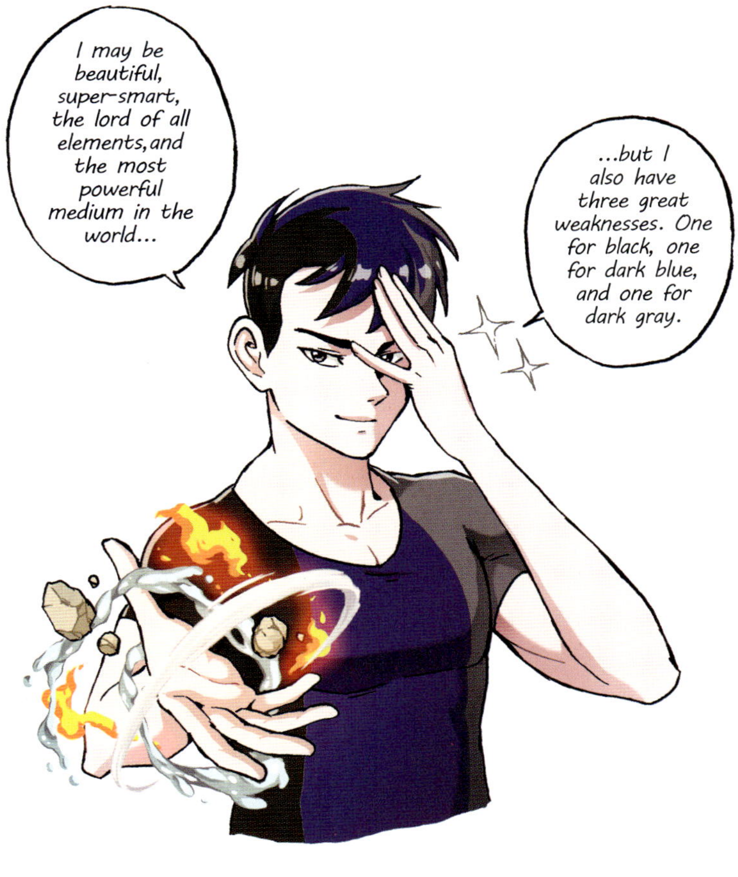

CHARACTER DIAMOND: HERO A

We know the theory, and we've practiced on examples. Now, let's create our own heroes with unique character diamonds! Firstly, Hero A gets five character traits.

Here are some final tips for creating character diamonds:

- Work out the character's motivation clearly.
- Distribute strengths, but also weaknesses.
- Also plan for friction between some of the points.
- Include at least one unusual point. A strange quirk, an exotic hobby, or something similar.
- Try to incorporate ideas from others. Ask your fellow human beings for a few characteristics and force yourself to integrate them. This will bring completely different impulses into the character and you will be forced to implement the ideas spontaneously and creatively.

Motivation: must trap 100 demon souls in his sword to free his own soul.

- Has a time limit before his soul is lost.
- Is under pressure because of this.

Is a kind of battle exorcist.

- Strong warrior and swordsman.
- Fights with a cyber sword that can wound demons and absorb and trap them.

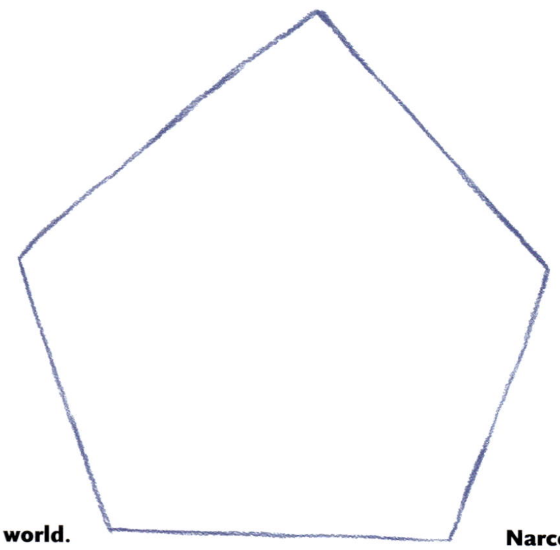

Very quick-tempered and overzealous.

- Always has ants in his pants.
- Wants to know everything; is curious.
- Can't stay focused on something for long; easily distracted.

Out of place in the modern world.

- Spent his life so far in a remote exorcist training facility far from civilization.
- Only knows strange, exotic exorcist culture with bizarre food, rituals, etc.
- Must first find his way in our world.

Narcoleptic.

- Can fall asleep unexpectedly and at any time.
- Underestimates his energy expenditure.

There he is, our Hero A. We started with just a look, a rough setting, and a genre, and now we have a character with a lot of soul – ironically, without a soul, as he has to reclaim it (but a connection is still there, so our hero can still be passionate and emotional). Recovering the soul sets everything in motion and brings a **time pressure** to the story, which is always good for an action title as it keeps the pace up.

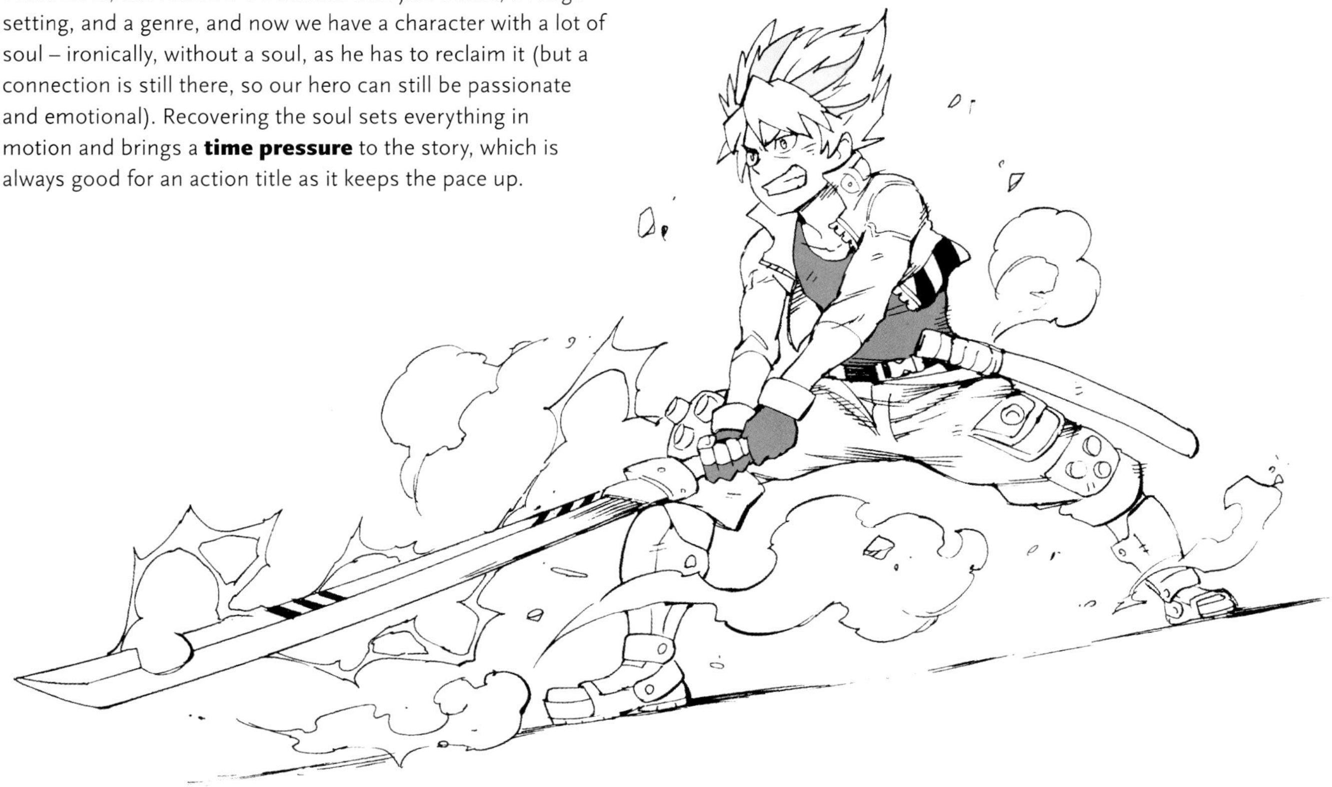

We also have some conflicts between his character traits. Hero A is under pressure because he only has a certain amount of time to trap 100 demon souls. Nevertheless, he is curious and easily distracted (a weakness that can also be a strength at times). Of course, this offers a lot of **comedy potential**. Then there's the narcolepsy, which suddenly pulls the hero out of the action and into sleep. A glaring weakness, offering even more comedy potential.

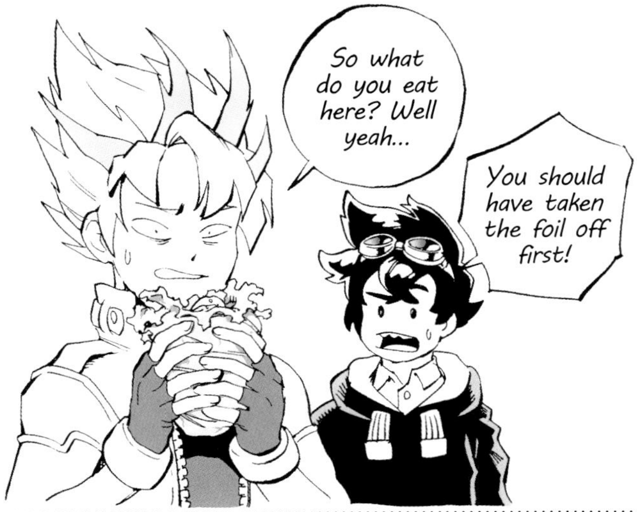

FISH OUT OF WATER

A unique element is that Hero A transitions from his familiar world to another, and we get to watch him learn the rules of the new culture. He will often appear helpless in the face of the unknown, which results in many interesting conflicts – he's like a fish out of water. This is an approach used, for example, in the popular *Isekai* genre. One of the greatest advantages of this device is that, as readers, we can experience the world of the manga alongside the hero, making the exposition – meaning the explanation of the setting, background information, and so on – feel much more natural.

CHARACTER DIAMOND: HERO B

Now let's create a character diamond for Hero B. As an equal protagonist alongside Hero A, we need to make sure that his motivation and his place in the world are not less relevant than his colleagues'. We also need to ensure that there is enough conflict potential between the two heroes' diamonds. Character traits and preferences should clash in a way that generates friction, leading to occasional flare-ups. These "frictions" can quickly escalate into an apocalyptic situation, especially in a *shōnen* battle manga. We'll start small for now, but who knows where the conflict potential between the two boys could lead if we let our little, spontaneously conceived series run long enough.

Motivation: seeks a path of peaceful coexistence between humans and demons.

- Ultimately, he wants to live a quiet and peaceful life.
- Knows that many demons are kind or can become kind.
- Also knows that other demons will stand in the way of this goal.

He is plagued by bad luck.

- He often stumbles (sometimes literally) from one mishap to the next.
- Sometimes, the bad luck is minor (like an inevitable fly in his drink), but sometimes it takes on catastrophic proportions (such as a building collapsing).

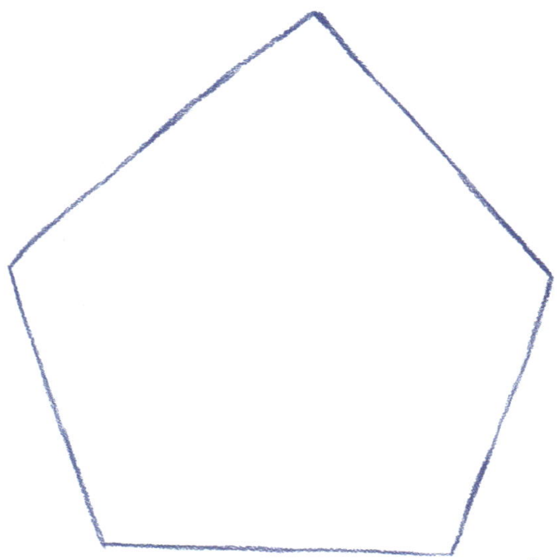

Carries 12 demons within him.

- Has the extraordinary ability to be a vessel for multiple demons.
- Lives in harmony with some of these demons.
- Some of the demons are dangerous and are mostly kept in check by Hero B.
- Hero B can let demons take control of his body, giving him access to their (sometimes supernatural) abilities.

He is weak, but brave.

- Despite many hardships, he stands up for people and his demon symbionts.
- Always finds ways out of sticky situations.
- Has lots of room to grow stronger.

Is sometimes like an old man.

- Due to his stressful everyday life plagued by constant bad luck and demons, he enjoys the brief moments of peace and quiet.
- Loves senior activities (drinking tea, crossword puzzles, feeding pigeons).

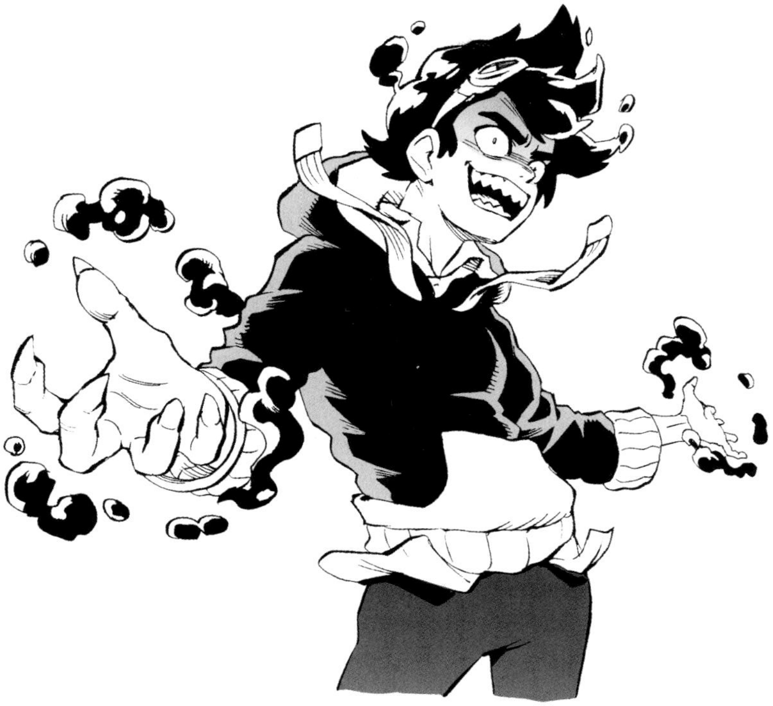

Allow me to introduce Hero B. In terms of character design, we are consistently continuing the approach we began with the visual design. Once again, it's all about contrasts. For instance:

- Hero A must exorcise demons in order to achieve his goal. Hero B carries 12 demons within him.
- Hero A sees demons as pure danger. Hero B sees them as companions.
- Hero A is bubbling over with a zest for action, which sometimes knocks him out with exhaustion. Hero B always finds himself involuntarily at the center of the action and can't imagine anything better than a moment of peace.
- Hero A is a well-trained fighter. Hero B is physically weak – but he can compensate for this by tapping into demon powers. More about that on the next double page.

FUNCTIONAL CLOTHING

We have already discussed how Hero A's clothing serves a practical purpose. That was clearer to see. A warrior who wears many protective elements but also carries his weapon openly on his body. Hero B, at first, just had a casual look. However, due to the character trait of his bad luck, the goggles and hoodie now serve a clear purpose. Both provide protection when Hero B once again finds himself in a sticky situation. Maybe he also has a tool in his hoodie pocket to fish the inevitable fly out of his drink...

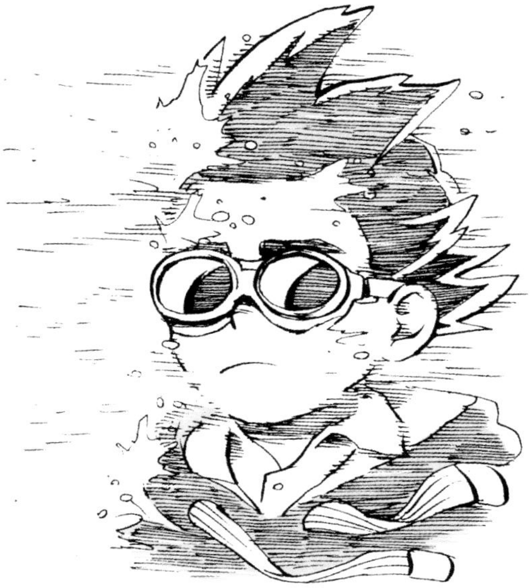

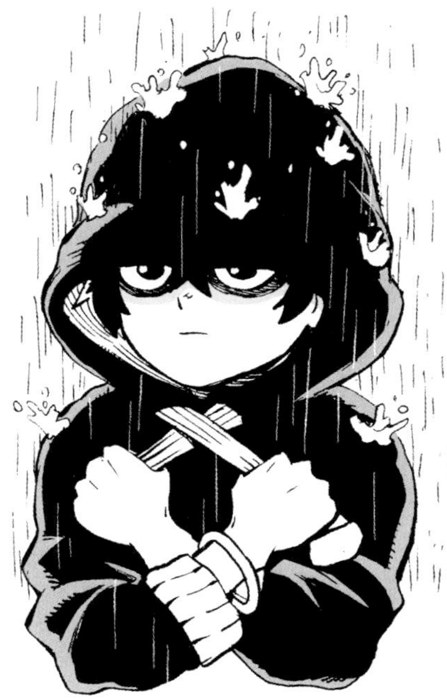

SUPERNATURAL POWERS

In the action genre, characters often have supernatural powers that are integrated into the plot, especially in battle scenes. Whether it's magic, supernatural beings, or ninja techniques, the powers should be logically structured and follow clear rules. In our example, this role is taken on by the demon symbionts.

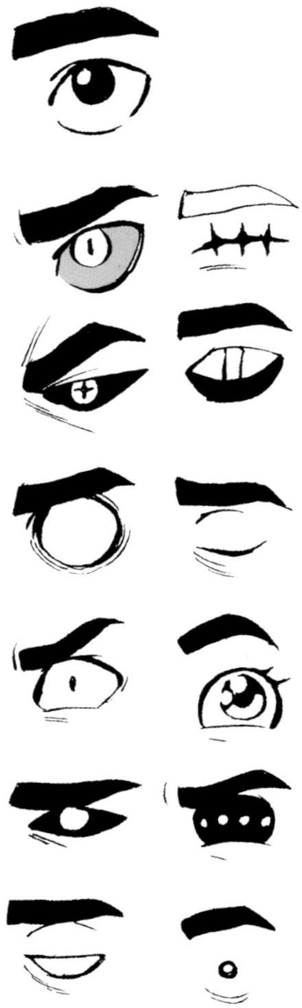

DEMON SYMBIONTS

Supernatural companions who occasionally take control of their host have a long tradition. What began with *Dr. Jekyll and Mr. Hyde* in novel form has become a staple of pop culture, especially through horror films and, of course, comics. In manga, this concept, which thrives on constant conflicts between characters sharing a body, has enjoyed decades of success. It also holds great potential for action scenes. Let's look at how we can integrate demon symbionts into a manga using Hero B's most prominent trait.

So, Hero B carries 12 demons inside him. This can be quickly written into the character diamond, and, naturally, it sounds exciting. Now, however, this expansive trait needs to be fleshed out with content. It would go beyond the scope of our example manga project to define 12 fully fleshed-out demons, each with their own skill set, but we can start by seeking inspiration with a first step.

We'll combine the exercise with a manga classic: **strange eyes**. This visual playground allows us to give the 12 demons – even before we truly get to know them – interesting eyes, which can then spark ideas about what kind of characters lie behind them.

On the left, you can see 13 eyes. At the top is the standard version: Hero B's eye in his normal human form. The four images below show the same crazed look as the example demon form from the previous page. There, it was established that transitioning into demon form also entails further visual adaptations (the sharp fingernails and wispy hair).

Some of the other eyes suggest more sinister demons, some are just more mysterious, and a few even seem to belong to funny symbionts. Appearances, however, may be deceptive. Finding out is a lot of fun. We'll give two of them a quick face here. What's the story behind the white-haired demon?

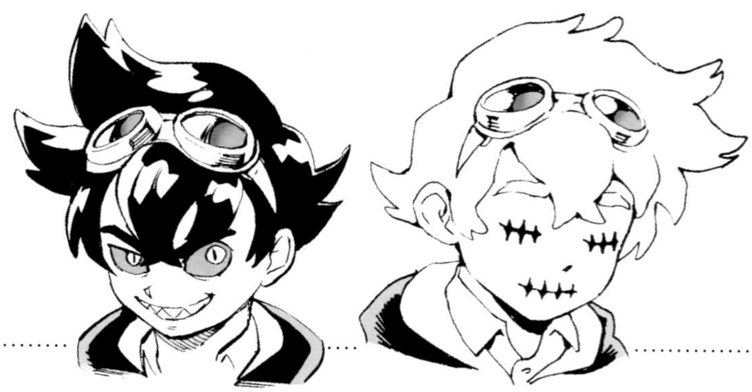

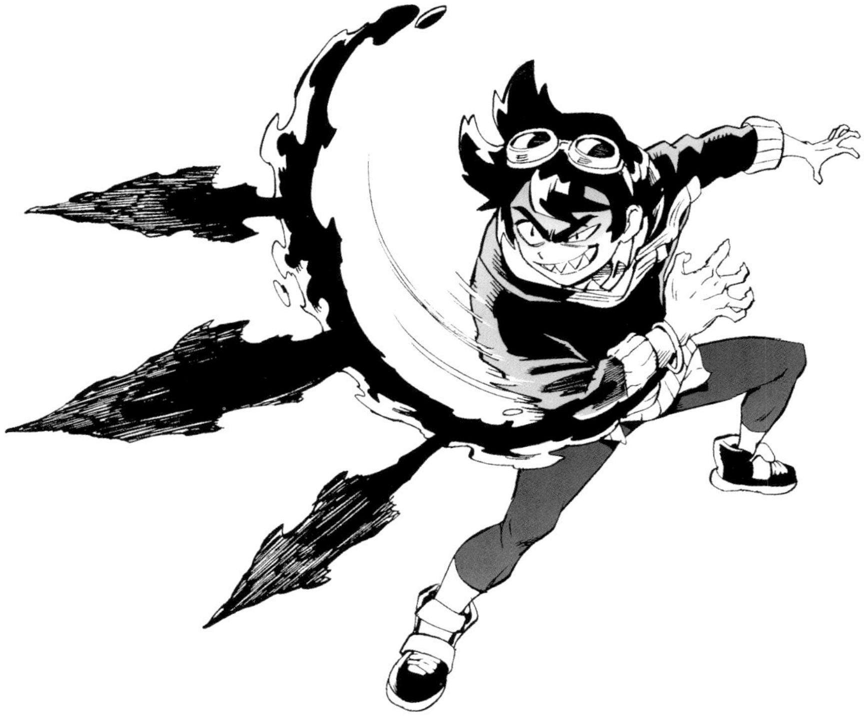

THE DEMONIC COST-BENEFIT FACTOR

Some of the demon forms and their abilities should, of course, be useful for attacks in a battle manga. This allows Hero B to have access to powers that would otherwise be inaccessible, a powerful bonus when facing enemies that would otherwise be too strong. Such power, however, always comes with a price. Perhaps the hero risks losing his body to the symbionts if he lets them take the helm for too long. Or maybe he suffers physical damage, shortens his lifespan, taints his soul, and becomes increasingly demonic himself. The question of how often to use the demon abilities introduces another exciting conflict that could escalate into the worst possible catastrophe.

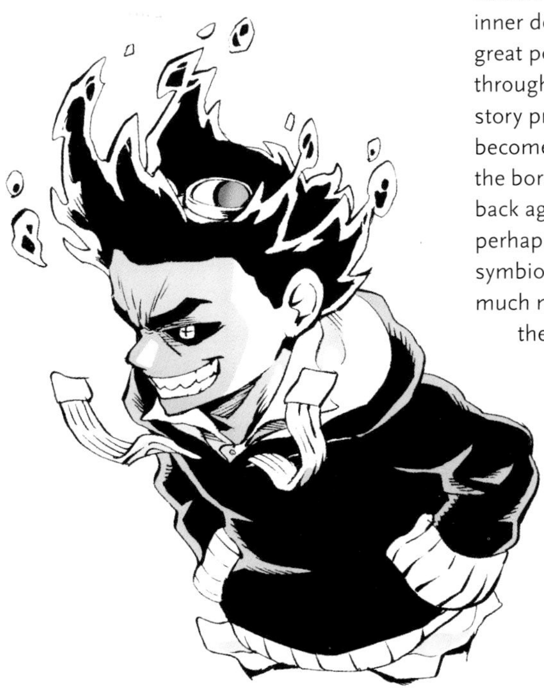

The beginning of a story like this will see the hero still struggling with himself, at odds with his inner demon, but relying on the great power within him to get through tough battles. As the story progresses, his goal is to become strong without relying on the borrowed power and to fight back against the demon within, perhaps even befriending it. With 12 symbionts, the situation becomes much more complex. Therefore, the different demons should be introduced and explored gradually. As a reader, knowing that there are still unknown demons within Hero B that will eventually make their grand appearance, adds another exciting element.

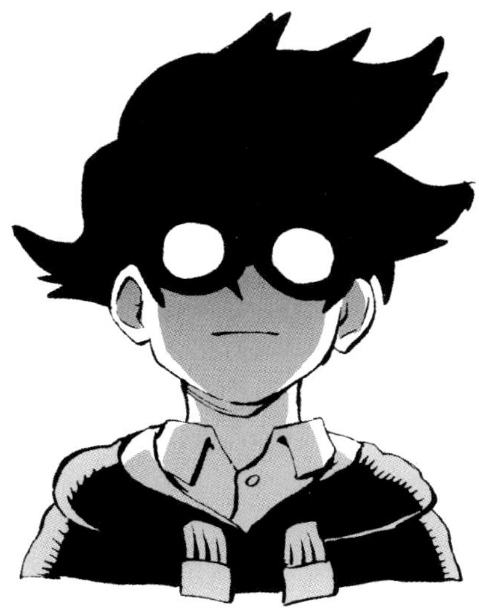

Is this one of the demon forms, or is Hero B just wearing his glasses? With mystery elements like this, there's a lot of room to play with the theme of demon possession.

THE MENTOR

Now we've established a hero duo for our little project, it's time to add an archetype essential to many action-packed stories: the mentor.

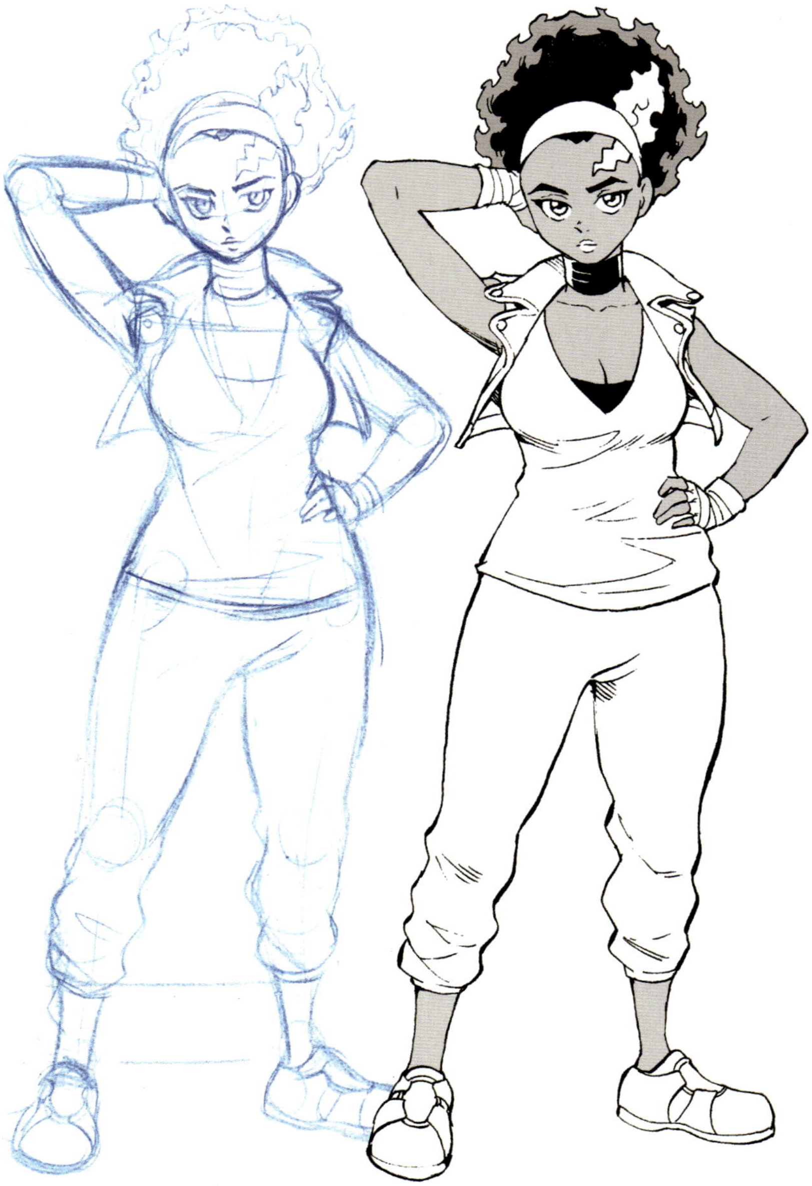

To further build on the **contrasts** between the protagonists, we will make this character a woman with a few years more life experience than the two teenage boys. She is also slightly taller than the heroes. She has dark skin, a different hairstyle, and her clothes are sportier.

She also has a mysterious scar on her forehead that seamlessly transitions into a white strand of hair. Why? First of all, because it looks cool and gives the character an immediate mysterious vibe. Her posture is confident to the point of superiority. The stern look accentuates this.

So much for the purely visual. On the following double page, we will also give this character some exciting traits by means of the character diamond.

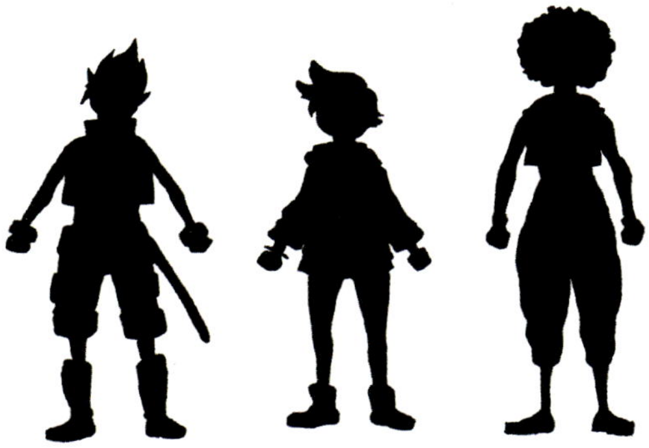

If we look at the extended silhouette comparison of the main character trio, we can still immediately recognize the character behind each shadow. Although the mentor has clear parallels to Hero A in the torso and arms (mainly due to the short vest), the other details are so different that there will never be any danger of confusion.

Mentors have always played a major role in stories. They impart knowledge and abilities and help the heroes on their journey to become strong enough to overcome the next big obstacle. The key stages in the interaction between the hero and the mentor are:
1 The Introduction: often, the hero has to convince the mentor to train them. Not infrequently, we see mentor figures embroiled in an existential crisis that must be overcome first.
2 The Training: training montages or entire training arcs – extensive educational storylines – are some of the scenes that a mangaka will have the most fun drawing. Questionable but creative training methods, totally exaggerated demands on the students, and eventually the realization that progress is actually being made – great progress, in fact – are among the most satisfying scenes in a hero's journey.
3 The Passing of the Baton: eventually, the student surpasses the mentor. The hero continues the teachings, while the mentor can now look for a new purpose in life. Many stories have the mentor die or retire at this point, but there are also plenty of counterexamples where the mentor continues to play an active role, and, for example, remains as a supporting character who gets involved in major events.

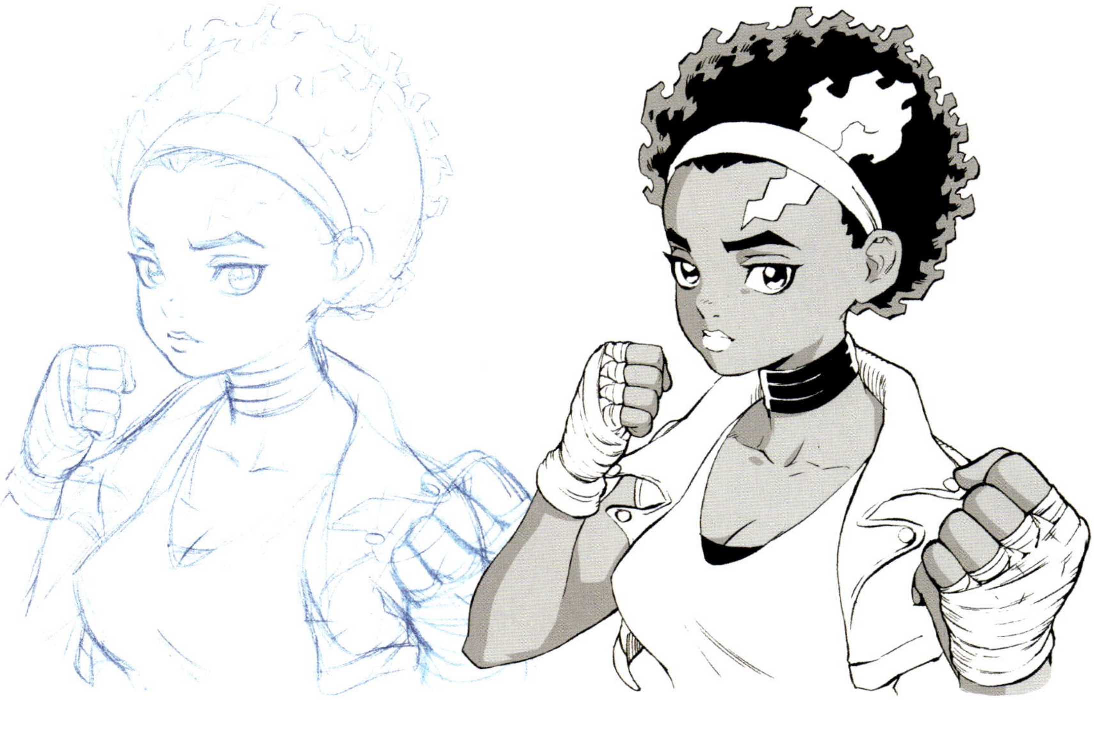

CHARACTER DIAMOND: MENTOR

Having covered the two hero boys, we now also have the character diamond for the mentor. Since this is a manga with a focus on combat and supernatural elements, we should design the mentor in such a way that she can impart knowledge and abilities in these areas. With her remaining qualities, we can and should focus heavily on entertainment value. Mentor characters in Japanese pop culture are often absolute fan favorites because they usually don't have to shoulder the heavy story burden, allowing them to act more relaxed and even be eccentric.

Motivation: wants to help the boys.

- We don't (yet) know why. But it's very important to her.
- Seems to want to resolve her own unfinished business through the boys.

Super-strong.

- Physically so powerful that she can break down the boundary between dimensions using pure muscle power.
- This makes her a kind of combat medium.
- She is the only "normal person" who can box ghostly apparitions.

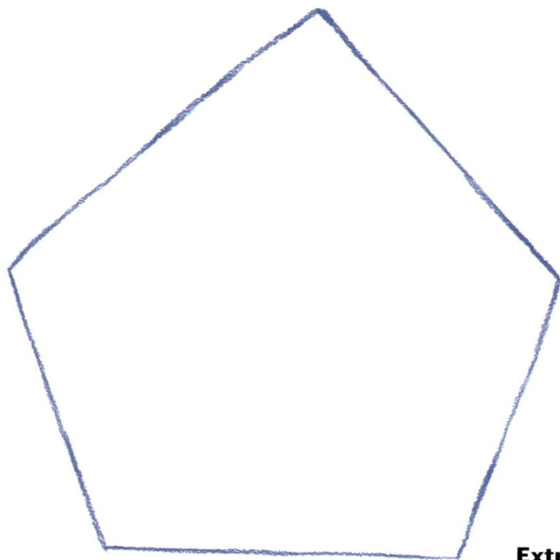

Mysterious past.

- Her scar and her motivation suggest that something terrible happened to her once, but she never goes into detail about it.
- She keeps dropping shocking hints and keeps running into people from her past, who hint at the most absurd anecdotes.
- Some things seem really bad and invite speculation; much of it, however, is so bizarre that it's just fun to read.

Vulgar.

- Has a really bad vocabulary.
- Swears a lot.
- Destroys friend and foe alike with devastating one-liners.
- Bad diction is also funny.

Extremely short-sighted.

- Too vain to admit that she has very poor eyesight. Therefore, she also refuses to wear glasses.
- Her poor vision is a weakness, but it also often leads to gags.

By now, you may have noticed how these diamonds work. We haven't discussed anything concrete about the plot of our sample project yet, only outlined a rough genre and theme, and defined the three most important characters both visually and in terms of substance. Even so, this is already enough for many scenes to almost write themselves. That's the big advantage of this model – if you always follow the rules, there will always be exciting interactions between the characters. With just three pentagonal diamonds, 15 traits already collide – some of them so absurd and conflict-laden that it's almost impossible not to draw entertainment value from it.

GATEWAY TO THE PAST

We don't know much about our mentor (as yet), but we do know that she knows a lot. This gives her another important function: **exposition**. That is, she can be the link to past events and characters that are relevant to the current events that Heroes A and B are facing.

However, make sure to avoid starting your project with what's called an **exposition dump**. These are mountains of (sometimes irrelevant) information about the world of your work that will overwhelm the readers. Let the heroes dive into the adventure knowing nothing at first, then use a character such as the mentor to give out exciting background information in bits and pieces.

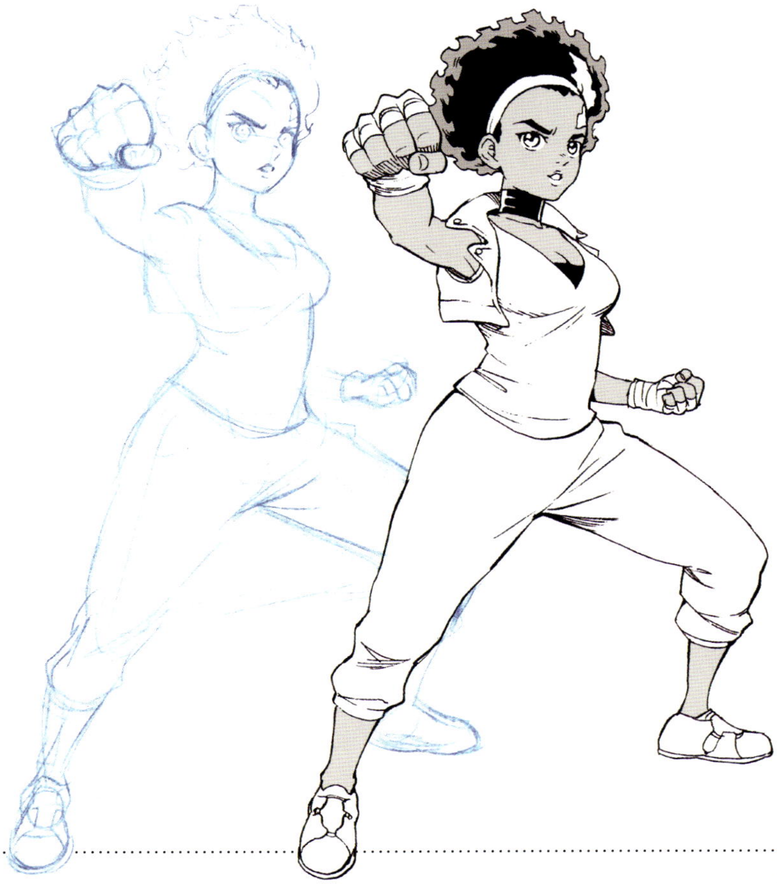

COMIC RELIEF

Four out of five corners of the mentor's character diamond have a strong potential for generating gags. We don't need to flesh out too much of the story to imagine how she'll pummel the two boys with the most ludicrous insults, or how she'll give the ghost who's confident in their invulnerability a good smack on their ectoplasmic cheeks. Or the absurd stories from her past, hinted at in the most inappropriate moments, and her short-sightedness, which makes her approachable in an endearing way.

All of this serves as comic relief, a jocular way to lighten up an otherwise serious plot. Hero A brings a lot of gag potential to the trio with his fish-out-of-water trope and his narcolepsy. Hero B adds to it with his constant bad luck, maybe a few quirky demons using him as a host, and his occasional grandad-like behavior. The action genre lends itself wonderfully to the use of humor to lighten up the plot. Serious tales are fine, but pure drama without any humor doesn't work, just like pure constant comedy without any serious moments.

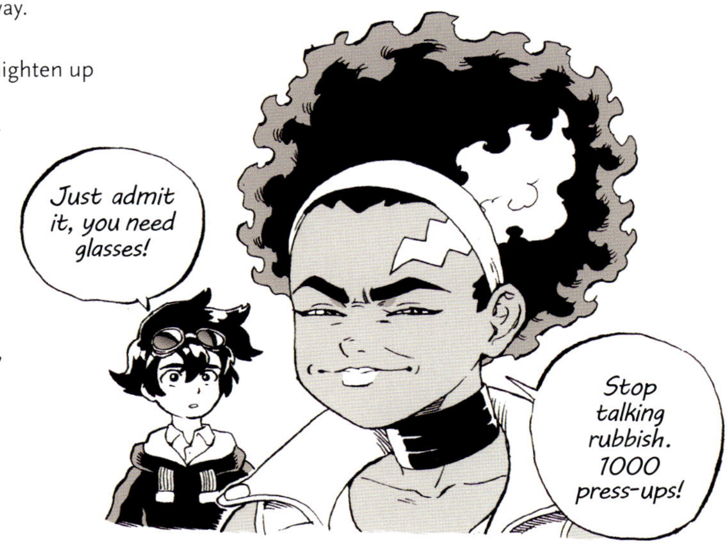

RIVALRY AMONG COMPANIONS

The action genre is often about the heroes needing to become stronger or better at what they do best. On the way to the top, enemies and other hurdles await to test their current level of skill and set the bar for the next level to aim for. A constant companion of the protagonist is usually a rival – not necessarily a villain, but rather an adversary with whom they compete for honor in a sporting manner. Through frequent duels, both become better and better, making them a first-rate duo when they finally team up against a common enemy.

In our example project, this kind of rivalry between Heroes A and B is also an essential driving force. It's assumed that, at the beginning, the two are hostile toward one another. We already know that Hero A urgently needs to exorcise demons in order to save his own soul. Then he arrives in a strange city and meets Hero B, who carries 12 demons inside him. Exorcising them with the cyber sword would bring Hero A a big step closer to his goal. A fight likely breaks out; the demons inside Hero B know how to defend themselves. It either ends in a draw or Hero A loses.

Perhaps this is followed by a phase in which Hero A keeps trying again and again but constantly fails. During this process however, the two heroes begin to understand each other's situations. Hero A realizes that not all demons deserve to be exorcised. Hero B, on the other hand, can relate to the life-threatening situation his persistent challenger is in and offers him an alternative path to reach his goal. Thus begins their journey together to hunt down malevolent demons who truly deserve to be exorcised, because that is the lowest common denominator in the motivation of both heroes.

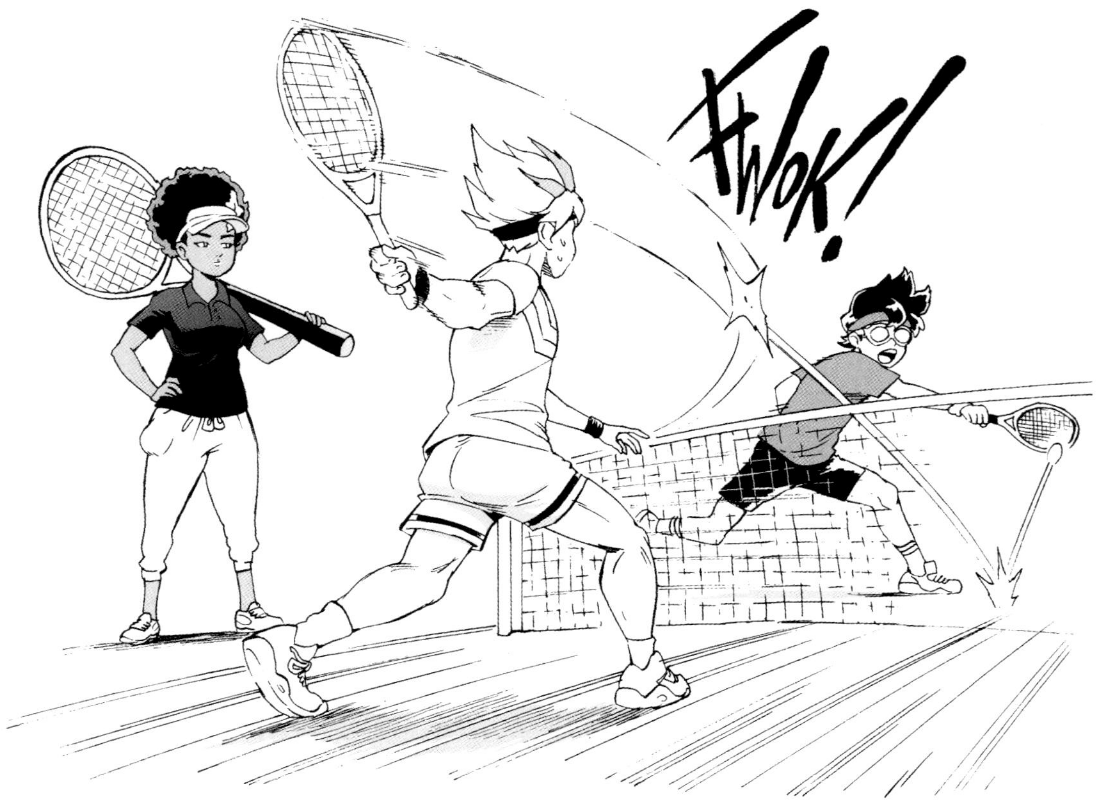

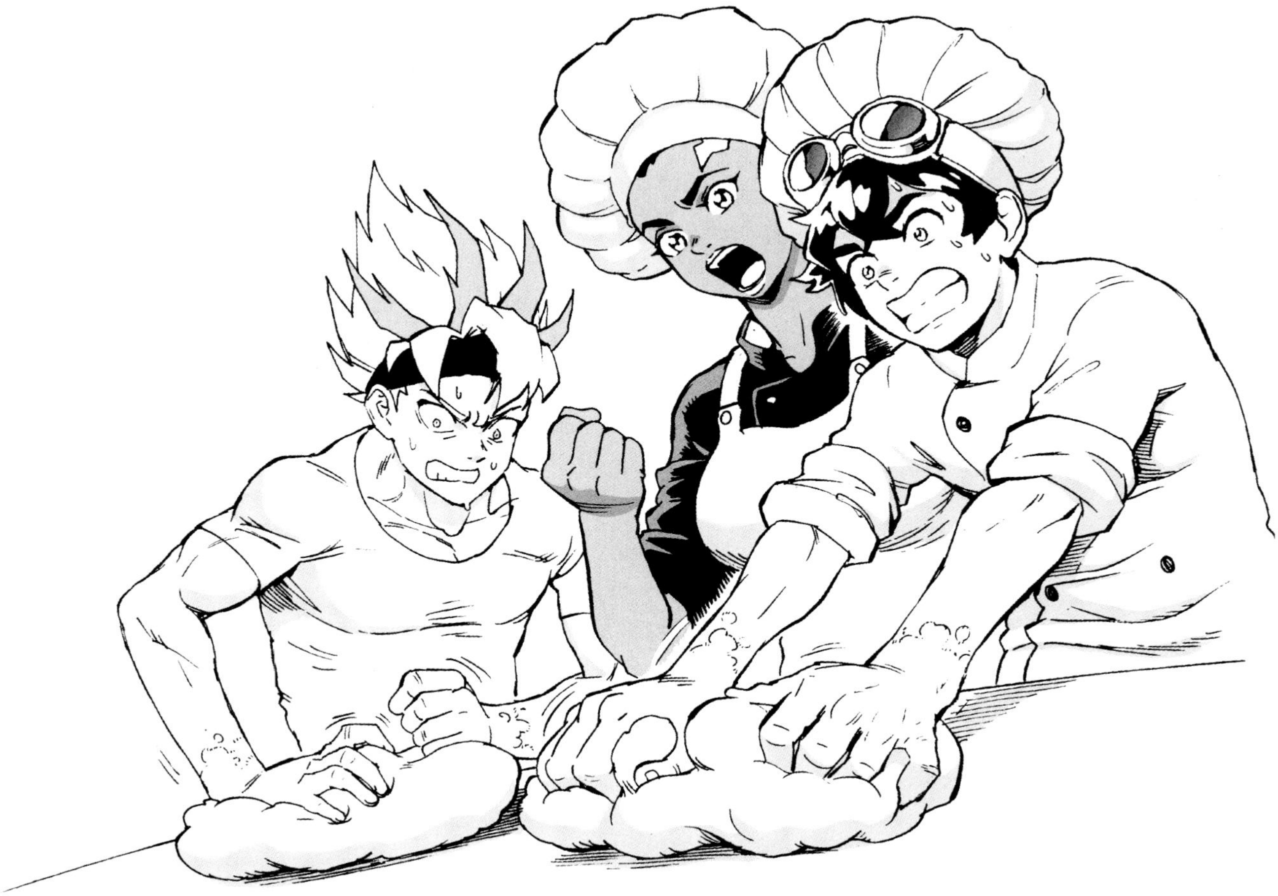

First come joint battles against adversaries (more on that on the next double page), as well as the first defeats and the realization of their own limits and weaknesses. The mentor helps the two to improve and rekindles the fire of their rivalry. The strengths and talents are split, and each wants to outdo the other. Fueled by healthy ambition, their abilities reach unimagined heights, and obstacles that once seemed insurmountable suddenly become a breeze.

That's roughly how the story could be sketched out if it's about cyber-samurai exorcists and multi-demon-possessed characters. But this basic framework also works in other genres and stories. The two heroes could just as well be tennis players on their way to the top of the world rankings, with the mentor as their coach – someone who's already been there and is now helping the next generation. Or they could be apprentice bakers, who want to bake the ultimate loaf of bread. The harsh words of their baker mentor drive them to knead the sourdough more fiercely than anyone has ever done before! Or they could be monster trainers fighting for the championship, pirates on a quest for the world's greatest treasure, or street footballers chasing their World Cup dream… You get where this is going.

If you change one or two corners of the character diamond or drop the characters into a different setting, it still works. The relationship between the main characters, along with their rivalry, is what keeps the whole story driving forward. And, even if you place the characters into a realistic sports setting or a down-to-earth craft profession, you could, in theory, keep all the stuff about 12 demons inside one hero and a missing soul in the other. In manga, even the most absurd things can work, as long as they're staged with lots of passion and energy.

DESIGNING VILLAINS

No other genre relies as much on distinctive adversaries as the action genre. Strong heroes must face even stronger opponents, and it is often the latter who are allowed to shine the most. While the good guys in the main roles usually have to act within a certain moral framework, the bad guys are simply allowed to do anything, which gives them more entertainment value. In this section, we want to briefly discuss the basics you should pay attention to when designing villains.

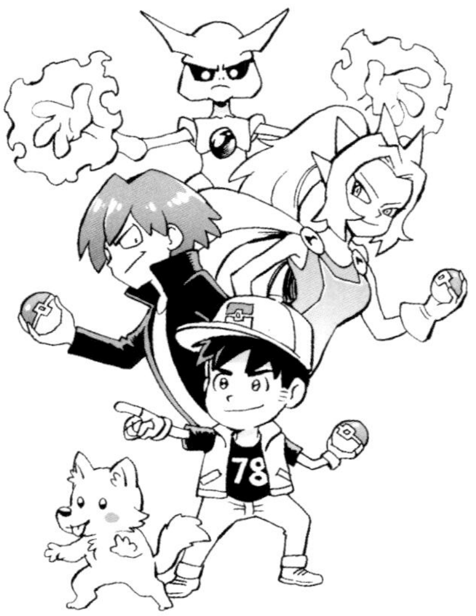

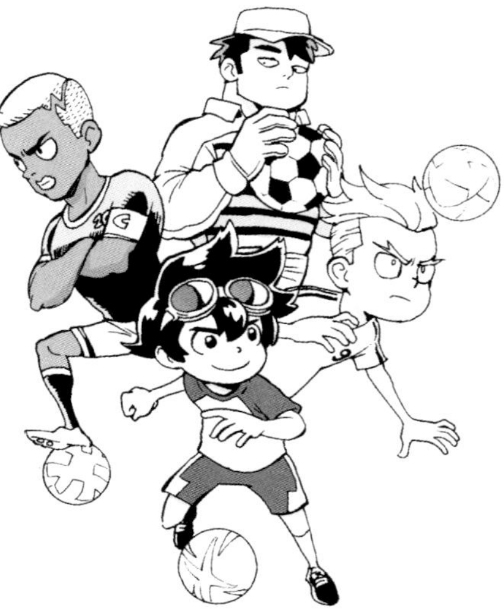

What kinds of opponents the heroes face generally depends on the protagonists' character concepts. In a story about a trainer of collectible monsters, they'll run into other trainers and powerful monsters. A footballer comes up against other footballers, whether in the battle for a championship or even just for a spot in the starting 11. A pirate fights other pirates who may be chasing the same treasure. Then there are marines, law enforcers, or sea monsters. A detective, naturally, tries to bring criminals to justice – some truly vile, others more of a lovable rogue type. In addition, there may be rival detectives, competing to deliver the most coherent solution to a case.

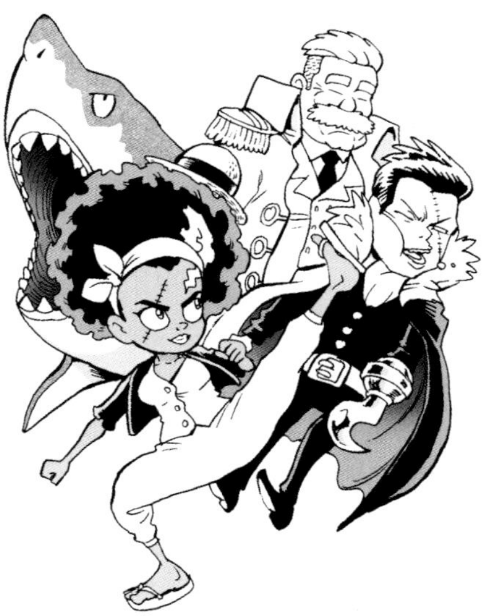

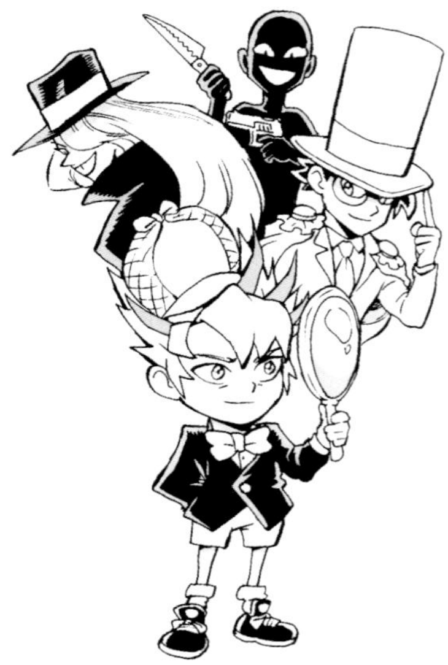

One of the most important functions of a good villain is to mirror the hero: a well-written opponent can show us what might have happened if one of our protagonists had taken a different path in life. This means that when the character diamonds of the hero and villain are put together, there should be at least one relevant corner that is directly comparable. Alternatively, the monster-collecting trainer could be arguing with the marine, or the detective could try to score a goal against the best goalkeeper in the league. But that wouldn't really help our heroes on their journey.

In terms of our project exercise, what this means is that our hero squad consists of mediums, who form a bridge to the world of spirits and demons – one even hosts supernatural symbionts, and the other is a cyber-samurai exorcist. The villains, then, should also come from within this world and context. Here is a list of a few possible candidates for standard villains for you to beat up along the way, and the Big Bads – the major antagonists of a given story arc.

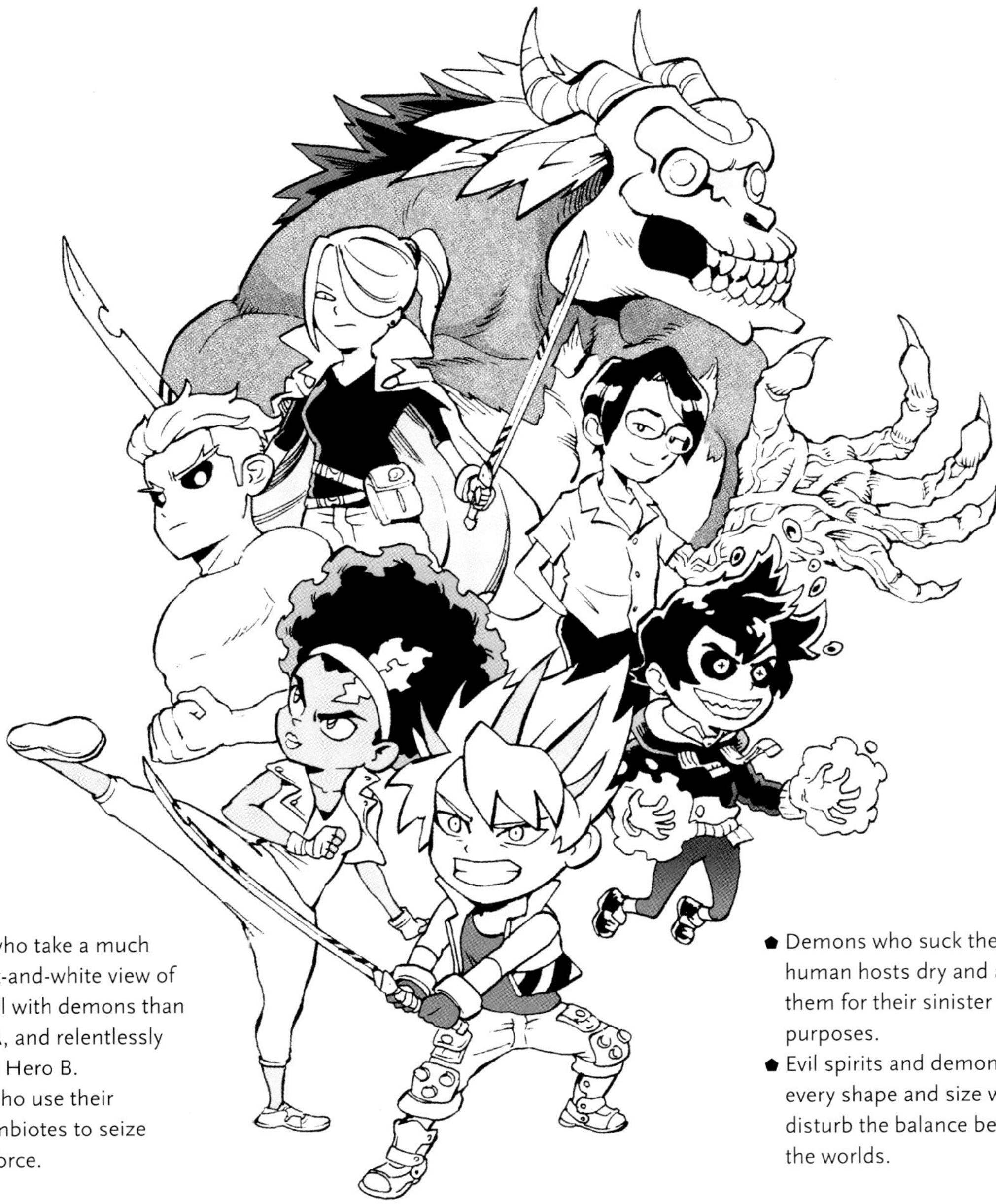

- Exorcists who take a much more black-and-white view of how to deal with demons than our Hero A, and relentlessly hunt down Hero B.
- Humans who use their demon symbiotes to seize power by force.
- Demons who suck their human hosts dry and abuse them for their sinister purposes.
- Evil spirits and demons of every shape and size who disturb the balance between the worlds.

MONSTROUS DESIGNS

With ghosts and demons among the potential array of villains, you can give free rein to your creativity. Absurdly grotesque distorted images of people, animal, or other everyday things. Terrifying horror beings that haunt your nightmares. Cool muscle monsters. A creative approach to the appearance and behavior of your adversaries adds enormous value to a manga. However, creating creatures far removed from classic mainstream monsters also brings with it a responsibility to develop rules for their creation. Here, too, you can work with a slimmed-down character diamond, but make it clear how your beings function: weaknesses, strengths, characteristics, etc.

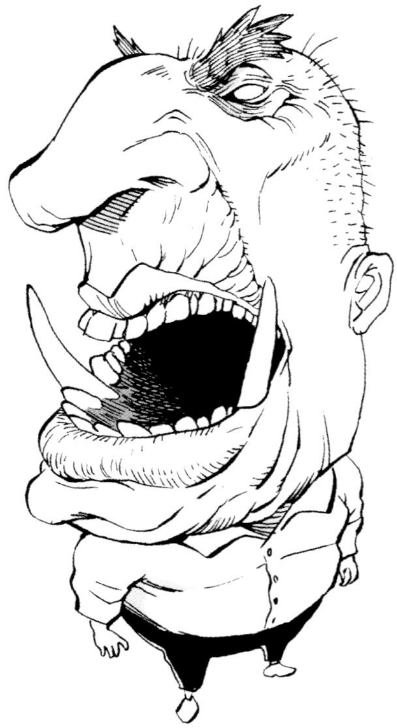

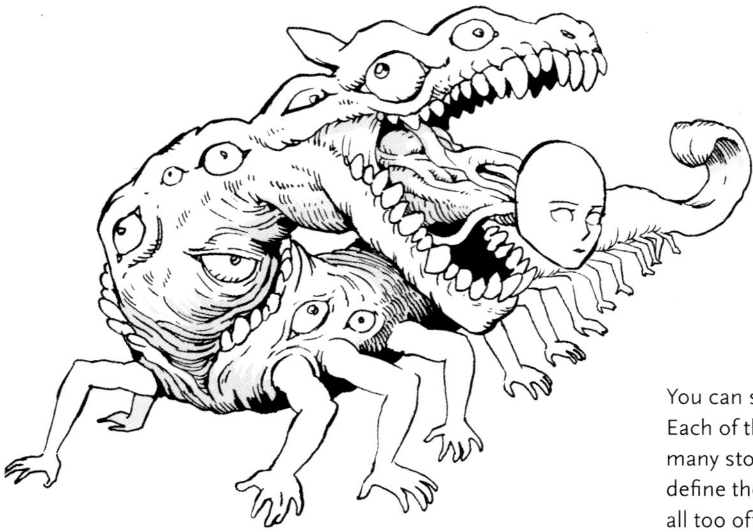

You can see three very different creature designs on this page. Each of them should follow their own rules. Unfortunately, many stories featuring enemy monsters miss the chance to define them in interesting ways. Sure, they may *look* cool, but all too often it's enough to just keep whacking the critters until they stay down. Boring!

So, aim for fewer designs but with more character. Let's take another look at the three monsters on this page. It'd be a shame if all three could just be taken apart with one strong swing of a sword or roasted with a demon fireball. Instead, ask yourself: what might the real danger posed by the dude with the giant skull be (and the related backstory)? *Why* exactly does the millipede monster have a mask on its tongue? The physical attributes alone should suggest a distinct fighting style. Are the eyes that are spread all over the monster's body weak points? Or are they just a distraction from the real one? And the strong guy on the right? Does he just smash things like a raging gorilla? Or does he surprise his enemies with a very intangible fighting style that directly attacks his opponents' psyche?

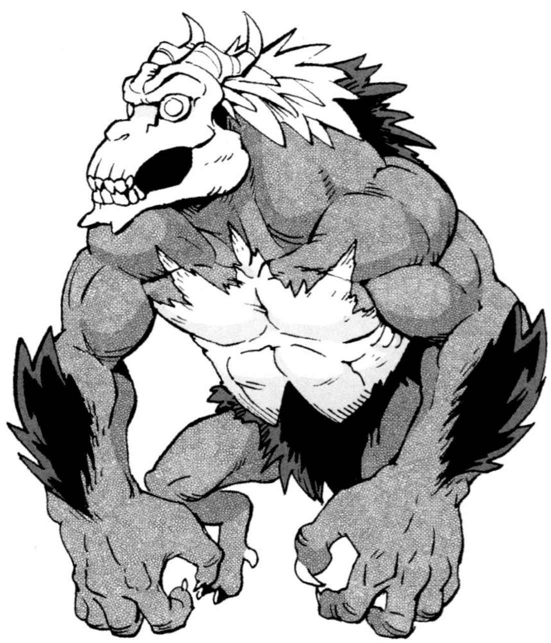

DEMON OVERLORD

Disgusting monsters are cool, and the fights against them can be staged in spectacular fashion, but the real antagonists usually show up in a more humanoid form. Often, they're even quite attractive, which makes them all the more interesting.

Here's an example of a Demon Overlord type antagonist, the kind of "Big Bad" who commands a horde of demonic minions. At first glance, he looks fairly human, but the demonic features definitely stand out, and of course, he's got one of those classic manga tricks up his sleeve: transformation! He can morph into a skeleton dragon in an instant (see bottom right)! And who knows what else he might turn into?

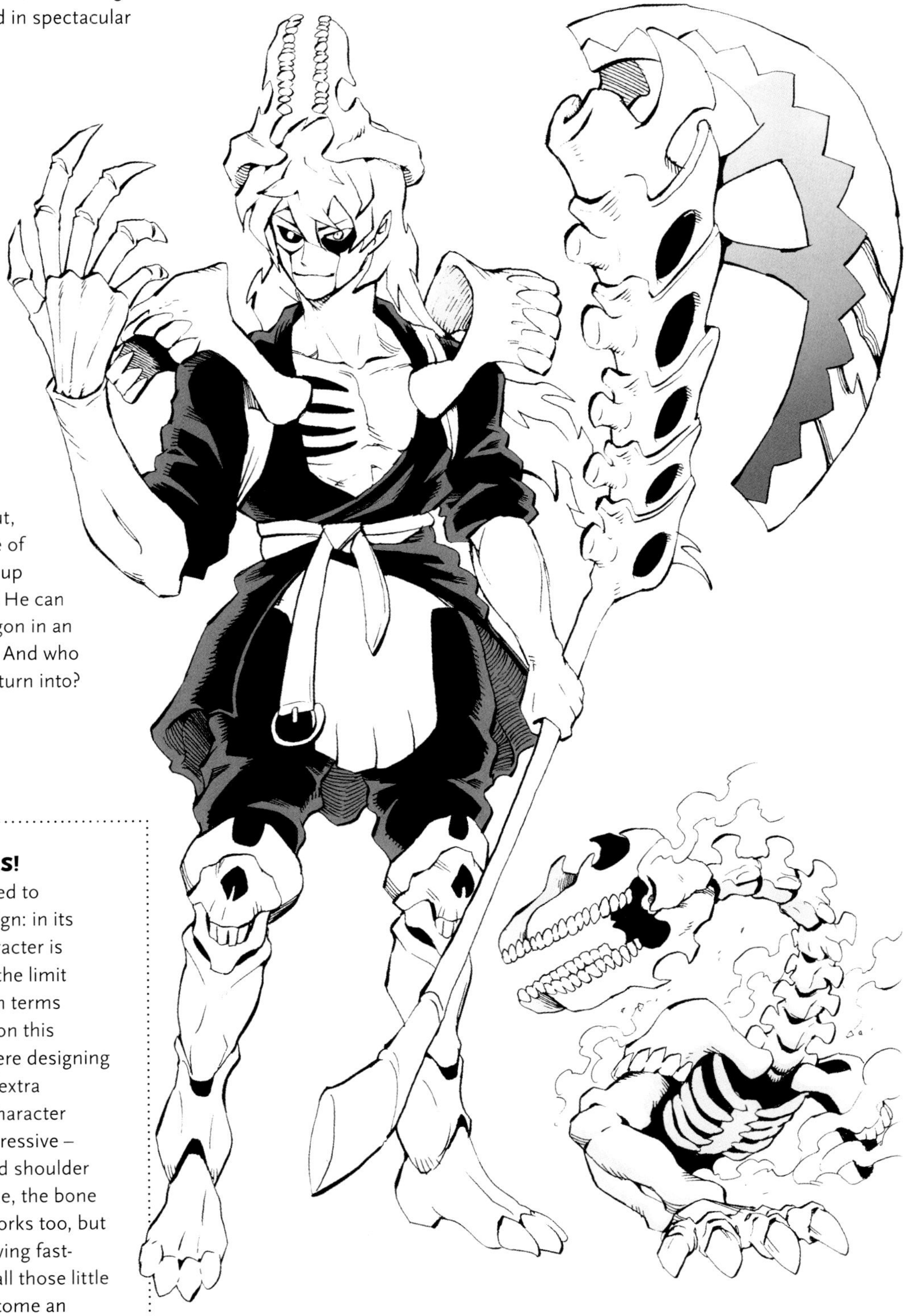

TOO MANY DETAILS!

Something else we need to consider with this design: in its current form, this character is probably already over the limit of what's reasonable in terms of detail. We touched on this previously when we were designing the two heroes. Every extra element can make a character more striking and impressive – the jawbone crown and shoulder plates, the spine scythe, the bone legs. The silhouette works too, but when it comes to drawing fast-paced action scenes, all those little details can quickly become an ordeal. If you're planning to draw a full-length manga, you should keep the design details manageable.

DEMON-HUMAN HYBRIDS

Here are a few more ideas for villains who look human at first, but who are demons. Without the shackles of human physiology, they can use all kinds of nasty techniques.

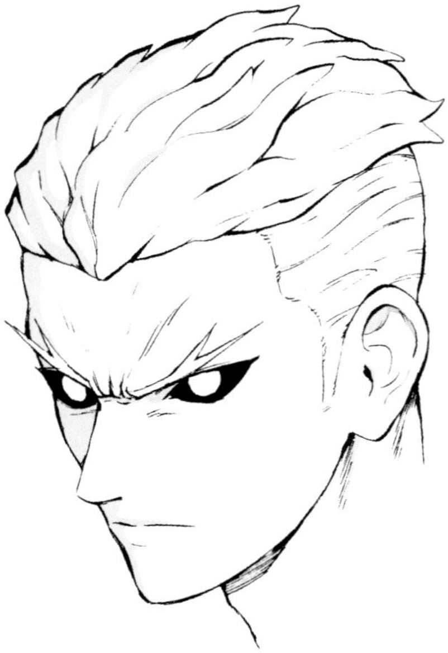

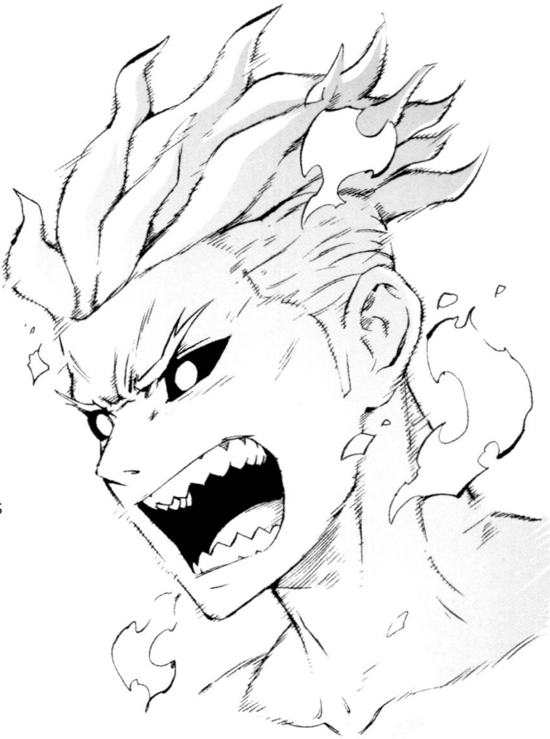

This villain can barely hide it when he loses his composure as flames flicker around his body. Later in the book, we see another trick he has up his sleeve.

This Spider-Lady has extra elbow joints and can sprout limbs.

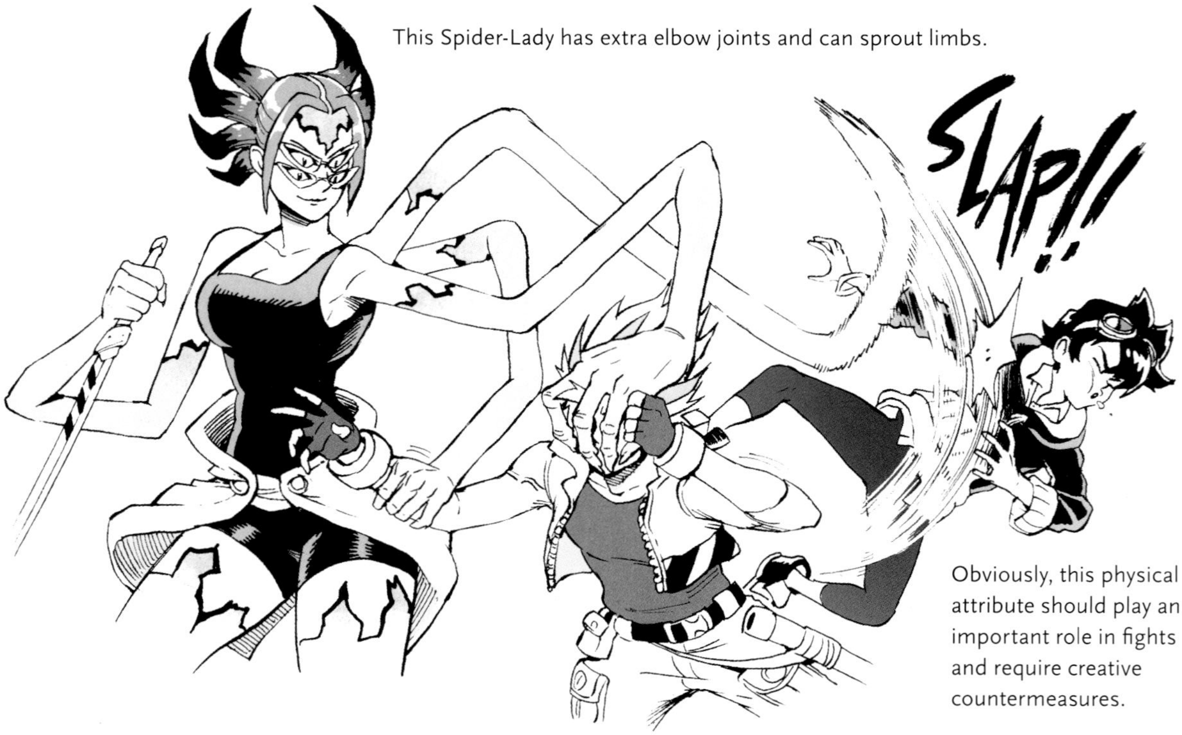

Obviously, this physical attribute should play an important role in fights and require creative countermeasures.

INSPIRATION FROM CLASSIC SOURCES

So, this tentacle-haired guy is really bad! Because he smokes! The leather jacket doesn't bode well either. He also seems to have a connection to the work of American horror writer H.P. Lovecraft, the master of cosmic horror who brought us the Kraken-dragon, deep-sea god Cthulhu (see the transformation of the antagonist below right), and many other monstrous entities from another world.

This is a creative buffet from which we are now all allowed to help ourselves, as Lovecraft's works are in the public domain. As 70 years have elapsed since his death, his copyright is expired and anyone can use his stories and characters. This applies to all works of fiction!

So, if you're looking for inspiration, you might find it in old books. Reinterpret a Grimm's fairy tale, throw literary legends like Dracula, Frankenstein, Hercules, Robin Hood, Shakespeare's Macbeth, Sherlock Holmes, Robinson Crusoe, or whoever you had to slog through in literature class into your stories and see what happens.

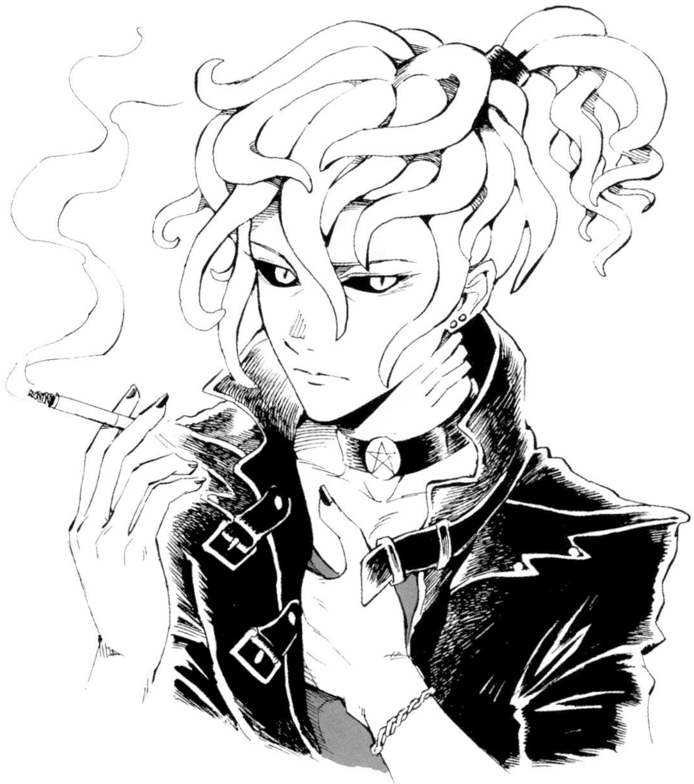

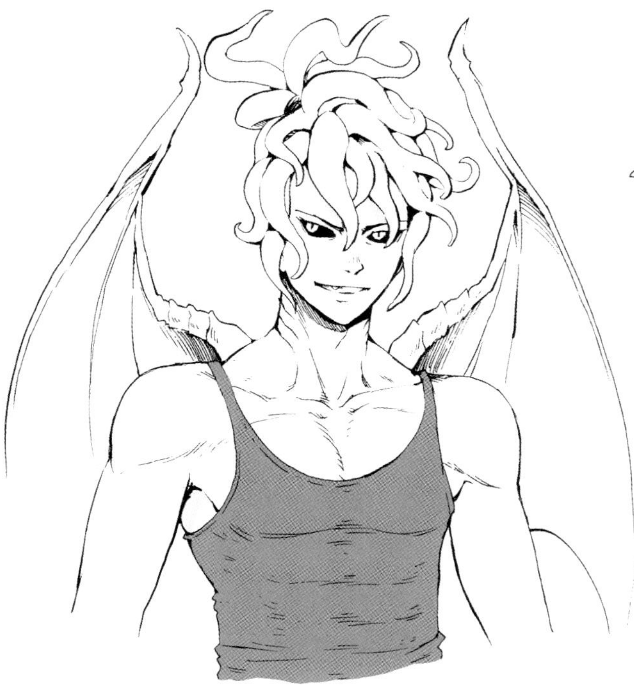

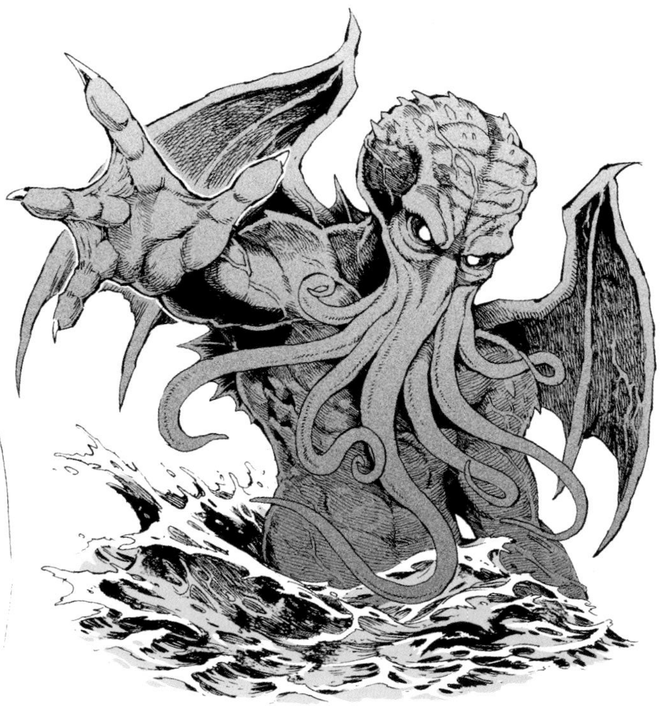

THE ANTIHERO

In really well-crafted stories, the boundaries between shining hero and villain often begin to blur. While the classic model manga still usually features hyper-enthusiastic, wildly optimistic heroes in leading roles, more complex and morally ambiguous protagonists are increasingly taking center stage. In this section, we will look at a type of character whose character diamond might read more like that of an antagonist, but who's absolutely capable of playing a leading role.

This figure should be seen as a kind of antithesis to our Hero B: a young man who, due to certain circumstances, has become the host for a demonic parasite. However, unlike Hero B, whose strong moral compass defines the nature of his symbiosis, this antihero is far less noble. He uses his powers selfishly, often without a second thought for the harm he might cause others. When the protagonist is a character like this, the usual sympathy points are naturally lacking at first. But if he is at the heart of the story and acts in ways that are consistent with his character diamond, readers will accept him and root for him.

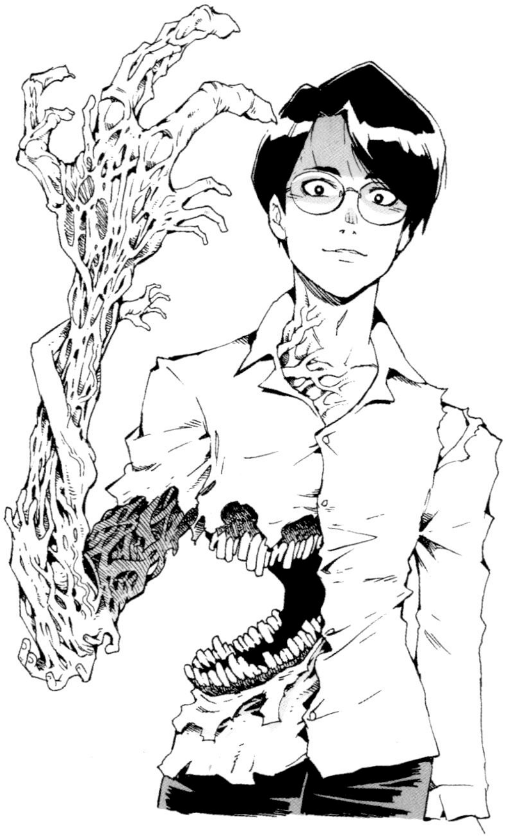

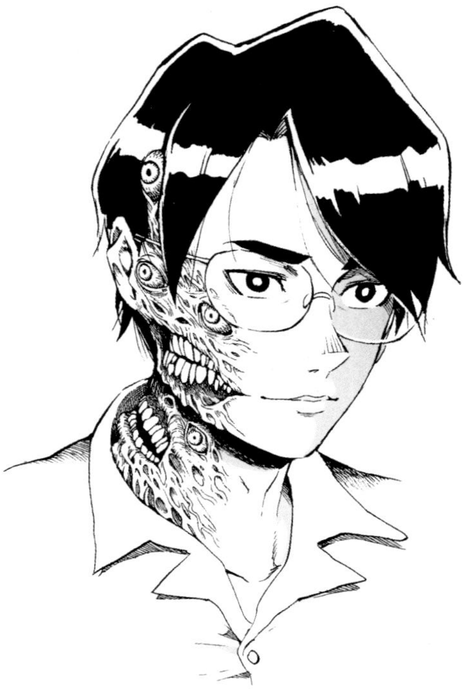

In keeping with his role as an antihero, the demon symbiosis manifests itself much more unpleasantly in this character than in Hero B. Creepy, but also fascinating!

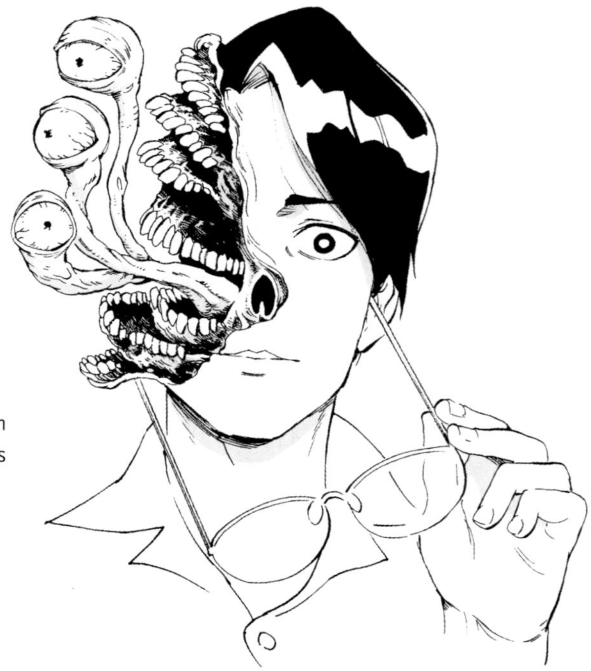

As you can see from the illustrative design of this double page, the antihero has a grotesque and rather gruesome design. His demonic possession state, which he can apparently control well, manifests itself in body transformations that can be used in a multitude of ways. For action scenes, this means you can draw on a cornucopia of creativity. Fights are certainly less chivalrous, but readers can expect gruesome techniques far removed from the classic punch-and-kick duels. Of course, the concept of the adaptive body can also be solved in a more friendly and aesthetic way.

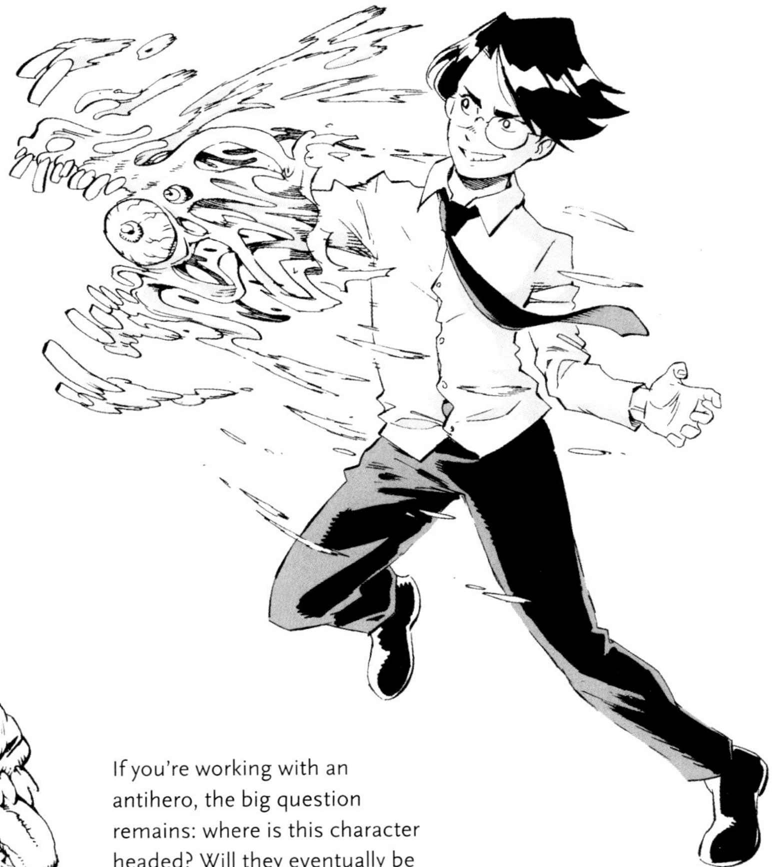

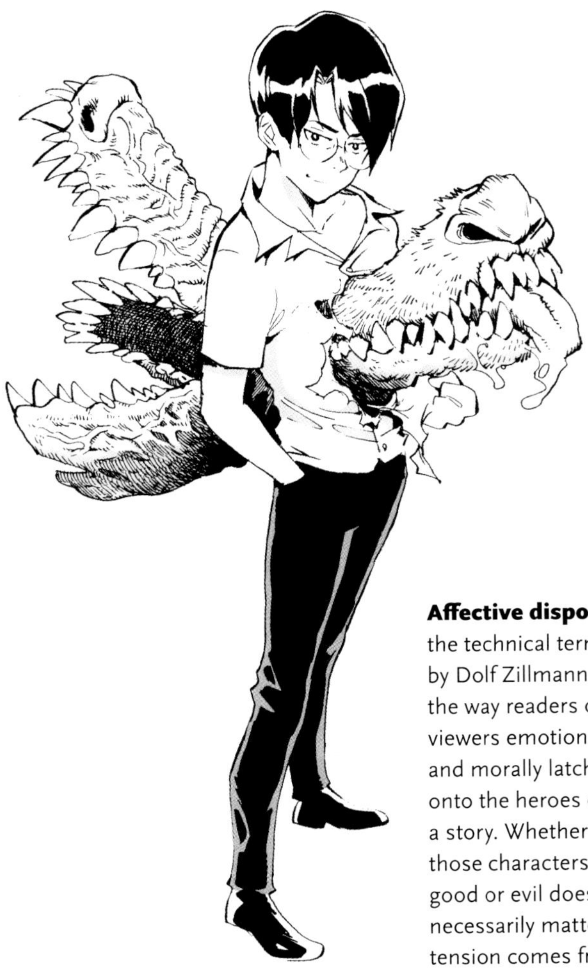

If you're working with an antihero, the big question remains: where is this character headed? Will they eventually be redeemed and become a true hero, or are they going down the road of villainy?

Affective disposition is the technical term coined by Dolf Zillmann for the way readers or viewers emotionally and morally latch onto the heroes of a story. Whether those characters are good or evil doesn't necessarily matter. The tension comes from the fact that, when characters are well thought-out, we automatically root for them.

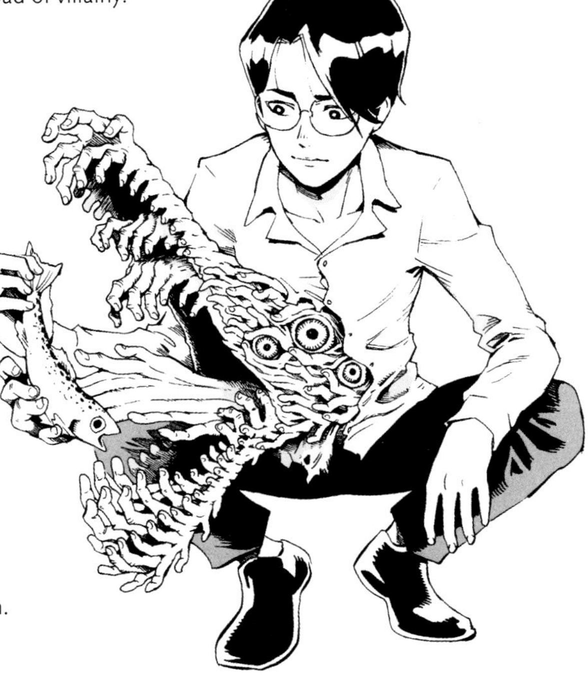

BUILDING WORLDS

We'll round off this big chapter on character design with a little detour into building worlds. How do the two go together? Well, the same basic principles apply when it comes to defining your story's setting as they do with designing characters. Before you dive in, you should determine clear rules for the setting you throw your characters into. Here, too, the more unique features your world has, the more interesting and distinctive it becomes, but as already discussed with the character diamond, if there are too many quirks, things can quickly get confusing.

The simplest setting you can choose is our real world – or rather, a version of it – but even then we need to define certain nuances, especially when it comes to action scenes. Crucially: how strictly do the laws of physics apply? It's always a bit more fun when you can loosen some of the corsets of science in fiction. For instance, characters can jump higher, hit harder, walk through fire longer, fall further, or take more bullets (without dying) than would be possible in our mundane reality.

However, no matter how much you adjust the settings on natural laws, the universe of your story must remain consistent. For our sample project, we should also ask: what are the consequences of there being demons and humans who can use their powers? How exactly do the rules work? What are the limits? Is this one of those manga where, with enough willpower and training, you can tap into supernatural abilities? Will I eventually leap onto a rooftop if I practice the high jump every day? That might sound trivial at first, but such questions should be thoroughly considered, and binding rules should be defined.

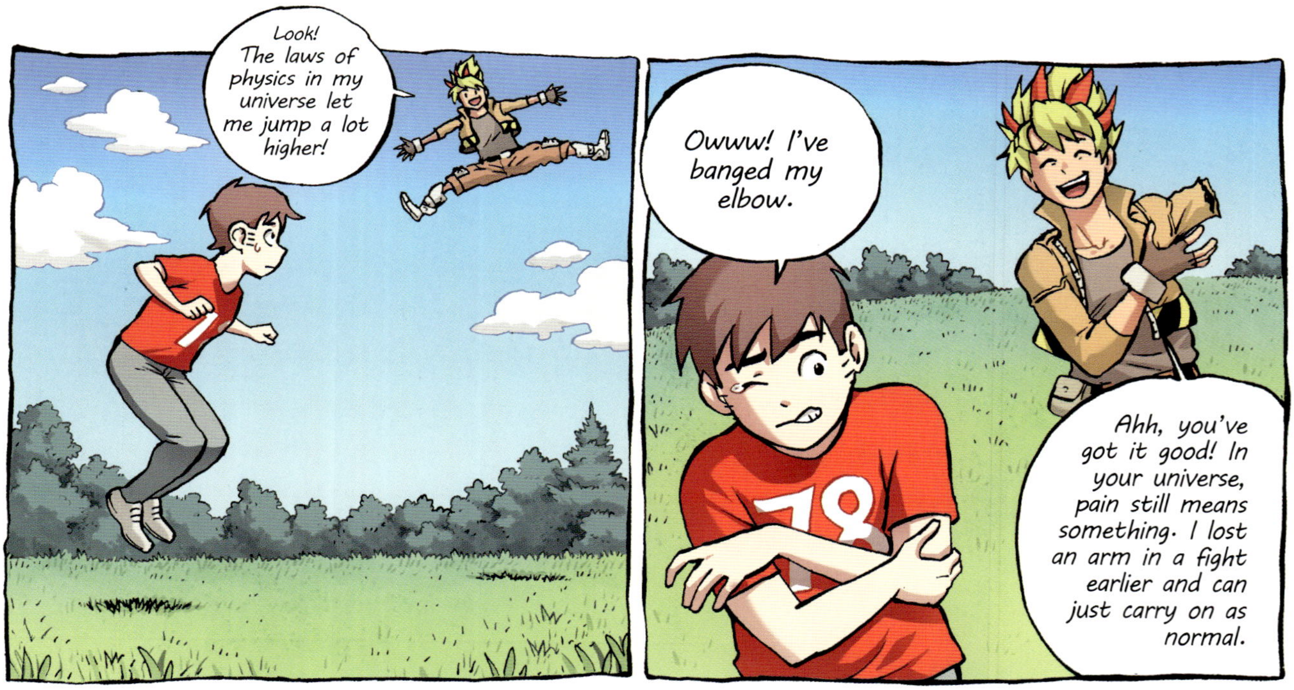

Many manga have their own set of rules for gags. In the context of comedic exaggerations, the established laws can also be suspended for that moment. However, this is a creative embellishment, an exaggeration. For example, a nosebleed can fill a bathtub without the character dying.

Don't worry! Despite the graph, this page hasn't wandered in from a math textbook. The following model is a very simple way of defining how a fictional world is organized by comparing it to our own. The zero point represents our reality – planet Earth, with the known universe surrounding it. Our laws of physics. Our writing of history. The X-axis shows how visually different a story's world is from ours. The further it moves from the center, the more fantastical it becomes: alien planets, other dimensions, a society where everyone wears hats all the time, and so on. The Y-axis has a label that refers to the scientific attributes. A visually fantastical world might still follow real-world laws; this would therefore be at or near the 0. The more bizarre the rules get, the further up the axis it goes. I like to informally call that the "bullshit factor". It might sound derogatory, but it actually encompasses all the creative playfulness that we love about Japanese pop culture. Things can be a bit over the top, or way, way over – as long as it's entertaining! Take a look at the sample chart we've filled in. Since this model is meant to encompass all types of stories, we've included some classic manga titles alongside others most people will recognize. You could certainly argue about where exactly each one falls on the grid, but the general idea should come across just fine.

Let me know if you want to sketch your own world into this grid – or build one together from scratch.

Have a look at the examples that have been entered into the system. As the model covers all stories, the manga classics have been supplemented by a few other titles that most people should be familiar with. Here and there it is certainly debatable which title belongs further to the left and further up, but the rough categorization should fit.

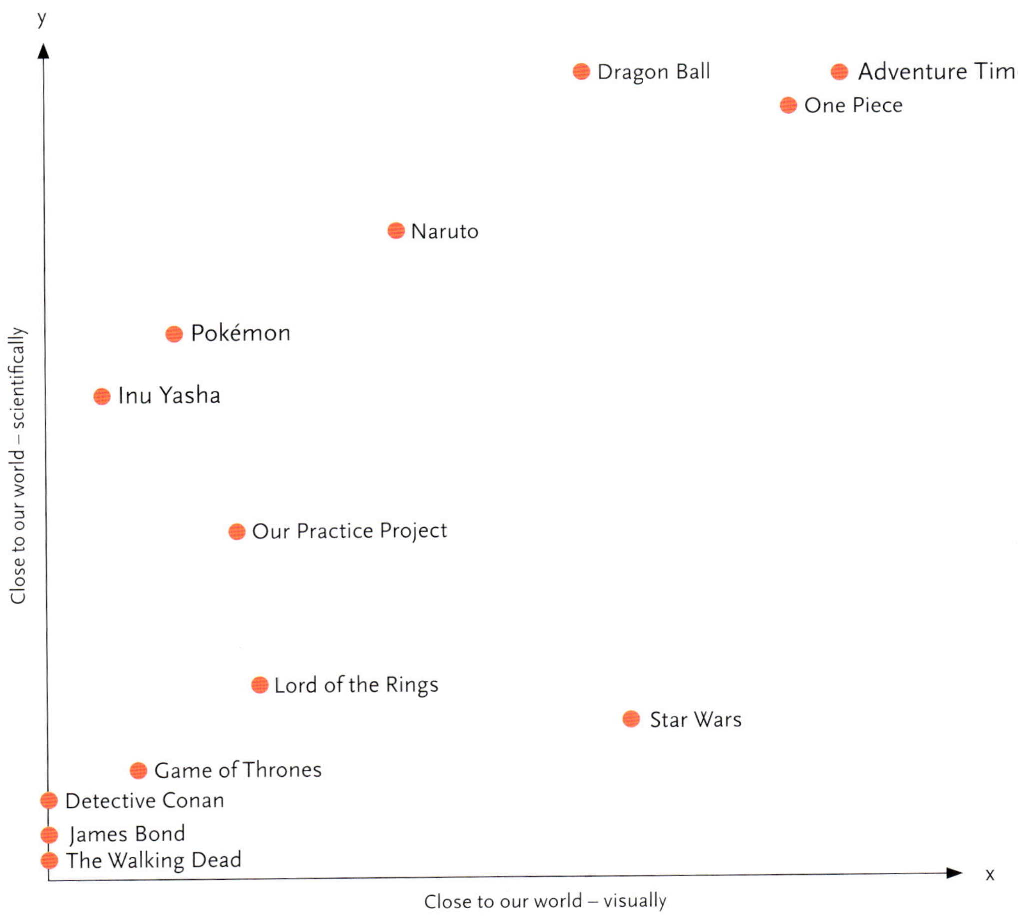

Most sports manga are set at or near the 0, but they are usually shifted slightly upward on the Y-axis so that the athletic performances can be staged more spectacularly. Classic action genres such as spy thrillers, gangster or war dramas, and even zombie horrors are also set there. With the latter example in particular, a slight shift upward on the Y-axis is enough for the walking undead to find their way into a world that is otherwise absolutely identical to ours.

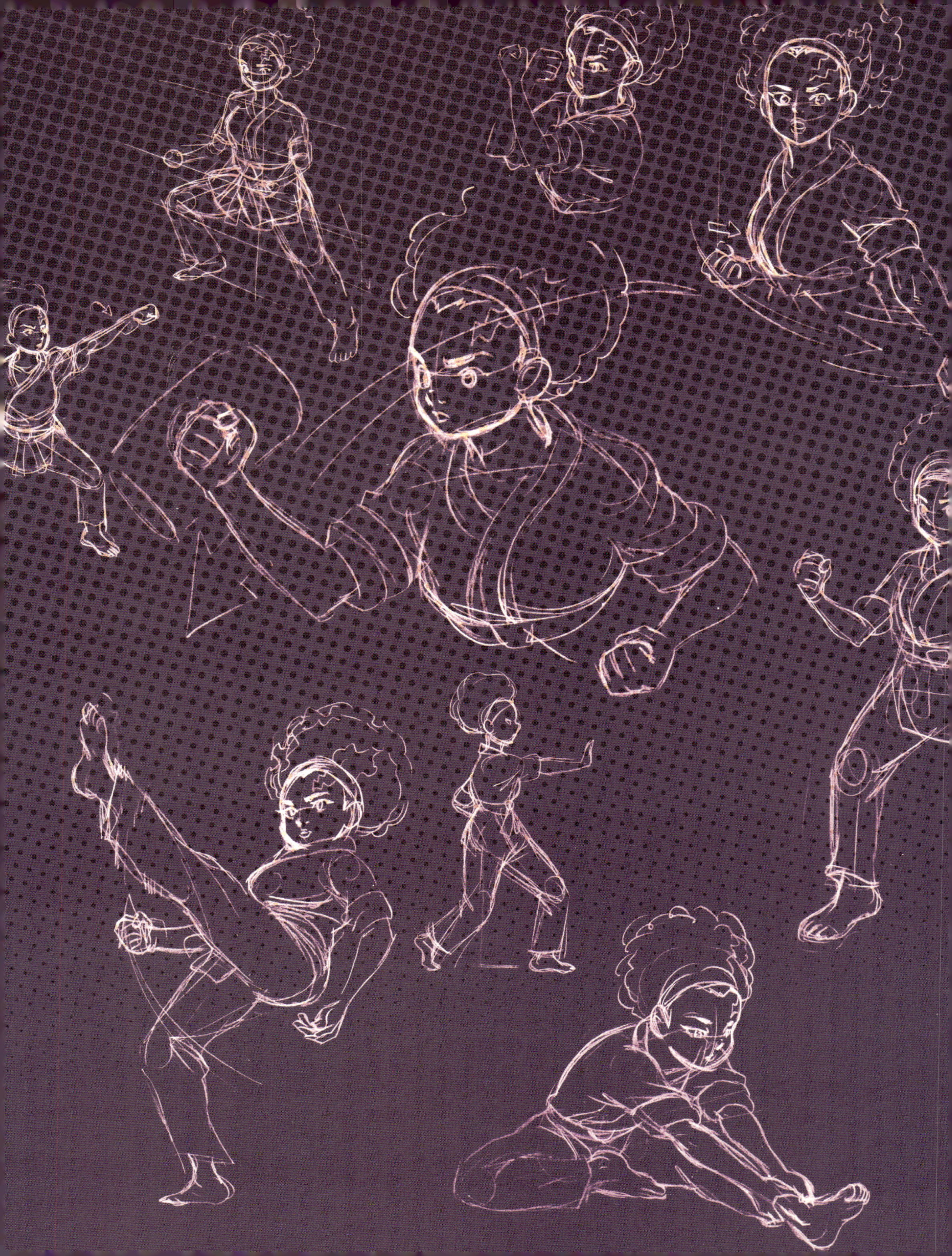

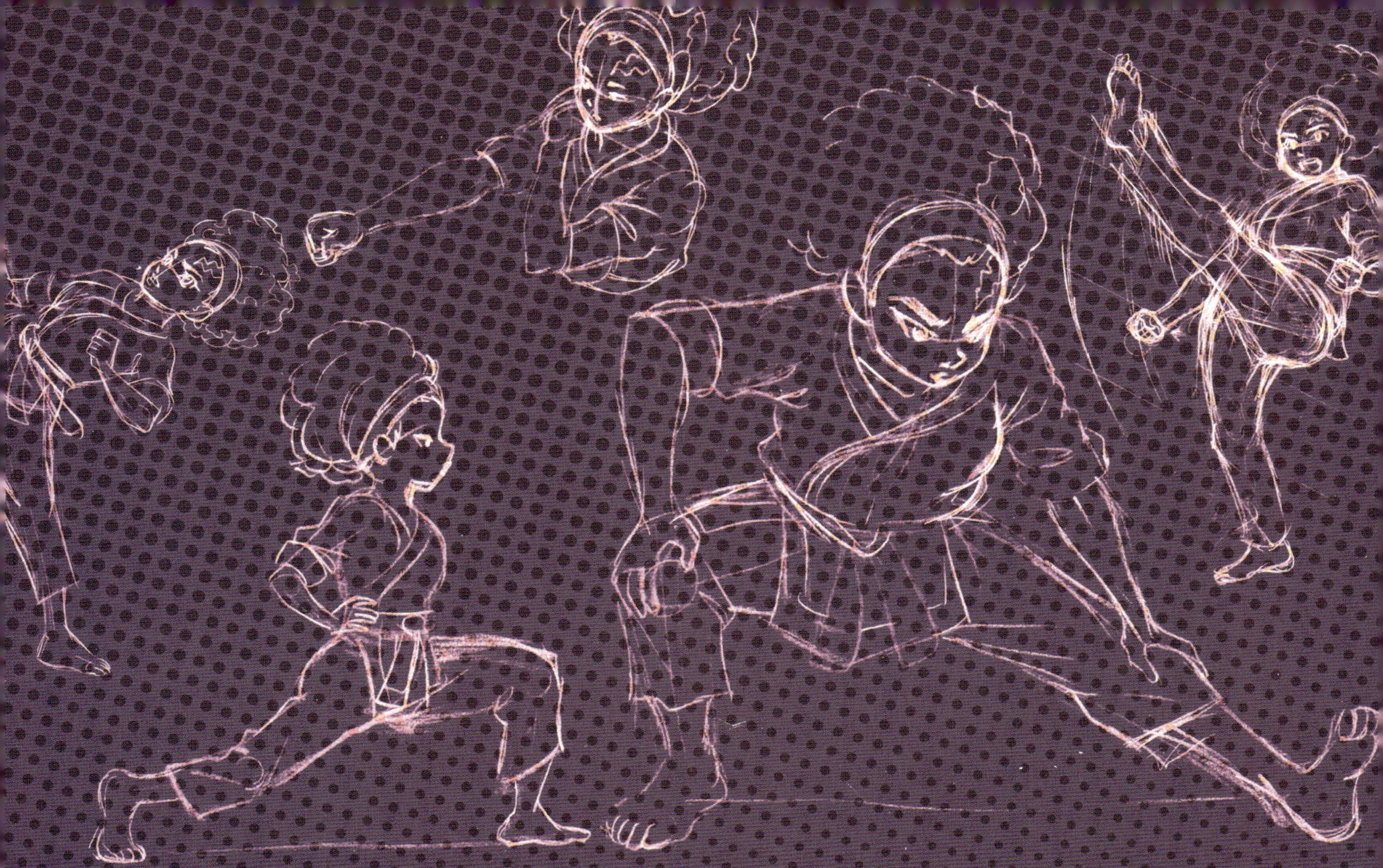

3. COMBAT TECHNIQUES

Yes, I know – you now want to know the most spectacular way to draw opponents throwing exaggerated energy punches at each other. Manga is synonymous with flamboyant special attacks and crazy perspectives, but for all the entertaining exaggeration, a realistic foundation is still necessary. This means that we first have to devote ourselves to classic martial arts before we shoot the moon out of space with apocalyptic moves. On the following pages, the master will therefore guide you through some beginner techniques of Kyokushin karate, so that you can get a feel for basic postures. Please excuse the verbal lapses of the honorable sensei.

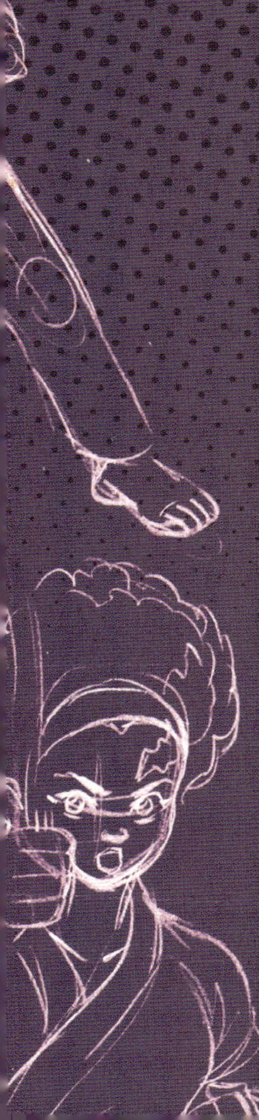

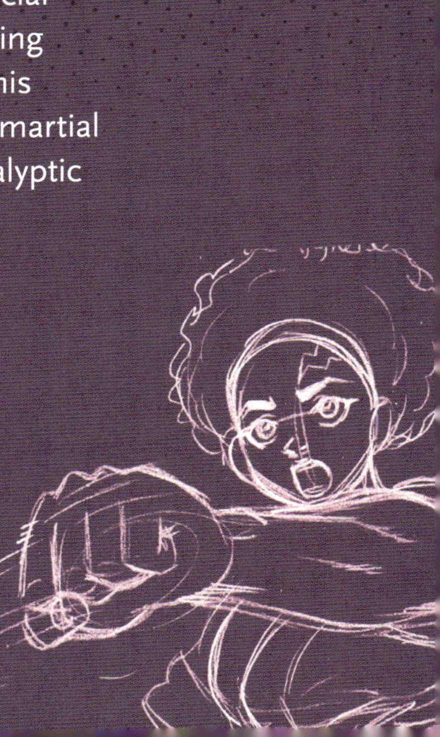

WARMING UP

Before the mentor shows their hits, kicks, and blocks, their body needs to be brought up to operating temperature, through stretching. The poses that you see here can be used in a variety of ways. For any kind of manga with a sporting theme (including fighting), you should also capture moments like these.

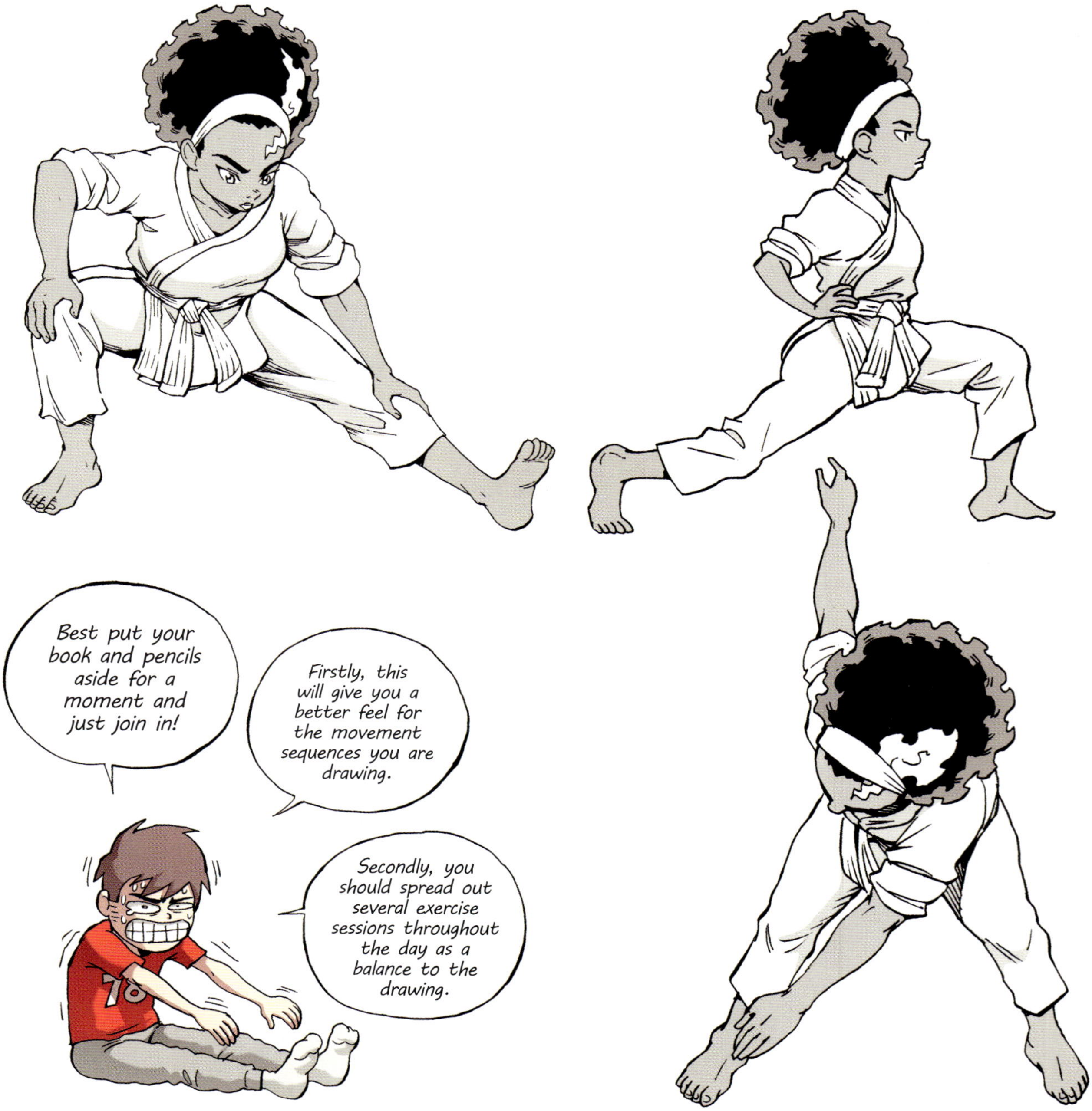

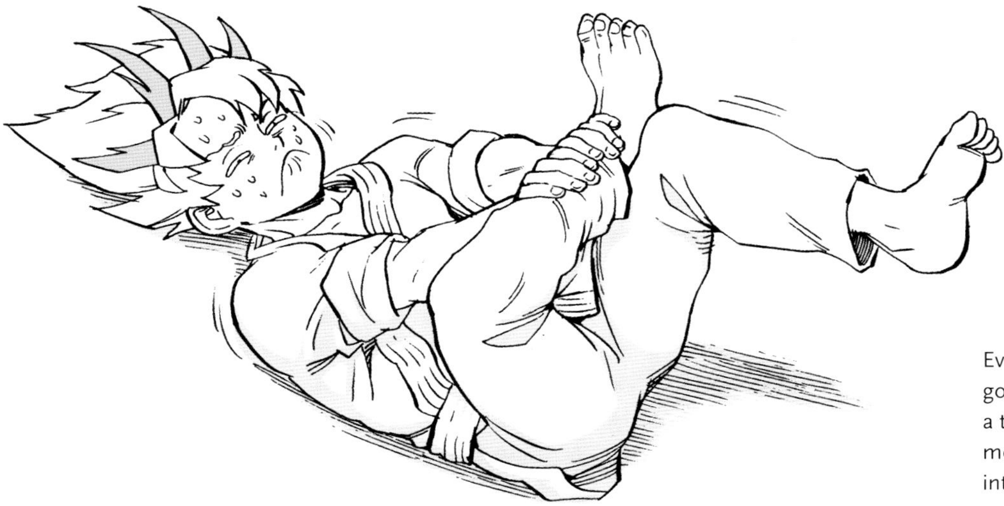

Even Hero A and Hero B have to go through the basics. In manga, a training session with the mentor would surely quickly drift into more abstruse exercises.

Drawing warm-up exercises has several advantages for us. One really superficial one: drawing complex postures improves our understanding of anatomy even more. On a narrative level, it grounds the characters as they prepare their muscles to avoid injuries. Even great warriors, like the legendary Son Goku in *Dragon Ball,* aren't above doing some dynamic stretching before an epic showdown with the Big Bad. The latter, on the other hand, usually just stands there looking cool, confident in his superiority. That already has an effect on the readers: it creates a connection to the hero and a sense of distance from the enemy. This means that you shouldn't underestimate the impact of such small gestures.

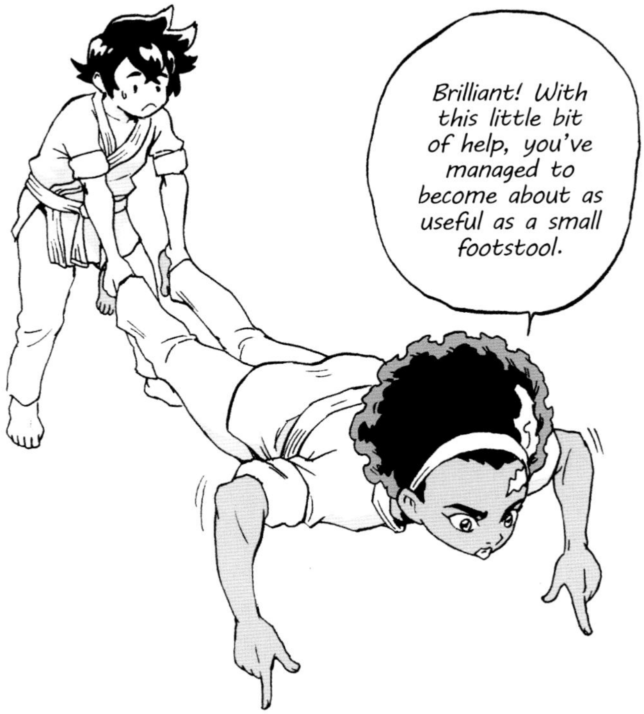

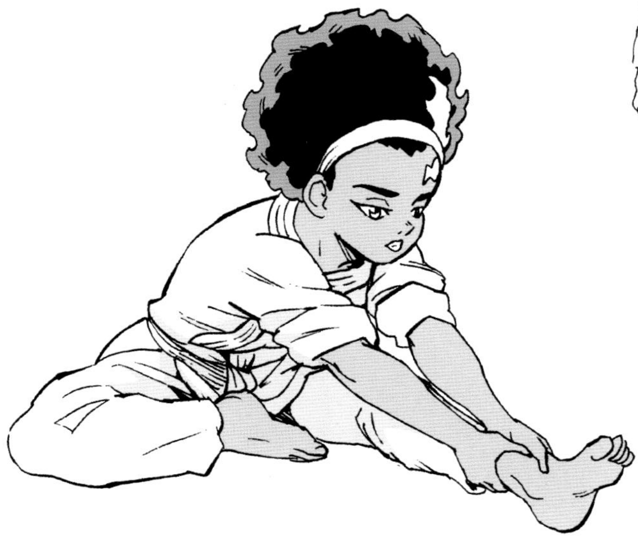

STRIKES

There are loads of martial arts and even more striking techniques. Of course, we can only scratch the surface here, but some basics are universal. For example, you place your thumb over the other fingers when clenching your fist, to avoid fractures.

This technique is called *Tettsui Oroshi Ganmen Uchi*, which roughly translates as, "Falling hammer blow to the face". In manga, it'd probably have some wildly over-the-top name like *"Final Megaton Hyper Hammer Strike!!"*

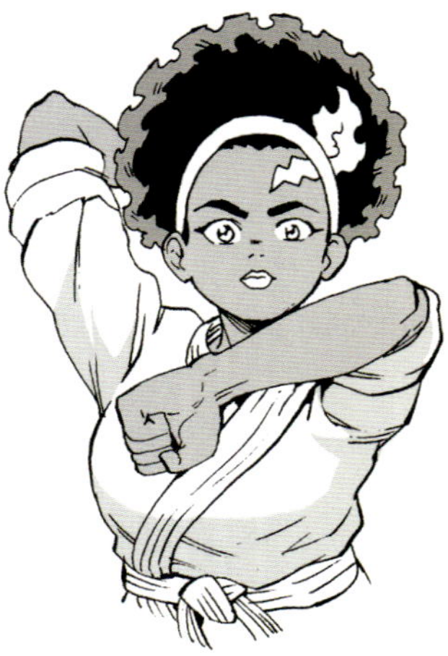

1. Blocking

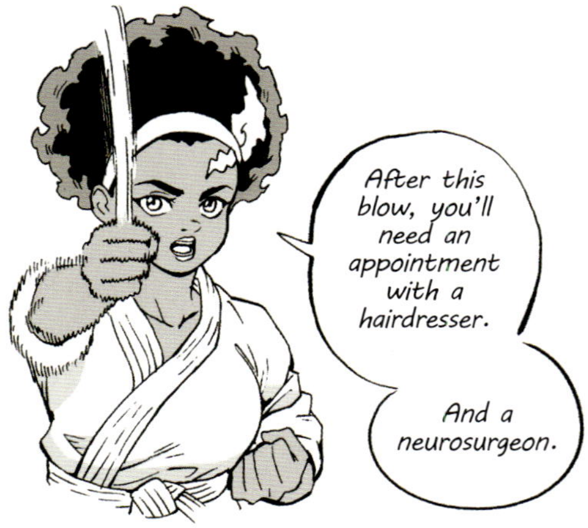

2. Striking

Here's the strike again from another angle. Note the striking surface on the underside of the fist. In karate, the official names of the techniques are usually quite clear descriptions of what is happening. If "Tettsui" appears, then an "iron hammer" fist is always involved.

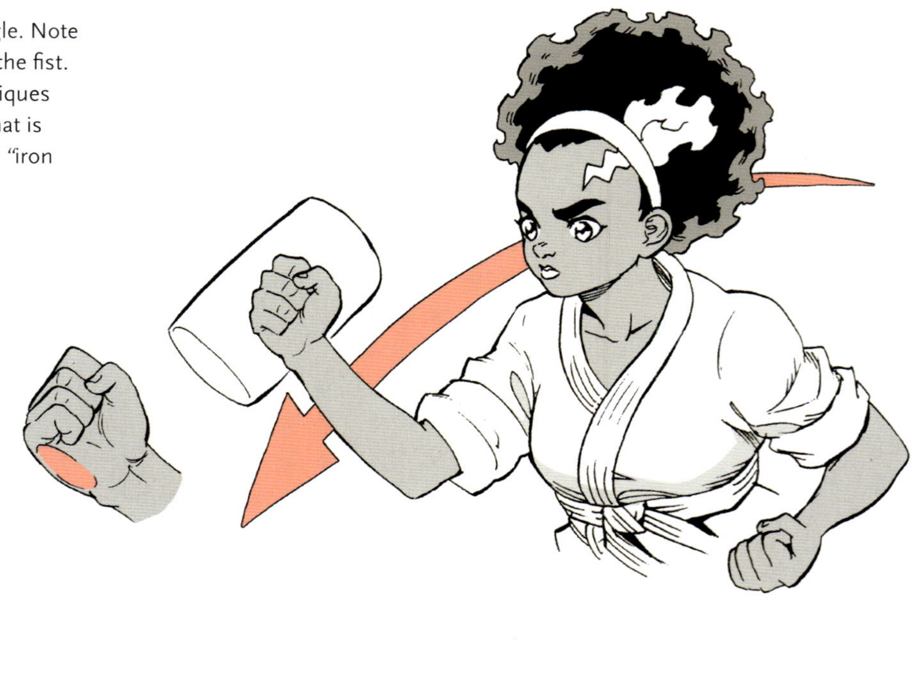

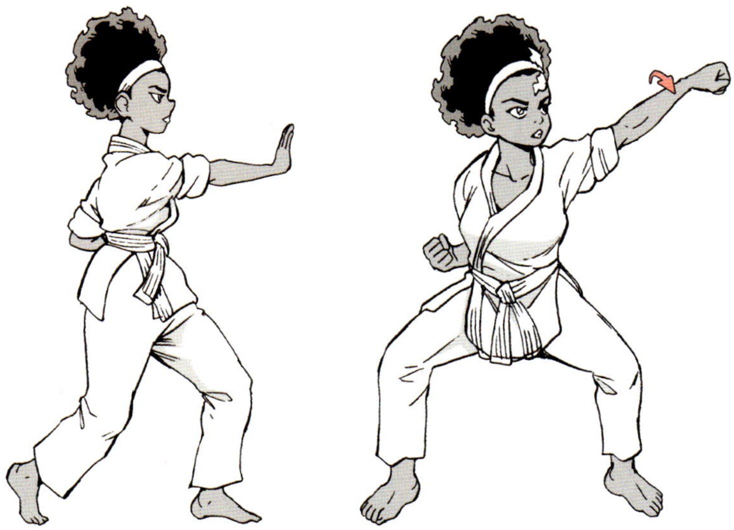

Using these three techniques from the *Jun Tsuki* sequence, we should explain the three recurring terms *Jodan*, *Chudan*, and *Gedan*.

Jun Tsuki means that the foot on the same side as the striking hand takes a step forward.

The mentor is demonstrating *Jun Tsuki Jodan. Jodan* means the attack is aimed at the neck or head.

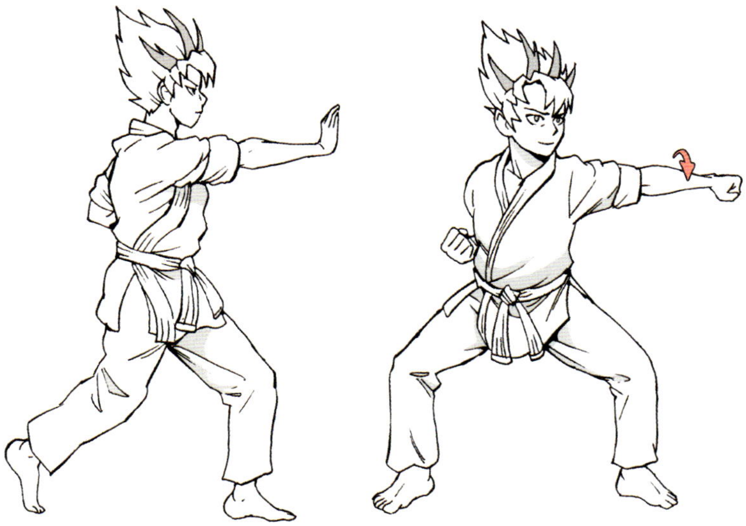

Hero A is demonstrating *Jun Tsuki Chudan. Chudan* means the attack is aimed at the body between the neck and the hips.

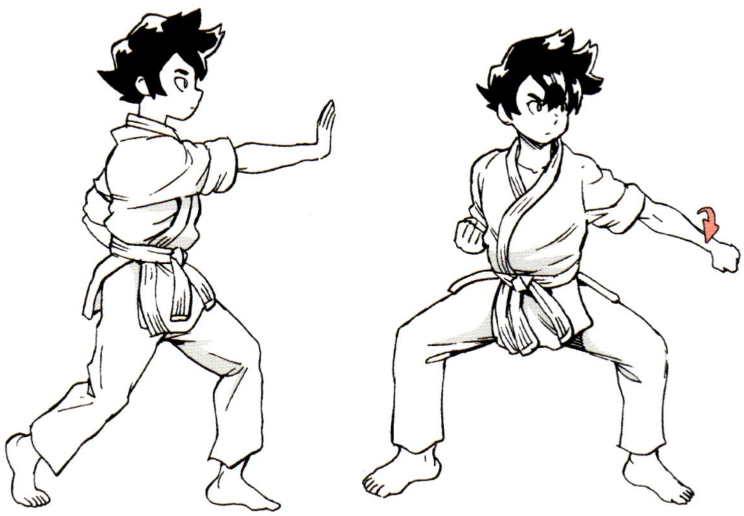

Hero B is demonstrating *Jun Tsuki Gedan. Gedan* means the attack is aimed at the body below the hips.

In all three techniques, the striking fist rotates 180 degrees as it shoots forward.

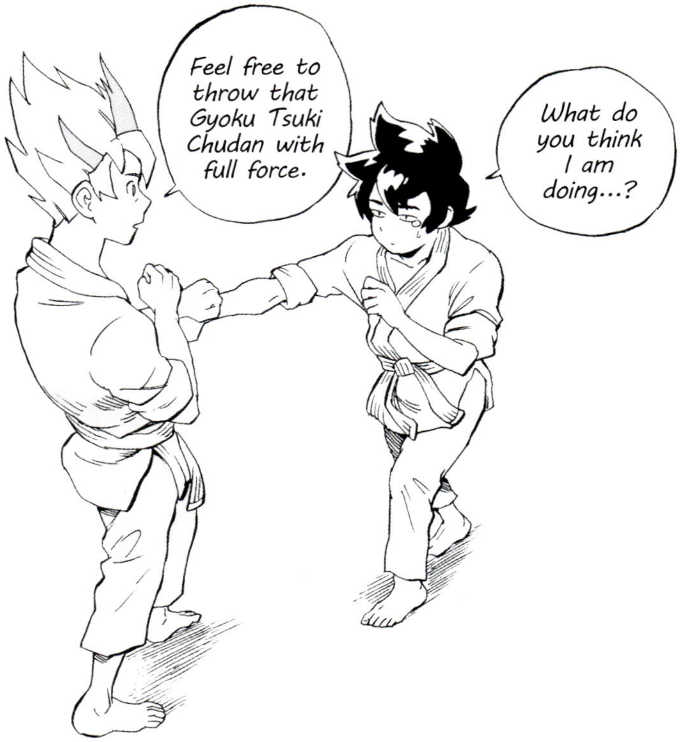

In karate, blocks usually flow straight into counterattacks. On top of that, blocking techniques tend to have a smooth, continuous motion that pushes the opponent back as you break free from their move – like here with the *Uchi Uke Gedan Barai*.

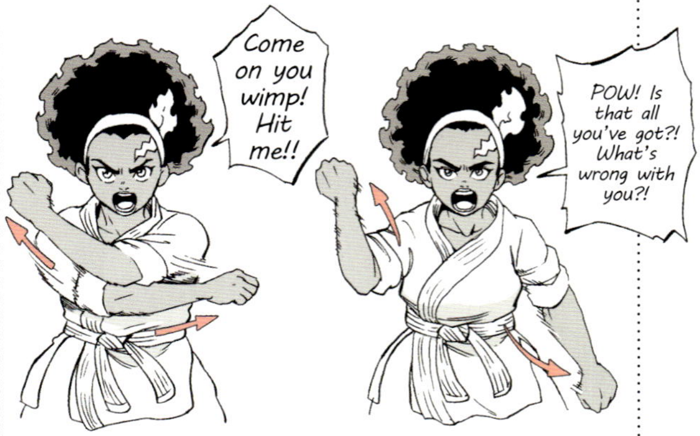

In the *Tettsui Mae Yoko Uchi Jodan*, the high frontal hammer strike, the striking hand initially rests at the neck, while the other arm keeps the opponent at a distance. Then, the fist snaps forward in a quarter-circle motion, hitting the opponent with the underside of the hand.

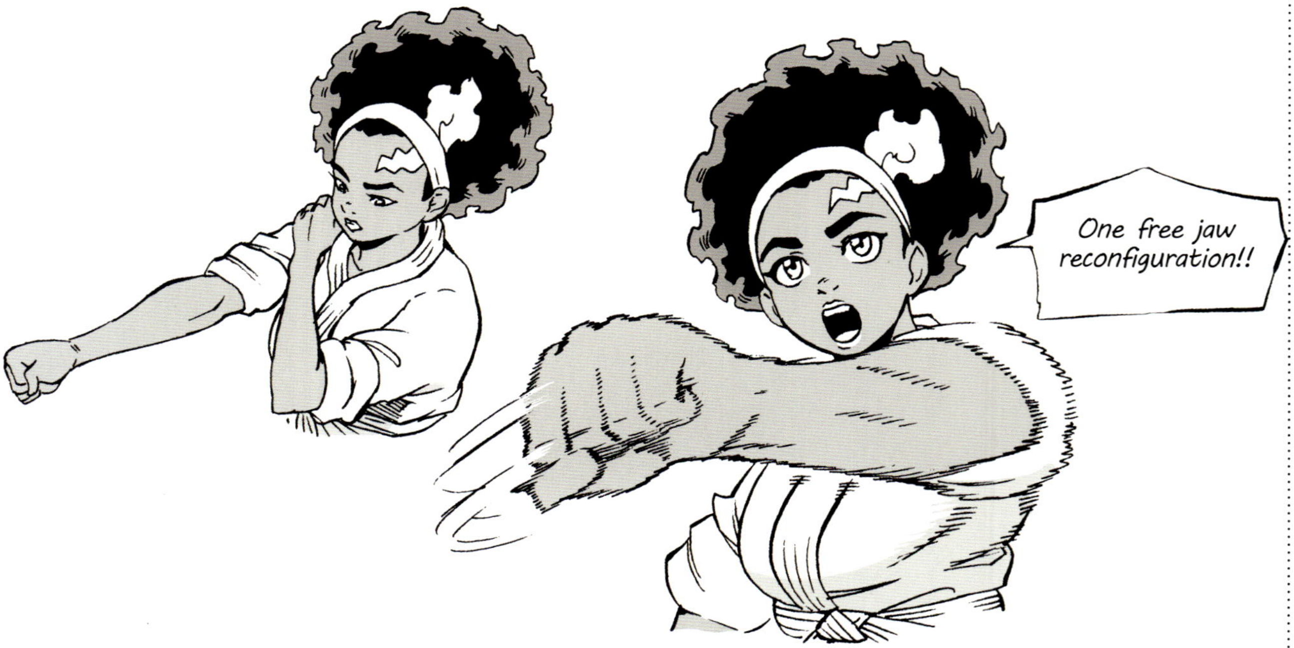

Tettsui Mae Yoko Uchi Gedan, the frontal hammer strike aimed at the lower part of the body. It's phrased politely, but we all have a pretty good idea of where these strikes might land...

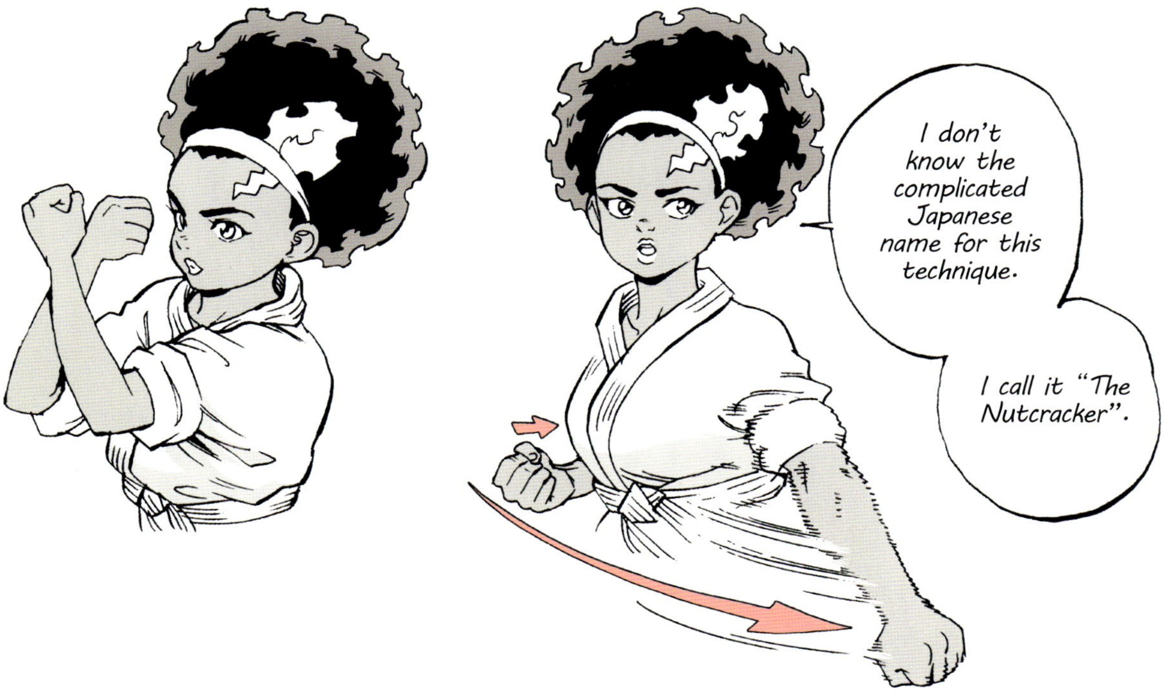

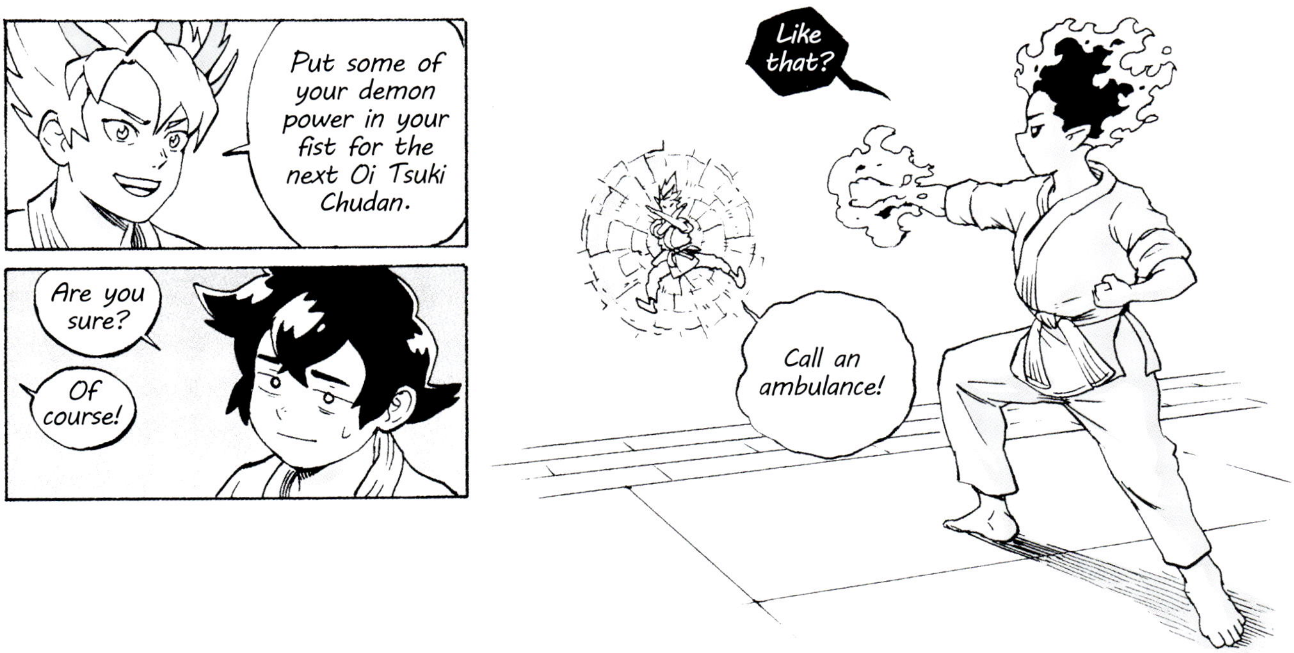

TAKING A HIT

There's no action without a few wounds! Your heroes, and all the other characters diving into the fray, are going to take some damage. That's unavoidable, and it has to be! Above all, your heroes need to keep falling (sometimes hard) so they can claw their way back up to those emotional highs.

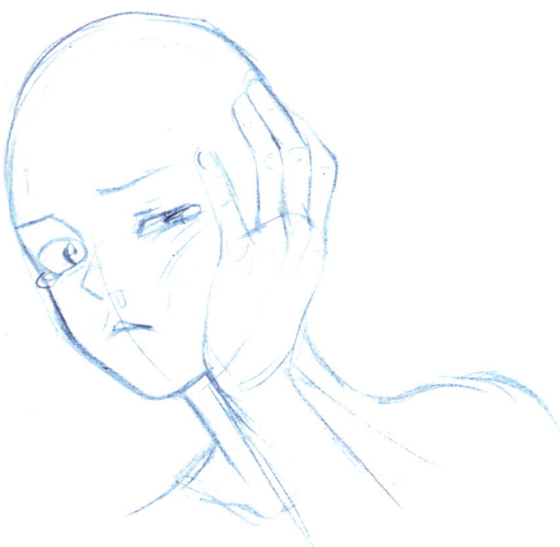

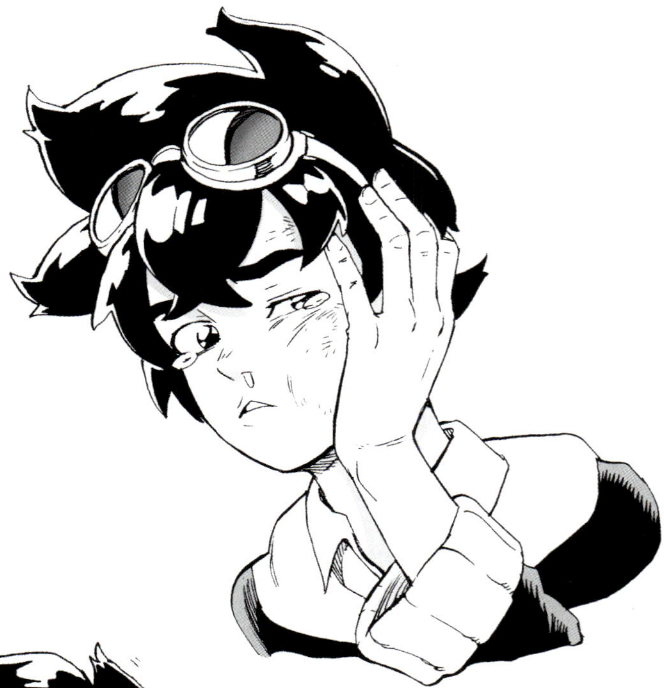

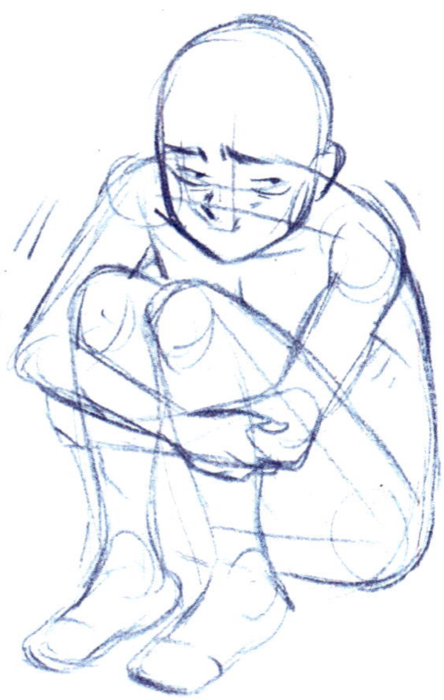

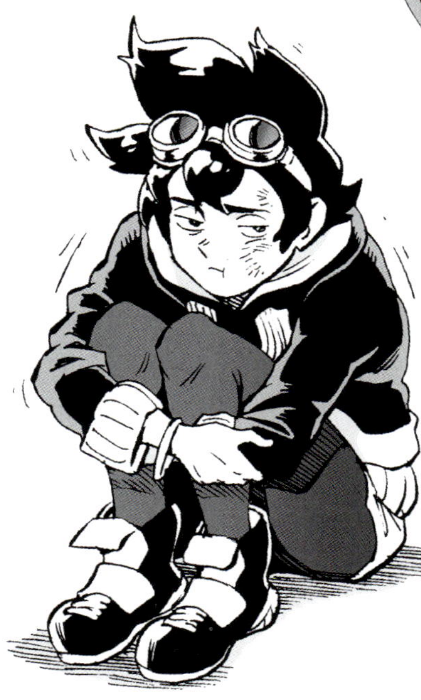

Let's start by looking at a crumpled reaction to a blow to the face. The preliminary sketches already show the frailty of the character who has been hit. The hand on the cheek in the close-up as well as the crouched, defensive posture say, "Please don't do it again."

Our Hero B was inked over the neutral preliminary sketches. In his human, rather helpless basic form, he has no desire for a confrontation, which is why he is a good model for this.

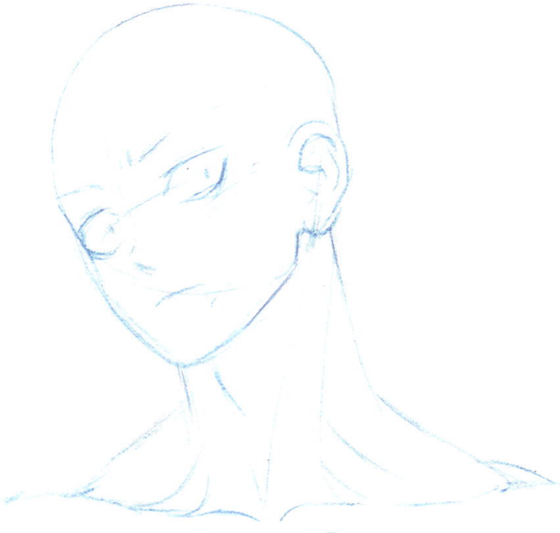

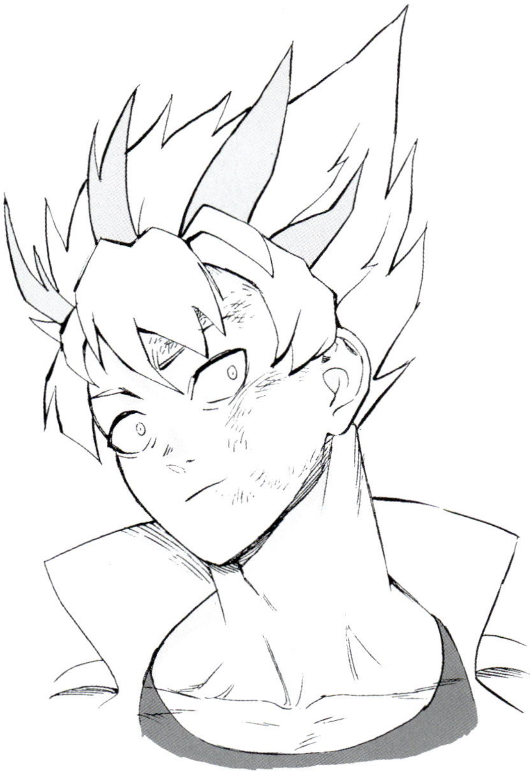

In contrast to the crumpled reaction to a blow and the accompanying admission of defeat, here we have the opposite. The view from the close-up makes it clear: this dance is just beginning! The character rises with a determined look, ready for the counterattack.

Hero A serves as an excellent model here, as this toughness and aggression perfectly reflect one of his character traits.

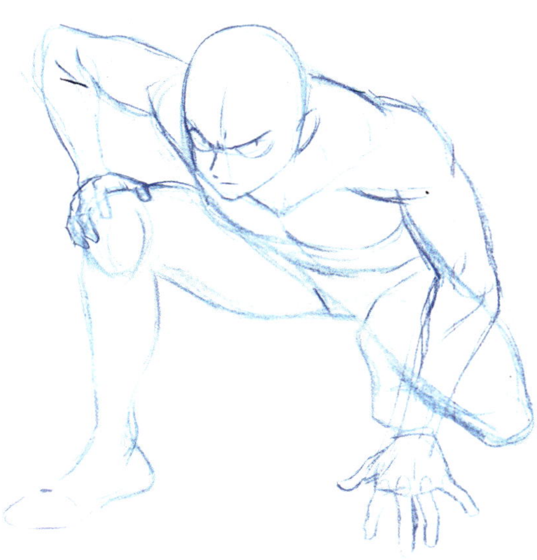

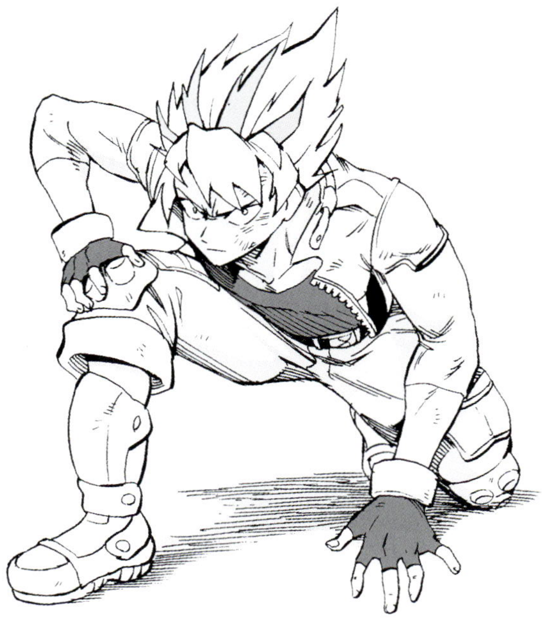

KICKS

For real impact in a fight, kicks are the best choice. They're usually a bit slower to execute than punches, but the power behind them makes up for it. Plus, kicks look cool!

In *Haisoku Mawashi Uchi Keage*, the kicking foot moves from the down and inward to upward and out in a circular motion. The leg remains extended.

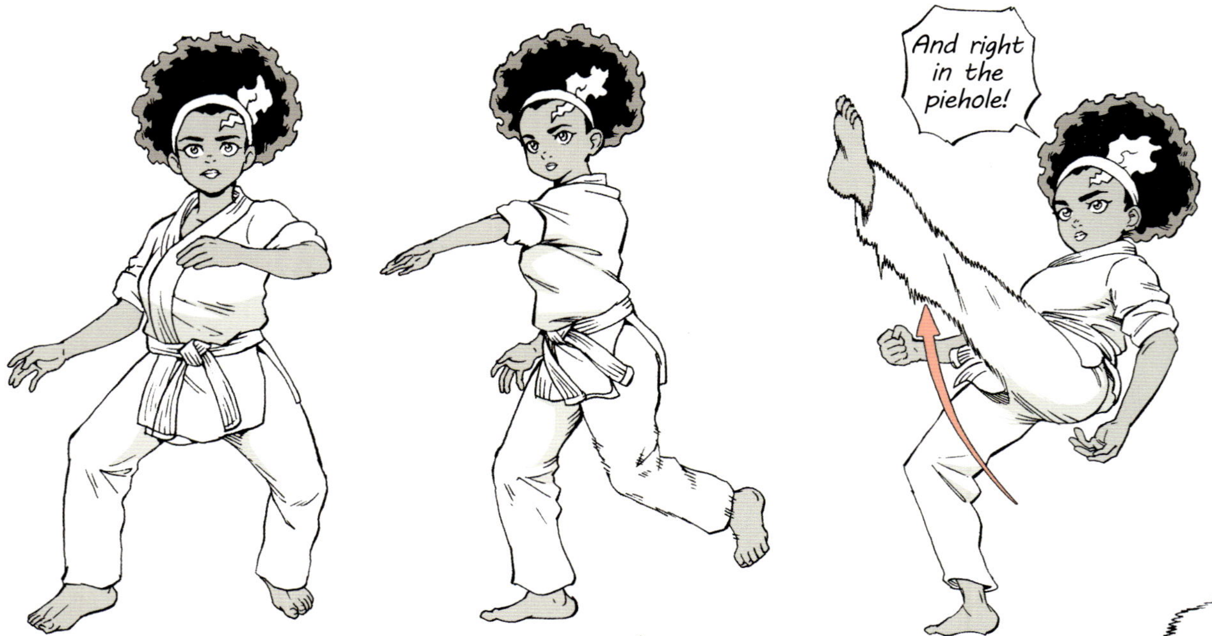

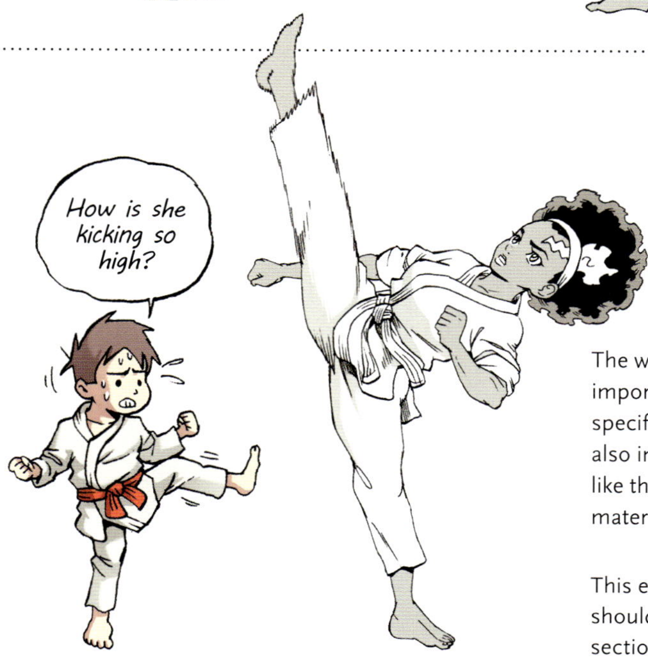

The weight shift is particularly important for kicks, and the specific position of the foot is also important. Even for details like this, study the reference material!

This exact pose, for instance, should look familiar from the section in Chapter 1: Anatomy with Reference Photos.

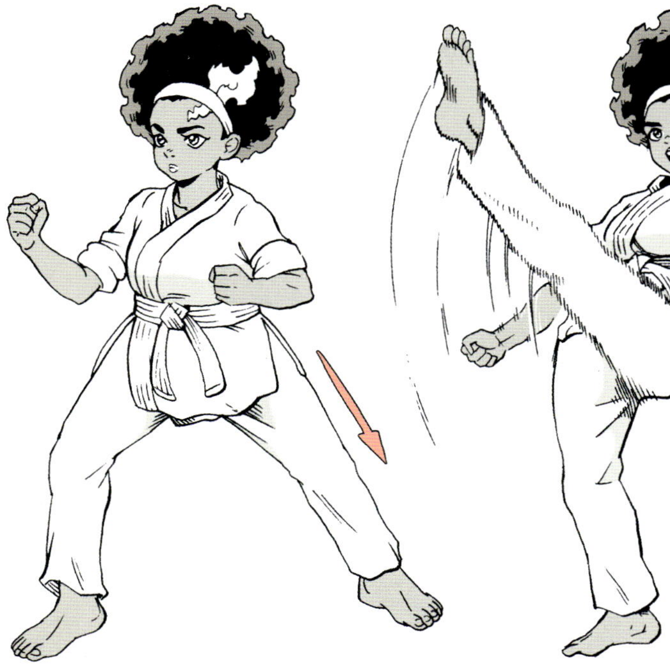

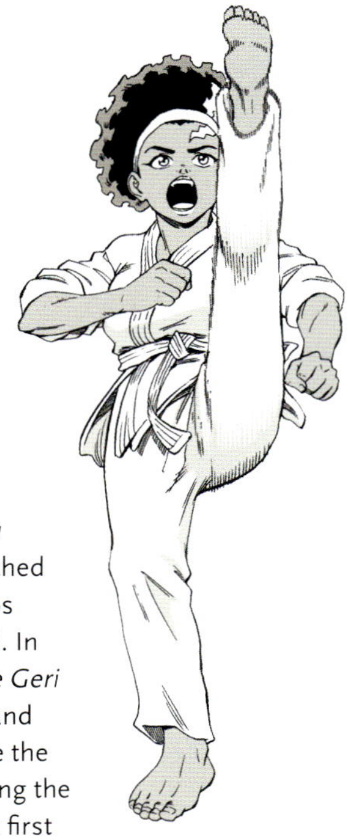

In the *Mae Chusoku Keage*, the leg stretched out at the back whips forward and upward. In the very similar *Mae Geri Jodan*, the starting and ending positions are the same, but when lifting the leg, the knee is bent first before the kick.

The rather dry presentation of techniques in this section can easily be jazzed up with more exciting perspectives, sound effects, and zoom or speed lines from the next chapters on effects and staging.

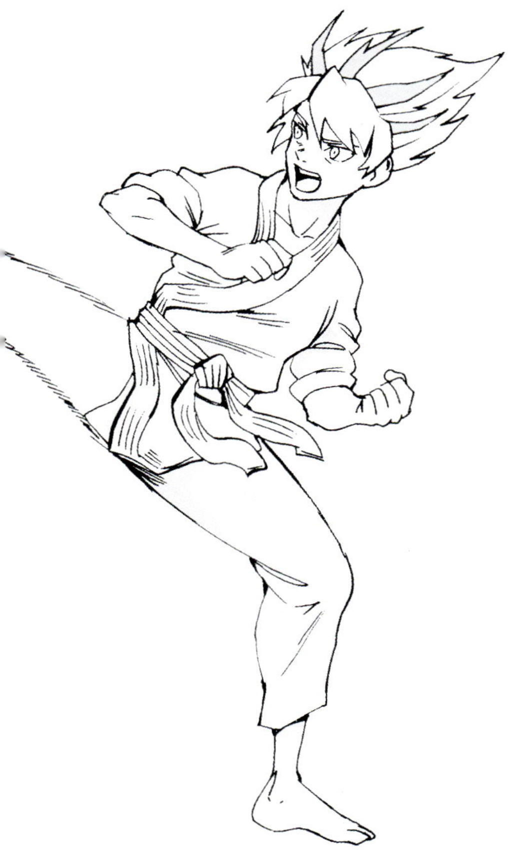

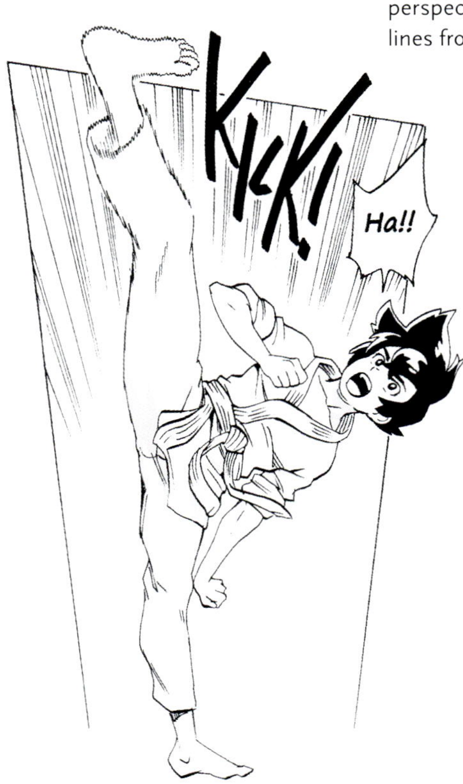

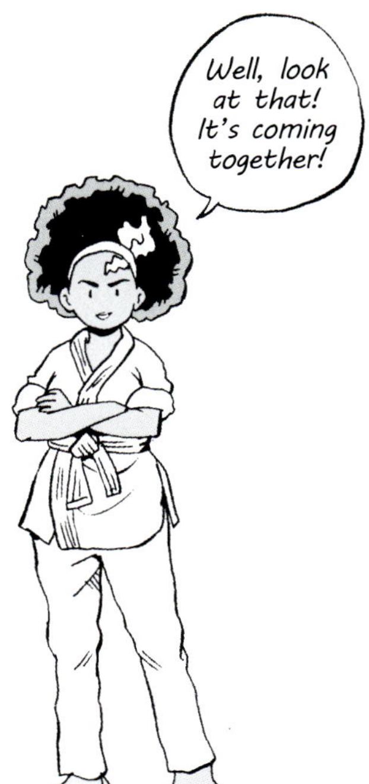

ONE-ON-ONE COMBAT

Time to ratchet things up a notch: let's put those techniques we've just learned into practice and unleash a few baddies on our team of heroes. On this double page, you can see a series of classic duel scenarios, pitting a villain against a hero.

As cool and impressive as manga fights may look, getting there takes work. For scenes like these, you should always start with a rough sketch to make sure everything lines up.

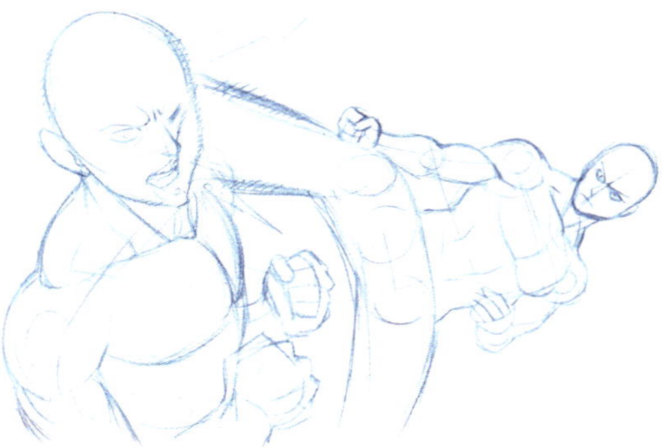

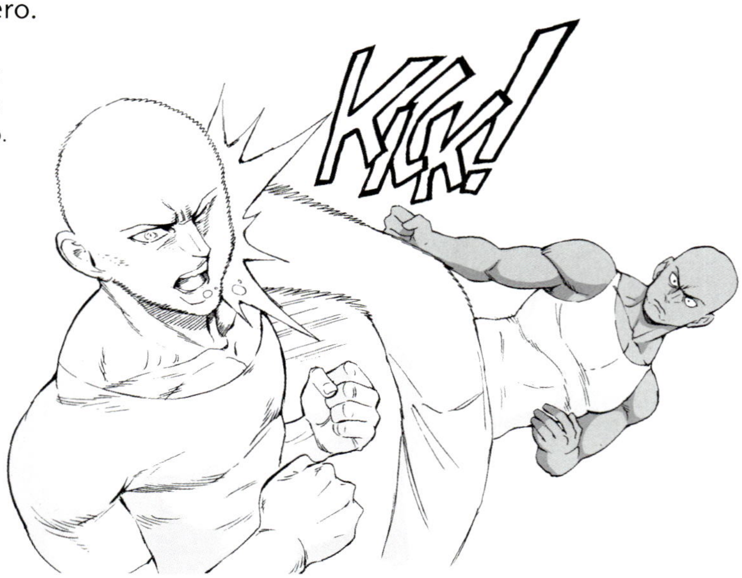

Left: It doesn't always have to be fists and feet delivering the blows.

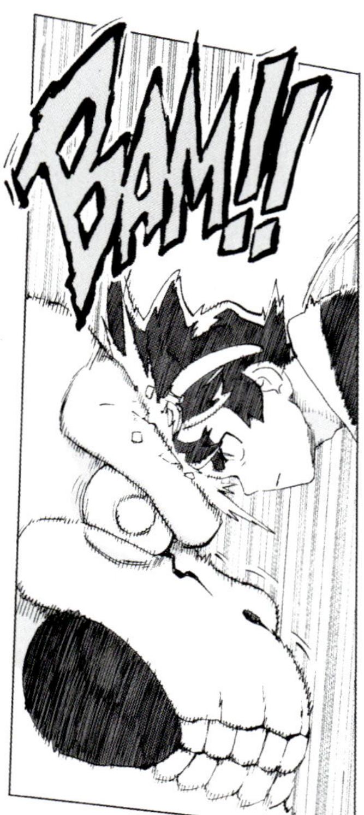

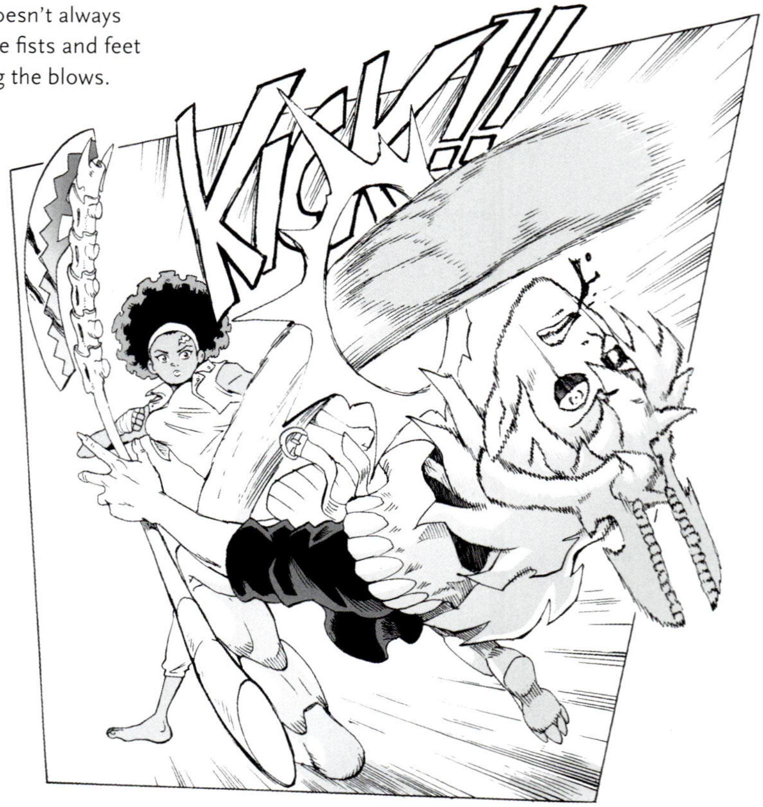

A prominent feature of manga is that it culminates in epic, cool poses, especially in individual action sequences (see also Chapter 5: Page Layout, Highlight Panels). A decisive blow should always look particularly effectual.

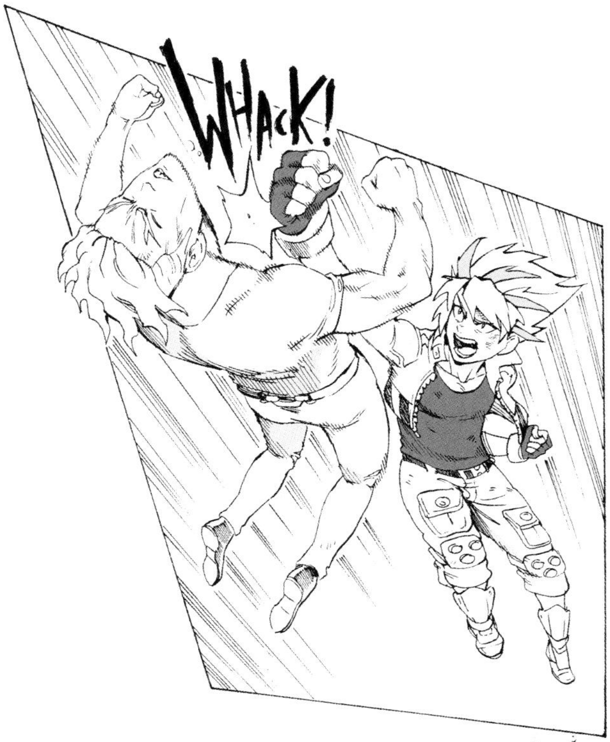

Below: here you can see another tool that manga often uses – a slight temporal offset. The strike itself is often not shown at all, but the moment afterward. The opponent flies away, the hero assumes his final pose.

Japanese-language sound effects give your action scenes even more authentic manga vibes. Search online for lists of suitable characters.

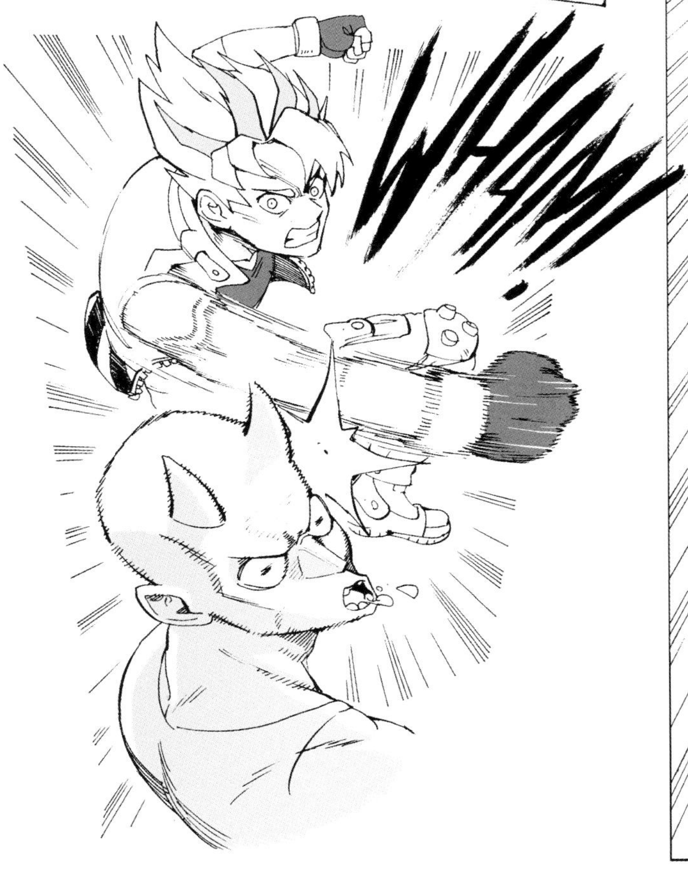

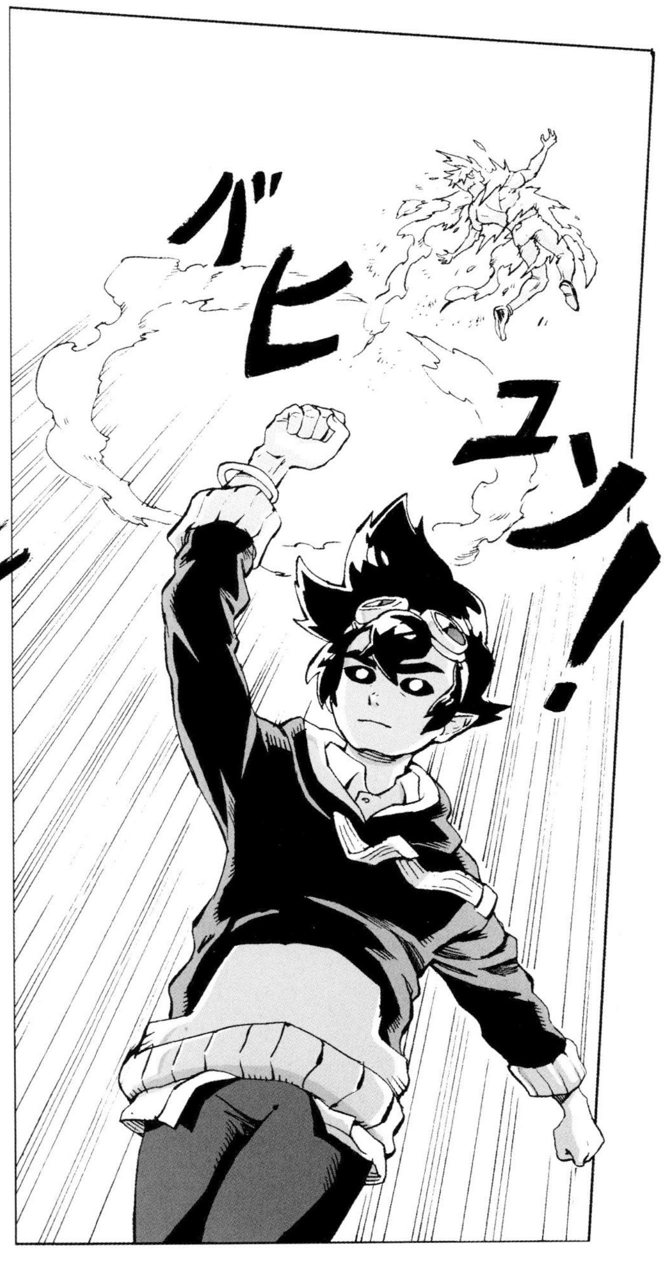

ON THE GROUND

Defeated! Heroes, their opponents, fighters, athletes – action manga always features tough defeats. Hands over the face, a hunched back, the head hanging low. Let's practice a few poses so that you can convey your characters into that emotional pit they need as motivation for their next victory.

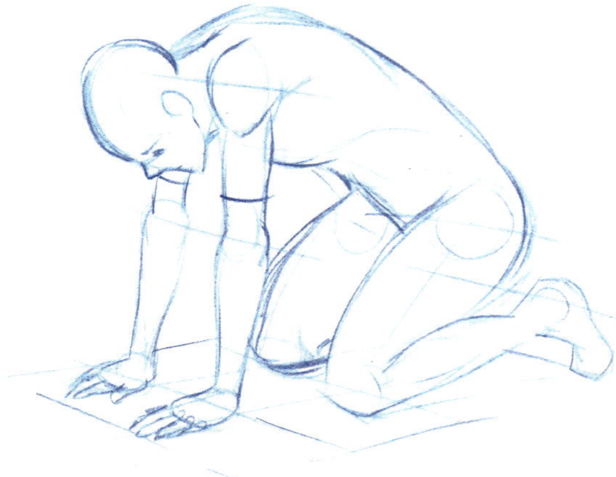

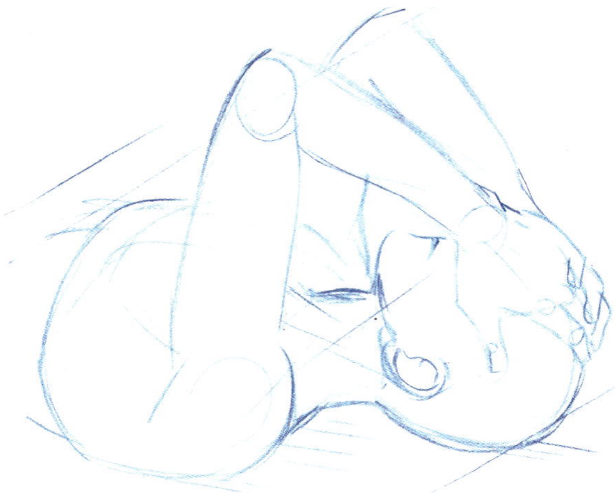

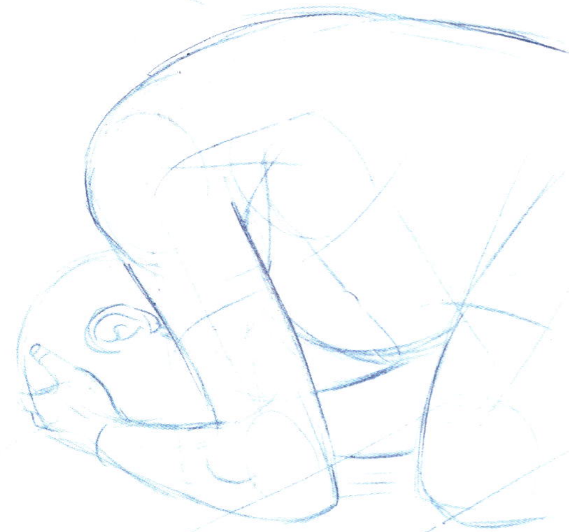

Note the many guide lines to place the figures in the space and, above all, to align the joints parallel to each other. And another... well..."fun fact" but not really that "fun": the reference for these poses was provided by some footballers after a defeat that resulted in elimination from a major tournament. So, the whole thing still had a positive purpose after all: a filled double page in this book...

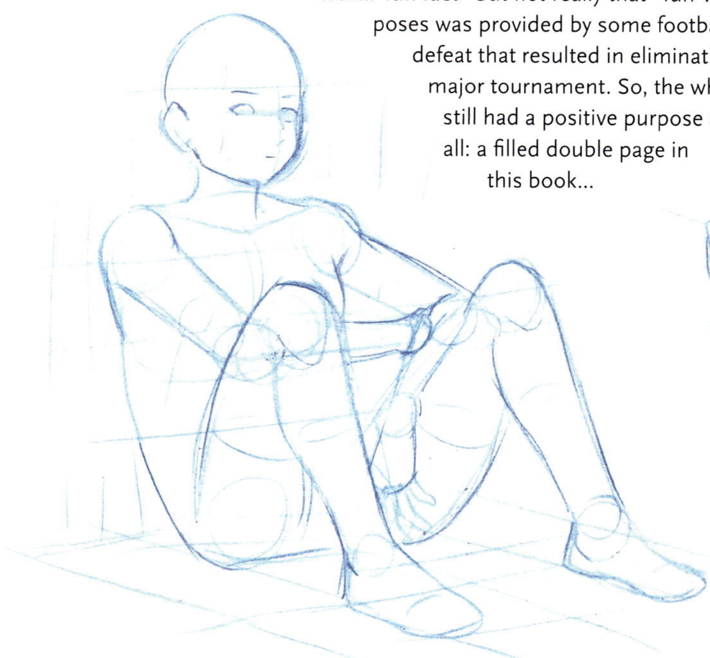

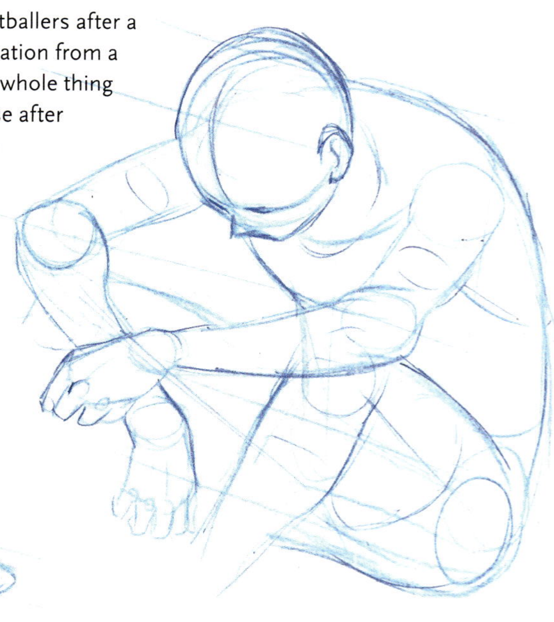

Once again, we ink in elaborate figures over the neutral preliminary drawings on the left. On the right, a female athlete who has perhaps just lost her long jump competition. Below are our three heroes and one of their enemies. You could almost feel some sympathy even for him. In fact, this low point for the bad guy would be a good moment for him to change sides. Only after a bitter defeat does a new window open up for him. Perhaps his opponents are surprisingly merciful to him and he realizes that his path may not have been the right one? Or maybe he will simply regroup and try again tomorrow.

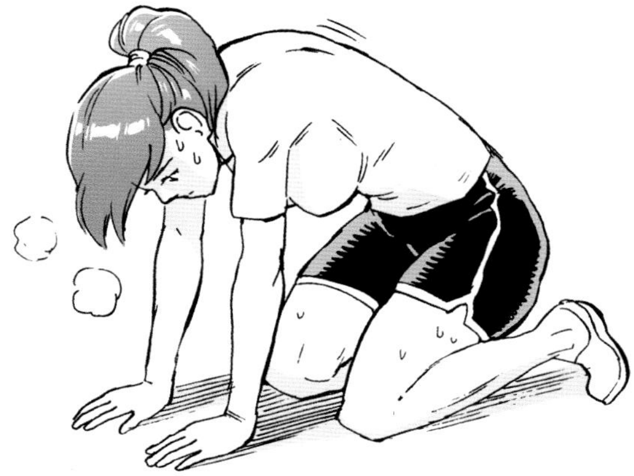

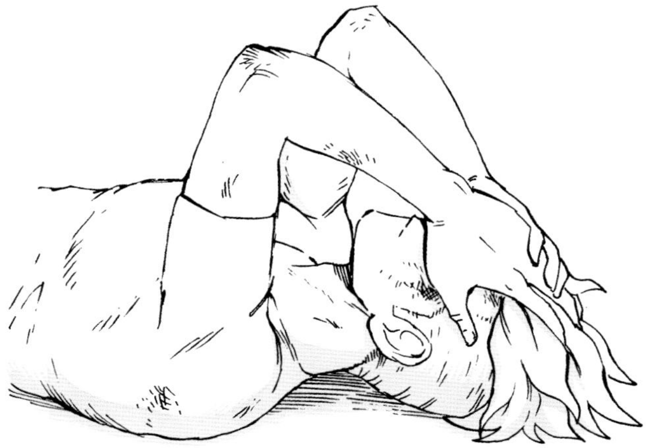

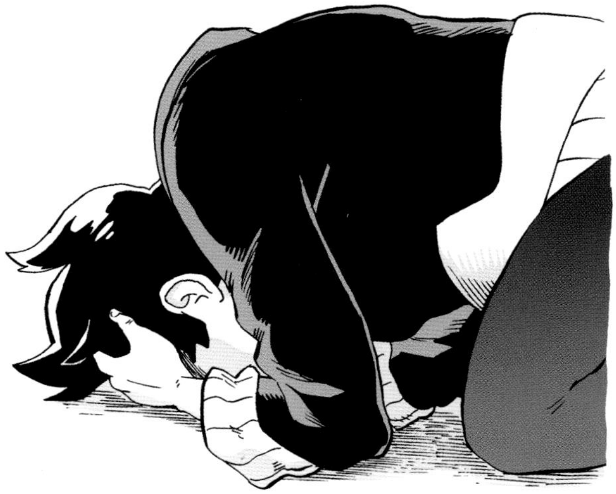

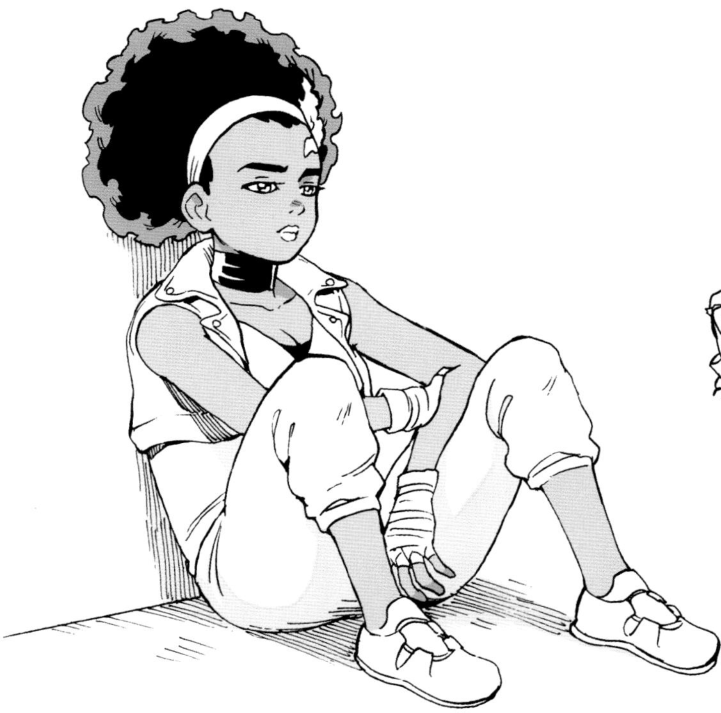

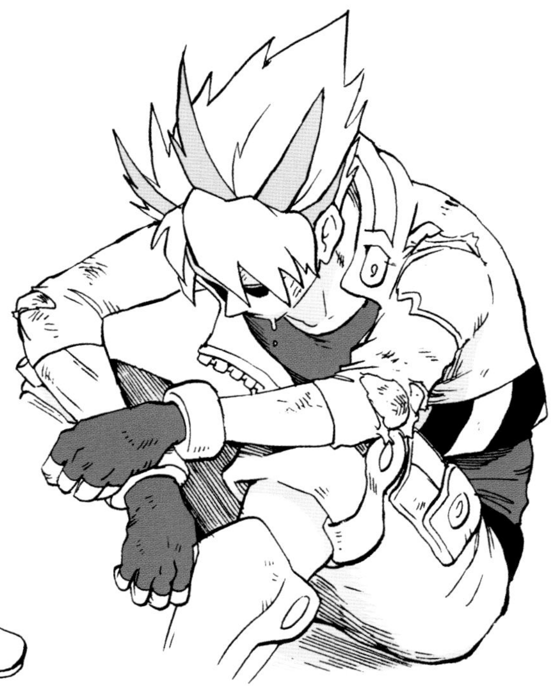

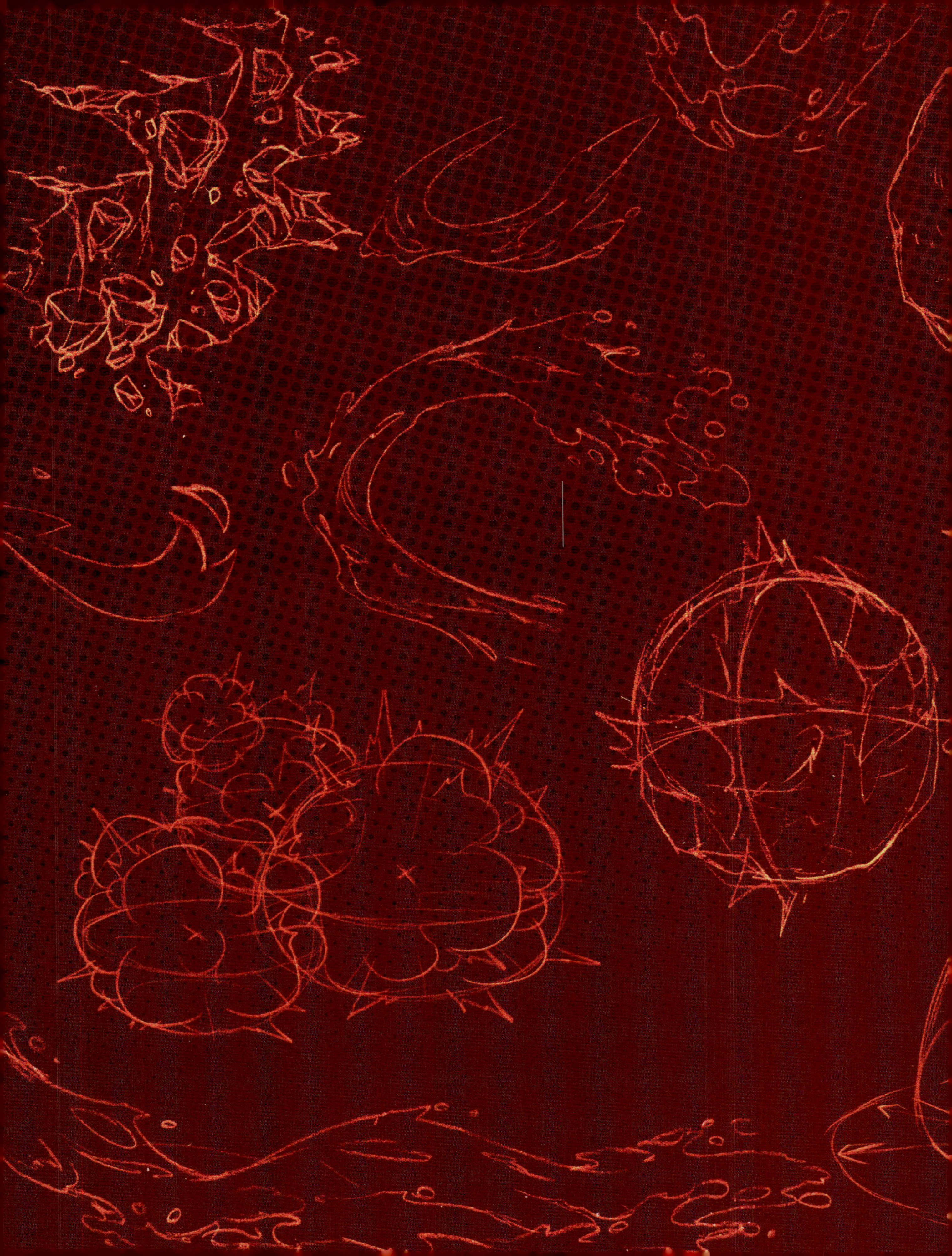

4. EFFECTS

We have now learned a lot about character design, anatomy and fighting techniques. Our foundations are in place – now it's time to refine them by adding some cool effects. In this chapter, you'll learn how to stage powerful explosions and shockwaves and use elements that spice up every action scene, giving physical attacks that popular "manga-overkill" effect through crackling bolts of lightning or swirling gusts of wind.

EXPLOSIONS

All good action stories have explosions! They may be large or small, of natural origin, or the result of a fantastic energy attack, explosions of fire or dust. The following pages seek to break down, in the simplest possible way and requiring only a very rudimentary understanding of physics, how these powerful effects can be spectacularly achieved.

1 Every explosion has a center, here shown by the cross. The circle around it serves as a guide – that's how far the flames should spread.

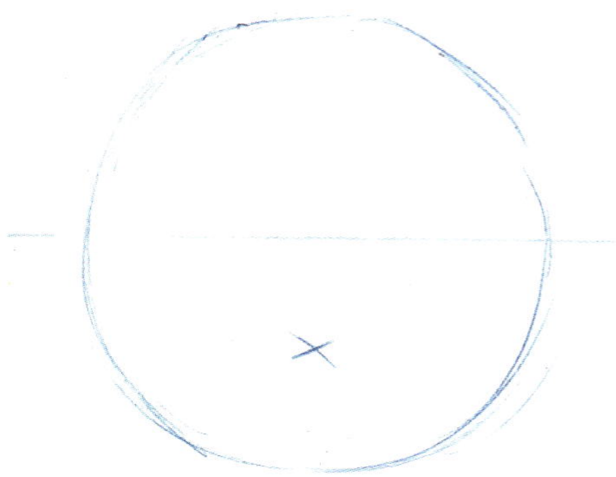

2 Now it's time to think in three dimensions: what we have here is a kind of sphere, forming fairly evenly around the center of the blast. The center itself isn't quite in the middle, since the explosion is happening on the ground.

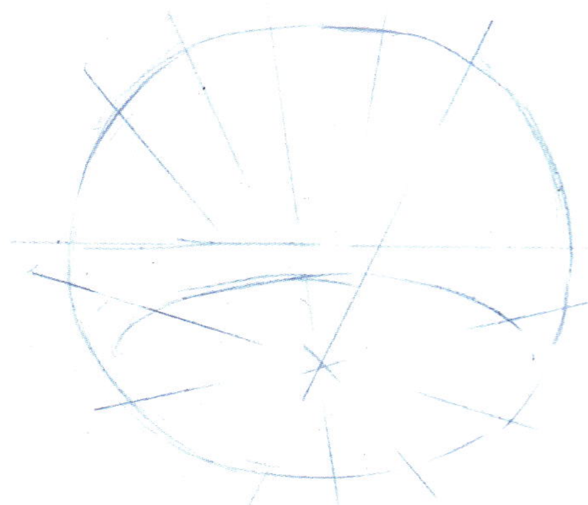

3 Next, draw some "blobs" around the explosion sphere, big and small, and make sure they're irregular, like a fluffy cloud. These will become the flames bursting outward.

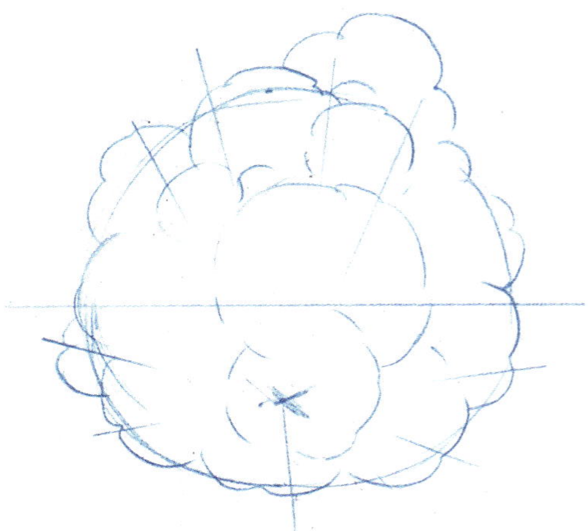

4 Time for the spikes! Draw long, uneven points sticking out between the blobs here and there. Those are the spots where the blast fire breaks out the strongest. The more spikes you add, the more powerful the explosion looks, but don't overdo it, otherwise it'll end up looking like a puffed-up porcupine.

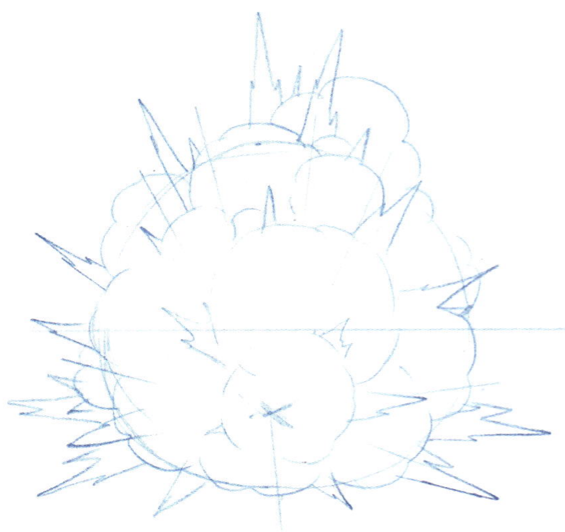

5 Now for the final touches! Don't worry, it takes a while to get a feel for how much detail an explosion can handle, and where it's better to leave gaps. The black areas give the flames more volume and really make the bursting "blobs" pop out.

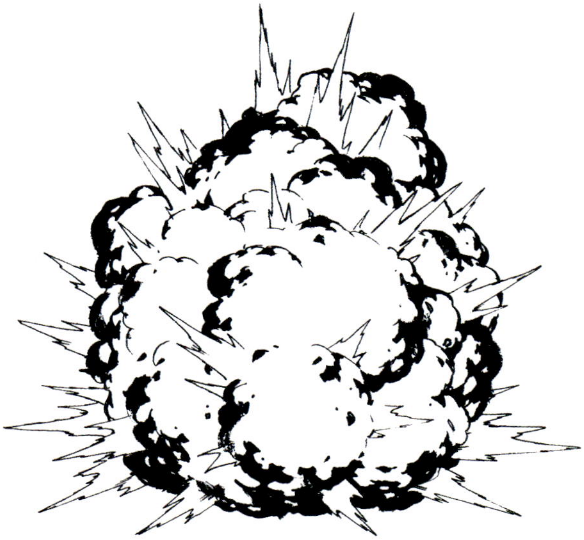

6 Here's a version in grayscale. Of course, you can also use screentone. The intermediate shades enhance the explosion's three-dimensional effect – once again, however, be careful! Including too many gradations can end up working against you.

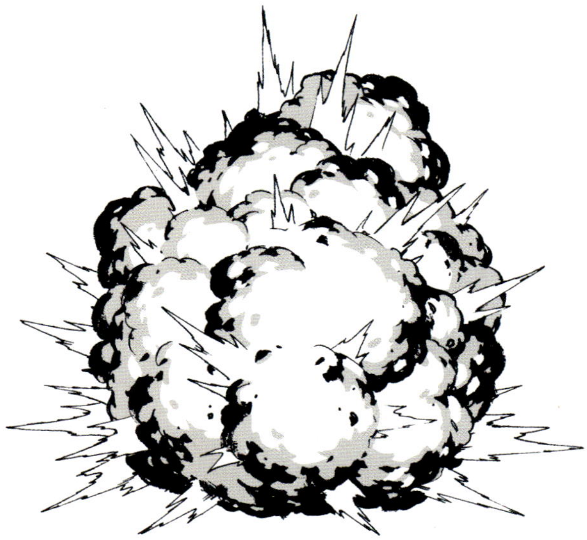

7 And now in color. The original black ink drawings have been lightened.

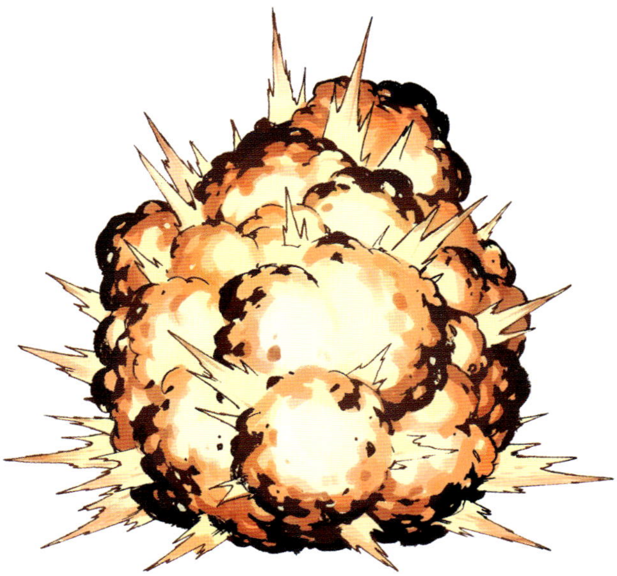

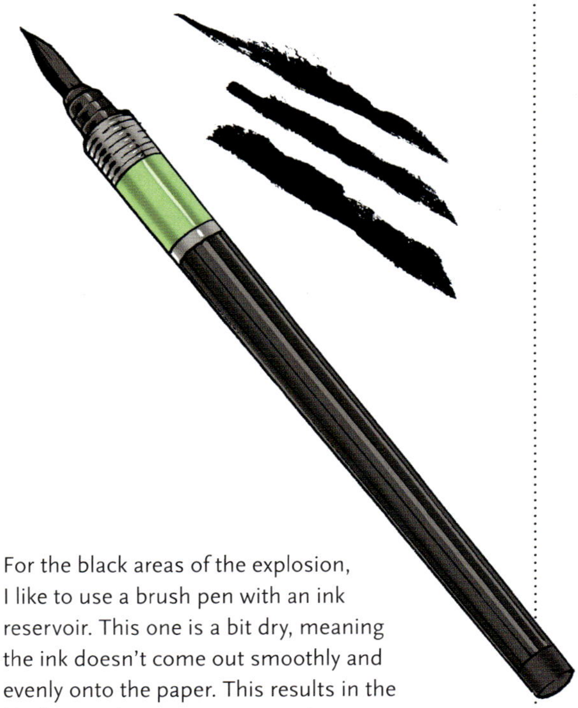

For the black areas of the explosion, I like to use a brush pen with an ink reservoir. This one is a bit dry, meaning the ink doesn't come out smoothly and evenly onto the paper. This results in the black areas being more textured, as you can see in the three example strokes to the right of the pen illustration.

EXPLOSIONS – VARIATION A

In this version, the flames are being pushed in one direction. The blast center is far to the left.

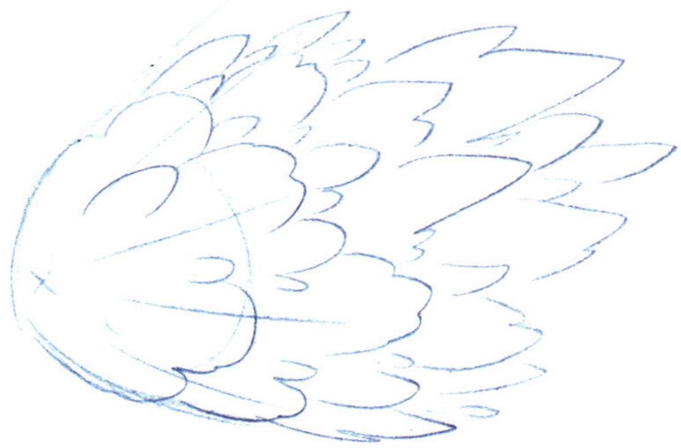

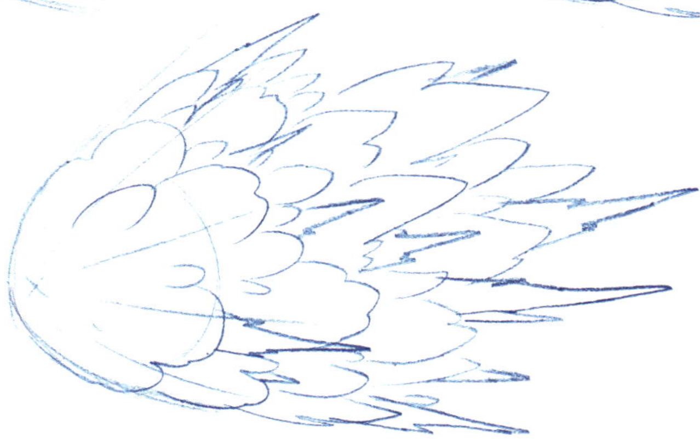

The blobs and spikes follow the movement of the explosion flames from left to right, and therefore stretch along the guide lines. The guide lines start at the blast center and then curve in an arc over an imaginary sphere.

Here's a simplified illustration, like a comet entering orbit.

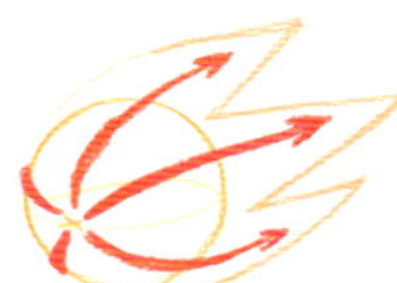

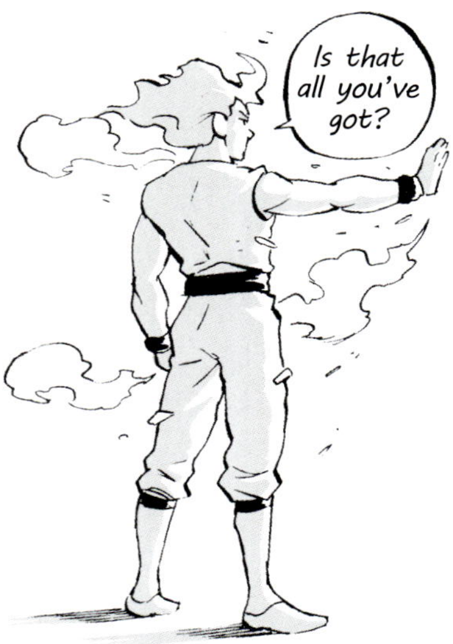

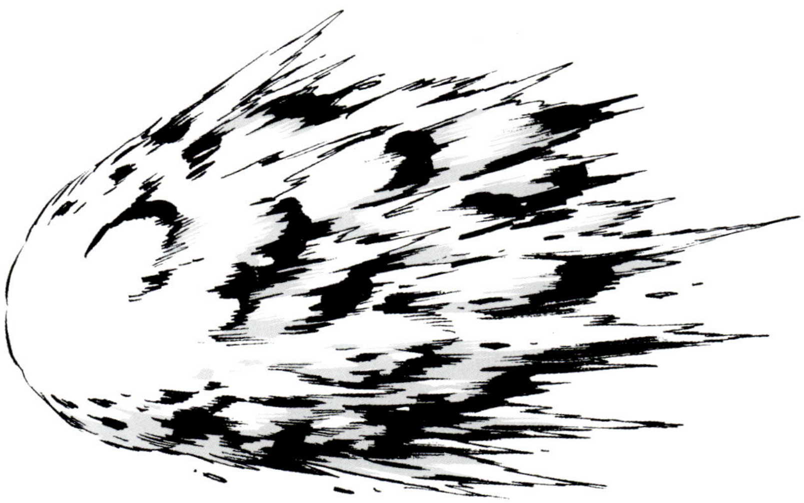

Explosions like this can occur, for example, when an explosive projectile is intercepted – as seen in the example above, where the character blocks an attack with some kind of energy barrier.

EXPLOSIONS – VARIATION B

Here you see an explosion in midair, where the flames can spread freely in all directions.

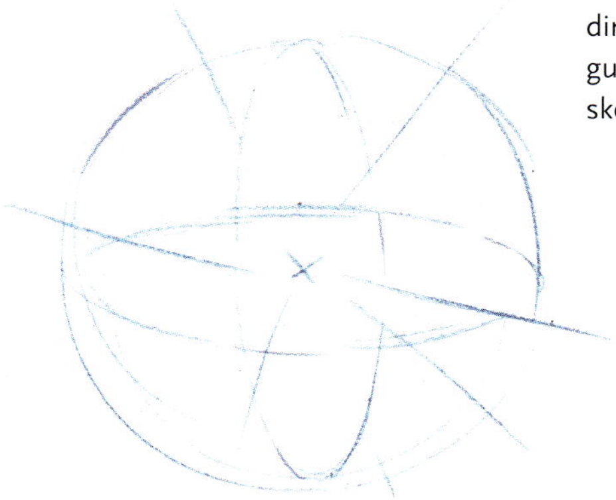

The blast center lies exactly in the middle of the sphere. To help convey the three-dimensionality, several guide lines have been sketched in.

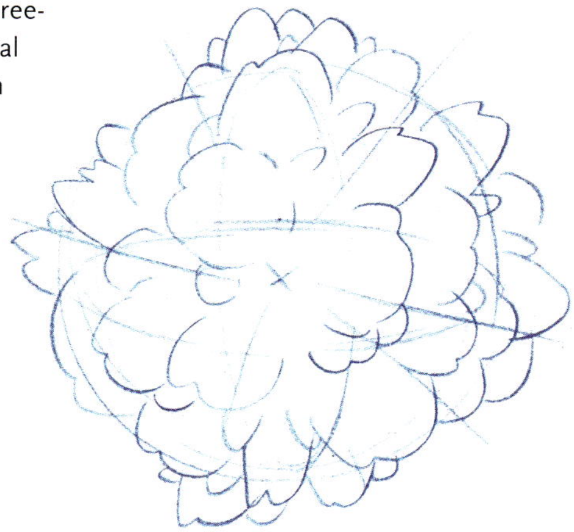

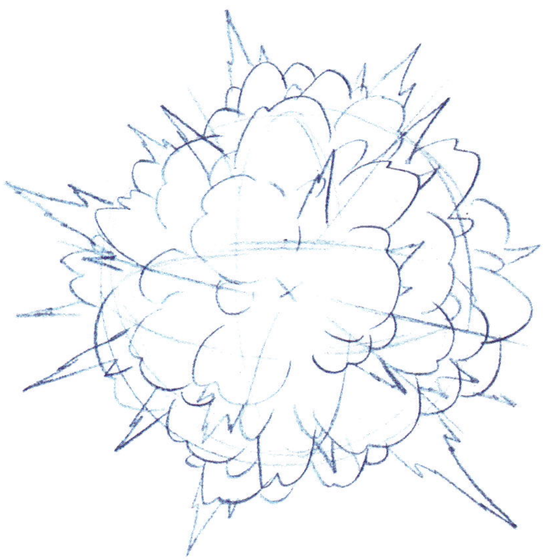

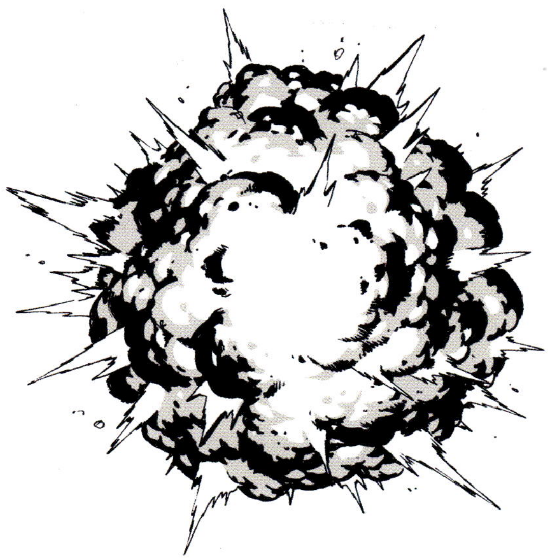

Since the ground doesn't "absorb" part of the explosion here and the flames spread out evenly, you can distribute the blobs and spikes fairly uniformly across the sphere.

For the black areas of this explosion, a brush pen with a very soft tip was used, one that lays down ink smoothly and evenly.

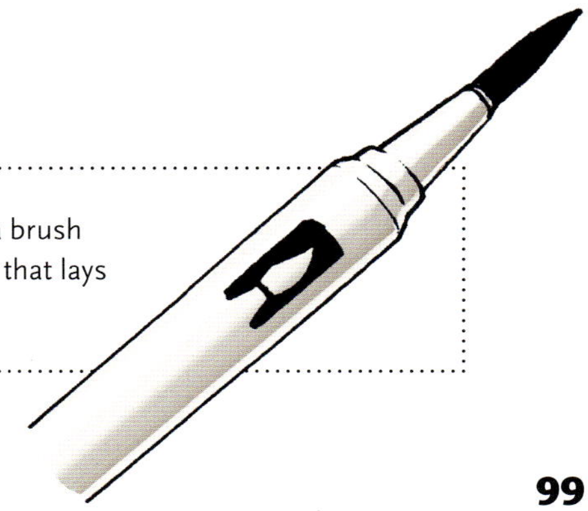

EXPLOSIONS – VARIATION C

This time you're looking at a chain of explosions, overlapping with each other, which leads to spectacular effects. Here there are four blast centers.

It's tricky to keep track of the physical dynamics of what's happening where and how, but if you start off with the trusty spheres and determine the spatial order of the explosions (which one is closest to us, etc., as highlighted here in color), you should be able to create effects that feel coherent.

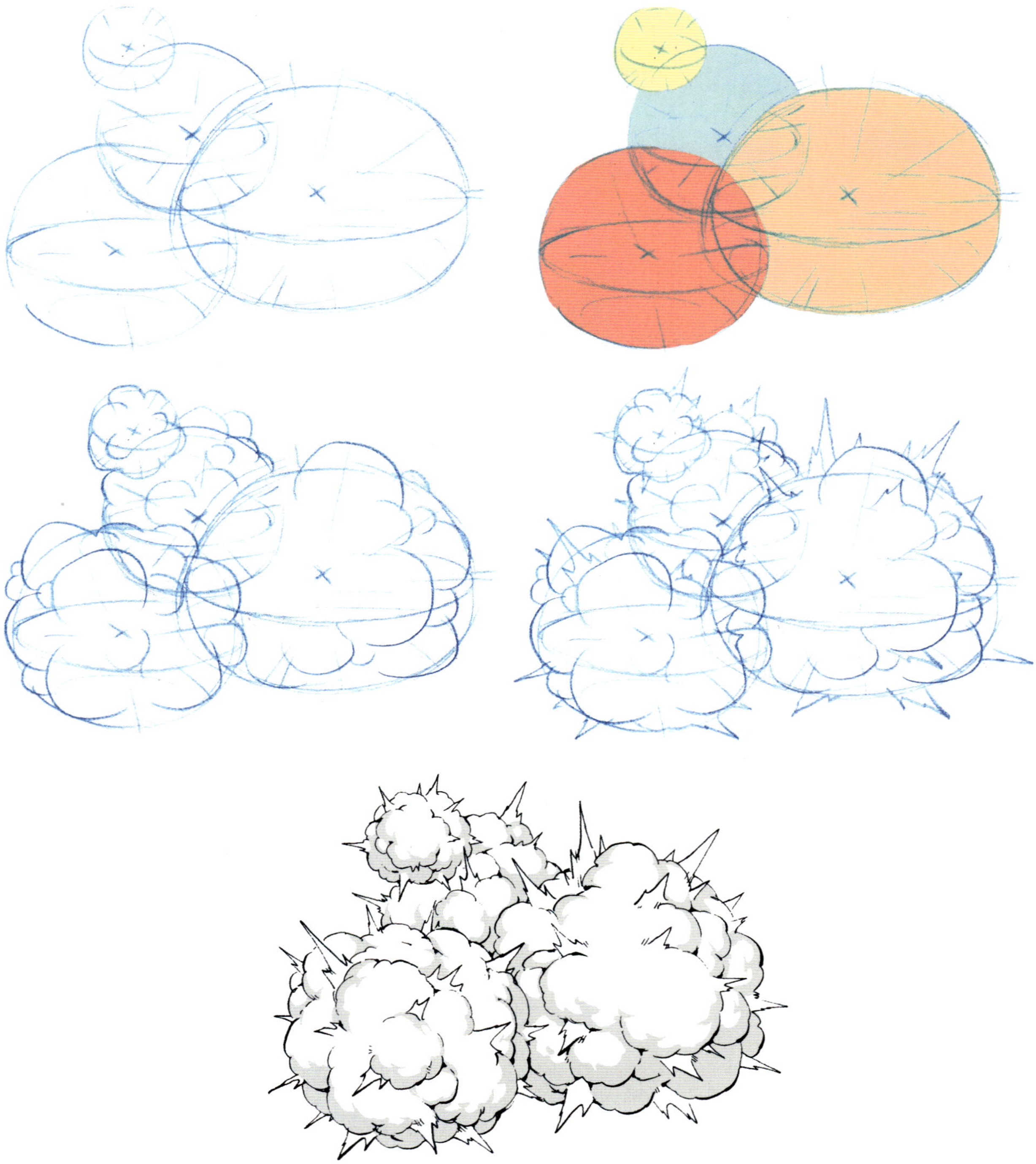

EXPLOSIONS – VARIATION D

Rubble and debris are flung away by the explosion. With these kinds of "particle effects" you can dramatically boost the quality of your explosion with relatively little effort.

This also offers another great way to enhance the sense of depth. For a better overview, the gray shading and black areas of the explosion flames have been omitted here.

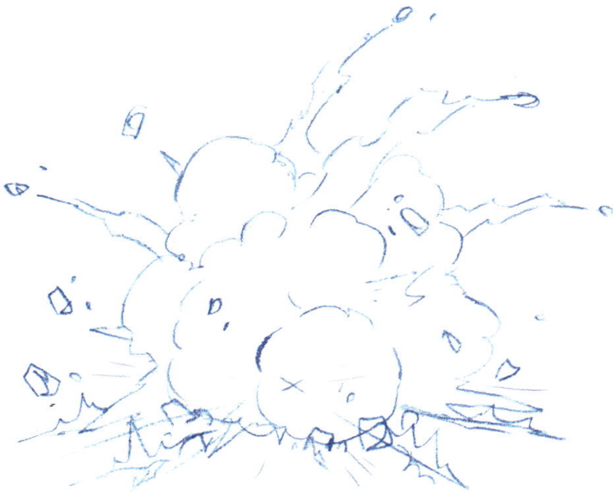

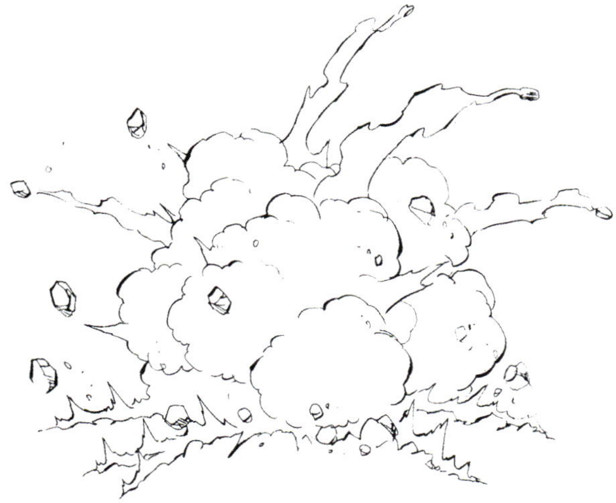

As an additional effect, the ground splits open. The cracks also radiate out from the blast center and branch outward.

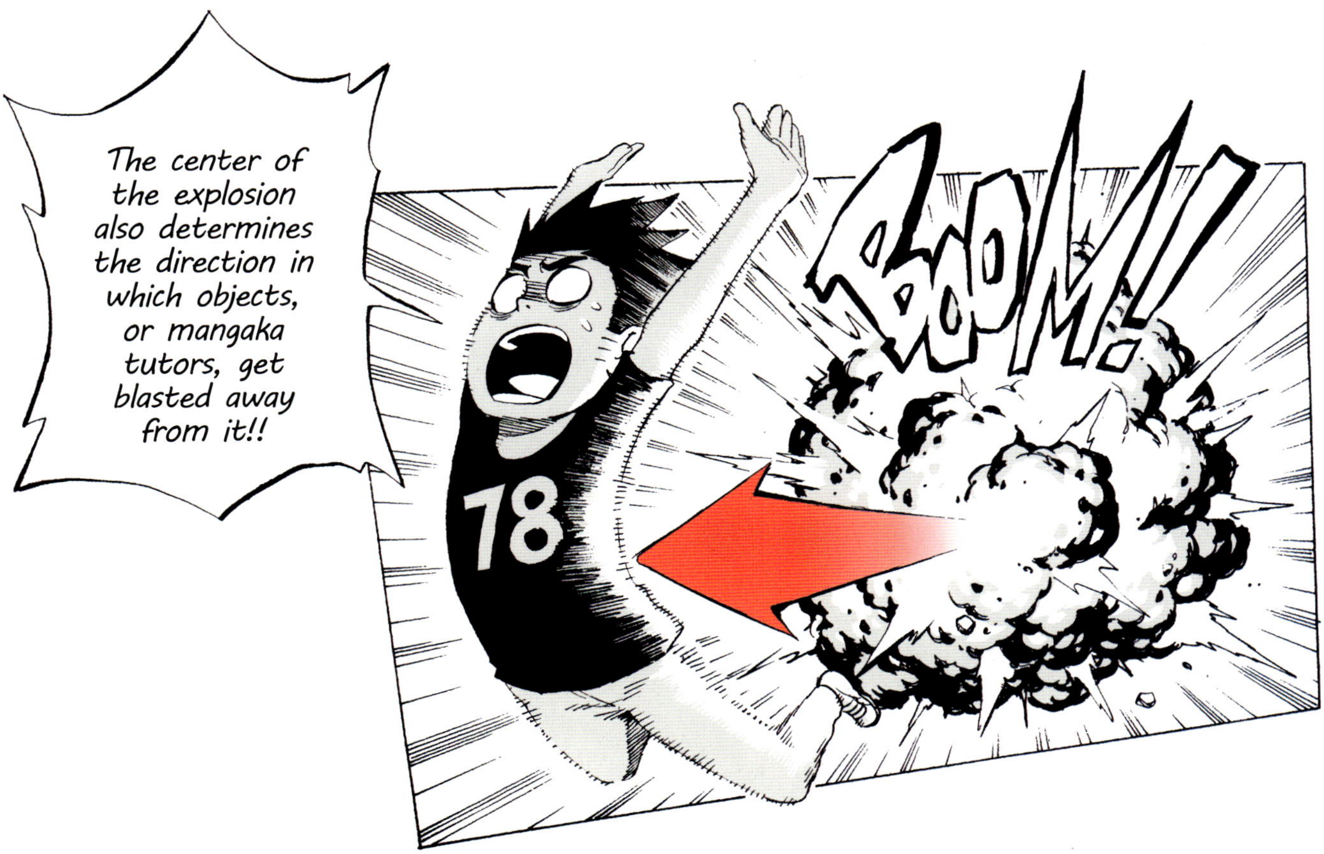

EXPLOSIONS – VARIATION E

In this version, the explosive flames shoot high into the air. A shockwave also spreads along the ground. We will look at shockwaves on the following double page.

The explosions on this page have no black areas to enhance the fire effect. This makes the explosions here look dustier.

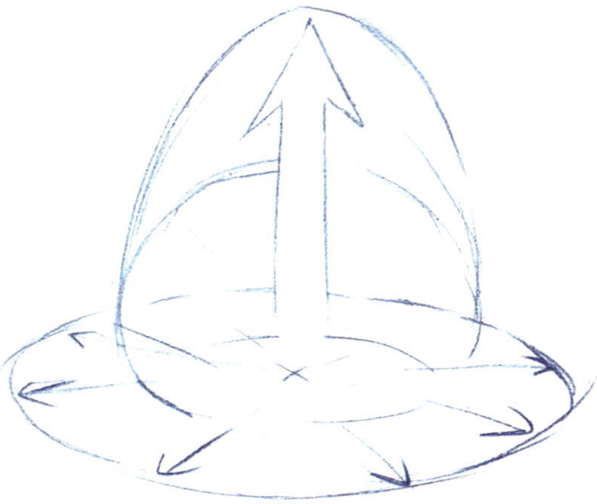

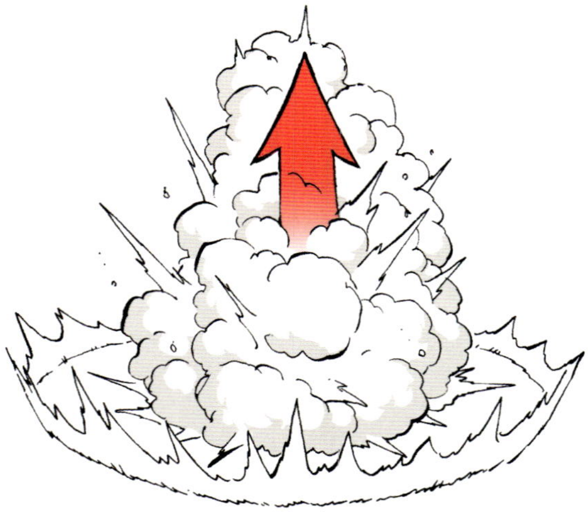

EXPLOSIONS – VARIATION F

1 A spherical explosion spreading out fairly evenly in all directions through the air, combined with a shockwave. It kind of looks like Saturn in the preliminary sketch.

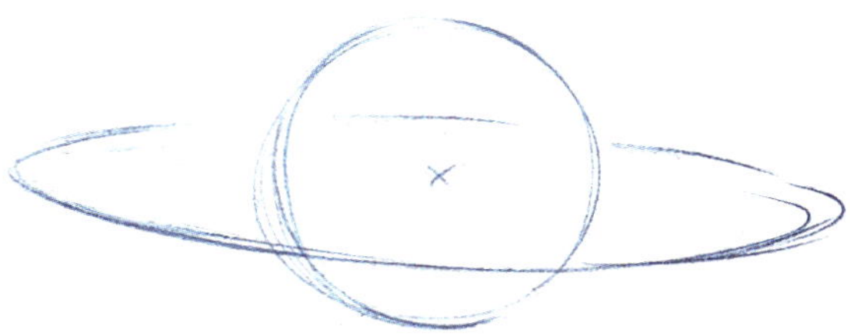

2 Using a vanishing point that also marks the blast center (i.e. the middle of the sphere), draw guide lines on the ring that will become the shockwave. The shockwave spreads across a two-dimensional plane, and these guide lines will help enhance the effect.

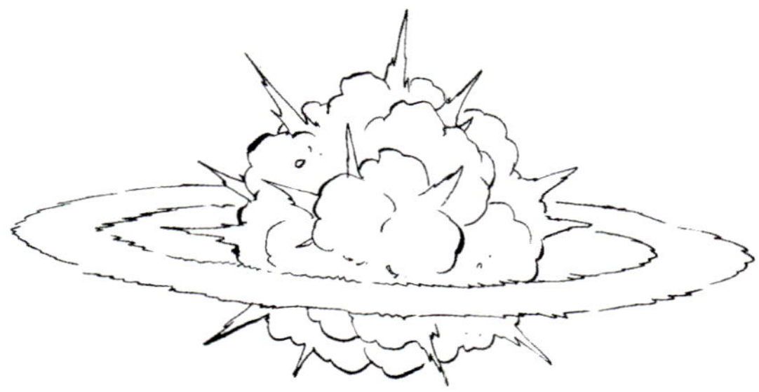

3 When inking the outline of the shockwave, you can now draw in slight ripples along the guide lines. This helps to illustrate the wave spreading outward from the center.

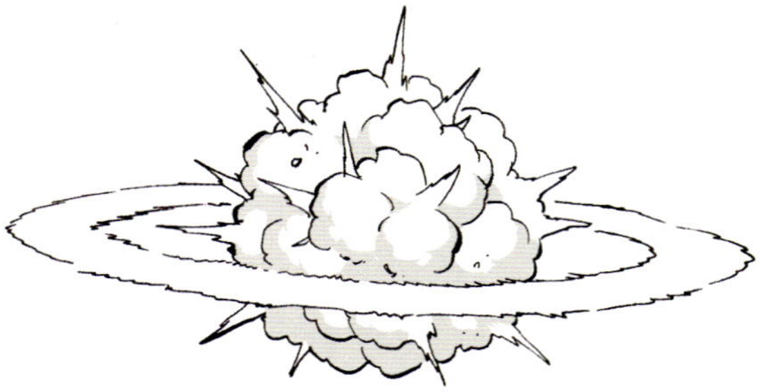

AFTER THE EXPLOSION

Finally, let's take a quick look at what you need to pay attention to when depicting a scene that comes after the explosion. There will be parts of the exploded structure (here a car and a tower block) that have been completely destroyed by the blast wave and the initial flames. Panes of glass, for example, are the first to break.

However, there are also materials that are more resistant and can at least survive for a while, such as the metal bodywork or reinforced concrete.

Fire escapes from all the cavities, and soot forms around these (shown by crosshatching in the car example).

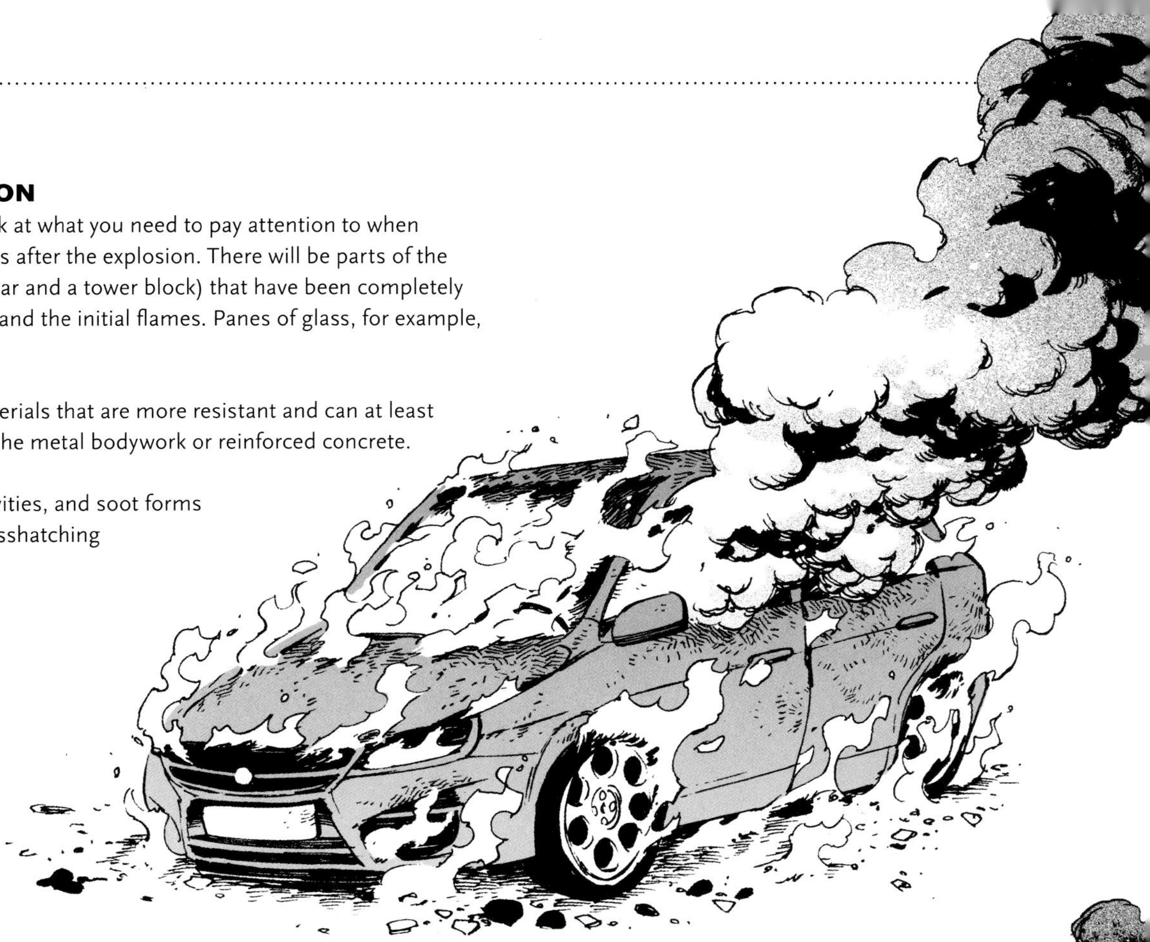

Fires produce thick columns of smoke. Use plenty of black when rendering these. Around the explosion site, you'll find lots of ash and other debris scattered about, some of which may still be burning.

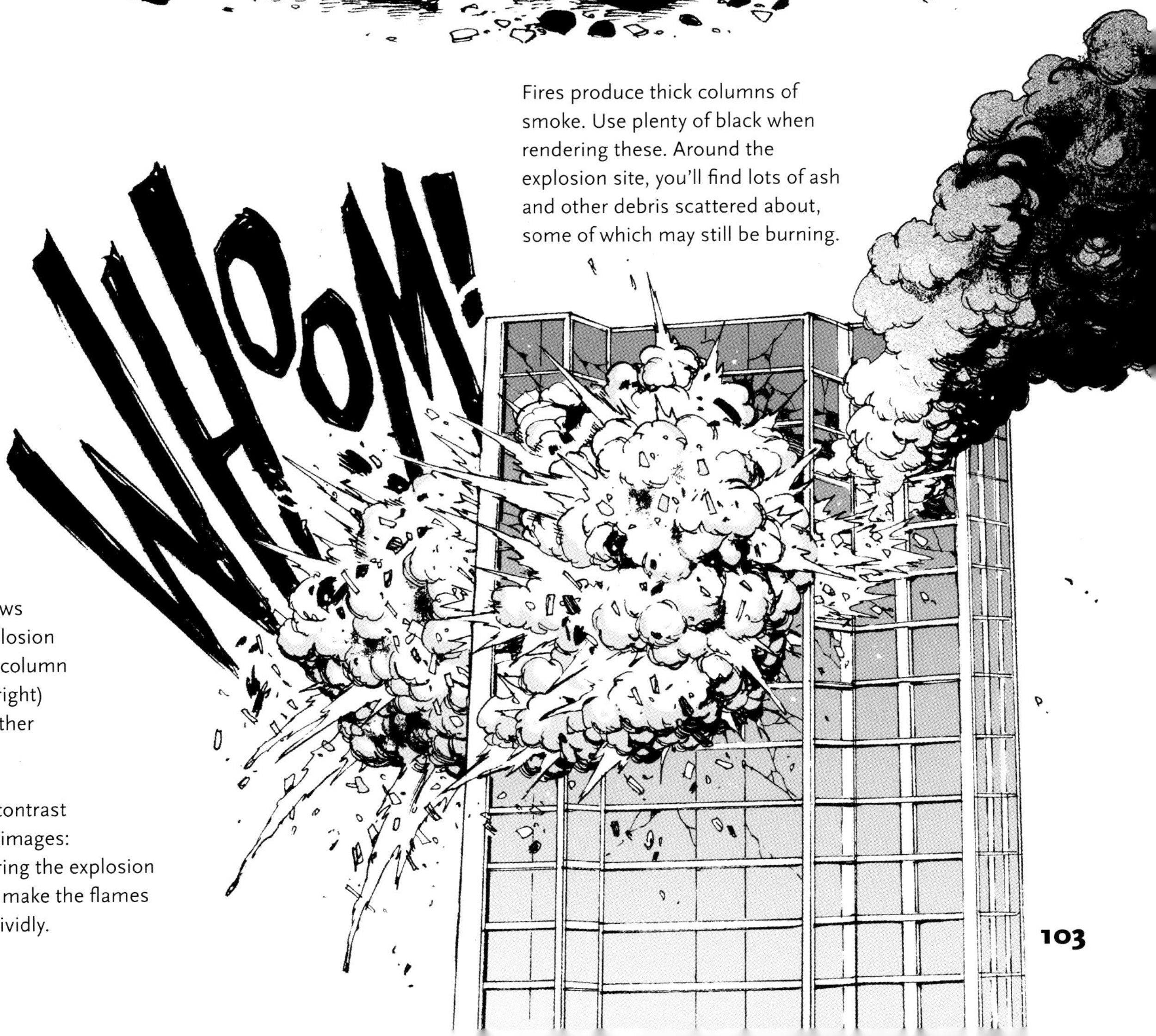

The tower block example also shows how an initial explosion (indicated by the column of smoke on the right) is followed by further explosions.

Take note of the contrast between the two images: the objects suffering the explosion are grayed out to make the flames stand out more vividly.

SHOCKWAVES

The use of shockwave effects is an efficient way of emphasizing the force of an impact or strike. Physically, we're once again close to what we saw with explosions on the previous pages: there's a central impact point from which the energy spreads outward. This time, however, it's not a spherical expansion through space, but rather a two-dimensional spread in concentric circles, usually across a solid surface. IMPORTANT: this only refers to how we graphically depict shockwaves, not how they actually radiate in real physics, where they spread out spherically – or even in a cone shape – through space.

1 For the shockwave, we draw two circles parallel to each other. In our example, the lower circle represents the plane where the energy is spreading.

2 The upper circle serves as a guide and marks the boundary up to which the energy wave extends. As seen in the sketches, the effect is, once again, very irregular.

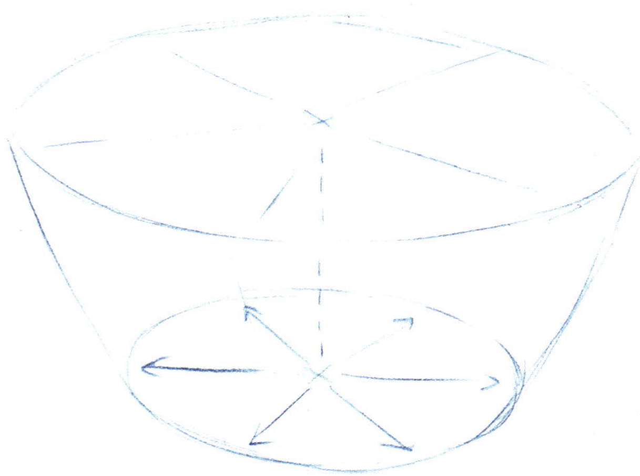

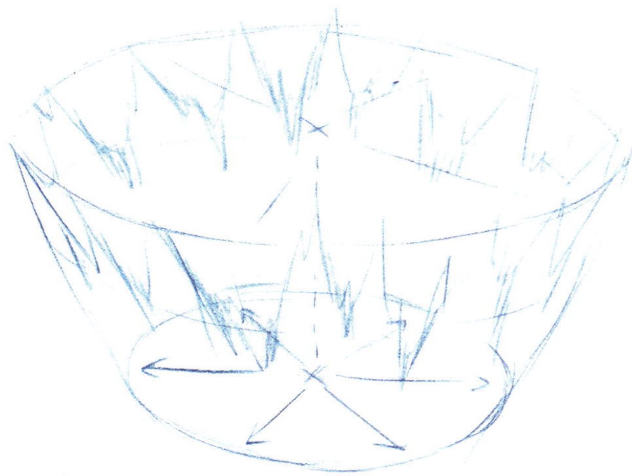

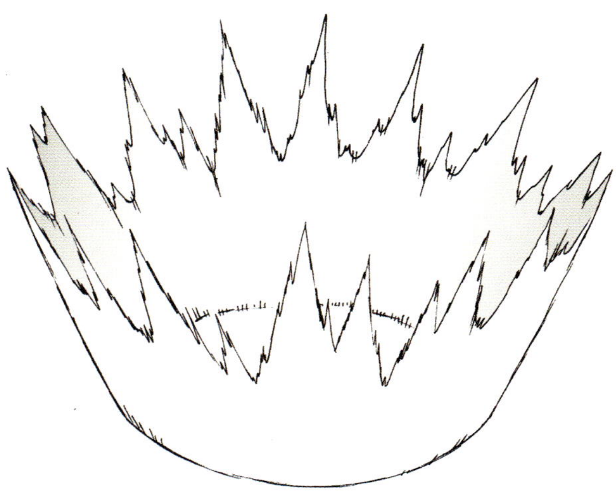

3 In its finished form, you can see that this effect can also be used, for example, for splashing water, or sand into which something has been thrown with great force.

Here, a series of shockwaves in frontal top view. Spatially, this is a bit less complex to pull off.

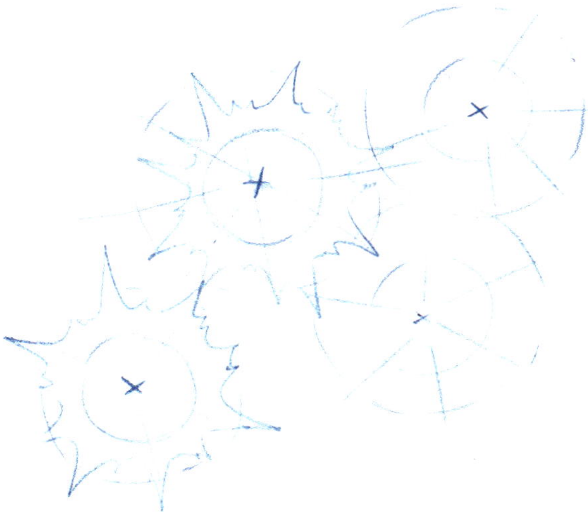

Several shockwaves, hitting with about the same intensity, suggests that the triggering impulses occurred more or less at the same time. See below for an example of this in practice.

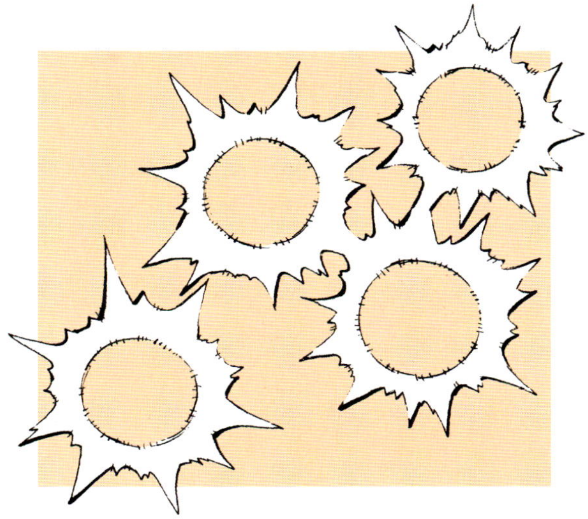

Our mentor demonstrates a common use of the shockwave salvo on the training wall: rapid-fire punching like a hail of bullets. You see it all the time in battle manga – fists flying at supersonic speed, so fast that the human eye can't keep up. Instead, it looks as though the number of arms has multiplied, with afterimages trailing behind. The same applies to the shockwaves. Of course, with only two arms punching, they can't all appear at once, but fortunately, you can exaggerate the speed a bit.

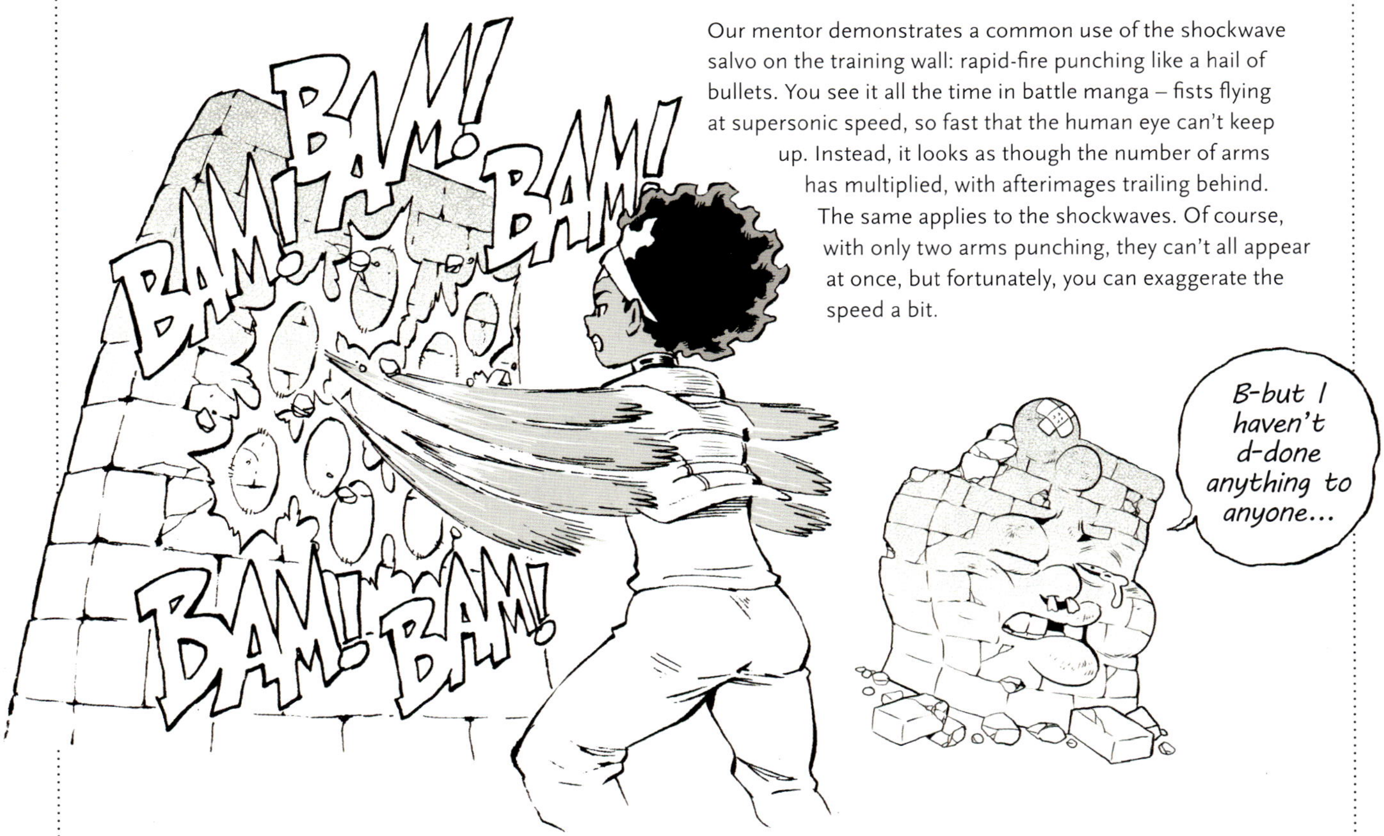

ROCKS

Cracking ground, crumbling rocks, and collapsing buildings – where there's action, there's rubble. We've already seen it used in previous chapters as a way to ramp up a powerful explosion or a scene of fists smashing a brick wall. Rocks can enhance action scenes in many ways, which is why we must give this solid element the attention it deserves.

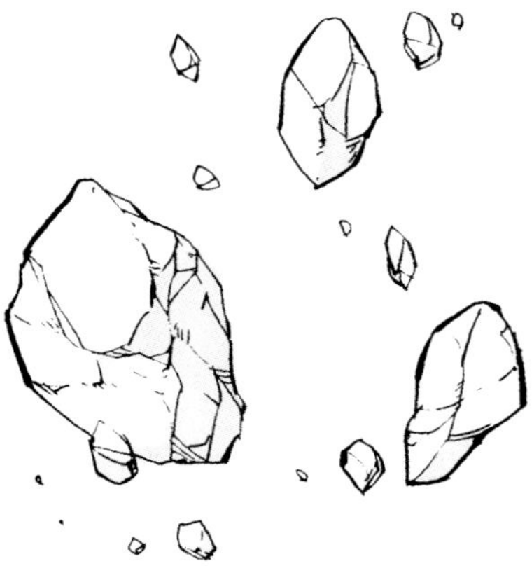

From small stones to earthquakes tearing up the scenery, the basic technique for drawing rocks is the same: work with clear, hard broken edges and use hatching to highlight the imperfections of the material. In these example images, gray shading was used to give the objects depth, always aligned to the fracture lines where the rock has broken.

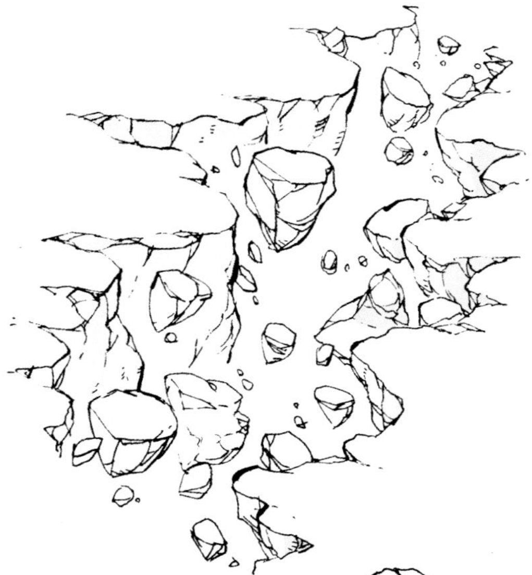

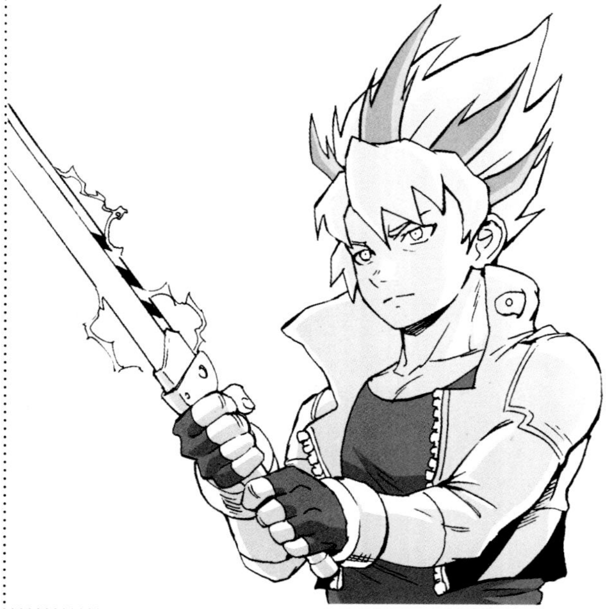

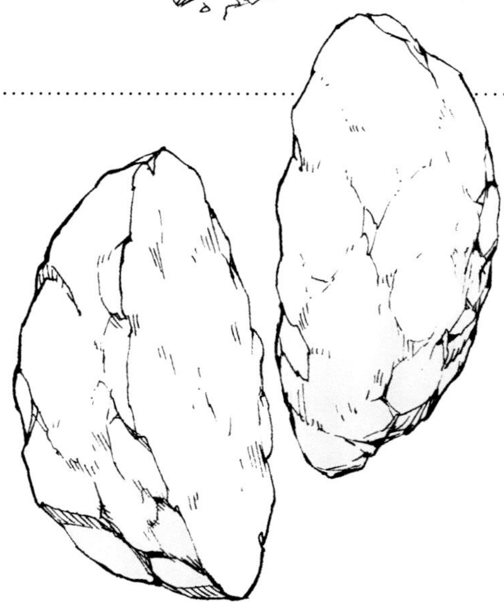

Rocks really don't have it easy in action manga. One classic move is to shatter them using one's bare hands to demonstrate strength, atomize them with energy beams, or, as we see Hero A doing here, cut them up with a weapon.

What's twice as impressive as a halved boulder? A quartered boulder! We are grateful for the boulder's noble sacrifice, because this dissection lets us get a much better look at the inner structure of split rock. The cut surfaces are a fair bit smoother than the outer ones, but not perfectly flat either.

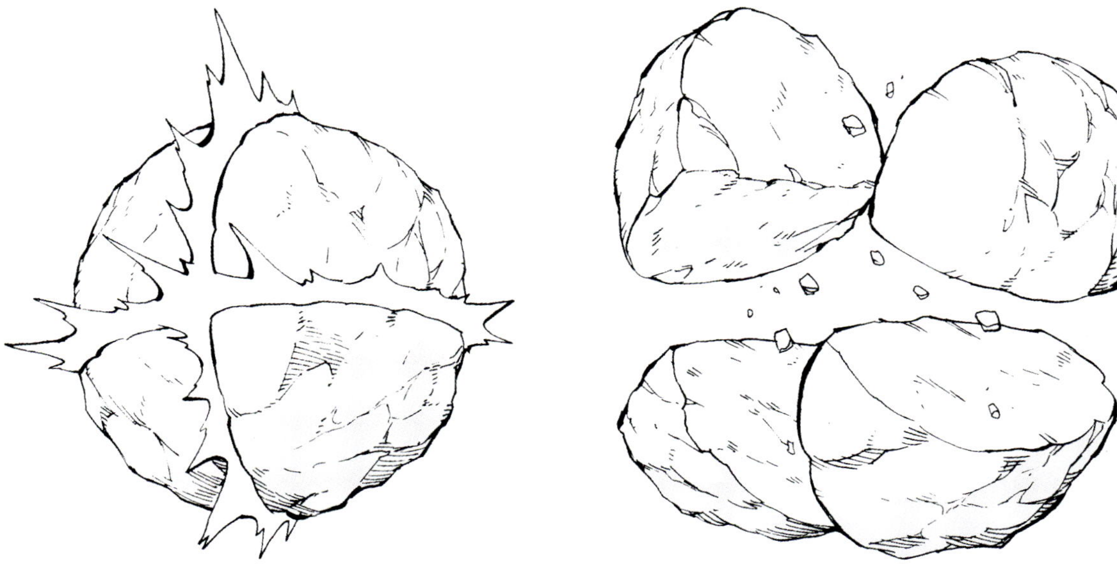

You can do a lot with flying rocks. A small one, thrown at the right moment, can help the hero distract the enemy in a tense game of cat-and-mouse. Go a few sizes up and you've got yourself a proper projectile for combat. Go *waaay* bigger and we're talking celestial weapons, like meteors or asteroids. To show the trajectory of a rock, regardless of its size, use guide lines in your preliminary sketches and work them into the final drawing using hatching. As you can see below, this has the same effect as with a fast punch or a high-speed kick: the direction of motion gets clearer, and the sense of speed is heightened.

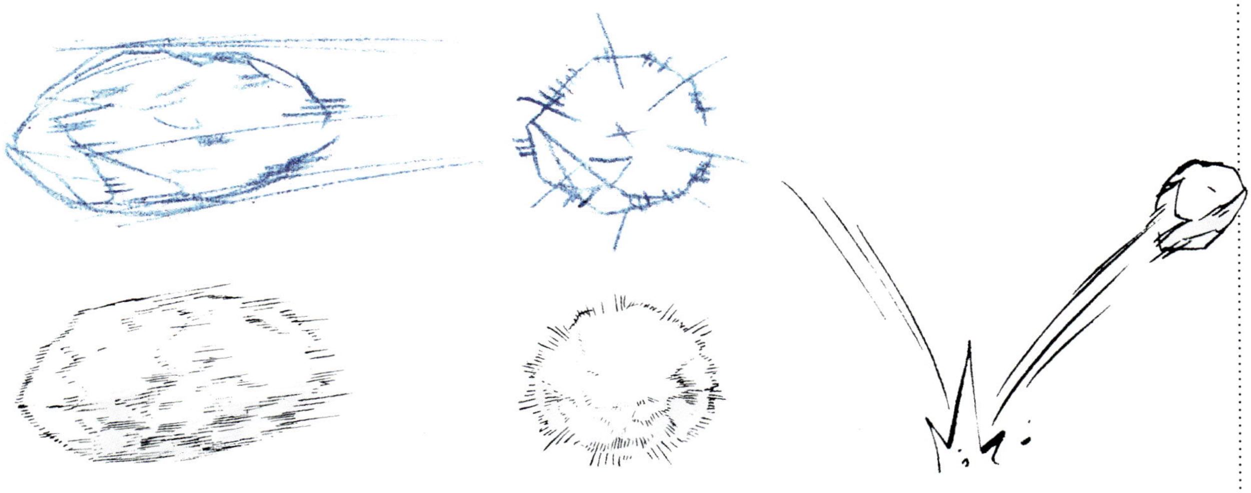

WIND

Since wind isn't something you can actually see, we have to make it visible through drawing. Think stirred-up dust, drifting smoke, the motion of clouds, or simply a clear, visual representation of air currents that you'd never see in reality. With the aid of the wind, we can inject a real sense of speed into a scene. Plus, no other element is quite as good at guiding the reader's eye across the page.

"Swoosh" effects like this one can be found in most action manga. They are drawn in a wide range of styles, but essentially it is a tattered ribbon that meanders through the panel in the dynamic scene's direction of flow. Thanks to its clear structure, it doesn't distract from the core content, but instead helps to draw the focus toward it.

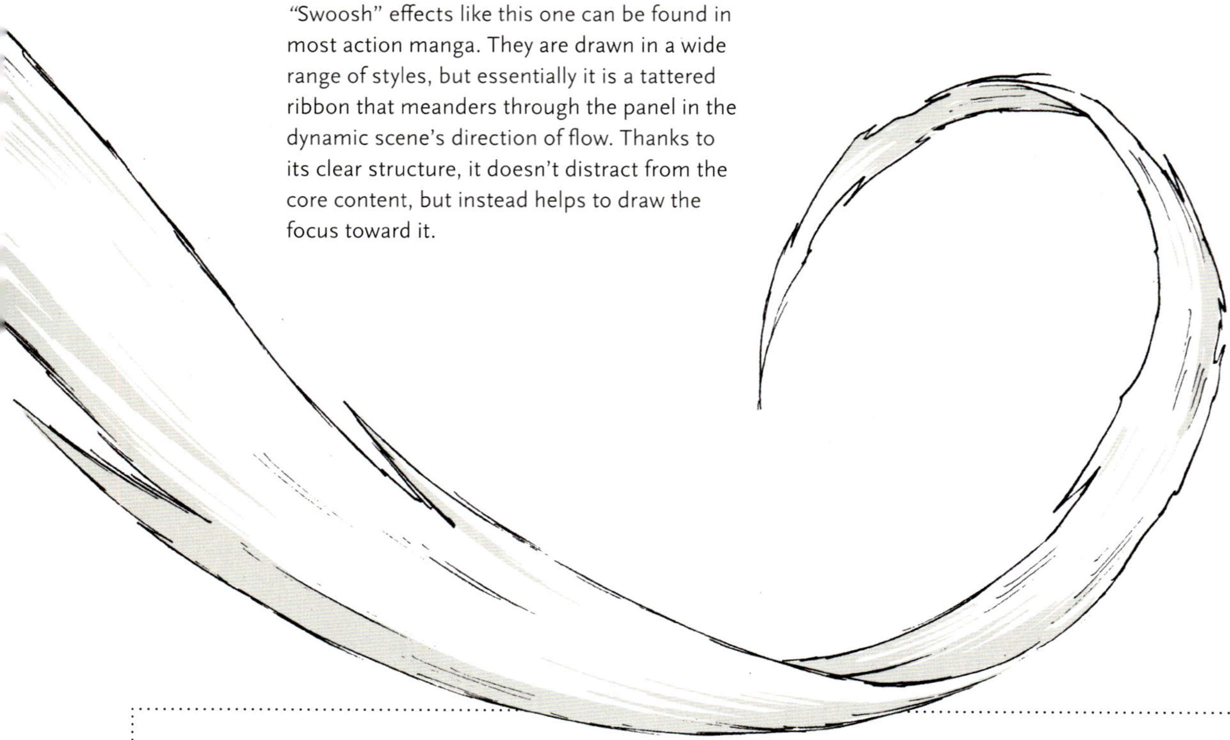

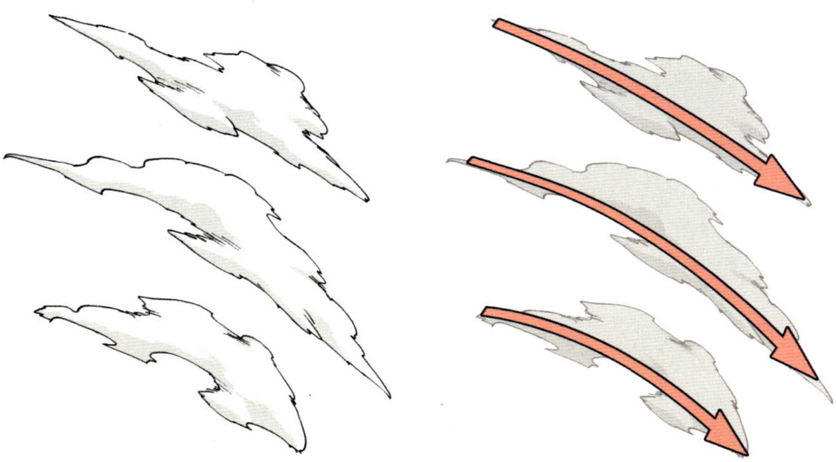

While the swoosh above looks more like a flat band, wind can also be shown by using more three-dimensional elements like the little cloud-like puffs you see here, which are a bit more segmented. What matters most is that the movement follows a clear direction. The best way to do this is to align the start and end points with a vector. In this case, it's shown by the red arrows.

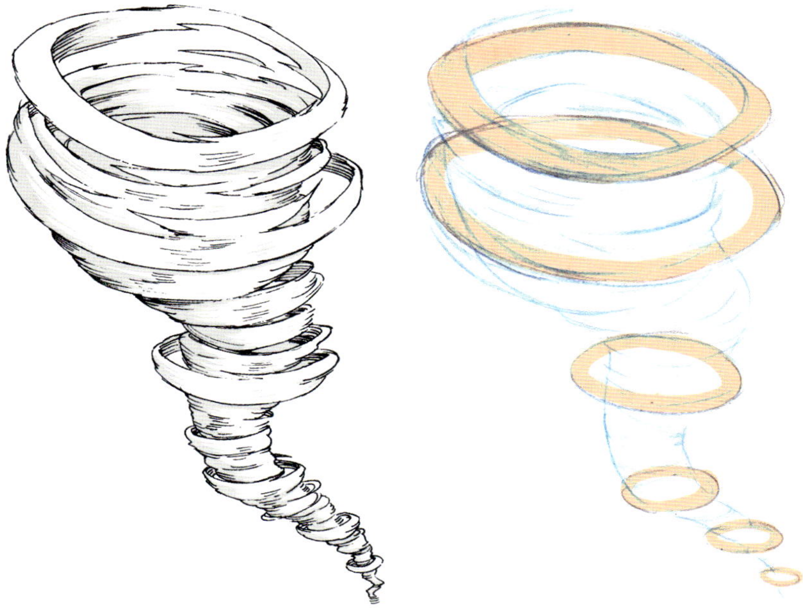

The whirlwind is even more vivid: the finished version on the left was drawn with more lines than necessary, just to show how even a force of nature like this can be broken down into simple shapes. The preliminary sketch with the rings highlighted in orange makes the geometry behind it even clearer. If you want to chase a tornado across your pages, then arrange some rings increasing in diameter from the ground upward, largely parallel, but not directly perpendicular to each other. Connect these rings, and you have the tornado's outline.

Of course, you can also use wind effects to power up attacks.

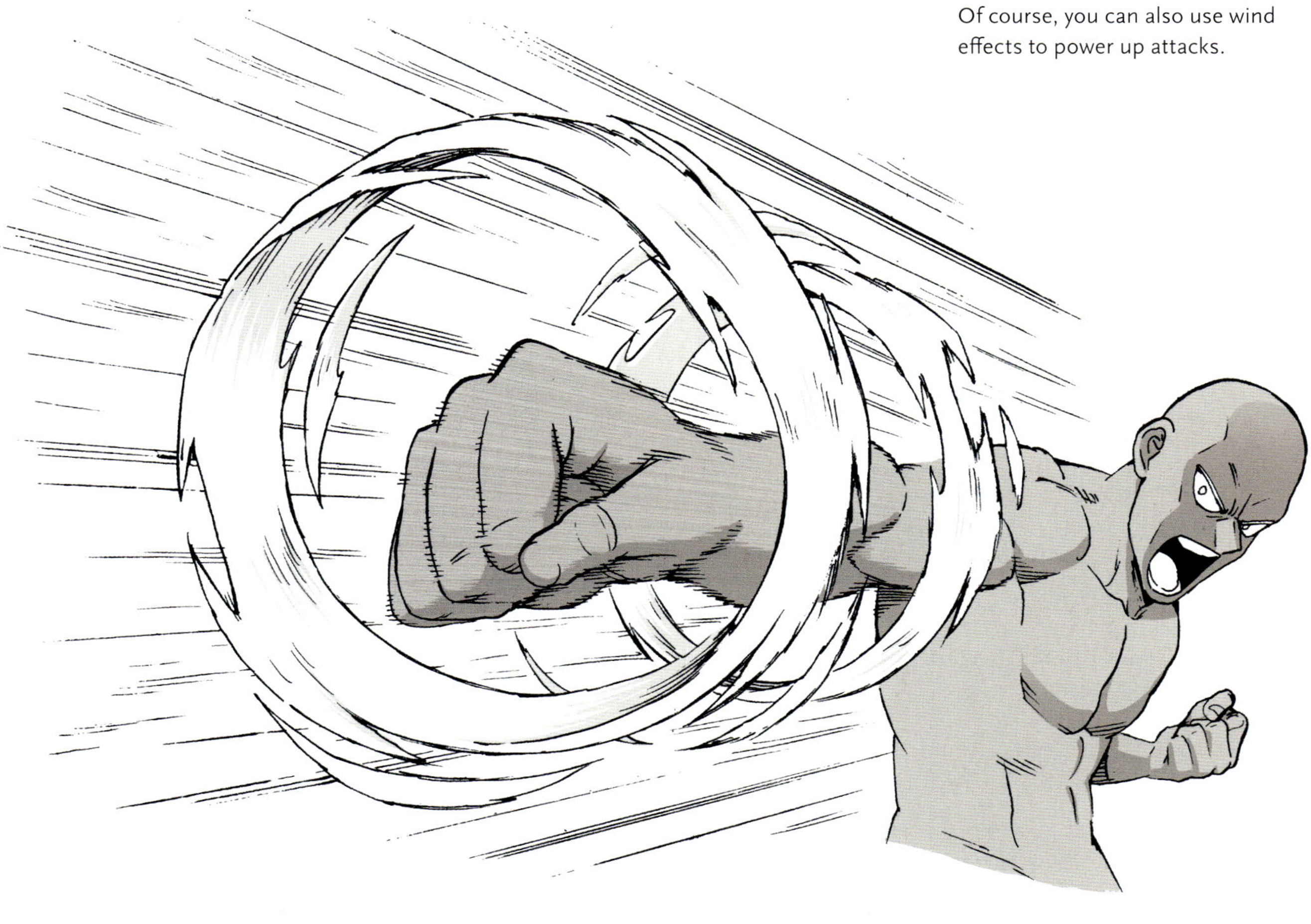

LIGHTNING

Hardly any other effect illustrates overwhelming power like lightning. It may be a real force of nature, a flickering aura around a warrior, or a magical or supernatural attack, but lightning always packs a punch! However, it must be well-executed... Let's take a look at a few techniques.

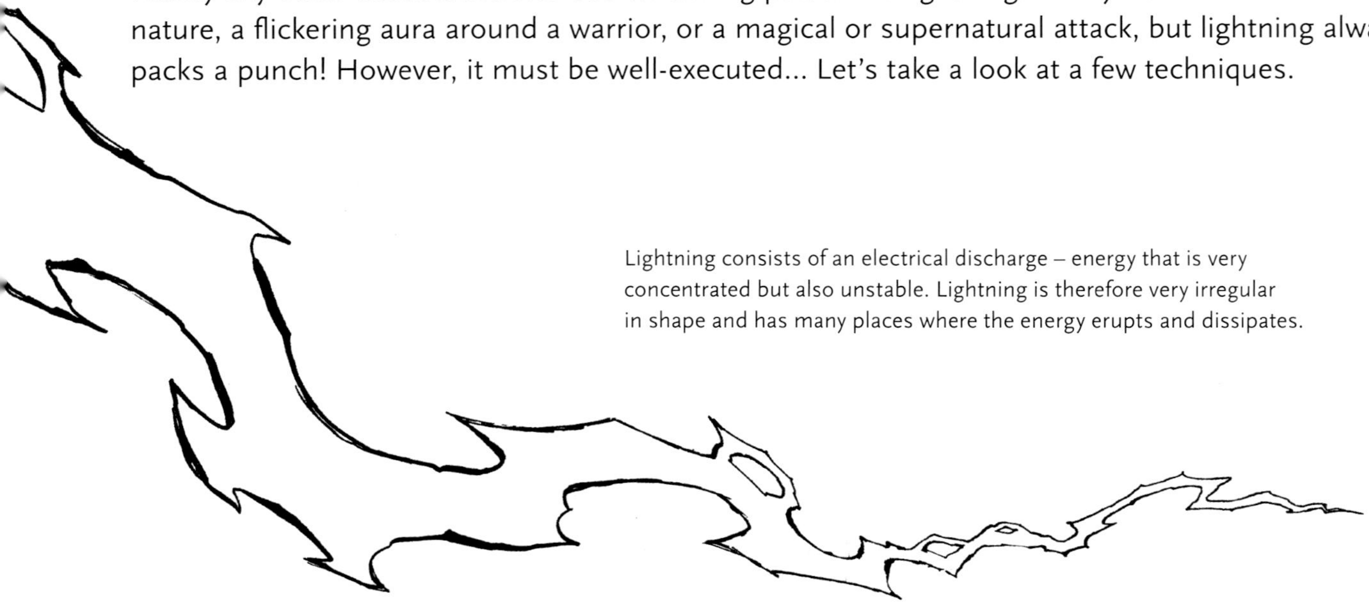

Lightning consists of an electrical discharge – energy that is very concentrated but also unstable. Lightning is therefore very irregular in shape and has many places where the energy erupts and dissipates.

Practice drawing lightning by drawing zigzag lines with a very loose wrist, then gradually add more detail and branching. In the examples below, the lightning bolts are drawn with pure black outlines, which softens the effect somewhat. More on this later. Let's concentrate on the shape first.

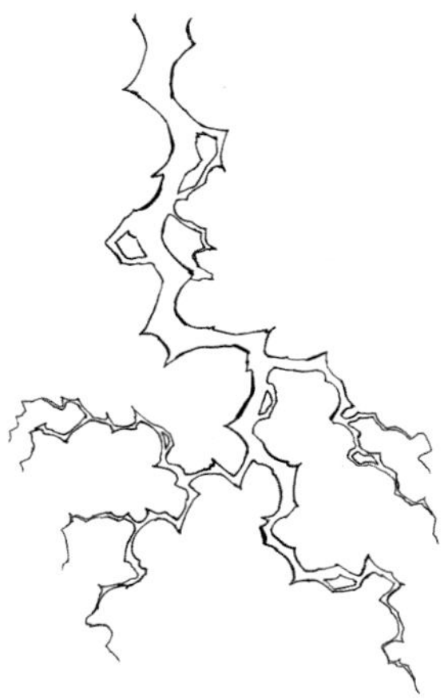

A standard lightning bolt as it emerges from the clouds to strike the earth during a thunderstorm. Small flashes of lightning flicker around it, and others branch off. If you turn the drawing upside-down, it could actually depict the silhouette of a withered tree.

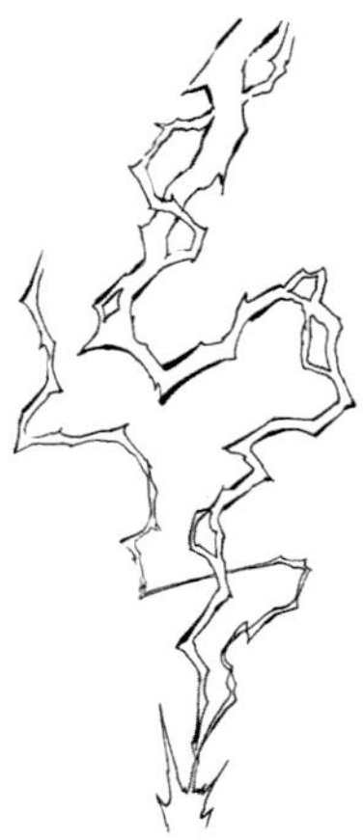

This bolt is a little more exciting: a second, smaller ray connects to the main bolt. This one also meanders more; it describes stronger curves on its way toward the point of impact, which emphasizes the unbridled and also raw unpredictability of the energy.

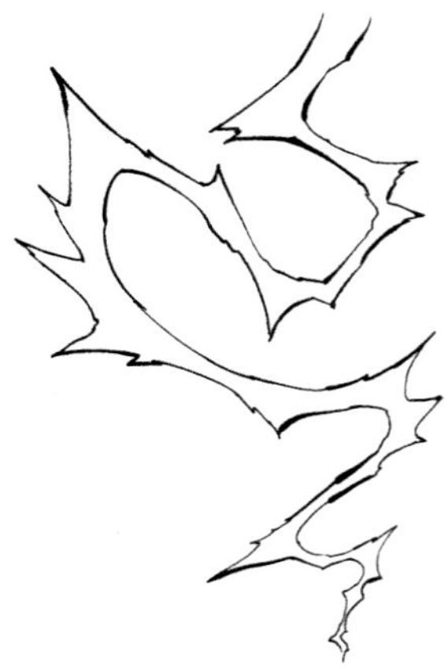

This example has a stronger sense of depth than the other two. You get the feeling that the jagged curves are jutting right out toward us.

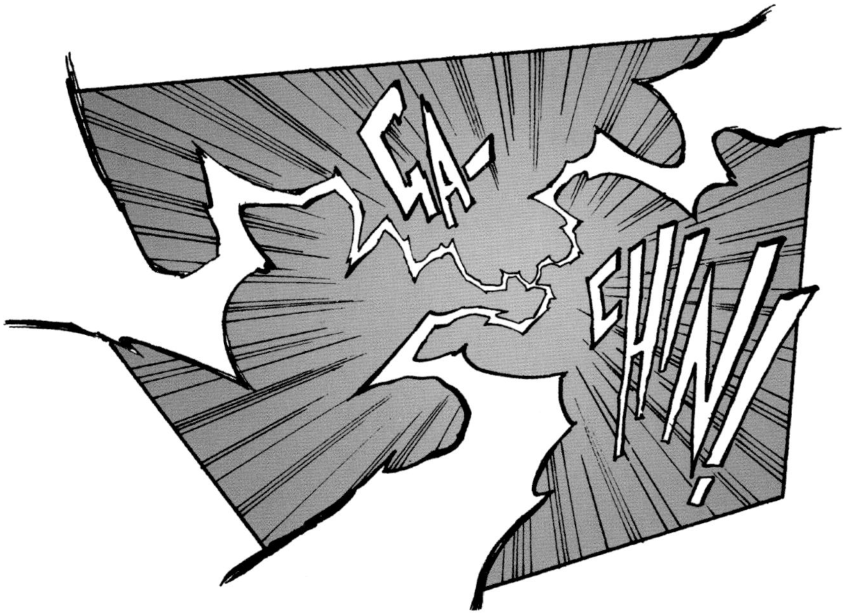

We can go even further in playing with spatial depth. The image to the left, for example, shows a perspective from the actual origin point of the lightning, looking straight down from above. Whatever's being struck down below appears especially tiny and powerless as a result.

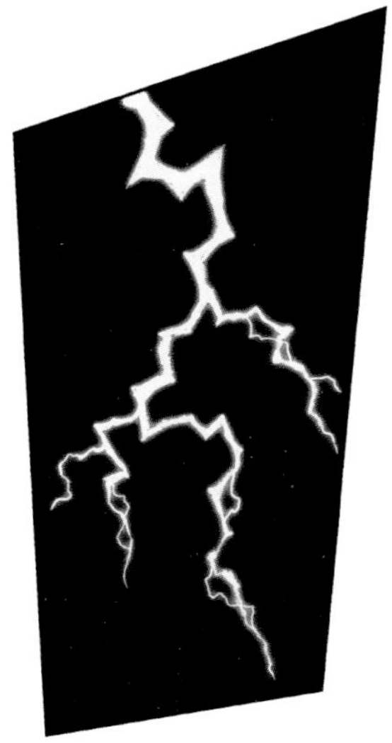

This illustration also highlights how much more dramatic lightning looks when it is standing out against a darker background. A well-placed sound effect can really boost the impact of the strike!

On the right, the bluish lightning bolt is drawn entirely without outlines. Instead, it glows with a light effect. Tricks like this are tough to do by hand, but a piece of cake in a graphics program.

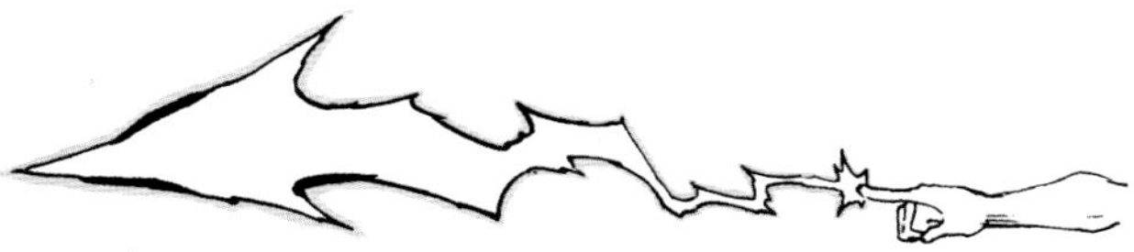

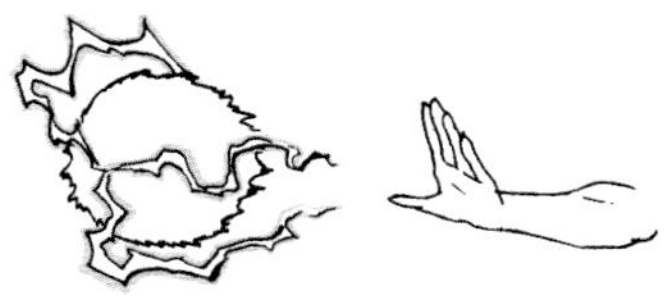

And now, time to get creative with the crackling electricity. Power up weapons, wrap characters in a mighty aura, and develop special lightning attacks that will make even Pikachu's cheeks go pale with envy!

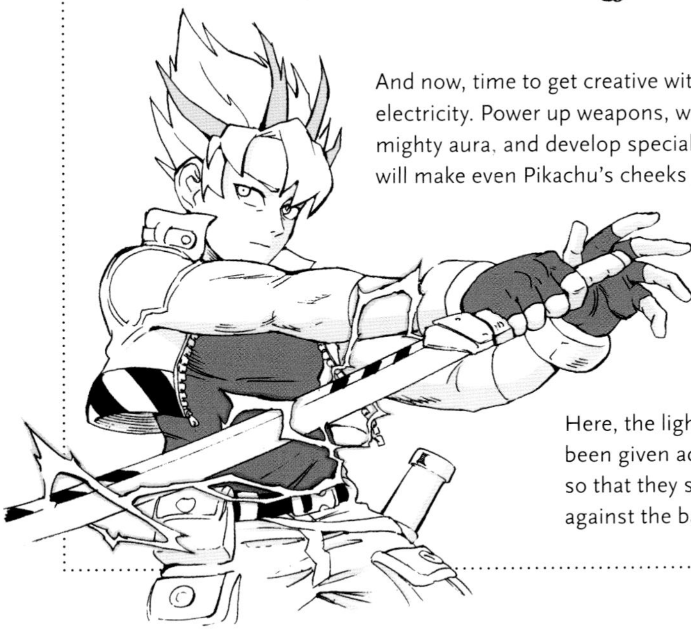

Here, the lightning bolts have been given additional outlines so that they stand out better against the background.

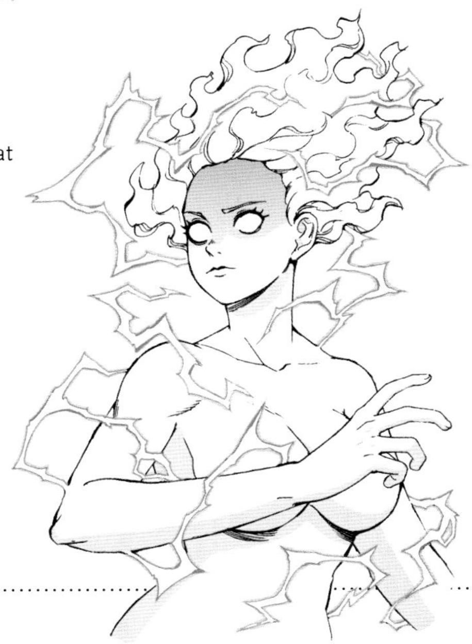

GIGA VOLT

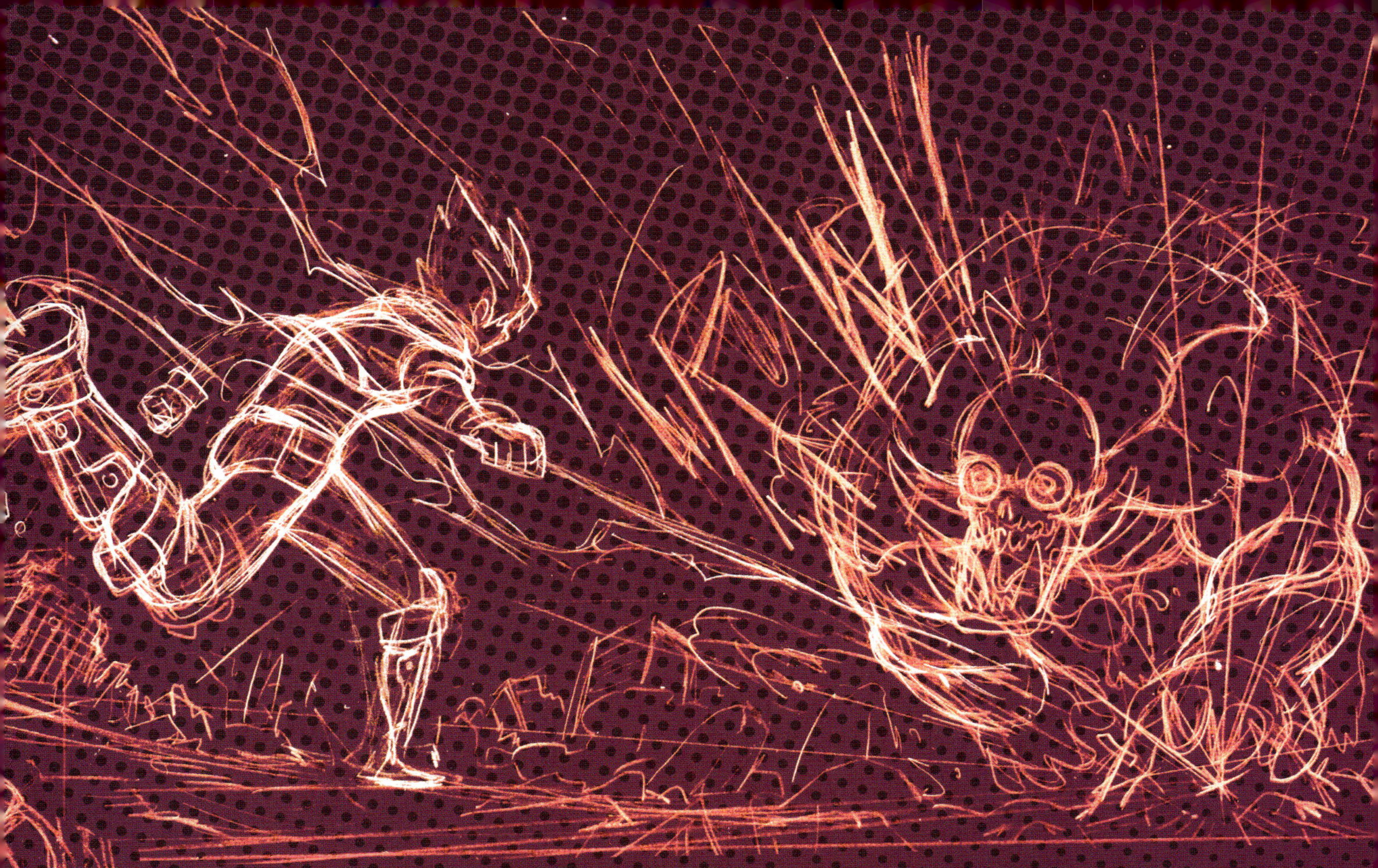

5. STAGING

What sets manga apart from other comics? The country of origin? The style? The reading direction? It's a debatable question, with plenty of possible approaches to the answer. For me, it all comes down to the staging. No other comic form feels quite as cinematic. Manga's static images somehow become a true flow. This is also why adapting manga into anime is so easy and natural. In this chapter, we'll look at a few key storytelling techniques that help create that effect, and later on, we'll break down a sample double page from our practice project.

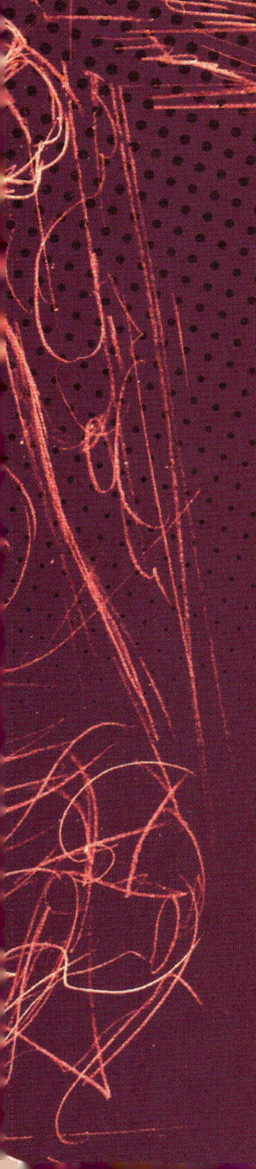

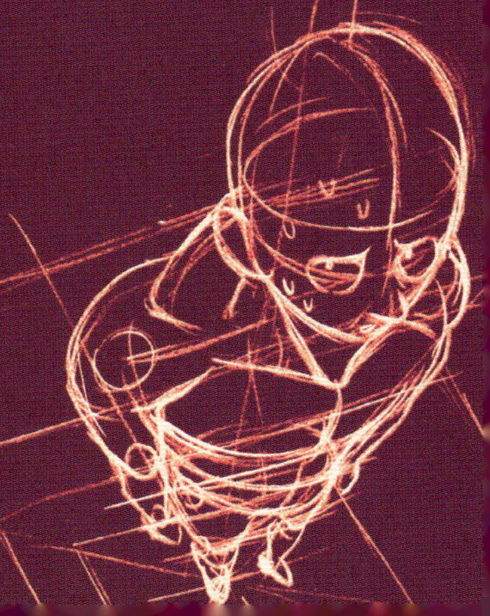

PERSPECTIVE

As artists, we determine the angle of our fictional camera and the effect we want to achieve. Through perspective, we can amplify emotions and highlight power dynamics.

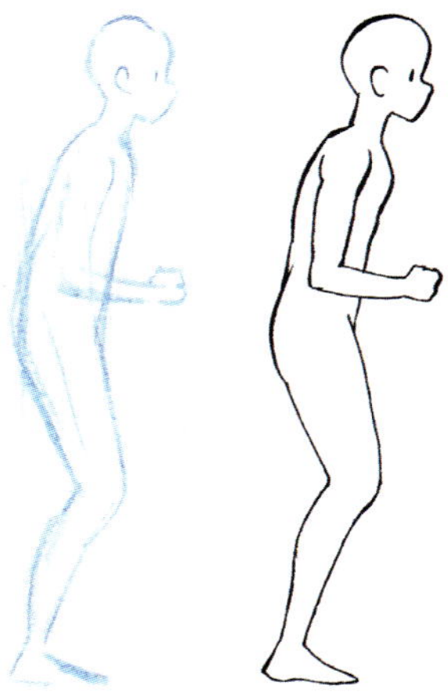

Let's take the example of a seemingly boring standing pose. The figure on the left might be standing at the edge of an exciting scene, or they might be facing an opponent or some other obstacle. Whatever the case, their body language is signaling tension, but the angle we're viewing them from doesn't help convey that. Our view of the figure is too normal and too distanced. While the essential information is communicated, no emotion is triggered.

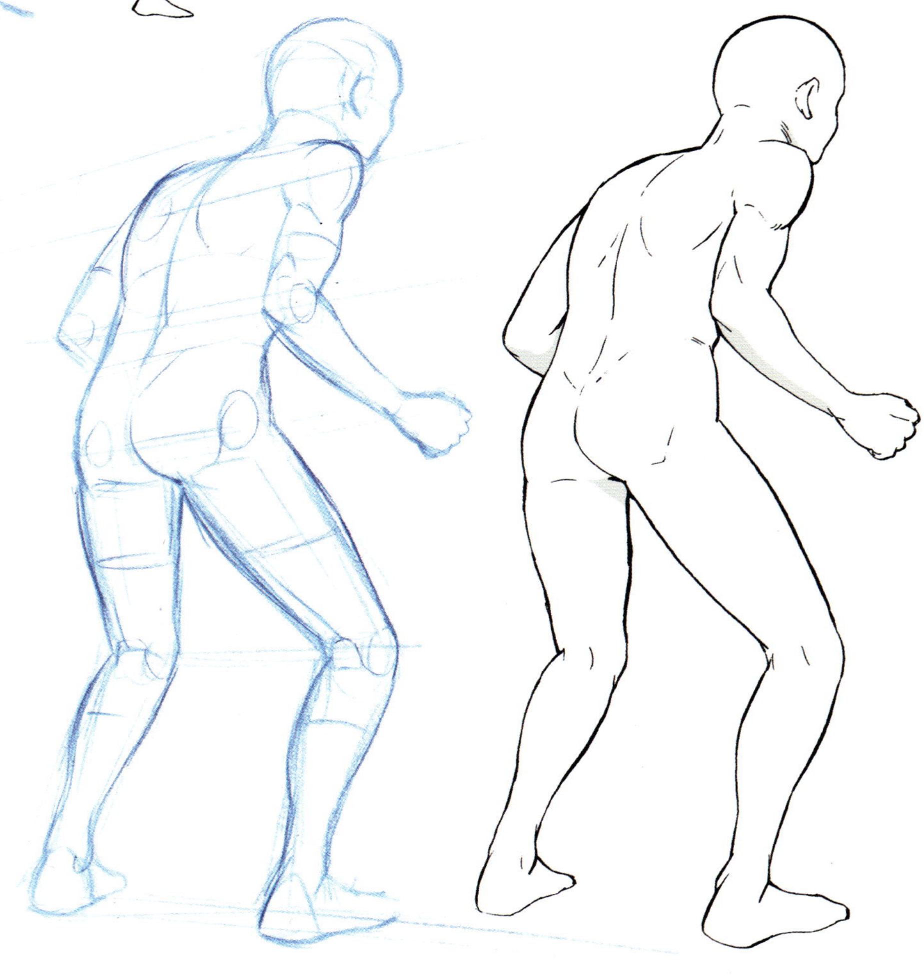

And now, for comparison, the more exciting viewing perspective: we are looking up at the figure from slightly below. We're closer, and a stronger sense of connection develops. The unusual angle takes us out of our comfort zone and we realize that the situation is particularly intense. We also see more of the tensed body.

You can see from the guide lines that the figure is already slightly distorted in space. Guide lines that would otherwise run parallel, such as those that align the pairs of joints at the same level, now lead to a vanishing point. This is also the great difficulty in achieving more interesting perspectives.

CAMERA ANGLE

The perspective depends entirely on the viewing angle; you can see some examples below. On the next double pages, we will delve into the various psychological effects of different perspectives.

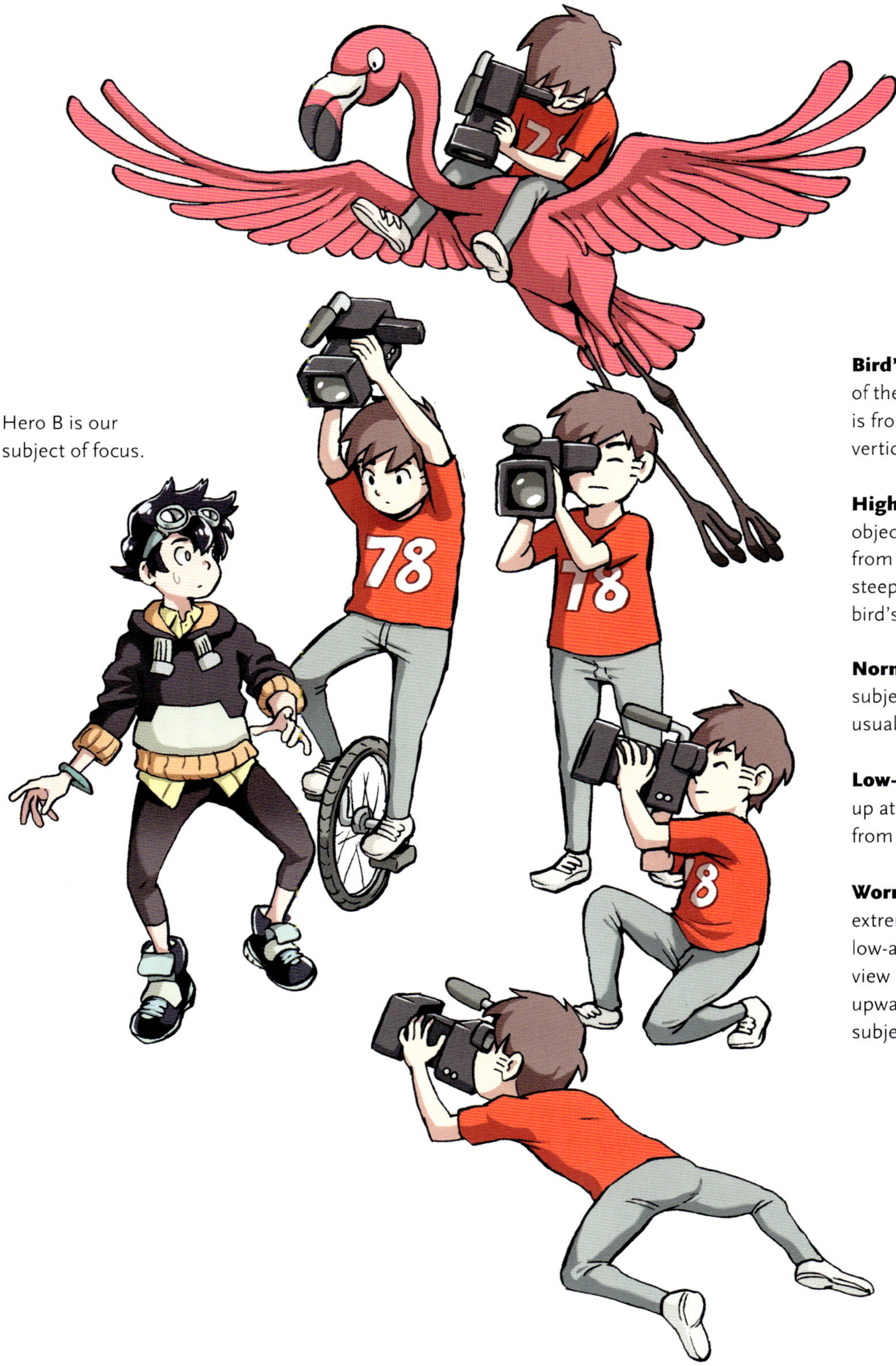

Hero B is our subject of focus.

Bird's-eye view: the view of the object or subject is from above, almost vertically downward.

High-angle view: the object or subject is viewed from above, but at a less steep angle than in the bird's-eye view.

Normal view: the object or subject is viewed from our usual eye level.

Low-angle view: looking up at the object or subject from below.

Worm's-eye view: an extreme form of the low-angle view, where the view is almost vertically upward at the object or subject.

LOW-ANGLE AND WORM'S-EYE VIEW

If we look at something or someone from below (i.e. we have to look up to see a person's head, the top of a mountain, and so on), this creates an effect of dominance. The person or thing "up there" feels (as yet) unreachable. The distance (whether spatial or metaphorical in a social, hierarchical sense) must first be overcome before our own gaze no longer has to go upward, but can be directed straight ahead.

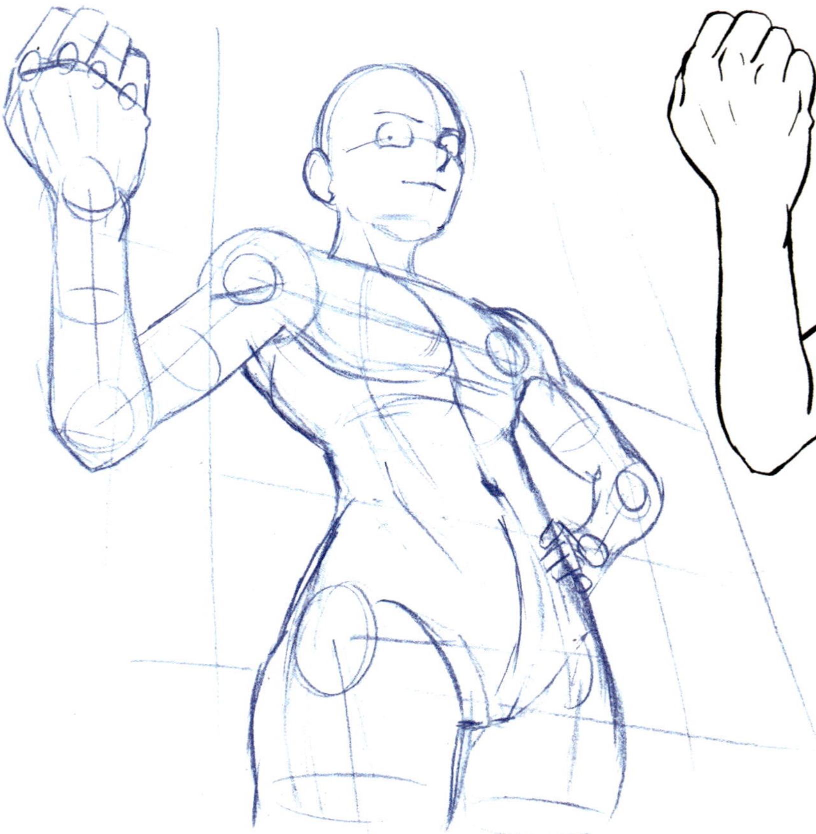

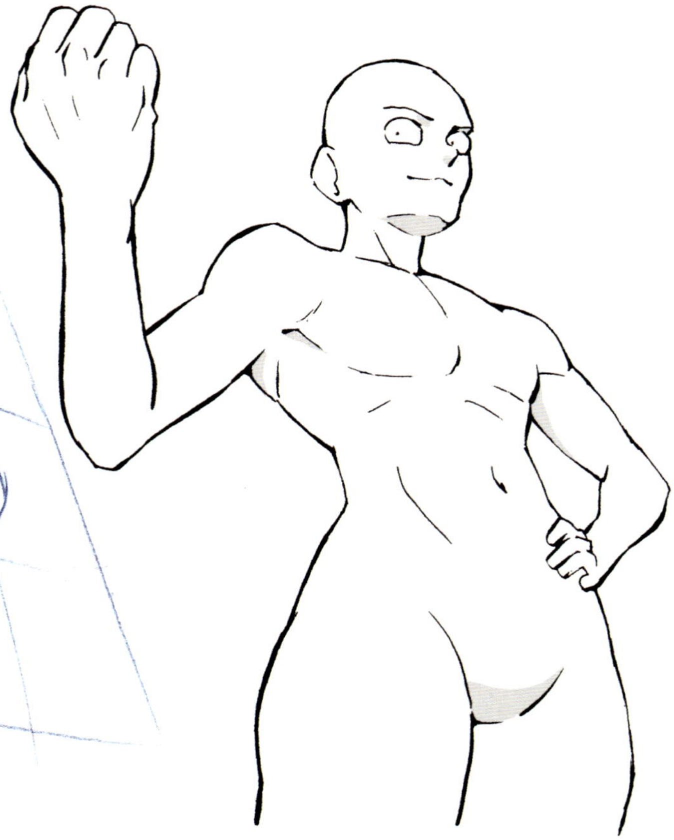

This is where drawing gets tricky, especially if you don't have any reference images available. We have to consider multiple vanishing points, which in the case of the example above, are all far outside the visible area. We have to apply perspectival distortion as accurately as possible while keeping the anatomical proportions consistent. It can be helpful to draw the figure in front of a grid of guide lines, as shown here, in order to get a rough overview of the perspective-related features.

Perspective takes work, and you won't get it perfectly correct the first time, but as you practice you'll improve at even the more complex perspectives and their distortion effects. And you will need these intense viewing angles, because manga, especially manga with lots of action, rely on this kind of visual sophistication more than any other medium. For the great masters, no angle is too steep and no distorted pose too extravagant. A word of encouragement: the human eye is usually so unused to extremely exaggerated viewpoints that it tends to overlook minor drawing errors.

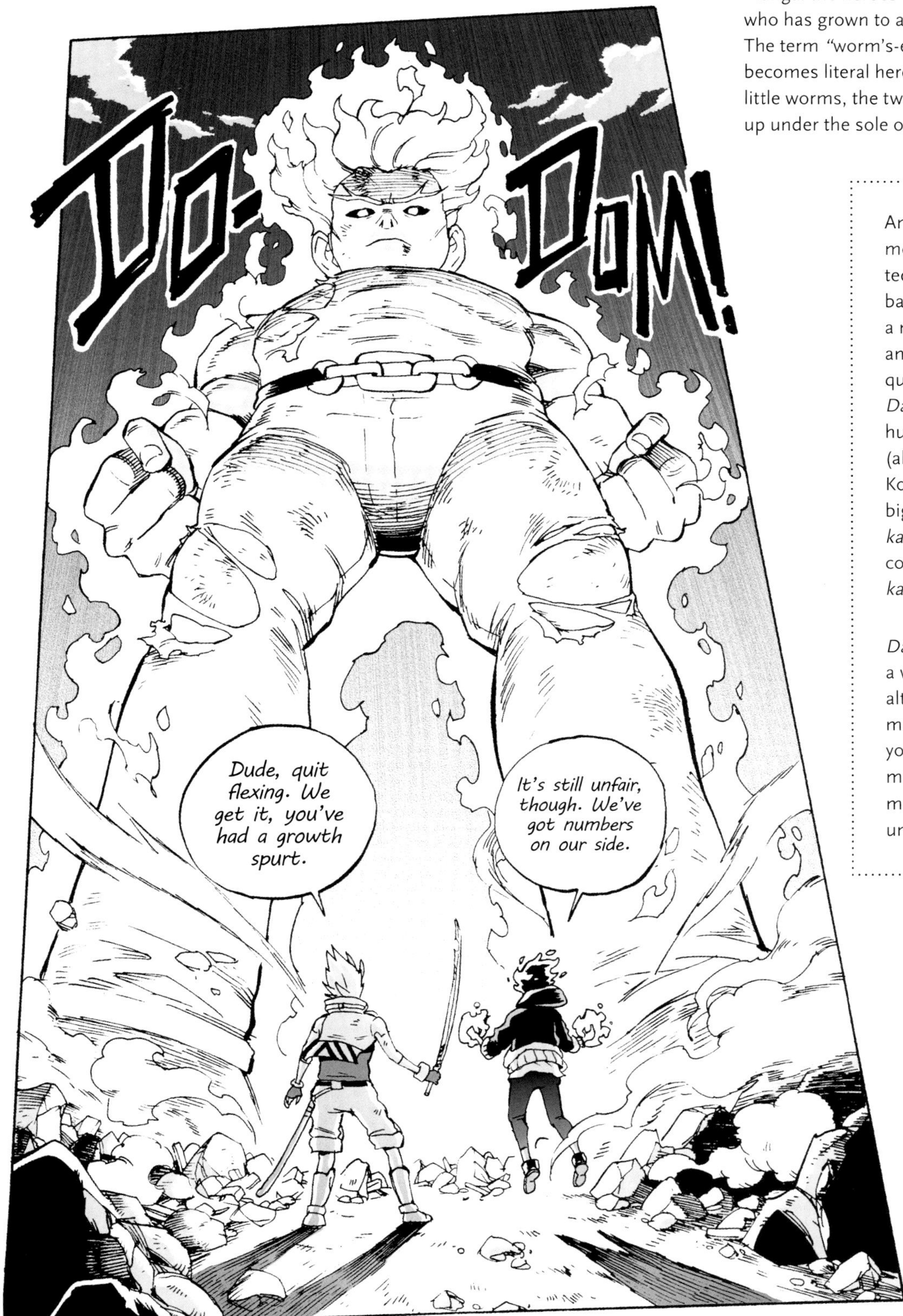

An extreme example that you can expect to appear at any time in classic *shōnen* battle manga: the heroes are facing an opponent who has grown to a gigantic size. The term "worm's-eye perspective" becomes literal here, because, just like little worms, the two of them could end up under the sole of the giant's shoe.

And here are a few more Japanese technical terms: the baddie on this page is a mixture of *daikaiju* and *kaijin*. *Kaiju* are quirky monsters. *Daikaiju* are *kaiju*, but huge, like Godzilla (aka Gojira) or King Kong (*dai* means big). Then there is the *kaijin* – the humanoid counterpart to the *kaiju*.

Daikaijin is not yet a widely used term, although it would make sense when you consider how many giant *kaijin* are making pop culture unsafe...

HIGH-ANGLE AND BIRD'S-EYE VIEW

When we view someone or something from above, it creates an impression of inferiority. This is particularly true of characters we're literally looking down on, as this often signals their diminished role in the social hierarchy of the scene – or a sense that this person has failed or been defeated. The high angle is just slightly above normal eye level, so the effect is still relatively mild. The effect intensifies with the bird's-eye view as the viewing angle gets steeper. In a "top shot", you're looking straight down on the scene. This can be used, for example, to evoke a feeling of conformity in a large crowd.

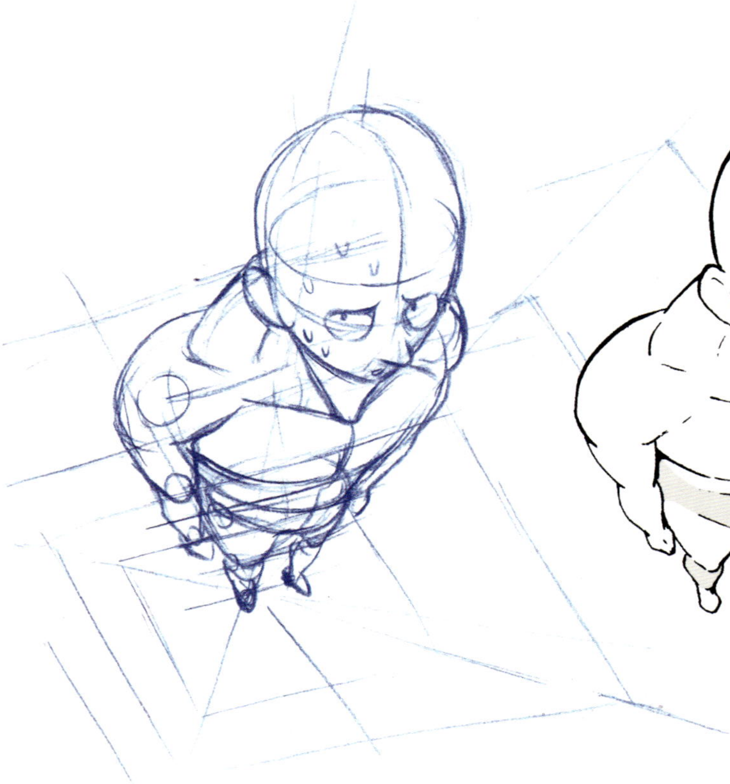

Here we have a bird's-eye view of this poor little chap. The angle is already steep enough to make him seem particularly pitiful and inferior. The facial expression further underlines this, but even without it the effect would work. You'll also notice here, once again, the complex mesh of guide lines that's needed to depict these kinds of perspective distortions.

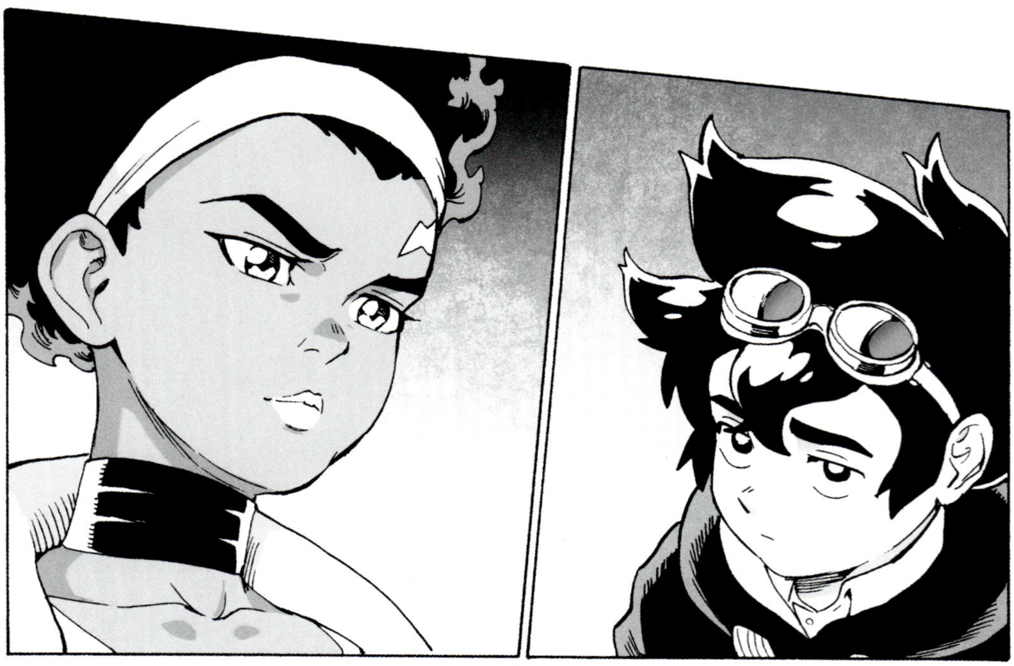

In direct comparison: from a low-angle and a high-angle view. We look up at the mentor, making her appear superior and strong. We almost share Hero B's view of her and can empathize with him. In turn, we share the view of him with his opposite number, creating the impression of inferiority and weakness.

Another function of the elevated camera angle, combined with a certain distance from the subject, is to provide an overview of the scene. The further away the view is, the more information the readers get about the location of the events. This is also referred to as an "establishing shot". It's an essential tool to stop readers getting confused. Who is in the scene? What is the spatial relationship between the characters? What other local factors are relevant? Try to include shots like these – especially at the beginning of a scene, or early on. Here's an example:

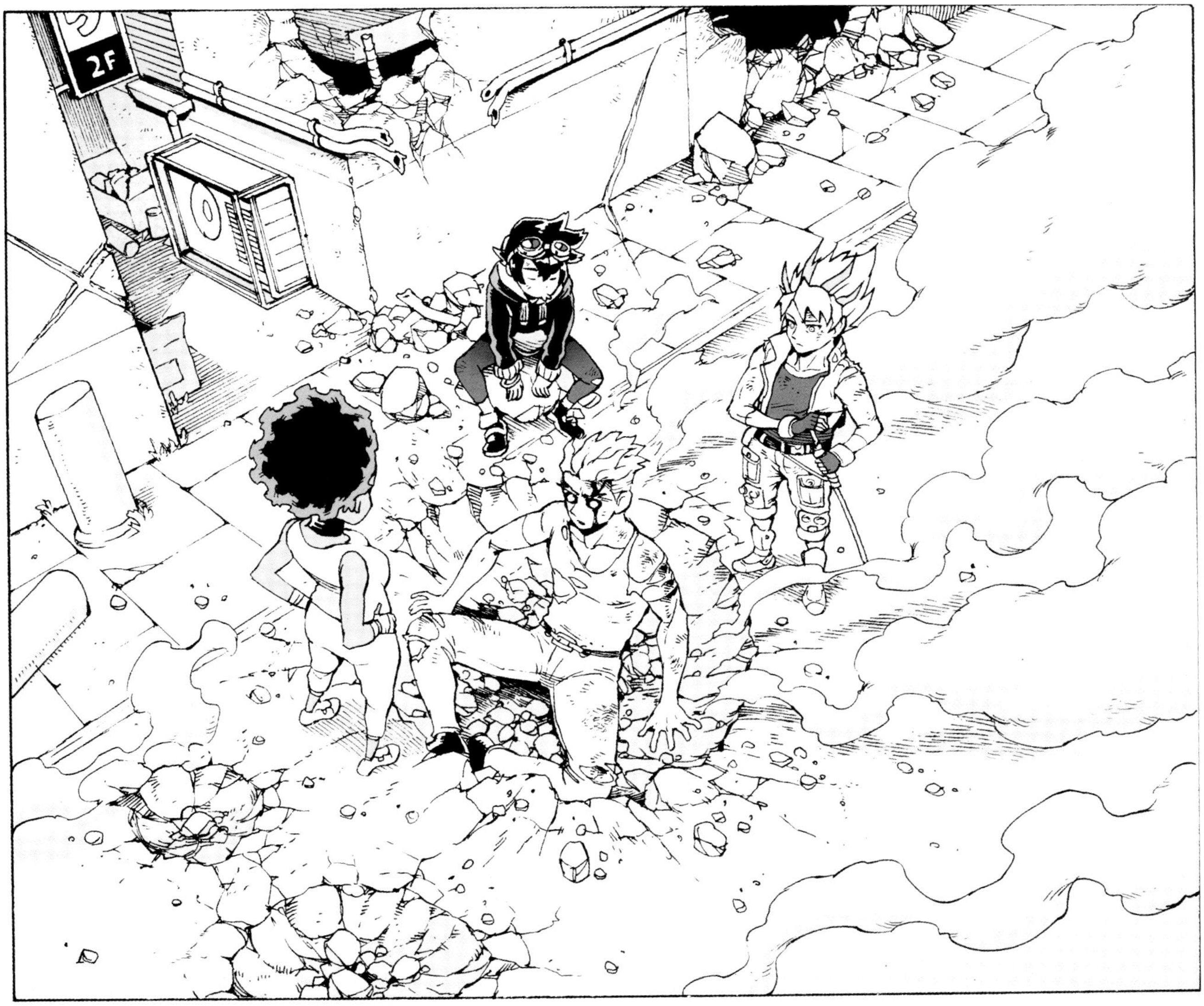

This image not only summarizes many lessons from the previous chapters, but also tells a story. In fact, it could be following on directly from the extreme image from the previous double page – we can deduce all the relevant actions that took place between the two images: the opponent has now been defeated and is no longer gigantic. He is the lowest down and therefore appears even more puny, while he is also sitting in a crater and is therefore spatially far below his adversaries. What's more, he is positioned at the so-called "Loser's Point", the center of the picture, which makes him appear lost and lonely from a psychological point of view.

In the background you can see extensive destruction, suggesting a fierce battle. Hero A has apparently destroyed a few things with his sword. Hero B is no longer in demon mode and is exhausted. The mentor has joined them and doesn't even have a scratch on her – a commanding appearance!

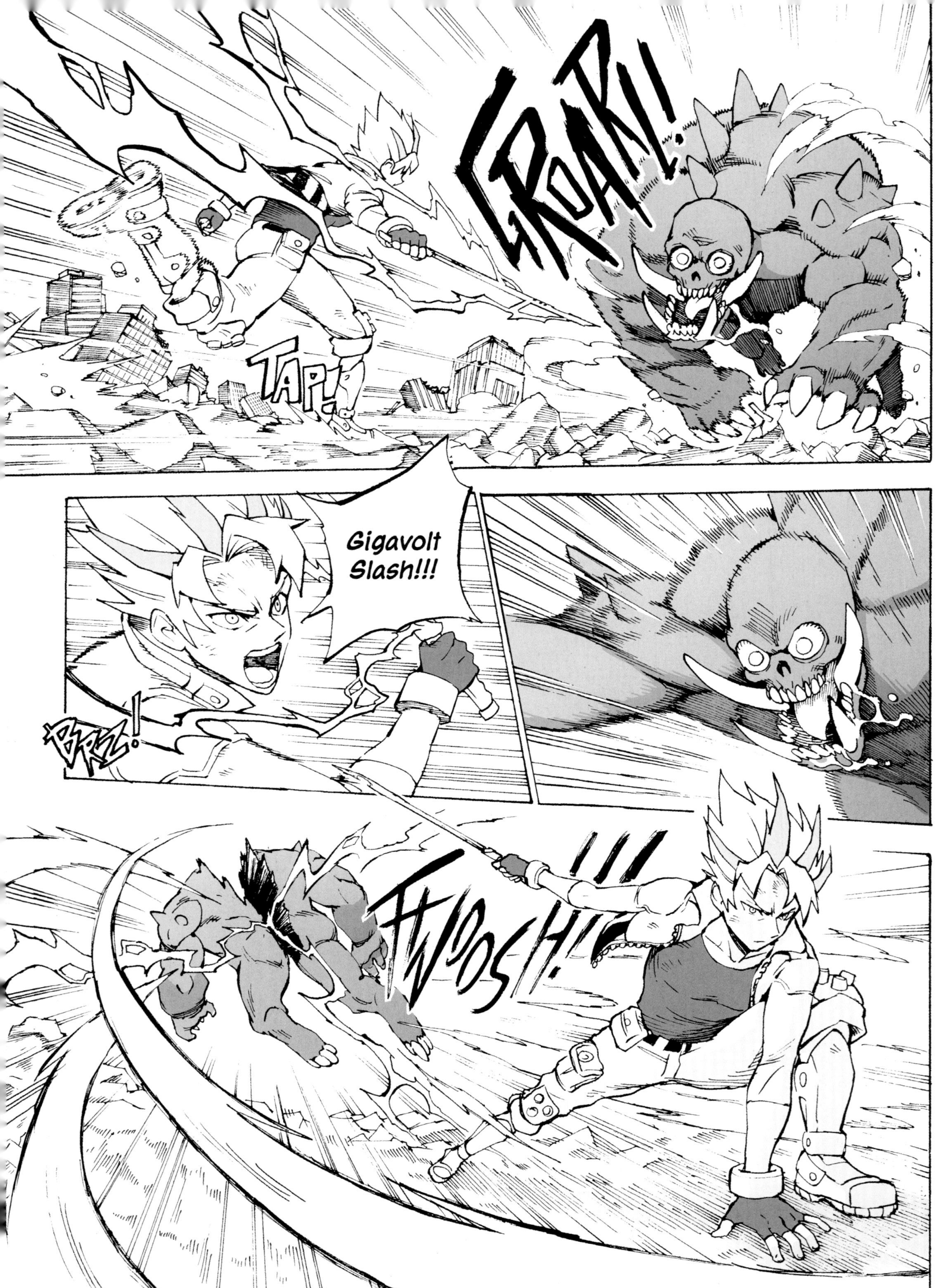
GROAR!!
TAP!
Gigavolt Slash!!!
BRZZ!
FWOOSH!!

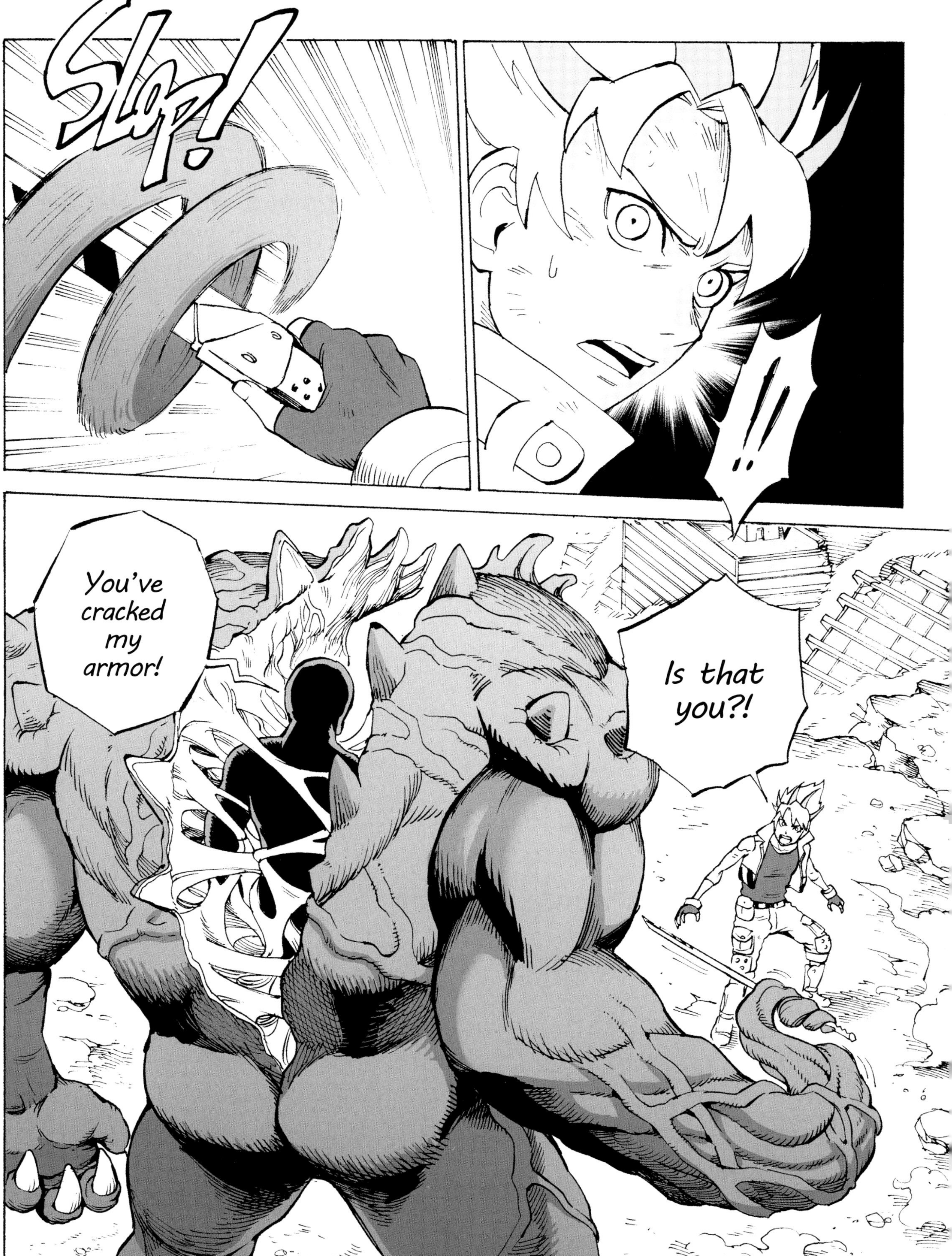
Slop!
!!
Is that you?!
You've cracked my armor!

PAGE LAYOUT

On the following pages, we'll take a closer look at the previous comic double page and highlight various factors that ensure a good page layout in manga. Some of these points apply only if you want to have your manga bound as a book, while others are generally relevant for all types of comics and manga.

THE PRINT AREA

The print area is the core section of your page. In the graphic below, print area regions are highlighted in red. This is where everything important happens. There is still space toward the edges of the page – about ½in (1–2cm). These outer areas are called margins. You can fill these spaces, but not with important information! For instance, try not to place your characters' heads in these areas – and it is certainly not a place for text. The area between the two pages (the gutter or inner margin, marked in yellow) should remain completely empty!

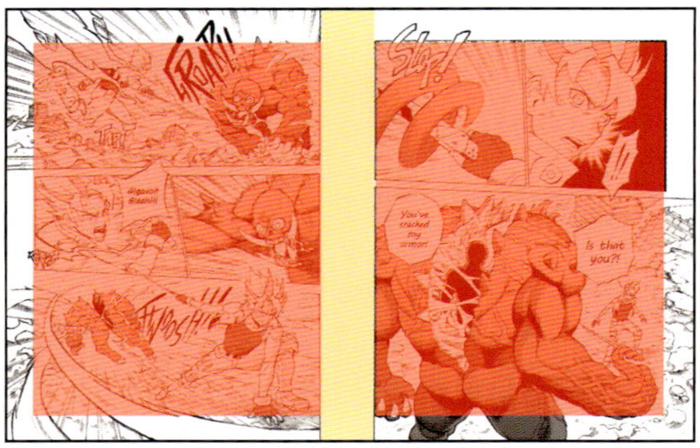

Why should you avoid placing important information outside of the print area? One reason is to create a clean page. By leaving areas of the page empty or only filling them with minor image details, you create rest zones. This reduces visual clutter, which ensures a more pleasant reading experience.

The second important reason is the printing of the final manga. Before everything can be bound between two covers, all the pages are trimmed at the edges to ensure a uniform final format. The outer edges of the manga pages are inevitably clipped in the process. Even the example double page you just saw has been subjected to this process, and all the edges are missing a fraction of an inch compared with the originals. However, because I made sure that everything important remains within the print area, you haven't missed anything relevant. Also, the previously mentioned inner margin should remain empty because this is where the spine fold is, and it will swallow up your artwork during the binding process.

PANEL ARRANGEMENT

Just in case you've never come across the term before, a panel is a single image in a comic. Typically, it's bordered by a panel frame, usually a black line. However, a panel can also be open on one or more sides (like the bottom one on the left-hand example page) or be bordered by the edge of the sheet. How you arrange the individual panels has a significant impact on the pacing of your story. Old-fashioned comics often use a system of keeping horizontal panel rows at the same height, which results in a neat appearance but lacks dynamism. We want more variety, particularly in emotionally charged action genres. So here's a tip: always plan for double pages and make sure that the opposite panel rows are never at the same height. This also helps prevent inexperienced readers from incorrectly interpreting rows of equal height and reading the top row of the left page first, followed by the top row of the right page.

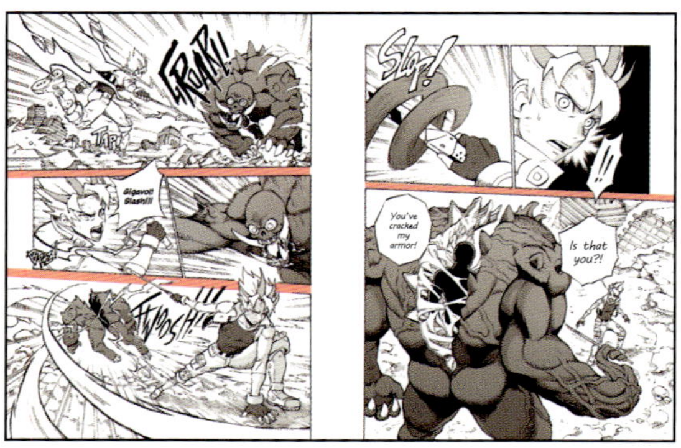

Additionally, make sure that the gutters (the gaps between panels) are thinner vertically and thicker horizontally. This makes it easier to read because it is based on how we read continuous text. There, the space between two lines is also greater than the space between two words.

FLOW

The be-all and end-all of a well-produced manga is its fluid readability. While American superhero comics, for example, scatter complicated text arrangements over a sometimes rather playful page layout, with both text and layout slowing down the reading flow, in manga everything is geared toward driving the reader through the books in record time.

First of all, it's important to note that our comic example is laid out in the Western reading direction (from left to right) because this also matches the reading direction of the rest of the book. Manga are traditionally read in the Japanese reading direction, i.e. from right to left. However, it doesn't really matter which you choose. The rules are always the same – just partially mirrored depending on the reading direction. Here, we will work with a Western reading direction.

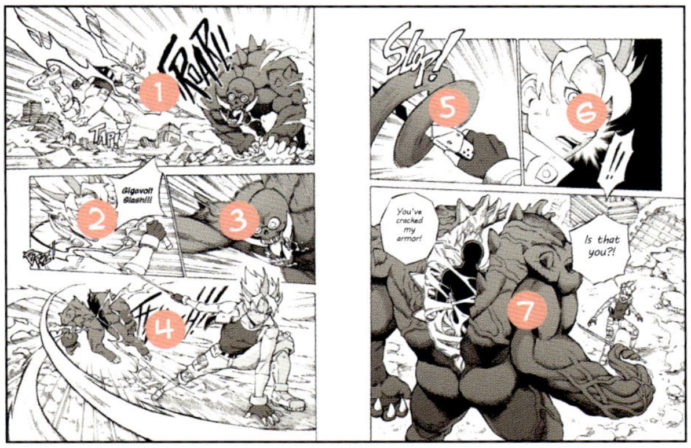

This is the order in which our sample double page should be read: seven panels that are clearly lined up in sequence. In the last image, there are two speech bubbles, but even there the priority is clear. Simple, isn't it? It is, if you stick to the basics. And yet beginners in particular tend to make a lot of mistakes in this area – often, this is even due to their misplaced aspiration to generate a distinctive page layout. Manga, however, is not really suitable for this approach! The order of the panels and speech bubbles should be clear. So, when drawing, always think about how you are guiding your readers through the content and whether there could be any stumbling blocks.

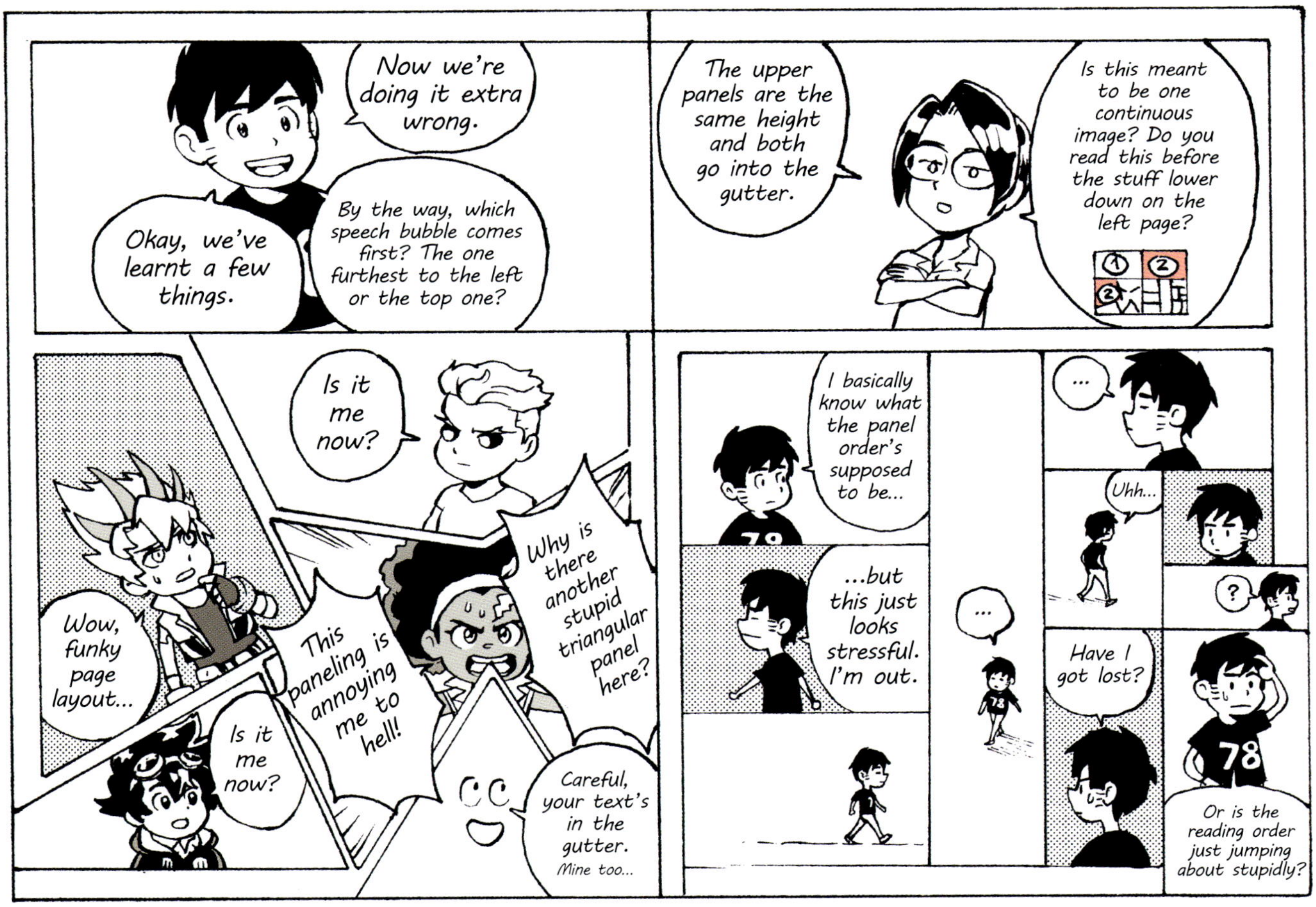

SPEED LINES AND ZOOM LINES

Few graphic tools direct the eye in manga as effectively as speed and zoom lines. These are usually a few straight lines that complement the image and can have a wide variety of effects. There is no precise or authoritative definition of the distinction between speed lines and zoom lines, but I use the terms as follows:

Speed lines are lines that run parallel to each other, regardless of whether they are vertical, horizontal, or diagonal.

Zoom lines are lines that run toward a vanishing point. They may be in the picture, but also outside.

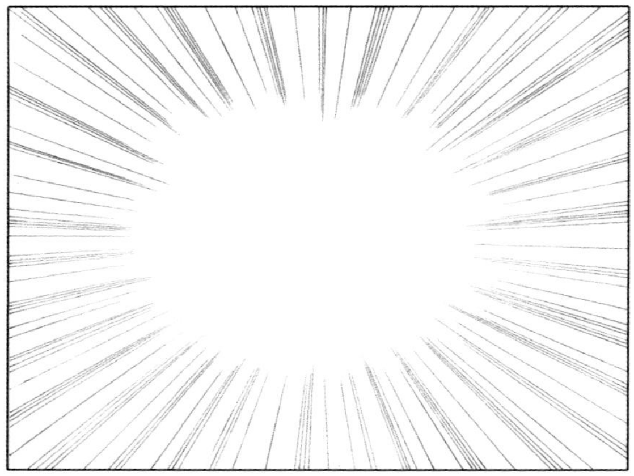

The distinction between the two can also be fluid. In our example double page, panel 2 also looks as if it is speed lines in the version defined above, but on closer inspection we can see that the lines do not run exactly parallel to each other, but converge toward a shared vanishing point that lies very far to the left, outside the panel.

Use the two line variations to simulate camera zooms, to illustrate speed, to draw attention to important scenes or objects, or to amplify expressions. For example, if a character shouts something, the underlying emotion is emphasized and you can always make it even clearer to the reader how relevant the image information is. However, make sure that these effects do not overlap in an image.

SOUND EFFECTS

The purely visual medium of comics lacks the emotionally powerful modality of sound, but you can at least evoke sounds in your readers' minds by using sound effects, such as onomatopoeic graphic indications of where each sound is coming from. Their shape and size can convey a lot about the volume and sound of the noises. This is why I'm a fan of hand-drawn sound effects, as they contain more character and information than clean digital fonts. The examples on the right also show this.

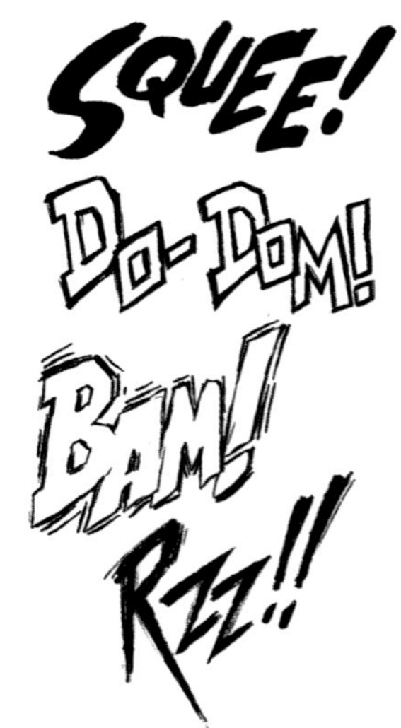

Sound effects are used a lot in Japanese, where they are even part of everyday language. They not only imitate sounds, but also describe them. You have probably seen words such as "wobble", "wink", or "crash" in comics before. So be creative and push the boundaries of this stylistic device! Sound effects should be placed so that they don't disrupt the visual flow (more on that on the next page). Position them so that they can be quickly matched to the relevant sound source. On the sample page on the right, this applies to the "TAP!" in the first panel. A small sound effect for a rather small noise in the overall context of the scene. If there are also zoom lines that lead to the sound source, the sound effect is aligned to these. Like the "GROARL!" also in panel one – its size makes it clear that it drowns out the "TAP"!

VISUAL FLOW

By now, it's clear that panel layout and speech bubble placement are crucial for guiding the reader's eye quickly across a (double) page, but there are many more tools at your disposal to achieve this. In a well-crafted (action) manga, you'll often find what I like to call hidden vectors. These are lines that result from the composition of the picture and which our eyes inevitably follow. If the vectors are arranged correctly, the eye moves directly from one vector to the next until it reaches the end of the double page, without any distracting elements. Let's take another look at the sample double page, this time with the vectors made visible.

We start by virtually running with Hero A from left to right. His movement pulls us with him, as does the alignment of the sword and the lightning effects, as well as the zoom lines in the background. These have a vanishing point that our eyes inevitably move toward. There we meet the monster, which catches our gaze and – together with its direction of movement – leads it from right to left again. We land in the second panel, where the vector is strongly influenced by Hero A's line of sight, his forward motion once again, the speed lines in the background, and another burst of lightning. The zoom lines in the next panel guide us toward the monster's gaze, which we follow to the bottom panel. There we land directly in the vanishing point of further zoom lines – which, along with wind effects and a suitably placed sound effect, lead us to Hero A. Even his outstretched leg helps our gaze to wander slightly upward again, to end up at his line of sight. This in turn leads us to the next page.

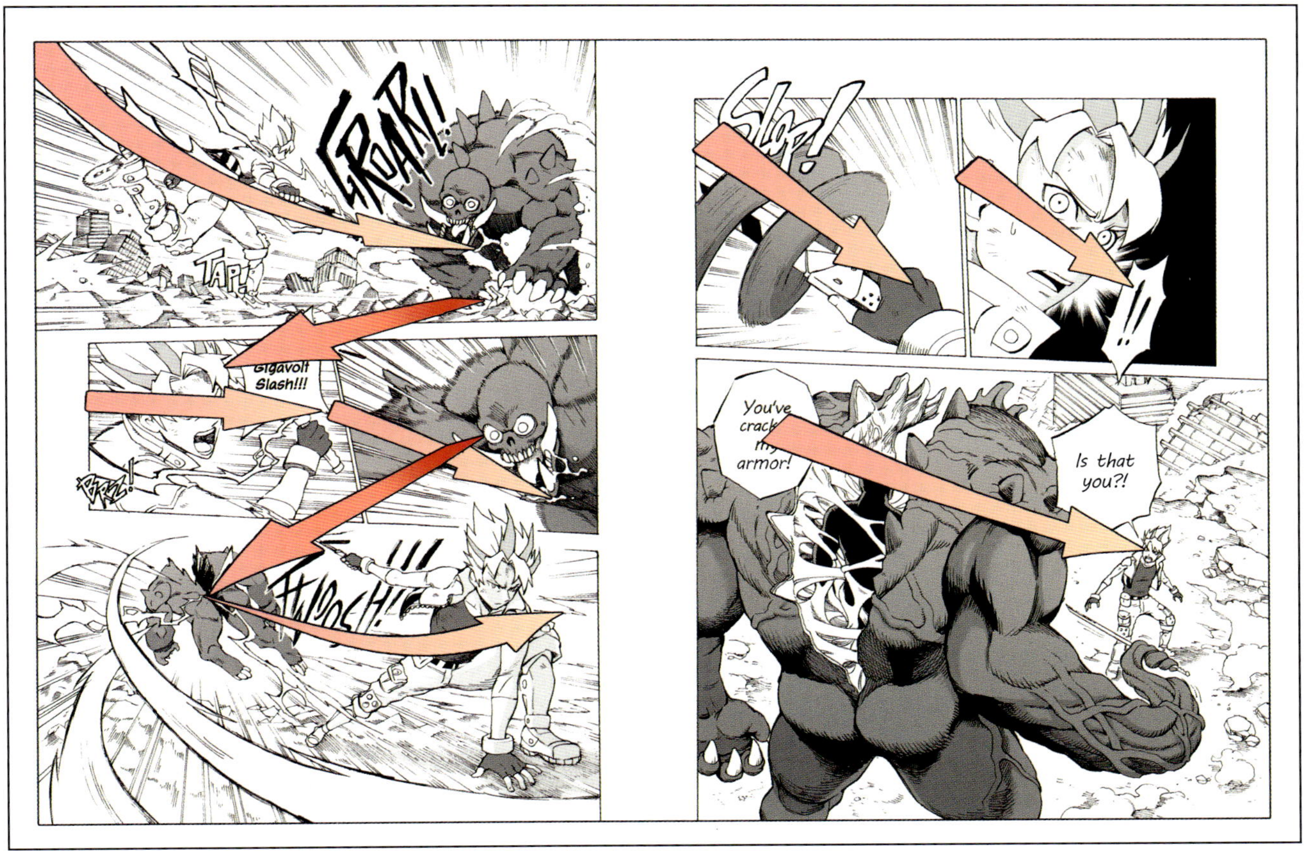

The following have a particularly strong effect on the reading vectors:

- Zoom and speed lines.
- General character movement and their line of sight.
- The arrangement of sound effects and speech bubbles, as well as other effects, like lightning and wind in this case.

SPEECH BUBBLES

In principle, what has been said about sound words can also be applied to speech bubbles. Their primary function is to convey the spoken text of the characters in the comic. However, they also have various secondary functions. These include guiding the eye, but also, for example, the importance of a line of text, which can be categorized based on the size of the speech bubble and the lettering it contains. Volume can also be emphasized by this means.

And just as I'm not a fan of digital font sound effects, I also don't like perfect speech bubble ovals that are drawn accurately in the software. This is because they take away another powerful aspect: the ability to depict the timbre, intonation, or other sonic nuances of the spoken word. It sounds a bit complicated again, but let's just take a look at a few examples:

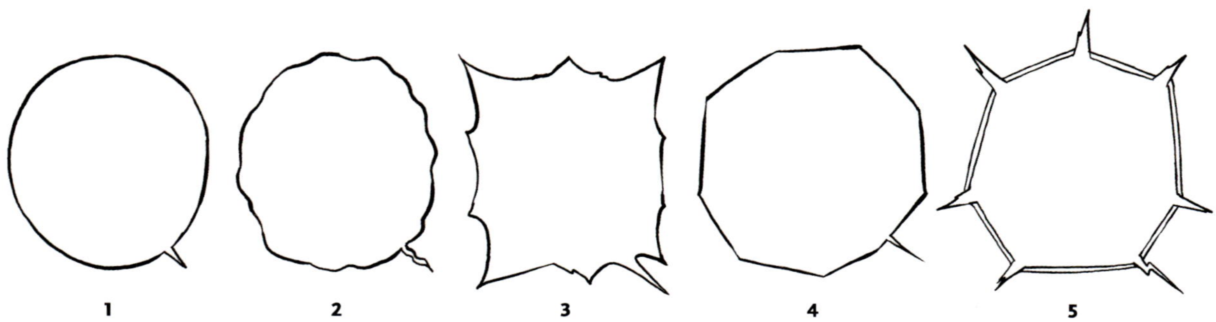

Even without context or dialogue, you should have a sense of what the different speech bubble shapes convey. These are the attributes that I assign to them:

1 Normal spoken text. The voice is calm. Therefore, this is also the standard form.
2 Trembling. This irregular form represents a shaky speech flow. The speaker could be anxious or exhausted.
3 The sound practically bursts out. The person is screaming. The fact that the spikes are not perfectly evenly distributed emphasizes the unbridled emotions. Like an explosion!
4 Angular and harsh. The person has a stern way of speaking. A small side note here: the great Akira Toriyama (illustrator of masterpieces such as *Dragon Ball* or *Dr. Slump*) used this speech bubble shape primarily for his villains, who usually expressed themselves very coldly. This also added a further contrast to the round speech bubbles of the heroes with their warmer timbres.
5 A machine voice. The double outline emphasizes the slight sonic effect. Then there are the small spikes around the edge, which could represent slight static in the voice output.

AVOID CROSSING THE AXIS

The rules for comics are similar to those for theater. Imagine the readers are sitting in the audience and looking at a stage. Naturally, everything should be clearly recognizable from the audience's perspective. Images in comics should also follow this rule.

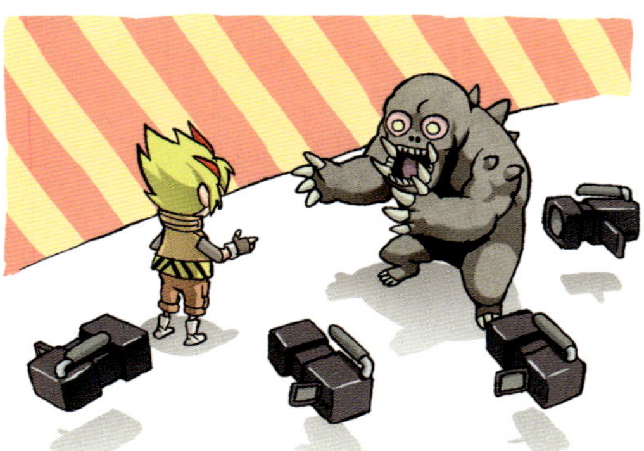

The medium of film has also adopted these rules for itself – a fact that, once again, emphasizes how closely manga is aligned with the laws of motion pictures. In film, we can imagine the different viewing angles of a scene like a multi-camera setup. The perspectives can switch back and forth in front of the stage, but there is a certain axis, established in advance, that must not be crossed. In the picture, this is the red and yellow striped area. If we start to capture the scene from this restricted area (i.e. cross the axis), it disrupts our visual expectations, arresting our reading flow. If we go back to our example double page, if Hero A storms from left to right in panel one, but from right to left in the second panel, this axis would have been crossed. That is a big no-no!

HIGHLIGHT PANELS

In manga, a single stand-out panel often provides a strong impetus for readers to want to dive into a double-page spread in the first place. They are usually somewhat more complex to produce, because they may, for instance, feature spectacular scenery or unusual perspectives. But the effort is worth it, because readers will want to get to this panel from the very first glance. So make a habit of building your page layouts around these special highlight panels and make them larger than the rest. Close-ups also have a special effect – especially close-ups of protagonists in highly emotional situations, for example in tears or horrified, or close-ups of a dark, brooding character laughing.

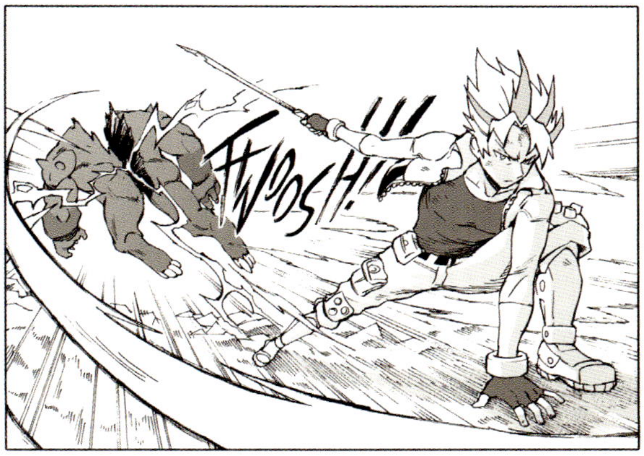

Never underestimate the power of highlight panels. In the bookshop, they can be a deciding factor in customers buying or not buying your manga. You know how it goes: you're unsure whether to get a (perhaps still unknown) manga. You grab a copy, flick through it – and you're hooked!

CLIFFHANGER

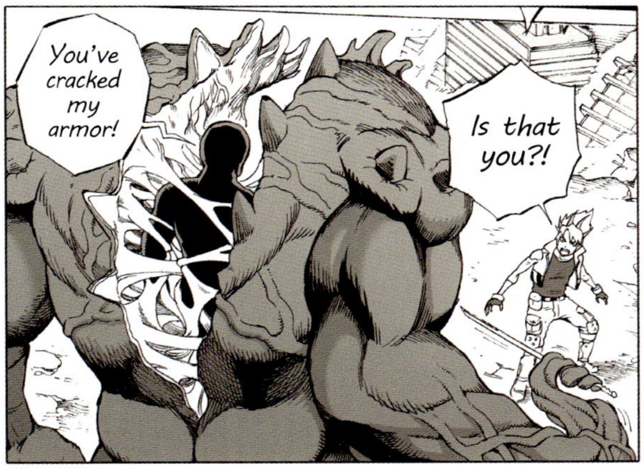

Now that we have an idea of how to guide the reader's eye quickly across a double page, as banal as it may sound, we also need to get them to turn the page quickly! The best way to do this is by not giving them a moment to rest. We end the last panel not with a potential exit point, but with a cliffhanger – a moment of tension. In our example, it turns out that the monster was just a shell –for a character that Hero A already knows. He is now one step ahead of us; he already knows the identity of his opponent. We want to be put in the picture as well, so we quickly turn the page.

Of course, it is difficult to create a final moment of tension on absolutely every double page, but sometimes a little thing like a character's reaction in the middle of a conversation can be enough. That said, if you realize that it just doesn't fit and you're disrupting your narrative flow by having to create tension at that moment, then don't do it. However, you shouldn't fail to include a cliffhanger when you close a chapter –or even an entire volume. Leaving readers with a moment of suspense can be the deciding factor in whether they continue reading your story, or buy the next volume at all.

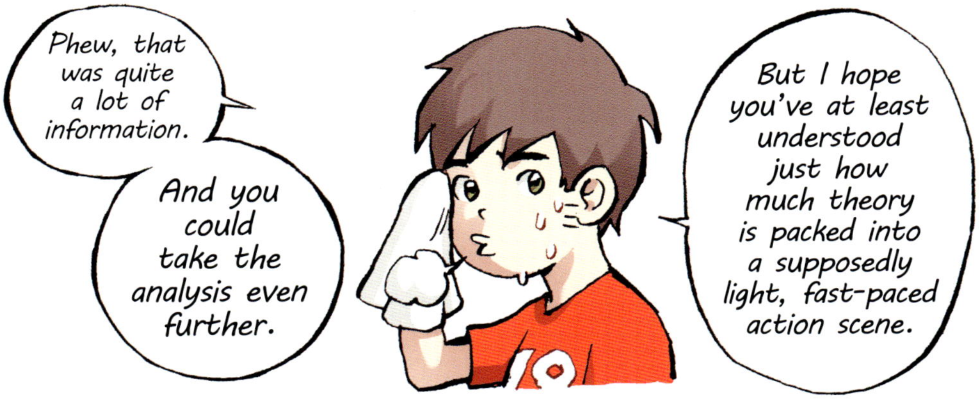

ABOUT THE AUTHOR

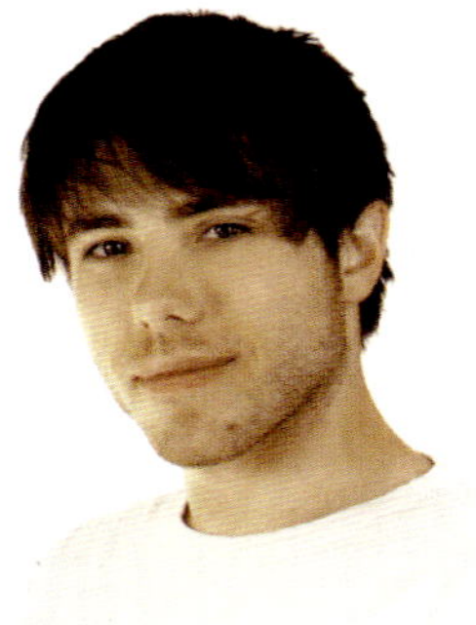

Born in the Ore Mountains in Germany, David Füleki made his debut as a mangaka at the age of 16. In his early days, he won numerous competitions and mainly published short stories in various anthologies. Alongside his media studies, he released his first major publications such as his debut paperback *Struwwelpeter: The Return* (Tokyopop) or series such as *Demon Mind Game*. He also regularly holds manga workshops on topics such as storytelling, character design, and practical aspects of working as a professional mangaka.

In recent years, David has mainly worked on large-scale projects such as the manga of top YouTubers GermanLetsPlay and Amir Yarahi, alias Kurono. He was also the official artist for the German national football team's appearance at the Tokyo Olympics, and worked with many of the world's most successful League of Legends e-athletes on the webcomic *Heroes of Rivalry*.

A DAVID AND CHARLES BOOK
Original title: *Action Manga zeichnen*, by David Füleki

EU GPSR Authorised Representative:
Logos Europe, 9 rue Nicolas Poussin, 17000, La Rochelle, France
Email: Contact@logoseurope.eu

David and Charles is an imprint of David and Charles, Ltd
Suite A, Tourism House, Pynes Hill, Exeter, EX2 5WS

Originally published in Germany in 2024
This edition first published in the UK and USA in 2026

A catalogue record for this book is available from the British Library.

ISBN-13: 9781446316948 paperback

This book has been printed on paper from approved suppliers and made from pulp from sustainable sources.

FSC MIX Paper | Supporting responsible forestry FSC® C136333

Printed in China through Asia Pacific Offset for:
David and Charles, Ltd
Suite A, Tourism House, Pynes Hill, Exeter, EX2 5WS

10 9 8 7 6 5 4 3 2 1

Publishing Director: Ame Verso
Senior Commissioning Editor: Nigel Browing
Text and Illustrations: David Füleki
Translation: Tankerton Translations
Designer: Giulia Sandri
Copy Editor: Katie Hardwicke
Editorial Assistant: Jenna McGill
Pre-press Designer: Susan Reansbury
Production Manager: Beverley Richardson

David and Charles publishes high-quality books on a wide range of subjects. For more information visit www.davidandcharles.com.

Share your art with us on social media using #dandcbooks and follow us on Facebook and Instagram by searching for @dandcbooks.

DEREK AUST - ROSSANA McKEANE PAGLIOLICO

COME PARLARE

leggere
ascoltare
scrivere

Guerra Edizioni

ISBN 88-7715-363-6

Gli autori ringraziano gli studenti e i professori che hanno gentilmente sperimentato gran parte del materiale. Inoltre ringraziano le rispettive famiglie e gli amici.

5. 4. 3.
2011 2010 2009

GUERRA EDIZIONI guru s.r.l.
Via A. Manna, 25
06132 PERUGIA (Italy)

Tel. +39 075 5289090 - Fax +39 075 5288244
e-mail: info@guerraedizioni.com
http: www.guerraedizioni.com

COME PARLARE

UNITÀ TITOLO	PAGINA	FUNZIONI COMUNICATIVE	STRUTTURE GRAMMATICALI
Unità 18*/** *Decisioni*	60	Arredare un appartamento	Condizionale Potere / Volere Pronomi oggetto diretto
Unità 19*/** *Programma di visita*	61	Discutere un programma di attività	Presente Condizionale
Unità 20*/** *Fare le valigie*	63	Decidere priorità	Dovere / Volere / Potere
Unità 21* *Cosa hai fatto?*	65	Parlare di cose fatte finora	Passato prossimo Espressioni di tempo Forma interrogativa
Unità 22* *Passato e presente*	66	Paragonare passato e presente	Presente Imperfetto
Unità 23** *Vero o falso?*	68	Spiegare Giustificarsi	Passato prossimo Imperfetto Stare + gerundio
Unità 24*/** *Fare la spesa*	70	Discutere di alimentazione	Presente Forma interrogativa
Unità 25*/** *Soldi, soldi!*	73	Discutere l'uso di soldi	Numeri Percentuali
Unità 26*/** *Sommersi dai divieti*	75	Discutere divieti e regolamenti	Forma impersonale
Unità 27** *Pubblicità*	78	Predire Analizzare un testo	Varie
Unità 28* *Ricordi di scuola*	80	Descrivere una immagine Inferire	Presente Futuro ipotetico
Unità 29/***** *Nuove tecnologie*	82	Discutere l'uso di Internet e altre tecnologie	Futuro
Unità 30** *Professioni*	86	Descrivere Paragonare Discutere pro e contro	Comparativo Congiuntivo Condizionale
Unità 31*/** *A che serve…?*	89	Discutere dell'utilità di certi oggetti	Condizionale Congiuntivo
Unità 32* *Mangiare e bere*	91	Paragonare abitudini alimentari Esprimere un parere	Infinito Preposizioni
Unità 33* *Cosa sai fare?*	94	Descrivere abilità e capacità	Sapere Imperfetto
Unità 34/***** *Cosa faresti se…?*	96	Ipotizzare	Condizionale Congiuntivo Imperfetto
Unità 35* *Apprendere una lingua straniera*	99	Discutere l'apprendimento di una lingua	Condizionale Forma impersonale

UNITÀ	PAGINA	FUNZIONI COMUNICATIVE	STRUTTURE GRAMMATICALI
Unità 36** *Problemi*	101	Esporre una preoccupazione Rassicurare	Comparativo Superlativo Imperativo
Unità 37/***** *Barzellette*	104	Raccontare una barzelletta	Varie
Unità 38* *Quante domande!*	108	Porre domande	Forma interrogativa Verbi irregolari
Unità 39*/** *Foto delle vacanze*	110	Descrivere una fotografia	Presente Passato prossimo
Unità 40*/** *Foto di famiglia*	112	Descrivere aspetto fisico e carattere Rapporti	Varie
Unità 41/***** *La mia zona*	114	Descrivere Paragonare Proporre miglioramenti	Pronomi relativi Condizionale
Unità 42*/** *Vero o falso?*	116	Negare Spiegare	Espressioni negative ed interrogative
Unità 43** *Spiegazioni*	118	Spiegare una situazione	Varie
Unità 44/***** *Scuola e università*	120	Discutere differenze Raccontare esperienze personali Spiegare una tabella	Imperfetto Comparativo
Unità 45*/** *Buonumore*	122	Descrivere una vignetta	Forma progressiva
Unità 46** *Salute e forma*	124	Fare un sondaggio Discuterne i risultati	Varie
Unità 47/***** *Vacanze*	126	Raccontare una vacanza Informarsi / protestare	Varie
Unità 48** *Cosa manca?*	130	Scegliere vocaboli corretti Esprimere accordo/ disaccordo	Potere
Unità 49*/** *C'è una persona che...?*	132	Fare un sondaggio	Presente Passato prossimo Frasi interrogative
Unità 50* *Caro diario*	134	Parlare dei propri impegni	Verbi servili Infinito dipendente
Unità 51*/** *Gioco 1*	136	Creare una situazione	Preposizioni Infinito passato
Unità 52*/** *Gioco 2*	137	Creare frasi	Tempi vari
Unità 53/***** *Buttiamo via!*	139	Giustificare una decisione Persuadere	Tempi vari

UNITÀ	PAGINA	FUNZIONI COMUNICATIVE	STRUTTURE GRAMMATICALI
Unità 54** *Abitudini*	141	Descrivere e confrontare	Verbi riflessivi
Unità 55* *Un giorno nella vita di...*	143	Descrivere una giornata tipica Scambiare ricordi	Presente Imperfetto
Unità 56* *Albero genealogico*	144	Descrivere la famiglia	Aggettivi Piacere Pronomi oggetto Pronomi relativi
Unità 57A** *Disegniamo*	145	Dare istruzioni Chiarire / correggere	Imperativo
Unità 57B** *I casi della vita*	147	Descrivere una vignetta	Presente Forma progressiva
Unità 58** *Sondaggio*	148	Scoprire cosa è successo Raccontare in modo particolareggiato	Passato prossimo Trapassato
Unità 59/***** *Ospiti*	150	Raccontare una visita Lamentarsi Consigliare	Passato prossimo Imperfetto Imperativo
Unità 60/***** *Il mio telefonino*	154	Scegliere un telefonino Paragonare Vantarsi	Comparativo Superlativo
Unità 61/***** *Cerco amici*	159	Discutere rapporti d'amicizia / sentimentali Rispondere a un annuncio	Varie
Unità 62*/** *Sei organizzato?*	162	Mantenere l'organizzazione domestica	Espressioni di luogo Preposizioni
Unità 63*** *Terapie alternative*	165	Ottenere / Dare informazioni Convincere	Futuro Imperativo
Unità 64/***** *In palestra*	168	Ottenere / Dare informazioni Consigliare Giustificarsi	Varie
Unità 65*** *Domeniche a piedi*	171	Completare informazioni attraverso la discussione Paragonare Proporre soluzioni	Varie
Unità 66/***** *Rimpianti*	175	Esprimere rimpianti	Passato prossimo Condizionale Congiuntivo
Unità 67/***** *Studenti e soldi*	177	Partecipare a un sondaggio Interpretare statistiche Fare una relazione	Percentuali
Unità 68/***** *Che avventura!*	181	Formulare ipotesi Creare una storia	Futuro ipotetico
Unità 69/***** *Studenti modello*	183	Discutere strategie di apprendimento	Forma impersonale Imperfetto

NOTA: il livello di difficoltà di ogni unità viene indicato da un asterisco - * = meno difficile, ** = più difficile ecc.

Guida per l'insegnante

Questo libro si rivolge a studenti di italiano a livello intermedio-avanzato. Molte delle attività si possono comunque usare/adattare a un livello più basso. Anche se l'obiettivo principale di *Come Parlare* è quello di sviluppare la competenza comunicativa dello studente, questo non può avvenire sempre fuori contesto; per tale ragione molte attività saranno basate su articoli di giornale o rivista autentici o su supporti visivi (immagini, disegni ecc.) Ogni unità è incentrata su un argomento che ha un rapporto diretto o indiretto con la vita quotidiana.

Le unità, che richiedono la partecipazione attiva di due o più studenti, sono indipendenti le une dalle altre e sono raggruppate dove possibile a seconda dell'argomento trattato. Si è cercato di indicare con un asterisco il livello di difficoltà di ogni unità in base alle strutture necessarie per svolgerla in modo efficace. Spetterà comunque all'insegnante decidere la sequenza di utilizzo in base allo stadio raggiunto dai propri studenti e decidere se è necessario svolgere tutte le attività presentate.

Le unità sono articolate, in generale, secondo il seguente schema:

Prima di parlare

Questa sezione ha lo scopo di creare aspettative, di motivare gli studenti alla comunicazione e prevede la riflessione individuale sulle domande poste o sulle attività suggerite.

Parliamo

In questa sezione, gli studenti saranno coinvolti in attività varie per sviluppare soprattutto l'abilità e le strategie di comunicazione. La gamma di attività e argomenti permetterà agli studenti sia di consolidare strutture e lessico già acquisiti che di impararne nuovi. A livello intermedio-avanzato è essenziale l'acquisizione di una sempre maggiore padronanza strutturale e lessicale, per essere in grado di discutere in modo approfondito una varietà di argomenti. Praticare le strutture fondamentali della lingua in un contesto e non isolatamente facilita l'acquisizione delle stesse. Si è cercato di predire le strutture di cui gli studenti avranno bisogno per svolgere le attività – vedi l'indice delle unità all'inizio del libro – ma il principale scopo delle attività è quello di stimolare la creatività e la spontaneità degli studenti.

Probabilmente vorranno utilizzare strutture e lessico non ancora acquisiti. Sarà il compito dell'insegnante, "direttore d'orchestra", provvedere a queste esigenze linguistiche. In molte unità gli studenti saranno esposti alle strutture e al lessico dei testi autentici e naturalmente una maggiore familiarità con gli stessi produrrà l'auspicabile impennata nella curva del loro apprendimento.

Espressioni utili

Una caratteristica del libro è quella di fornire una consistente scelta di espressioni utili per permettere a tutti gli studenti di esprimere le loro idee e di comunicare in diversi contesti.

Naturalmente gli studenti non dovranno usare tutte le espressioni presentate ma selezionare quelle più appropriate alle loro esigenze comunicative. L'esperienza dimostra che gli studenti hanno la necessità di usare più volte determinate espressioni per rafforzare la loro abilità comunicativa e per sviluppare ulteriormente la padronanza della lingua. L'uso frequente e ripetuto di tali strutture assicurerà un costante miglioramento.

È importante che l'insegnante analizzi le varie espressioni con gli studenti e fornisca, se del caso, alcuni esempi per assicurarsi che esse vengano capite ed usate in modo appropriato.

Vocabolario

La maggior parte delle unità si conclude con un elenco lessicale legato all'argomento trattato.

CONSIGLI GENERALI

1. Il livello di difficoltà di ogni unità viene indicato nell'indice da un asterisco - * = meno difficile, ** = più difficile ecc. L'indice inoltre indicherà le principali strutture grammaticali necessarie per svolgere le attività di conversazione.

2. A volte il contenuto di alcune unità pare molto simile ma in genere l'una sarà più generale e l'altra più specifica, oppure l'una si rivolgerà a un tipo di studente piuttosto che a un altro. In tal caso sarà consigliabile usare una delle unità dopo un certo intervallo di tempo. Ciò servirà per ripassare lo stesso argomento ma in un contesto leggermente diverso. Gli autori ritengono che possa essere un'esperienza estremamente motivante per gli studenti rifare la stessa attività dopo alcuni mesi in quanto si possono rendere conto del miglioramento ottenuto. È importante attirare la loro attenzione sul motivo della ripetizione della stessa attività.

3. L'esperienza degli autori suggerisce che l'eccessiva correzione degli errori è controproducente. A volte è possibile correggere subito lo studente ma interrompere troppo sovente può essere scoraggiante e demotivante; è preferibile spiegare quelli più comuni alla fine dell'attività senza riferimenti particolari a chi ha fatto gli errori. Dopotutto, sbagliando s'impara. Anche se lo scopo del libro è quello di aiutare gli studenti a parlare correntemente e correttamente l'italiano è necessario far notare agli studenti che la lingua parlata, essendo spontanea, spesso non è corretta dal punto di vista grammaticale, sintattico e lessicale. I parlanti, anche alla radio o alla televisione, esitano, si correggono, si ripetono, ma questo fa parte del bagaglio linguistico che gli studenti devono imparare non solo a capire ma anche ad utilizzare per parlare italiano in modo naturale.

4. Fin dall'inizio è importante incoraggiare gli studenti a parlare sempre in italiano. Le strategie di comunicazione a pagina 39 saranno molto utili a questo proposito.

5. Quasi tutte le attività richiedono il coinvolgimento di due o più studenti e offrono la possibilità di lavorare con più di un interlocutore o più di un gruppo. Spetterà all'insegnante decidere la composizione dei vari gruppi. Gli studenti, lavorando in coppia o a gruppi, possono confrontare e discutere le loro risposte, scambiare opinioni ecc. prima di procedere a un eventuale riscontro con l'insegnante.

6. Molte unità offrono una grande scelta di attività e non occorre svolgerle tutte in classe. Certe attività, per esempio, che richiedono la lettura di articoli di giornale o rivista potrebbero essere preparate a casa. Inoltre per dibattiti/role-play/discussioni, gli studenti avranno bisogno del tempo necessario per preparare gli interventi e trarne così il massimo vantaggio. È bene tener presente che soffermarsi eccessivamente su un argomento può condurre al disinteresse.

7. Alcune attività incoraggiano gli studenti a cercare di capire dal contesto il significato delle parole che non conoscono: l'utilizzo del dizionario monolingue anziché bilingue è consigliabile. È importantissimo usare la lingua italiana in classe invogliando così gli studenti che conoscono la parola o l'espressione in questione a spiegarla in italiano agli altri.

8. Le 'Espressioni utili', oltre alla loro funzione nelle attività orali, servono anche in seguito alla conversazione per il rinforzo dell'italiano scritto.

9. Dal momento che le attività all'interno di ogni singola unità sono integrate e basate su un argomento centrale (cibo, lavoro, tecnologia, vacanze, salute ecc.), gli studenti dovrebbero essere incoraggiati a preparare una mappa delle idee alla fine di ogni unità. La tecnica consiste nel raggruppare i vocaboli già conosciuti o appena acquisiti di uno stesso argomento, facilitandone la memorizzazione. Ogni volta che gli studenti dovranno ripassare, discutere o scrivere qualcosa su un determinato argomento, avranno così a disposizione una serie di schemi di facile consultazione. Questi schemi possono essere aggiornati continuamente. Vedere COME LEGGERE, Unità 10, Attività Supplementari B oppure COME ASCOLTARE Unità 5B Postascolto.

10. Di tanto in tanto sarebbe molto utile chiedere agli studenti di usare la forma di cortesia 'Lei' in certe attività in modo che si abituino anche a un registro linguistico più formale.

Unità 1

L'insegnante può chiedere a un componente di ciascun gruppo di leggere l'articolo come se fosse annunciatore alla radio.

Attività alternativa. Gli studenti lavorano a gruppi di 4. Ogni membro del gruppo legge un articolo differente e ne comunica i fatti salienti agli altri.

A coppie o in gruppo si scambiano le esperienze personali riguardo ai viaggi – in macchina / treno / aereo. Prima di iniziare sarebbe una buon'idea che gli studenti aggiungessero altre parole/espressioni utili all'elenco di vocabolario.

Unità 2

Prima di parlare Naturalmente si possono suggerire altri argomenti. Ci saranno altre unità che tratteranno in altro modo gli argomenti scelti ma la ripetizione è a volte molto utile come detto sopra. Gli studenti potrebbero preparare l'argomento scelto a casa prima di presentarlo in classe.

Attività alternativa. Scegliere uno degli argomenti e dividere la classe in due gruppi A e B. Il gruppo A fa un brain-storming sui possibili vantaggi e il gruppo B sugli svantaggi dell'argomento scelto. È necessario fissare un tempo limite (es. 5 minuti). Ognuno deve fare una lista sia dei vantaggi che degli svantaggi. Poi a coppie A e B confrontano e discutono le loro liste.

Unità 6

Istruzioni per l'insegnante:

1. Questa è un'attività creativa e divertente. Fotocopiare un numero sufficiente di fogli per la classe.
2. Preparare un mazzo di 12 carte per ogni gruppo.
3. Nominare una persona in ogni gruppo che tiene e gira le carte una per volta – la prima espressione in cima al mazzo di carte è *un giorno del mese scorso* e l'ultima carta contiene la parola *un appartamento.* Nemmeno la persona che tiene le carte vede quello che c'è scritto finché la carta non viene girata e posata sul banco.
4. Spiegare le regole del gioco, cioè, a vicenda, ogni membro del gruppo deve costruire una frase che contiene la parola/espressione sulla carta e ripetere o modificare, se necessario, tutte le frasi precedenti. Questo vuole dire che l'ultima persona dovrà raccontare tutta la 'storia' dall'inizio.
5. Le storie create dai vari gruppi spesso risultano molto diverse.
6. Questa attività può essere utilizzata a vari livelli poiché l'insegnante ha la possibilità di specificare un determinato periodo usando un avverbio di tempo. ad esempio, *oggi, domani, la settimana prossima.*
7. Alla fine ogni gruppo può raccontare la sua storia e poi scriverla ed appenderla alla parete della classe. Una giuria potrebbe premiare quella più originale/creativa.
8. Questo è un esempio di come potrebbe funzionare: 1. Un giorno del mese scorso sono andato in città. 2. Un giorno del mese scorso sono andato in città per imbucare una lettera a un amico italiano. 3. Un giorno del mese scorso sono andato in città per imbucare una let-

tera a una ragazza italiana (qui bisogna modificare la frase precedente) che avevo conosciuto durante le mie vacanze a Firenze. 4. Un giorno del mese scorso sono andato in città per imbucare una lettera a una ragazza italiana che avevo conosciuto durante le mie vacanze a Firenze. In questa lettera volevo comunicarle una bella notizia *o* *un'altra versione*; Un giorno del mese scorso ho ricevuto una lettera da una ragazza italiana che avevo conosciuto durante le mie vacanze a Firenze. In questa lettera c'era una bella notizia... ecc. ecc.

9. Si potrebbe anche suggerire ai gruppi di creare la storia in un certo stile, esempio: versione romantica, avventurosa, surreale, comica ecc.
10. Si è acclusa una versione in bianco che l'insegnante potrà utilizzare a piacimento.

1 UN GIORNO DEL MESE SCORSO	2 LETTERA	3 RAGAZZA ITALIANA	4 BELLA NOTIZIA
5 FELICE	6 SPOSARSI	7 PRIMA	8 CORSO UNIVERSITARIO
9 ANCORA UN ANNO	10 RISPARMIARE	11 COMPRARE	12 UN APPARTAMENTO

1	2	3	4
5	6	7	8
9	10	11	12

Unità 7

Distribuire ad ogni gruppo uno dei seguenti fogli.

Gruppo A: in vacanza – sulle spiagge semideserte – andavamo spesso a cenare – abbiamo portato – gatti

Gruppo B: in Sardegna – nelle gelaterie all'aperto – al mattino e alla sera – ancora autentica e selvaggia – gli animali

Gruppo C: tre cani – sotto i tavoli dell'agriturismo – nuotavano e correvano – abbiamo pulito

Gruppo D: contenti – la vacanza – spazi per tutti – se ne stavano in pineta all'ombra – cuccioli

Unità 9

Qui sotto sono i brani da fotocopiare e distribuire agli studenti per **Prima di parlare 1**.

PAGARE PER VEDERE VENEZIA

Brano A

Vicesindaco Vianello, è lei l'inventore del "serenissimo balzello" da 1.000 lire?
"Sì, confesso: l'idea è mia. *Mi sono fatto carico* di *una proposta che suscita perplessità* e reazioni, perché di fatto io sono la "vittima" designata a gestire i servizi di Venezia: dalla pulizia della città ai trasporti, dai wc pubblici alla vigilanza urbana. Per la gente *sono servizi scontati* e nessuno si sofferma mai a *riflettere sui costi* che, per una città unica al mondo qual è Venezia, sono onerosissimi".

Brano B

Allora è un problema di quadratura di bilancio delle case comunali?
"Venezia ha poco meno di 300 mila abitanti, terraferma compresa; 300 mila persone che contribuiscono con le tasse al mantenimento della città. Sono però ben 12 milioni i turisti che arrivano ogni anno e noi *non siamo più in grado di sostenere,* con la fiscalità generale, *una rete di servizi,* per qualità e quantità, idonea a 12 milioni di presenze aggiuntive. Solo per rimuovere i rifiuti lasciati dai turisti spendiamo 18 milioni e mezzo all'anno. Non possiamo tassare di più i veneziani per *fronteggiare problemi d'importazione"*.

Brano C

Dunque 1.000 lire per tutelare i residenti?
"Sì, ma per trattare meglio anche i turisti".
Perché tanto *clamore* allora?
"Qualunque cosa accada a Venezia suscita sempre una vasta eco. Mille lire, da pagare su *un pernottamento* o in aggiunta al conto del ristorante, sono *davvero un piccolo "obolo"*, dal quale oltre al risultato economico mi aspetto maggior senso di responsabilità e consapevolezza da ristoratori e albergatori. Una città vive non perché il Comune cattivo fa l'esattore, ma perché *tutti si rimboccano le maniche* e *si danno da fare* per trovare le risorse necessarie".

Brano D

Nessun problema dal punto di vista giuridico?
"La proposta è legittima perché si tratta di un contributo al mantenimento della città e non di una tassa d'ingresso, che invece sarebbe incostituzionale".
L'idea di far pagare qualcosa in più ai turisti non crea un alone di *città "respingente"*?
"No. Noi diciamo solo al turista: "Amico, se tu non ci fossi noi potremmo pulire piazza San Marco una volta al giorno e invece dobbiamo farlo cinque volte. Per piacere, poiché Venezia è *un bene universale,* dacci un piccolo contributo per conservarla meglio". (Famiglia Cristiana – N35/1999)

Unità 10

Parliamo 4 . Gli studenti possono essere raggruppati in modo differente (questo può essere fatto dopo aver assegnato ad ogni studente dei vari gruppi una lettera, A B C D, mettendo insieme tutti gli studenti dei vari gruppi con la lettera A, poi quelli con la lettera B, ecc.). È importante a volte riformare i gruppi in questo modo affinché gli studenti abbiano l'occasione di riportare quello che hanno detto gli altri.

Unità 11

Parliamo 2 Per la riformazione dei gruppi vedere la spiegazione in Unità 10.

Unità 12

Questo è un buon esempio di un argomento che si può ripetere a intervalli durante il corso. È adatto a studenti di vari livelli e tratta di un argomento molto comune.

Unità 14

Prima di parlare. Naturalmente gli studenti dovrebbero essere incoraggiati ad esprimere altri fastidi personali non contenuti nella lista – se vogliono!

Unità 15

Gli studenti possono immaginare di telefonarsi. Possono sedersi schiena contro schiena. Qui si presenta l'occasione di insegnare espressioni informali che si usano al telefono, es. *stammi a sentire un attimo.*

Unità 16

È meglio che ogni studenti pensi all'oggetto / apparecchio che vuole descrivere. Si possono preparare dei fogli contenenti una parola ciascuno (esempi: *dizionario / cacciavite / telecomando*) nel caso in cui allo studente manchi un'idea.

Unità 17

Qui sotto sono gruppi di parole/espressioni che si possono usare. Ogni gruppo di parole/espressioni deve essere scritto su un foglio di carta e distribuito ai vari gruppi. Se un gruppo non vuole mimare la storia tocca a qualcuno raccontarla. Si dovrebbe incoraggiarli a mimare perché può rendere l'attività ancora più divertente.

- un gatto randagio / le vacanze / la mia amica
- l'incidente / il matrimonio / gli sposi
- una multa / fare la spesa / dimenticare
- distratto / le pantofole / i miei colleghi
- una festa di compleanno / sbagliare la casa / imbarazzato
- un esame / il telefonino / dichiarazione d'amore
- discoteca / uno strappo / amica
- direttore di banca / prestito / affitto

Attività alternativa. Distribuire le stesse parole/espressioni ad ogni gruppo. Sarebbe interessante confrontare le loro creazioni. Potrebbero risultare molto simili oppure molto diverse. Gli 'osservatori' possono fare da giuria e nominare la storia più creativa.

Unità 19

Chi conosce bene la zona sarà senz'altro in grado di dare molti suggerimenti. Comunque sarebbe una buon'idea fotocopiare alcune pagine del giornale locale (spettacoli, visite, mostre, ecc.) e distribuirle ai vari gruppi. Ciò renderà l'attività più autentica.

Unità 24

Forse sarà necessario adattare leggermente l'attività se si tratta di una classe di adulti perché forse sceglieranno prodotti simili. Possono immaginare di andare a fare la spesa con i figli. Cosa metterebbero loro nel carrello?

Unità 27

Vedere anche COME ASCOLTARE, Unità 8 che tratta della pubblicità.

Unità 28

Le attività che dipendono da immagini incoraggiano gli studenti ad essere molto creativi perché non ci sono risposte specifiche alle domande e perciò risultano molto motivanti.

Unità 30

Per ulteriori attività sul Lavoro e Professioni vedere anche COME ASCOLTARE , Unità 7 e COME LEGGERE, Unità 4.

Unità 31

Chi ha una classe composta da pochi studenti può, se necessario, togliere uno degli elenchi di parole in **Prima di parlare**.

Unità 37

Questa è la barzelletta da raccontare. È chiaro che l'insegnante può raccontare un'altra barzelletta o un altro aneddoto. In questo caso darà una lista di parole chiave.

> Un giorno d'inverno sono andato a fare un giro in macchina. Guidavo lungo una strada stretta stretta in piena campagna quando tutto ad un tratto ho avuto un guasto al motore. Sono sceso dalla macchina e ho aperto il cofano per dare un'occhiata anche se non mi intendevo molto di motori. Purtroppo, proprio in quel momento, ha cominciato a piovere a dirotto. Ho guardato il motore per alcuni minuti ma non sono riuscito a scoprire il problema. Poi ho sentito una voce dietro di me che diceva che il guasto aveva a che fare con il carburatore. Mi sono girato ma non ho visto nessuno. Poco dopo ho sentito di nuovo la stessa voce. "È il carburatore". Mi sono girato ma non c'era nessuno. Mi sono accorto che un cavallo dietro alla siepe mi fissava ma altrimenti non c'era un'anima viva. Comunque, ho aggiustato un po' il carburatore, sono salito sulla macchina e ho acceso il motore che si è messo subito in moto. Che fortuna! Ho ripreso il mio viaggio ma dopo una quindicina di minuti mi sono fermato ad una stazione di servizio nel prossimo paesino per fare il pieno. Quando il benzinaio è arrivato gli ho raccontato quello che mi era successo. Lui pensava che fossi pazzo da legare e mi ha invitato a sedermi e ed è andato a prendermi un bicchiere d'acqua. Dopo che avevo bevuto il bicchiere d'acqua il benzinaio mi ha chiesto di raccontare un'altra volta questa storia. Allora per la seconda volta gli ho detto che guidavo lungo questa strada stretta stretta in piena campagna quando tutto ad un tratto ho avuto un guasto al motore. Sono sceso dalla macchina e ho aperto il cofano per dare un'occhiata anche se non mi intendevo molto di motori. Purtroppo, proprio in quel momento, ha cominciato a piovere a dirotto. Ho guardato il motore per alcuni minuti ma non sono riuscito a scoprire il problema. Poi ho sentito una voce dietro di me che diceva che aveva a che fare con il carburatore. Mi sono girato ma non ho visto nessuno. Poco dopo ho sentito di nuovo la stessa voce. "È il carburatore". Mi sono girato ma non c'era nessuno. Mi sono accorto che un cavallo dietro alla siepe mi fissava ma altrimenti non c'era un'anima viva. Comunque, ho aggiustato un po' il carburatore, sono salito sulla macchina e ho acceso il motore che si è messo subito in moto. "Ho capito", ha detto il benzinaio "ma mi dica una cosa: il cavallo era di color nero o bianco? Perché, se mi ricordo bene ci sono due cavalli in quel campo di cui parla". - "Sono sicurissimo che il cavallo era bianco". - "Meno male" ha risposto il benzinaio, "ha avuto proprio fortuna perché quello nero non si intende per niente di motori!".

Unità 38

Lo scopo di questa unità è quello di far capire agli studenti quante domande si possono fare con un numero limitato di forme interrogative, verbi e parole. Sarà inoltre interessante osservare il numero di dialoghi / conversazioni differenti che si possono creare. È molto importante che gli studenti abbiano l'occasione di porre domande e non solo rispondere alle domande dell'insegnante.

Unità 41

Se possibile sarà meglio organizzare le coppie in modo che vengano da zone differenti.

Non è essenziale però perché due abitanti della stessa zona possono avere opinioni del tutto contrastanti.

Attività supplementare: Chi pensa di abitare in una zona ideale deve convincere gli altri componenti del gruppo a traslocare in quella zona.

Unità 43

A volte sarà necessario presentare un dialogo per contestualizzare quelle espressioni che nessun componente della classe è in grado di comprendere. Sarebbe utile ricorrere ogni tanto a questo genere di attività affinché gli studenti abbiano l'occasione di apprendere frasi idiomatiche, proverbi ed altre espressioni che si usano quotidianamente nel linguaggio sia informale che formale.

Unità 45

Queste sono le frasi originali che descrivono le vignette:

A - Adesso è ancora niente, vedrai nelle ore di punta.
B – Chissà che origine ha questa isoletta...
C – Capo, lo ammetto, ho fatto uno sbaglio...
D – È come temevo: vede, c'è una perdita d'acqua...

Unità 47

Attività supplementare: gli studenti possono preparare a casa il diario di una vacanza prima di presentarla oralmente in classe ai loro compagni.

Unità 48

Ecco l'articolo di giornale che bisogna fotocopiare e distribuire agli studenti quando hanno finito l'attività **Parliamo**.

Firenze, un'altra rapina in una villa in campagna

Continuano le rapine nelle ville. L'ultima della serie è avvenuta domenica notte in Toscana. Almeno 4 banditi, armati di pistola e col volto coperto, hanno fatto irruzione in una villa nei pressi di Figline Valdarno (Firenze). I malviventi che sono riusciti ad aprire una cassaforte, hanno preso denaro e gioielli per centinaia di milioni. Avevano atteso che rincasasse l'ingegner M.B., di 34 anni, con la madre. L'uomo è stato aggredito, ha tentato di reagire, ed è stato duramente picchiato (40 giorni di prognosi). Poi madre e figlio sono stati chiusi in uno sgabuzzino. (Corriere della sera, 19/1/2000)

Questo genere di attività incoraggia la riflessione sulle strutture grammaticali e sui termini che occorrono sapere per discuterle.

Unità 52

Domande sull'Italia

L'insegnante potrà usare alcune di queste domande o farne altre più adatte al livello e alle esigenze di programma della propria classe.

1. Qual è la capitale d'Italia?
2. Qual è la più grande isola italiana?
3. Come si chiama il cantante italiano il cui nome indica un ingrediente che si usa in cucina?
4. Chi ha dipinto la Cappella Sistina?
5. Dove si trova la Cappella Sistina?
6. Quale regista italiano ha vinto un Oscar?
7. In quale città si trova la Mole Antonelliana?
8. Come si chiama la maggiore compagnia aerea italiana?
9. Cosa è il Pendolino?
10. In quale città si trova il Museo degli Uffizi?
11. Quali sono gli ingredienti del pesto?
12. In quale regione italiana si parla anche il tedesco?
13. Per che cosa sono famosi questi italiani:
    Dolce & Gabbana, il Senatore Agnelli, Emma Bonino, Francesca Archibugi, Giuseppe Tornatore, Marconi, Beniamino Gigli, Renzo Piano, Vittorio Storaro, Salvatore Ferragamo.

Attività alternativa: Sostituire i verbi nelle caselle con quelli che richiedono una preposizione davanti a un infinito o un sostantivo, per esempio, *decidere di, mettersi a, dipendere da, fidarsi di.* Non includere la preposizione. Toccherà agli studenti fornire la preposizione appropriata quando costruiscono la loro frase.

Unità 57 Parte A

Per materiale di ascolto relativo a questa Unità vedere COME ASCOLTARE, Unità 3.

Unità 57 Parte B

Queste sono le vignette da fotocopiare e distribuire agli studenti. Dare solo una delle vignette a caso a ciascun componente di ogni gruppo.

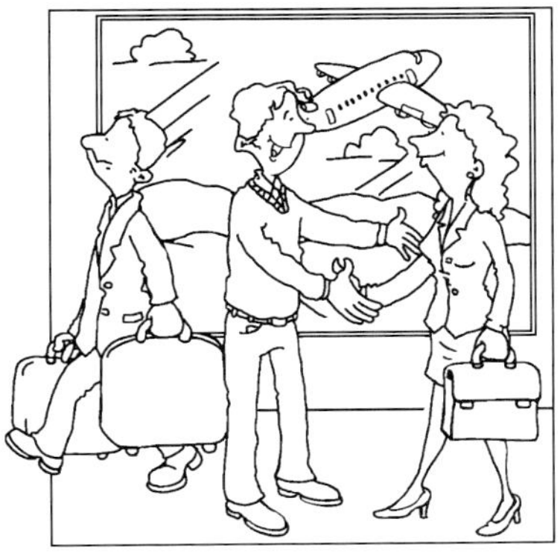

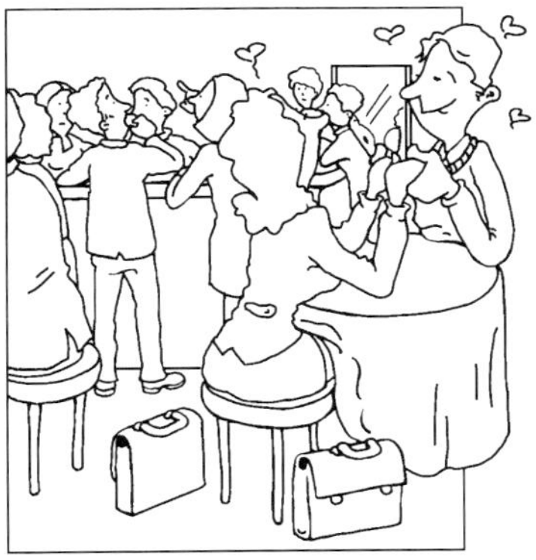

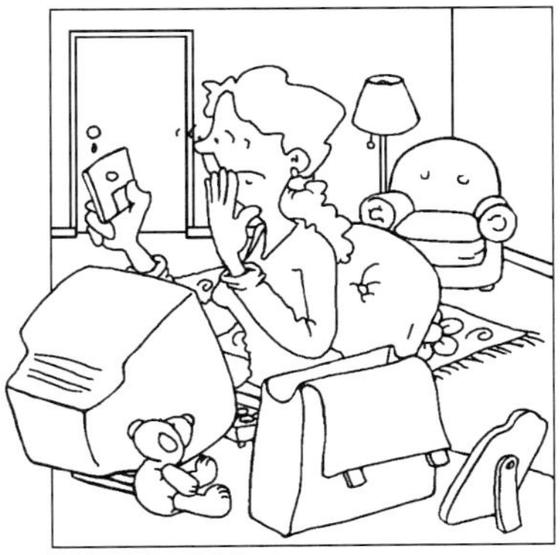

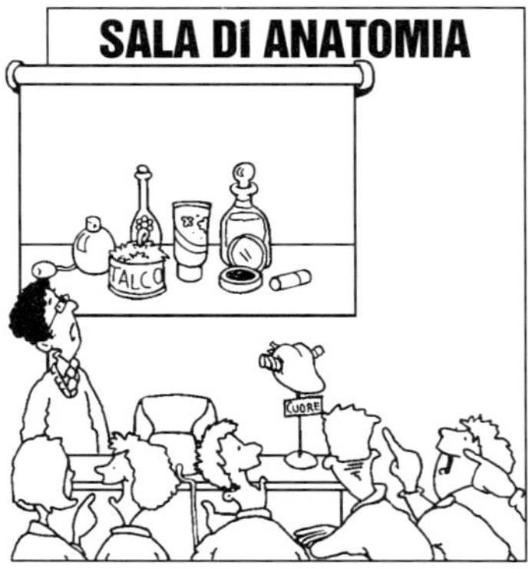

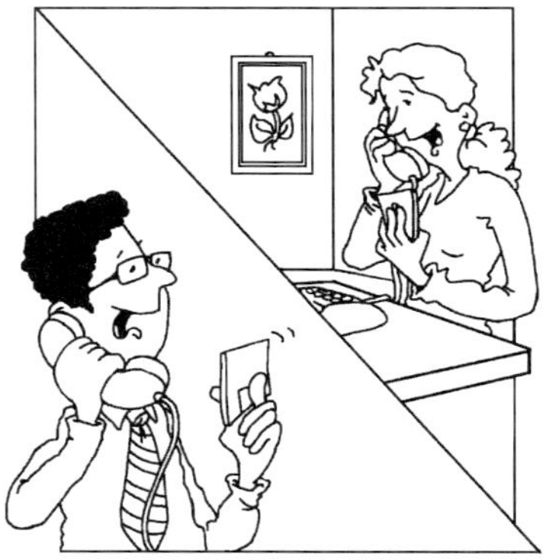

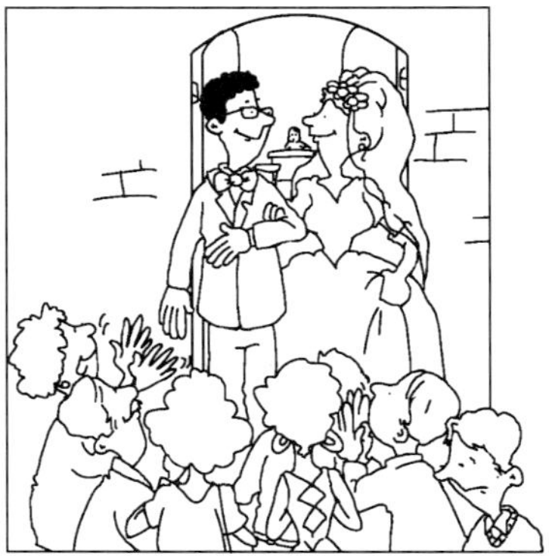

Lo scopo dell'attività è di liberare la fantasia degli studenti attraverso la libera interpretazione di una serie di 6 immagini che costituiscono una breve narrativa.

Le immagini sono fotocopiabili e, presentate individualmente, si prestano a più possibilità d'uso, come negli esempi 1 - 3. Prima di distribuire le carte l'insegnante annuncerà che ogni carta rappresenta una parte di una storia completa che sarà ricostruita collettivamente.

1. Classe divisa in sei gruppi. Tagliare le carte, mescolarle e darne una sola a ogni gruppo. Ogni gruppo discuterà la propria immagine, cercando allo stesso tempo di immaginare le circostanze della storia. A turno, il portavoce di ogni gruppo dovrà descrivere l'immagine in modo particolareggiato. Dopo avere ascoltato tutti i gruppi la classe deciderà in quale sequenza mettere le immagini e la storia sarà ricostruita collettivamente.

2. Classe divisa in gruppi di sei persone. Tagliare le carte, mescolarle e distribuirle a caso, una per ogni persona nel gruppo. Il gruppo discuterà le varie possibilità di sviluppo della storia. Il portavoce di ogni gruppo racconterà la propria versione.

3. Individualmente o a coppie. Ogni studente o coppia riceve una carta, di cui dovrà preparare una descrizione particolareggiata. Circolando in classe e scambiando informazioni sulle varie carte (è consigliabile prendere qualche appunto), ogni studente o coppia otterrà informazioni sulle altre cinque carte e formulerà un'ipotesi di sviluppo della storia. A turno si presenterà la propria versione. Il gioco può continuare fino a quando tutti avranno fornito la propria versione. Si può anche suggerire a chi ha già finito da tempo di scrivere la propria versione che sarà esposta al muro o alla lavagna luminosa.

Il gioco può anche avere un elemento competitivo se si pone un certo limite di tempo. Vince il primo studente o la prima coppia che riuscirà a creare una storia.

Unità 64

Alla pagina seguente si trova un altro articolo che si può usare.

In palestra sul posto di lavoro

Molte aziende hanno spazi attrezzati per i dipendenti: meno stress e più efficienza

MILANO — Relax e ginnastica. A spese dell'azienda, anzi dentro l'azienda. E' incominciata in sordina, ma è già una moda. L'imprenditore mette i locali e l'attrezzatura — basta una stanza in fondo al corridoio per ricavare una piccola palestra — il dipendente durante le pause pranzo ne approfitta per ritemprarsi dalle fatiche e dallo stress.

Negli Usa — dove il fitness sul luogo di lavoro è stato introdotto da 43 società su cento — ormai è normale: assenteismo ridotto e spese mediche tagliate del 40 per cento. Da noi la rivoluzione sul lavoro è appena cominciata, ma i segni del nuovo clima si possono trovare un po' ovunque.

«Se fino a ieri la massima aspirazione era avere l'auto, il telefonino e il viaggio all'estero con la moglie, oggi preferiscono la palestra sul luogo di lavoro — dice Massimo Villani, direttore del personale della Nike di Bologna — Quando abbiamo aperto, due anni fa, la palestra non era terminata e i 160 dipendenti fremevano. Oggi la struttura è perfettamente funzionante — 100 metri quadri ai quali se ne aggiungeranno altri 250 — suddivisi nelle tre aree classiche del fitness: cardiovascolare per il riscaldamento, isotonica per il risveglio del tono muscolare e stretching per l'attività aerobica. Come nella casa madre americana e nelle filiali europee rimane aperta fino alle 22.30 inclusa la domenica. E ora i dipendenti hanno decisio di "autotassarsi" per organizzare corsi di stretching».

Si fa ginnastica nelle pause pranzo e la sera fino alle 20.30 anche nel nuovo stabilimento Tod's di Diego della Valle, a Brancadoro, 60 chilometri da Ancona. La palestra è frequentata ogni giorno da circa 100 persone (un terzo dei dipendenti) in prevalenza donne. «La filosofia dell'azienda è quella di offrire un modello moderno di benefit, sotto forma di strutture di supporto ai collaboratori», spiega l'imprenditore marchigiano. Molto apprezzato dai lavoratori è anche lo spazio fitness dell'industria chimica Mapei di Milano con vista panoramica sulla città. «Da noi è il capufficio a raccomandare di andarsi a rilassare in palestra — dice Adriana Spazzoli, responsabile marketing — lo sport favorisce la socializzazione e tiene alto il morale della squadra». La pensano allo stesso modo alla Fila Sport di Biella che nell'area per la ginnastica hanno ricreato anche una parete per il free climbing.

Ed è solo l'inizio, assicurano gli esperti. «Gli imprenditori italiani si stanno attrezzando per prevedere anche il programma di educazione alimentare come già accade alla Adidas di Londra, dice Franco Cicognani, responsabile della comunicazione della TechnoGym di Gambettola, l'azienda di attrezzi professionali alle porte di Cesena che ha esportato in tutto mondo il loro programma di fitness.

Il partito dei salutisti è trasversale. Dallo studio legale Consolo di Roma, che negli uffici ai Parioli ha allestito una palestra con tanto di sauna e solarium, alla Rai di Saxa Rubra, che sull'esempio della Bbc, sta costruendo una vasta zona benessere. Alle porte di Firenze nell'azienda di abbigliamento giovane Patrizia Pepe la palestra è stata concepita accanto alla mensa dalla quale è separata solo da un'ampia vetrata. «Un invito ai lavoratori a restare in forma — dicono i responsabili — Non ci crederete ma l'esperimento funziona».

Maria Teresa Veneziani

La palestra in azienda

Investimento minimo
per 15-20 persone **50-60** milioni

Progetto Sala attrezzi
Stanza areata, luminosa e insonorizzata di circa 100 metri quadrati, pavimento in parquet

Area Cardiovascolare
(per allenare il cuore e bruciare i grassi)

- 2 tapis roulant
- 3 bike (di cui una orizzontale)
- 1 step simulatore di scalini
- 1 top xt cross trainer arm ergometro (per allenare i muscoli superiori del tronco)

Area Stretching
(per allungare i muscoli e scaricare la tensione) tappetini vari

Area Forza e Pesi
(per tonificare i muscoli)

- Panche e manubri
- 1 leg press (macchina per quadricipiti)
- 1 leg estension (lavora sui quadricipiti superiori)
- 1 standing gluteus (per rassodare i glutei)
- 1 abdominal (agisce sugli addominali)
- 1 lowel back (rinforza i muscoli della schiena)
- 1 chest Press (tonifica i pettorali)

Unità 70

Prima di svolgere **Parliamo 2 e 3** gli studenti possono copiare altre tabelle nel quaderno oppure l'insegnante può fare un numero sufficiente di fotocopie della tabella e distribuirle agli studenti. Per materiale di ascolto sui corsi di lingua e sul sistema scolastico italiano vedere COME ASCOLTARE, Unità 10.

Unità 71

Qui sotto sono i brani da fotocopiare e distribuire agli studenti per l'attività **Prima di parlare 2**:

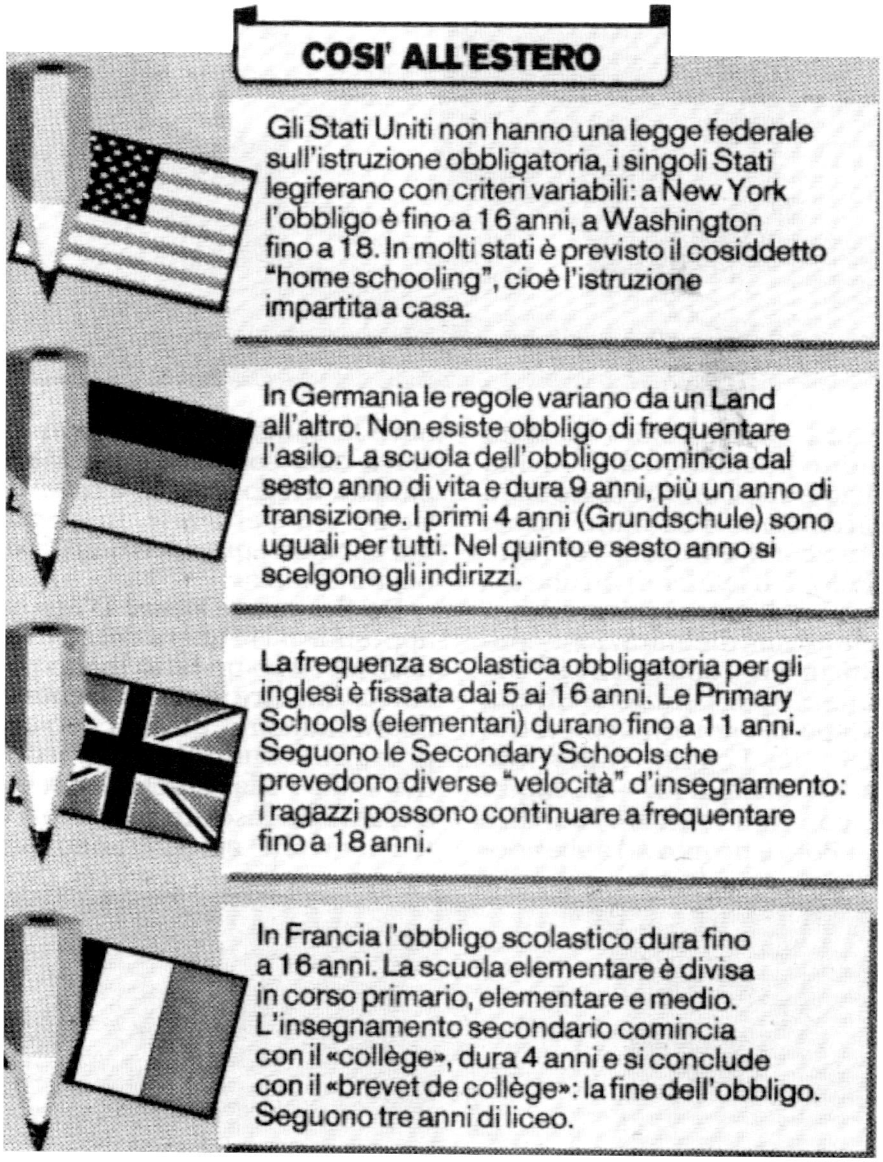

COSI' ALL'ESTERO

Gli Stati Uniti non hanno una legge federale sull'istruzione obbligatoria, i singoli Stati legiferano con criteri variabili: a New York l'obbligo è fino a 16 anni, a Washington fino a 18. In molti stati è previsto il cosiddetto "home schooling", cioè l'istruzione impartita a casa. — **Studente A**

In Germania le regole variano da un Land all'altro. Non esiste obbligo di frequentare l'asilo. La scuola dell'obbligo comincia dal sesto anno di vita e dura 9 anni, più un anno di transizione. I primi 4 anni (Grundschule) sono uguali per tutti. Nel quinto e sesto anno si scelgono gli indirizzi. — **Studente B**

La frequenza scolastica obbligatoria per gli inglesi è fissata dai 5 ai 16 anni. Le Primary Schools (elementari) durano fino a 11 anni. Seguono le Secondary Schools che prevedono diverse "velocità" d'insegnamento: i ragazzi possono continuare a frequentare fino a 18 anni. — **Studente C**

In Francia l'obbligo scolastico dura fino a 16 anni. La scuola elementare è divisa in corso primario, elementare e medio. L'insegnamento secondario comincia con il «collège», dura 4 anni e si conclude con il «brevet de collège»: la fine dell'obbligo. Seguono tre anni di liceo. — **Studente D**

La Repubblica 15/1/1997

Unità 72

I titoli dei film che corrispondono alle persone o occasioni descritte in **Prima di parlare 2**.

a. Onegin
b. East is East
c. Agnes Brown
d. La Via Degli Angeli
e. Tarzan
f. Tutti gli uomini del deficiente
g. Mifune
h. Se scappi ti sposo
i. Summer of Sam

Unità 77

Per ulteriore materiale di ascolto e di lettura sull'argomento delle *Vacanze* vedere rispettivamente COME ASCOLTARE, Unità 4 e 14 e COME LEGGERE, Unità 10.

Unità 78

... SI RISOLVONO COSÌ

D — **È** indispensabile che ognuno possieda il suo cesto dei panni sporchi e ripulisca la cucina appena ci si alza da tavola. Per i turni, invece, il trucco è prevedere due date settimanali ciascuno, in modo che se qualcuno fa il furbo il lunedì, non possa farlo anche il giovedì. Un consiglio ai super ordinati: calma e tolleranza, non rinfacciate agli altri di essere gli unici a conoscere la civiltà se non volete rischiare la cacciata di casa! Ovviamente il discorso inverso vale per chi della confusione e del disordine ha fatto la sua filosofia di vita!

H — **È** necessario diminuire i consumi: staccare il boiler quando la casa resta vuota per qualche giorno, evitare le lampadine da troppi watt in corridoi e bagni, non attaccare la lavabiancheria per due camicie e un pigiama. Ogni quota di pagamento, invece, deve subire un aumento di 2/3 mila lire, a seconda del numero degli inquilini: così chi va a pagare la bolletta possa usufruire di una colazione gratis alla faccia dei più pigri!

B — **L**'unica soluzione per evitare l'ira dei compagni è ricomprare in giornata ciò che viene consumato «a sbafo». Meglio perciò conservare lontano dalla cucina le leccornie (non deperibili) che concedete esclusivamente a voi stessi. Inoltre non perdete occasione per rammentare a chi fa la spesa ai superdiscount che è tenuto a consumare i suoi prodotti e non comprare la pasta che scuoce e poi mangiare la De Cecco degli altri!

E — **L**egge numero uno: il prestito deve essere a completa discrezione del proprietario. Esempio: se Luca è un pirata della strada è meglio non prestargli niente mentre Angela, che rispetta i limiti di velocità e non dimentica mai di mettere l'antifurto, merita maggiore fiducia. Se siete come Luca meglio non insistere quando alla prima richiesta vi hanno risposto di no, poiché potrebbero soprassedere per una volta, ma poi rifarsi meschinamente sul vostro impianto stereo da un milione di dollari che troneggia in salotto.

L **L**'unica via d'uscita, qui, è il buon senso. Qui si va su un terreno minato, perché certo non si può andare d'accordo con tutti. Allora se tra gli invitati c'è qualcuno che non va giù... occorre far buon viso a cattivo gioco. Chiedendo che i compagni di appartamento mostrino la stessa comprensione verso i vostri amici.

A **C**ontro i disordinati cronici esiste solo l'intimidazione, della serie: «Qualsiasi cosa trovo sul mio letto sarà buttata via». Ma quando avete già dato al pattume di tutto, potrete proporre ai vostri coinquilini di comprare una cesta, necessariamente con coperchio, dove sarà riposta ogni cosa che non sta al suo posto. A chi invece ha il brutto vizio di ordinare le vostre cose come voi non fareste mai, si deve imporre di annotare ogni cosa sulla lavagna all'ingresso.

F **I**ntanto bisogna chiedere sempre l'autorizzazione prima di calare le mani nei cassetti o sulle mensole degli altri. Per quel che riguarda i vestiti, però, il vizio è sempre quello di prendere T-shirt fresche di bucato e restituirle in condizioni pietose. Quindi ciò che è pulito e stirato, così deve essere restituito. Per Cd e libri, invece, se al primo reclamo del proprietario non avete ancora provveduto, al secondo non potrete far altro che ricomprare l'oggetto, anche se dello smarrimento non siete voi i diretti responsabili.

I **A** chi dà fastidio il fumo di sigarette la convivenza con i fumatori deve basarsi su delle regole ben precise: caricare sul badget vagonate di deodoranti antifumo; obbligare i fumatori a perlustrare la casa prima di andare a letto per svuotare tutti i portacenere; vietare di accendere Marlboro e Camel in camera e imporgli di aprire sempre le finestre dopo una ricca fumata. Avvisateli che non usando queste accortezze gli butterete puntualmente le bionde: se si tratta di fumatori incalliti, solo grazie alla paura di restare senza sigarette vi staranno a sentire.

G **P**rima regola: nessuna telefonata, quando tutti gli altri sono in casa, deve superare i 20 minuti; se ciò non avviene e non ci sono motivi evidenti perché questa continui, chiunque necessiti dell'apparecchio può sentirsi autorizzato a staccare la spina. Seconda regola: i malati di Internet addiction devono poter chattare quanto vogliono, ma esclusivamente nelle ore notturne. A chi porta in giro il cordless (perdendolo), infine, bisogna vietare di usarlo, ma solo fino a quando avrà imparato la lezione!

C **O**gnuno è artefice del suo lavaggio: questa regola è fondamentale, affinché il carico con quel fazzoletto rosso che colora di rosa confetto tutto il bucato non vi venga rinfacciato fino alla scadenza del contratto di affitto. Ricordate di non allontanare mai il tubo di scarico dal lavabo vicino, poiché una sciocca dimenticanza potrebbe costarvi ore di lavoro: se attaccate la lavatrice, magari prima di uscire, al ritorno, potreste ritrovarvi in una piscina di acqua sporca!

a cura di *Francesca Candreva*

Lo scopo dell'attività **Prima di parlare 2** è di abbinare il problema alla corretta soluzione. L'insegnante dovrà fotocopiare il testo e presentarlo alla classe in ordine diverso. È molto importante permettere agli studenti di trovare loro stessi suggerimenti e soluzioni prima di presentare il testo. Questa attività si presta a numerose variazioni.

TITOLI DI GIORNALE

Prima di parlare 1. *Le seguenti parole/espressioni sono state tratte da quattro articoli di giornale, i cui titoli sono elencati qui sotto. Secondo te, in quale degli articoli troverai queste parole/espressioni? Scrivi nella casella la lettera che corrisponde al titolo. Attenzione, forse troverai le stesse parole/espressioni in più articoli.*

1 ❑ il prossimo collegamento potenza presunta veicoli

2 ❑ vigili del fuoco campagna di prevenzione snobba infortunati

3 ❑ persone ferite motori sostituiti da autobus disagi traffico

4 ❑ incidenti stradali dimezzato passeggeri caselli deviati

a. Strade: super multe a chi non mette cinture e casco
b. Nebbia: tamponamenti a catena sulla A-13
c. Aerei: Il Roma-New York rientra a Fiumicino per avaria
d. Treni: Roma Termini chiusa anche domani

Parliamo 1 *A coppie discutete la vostra scelta.*

Espressioni utili

- Secondo me questa parola/espressione è stata tratta dall'articolo *a* perché ...
- Non c'è dubbio / è ovvio che questo articolo tratta di ... e quindi ...
- Non sono al cento per cento sicuro/a ma penso che appartenga all'articolo ...
- A giudicare dal titolo non sono convinto/a che abbia un collegamento con ...
- Non ha nulla a che fare con ...
- Si può usare questa parola sia per descrivere ... che per parlare di ...

Prima di parlare 2 e Parliamo 2 *Lavorate a gruppi di 4. Ognuno sceglie uno dei titoli qui sopra e riflette sul contenuto dell'articolo. Poi a vicenda ogni studente racconta la propria versione dell'articolo. Gli ascoltatori possono fare domande per chiarire alcuni punti. Infine leggete gli articoli originali a pagina 229.*

Vocabolario

allacciare
andare in tilt
avvenire
il casello
la cintura di sicurezza
il codice stradale
coinvolgere
il collegamento
il disagio
è vietato
l'episodio
lanciare una campagna
il maltempo
obbligatorio
provocare
rispettare
i tamponamenti a catena
sostituire
sorvolare
sopprimere
lo scalo di partenza
la sede stradale
tremare

Unità 2

VANTAGGI E SVANTAGGI

Prima di parlare *Lavorate a gruppi di 3 o 4. Ognuno sceglie un argomento differente tra quelli elencati qui sotto e fa un elenco dei suoi vantaggi e svantaggi entro un limite di tempo stabilito dall'insegnante.*

- l'Internet
- l'auto
- la posta elettronica
- le isole pedonali
- i grandi supermercati fuori città / gli ipermercati

Parliamo *A vicenda ognuno deve presentare l'argomento scelto. Gli 'ascoltatori' possono interrompere se vogliono fare domande o contraddire vari punti di vista avanzati nel corso della presentazione.*

Espressioni utili

- Quali sono, secondo te, i vantaggi e gli svantaggi di ...?
- A mio parere / Secondo me ci sono più vantaggi che svantaggi
- Per quanto riguarda ...
- Quello che mi dà fastidio / mi fa arrabbiare ...
- Dipende da ...
- In genere / Inoltre / Infine ...
- Personalmente preferisco ...
- Ogni volta che uso ...
- Non sono (assolutamente) d'accordo
- Allora, secondo te, sarebbe possibile ... / si dovrebbe ...
- Ma hai preso in considerazione il fatto che / il punto di vista di ...?
- Non pensi piuttosto che ...?
- Sì, d'accordo, ma stai dimenticando ...
- Rifletti un attimo ...

Vocabolario

attraversare
camminare
il carrello
la coda
comodo / comodamente
la convenienza
dipendere (da)
evitare
i gas di scarico
girare in città
l'indipendenza
indispensabile
infine
informarsi (su)
l'ingorgo
innanzitutto
inoltre
l'inquinamento
mantenersi in contatto (con)
il messaggio
ottenere informazioni
respirare
risparmiare
sicuro
spostarsi
il tempo reale
tranquillamente
la velocità di comunicazione
la vendita all'ingrosso

BUONE INTENZIONI

Prima di parlare *In un prossimo futuro o a partire dal Capodanno ci sono delle cose/attività che hai intenzione di svolgere o alle quali vuoi rinunciare? Può darsi che ce ne siano alcune nell'elenco qui sotto. In caso affermativo indicale con una crocetta. Sotto l'elenco troverai uno spazio per scrivere altre tue intenzioni.*

- ❖ mangiare più prodotti biologici
- ❖ viaggiare di più
- ❖ fare più sport per mantenersi in forma
- ❖ guardare meno la televisione
- ❖ fare un corso intensivo di lingua in Italia
- ❖ smettere di fumare
- ❖ pitturare la casa
- ❖ andare in pensione
- ❖ uscire più spesso la sera
- ❖ imparare a suonare (bene) uno strumento

Inoltre ho intenzione di... 1. ....
2. ....
3. ....

Parliamo 1 *Adesso a coppie o in gruppo parlate delle vostre intenzioni, spiegandone i motivi come negli esempi.*

Esempi:

a. A partire dal mese prossimo ho intenzione di fare più sport per mantenermi in forma. In questi ultimi mesi sono diventato veramente pigro e non ho fatto proprio nulla. Al fine settimana rimango a letto fino a tardi e poi non ho voglia di andare in piscina o di fare una passeggiata. Ormai incomincio ad ingrassare e quindi è ora di fare qualcosa.

b. A settembre ho intenzione di imparare a suonare bene la chitarra. È sempre stata una cosa che volevo fare fin da giovane. Ho iniziato a suonare all'età di 16 anni ma mi mancava la pazienza di esercitarmi regolarmente e poi quando ho iniziato a lavorare rimandavo sempre a un altro giorno l'esercitazione e alle fine ho smesso. Adesso sono meno impegnato con il lavoro e ho deciso di riprendere l'attività ma questa volta prenderò lezioni da un professore di musica.

Parliamo 2 *Ormai sono passati alcuni mesi da quando avevi deciso di mettere in pratica certe buone intenzioni. Immagina che non siano state tutte realizzate. Quali per esempio? Spiega a un compagno di classe i motivi dell'insuccesso come nell'esempio.*

Esempio:

L'anno scorso avevo intenzione di smettere di fumare perché mi sono reso conto che fumavo troppo, a volte addirittura due pacchetti di sigarette al giorno. Cominciavo a respirare forte quando salivo le scale a casa e un bel giorno mi sono detto che non potevo andare avanti così. Ho trent'anni. Mi sono guardato allo specchio e mi sono chiesto: "Oddio, come sarà fra altri dieci anni?". Ho detto "Basta!" e infatti sono riuscito a smettere per due settimane ma poi alcuni miei amici, fumatori incalliti anche loro, continuavano ad offrirmi una sigaretta dopo l'altra e alla fine ci sono ricascato.

Espressioni utili

- Ai primi/All'inizio di gennaio avevo intenzione di ...
- Ho fatto di tutto per ... ma, putroppo ...
- A partire dal mese di febbraio avevo programmato di ...
- Mi ero ripromesso di smettere di fumare ma, all'ultimo momento ...
- Nonostante / Malgrado il mio tentativo di ...
- Mi sono proprio sforzato/a di ... ma, come puoi immaginare ...
- Ho provato a ...
- Devo fare una piccola confessione. Ti ricordi che ...?
- Avevo una gran voglia di ... ma, per mia sfortuna, non ho potuto rinunciare a questo vizio

Vocabolario

l'ambizione
la costanza
la dieta
divertirsi
fare attenzione (a)
fare male (a)
l'impegno / impegnato
nocivo
passivo
la pigrizia
progettare / programmare (di)
realizzare
rendersi conto (di)
ricadere
rilassarsi
sano
sforzarsi (di) / lo sforzo
stressante
la vita sedentaria

Unità 4

CHE TIPO SEI?

Prima di parlare 1 *Che tipo sei? Dall'elenco di aggettivi qui sotto annota tutti quelli che, secondo te, descrivono il più accuratamente possibile il tuo carattere. Naturalmente puoi includere aggettivi che non sono contenuti nell'elenco.*

timido	ambizioso	(im)paziente	sportivo	pigro	impulsivo
pignolo	loquace	spensierato	tirchio	diligente	estroverso
curioso	capriccioso	gentile	coraggioso	sicuro di sé	lunatico
socievole	(dis)ordinato	pauroso	affettuoso		

Prima di parlare 2 *Indica con una crocetta se fai le seguenti attività spesso, raramente o mai.*

	spesso	raramente	mai
cucinare			
lavare i piatti			
aiutare in cucina			
fare la spesa			
passare l'aspirapolvere			
lavare i vetri			
spolverare i mobili			
lucidare i pavimenti			
stirare			
guardare la televisione			
ascoltare musica			
invitare amici a cena			
organizzare feste a casa			
fumare			
bere alcolici			
mettere in ordine			

Parliamo 1 *Lavorate a gruppi di 4/5. Ognuno ha intenzione di dividere un appartamento con un'altra persona ma naturalmente è importante scegliere una persona idonea. Ognuno deve intervistare gli altri compagni tenendo conto del carattere (**Prima di parlare 1**) e delle varie attività menzionate (**Prima di parlare 2**). Lo scopo dell'attività è di conoscere il meglio possibile gli altri componenti del gruppo, facendo tutte le domande che ritenete siano importanti.*

Espressioni utili

- Allora mi hai detto che sei pigro/a. Cosa intendi dire con questo, rimani a letto fino a tardi? – Beh, intendo dire che ...
- Sei un tipo disordinato/a. Vuol dire che lasci la casa sempre in disordine?
- In che modo sei pignolo/a? In tutte le cose o solo quando si tratta del mangiare per esempio?
- Ti piace fare le faccende domestiche? Quali per esempio? A dire il vero, l'idea di ... non mi è mai venuta in mente
- C'è qualcosa che non ti piace fare in casa?
- Saresti disposto/a a ...?
- Ci sono delle cose che ti danno fastidio quando sei in compagnia di altre persone? Quali per esempio?
- Ti dà fastidio se qualcuno fuma o beve alcol?
- Cosa ne diresti se io ascoltassi la musica a volume molto alto? Sarebbe insopportabile ...
- Non potrei mai abitare con una persona che ...

Parliamo 2 *Fatte le interviste, i gruppi verranno riorganizzati in modo che ognuno lavori con 4/5 compagni diversi. Tocca ad ogni studente comunicare agli altri la scelta del/della partner ideale in base alle interviste. Bisogna inoltre giustificare la propria scelta e spiegare perché non sono state scelte le altre 3/4 persone.*

Parliamo 3

Studente A – Lei è il proprietario di una casa troppo grande per Lei e desidera affittarne una parte. Una persona ha risposto al Suo annuncio e oggi vi incontrate. Stabilisca innanzitutto se la persona è di Suo gradimento.

Studente B – Per motivi di lavoro Lei si è trasferito in una nuova città ed è alla ricerca di una sistemazione provvisoria. Ha risposto all'annuncio di una persona che desidera affittare parte della propria casa. Oggi vi incontrate. Stabilisca innanzitutto se la persona Le è congeniale.

Espressioni utili

- Vedo che ha un bel quadro. Lei si interessa d'arte?
- Le confesso, non mi piace ...
- Le darebbe fastidio se io facessi ...?
- Che bel trombone! Lei fa pratica sovente?
- Sarebbe disposto/a a ...?
- Lei mi sembra una persona ...
- Mi chiarisca una cosa ...

Vocabolario

abituarsi (a)
(in) affidabile
altruista
l'atteggiamento
attento
comportarsi / il comportamento
comprensivo
contare (su)
il difetto
il disordine / disordinato
egoista
le faccende domestiche
fidarsi (di)
insopportabile
nei confronti di
pignolo
scegliere
sensibile
sopportare
tollerare / tollerante
il vizio / viziato

Unità 5

DESIDERI

Prima di parlare *Scrivi brevemente almeno cinque desideri che vorresti realizzare in futuro. Se vuoi, puoi precisare quando speri di realizzare questi desideri, come negli esempi:*

Esempi:

Desiderio		**Quando:**
1.	andare in Cina	l'anno prossimo, in primavera
2.	avere un cane	fra qualche mese

Parliamo 1 *A coppie o in gruppo confrontate i vostri desideri, spiegandone il più dettagliatamente possibile il motivo, come negli esempi:*

Esempi:

1. L'anno prossimo mi piacerebbe andare in Cina. Ho visitato molti paesi in Europa in questi ultimi anni ma adesso ho tanta voglia di visitare un paese del tutto diverso. Alcuni miei amici ci sono già stati e mi hanno raccontato tutto. Ho iniziato a leggere diversi libri e ho già a casa un mucchio di informazioni e depliant che mi hanno spedito le agenzie di viaggio. Ogni mese metto da parte un po' di soldi per le vacanze e spero di averne abbastanza per partire l'anno prossimo per almeno un paio di settimane. Se vincessi un sacco di soldi al Superenalotto la questione dei soldi sarebbe subito risolta.

2. Io vorrei avere un cane fra qualche mese. Fin da piccolo ho sempre avuto gatti in casa ma mai un cane. Amo tanto i gatti ma loro sono molto indipendenti. Non ho bisogno di portarli a passeggio. Vanno e vengono quando vogliono mentre un cane dipende molto di più dal padrone. Ultimamente sono diventato molto pigro, non ho voglia di uscire quando torno a casa dal lavoro e questa voglia di uscire diminuisce man mano che le giornate si accorciano durante l'inverno. Quando avrò un cane sarò costretto ad uscire, che faccia caldo o freddo, che piova o meno, che sia buio o chiaro. Sarò costretto a fare un po' di 'ginnastica' e avrò un bel cane che mi terrà compagnia.

Parliamo 2 *A coppie raccontate alcuni desideri che siete riusciti a realizzare in questi ultimi anni.*

Espressioni utili

- L'anno scorso ho realizzato una mia ambizione che avevo sin da giovane ...
- Qualche mese fa ho avuto la fortuna di ...
- Fin da giovane ho sempre voluto ... e finalmente ...
- Una cosa che ho sempre sognato di fare è ...

Vocabolario

avere una passione (per)
cambiare vita
dedicarsi (a)
essere appassionato (di)
fare una crociera
girare il mondo
lavorare meno
preoccuparsi (di)
riprendere gli studi
sognare / il sogno
il volontariato

Unità 6

GIOCO DI PAROLE

Parliamo 1 *Lavorate a gruppi di 4. L'insegnante darà a ogni gruppo un mazzo di 12 carte che non devono essere rivelate inizialmente. Una persona tiene il mazzo, gira una carta per volta e la posa sul banco. La prima persona che parla deve costruire una frase che contiene la parola/espressione sulla carta. La persona seguente deve ripetere la prima frase e aggiungerne un'altra che contiene la parola/espressione sulla seconda carta. Attenzione! La frase precedente può essere modificata a seconda del senso delle parole/espressioni sulle carte successive. Una per volta le carte vanno posate e lasciate in ordine sul banco.*

Parliamo 2 *Ogni gruppo sceglie una persona che racconterà la storia inventata.*

DI COSA SI TRATTA?

Prima di parlare. *Lavorate a gruppi di 3. Ogni gruppo riceverà dall'insegnante alcune parole/espressioni tratte da una lettera scritta a un Forum su Internet. Ogni studente deve riflettere sulle possibilità che queste parole offrono prima di iniziare la discussione con il proprio gruppo.*
I gruppi devono cercare di ricostituire, in base a queste parole/espressioni, il contenuto della propria lettera.

Parliamo 1 *Ogni gruppo deve cercare di mettersi d'accordo sull'eventuale contenuto della lettera in base alle parole/espressioni a disposizione.*

Espressioni utili

- Cosa c'entra questa parola / espressione?
- È ovvio / chiaro che questa lettera tratta di ...
- Secondo me / A mio parere ...
- Mi dispiace ma non ne ho la più pallida idea
- Non sono d'accordo con la tua versione, innanzitutto perché ...
- Ti dispiace ripetere quello che hai detto?
- Bisogna tener presente che ...
- Quello che hai detto mi pare molto logico, però ...

Parliamo 2 *A vicenda ogni gruppo racconta la sua storia e comunica le parole/espressioni sulle quali è basata. I vari gruppi devono tener conto di queste parole/espressioni utilizzate in modo da poter, se necessario, modificare la loro versione della storia.*

Parliamo 3 *Il portavoce di ogni gruppo racconta la propria versione. Gli ascoltatori possono accettare questa versione o proporne un'altra, giustificando il motivo di qualsiasi cambiamento. Finita questa attività, leggete la lettera originale a pagina 233.*

Vocabolario

abbaiare
abbandonare
l'agriturismo
andare in villeggiatura
disturbare
graffiare
il guinzaglio
miagolare
mordere
la museruola
pulire
il rispetto
il soggiorno
sporcare
la tolleranza

STRATEGIE DI COMUNICAZIONE

Prima di parlare *Consulta l'elenco di parole ed espressioni utili qui sotto, che dovrai utilizzare durante l'attività* ***Parliamo****. Se necessario, chiedi all'insegnante di spiegare l'uso delle espressioni che non riesci ad usare correttamente in una frase.*

Espressioni utili

- La prima cosa che vorrei dire è che ...
- Oltre ad essere (utile/importante/indispensabile) ...
- Da una parte ... dall'altra ...
- Sotto molti aspetti ...
- Mi è venuta in mente un'altra cosa ...
- Volevo dire un'altra cosa a questo proposito ...
- A parte questo, bisogna anche tener presente ...
- Intendo dire con questo che ...
- Mi segui/capisci ...?
- A dire il vero ...
- Per il momento mi è sfuggita la parola, pazienza ...
- Se posso fare un altro esempio ...
- Adesso ho perso il filo del discorso ...
- Dunque, per concludere ...
- Tutto sommato ...
- Penso di aver detto tutto ...
- Spero di essere stato chiaro

Parliamo *A coppie o in gruppo. Ognuno deve scegliere un argomento dall'elenco qui sotto e parlare ininterrottamente per almeno 2/3 minuti utilizzando il massimo numero possibile delle parole/espressioni qui sopra. Il compagno o i compagni possono indicare con una crocetta tutte le espressioni che vengono usate (in modo appropriato) nel corso della presentazione.*

a. il walkman
b. l'Internet
c. imparare una lingua straniera
d. la segreteria telefonica
e. le faccende domestiche
f. mantenersi in forma
g. lavorare fino a 65 anni
h. i mezzi di trasporto pubblici
i. la censura
l. il Superenalotto
m. i videogiochi
n. le discoteche
o. andare in pensione

Vocabolario

a volte
al giorno d'oggi
comunque
contare (su)
diffuso
dipendere (da)
in confronto a
in futuro
in passato
infine
innanzitutto
malgrado
ovviamente
per cui
perciò
prendere in considerazione
quindi
sicuramente
lo svantaggio
tenere conto (di)
il vantaggio

Unità 9

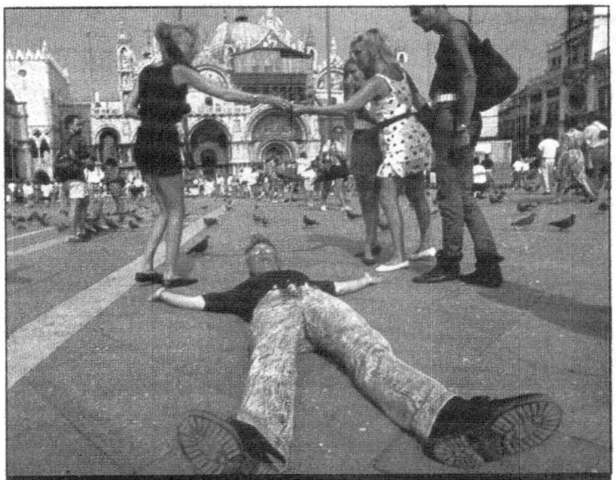

Turisti a Venezia.

Prima di parlare 1 *Leggi il brano (A, B, C o D) che ti verrà assegnato dall'insegnante e completa, dove possibile, la tabella, scrivendo le informazioni ottenute come nell'esempio.*

Vicesindaco Vianello	
I servizi di Venezia	
I costi di questi servizi	
300 mila	
12 milioni	**i turisti che arrivano ogni anno a Venezia**
1.000 lire	
Il risultato economico	
Il punto di vista giuridico	
La tassa d'ingresso	
Una volta al giorno	
Cinque volte	
Un piccolo contributo	

Parliamo 1 *Adesso bisogna parlare con coloro che hanno letto gli altri brani in modo da poter completare la tabella. Se incontri un compagno che ha letto lo stesso brano verifica se hai annotato gli stessi dettagli prima di andare avanti. Non si tratta di leggere ad alta voce i brani ma piuttosto di comunicare le informazioni oralmente con parole tue.*

Parliamo 2 *Un partecipante si offre di ricostituire l'articolo riferendosi alle informazioni sulla tabella. Gli ascoltatori possono confermare o contraddire i fatti presentati, giustificando il motivo della loro interruzione.*

Parliamo 3 *A gruppi discutete quale titolo dareste voi a questo articolo.*

Prima di parlare 2 *Ora leggete l'articolo intero a pagina 234.*

Parliamo 4 *A gruppi discutete le vostre reazioni all'idea di chiedere ai turisti di dare un piccolo contributo ai costi del mantenimento della città. Se la stessa cosa succedesse nel vostro paese, sareste a favore di imporre una "tassa turistica"?*

Parliamo 5 *A coppie spiegate, a vicenda e in altri termini in italiano, il significato delle parole/espressioni sottolineate nell'articolo a pagina 234.*

Espressioni utili

- Secondo me, questa parola vuol dire ...
- A mio parere, questa frase significa ...
- Non sono sicuro/a al cento per cento ma penso che significhi ...
- In questo contesto il significato non è molto chiaro
- A dire il vero, non ne ho la più pallida idea
- A questo punto sarebbe meglio consultare il dizionario

Vocabolario

attirare l'attenzione (su)
conservare
fare l'esattore
l'imposta
in aggiunta a
l'inquinamento
mantenere pulita la città
mettere in rilievo
il patrimonio culturale
proteggere
riferirsi (a)
salvaguardare
soffermarsi (a)
suscitare
tassare

CONSIGLI

Prima di parlare 1 *A gruppi di tre. Lo studente A legge la prima lettera, lo studente B la seconda e lo studente C la terza. Preparatevi a riassumere il contenuto della vostra lettera.*

Studente A

Il mio sogno è il part-time

Vi scrivo per sottoporre a voi e alle lettrici *una questione che mi sta molto a cuore,* e che di recente ha coinvolto in un'appassionata discussione fra amici anche molti papà. Riguarda la famiglia e il lavoro. Terminata la maternità, che cosa faccio? La cosa apparentemente più normale e comoda (ma non economicamente) è tornare al lavoro, *piazzare il bambino* all'asilo nido per due anni, poi alla scuola elementare, solo parzialmente a tempo pieno. Mi tocca, perciò, cercare una babysitter. Idem per gli anni di scuola media e per i periodi di vacanza, visto che le ferie mie e di mio marito non durano due mesi. Al liceo mio figlio potrebbe *cavarsela da solo,* poi cercare un lavoro e sposarsi. A questo punto quanto lo avresti visto in tutto? Qualche settimana? Ti consoli pensando che è una questione di qualità e di quantità del tempo, ma stai male lo stesso. Una soluzione ci sarebbe: lasciare il lavoro. Ma il lavoro è un diritto, e poi la situazione economica della famiglia non mi permette una scelta simile. Soluzione di compromesso: lavoro part-time. *Rinunciare a due soldi in più* e guadagnare tempo per le cose che ci interessano, per la famiglia. Ma è un'illusione: i datori di lavoro sostengono che il part-time a loro costerebbe troppo, innanzitutto per i contributi. Ho sentito in tv le proposte dei parlamentari: più all'asilo nido, scuole a tempo pieno per più anni. Ma così ci aiutano a piazzare i figli, non a far crescere la famiglia! Perché invece non si insiste sulla possibilità del lavoro part-time per le lavoratrici madri che lo richiedano? Ci sarebbe meno disoccupazione, le aziende eviterebbero il problema dell'"addetto in ferie", perché a occuparsi di un lavoro si sarebbe in due. La società sarebbe più libera e felice. Mi sforzo di trovare *l'altra faccia di questa medaglia dorata*. Ma non la trovo.

Paola Belotti, Bergamo (Anna n. 46, 16/11/1998)

Studente B

È vero, l'alcol è una droga

Ho letto con immenso piacere il servizio "La vera droga è l'alcol". Ve ne sono grata perché questo problema mi ha toccato da molto vicino e informare, specie i giovani, di quanto è distruttivo l'alcol è indispensabile e quanto mai urgente. A differenza delle droghe, siano esse leggere o no, l'alcol è più sottilmente pericoloso, non dà subito dipendenza ma poco alla volta. Quando si capisce che non se ne può più fare a meno è già troppo tardi. E da soli non se ne esce. Per mia esperienza devo il pieno ritorno alla normalità al CAT (Club alcolisti in trattamento), che si basa sul recupero di tutta la famiglia, non del solo alcolista. Voglio precisare che conosco molto bene quanto non sia facile ammettere e tantomeno parlare di questo problema (la maggior parte delle persone non sa cosa vuol dire vivere con un alcolista), ma fare un piccolo passo e accostarsi al CAT (o comunque a un gruppo di auto aiuto) è sicuramente di giovamento a tutti. Noi ci riuniamo tutti i sabato pomeriggio, alle 15,30, nella sede dell'associazione "Tetto fraterno", a Erba, in provincia di Como. Per contattarci il numero di telefono è 031/282609.

Maria Teresa Ferrero (Anna n46, 16/11/1998)

Studente C

La mia preoccupazione è la forma e la salute

Lavoro in ufficio e quasi tutto il giorno sto seduto davanti al computer. Il lavoro che faccio è molto ripetitivo. Quando torno a casa mi faccio qualcosa da mangiare e dopo mi metto a guardare la televisione e quasi quasi non mi alzo più dalla poltrona tutta la sera. Anzi mi muovo verso le undici e mezza per andare a dormire. Mi rendo conto che sto diventando sempre più pigro e tutti i miei amici mi dicono in continuazione che devo fare qualcosa. Sono ancora molto giovane, ho 23 anni, ma già ho dolori dappertutto, mi fa male la schiena, mi fanno male le spalle e le braccia, un po' di pancia comincia a farsi vedere. È deprimente. Che cosa mi consigliate?

Parliamo 1 *A gruppi di tre. A vicenda riassumete i punti più importanti della lettera che avete letto. Cosa pensate dei problemi esposti in queste lettere?*

Parliamo 2 *A gruppi di tre. A vicenda spiegate in altri termini in italiano le espressioni in corsivo o sottolineate nella lettera che avete letto. (Vedete* ***Espressioni utili*** *a pagina 42 Unità 9)*

Prima di parlare 2 *Leggi attentamente l'elenco di* ***Espressioni utili*** *a pagina 45. È importante saperle usare in modo appropriato prima di svolgere l'attività* ***Parliamo 3****.*

Espressioni utili

- Cosa faresti tu al mio posto / nel mio caso?
- Hai qualche suggerimento?
- Se permetti, ti do un consiglio ...
- Chi vuole affrontare il problema deve ...
- Una cosa essenziale è ...
- (Non) si deve / dovrebbe dimenticare di ...
- Bisogna / È importante/necessario fare ...
- Secondo me non si dovrebbe mai ...
- La cosa più importante, secondo me, è ...
- Quello che faccio io ...
- Personalmente, non condivido l'opinione di quelli che dicono che ...
- Una cosa da evitare /che si può fare è ...
- Qualcuno mi ha detto che ...
- Sarebbe un'ottima idea fare ... / se si potesse fare ...
- Se io fossi in te non farei ...
- Non c'è alcun dubbio che ci sia ...
- Hai mai pensato di fare ...?
- Inoltre si potrebbe ... / potresti ...
- Non ho molta esperienza in fatto di ... ma ...

Prima di parlare 3 *Lavorate a gruppi di 3 o 4. A volte succede che qualcosa vada (tutto) storto (come nelle lettere che avete appena letto) e bisogna chiedere qualche consiglio. A vicenda ogni membro del gruppo deve comunicare il 'problema' agli altri. Ovviamente tocca a ognuno identificare un 'problema personale' forse attinente a una o più delle problematiche elencate.*

❖ gli studi in genere o l'apprendimento di una materia specifica
❖ lo stato d'animo
❖ i rapporti sentimentali
❖ i rapporti con colleghi di lavoro
❖ i parenti
❖ la difficoltà di trovare un lavoro stabile
❖ la forma e la salute

Parliamo 3 *Dopo una breve presentazione del problema tocca agli altri componenti del gruppo dare dei consigli, i quali naturalmente possono essere accettati o rifiutati. Prendete nota dei consigli accettati e quelli respinti.*

Parliamo 4 *I gruppi verranno riformati in modo che ognuno abbia l'occasione di ripresentare il proprio problema e l'esito della conversazione con il gruppo precedente. È importante presentare ai nuovi interlocutori i consigli accettai e quelli respinti, spiegandone i perché.*

Espressioni utili

- Tutto sommato, i consigli che mi hanno dato sono stati molto utili. Eccone alcuni.
- L'idea avanzata/proposta da X mi è sembrata ottima perché ...
- Un ottimo consiglio è stato quello di ...
- Invece di accettare questo consiglio sarebbe molto meglio ...
- Non è un buon consiglio quello che mi ha dato ... sarebbe meglio ...
- Non mi ha convinto per niente l'idea di fare ...
- Se io accettassi di ...
- Secondo me, sarebbe molto meglio se io andassi ... / lui facesse ...
- Non mi va l'idea di ...
- Come si fa ad accettare un consiglio del genere ...?
- Qualcuno mi ha suggerito di ... ma come dice il proverbio, tra il dire e il fare c'è di mezzo il mare.

IMMAGINI

Prima di parlare *Guarda le tre immagini qui sotto e rifletti sul contenuto degli articoli ai quali si riferiscono. Se preferisci, puoi scrivere dei brevi appunti che serviranno per descrivere ogni immagine.*

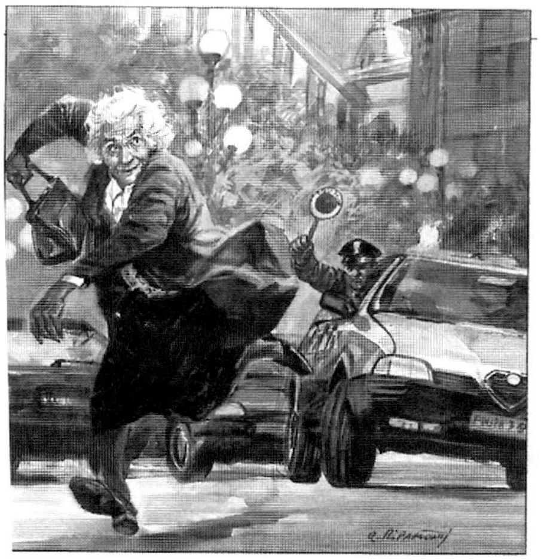

A

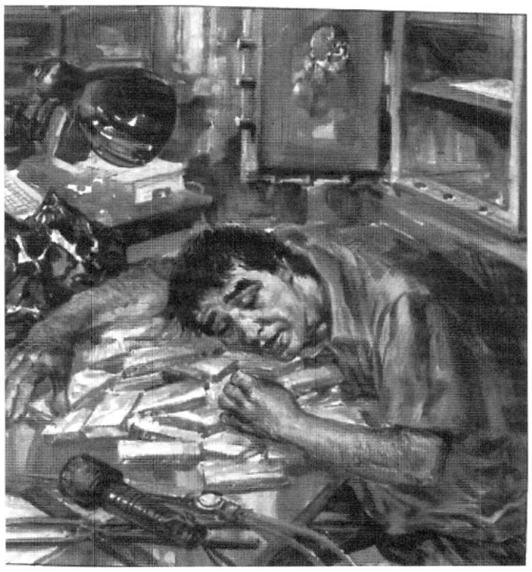

B

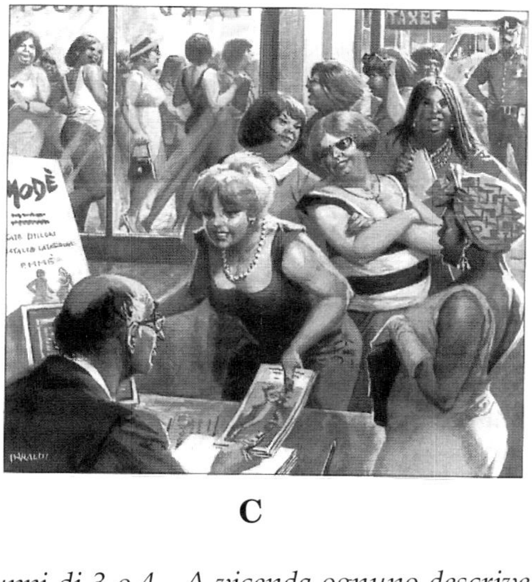

C

(Famiglia Cristiana n. 35/1999)

Parliamo 1 *Lavorate a gruppi di 3 o 4. A vicenda ognuno descrive una delle immagini e ipotizza su quanto può essere successo. Gli ascoltatori possono accettare la versione presentata o respingerla interamente o in parte, suggerendo una versione diversa o aggiungendo altri dettagli. Alla fine bisogna cercare di mettersi d'accordo sulla versione finale per ciascuna delle immagini.*

Espressioni utili

- In questa immagine è chiaro che ...
- In questa immagine invece ...
- Sono sicuro/a convinto/a che ...
- A giudicare dalla reazione di ...
- Se dai un'occhiata a ...
- Ho l'impressione che ...
- Se non sbaglio questa persona ...
- Può darsi che queste donne stiano guardando ...
- Sembra/Pare che questo signore faccia ...
- Dopo aver parlato ... / essere andato/a ...

Parliamo 2 *I gruppi verranno riformati. Adesso bisogna ripresentare le versioni accettate dai vari gruppi, che potranno essere modificate, se necessario, in base a quello che dicono i componenti dei nuovi gruppi.*

Ora leggete le versioni originali a pagina 235. Chi è riuscito ad indovinare più o meno il contenuto degli articoli?

Parliamo 3 *Lavorate a gruppi di tre e assumete il ruolo di una di queste persone. A vicenda raccontate l'avvenimento come foste voi i protagonisti. Gli 'ascoltatori' vorranno forse esprimere le loro reazioni.*

Espressioni utili

- Incredibile!
- Roba da matti!
- Puoi immaginare la sorpresa ...
- Che peccato!
- Che vergogna!
- Ma cosa hai fatto?
- Non ci credo
- Ma non è possibile
- Che spavento!
- Ma cosa dici?

Vocabolario

addormentarsi
arrabbiarsi
l'avvenimento
il capoufficio
la cassaforte
il commissariato
la coda
la denuncia
il divieto
l'episodio
in cerca di
presentarsi
scappare a gambe levate
succedere
tutto ad un tratto

UNA GIORNATA TIPICA

Prima di parlare *Leggi i seguenti brani in cui due persone raccontano come passano una giornata tipica durante la settimana. Nota le parole ed espressioni in corsivo.*

1

Durante la settimana mi alzo *piuttosto* presto, *intorno a*lle sei e mezza perché lavoro in una città che dista una ventina di chilometri da casa mia. Devo prendere il treno delle sette e un quarto e *ci vogliono almeno* cinque o sei minuti per raggiungere la stazione a piedi. Mi preparo in fretta e *ho appena il tempo di* fare una colazione molto leggera, un caffè e un po' di pane con burro o qualche biscotto. *Questo mi basta* perché *non ho tanta voglia di* mangiare a quell'ora della mattina, preferisco fare uno spuntino in ufficio *verso* le dieci, le dieci e mezza. *Purtroppo* il treno delle sette e quindici è pieno zeppo di pendolari e sono *proprio* fortunato se *riesco a* trovare un posto a sedere. È lo stesso quando torno a casa alle cinque, l'ora di punta. Incomincio a lavorare alle otto e mezza. *Però*, non ho un orario fisso, *anzi* è molto flessibile, basta fare le quaranta ore alla settimana. *All'ora di pranzo*, delle volte vado alla mensa dove si possono mangiare tre piatti a un prezzo molto modico. È un ambiente molto simpatico e *si ha l'occasione di* chiacchierare con i colleghi. Quando arrivo a casa *mi metto in poltrona* per una mezz'oretta per rilassarmi e per guardare il telegiornale. *Poi* ceno con la mia famiglia e parlo con mia moglie e i miei figli di come hanno passato la loro giornata. Esco raramente durante la settimana perché *mi sento troppo stanco*. Preferisco stare a casa, *soprattutto* in inverno, e guardare un po' di TV, ascoltare qualche Cd *oppure* leggere il giornale o un romanzo. *Molto spesso* mi addormento sulla poltrona e dormo *a volte* per due ore prima di andare a letto. Ecco una mia giornata tipica durante la settimana. Svegliati, ho finito di parlare!

2

Allora, io frequento il terzo anno di una scuola secondaria. Durante la settimana mi alzo sempre alla stessa ora, *cioè* alle sette e un quarto. Mi faccio la doccia e *dopo essermi vestito* vado in cucina per fare colazione. Mangio cereali e bevo un succo di frutta. Parto di casa alle otto e cammino fino alla fermata dove aspetto lo scuolabus che arriva alle otto e dieci. A quell'ora della mattina il traffico è molto intenso e *ci vogliono* sempre trenta minuti per fare un viaggio di solo cinque chilometri. Le lezioni cominciano alle nove e finiscono alle quattro meno quindici. Il mio orario scolastico è molto pesante e ho poco tempo libero durante il giorno. *Se per caso, ho un'ora buca*, vado in biblioteca per studiare o fare un po' di compiti. C'è una pausa alla mattina, *giusto il tempo per* fare uno spuntino prima di andare avanti. *Finita la scuola*, arrivo a casa intorno alle quattro e mezza. *Alla sera* ho *un sacco di* compiti da fare per il giorno successivo *e quindi mi rimane pochissimo tempo per* fare altre cose. Preferisco *lavorare sodo* durante la settimana e *in genere questo vuol dire che* sabato e domenica sono libero di fare quello che voglio. Ecco ho finito. Questa è per me una tipica giornata di scuola. Spero di non averti annoiato troppo!

Unità 13

MOMENTI SIGNIFICATIVI

Prima di parlare *Completa le seguenti frasi:*

a. Le date più significative per me sono ....

b. Un anno indimenticabile è stato il 1999 / il 2000 ....

c. La stagione dell'anno che mi piace di più è ....

d. La parte del giorno che preferisco è ....

e. Il giorno delle settimana che preferisco è ....

f. Un avvenimento indimenticabile è stato ....

Parliamo *A coppie o a gruppi. A vicenda, interrogatevi sul modo in cui avete completato le frasi, chiedendo una spiegazione dettagliata, come negli esempi qui sotto:*

Esempi:

1. C'è un proverbio in italiano che dice 'chi dorme non piglia pesci'. Devo confessare che per me questa è una descrizione perfetta perché preferisco stare a letto e lasciare i pesci in pace. In altre parole, non sono per niente una persona mattiniera. Posso ammirare fino a un certo punto coloro che riescono ad alzarsi di buon'ora e fare un sacco di cose nel giro di alcune ore perché si sentono molto svegli, io invece, anche se mi devo alzare prestino a volte per andare al lavoro, incomincio a svegliarmi verso le nove, le nove e mezza. Prima di quest'ora è meglio non chiedermi nulla. Di solito sono di cattivo umore, non ho voglia di parlare né di scherzare. Più tardi divento un'altra persona. Sono sempre stato così. Quello che mi dà fastidio è quando qualcuno mi chiede 'che cos'ha oggi?' oppure 'ti sei alzato col piede sbagliato?' Ormai i miei colleghi ed i miei migliori amici mi capiscono e tendono a starmi alla larga finché non mi sveglio del tutto.

2. Una data molto significativa per me è stata il 2 agosto dell'anno scorso, giorno in cui ho ricevuto i risultati degli esami di maturità. Ero al settimo cielo quando ho aperto la lettera e ho visto che avevo superato gli esami con dei bellissimi voti. Durante quest'ultimo anno avevo fatto tanti sacrifici perché spesso quando i miei amici uscivano a divertirsi io rinunciavo alla maggior parte delle distrazioni per stare in casa a studiare. Per fortuna ne è valsa la pena perché adesso ho realizzato un'ambizione, cioè la possibilità di andare all'università. Anche i miei genitori erano felicissimi e hanno organizzato una grande festa a casa alla quale hanno invitato parenti e alcuni dei miei più cari compagni di scuola. È stata una serata indimenticabile.

Espressioni utili

- Vorrei accennare ad alcune date significative. La prima ...
- Mi ricordo in particolare l'anno in cui ...
- Aspetto sempre con ansia l'arrivo della primavera. Per me è una stagione meravigliosa perché ...
- Sabato per me è il giorno più bello della settimana per parecchie ragioni
- Questo avvenimento risale a ...
- Non dimenticherò mai il giorno del mio primo ...

Vocabolario

l'anniversario
(non) essere al corrente di
cogliere l'occasione (per)
con mia grande sorpresa
divertirsi un mondo
festeggiare
mettersi d'accordo (per) (con)
ricordare
la ricorrenza
riunirsi
sbalordito
significativo
venire in mente (a) (di)

Unità 14

CHE FASTIDIO!

Prima di parlare *Nell'elenco qui sotto indica con una crocetta le cose che ti danno fastidio, aggiungendone altre se vuoi.*

a. Mi metto in agitazione quando qualcuno arriva inaspettatamente a casa mia.
b. Mi danno fastidio le persone che non rispondono ai messaggi che lascio alla segreteria telefonica.
c. Non sopporto le persone che parlano sempre e non lasciano parlare gli altri.
d. Mi secca fare il giro dei negozi senza uno scopo ben preciso.
e. Mi irritano quelli che arrivano in ritardo a un appuntamento.
f. Mi dà ai nervi l'indecisione degli altri.
g. Mi disturba lo squillo incessante dei cellulari quando viaggio in treno.
h. Mi dà fastidio se qualcuno mi dice in anticipo quello che mi ha comprato per il mio compleanno.
i. Mi mandano in bestia i maleducati che rifiutano di mettersi in coda e cercano di passare davanti.
l. Trovo insopportabile l'atteggiamento di quelli che buttano via i rifiuti per strada.

Parliamo *A coppie o a gruppi discutete in modo dettagliato le cose che vi danno fastidio. Potete inoltre discutere le cose nell'elenco qui sopra che non vi danno fastidio, spiegandone il perché.*

Espressioni utili

- Non sopporto proprio ...
- Mi dà fastidio ...
- Mi secca ...
- Mi irrita ...
- Mi scoccia ...
- Quello che non sopporto affatto è ...
- Una cosa in particolare che mi dà ai nervi ...
- Fino a un certo punto posso capire ...
- Ho difficoltà ad accettare ...
- Mi rendo conto che ...
- Non riesco a capire perché sia così difficile ...
- A dire il vero, mi fa sempre molto piacere se ...
- Non mi disturba affatto se qualcuno ...
- A che cosa serve arrabbiarsi ogni volta che ...

Vocabolario

aspettare il proprio turno
l'atteggiamento
comportarsi / il comportamento
il disturbo
inaspettato
insistere / insistente
insopportabile
lasciare in pace
maleducato
la mancanza di rispetto
martellante
nei confronti di
pensare alle conseguenze
rispettare
il rumore / rumoroso
una scocciatura
scortese
la sorpresa
spiacevole

Unità 15

INVITI

Prima di parlare *Leggi alcune volte le seguenti conversazioni telefoniche.*

1

- Pronto, chi parla?
- Sono Anna.
- Ciao Anna, sono Gianni. Come va?
- Non posso lamentarmi, grazie e tu stai bene? È una vita che non ci sentiamo.
- Devi scusarmi ma sono stato molto impegnato con il lavoro. Senti, cosa ne dici di andare in pizzeria venerdì sera?
- Che buon'idea! C'è qualcun altro che viene?
- Volevo invitare Marco e Daniela ma, purtroppo, hanno già qualcosa in programma ma devo ancora sentire Elena e Enrico.
- A che ora pensi di andare?
- Verso le otto.
- Possiamo fare un po' più tardi? Lavoro fino alle sette venerdì sera e non sono a casa prima delle sette e mezza.
- Per me va benissimo. Mi puoi dare un colpo di telefono quando arrivi a casa e ti vengo a prendere con la macchina?
- D'accordo. A venerdì allora. Salutami tanto i tuoi.
- Senz'altro, ciao a presto.

2

- Pronto, chi parla?
- Ciao Silvia, sono Franco. Senti, ti va di andare a una festa di compleanno domani sera? Il mio amico Leonardo compie ventun anni.
- Mi dispiace ma domani sera sono già impegnata, vado al cinema con mia sorella.
- Ma dài Silvia, puoi andare al cinema un'altra sera, no?
- Purtroppo, domani è l'ultima occasione di vedere questo film e ho promesso di andare. Non posso cambiare idea adesso.
- Che peccato! A che ora finisce il film?
- Verso le undici.
- Perché non vieni alla festa dopo? Puoi anche portare tua sorella, se vuoi.
- No grazie, sarà troppo tardi e poi il giorno successivo mi devo alzare presto per andare a lavorare.
- Va bene. Buon divertimento al cinema, allora.
- Grazie, buona notte. Ci sentiamo presto.

Parliamo 1 *La settimana prossima vuoi uscire tutte le sera tranne che due – tocca a te determinare quali sere. Ogni sera vuoi fare qualcosa di differente, per esempio, andare al cinema / al ristorante / in discoteca / al bar / a teatro / a una festa / a un concerto. Devi fissare un appuntamento con cinque compagni diversi. Se qualcuno rifiuta l'invito devi andare avanti finché non hai completato la griglia.*

Giorno x = impegnato	Attività	Con chi	Ora
lunedì			
martedì			
mercoledì			
giovedì			
venerdì			
sabato			
domenica			

Espressioni utili

Invitare qualcuno

- Perché non andiamo ...?
- Hai voglia di ...?
- Ti piacerebbe ...?
- Vuoi ...?
- Cosa ne dici di ...?

Accettare un invito

- D'accordo
- Mi pare / Mi sembra una buon'idea
- Che buon'idea!
- È un'idea geniale
- Con piacere
- Molto volentieri
- Sì, perché no?

Rifiutare un invito

- Che peccato!
- Mi dispiace, ma sono impegnato/a ...
- Non posso (andare/venire) ...
- Ho già altri impegni ...
- Ho già qualcosa in programma per quella sera/quel giorno ...
- Forse un'altra volta ...
- Non mi va di uscire ...
- Non ho (abbastanza) soldi ...
- Sono (completamente) al verde ...
- Sarà per un'altra volta ...

Parliamo 2 *A coppie descrivete in modo dettagliato gli appuntamenti che avete fissato. Inoltre, spiegate i motivi per cui non siete potuti uscire due sere.*

Vocabolario

l'agendina
annoiarsi
avere bisogno (di)
avere molto da fare
avere qualcosa in programma
cambiare idea
convincere / convinto
dài!
disdire un impegno
divertirsi un mondo
essere libero / impegnato / solo / spiacente / stanco
farcela
pensarci
proporre
rientrare presto / tardi
rilassarsi
la stanchezza

INDOVINIAMO

Prima di parlare *Pensa a un oggetto oppure guarda la parola/espressione sul foglio che ti darà l'insegnante e rifletti sul come puoi descriverlo. Toccherà ai tuoi compagni di classe indovinare 'l'oggetto'. La seguente descrizione serve da esempio.*

Esempio:

Questo apparecchio è molto diffuso al giorno d'oggi. Ecco alcune situazioni in cui l'utilizzo di questo apparecchio è senz'altro molto efficace. Se ad esempio si viaggia da soli in macchina, soprattutto di sera o di notte, e si buca la gomma o si ha un guasto al motore, questo apparecchio può essere indispensabile. Si può stare tranquilli nella macchina e aspettare che arrivi qualcuno. In caso di un incidente o di qualsiasi emergenza questo apparecchio può in un certo senso salvare la vita a qualcuno.

- Secondo me, l'apparecchio di cui parli è un cellulare.
- Sì, hai ragione, bravo! Adesso tocca a te descrivere il tuo oggetto.

Parliamo *Lavorate a gruppi di 3 o 4 e, a vicenda, descrivete la parola/espressione sul foglio assegnatovi dall'insegnante. L'obiettivo di questo gioco è di non rendere troppo ovvia la descrizione e di evitare naturalmente l'uso della parola/espressione sul foglio.*

Espressioni utili

- Dunque, questo oggetto / apparecchio mi serve quando ...
- Ho bisogno di questo coso quando ...
- Lo uso quando ...
- Non lo userei mai per fare ...
- Ecco una situazione in cui mi serve:
- Ha una forma rettangolare / rotonda / quadrata / ovale ...
- È una cosa molto / abbastanza leggera / pesante ...
- È fatto di plastica / pelle / metallo ...
- Al giorno d'oggi la maggior parte della gente lo usa per ...
- Nel caso che ci sia ... / di incendio ...

Unità 1

UNA STORIA

Prima di parlare *Lavorate a gruppi di 3 o 4. Guardate le parole sul foglio assegnatovi dall'insegnante e cercate di creare una storia ispirata a queste parole. Forse sarebbe una buon'idea scriverne i punti chiave. In seguito riflettete sul come potete mimare questa storia davanti agli altri gruppi.*

Parliamo 1 *Tocca a uno dei gruppi mimare la storia creata. Gli spettatori devono indovinare di che cosa si tratta. Finita questa scenetta, i vari gruppi possono discutere la loro versione prima che sia comunicata da un portavoce nominato da ciascun gruppo.*

Espressioni utili

- C'era una volta ...
- Questa storia tratta di ...
- All'inizio di questo episodio ...
- Noi abbiamo pensato che si trattasse di ...
- Nel nostro gruppo siamo tutti d'accordo che si tratta di ...
- La fine della storia era poco/molto chiara
- Scusate, ma perché avete mimate un automobilista ...?
- Non c'entrava per niente!

Parliamo 2 *Il gruppo che ha mimato la storia conferma se qualcuno è riuscito ad indovinarla. Nel caso in cui nessuno abbia indovinato la storia, tocca a un membro del gruppo raccontarla.*

Parliamo 3 *Adesso è il turno del prossimo gruppo mimare la sua storia e spetta agli altri indovinarla.*

DECISIONI

Prima di parlare *Immagina di aver comprato un appartamento completamente vuoto. Purtroppo non ti restano abbastanza soldi per arredarlo completamente e quindi puoi acquistare solo dieci mobili/apparecchi domestici/articoli differenti. Fai un elenco, in ordine di importanza, di quello che compreresti.*

Parliamo 1 *A coppie o a gruppi. A vicenda nomina gli eventuali acquisti, giustificandone la scelta e l'ordine di importanza. In base alla scelta del compagno o dei compagni puoi modificare il tuo elenco. Sei d'accordo con la scelta degli altri o ci sono delle cose delle quali, data la mancanza di soldi, potresti fare a meno?*

Parliamo 2 *Adesso i gruppi vengono riorganizzati. Confronta il tuo elenco con quello dei nuovi compagni.*

Espressioni utili

- La prima cosa che comprerei è ...
- Non potrei fare a meno di ...
- Chi può rinunciare a ...?
- Una cosa assolutamente indispensabile per me è ...
- E tu, che cosa compreresti in ordine di importanza?
- Data la mancanza di soldi ...
- Avrei senz'altro bisogno di ...
- Nessuno, secondo me, potrebbe vivere senza ...

Vocabolario

l'armadio
l'arredamento
il cassettone
il divano
il forno a microonde
la lampada
la lavastoviglie
la lavatrice
la poltrona
le posate
le stoviglie
il tavolo

Unità 19

PROGRAMMA DI VISITA

Prima di parlare *Fra poco ospiterai per una settimana due amici italiani (padre/madre e figlio/a di diciotto anni) che visitano la tua regione per la prima volta. Vuoi organizzare un vario programma di attività per il loro soggiorno. Hai già in mente di proporre alcune cose ma decidi di chiedere qualche consiglio ai tuoi amici (= 3 compagni di classe). Forse sarebbe una buon'idea consultare le pagine di spettacoli, mostre ed altre attività sul giornale cittadino/regionale.*

Espressioni utili

- Allora, il primo giorno ho pensato di ...
- Sono d'accordo fino a un certo punto, però ...
- Questa è un'idea geniale
- Questo andrebbe bene se facesse bello
- Secondo me, questa non è una buona idea perché ...
- Cosa ne dici se martedì sera ...
- Se tu avessi 18 anni, non ti piacerebbe piuttosto ...?
- Mettiamoci nei loro panni ...
- Una sera ho pensato di ...
- So che a loro piace molto ...
- A quanto parte sono tutti e due appassionati di ...
- Può darsi che un giorno / una sera siano stanchi / abbiano voglia di ...
- Sono sicuro/a che a loro piacerebbe l'idea di ...
- Se a loro non piace questa idea puoi sempre ...
- Se cosa farai se piove ...?
- Se io fossi in te, li porterei ...
- Mi è venuta in mente un'altra cosa
- Pensi che questa sia una buona soluzione?

Parliamo 1 *Comunica il tuo programma ai tuoi amici, chiedendo loro qualche consiglio in merito. Puoi modificare o meno il programma in base ai loro consigli.*

Parliamo 2 *Confronta il tuo programma con quello degli altri compagni che faranno da ospiti, discutendo le eventuali differenze.*

Vocabolario

l'abitudine
accogliente
accogliere a braccia aperte
assaggiare
avere nostalgia di casa
caratteristico
i dintorni
essere disponibile
fare conoscere (a)
fare un giro
fare una buona impressione (a)
fare uno sforzo (per)
girare per i negozi
un giro turistico della zona
una gita in pullman
incantevole
informarsi
le attrazioni turistiche
noleggiare
organizzare
l'ospitalità
il paesaggio
la pianta della città
i piatti tipici
portare in giro
riposarsi
suggerire (di)
suggestivo
trovarsi

Unità 20

FARE LE VALIGIE

Prima di parlare *Tu e tre amici avete deciso di andare in macchina in Italia per due settimane a luglio. La macchina in cui viaggerete non è molto grande perciò ognuno può portare solo uno zaino oppure una valigia poco ingombrante. Tocca a ogni passeggero fare un elenco delle cose che intende portare.*

Parliamo 1 *A coppie o in gruppo confrontate il vostro elenco discutendo le eventuali differenze.*

Espressioni utili

- Devo assolutamente portare ...
- Non potrei fare a meno di ...
- Data la mancanza di spazio dovrò rinunciare a ...
- Avrò senz'altro bisogno di ...
- A che cosa serve ...?
- Perché hai bisogno di ...?
- Secondo me, sarebbe meglio ...

Parliamo 2 *Se ci fosse più spazio nella macchina che cosa aggiungeresti all'elenco di cose che hai deciso di mettere nella valigia? Confronta nuovamente il tuo elenco con quello degli altri, discutendo le eventuali differenze.*

Parliamo 3 *Due amici decidono di rimanere in Italia per altre due settimane. Che sollievo! Ci sarà molto più spazio nella macchina e potrete comprare tutte quelle cose che avete ammirato in Italia e che sono particolarmente originali, utili o introvabili nel vostro Paese. Fate un elenco di questi articoli, giustificandone la scelta.*

Parliamo 4 *Confrontate il vostro elenco con quello di un'altra coppia discutendo le eventuali differenze. Chi riporta al proprio Paese gli oggetti più interessanti?*

Vocabolario

gli accessori
un articolo di abbigliamento
un articolo di pelletteria
gli articoli di toeletta
la biancheria intima
la chitarra
i cosmetici
la crema solare
la felpa
la gastronomia
la giacca a vento
la macchina fotografica
la maglietta
un oggetto regalo
gli oggetti di pronto soccorso
i pantaloncini corti
i pattini a rotelle
il romanzo
i sandali
le scarpe da tennis / gli scarponcini da montagna
scattare
la tavola surf
lo zaino

Unità 21

COSA HAI FATTO?

Prima di parlare *Scrivi su un foglio dieci frasi che indicano certe cose che hai fatto in vita tua finora, come negli esempi qui sotto. Non devi precisare* ***quando*** *hai fatto queste cose.*

a. Sono andato/a in Egitto.
b. Ho frequentato un corso intensivo d'italiano.
c. Ho comprato un computer.
d. Ho venduto la macchina.
e. Ho imparato a suonare la chitarra.
f. Ho cambiato lavoro.
g. Ho superato un esame.

Parliamo 1 *A coppie. Scambiate i fogli. Siete tutti molto curiosi e quindi avete voglia di fare un sacco di domande per conoscere a fondo i motivi di ogni asserzione scritta sul foglio.*

Parole ed espressioni interrogative

- Quando ... ?
- In che mese ...?
- In che anno ...?
- Con che cosa ...?
- Perché ... / Come mai ...?
- Per quale motivo ...?
- Come ...?
- Quanto ...?
- Quante volte ...?
- Dove ...?
- A / Con / Per / Di chi ...?
- Chi ....?
- Che cosa ...?
- Per quanto tempo hai studiato ...?
- Da quanto tempo studi ...?

PASSATO E PRESENTE

Prima di parlare *Ci saranno sicuramente molte cose che fai adesso che non facevi in passato o, al contrario, cose che facevi in passato ma non fai più adesso. Fanne un elenco nella tabella qui sotto. I primi due servono da esempi.*

Ora	In passato
mangio molta frutta	fumavo due pacchetti di sigarette al giorno
guido la macchina	suonavo il pianoforte

Parliamo *A coppie o in gruppo parlate in modo dettagliato di quello che avete scritto nella tabella, confrontando sempre il passato e il presente, come negli esempi qui sotto.*

Esempi:

Adesso mangio molta frutta perché tutti gli esperti di alimentazione dicono che la frutta fa bene alla salute perché contiene diverse vitamine eccetera. Cerco di mangiare due o tre frutti diversi durante la giornata, una mela, una banana, un po' di uva. Quando ero più giovane mangiavo la frutta ma raramente, certo non ero abituato a mangiarla ogni giorno. Ricordo che a casa dei miei c'era sempre sulla tavola una grande fruttiera piena di mele e di pere, roba che cresceva nel nostro giardino, mentre io sognavo frutti più esotici, cioè ananas, mango, pompelmo...

Ho cominciato a fumare all'età di quindici anni e per parecchi anni fumavo almeno quaranta sigarette al giorno. Non potevo fare a meno delle sigarette. Avevo praticamente una sigaretta in bocca qando mi alzavo la mattina e durante il giorno ne fumavo una dopo l'altra. È diventato proprio un vizio al quale non potevo rinunciare. Un giorno qualche mese fa mi sono reso conto che mi mancava il fiato anche quando camminavo lungo la strada, altro che salire su per le scale! Avevo appena compiuto 35 anni. Quel giorno ho deciso di smettere e da quel momento non ho mai messo un'altra sigaretta in bocca. Ho cominciato a fare un po' di ginnastica, vado in palestra due o tre volte alla settimana e adesso mi sento molto meglio. Anche le cose che mangio hanno un gusto migliore e i miei amici mi hanno fatto notare un altro vantaggio: non puzzo più di tabacco!

Espressioni utili

- In passato ...
- Una volta ...
- Quando ero più giovane ...
- All'età di ... anni ... / Quando avevo ... anni ...
- Alcuni anni fa non potevo permettermi di comprare ...
- Avevo l'abitudine di ...
- Ero abituato/a a...
- Ora / Adesso invece ...
- Ho smesso di ...
- Ho deciso di smettere perché ...
- Mi sono reso/a conto che ...
- Qualcuno mi ha consigliato di ...
- È stata una decisione improvvisa / maturata nel tempo ...

Vocabolario

l'adolescente
il bambino
cominciare (a)
il giovane
la decisione
il periodo
rinunciare (a)
lo sforzo
smettere (di)
la vita
la volontà

Unità 23

VERO O FALSO?

Prima di parlare 1 *Leggi la seguente conversazione fra Pierino e la sua maestra. Pierino ha l'abitudine di arrivare a scuola in ritardo e ha sempre una spiegazione abbastanza convincente! Secondo te, questa spiegazione è vera o falsa?*

- Buon giorno, Pierino.
- Buon giorno, maestra.
- Come mai sei arrivato con una mezz'ora di ritardo oggi?
- Le chiedo scusa, signora maestra, ma quando sono uscito stamattina tutte le strade e i marciapiedi erano coperti di neve e lei sa benissimo che io vengo a scuola sempre a piedi. Allora, ogni volta che io facevo un passo in avanti scivolavo e andavo due passi indietro.
- Ma come hai fatto allora ad arrivare a scuola?
- Perché mi è venuta un'idea geniale, signora maestra, mi sono girato per tornare a casa.
- Mi dispiace Pierino ma questa volta non ti credo, è un'altra delle tue solite storie!

Prima di parlare 2 *Scegli una delle situazioni elencate qui sotto e prepara una spiegazione convincente. La storia che racconterai in seguito può essere vera o inventata. Se preferisci, puoi scegliere una situazione che non è contenuta nell'elenco.*

- ❖ perdere le chiavi della casa / della macchina
- ❖ vivere all'estero per alcuni anni
- ❖ incontrare una persona molto famosa, per esempio un divo / una diva del cinema
- ❖ sposarsi a 18 anni
- ❖ essere in grado di parlare bene tre lingue straniere
- ❖ superare tutti gli esami a scuola
- ❖ possedere una casa all'estero
- ❖ slogarsi la caviglia
- ❖ fare autostop
- ❖ scrivere una lettera d'addio
- ❖ chiedere un prestito alla propria banca

Parliamo 1 *A gruppi. A vicenda ognuno deve raccontare la propria storia. Toccherà ai compagni decidere se le storie sono vere o inventate, spiegando i motivi della loro decisione.*

Espressioni utili

Un giorno della settimana scorsa ...
Siccome sono molto distratto/a ...
Ho sempre l'abitudine di ...
Un paio di anni fa mi è capitato di ...
Non dimenticherò mai il giorno/il momento in cui ...
Questo episodio mi è successo ...
Quando avevo ... anni ho preso una cotta per ...
All'età di ... anni ero in grado di ...
Un bel giorno ho deciso di ...

Prima di parlare 3 *Scegli una delle situazioni qui sotto e preparati a raccontare una storia ispirata da quella situazione.*

1. Un poliziotto ti ha visto camminare nel parco alle due di notte, in tuta da immersione subacquea.
2. A poche ore dal tuo matrimonio, un amico ti ha visto in un ristorante con un altro uomo / un'altra donna.
3. Un giorno sei arrivato/a in classe indossando le pantofole.
4. Arrivi in ufficio / a scuola indossando sempre il pigiama / la camicia da notte e portando le pantofole in mano.
5. L'insegnante / il tuo direttore/capo ti ha visto in città quando dovevi essere a scuola / al lavoro.
6. Ti addormenti durante la lezione d'italiano.
7. In treno / metropolitana / autobus uno sconosciuto ti fa una serenata.

Parliamo 2 *Racconta la tua storia al resto del tuo gruppo o alla classe.*

Unità 24

FARE LA SPESA

Prima di parlare *Vai a fare la spesa settimanale al supermercato. Dall'elenco di alimentari e bevande qui sotto quali metteresti nel tuo carrello? Scegli dieci prodotti differenti e mettili in ordine di importanza inserendo un numero da uno a venti nella casella accanto al prodotto. Naturalmente puoi aggiungere alla tua lista prodotti che non sono contenuti nell'elenco.*

	patatine
	biscotti
	insalata
	bevande alcoliche — vino, birra
	bibite — coca cola, aranciata
	frutta
	carne
	alimenti surgelati
	verdure
	gelato
	burro
	pesce
	pasta
	riso, cibi precotti
	dolci — biscotti, torta, budini, Nutella
	merendine, latte
	acqua minerale
	formaggi
	pane
	cibi in scatola

Parliamo 1 *A coppie confrontate la lista di prodotti scelti discutendo le eventuali differenze.*

Espressioni utili

- A casa nostra, mangiamo/beviamo molto/a ...
- Tendo a scegliere prodotti ... perché ...
- Non compro mai ...
- Personalmente non mi piace per niente ...
- Ho un debole per ...
- Una volta alla settimana mangiamo/si preparano i tortellini freschi ...
- Compro spesso/sempre ...
- Se il supermercato ha un'offerta speciale ...
- Sto molto attento/a quello che mangio e quindi ...
- Guardo sempre l'etichetta ...
- Sono a dieta e perciò ...
- Nella mia famiglia siamo abituati a ...
- A mio figlio/mia figlia/mio marito/mia moglie piace/piacciono soprattutto ...
- A casa vostra, cosa mangiate?

Parliamo 2 *Se la tua lista è molto diversa da quella del compagno cerca di convincerlo a modificarla.*

Espressioni utili

- Non penso (che) sia una buon'idea nutrirsi di ...
- Dovresti fare più attenzione a quello che ...
- Secondo me dovresti mangiare più olio che burro
- Se (io) fossi in te ...
- Non è molto sano mangiare ...
- A mio parere sarebbe meglio ...
- Non sai che questo prodotto contiene ...?
- Non fai mai caso alle etichette ...?
- Non hai mai assaggiato ...?
- Faresti meglio a ...

Parliamo 3 *A coppie o a gruppi rispondete alle seguenti domande.*

1. Quante volte alla settimana fai la spesa?
2. Dove preferisci fare la spesa, al supermercato o in un piccolo negozio? Perché?
3. Mangi molti prodotti biologici? Quali per esempio? Perché li preferisci? In caso negativo, perché non li compri?
4. Ti ritieni molto pignolo/a quando si tratta di comprare il cibo? Tendi a guardare attentamente l'etichetta / gli ingredienti o basi la tua scelta dei prodotti sul costo?
5. Se abiti con altri, chi decide quali alimenti acquistare e come raggiungi un accordo con altri?

Vocabolario

abbassare
l'alimentazione
a portata di mano
aumentare
il/la cliente
il codice
la concorrenza
nel congelatore
conveniente
nella dispensa
in frigorifero
frutta/verdura non trattata/biologica
ingannare
l'ingrediente
un'offerta speciale
persuadere / persuasivo
il prezzo
i prodotti di marca
la pubblicità martellante
il reparto
resistere (a)
lo scaffale
la scelta
lo sconto
tendere (a)
la tentazione

Unità 25

SOLDI, SOLDI!

Prima di parlare *Rifletti a come spendi ora la maggior parte dei tuoi soldi nel giro di sei mesi. Grosso modo, su che cosa spenderesti di più? Dall'elenco qui sotto metti in ordine di importanza le spese essenziali e quelle meno necessarie, indicando la tua graduatoria con i numeri nelle caselle. Se vuoi, puoi includere nella tua lista cose che non sono contenute nell'elenco.*

- [ ] il cellulare
- [ ] la casa – apparecchi elettrodomestici/mobili
- [ ] i divertimenti – cinema/teatro/discoteca
- [ ] giornali/libri/riviste/Cd
- [ ] spese di trasporto – la macchina/il treno/l'autobus
- [ ] l'abbigliamento
- [ ] i cosmetici/la forma
- [ ] le vacanze
- [ ] mangiare fuori
- [ ] l'alcol/le sigarette
- [ ] le attività sportive
- [ ] il computer
- [ ] l'alimentazione
- [ ] i viaggi di studio
- [ ] la partecipazione a convegni / conferenze

Altro:
....
....
....

Parliamo *A coppie o a gruppi confrontate la lista, spiegandone la scelta.*

Espressioni utili

- Ogni mese spendo molto per ...
- Spendo invece pochissimo per ...
- Per me, il cellulare è indispensabile e quindi ...
- Spendo almeno il 20% del mio stipendio ...
- È una percentuale alta ... / bassa ...
- Cerco di andare in vacanza due volte all'anno perciò ...
- Ho una gran passione per la lettura / la musica, allora ...
- Non c'è dubbio un'alta percentuale del mio stipendio è destinata ...
- Non posso resistere alla tentazione di comprare vestiti firmati, ecco perché ...
- Mi sposto molto in macchina per cui ...
- Dato / Visto che uso ogni giorno l'Internet ...
- Non mi interessa / interessano molto ...
- In fondo alla mia classifica di spese è ... sono ...
- Se dovessi rinunciare a qualcosa, preferirei ...
- E tu quanto spendi per ... / su ...?
- L'estratto conto della banca è sempre una brutta sorpresa
- ... per me ... è sempre una spesa prioritaria

Vocabolario

avere le mani bucate
comprare / spendere il minimo necessario
costare un occhio della testa
fare a meno (di)
i guadagni
la maggior parte
mettere da parte
mettere qualcosa da parte per i tempi di magra
la paghetta
risparmiare
uno/una spendaccione/a
sperperare
una spesa stravagante / ragionevole / imprevista / prioritaria
tirare la cinghia

Unità 26

SOMMERSI DAI DIVIETI

Prima di parlare 1 *Leggi attentamente il seguente elenco delle proibizioni/obblighi più comuni in Italia.*

- Le nuove etichette per vino e birra con la scritta: "Bere fa male"
- I divieti anti fumo
- Obbligo della cintura di sicurezza in macchina
- Divieto di viaggiare in due sul motorino
- Film vietato ai minori di 18 anni
- Divieto di parlare al conducente sui mezzi pubblici
- Divieto di imbrattare i muri
- Divieto di ingresso con gli animali nei locali pubblici
- Obbligo di casco in moto
- Divieto di camminare sull'erba e sulle aiuole nei giardini pubblici

Parliamo 1 *A coppie o a gruppi discutete il pro e il contro di questi divieti/obblighi.*

Espressioni utili

- Secondo me, è assolutamente indispensabile ...
- (Non) è giusto che il governo / lo Stato obblighi / le autorità obblighino ...
- (Non) credo che sia una buon'idea vietare ...
- È ridicolo/assurdo (che) ...
- In ogni società civile bisogna (che) ...
- Fino a un certo punto è necessario (che) ...
- Come cittadini dobbiamo rispettare ...
- A mio parere, il proliferare dei divieti ...
- Se vogliamo combattere la piaga dell'alcolismo ...
- A dire il vero, non sono convinto/a che sia necessario ...
- Bisogna prendere in considerazione ...
- Se non ci fossero queste norme ...
- È importante tener conto dei vantaggi/degli svantaggi ...
- Prendiamo il caso di ...
- Se per esempio ... /Faccio un esempio ...

Parliamo 2 *Nel tuo Paese esistono le stesse proibizioni? Aggiungeresti altri divieti all'elenco qui sopra? In caso affermativo, quali per esempio? Ci sono dei divieti nel tuo Paese che non vengono rispettati dalla maggioranza della gente? Quali? Confronta le tue idee con quelle degli altri compagni, discutendo le eventuali differenze.*

Prima di parlare 2 *Scrivi un elenco di regole che vengono imposte a casa, a scuola, oppure al lavoro.*

Parliamo 3 *A coppie confrontate il vostro elenco di regole discutendo le eventuali differenze.*

Espressioni utili

- A casa / scuola sono obbligato/a a ...
- Quando sono in ufficio / in fabbrica sono costretto/a a ...
- In un parco pubblico non si può ...
- A casa (non) devo (mai) ...
- A scuola è vietato / proibito ...
- Al lavoro non si può / deve ...

Parliamo 4 *Quali delle regole ritieni siano essenziali e quali no? In che modo reagisci a queste regole? A coppie scambiate le vostre opinioni.*

Espressioni utili

- Secondo me, la regola riguardante ... è essenziale ...
- Il divieto concernente ... invece non serve a nulla ...
- Non rispetto mai questa regola perché ...
- Se non ci fosse questo regolamento ...
- In un Paese civile è importante (che) ...

Vocabolario

l'abuso di alcolici
avere il diritto (di)
l'avvertimento
la buona educazione
cancellare le scritte
cogliere in flagrante
convivere civilmente
correre il rischio (di)
creare problemi
danneggiare irrimediabilmente
il deterrente
deturpare i monumenti
educare
essere favorevole (a)
imporre
in difesa dei beni culturali
introdurre pene più aspre
la maleducazione
la mancanza di rispetto
mettere in pericolo
la multa
per moda
proteggere
ridicolo
ripulire
rispettare
salvare la vita (a)
scoraggiare / scoraggiante
sensibilizzare l'opinione pubblica
la tolleranza
la tutela del patrimonio artistico
le vernici spray

PUBBLICITÀ

Prima di parlare *Leggi attentamente le seguenti frasi tratte da quattro annunci pubblicitari diversi apparsi sui giornali.*

a. Per chiamare la Spagna c'è un numero in più

b. I bambini a 5 anni, in Sardegna, pagano meno di 7.000 lire al giorno

c. Leggere conviene

d. L'arte di assicurarsi – Ras è sponsor della mostra su SALVATORE FIUME

Secondo te:

1. Chi sono gli inserzionisti di questa pubblicità?
2. Qual è lo scopo di ogni pubblicità?
3. A chi sono indirizzati i quattro annunci?
4. Quali pubblicità dipendono dai giochi di parole?

Parliamo 1 *A coppie o a gruppi confrontate le vostre risposte.*

Espressioni utili

- Secondo me, questa pubblicità di ...
- Non sono al cento per cento sicuro/a ma penso che ...
- A giudicare da questa frase direi che ...
- Questa pubblicità riguarda/concerne ...
- Sono sicuro/a che ...
- A dire il vero non ne ho la più pallida idea
- Quello che trovo interessante è che ...

Parliamo 2 *Dopo aver guardato le quattro inserzioni a pagina 235, quale, secondo te, è la più efficace? Confronta la tua scelta con quella degli altri.*

Vocabolario

l'acquirente
approfittare (di)
attirare l'attenzione
il consumatore
evidenziare
il gioco di parole
incoraggiare
influire (su)
i lati negativi/positivi
l'obiettivo
ricorrere (a)
la rima
la ripetizione
lo slogan
spingere
le tecniche pubblicitarie

Unità 28

RICORDI DI SCUOLA

Prima di parlare 1 *Guarda la prima immagine e poi preparati a rispondere alle domande.*

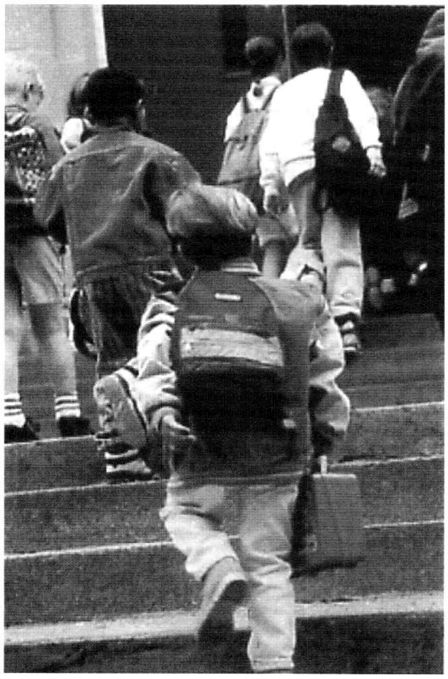

1. Dove ha luogo questa scena?
2. In quale periodo dell'anno?
3. Quanti anni avranno questi ragazzi?
4. Che cosa stanno facendo?
5. Come ti sembrano – felici, calmi, preoccupati? Giustifica la tua risposta.
6. Cosa ti viene in mente quando guardi questa scena?
7. Qual è il legame fra questa immagine e la seconda nella pagina seguente?

Parliamo 1 *A coppie confrontate le vostre risposte alle domande.*

Espressioni utili

- Questa scena ha luogo davanti a ...
- È difficile dire con precisione ma direi che ...
- Questi ragazzi avranno sui ... anni
- Questo a sinistra / in primo piano sta per ...
- Quell'altro invece ...
- Hanno tutti un'aria ...
- Il ragazzo al centro dell'immagine mi sembra ...
- Questa immagine mi fa ricordare il periodo in cui ...
- Quando ho visto la prima immagine mi è subito venuto in mente ...
- Per quanto riguarda il legame fra le due immagini io direi che ...

Prima di parlare 2 *Guarda la seconda immagine e poi preparati a rispondere alle stesse domande in **Prima di parlare 1**.*

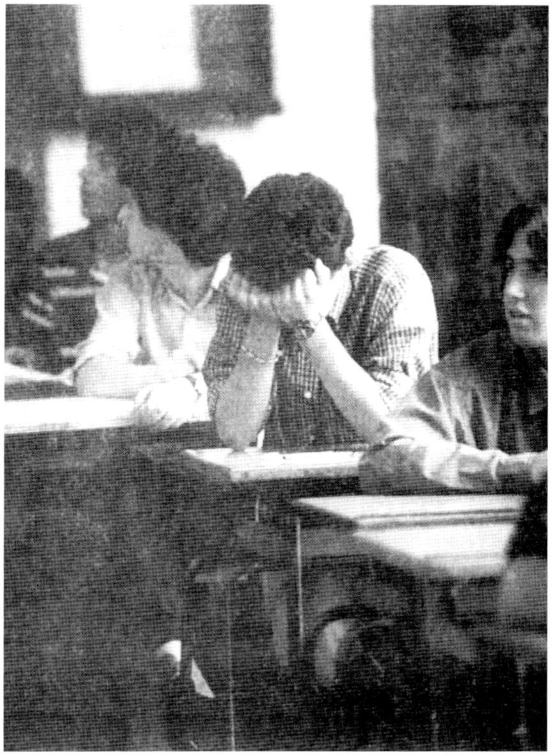

Parliamo 2 *A coppie confrontate le vostre risposte.*

Parliamo 3 *A coppie discutete quali sono state per voi le maggiori differenze fra la scuola elementare e quella secondaria. Raccontate le buone e le brutte esperienze.*

Prima di parlare 3 *Immagina di essere il ragazzo nella seconda fila. Che cosa sta pensando? Preparati a raccontare la sua giornata nei due giorni precedenti alla fotografia.*

Parliamo 4 *A coppie. A vicenda, raccontate che cosa ha fatto questo ragazzo nei due giorni precedenti, discutendo le eventuali differenze.*

Vocabolario

ambizioso
la bocciatura
il comportamento
comportarsi
dare un esame
diligente
essere bravo (in)
frequentare
indimenticabile
noioso
la pagella
preoccuparsi
superare un esame
il voto

NUOVE TECNOLOGIE

Prima di parlare 1 *Studia il grafico 'Il boom in Italia' e preparati a commentarlo. Sei sorpreso dalla rapida crescita dei navigatori in Italia? Chi usa l'Internet di più? Ci sono differenze geografiche, d'età o di sesso? Ci sono similarità con il vostro Paese?*

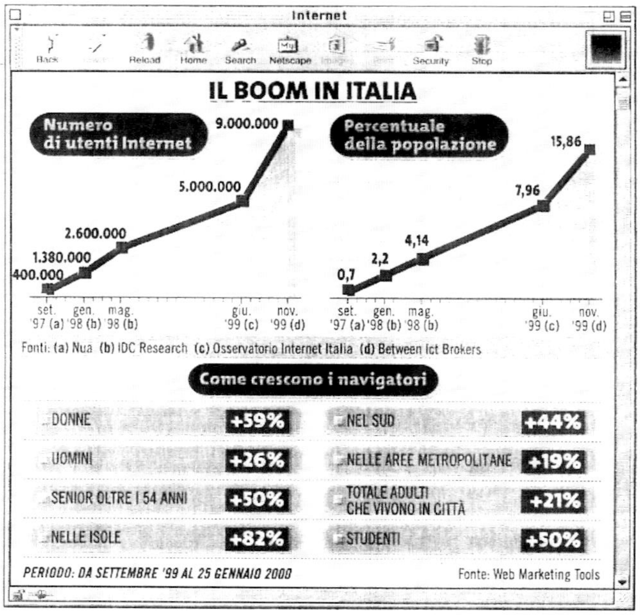

(Espresso, 10/2/2000)

Espressioni utili

- Secondo questo grafico ...
- C'è stato un aumento del ... percento da ... a ...
- La percentuale di coloro che ...
- Sembra che ci sia una disparità fra ... e ...
- È interessante / sorprendente / prevedibile ...

Parliamo 1 *A coppie o a gruppi. Scambiate le vostre osservazioni e cercate di dare un'interpretazione ai dati.*

Prima di parlare 2 *In che modo l'Internet esercita un'influenza sulla tua vita attuale? Se navighi in rete regolarmente, fai una lista degli usi che ne hai fatto finora.*

Parliamo 2 *Confronta i tuoi usi di questa tecnologia con quelli di altri due compagni di classe, discutendo le eventuali differenze.*

Espressioni utili

- Ultimamente ho navigato molto in rete ...
- L'Internet mi serve soprattutto ...
- Se per esempio ho bisogno di ...
- Personalmente non ho l'Internet però mio figlio / mia figlia ...
- Navigo quotidianamente alla ricerca di ...
- Ormai per il mio lavoro l'Internet / saper navigare in rete è diventato indispensabile. Ti faccio un esempio ...
- Navigo solo ogni tanto ma uso spesso la posta elettronica per contattare / rimanere in contatto con ...
- A dire la verità, non sono molto pratico/a di computer per cui ...

Parliamo 3 *La classe viene divisa in due gruppi A e B. Il gruppo A deve riflettere su tutti i vantaggi e gli aspetti positivi della navigazione in rete, mentre il gruppo B penserà a eventuali svantaggi o aspetti negativi, citando esperienze personali, positive o negative che siano.*

Parliamo 4 *Ora lavorate in coppia – uno studente del gruppo A e uno studente del gruppo B. Confrontate gli elenchi di svantaggi e svantaggi, accennando inoltre alle esperienze personali dei vari membri dei gruppi.*

Prima di parlare 3 *Leggi la prima parte dell'articolo intitolato* **Futurshow, il domani comincia oggi.**

Futurshow, il domani comincia oggi

Lavoro, salute, casa, tempo libero: 300 stand a Bologna per scoprire come vivremo

BOLOGNA – Fra mille anni vivremo così. *Lavoreremo in macchina prima di arrivare in ufficio e riposeremo in ufficio prima di tornare per lavorare. Ci accomoderemo nel nostro salotto davanti a megaschermi da cinema e andremo in vacanza navigando su Internet.* È il 2998, almeno secondo il Futurshow di Bologna, fiera multimediale che da oggi al 7 aprile sposterà in avanti le coordinate spazio-tempo per cercare di entrare nell'era cyber.

Sotto lo slogan un po' minaccioso "chi non c'è non ci sarà", l'edizione di quest'anno è riassunta nell'idea che "*le tecnologie liberano il nostro tempo*": teleguidati, tele-educati, telecurati, *dovremmo ridurre le ore che passiamo imbottigliati nel traffico per poterci dedicare a noi stessi.* La visione è certa ottimistica, ma stand dopo stand (gli espositori sono 300) il Futurshow prova a creare un percorso che immerga nel millennio a venire.

Corriere della Sera, 3/4/1998

Parliamo 5 *A coppie o a gruppi discutete le idee in corsivo nell'articolo.*

Espressioni utili

- Non c'è alcun dubbio che l'avvento delle nuove tecnologie influirà molto su ...
- Infatti molte ditte, agenzie di viaggi per esempio, sono già state costrette a ...
- Ormai donne e uomini di affari e liberi professionisti lavorano in treno / in aereo / in albergo usando il loro computer portatile o il palmare
- Se le varie tecnologie ci permetteranno di avere più tempo libero ...
- Se si potesse lavorare da casa ...
- Se potessimo approfittare delle tecnologie per migliorare la qualità della vita ...
- Quello che mi preoccupa ...
- Non riesco a capire come andrà a finire ...
- Sarà molto interessante vedere quello che succederà ...

Prima di parlare 4 *Lavorate in gruppi di tre, A,B,C. Lo studente A legge il primo brano, lo studente B il secondo e lo studente C il terzo. Questi brani fanno sempre parte dell'articolo intitolato* **Futurshow, il domani comincia oggi.**

Studente A

Commercio on line – L'opportunità è quella di poter concludere affari o anche solo comprarsi un vestito nuovo senza doversi preoccupare di distanze, lingue, fusi orari o monete. In Italia non esistono ancora molte applicazioni concrete, ma a Bologna un convegno (il 6 aprile) farà il punto sull'electronic-business e varie aziende mostreranno al pubblico come sia già possibile acquistare all'estero attraverso Internet.

Ambulatorio in rete – Al Futurshow sarà presentato il sito "Hospital Today", un ospedale virtuale dove i "pazienti" possono consultare medici specialisti, dall'oncologo al sessuologo. Selezionato il reparto desiderato, inizia il dialogo con il dottore di turno per avere un primo consulto.

Studente B

La macchina ufficio – Da fuori assomiglia a una normale monovolume, non fosse per quell'antenna parabolica piazzata sul tetto. La Web Car, secondo i suoi progettisti, permetterà a una squadra di 3-4 persone di lavorare viaggiando o durante gli spostamenti da un appuntamento all'altro. È equipaggiata come un'astronave: mappa computerizzata che indica il percorso più veloce nelle strade cittadine; un paio di personal portatili collegati a Internet per controllare la posta elettronica o collegarsi con l'ufficio; telefono satellitare per la connessione alla Rete e per chiamare da qualunque punto.

Studente C

La casa digitale – Le abitazioni del Duemila saranno dotate di sistemi a comando vocale che aprono le porte, alzano le serrande, rispondono al telefono. Megaschermi permetteranno di vedere i film come al cinema.

Sfide e videogiochi – Nei cinque giorni della fiera si svolgerà un vero e proprio campionato di videogames su consolle di tutte le marche: dal basket al tennis, dal calcio al rally.

Parliamo 6. *Ora tocca ad ognuno comunicare i punti più importanti del brano che ha letto e compilare la seguente tabella.*

Commercio on line
Ambulatorio in rete
La macchina ufficio
La casa digitale
Sfide e videogiochi

Parliamo 7 *A coppie o a gruppi discutete il pro e il contro delle possibilità sopraccitate.*

Vocabolario

le abitazioni dotate di sistemi a comando vocale
l'aggiornamento culturale
alzare le serrande
chiudere l'accesso a quanto può nuocere
la conoscenza di Internet
contattare nuovi amici
l'era cyber
essenziale
essere in grado (di)
impradronirsi di un nuovo mezzo di comunicazione
informarsi
malgrado
il megaschermo
navigare su Internet
oltre a
le opportunità offerte dalla Rete
ormai
l'ospedale virtuale
ottimistico
una sorta di ufficio mobile
uno strumento indispensabile nella vita di tutti i giorni
l'utente
la visione

Unità 30

PROFESSIONI

Prima di parlare *Secondo te, quale delle seguenti persone dovrebbe essere pagata meglio? Scegli un gruppo di professioni e metti ogni mestiere in ordine a seconda della paga che dovrebbe percepire. Devi giustificare la tua scelta. Le professioni si riferiscono sia a donne che a uomini.*

❑ anestesista
❑ calciatore
❑ cameriere
❑ agente immobiliare

❑ pompiere
❑ segretario bilingue
❑ medico
❑ poliziotto

❑ buttafuori di discoteca
❑ avvocato
❑ minatore
❑ assistente sociale

❑ ispettore delle tasse
❑ operaio
❑ pilota d'aereo di linea
❑ postino

❑ infermiere
❑ camionista
❑ cantante rock
❑ guardia carceraria

❑ insegnante elementare
❑ professore di liceo
❑ istruttore di guida
❑ consulente finanziario

Espressioni utili

- Per determinare la paga di qualsiasi dipendente / lavoratore / libero professionista bisogna prendere in considerazione / tener conto di ...
- Per quanto riguarda il lavoro di un / una ...
- È normale / logico che ...
- Per poter svolgere questo mestiere / questa professione bisogna aver conseguito una laurea e perciò ...
- Per diventare ... ci vogliono parecchi anni di studio e occorre fare tanti sacrifici. Per questa ragione penso che ...
- In confronto al mestiere di un/una ... questo lavoro non è per niente difficile / arduo / faticoso / sedentario / stressante e quindi ...
- Chi esercita una professione del genere non merita di essere pagato più di ...
- Uno non ha bisogno di titoli di studio per diventare ... e quindi ...
- Questo mestiere comporta molte responsabilità per cui ...
- È giusto che X guadagni più di Y, innanzitutto perché ...
- Si dà troppa / troppo poca importanza a ...
- Dato/Visto che ...
- Oggigiorno c'è una certa percentuale di dipendenti, soprattutto nel settore privato, i cui salari sono saliti vertiginosamente rispetto a quelli della maggior parte dei dipendenti impiegati nel settore pubblico. A mio parere ...
- C'è un enorme divario fra ...

Parliamo 1 *A coppie confrontate il vostro elenco discutendo le eventuali differenze.*

Parliamo 2 *Lavorate in coppia e scegliete un gruppo di professioni differenti. A vicenda, spiegate le caratteristiche personali e i requisiti necessari per poter esercitare ognuna delle professioni. Servitevi dei due elenchi qui sotto ma naturalmente potete usare parole ed espressioni che non sono contenute nelle liste.*

Caratteristiche personali

- abituato a lavorare in autonomia
- altruismo
- ambizioso
- bella presenza
- buon livello culturale
- buona predisposizione ai contati umani
- capacità organizzative
- coraggio
- dinamico / dinamismo
- doti di grande affidabilità, serietà ed adattabilità
- doti di leadership
- energico / energia
- entusiasta / entusiasmo
- flessibile / flessibilità
- intraprendente / intraprendenza
- motivato / motivazione
- predisposizione al lavoro di gruppo
- spiccate capacità creative

Requisiti

- auto propria
- conoscenza PC / padronanza nell'uso dei PC
- esperienza commerciale
- la capacità di resistenza allo stress
- la disponibilità di spostamenti nel proprio Paese e all'estero
- possesso di un diploma o di una laurea
- precedente esperienza nel settore
- una buona / ottima / perfetta conoscenza di almeno una lingua straniera parlata e/o scritta
- una significativa esperienza di lavoro

Parliamo 3 *Tenendo conto del tuo carattere e curriculum vitae, quali dei mestieri sopraccitati saresti in grado di fare e quali non ti piacerebbe fare per niente? Giustifica la tua scelta.*

Parliamo 4 *A coppie parlate di un lavoro che fate attualmente o di uno che avete fatto in passato. Descrivete questo lavoro in modo dettagliato, prendendo in considerazione l'orario, le varie mansioni, i colleghi, la ditta o il datore di lavoro, i vantaggi e gli svantaggi o altri fattori che ritenete siano importanti.*

Parliamo 5 *Lavorate a gruppi di 3 o 4 e a vicenda, usando le parole ed espressioni qui sotto, descrivete le caratteristiche e i requisiti che bisogna avere per una certa professione, senza nominarla. I compagni del gruppo devono cercare di indovinare la professione che viene descritta.*

Espressioni utili

- A mio avviso il/la candidato/a ideale dovrebbe avere/possedere ...
- Sarebbe gradito/a ma non indispensabile ...
- Siccome questa posizione comporta responsabilità ecc. ...
- Non si può assumere chi non è in possesso di ...
- Questo posto di lavoro richiede ...
- A che cosa serve ...?
- Bisogna avere/possedere/essere ...
- È logico/ovvio che ...
- Bisogna selezionare una persona che abbia/sia ...

Vocabolario

acquisire delle competenze
all'inizio della carriera
l'ambizione
l'annuncio / l'inserzione
arrotondare lo stipendio
assumere
attraverso
aumentare
le capacità
il colloquio di lavoro
dare le dimissioni
l'esperienza
fare domanda
fare i turni
la formazione professionale
impegnativo
infatti
l'iniziativa
l'intraprendenza / intraprendente
lavorare a tempo pieno
lavorare part-time
il lavoro fisso / interinale / stressante / gratificante
la motivazione
offerta del lavoro
l'orario
rendersi conto (di)
la ricerca di un posto di lavoro
il salario
sicuro di sé
la soddisfazione/soddisfacente
lo spirito imprenditoriale
gli straordinari
trovarsi di fronte (a)

Unità 31

A CHE SERVE?

Prima di parlare *A coppie. A ogni coppia verrà assegnata una lettera, A, B, C o D dall'insegnante. Tocca a ogni coppia annotare tutti i possibili usi degli apparecchi / oggetti / articoli nel suo elenco.*

A	B
l'orologio	il forno a microonde
la segreteria telefonica	il videoregistratore
il dizionario	la patente di guida
la carta di credito	il filofax

C	D
il pettine	le forbici
l'agenda elettronica	la pila
il frigorifero	lo zainetto
la valigia	il martello

Parliamo 1 *Le coppie che hanno la stessa lettera si riuniscono e procedono alla discussione dei vari usi degli oggetti. Ognuno può aggiungere alla lista usi che ha trascurato precedentemente.*

Espressioni utili

A che cosa serve ...? Hai qualche idea?
L'uso principale di questo oggetto ... è senz'altro ...
Ovviamente usiamo tutti quanti l'orologio per ...
Il dizionario serve soprattutto quando ...
Questo articolo è utile / essenziale / indispensabile ...
Non dobbiamo dimenticare ...
Mi è venuto in mente un altro uso importante / poco comune
Ormai usiamo ogni giorno ...
Per il momento non riesco a pensare ad altri usi

Parliamo 2 *Formate un nuovo gruppo composto da uno studente per ogni gruppo dell'attività precedente (A,B,C e D). A vicenda, ognuno deve comunicare gli usi degli oggetti nel suo elenco. Naturalmente, gli altri tre compagni possono suggerire altri usi che ritengono siano importanti.*

Parliamo 3 *A coppie o a gruppi. Tocca ad ognuno scegliere almeno tre articoli differenti dagli elenchi nella sezione* ***Prima di parlare*** *e spiegare che uso ne fa personalmente.*

Espressioni utili

- Al giorno d'oggi come si può sopravvivere senza ...?
- Non potrei fare a meno di ... Ti/vi faccio qualche esempio
- Uso ogni giorno ...
- Mi è assolutamente indispensabile ...
- Trovo molto utile il videoregistratore sotto vari aspetti, per esempio ...
- Come si farebbe senza ...?
- Ho sempre bisogno di ...
- La carta di credito mi serve quando ...
- Poiché mi sposto molto in macchina per motivi di lavoro ...
- Quando mi hanno regalato ... non pensavo fosse così utile per ...

Parliamo 4 *Come sarebbe la tua vita se dovessi fare a meno degli oggetti elencati qui sopra? Confronta le tue idee con quelle di due o tre compagni di classe.*

Vocabolario

a volte / di tanto in tanto / ogni tanto
l'appuntamento
avere fretta
il canale
il conducente
conservare
esaurito
il fai-da-te
guidare
l'impegno
invece di
mancare
la manutenzione
non avere voglia (di)
pagare in contanti
per motivi di lavoro
raramente
riparare
tagliare
tradurre
verificare il significato

Unità 32

MANGIARE E BERE

Prima di parlare 1 *Completa la seguente tabella riguardante i pasti e gli spuntini che fai durante una giornata tipica, l'orario approssimativo e il luogo dove mangi. Il primo è già fatto come esempio.*

	Nome	Colazione	Pranzo	Cena	Spuntini
1	Maria	caffelatte, pane, burro, marmellata 07.15 a casa	caffè, un panino 12.30 in ufficio	carne, patate, verdura, due bicchieri di vino 19.00 a casa	caffè, una pasta 10.30 in un bar
2					
3					
4					
5					

Parliamo 1 *Intervista 4 compagni di classe e completa la tabella per ognuno di loro. Cerca però di approfondire l'argomento, chiedendo loro se:*

- fanno colazione ecc. sempre alla stessa ora
- se a volte saltano la colazione o il pranzo (e perché)
- se tendono a mangiare le stesse cose a colazione/pranzo
- preparano loro i pasti
- hanno un piatto preferito

Espressioni utili

- Di solito faccio colazione alle ...
- A volte però ...
- Al fine settimana invece ...
- Tendo a mangiare ...
- A colazione mangio solo ...
- A colazione non ho voglia di ...
- Da bere, dipende, delle volte ... altre volte ...
- A pranzo mi accontento di ...
- Generalmente, all'ora di pranzo, mi fermo in qualche bar ...
- Pranzo alla mensa universitaria/aziendale ...
- In genere ceno verso ...

Parliamo 2 *I gruppi vengono riformati. Tocca ad ognuno riferire i risultati del sondaggio, esprimendo inoltre opinioni sulle abitudini alimentari delle persone intervistate, cioè se hanno una dieta equilibrata o se, al contrario, mangiano troppa carne, bevono troppo alcol ecc.*

Prima di parlare 2 *Leggi il seguente brano*

GENTE *Un nonnino sardo ha attraversato nella sua vita tre secoli*

"Ho 111 anni e sono vissuto nell'800 e nel '900: ora vado alla scoperta del nuovo millennio"

Ma a parte i due bicchieri di vino rosso e a parte la gioia di seguire la televisione, quali sono gli altri "segreti" per vivere 111 anni?

"Voi di città dovreste vivere come ho vissuto io i miei primi ottant'anni: in campagna, senza troppi bagordi, amando gli animali e bevendo due bicchieri di vino rosso a pasto. Il vino rosso fa sempre buon sangue. Al mattino faccio colazione con una bella "chicchera" di caffé caldo e pane abbrustolito o biscotti al miele preparati dalle mie figlie e dalle mie nuore.

«SONO UNA ROCCIA»

"A mezzogiorno non disdegno un pezzetto di porceddu, cioè di maiale, o di agnello arrosto o in padella in umido, se c'è, oppure qualche buona fetta di salsiccia o salame, qualche olivetta, o un primo piatto di pasta fatta in casa da mia figlia Laura. La sera, a cena, una minestrina. Poi seguo se ho voglia i notiziari sardi alla TV e quindi vado a letto. Così sto bene e mi sento una roccia, esattamente come la Torre Eiffel. Anzi, come la Torre Eiffel anch'io sono diventato un "monumento" qui a Tiana e in tutta la Sardegna, essendo, così dicono, il più longevo di tutta l'isola. Vengono a farmi visita da ogni luogo, curiosi, studiosi, poeti, pittori. Tutti mi chiedono il segreto per vivere a lungo e io rispondo così: amate il prossimo e bevete un buon bicchiere di vino".

(Gente n. 4 27/1/2000)

Parliamo 3 *A coppie o a gruppi discutete il contenuto dell'articolo. Secondo voi, fino a che punto possiamo attribuire la longevità alla dieta che seguiamo? In base a quello che dice il nonnino avete intenzione di cambiare in qualche modo la vostra dieta? Se sì, in che modo? Se no, perché no?*

Vocabolario

accontentarsi (di)
affamato
avere paura (di)
avere un debole (per)
i cibi che fanno ingrassare
concedersi
dimagrire
evitare (di)
fare merenda
fare uno spuntino
goloso
ingrassare
lavorare a digiuno
limitarsi (a)
mangiare come un lupo
un mangione / una mangiona
pignolo
resistere alla tentazione (di)
saltare un pasto
stare a dieta
stare attento (a)

Unità 33

COSA SAI FARE?

Prima di parlare *Completa le due colonne qui sotto in cinque minuti di tempo elencando le cose che sai fare e quelle cose che non sai fare ma che vorresti imparare a fare in futuro. I primi sono stati scritti come esempi.*

<u>So</u>	<u>Non so e vorrei imparare a ...</u>
giocare a tennis	suonare uno strumento
sciare	guidare
....	....
....	....

Parliamo 1 *Adesso confronta le tue liste con quelle di un compagno di classe. Per le cose che il compagno sa fare puoi chiedere "quando e perché hai imparato a ...?". Per quelle cose che non sa fare puoi chiedere "perché vorresti imparare in futuro e perché non hai imparato a farlo?"*

Espressioni utili

- Ho imparato a ...
- Fin da piccolo/a ho sempre voluto ...
- È bello sapere ...
- Secondo me, è molto utile sapere / potere / essere in grado di ...
- Se uno non sa ...
- Mi sarebbe piaciuto imparare a ...
- Avrei voluto imparare a ...
- Purtroppo, quando avevo ... anni ...
- A quell'età non avevo i soldi per ...
- Non potevo permettermi di ...
- Se avessi avuto abbastanza tempo / soldi avrei preso lezioni di ...

Parliamo 2 *Ora cambia compagno e riferisci alla nuova persona quello che ti ha detto il tuo compagno precedente.*

Vocabolario

l'ambizione
l'abbonamento
ammirare
assiduamente
l'attrezzatura
capace (di)
la capacità
il circolo del tennis
il costo
dedicarsi (a)
dotato
esercitarsi
una gran voglia (di)
invidiare
l'istruttore
la motivazione
l'occasione
l'opportunità
per caso
la pratica
la quota d'iscrizione
il talento
un tipo sportivo
la volontà

COSA FARESTI SE ...?

Prima di parlare 1 *Leggi il seguente articolo.*

Londra, vince 20 miliardi e si lamenta: «Troppi soldi»

LONDRA. Un'anziana signora inglese ha vinto 6,8 milioni di sterline (circa 20 miliardi di lire) alla "National Lottery", l'equivalente del Superenalotto, e invece di pensare a come spendere e investire il suo "tesoro" ha lanciato l'idea di un tetto alle vincite sottolineando che la sua l'ha letteralmente "terrorizzata". È successo a una signora di 73 anni che più di 50 anni fa frequentò la stessa scuola dell'ex premier Margaret Thatcher e che è stata l'unica a centrare il "jackpot": 6.862.953 sterline. La signora ha tenuto una conferenza stampa a Londra, sorprendendo moltissimo i giornalisti. Invece di parlare di crociere e investimenti, infatti, l'arzilla vechietta ha esordito: "Sono terrorizzata da questa vincita, non voglio che la mia vita venga rovinata da una cosa del genere". E ancora: "Vorrei non essere stata l'unica a vincere. Forse dovrebbe esserci un tetto alla somma che una singola persona può vincere". Dichiarazioni, queste, che hanno addirittura indotto a una risposta i dirigenti della "National Lottery", forse preoccupati per quel senso di "terrore" che possono dare 20 miliardi o per quel proposto "tetto" alle vincite. È una reazione iniziale normale - ha commentato un portavoce della National Lottery -. Tra qualche settimana la sua sensazione potrebbe essere completamente diversa".

La stampa, 18/7/99

Parliamo 1 *Cosa faresti tu se vincessi un'ingente somma di denaro al Superenalotto o al Totocalcio? Cosa pensi della reazione della signora che ha vinto? A coppie confrontate le vostre idee e opinioni.*

Espressioni utili

- Se vincessi un'ingente somma di denaro ...
- Mi comprerei subito ...
- Coglierei l'occasione per ...
- (Non) vorrei smettere di lavorare

- Io invece ...
- Darei subito il dieci per cento/la metà ...
- Anch'io penso che sia una buon'idea imporre un tetto alle vincite
- Secondo me, sarebbe molto meglio se ...
- Capisco benissimo la reazione di questa signora
- Conosco una persona/una famiglia che ha vinto ...
- Non conosco nessuno che abbia vinto ... e quindi ...
- Se la vincita di tanti miliardi ti terrorizzasse, potresti sempre ...
- Basta tener presente tutte le organizzazioni benefiche che hanno bisogno di soldi per ...

Prima di parlare 2 *Completa per iscritto tutte le seguenti frasi.*

Cosa farei se:

- non avessi abbastanza soldi per andare in vacanza quest'estate ...
- uno sconosciuto mi invitasse a cena a casa sua ...
- il mio televisore non funzionasse ...
- avessi difficoltà a comunicare bene in italiano ...
- il professore / la professoressa arrivasse sempre in ritardo ...
- trovassi un portafoglio nella strada ...
- i miei vicini facessero molto rumore fino alle ore piccole ...
- avessi la possibilità di lavorare all'estero ...
- dimenticassi di presentarmi a un colloquio di lavoro ...

Parliamo 2 *A coppie o a gruppi parlate del modo in cui avete completato le frasi, discutendo le eventuali differenze.*

Prima di parlare 3 *Fai un elenco degli aspetti positivi e negativi del Paese o della zona in cui vivi, come negli esempi.*

Aspetti positivi	Aspetti negativi
il volontariato	il traffico

Parliamo 3 *A coppie confrontate il vostro elenco. Prima di tutto parlate degli aspetti positivi. Poi discutete gli aspetti negativi spiegando quello che fareste voi per migliorare la situazione oppure, in caso di emergenza, se foste il primo ministro del Paese o il sindaco della città.*

Esempio:

Se succedesse una calamità naturale, ad esempio un terremoto, **mobiliterei** l'esercito e **cercherei** di ottenere la collaborazione delle organizzazioni volontarie più adatte a questo tipo di disastro.

Vocabolario

gli abitanti	prendere una decisione
dedicarsi (a)	programmare (di)
essere deciso (a)	realizzare un sogno
investire	riflettere
mettere da parte	l'unica preoccupazione

Unità 35

APPRENDERE UNA LINGUA STRANIERA

Prima di parlare *Vuoi imparare a parlare il più perfettamente possibile una lingua straniera. Che cosa devi fare per poter raggiungere questo scopo? Scrivi un elenco di cose che devi fare e perché.*

Parliamo 1 *A coppie confrontate le vostre idee discutendo le eventuali differenze.*

Espressioni utili

- Devo senz'altro ...
- Sarà necessario ...
- Bisogna dedicare più tempo a ...
- Avrò bisogno di ...
- Non c'è alcun dubbio che ...
- A parte questo sarà importante/essenziale ...
- Sarà una buon'idea ...

Parliamo 2 *Sarà possibile effettuare tutte le idee che hai proposto? Discutine con un compagno.*

Espressioni utili

- Per me, non sarà difficile ...
- Anche se avrò difficoltà a ...
- Se faccio uno sforzo ...
- Farò di tutto per ...
- Non mi sarà possibile ...
- Detto questo però ...
- Per me, il guaio è che ...
- Secondo me, sarebbe impossibile ...
- Dati i miei impegni attuali ...

Vocabolario

abbonarsi (a)
acquisire
approfittare (di)
l'ascolto
avere una padronanza (di)
concentrarsi (su)
consultare un dizionario
la costanza
l'errore
fare dei sacrifici
la grammatica
imparare a memoria
iscriversi (a)
leggere di tutto
le lezioni individuali
migliorare
una persona di madrelingua
rendersi conto (di)
ripetere più volte
rinunciare (a)
sforzarsi di parlare
superare
un vocabolario più ampio
la (buona) volontà

Unità 36

PROBLEMI

Prima di parlare 1 *Secondo te, quali sono i maggiori problemi che dobbiamo affrontare attualmente e in futuro? Cerca di mettere in ordine di importanza quelli elencati qui sotto e poi annota alcune delle principali cause di ogni problema e eventuali soluzioni. Forse vorrai aggiungere altre preoccupazioni che non sono contenute nella lista.*

- ❖ la disoccupazione
- ❖ il divario fra i ricchi e i poveri
- ❖ la minaccia nucleare
- ❖ la droga
- ❖ i problemi ambientali
- ❖ la criminalità
- ❖ la disgregazione della famiglia
- ❖ il terrorismo

Parliamo 1 *Confronta la tua lista con quella di 2 o 3 compagni di classe, discutendo in modo approfondito le principali cause e eventuali soluzioni di queste preoccupazioni.*

Espressioni utili

- Secondo me, uno dei problemi maggiori è ...
- Per quanto riguarda ...
- Quanto a ...
- Bisogna rendersi conto che ...
- Da una parte ... dall'altra ...
- È importante affrontare il problema ...
- A mio parere la migliore soluzione sarebbe quella di ...
- Come si fa a risolvere ...
- Va ricordato che ...
- Dobbiamo tener presente ...
- Per superare queste difficoltà ...

Prima di parlare 2 *Alcuni italiani esprimono ansia, preoccupazione o disapprovazione attraverso lettere ai giornali. Leggete i contributi qui sotto.*

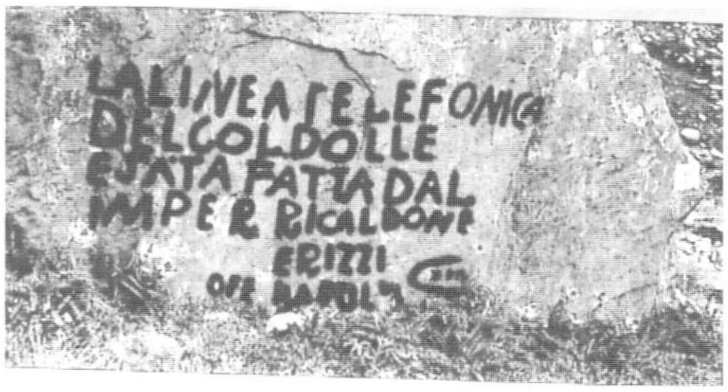

Una pubblicità che scredita chi l'ha fatta

Vi invio una fotografia che ho scattato sul sentiero n. 5 che da Alagna (Val Sesia) porta al Col d'Olen. In essa si vede un pessimo, abusivo e sgrammaticato esempio di iniziativa pubblicitaria, oltre che di inquinamento paesaggistico. La scritta, alta circa un metro e mezzo su un masso erratico di alcune decine di tonnellate fiancheggiante il sentiero, dice: "la linea telefonica del Col d'Olen è stata fatta dall'impresa ecc. ...".

(Qui, TCI, maggio 1999)

LA POSTA

Pantelleria, un'isola meravigliosa rovinata dai rifiuti

Sono diversi anni che passo le ferie a Pantelleria. L'isola è meravigliosa, ma i rifiuti di ogni genere che si trovano in alcuni punti della costa e anche all'interno sono sempre tanti. Non penso che siano i turisti a buttare a mare lavatrici, letti, materassi. Perché l'amministrazione comunale non provvede a mettere ordine nella raccolta dei rifiuti ingombranti?

(Qui, TCI, aprile 1999)

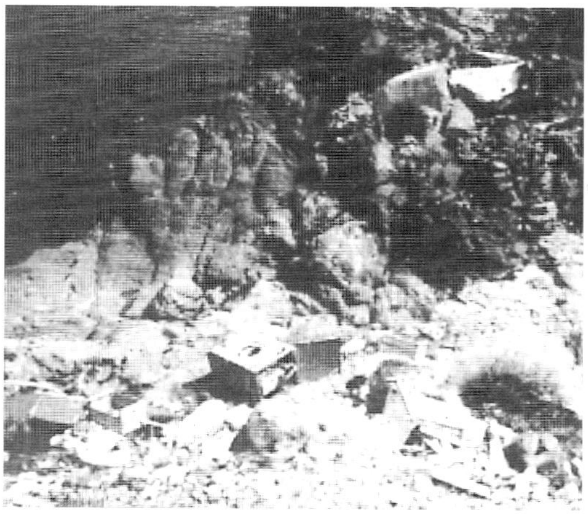

Il calcio soffoca gli altri sport

Di calcio in TV ce n'è molto, e soffoca gli altri sport, ce ne sono di molto belli e interessanti che meriterebbero altrettanta attenzione. Ma il vero problema non è la quantità di calcio giocato che si vede: spesso è anche bello guardare una partita. Quello che trovo veramente eccessivo sono i dibattiti televisivi sul calcio, in particolare sugli errori arbitrali e il potere delle squadre: le polemiche sono eccessive, distraggono l'attenzione da problemi reali e non dovrebbero ricevere tutta questa attenzione. Ci sono troppi dibattiti sul calcio e soprattutto troppa attenzione a questi fatti al di fuori del mondo calcistico. Invece capisco, e in parte condivido, l'attenzione sul problema doping, che è un gravissimo fenomeno che coinvolge la salute dei giocatori oltre all'etica sportiva, ma su quest'argomento la discussione dovrebbe essere originata da dati e riscontri oggettivi e non solo da interviste ad effetto. Saluti,

Davide Corticelli (Pino Torinese) (La Stampa, 9 marzo 2000 Forum)

La Tv non rispetta i bambini

Chiara Cerboni Baiardi

cbaiardi@yahoo.it

Sono la madre di una bambina di sei anni. Non è la prima volta, ma anche oggi mi è capitato di vedere durante una interruzione pubblicitaria di "Solletico" (Raiuno) il provino di un film violento, assolutamente inadatto alla visione di un bambino! Sono indignata.

Parliamo 2 *A coppie.*

Studente A Tu condividi il punto di vista dell'autore di una delle lettere. Esponi il problema allo studente B, aggiungendo altri argomenti a supporto.

Studente B Il tuo amico ti espone un problema che ritiene preoccupante. Tu non condividi questa preoccupazione: secondo te, il suo atteggiamento è esagerato. Cerca argomenti per rassicurare l'amico

Espressioni utili

- Questo è uno dei problemi più gravi del nostro tempo ...
- Parliamo di cose serie ...
- È inutile negare che ci sia ...
- Perché non si provvede a ...?
- È un problema che mi angoscia ...
- È forse meno diffuso di quanto sembri ...
- Non merita il dibattito
- Cerca di non essere troppo pessimista
- Ci sono problemi più pressanti

Vocabolario

l'abusivismo / abusivo
allarmistico / allarmante
l'iniziativa
inadatto
indignarsi / l'indicazione / indignato
ingombrare / ingombrante
l'inquinamento
il paesaggio
prendere posizione
la questione
i rifiuti
la violenza

BARZELLETTE

Prima di parlare 1 *Il professore racconterà una barzelletta. Ascoltala attentamente ma nello stesso tempo annotane i punti principali.*

Parliamo 1 *A coppie cercate di ricostruire questa barzelletta, usando dove necessario le seguenti parole ed espressioni utili.*

un giorno d'inverno	*fare un giro in macchina*	*in piena campagna*
tutto ad un tratto	*cofano*	*dare un'occhiata a*
intendersi di	*proprio in quel momento*	*riuscire a*
avere a che fare con il carburatore	*girarsi di nuovo*	*accorgersi di / che*
altrimenti	*anima viva*	*mettersi in moto*
riprendere il viaggio	*fare il pieno*	*pazzo da legare*

Parliamo 2 *Un "volontario" di una delle coppie prova a raccontare tutta la storia. Gli altri studenti possono interromperlo se trascura qualcosa o sbaglia dei dettagli importanti.*

Espressioni utili

- Scusami se ti interrompo ma ...
- Fermati un attimo perché hai dimenticato di dire una cosa essenziale/importante
- Per favore, ripeti l'ultima cosa che hai detto
- Mi dispiace ma ti sei sbagliato. Non c'entra per niente ...
- Un momento, c'è un'altra cosa che vorrei chiarire ...
- A mio parere non è vero che ...
- Scusa ma l'ultima cosa che hai detto non ha senso
- Ha ragione ... quando dice che ...

Prima di parlare 2 *A coppie. Lo studente A legge la prima barzelletta e lo studente B la seconda, tenendo conto dei fatti principali e sottolineando le parole o espressioni chiave.*

1

Un bellissimo giorno d'estate un impiegato di uno zoo inglese ha deciso di portare una decina di pinguini al mare. Erano contentissimi quando il guardiano gli ha comunicato questa notizia e la notte prima della gita non sono riusciti a dormire bene, tanto erano felici. Il giorno della gita si sono alzati presto, e dopo aver fatto una bella colazione abbondante si sono preparati per partire, mettendo il costume da bagno, la crema solare, gli occhiali da sole, il secchiello e la paletta nello zainetto. Sono partiti in pulmino intorno alle dieci e sono arrivati al mare una mezz'ora più tardi. Hanno passato quasi cinque ore in spiaggia e si sono divertiti un mondo. C'era chi stava sempre in acqua, chi giocava a pallone o a pallavolo e chi prendeva il sole. Hanno mangiato i panini che avevano portato con loro e si sono tutti comprati un bel gelato con i soldi che avevano risparmiato. Quando è giunto il momento di risalire a bordo del pulmino si sentivano un po' tristi perché il giorno di libertà era quasi al termine. Sulla via di ritorno il guardiano ha deciso di passare per la città. Purtroppo proprio in centro città si è bucata una gomma. Il guardiano non sapeva cambiare la ruota e perciò ha telefonato a una autorimessa ma tutti i meccanici erano occupati e hanno risposto che doveva aspettare un'ora. A questo punto il guardiano ha cominciato a preoccuparsi perché faceva un caldo da morire e non poteva lasciare i pinguini chiusi nel pulmino. Sudavano, avevano sete e rischiavano di morire. Per fortuna ha visto arrivare un altro pulmino e ha fatto segno all'autista di fermarsi. Ha spiegato la vicenda e ha chiesto all'autista di portare i pinguini allo zoo. Questo signore ha accettato e il guardiano gli ha dato dieci sterline. Allora i pinguini sono scesi da un pulmino e saliti a bordo di un altro. Dieci minuti dopo il guasto sono partiti di nuovo per lo zoo.

Un'ora più tardi è arrivato un impiegato dell'autorimessa per cambiare la ruota e finalmente il guardiano è partito per lo zoo anche lui. All'entrata dello zoo ha chiesto se i pinguini fossero arrivati sani e salvi ma hanno detto di no, che non li avevano visti. "Ma cos'è successo?" si è domandato "sarebbero dovuti arrivare qua un'oretta fa". Ha girato il pulmino ed è ripartito in direzione della città. Arrivato in centro non poteva credere ai suoi occhi. In lontananza ha visto il signore, al quale aveva dato le dieci sterline per portare i pinguini allo zoo, camminare in mezzo alla strada e tutti i pinguini lo seguivano. Ha fermato il pulmino, è saltato giù e si è avvicinato al signore. Gli ha detto "Scusi, cosa sta succedendo? Le avevo dato dieci sterline per portare i pinguini allo zoo". Il signore gli ha risposto "Lo so e ho fatto quello che mi ha chiesto, li ho portati allo zoo ma siccome mi sono rimaste ancora cinque sterline, adesso li porto al cinema".

2

Un giorno della settimana scorsa sono andato al cinema a vedere un film comico che, secondo tutti i miei amici, era bellissimo. Sono arrivato un quarto d'ora prima dell'inizio dello spettacolo ma, siccome faceva freddo fuori, ho deciso di comprare il biglietto per la platea ed entrare. La sala era quasi vuota. Dietro di me ho notato un signore che era comodamente sdraiato e occupava tre poltrone. Quando più gente cominciava ad entrare nel cinema una maschera si è avvicinata al signore sdraiato e gli ha gentilmente chiesto di sedersi bene perché aveva pagato per una poltrona e ne occupava tre. Ho sentito rispondere solo "Ah, ah". Ormai la sala era quasi piena e la maschera è tornata di nuovo e ha chiesto al signore di alzarsi e di sedersi per bene. La gente che arrivava aveva bisogno di queste poltrone. Ancora una volta il signore ha risposto nello stesso modo di prima: "Ah, ah!!" La maschera ha perso la pazienza e ha minacciato di chiamare il direttore. L'uomo ha risposto "Ah, ah" come se avesse difficoltà a dire altro. Ormai la sala, era piena zeppa tranne che le due poltrone in più che occupava il signore 'muto'. La maschera ha chiamato il direttore, il quale è arrivato in un batter d'occhio e ha chiesto al signore di alzarsi, dicendo che il suo comportamento non era assolutamente accettabile. Il signore ha risposto con l'ormai famoso "ah, ah". Va bene, ha detto il direttore, adesso chiamo la polizia. Due poliziotti sono arrivati subito sul posto e hanno detto al signore di alzarsi e di accompagnarli in questura. Il signore forse non aveva un grosso vocabolario perché di nuovo ha risposto come prima "Ah, ah". Uno dei poliziotti gli ha chiesto il nome. "Ah, ah" è stata la risposta. Il poliziotto gli ha fatto un'altra domanda: "Da dove viene Lei?" Finalmente il signore è riuscito a pronunciare qualche parola a bassa voce e balbettando "da... da... dal... dalla... dalla ga... dalla gal... dalla galleria".

Parliamo 3 *Adesso, a vicenda, provate a raccontare la barzelletta che avete letto. Sarà possibile a volte cambiare alcuni dettagli ma non quelli più importanti.*

Parliamo 4 *Lavorate in piccoli gruppi e, a vicenda, ognuno deve raccontare una barzelletta che conosce bene. Alla fine scegliete la migliore barzelletta e decidete chi avrà il compito di raccontarla a tutta la classe.*

Parliamo 5 *A vicenda tocca alla persona scelta raccontare la barzelletta migliore del proprio gruppo. I membri della classe voteranno poi la barzelletta più divertente, che verrà premiata!*

Vocabolario

a causa di
arrivare sul posto
avvenire
balbettare
in un batter d'occhio
la battuta finale
cadere
dato che
di conseguenza
fare un caldo da morire
farsi una bella risata
fissare
giungere
la gomma bucata
un guasto
in altri termini
la maschera
meno male
minacciare (di)
non poter credere ai suoi occhi
la paletta
pieno zeppo
piovere a dirotto
la platea
la poltrona
la questura
ridere di cuore
ridere fino alle lacrime
rischiare (di)
la ruota
sano e salvo
scherzare
scoppiare a ridere
scoprire
il secchiello
siccome
la siepe
il significato
stare in pensiero
tranne
trattenersi dal ridere
la vicenda

Unità 38

QUANTE DOMANDE!

Prima di parlare *Sei curioso? Ti piace sapere i fatti degli altri? Ecco il tuo gioco ideale! Usando i verbi al presente indicativo (o altri modi e tempi) e il vocabolario qui sotto scrivi in cinque minuti di tempo tutte le domande possibili che puoi rivolgere ai compagni di classe.*

fare — faccio fai fa facciamo fate fanno
andare — vado vai va andiamo andate vanno
stare — sto stai sta stiamo state stanno
dare — dò dai dà diamo date danno
venire — vengo vieni viene veniamo venite vengono
dire — dico dici dice diciamo dite dicono

cosa?
chi?
(da) dove?
(con/per) chi?
come?
a che ora?
perché?
quando?

a Roma
in Toscana
a scuola
all'estero
al fine settimana
a teatro
a casa (mia/tua/sua)
in ufficio

ieri / l'altro ieri
due giorni fa
dopodomani
questo sabato
dopo la lezione
durante le vacanze estive
domani sera
stasera
a Natale

Regole del gioco

L'intenzione del gioco è di sfruttare al massimo le possibilità della domanda iniziale, come indicato nell'esempio. Non è permesso ripetere domande che sono state poste da altri studenti precedentemente! Un gioco ideale per persone curiosissime!!

Parliamo *Lavorate a gruppi di 4. Lo studente A fa una domanda allo studente B che deve rispondere in modo appropriato. Gli studenti C e D possono fare domande supplementari, come nell'esempio.*

– Cosa fai stasera?

– Vado al cinema.
– Con chi vai?
– Vado da solo?
– Cosa vai a vedere?
– Vado a vedere l'ultimo film di Giacomo Bondi.
– A che ora vai?
– Verso le zero zero sette.

Unità 39

FOTO DELLE VACANZE

Prima di parlare *Ognuno deve portare in classe una decina di foto delle ultime vacanze o di una vacanza precedente. Come descriveresti queste foto a un compagno di classe?*

Parliamo 1 *A coppie descrivete il più dettagliatamente possibile le foto che avete scelto. Naturalmente potete anche fare domande a chi presenta la fotografia per saperne di più.*

Espressioni utili

- Ho fatto / scattato questa foto ...
- L'anno scorso sono andato / a in Austria / negli Stati Uniti ...
- Mi ricordo che quel giorno ...
- Guarda questo paesaggio ....
- Chi è la persona seduta ...?
- Allora la persona a destra / al centro / in primo piano ...
- Per quanto tempo ti sei fermato / a ...?
- Mi piace molto questa foto perché ...
- Cos'hai fatto quel giorno?
- E alla sera?
- È stata la tua prima visita a ...?
- Ti piacerebbe ritornare?
- Perché questa persona ha l'aria così seria / scocciata ...?
- Come vedi, indosso la felpa / il casco / la tuta da sub perché ...

Parliamo 2 *In gruppi di 4. Mescolate le fotografie che appartengono ai componenti del gruppo e mettetele a faccia in giù. A turno, cercate di ricordare le foto che erano state descritte precedentemente e descrivetele. Confrontate la nuova descrizione con quella originale. Avete avuto buona memoria?*

Espressioni utili

- Ricordo che nella foto di ... c'era ...
- Mi sembra che tuo fratello indossasse ...
- Non c'erano anche ...?
- Hai ottima memoria!

Vocabolario

affittare
andare d'accordo
cogliere l'occasione (per)
un/una (ex) collega
deludere / deludente
la diapositiva
fare un caldo / un freddo da morire
inginocchiato
in piedi
la luce
magnifico
molto / tanto da fare
il momento / giorno in cui
noleggiare
il paesaggio
un parente alla lontana
in primo piano
quello con gli occhiali da sole
quello che abbraccia ... / che si appoggia a ...
scattare una foto
sdraiato
seduto
lo sfondo / sullo sfondo
il soggiorno
sviluppare le foto
la tintarella
un viaggio organizzato / di nozze / d'affari
una visita guidata
lo zoom

Unità 40

FOTO DI FAMIGLIA

Prima di parlare *Ognuno deve selezionare alcune foto di famiglia da portare in classe, preferibilmente alcune foto recenti ed altre fatte parecchi anni fa. Bisogna riflettere sul come descrivere queste foto a un compagno di classe, tenendo conto di alcuni dei seguenti punti:*

- età
- legami di parentela, rapporti
- professione
- stato civile
- domicilio
- descrizione del carattere
- occasione in cui la foto è stata scattata

Parliamo 1 Le fotografie saranno mescolate e distribuite a caso. Ogni studente descrive la foto assegnata (età, legami di parentela ecc.) ovviamente immaginando le informazioni. Il proprietario della foto descritta non deve intervenire per correggere le inesattezze.

Espressioni utili

- Ho fatto / scattato questa foto nel (1975) ...
- Questa è una foto di ...
- La ragazza con i capelli ...
- Quello/a con gli occhiali è ...
- In questa foto mia sorella aveva ... anni ...
- Frequentava il secondo anno della scuola ...
- La persona / seduta / in piedi / accanto a ...
- Purtroppo questa persona è morta ...
- Questo è il mio zio che vive ...
- (Non) ci vediamo da ...
- Questa qui è sempre mia sorella ...
- Vedi la differenza, è molto più alta ...
- Adesso ha ... anni ...
- È sposato/a e ha ... figli
- Lui/lei lavora come ...
- Mio fratello non abita più con noi ...
- Per motivi di lavoro ...

Parliamo 2 *Ogni studente riprende la propria fotografia. A coppie o a gruppi ogni studente darà la versione reale per ogni foto.*

Espressioni utili

Hai indovinato l'età ma hai completamente sbagliato ...
Il suo carattere è esattamente l'opposto ...
Ci sei andato/a vicino ...
Sei un mago!
Come hai fatto a indovinare ...?
Mi dispiace, tutto sbagliato!

Vocabolario

abbastanza / piuttosto
abbronzato
alto
avere sui trent'anni
i baffi / baffuto
la barba
basso
la bocca aperta
calvo
i capelli ricci/lisci/ondulati
celibe
mio/mia cognato/a
di statura media
un'espressione sorridente / annoiata
il mio fratellastro
mio genero
grassoccio
le lentiggini / lentigginoso
la mia madrina
magro
la mia matrigna
nubile
mia nuora
gli occhi socchiusi / spalancati
l'orecchino
il mio padrino
paffuto
il pallido
il mio patrigno
portare bene /male gli anni
robusto
sbadigliare
lo sguardo fisso
snello
la mia sorellastra
sorridente
triste
vedovo/a
il viso

(Vedi anche Unità 4 pagina 31 per vocabolario che descrive il carattere)

Unità 41

LA MIA ZONA

Prima di parlare *Rifletti per qualche minuto sulla zona in cui abiti e poi fai un elenco di tutto quello che ti piace e quello che non ti piace del quartiere. Ecco alcuni aspetti che puoi prendere in considerazione.*

abitanti; negozi; scuole; mezzi pubblici; svaghi per bambini, giovani e adulti; parchi; attrezzature sportive; lavoro; ambiente; case/appartamenti; criminalità

Quello che mi piace	Quello che non mi piace
....	....
....	....

Espressioni utili

- Mi piace tanto la zona in cui vivo perché ...
- Da quando ci sono arrivato/a ...
- Un vantaggio di abitare qui ...
- Sono contento/a di aver traslocato qui ...
- In confronto alla zona in cui abitavo prima, questo quartiere ...
- Un lato molto positivo ...
- Purtroppo c'è una mancanza di ...
- Se ci fosse/fossero ...
- Sarebbe un posto ideale se ...
- C'è molto da fare ...
- Non ci sono molte possibilità di svago ...
- Non c'è tanto da fare ...
- Per quanto riguarda ...
- Quanto ai lati negativi ...
- Devo dire che non mi piace affatto ...
- Devo dire che il Comune non fa molto per migliorare ...
- Certi problemi sono comuni a tutti i quartieri, però ...
- Se avessi saputo che ... non avrei traslocato in questa zona ...

Parliamo 1 *A coppie. In base ai due elenchi a pagina 114 confrontate la zona in cui abitate discutendo le eventuali differenze.*

Parliamo 2 *A coppie. Se aveste la possibilità di migliorare la vostra zona che cosa fareste?*

Parliamo 3 *A coppie. Se avete vissuto in passato in un'altra zona, paragonatela con quella in cui vivete attualmente.*

Espressioni utili

- Dalla descrizione che hai fatto ...
- La zona in cui tu abiti (non) mi sembra molto differente ...
- Mi pare che nel tuo quartiere ci sia ... più/meno ...
- Se fossi assessore comunale la prima cosa che farei sarebbe di cambiare ...
- In confronto alla zona in cui abitavo prima, questa è ...
- Se ricordo bene, neanche là c'era .../era possibile ...

Vocabolario

abitare in centro/in periferia/
in piena campagna
a differenza di
la carenza
una casa colonica
il centro commerciale
il centro sportivo polivalente
il costo della vita
i disagi
la disoccupazione giovanile
distare
la fabbrica
il grattacielo
in confronto a
l'inconveniente
migliorare
il modo di vivere
il palazzo / il condominio
parcheggiare
il pendolare
la percentuale
la qualità della vita
un quartiere popolare / residenziale
rumoroso
la scelta
i servizi comunali
stabilirsi
il tenore di vita
trasferirsi
trovare lavoro
i vicini
una villa
una villetta a schiera
la zona industriale

VERO O FALSO?

Prima di parlare *Leggi le affermazioni seguenti e indica con una crocetta quelle che sono false.*

1. Stamattina mi sono fatto/a un panino alla Nutella per colazione.
2. Oggi mi sono alzato/a prima delle sei e mezza.
3. Ieri mattina sono andato/a a scuola / al lavoro in bicicletta.
4. Ieri l'altro ho studiato/lavorato per tre ore di fila senza nemmeno una pausa.
5. Sabato scorso sono rimasto/a a letto fino al due del pomeriggio.
6. Domenica pomeriggio sono andato/a a fare un giro in macchina con i miei amici.
7. Non ho mai studiato una lingua straniera a scuola.
8. L'estate scorsa sono andato/a in vacanza in Spagna.
9. Per il mio ultimo compleanno ho organizzato una festa a casa mia alla quale ho invitato i miei migliori amici.
10. Oggi a pranzo ho comprato un panino alla mozzarella e peperoncino al chioschetto vicino a scuola.
11. Nell'intervallo fra la lezione di storia e quella di matematica ho bevuto una coca cola in lattina.
12. Oggi indosso un vestito carino perché ho bisogno di tirarmi su il morale.

Parliamo 1 *A coppie spiegate in modo dettagliato tutte le affermazioni che sono false, come nell'esempio:*

Esempio:

Non è vero che mi sono alzato prima delle sei e mezza. Non mi sono mai alzato a quest'ora in vita mia, alle sei e mezza di sera sì ma alle sei e mezza di mattina, scherziamo? Se mi alzassi così presto sarei distrutto per il resto della giornata. Normalmente mi alzo intorno alle sette e un quarto dato che ci vogliono solo dieci minuti, un quarto d'ora per arrivare a scuola/al lavoro da casa mia. E poi, per prepararmi e fare colazione mi occorre al massimo un quarto d'ora. E tu, ti sei alzato prima delle sei e mezza oggi? Ti sei mai alzato prima delle sei e mezza? Quando? Per quale motivo?

Espressioni utili

- Questa affermazione è vera
- Questa affermazione è (completamente) falsa
- Se ricordo bene ...
- Siccome l'ufficio/la scuola è molto lontano/a da casa mia ...
- Per me, non è possibile andare al lavoro/ a scuola in bicicletta/a piedi perché ...
- È vero che ...
- Fino a un certo punto è vero che ...
- A dire la verità non mi alzo mai prima delle ...
- Purtroppo l'estate scorsa ...
- Di solito a pranzo mi accontento di uno spuntino molto leggero, per esempio ...

Parliamo 2 *Ora potete parlare delle affermazioni che sono vere rivolgendovi il maggior numero di domande possibili in modo da poter ottenere ulteriori informazioni, come nell'esempio:*

Esempio:
- È vero che ho fatto colazione prima di uscire.
- A che ora hai fatto colazione?
- Che cosa hai mangiato?
- Che cosa hai bevuto?
- Chi ha preparato la colazione?
- Fai colazione sempre alla stessa ora?
- Sei abituato a mangiare e a bere le stesse cose?
- Potresti fare a meno della colazione?

Altre parole/espressioni interrogative:

Dove?	Con chi?	Quale?	Come?	Quando?	Quanto?
Perché?	Come mai?	Da quanto tempo?			

Vocabolario

(non) farcela (a)
appunto
assaggiare
avere voglia (di)
dipende (da)
è il massimo!
esatto
indimenticabile
intorno a
lavorare senza sosta
ma scherzi!
neanche per sogno!
per carità!
provare
rimpiangere (di)
saltare la colazione
stanco morto
stare a digiuno
stufarsi (di)
una festa da sballo

Unità 43

SPIEGAZIONI

Prima di parlare *Guarda le seguenti parole/espressioni e pensa al contesto o alla situazione in cui vengono usate.*

- ❖ Grazie – Altrettanto
- ❖ Piacere di conoscerLa
- ❖ Salve!
- ❖ Cin cin
- ❖ Sogni d'oro
- ❖ Auguri
- ❖ A più tardi
- ❖ Si accomodi
- ❖ In bocca al lupo
- ❖ Mi dica
- ❖ Vuole assaggiare?
- ❖ Ci mancherebbe altro!
- ❖ Alla cassa
- ❖ Neanche per sogno

Parliamo 1 *A coppie cercate di spiegare una situazione (o situazioni) in cui vengono usate le parole/espressioni.*

Espressioni utili

- Si usa questa espressione ...
- Ho sempre usato questa parola quando ...
- Un contesto in cui viene usata spesso questa parola ...
- Se per esempio ...
- A mio parere ...
- Penso che si possa usare questa espressione ...
- Allora ti faccio un esempio ...
- Sono sicuro/a che ...
- Per quanto ne so io ...
- Se non sbaglio ...
- Non sono al cento per cento sicuro/a ...
- A dire la verità, non ne ho la più pallida idea
- Non so spiegare bene come ...
- Ho sentito usare parecchie volte questa parola, però ...

Parliamo 2 *A coppie cercate di creare dei dialoghi in cui vengono usate le parole/espressioni elencate in **Prima di parlare**.*

Esempio:

- Ciao Stefano.
- Salve Marcella, ti vedo un po' giù, come mai?
- Che ti devo dire, è la solita storia, problemi di lavoro..colleghi deficienti.
- Ma non mi avevi detto che volevi cambiare ufficio?
- Sì, appunto, ho un colloquio per il trasferimento proprio domani.
- Finalmente! Allora, Marcella, in bocca al lupo!
- Grazie Stefano, ti farò sapere come è andato, ciao.

Altri contesti possibili:

- ❖ In banca
- ❖ Celebrazione in famiglia
- ❖ Riunione d'affari
- ❖ Cena romantica
- ❖ In viaggio
- ❖ Fra amici
- ❖ Incontro in autobus / per la strada
- ❖ In spiaggia, sotto l'ombrellone

Vocabolario

aiutare
al posto di
una buona / cattiva educazione
comune
convincere
cortese
educato
un'espressione di uso corrente
essere in compagnia (di)
fare la conoscenza (di)
fare le presentazioni
fare un favore a qn
formale
incontrare
informale
invece di
maleducato
un modo di dire
offrire
per cortesia
prestare
prima di
reagire / la reazione
rispondere / la risposta
la situazione
lo stesso significato (di)

SCUOLA E UNIVERSITÀ

Prima di parlare *Leggi la seguente lettera e sottolinea i punti che ritieni interessanti.*

Gli strumenti scolastici sono inadeguati

Gentile dottoressa Palombelli, ho i problemi di un giovane disoccupato italiano che è stato costretto ad andare all'estero a migliorare l'inglese. Una tesi la leggono 10 persone; inoltre studiamo troppa teoria e pochissima pratica nell'università italiana. Siamo poco vendibili sul mercato internazionale. Non voglio essere un "rivoluzionario" perché le sto raccontando la mia esperienza personale. Oggi nel mondo del lavoro è richiesto il Toefl di inglese e Word, Excel and Power Point per il computer.
Durante tutta la mia carriera scolastica e universitaria non ho mai usato il computer. L'inglese l'ho praticamente accantonato all'università. Alle medie le ore di musica sono come quantità le stesse che quelle d'inglese. Oggi il latino è poco utilizzabile sul mercato. Adesso le ho descritto in poche righe gli ultimi dieci anni della mia vita scolastica.
Come vede, chiedo solo che gli studi che si compiono siano maggiormente vendibili sul mercato nazionale ed internazionale. Lei ha circa 20 anni più di me e in vent'anni la situazione del mercato del lavoro per i giovani è completamente cambiata. Invece la scuola e l'università no.
Per esempio, nella facoltà di giurisprudenza, istituzioni di diritto privato si studia ancora sul testo Torrente che si usava 35 anni fa.
Nella facoltà di medicina, per la neuropsichiatria infantile si studia ancora la psicoanalisi classica, e rispetto agli Usa siamo indietro di 40 anni.
Come vede, non sono un rivoluzionario, sono solo un giovane neolaureato che le fa un resoconto della situazione di noi giovani.

(La Repubblica 26/10/1999)

Parliamo 1 *Quali aspetti avete trovato particolarmente interessanti / sorprendenti nella lettera dello studente italiano? A coppie confrontate i punti che avete sottolineato discutendo le eventuali differenze.*

Parliamo 2 *A coppie raccontate la vostra esperienza scolastica/universitaria, tenendo conto, se volete, delle seguenti domande:*

1. Lo studio di una lingua straniera è/è stata un'esperienza positiva o negativa? Siete stati costretti ad andare all'estero a migliorare la lingua/le lingue che studiate/avete studiato?

Parlate del modo in cui imparate/avete imparato una lingua straniera, tenendo conto dei metodi adottati.

2. Il vostro programma di studi è/è stato molto pratico o troppo teorico oppure riunisce/riuniva entrambi i metodi?
3. Dato il vostro programma di studi, vi ritenete vendibili sul mercato nazionale ed internazionale?
4. Usate/avete usato il computer? Per fare che cosa?
5. Studiate/avete studiato materie poco utilizzabili nel mondo del lavoro? Quale/quali?
6. La scuola/l'università che frequentate/avete frequentato risponde/ha risposto, secondo voi, alle esigenze del mercato/del mondo del lavoro?
7. Avete mai partecipato a viaggi di studio, stages o visite didattiche? Raccontate i lati positivi e/o negativi dell'esperienza.

Vocabolario

l'abilità
accantonare
aggiornarsi
bilingue
la carriera
cercare un posto di lavoro
compiere
un corso di avviamento professionale
costringere
la disciplina
la domanda di assunzione
un'esperienza (in)utile
la formazione professionale
l'insegnamento
la maggior parte
il metodo migliore
mantenere i contatti
motivato
un neolaureato
l'orientamento professionale
per fortuna
il resoconto
rilevante
rispetto a
un soggiorno all'estero
spingere
il tirocinio
i titoli di studio
la valenza / valido
vendibile

Unità 45

BUONUMORE

Prima di parlare *Ti piacciono le barzellette? Sai raccontarle? Guarda le seguenti vignette e cerca di immaginare la conversazione che si svolge in ogni situazione. Poi scrivi una frase che, secondo te, riassuma in poche parole il significato di ogni vignetta.*

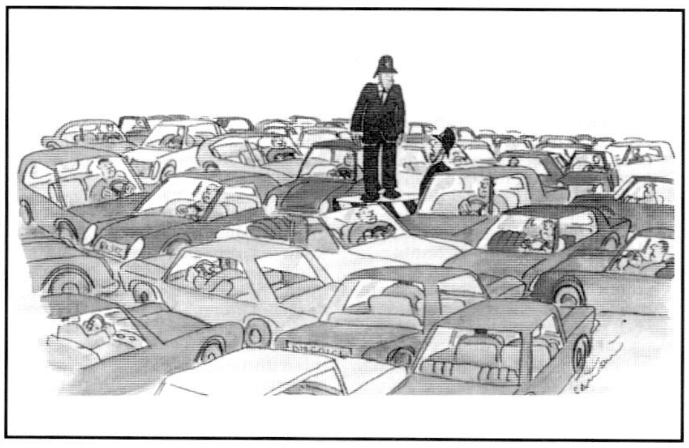

A

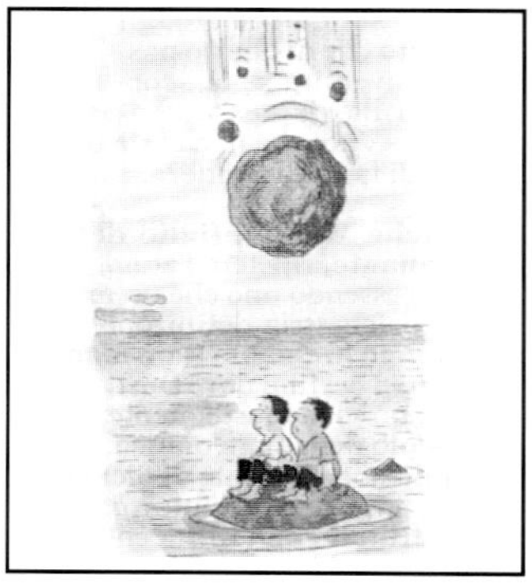

B

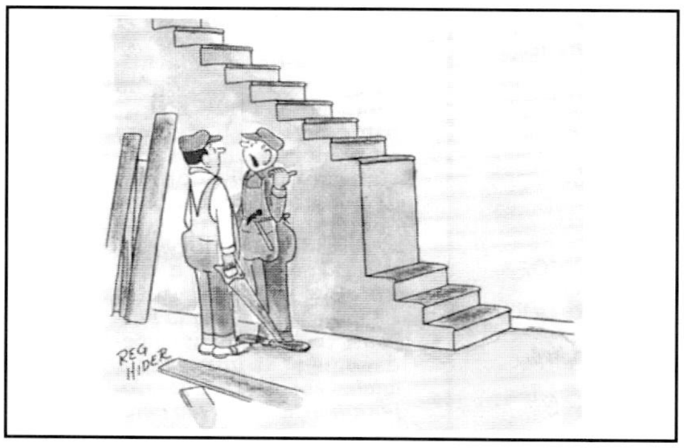

C

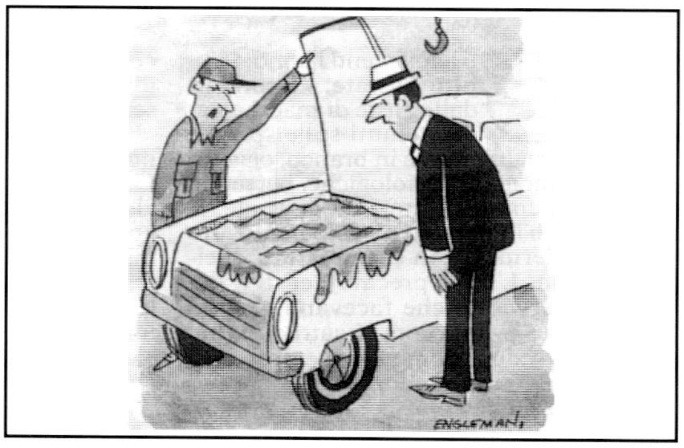

D

Parliamo 1 *A coppie o in gruppo scambiate le frasi sulle varie vignette. Qual è la frase più azzeccata?*

Espressioni utili

- Sembra che il signore/la signora sia .../stia facendo ...
- Il signore non può credere ai suoi occhi ...
- Il capo si è arrabbiato quando ...
- Il signore/la signora sta dicendo che ...

- L'operaio sta spiegando che ...
- Il marito è irritato perché ...
- Questi due signori stanno parlando (di) ...

Prima di parlare 2 *Quale vignetta vi ha fatto ridere di più e perché? Quale non avete apprezzato? Perché?*

Espressioni utili

- Questa mi fa ridere perché ...
- ... è una situazione comica/assurda
- ... i personaggi sono buffi
- ... c'è un senso dell'assurdo
- Non capisco cosa ci sia da ridere qui ...
- Non mi piace perché incoraggia lo stereotipo di ...

Parliamo 2 *Commentate ogni vignetta a coppie o in gruppo.*

Vocabolario

la barzelletta
la battuta
la comicità / comico
la discriminazione
divertente
la freddura
illustrare
la mancanza di senso dell'umorismo
il pregiudizio
la satira di costume
spiritoso
lo stereotipo

Unità 46

SALUTE E FORMA

Prima di parlare 1 *In dieci minuti di tempo scrivi un elenco di tutte le cose che si dovrebbero fare per mantenere salute e forma.*

Esempio: Si dovrebbe fare una bella camminata almeno due volte alla settimana

1. ....
2. ....
3. ....
4. ....
5. ....
6. ....
7. ....
8. ....

Parliamo 1 *A coppie o a gruppi confrontate il vostro elenco discutendo le eventuali differenze.*

Prima di parlare 2 *Ora passiamo dalla teoria alla pratica! Di tutti i consigli che hai elencato, quali riesci a seguire in realtà? Indicali con una crocetta e scrivi se li segui* ***ogni giorno, abbastanza regolarmente*** *o* ***raramente.***

Parliamo 2 *Spiega a un compagno di classe i risultati del tuo sondaggio, sottolineando la frequenza di ogni attività. Poi il tuo compagno ti comunicherà i suoi risultati. Perché non riesci a seguire gli altri consigli / suggerimenti se li ritieni importanti?*

Espressioni utili

- Sono abbastanza soddisfatto/a di quello che faccio
- Mi rendo conto che dovrei ...
- So benissimo che ...
- Anche se dovessi ...
- Una volta alla settimana mi sforzo di .../ cerco sempre di ...

- Tutti mi dicono che ...
- Faccio uno sforzo per ...
- Purtroppo non riesco sempre a ...
- Per motivi di lavoro/di studio ...
- Ultimamente sono stato/a molto impegnato/a per cui ...
- A partire dall'anno scorso ...
- D'inverno non ho voglia di ...
- Quando fuori fa un freddo da morire ...
- Mi manca la volòntà/la costanza/il tempo
- Quante scuse!
- D'accordo, sono pigro/a!

Vocabolario

l'acqua naturale / minerale / di sorgente
avere voglia (di)
gli antibiotici
bere alcolici in moderazione
camminare di buon passo
correre
la dieta
esagerare
evitare
fare ginnastica
la flessibilità
godersi la vita
i grassi
l'obesità
il pericolo
il piacere della buona tavola
praticare uno sport
la resistenza
respirare profondamente
rinunciare (a)

Unità 47

VACANZE

Prima di parlare 1 *Pensa alla vacanza più memorabile che tu abbia fatto finora. Scrivi un breve elenco degli aspetti che l'hanno resa indimenticabile.*

Parliamo 1 *A coppie raccontate il più dettagliatamente possibile la vostra memorabile vacanza.*

Espressioni utili

- Quando avevo ... anni ...
- Sono partito/a a metà di luglio ...
- Ho trascorso ...
- Ho incontrato ...
- La cosa più emozionante è stata ...
- Il tempo è stato/era ...
- Ho dei bei ricordi di questa vacanza soprattutto perché ... per non parlare di ...
- A differenza delle altre vacanze che ho avuto ...
- Non dimenticherò mai il giorno in cui ...
- Quanto alla sistemazione ...
- Il posto era bellissimo/suggestivo/incantevole ...
- Quello che non dimenticherò mai è ...
- C'erano mille possibilità/attività, per esempio ...
- C'era tanto da vedere/fare, per esempio ...
- Quello che mi ricordo particolarmente ...
- Questa esperienza mi ha arricchito ...
- Ho imparato che ...

Prima di parlare 2 *Leggi attentamente il seguente articolo.*

Un golfo selvaggio e suggestivo. Ma adatto anche per vacanze familiari

Una natura incantevole abbraccia calette, insenature e spiagge del golfo di Policastro, a pochi chilometri dalle antiche testimonianze di Paestum e Velia. Scario, affacciatasi su un lembo di costa in provincia di Salerno, all'interno del parco Nazionale del Cilento, è la base ideale per una vacanza con bambini. Il Parco è un vero e proprio scrigno di bellezze naturali diverse: dalla pianura costiera alla collina per finire nell'asprezza del massiccio montuoso. Un paesaggio generoso e al tempo stesso avaro, che conferisce fascino e mistero a un territorio che è riuscito a conservare intatti ambiente e tradizioni. In quest'area, uno dei tratti costieri più belli del Mediterraneo, sorge il villaggio La Francesca e, alle spalle, il Monte Bulgheria, bastione calcareo ricoperto dai boschi mediterranei dove abbonda la profumatissima lavanda. A due passi c'è la Grotta Azzurra di Capo Palinuro, raggiungibile in barca. In zona si possono visitare anche la Grotta del Sangue - chiamata così per la colorazione rossastra naturale che si riflette sul fondo di roccia bianca - e la Grotta dei Monaci, al cui interno la natura e il tempo hanno modellato forme che ricordano quelle di monaci benedettini raccolti in preghiera. Passeggiate in riva al mare, itinerai naturalistici, ma anche bagni in spiagge sempre diverse (facilmente raggiungibili via mare) e scorpacciate di pesce freschissimo. Non c'è che l'imbarazzo della scelta. Il Villaggio La Francesca (tel. 0974986068), all'interno del Parco del Cilento, ha una spiaggetta privata, riparata, dove il mare è sempre calmo. Nel Villaggio i bambini hanno a disposizione numerosi spazi per giocare: uno staff di animatori organizza per loro giochi e attività di vario tipo. Un bungalow a 4 letti per una settimana, dal 4 al 30 settembre, parte da L. 480.000.

Parliamo 2 *A coppie discutete se questa vacanza vi attrae o no, spiegando perché.*

Parliamo 3 *Lavorate in gruppi di 3 o 4. Ognuno deve assumere uno dei seguenti ruoli: agente di viaggio, cliente (esigente e pignolo), direttore del Villaggio La Francesca (al telefono), compagno/a del/della cliente.*

3a Prima della vacanza – informarsi. Il cliente vuole assicurarsi che i servizi del villaggio rispondano alle sue esigenze. L'agente risponde e rassicura, telefonando al direttore del villaggio quando è in difficoltà.

3b Dopo la vacanza – protestare. Tutto è andato storto e il cliente è furibondo. L'agente risponde diplomaticamente e telefona al direttore del villaggio per trasmettere le lamentele e avere schiarimenti.

Prima di parlare 3

Studente A *Leggi la pubblicità di questo Villaggio e comincia a fare lavorare la fantasia. Sei lì e ti stai godendo una meritata vacanza. L'unico problema sono i contatti con il mondo esterno: sia la tua famiglia che i tuoi colleghi di lavoro ti hanno raccomandato di telefonare e di raccontare tutto. Pensa a come descrivere una tua giornata tipica al Villaggio ...*

Studente B *Sei un parente / un collega della persona che è andata in vacanza. Schiatti dalla curiosità di sapere come sta andando la sua vacanza al Villaggio e sei anche leggermente invidioso... Hai anche una mezza idea di andarci anche tu ...*

Il villaggio

Si trova sulla costa nord orientale della Sicilia tra Capo d'Orlando e Capo Calavà e dista circa 2 km da Gioiosa Marea. Il villaggio, immerso nella ricca vegetazione e circondato da numerosi giardini fioriti, sorge su un terrazzo naturale, dominante la baia sottostante con un panorama incantevole sul mare aperto e sulle Isole Eolie.

La spiaggia

Di sabbia e ciottoli, dista circa 400 metri ed è attrezzata con sdraio, ombrelloni e lettini. Servizio di navetta continuo e gratuito.

Servizi e strutture

Reception aperta 24 ore su 24 con servizio cassaforte e cambio, ristorante con prima colazione, pranzo e cena a buffet, due bar, snack bar, boutique, bazar, parcheggio interno limitato gratuito, discoteca, anfiteatro, sala TV, ufficio turistico per escursioni, noleggio auto.

Attività sportive e ricreative

Due piscine a disposizione degli ospiti, una per adulti e una per bambini, campo da tennis, pallavolo, ping-pong, windsurf, canoe, pedalò, ginnastica, aerobica, sci nautico, deltaplano ed equitazione esterni al villaggio, escursioni in battello.

Animazione

L'équipe del villaggio organizza giornalmente giochi, tornei sportivi e manifestazioni. La sera in anfiteatro oltre al ballo, spettacoli, cabaret, show. Tutte le attività sono garantite dal 19 giugno al 17 settembre.

Bambini

Miniclub dai 3 ai 10 anni con area riservata alle numerose attività giornaliere. È prevista l'assistenza anche durante il pranzo in un apposito spazio, con specifico menu (luglio e agosto).
A richiesta servizio di baby sitter.

Assistenza medica

Guardia medica e farmacia a 2 km dal villaggio.

Animali

Non sono ammessi.

Carte di credito

Sono accettate: VISA, CartaSi.

Come raggiungere il villaggio

Formula Transfer
Una combinazione speciale organizzata dal Touring comprensiva di viaggio aereo per Catania e trasferimento fino al villaggio.

Per chi raggiunge il villaggio con mezzi propri:

- **In aereo.** L'aeroporto più vicino è quello di Catania che dista 150 km.
- **In auto.** Autostrada Messina-Palermo uscita Patti e proseguimento in S.S. 113 in direzione Palermo.
- **In treno.** La stazione più vicina è quella di Patti che dista circa 13 km.

È possibile richiedere il servizio transfer (da pagare in loco) dall'aeroporto e dalla stazione ferroviaria. Le relative tariffe saranno comunicate al momento della prenotazione.

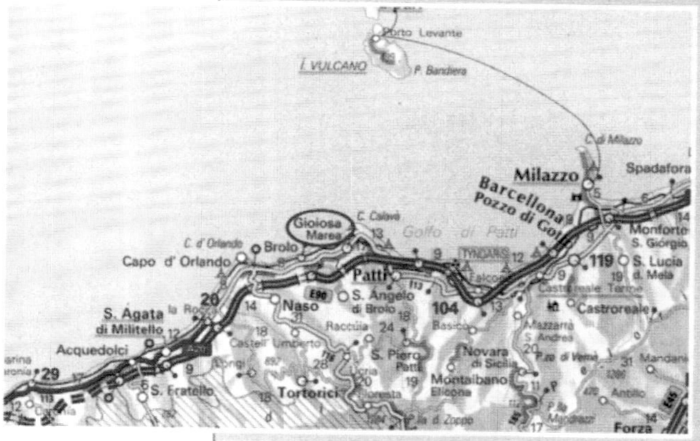

Le camere

Le camere vengono assegnate il giorno di arrivo dalle ore 17 e devono essere lasciate libere entro le ore 10 del giorno di partenza.

Cottage
Villette indipendenti doppie, triple e quadruple, con servizi, telefono diretto, ventilatori a pale e quasi tutte con vista mare.

Camere
Situate nel corpo centrale, con servizi, telefono diretto, ventilatore a pale e quasi tutte con vista mare.

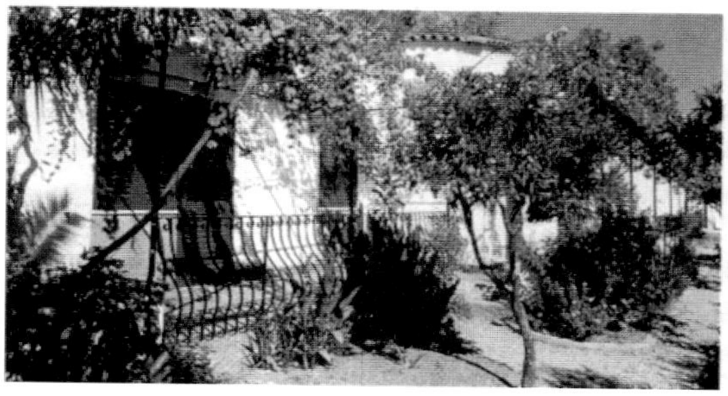

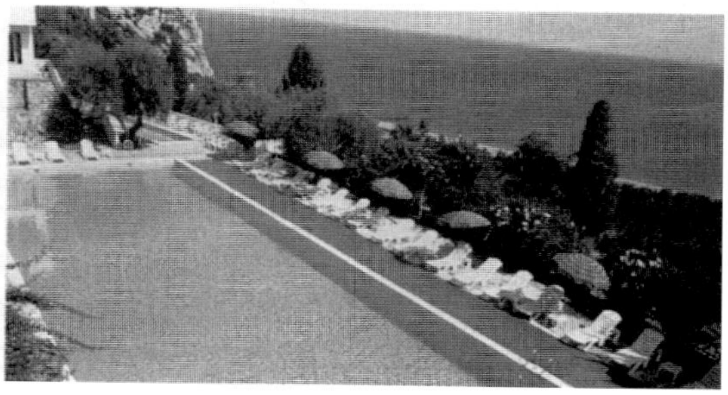

Parliamo 4

Prima telefonata: Alla tua famiglia. Loro si aspettano un racconto particolareggiato di come passi la giornata. Vuoi rassicurarli (sono un po' ansiosi) ma allo stesso tempo vuoi evitare che decidano di venire anche loro. Sarebbe la fine della tua immagine cool!

Seconda telefonata: A un collega. Anche il tuo collega si aspetta un racconto dettagliato. In questo caso vuoi esagerare un po' le cose, ben sapendo che la tua descrizione farà il giro dell'ufficio!

Dopo avere fatto una telefonata scambiate i ruoli.

Vocabolario

abbronzarsi
l'agenzia di viaggi
l'agriturismo
l'alta stagione
ammirare
andare in crociera
l'animatore
apprezzare
approfittare (di)
la bassa stagione
la borsa da viaggio
il clima
cogliere l'occasione (per)
la compagnia
divertirsi un mondo
i documenti di viaggio
fare vela / windsurf
fare sci alpino / di fondo / di discesa / estivo
il Ferragosto
le ferie
l'incontro
l'insenatura
l'isola
ai laghi
lamentarsi
un lembo di costa
al mare
in montagna
noleggiare
l'operatore turistico
l'ostello della gioventù
organizzare
il paesaggio
la pianura
il patrimonio artistico/culturale
pignolo
prenotare
raggiungibile
la ricettività turistica
il rifugio di montagna
rilassarsi / rilassante
riposare
selvatico
scoprire
la scorpacciata
scottarsi
in spiaggia
tener conto (di)
la testimonianza
il traghetto
il tratto costiero
il turismo culturale / di massa
le vacanze tutto compreso / di sopravvivenza
il villaggio vacanze

COSA MANCA?

Prima di parlare *Leggi il seguente articolo di giornale e cerca di indovinare, secondo il senso, le parole che sono state tolte.*

Firenze, un'altra ... (1) ... in una villa in ... (2) ...

Continuano le rapine nelle ville. L'ultima della serie è ... (3) ... domenica ... (4) ... in Toscana. Almeno 4 banditi, ... (5) ... di pistola e col ... (6) ... coperto, hanno fatto irruzione in una villa nei pressi di Figline Valdarno (Firenze). I malviventi che sono ... (7) ... ad aprire una cassaforte, hanno preso ... (8) ... e ... (9) ... per centinaia di milioni. Avevano ... (10) ... che rincasasse l'ingegner M.B., di 34 anni, con la ... (11) ... L'uomo è stato aggredito, ha tentato di ... (12) ..., ed è stato duramente picchiato (40 ... (13) ... di prognosi). Poi ... (14) ... e figlio sono stati ... (15) ... in uno sgabuzzino.

(Corriere della sera, 19/1/2000)

Parliamo *Lavorate a gruppi di 3 o 4. Dopo aver discusso i vari suggerimenti, cercate di mettervi d'accordo su tutte le parole che mancano. Poi l'insegnante vi farà vedere la versione originale.*

Espressioni utili

- Non ho alcun dubbio che la parola mancante qui è ...
- Una cosa è certa, la parola mancante non può essere ...
- Non sono al cento per cento sicuro/a ...
- Dal punto di vista grammaticale quello che dici non è possibile ...
- Qui ci vuole un verbo/un sostantivo ...
- Secondo me, ci sono varie possibilità, ad esempio ...
- Se non sbaglio si possono usare parecchie parole che hanno lo stesso significato ...
- Capisco benissimo perché pensi che sia ..., però ...
- Pensavo che fosse ... ma pensandoci meglio sono convinto/a che ...
- Hai perfettamente ragione
- A mio parere hai intuito/indovinato bene
- A dire il vero non ne ho la più pallida idea

Vocabolario

l'aggettivo
l'avverbio
concordare
la congiunzione
la desinenza femminile / maschile / singolare / plurale
il modo indicativo / congiuntivo
il sostantivo
la preposizione semplice / articolata
il pronome
il tempo presente / l'imperfetto / il passato prossimo / il futuro
un verbo di prima / seconda/ terza coniugazione
un verbo regolare / irregolare

C'È UNA PERSONA CHE...?

Prima di parlare *Leggi attentamente le seguenti frasi*

Trova una persona che:

	Persona 1	Persona 2	Persona 3	Persona 4
vive in campagna				
parla correntemente due lingue straniere				
è stata in Italia più di una volta				
ha vissuto all'estero				
non fa mai colazione				
non ha mai avuto un animale domestico				
preferisce ascoltare la radio che guardare la televisione				
beve vino quasi ogni giorno				
pratica uno sport				
ha una passione per la lettura				
tiene una tartaruga in giardino				
dorme senza cuscino				
ha partecipato a un quiz televisivo				
ha vinto al Totocalcio				

Parliamo 1 *Adesso fai il giro della classe e cerca di intervistare almeno 4 persone, annotando brevemente le loro risposte e scrivendo i nomi degli intervistati.*

Parliamo 2 *A vicenda ognuno deve parlare il più dettagliatamente possibile di una persona che ha intervistato.*

Parliamo 3 *Ognuno sceglie un membro della classe che non conosce bene e conduce la stessa intervista in modo più approfondito.*

Espressioni utili

- Allora, da quanto tempo vivi in/a ...?
- Quali lingue straniere ...?
- Quando hai imparato a ...?
- Quante volte sei stato/a in ...?
- Dove sei stato/a esattamente?
- Per quanto tempo ...?
- Per quali motivi ...?
- Come mai non fai colazione?
- Perché non hai avuto ...?
- Non ti piacciono gli animali?
- Quali sport pratichi?
- Ho notato che hai una passione per ...
- Qualcuno mi ha detto che ...

Vocabolario

abituarsi (a)
adorare
allergico
le attualità
essere appassionato (di)
fare bene alla salute
fin da giovane
iniziare (a)
mancare
la pace
il programma
una questione di abitudine
il radiogiornale
servire
stufarsi (di)
il telegiornale
le telenovele
tenersi aggiornato
un topo di biblioteca
utile
la vita solitaria

Unità 50

CARO DIARIO

Prima di parlare *Copia questa pagina di diario nel tuo quaderno e completala nelle prossime due settimane. Non è necessario scrivere qualcosa per ogni giorno ma forse, per alcuni giorni puoi annotare due o tre attività / appuntamenti differenti, come negli esempi.*

Mese ....

1 cena da Maria? ....
2 ....
3 dentista 10.00/compleanno di Costantino ....
4 ....
5 ....
6 ....
7 ....
8 ....
9 ....
10 ....
11 ....
12 ritirare i biglietti all'agenzia di viaggi
13 ....
14 ....

Parliamo *Ora confronta il tuo diario con quello di un compagno di classe, spiegando dettagliatamente gli impegni che hai elencato.*

Espressioni utili

- Il primo del mese devo andare ...
- Il tre febbraio/marzo ... ho fissato un appuntamento con ...
- Non ho ancora niente in programma per ...
- Questo appuntamento deve essere ancora confermato. Ecco perché ...
- Il dodici devo ricordarmi di ritirare i biglietti dall'agenzia ...
- All'inizio della settimana prossima, cioè l'otto, spero di ...
- Il cinque del mese ho intenzione di ...
- Il dieci, salvo imprevisti, sono deciso/a a ...
- Sono sicuro/a di avere qualche impegno la mattina del dieci ma ...
- Se non sbaglio devo andare da qualche parte la sera del nove ...
- Non ho ancora scritto niente sul diario ma se ricordo bene ...

Vocabolario

accettare
andare all'aria
l'anniversario
annullare
cambiare idea
capitare
confermare
dimenticarsi (di)
disdire
festeggiare
gli impegni di lavoro / di studio / professionali
inaspettatamente
invitare
mandare un e-mail
mensile
mettersi d'accordo
l'onomastico
organizzare
per caso
per fortuna
per via di
il progetto / progettare (di)
il programma
quotidiano
recarsi (a/da)
ricevere un messaggio
ricordarsi (di)
rifiutare
rimandare (a)
rinunciare (a)
riorganizzare
la riunione
settimanale
sfortunatamente

Unità 51

GIOCO 1

Prima di parlare *Leggi attentamente le seguenti frasi facendo particolare attenzione alle parole sottolineate.*

Dopo essere tornato/a a casa dal lavoro ho fatto subito la doccia. Poi, invece di accendere la televisione per guardare il telegiornale delle 18.00, una mia abitudine giornaliera, mi sono messo/a a leggere il giornale. Dopo aver letto il giornale dall'inizio alla fine ero così stanco/a che mi sono addormentato/a. Dopo essermi svegliato/a mi sono reso/a conto che era ora di andare a letto. Prima di andare a letto mi sono preparato/a un bel tè caldo. Che serata! Sono andato/a a letto senza nemmeno mangiare.

Parliamo 1 *Lavorate a gruppi di 4. A vicenda ognuno deve creare una situazione in cui è possibile usare le preposizioni* ***senza, invece di, prima di, per, dopo,*** *seguite da un infinito. Notate in particolare la struttura* ***dopo avere/essere*** *ecc. Non importa in quale ordine vengono usate le preposizioni. Forse è meglio scegliere un argomento specifico, per esempio vacanze, cibo, passatempi, studi ecc. in modo da avere un contesto in cui usare le varie preposizioni. Ogni studente può avere un massimo di tre minuti di preparazione prima di parlare.*

Parliamo 2 *I gruppi vengono riorganizzati in modo da poter scambiare i vari esempi che sono stati creati.*

Regole del gioco

a. Due punti per ogni frase corretta che contiene una delle preposizioni sopraccitate più l'infinito.
b. La preposizione **dopo** ognuna delle seguenti frasi: dopo aver(e) ...; dopo essere ...; dopo essersi ... vale tre punti.
c. Quando si usa la stessa preposizione o la stessa struttura es. **dopo aver...** una seconda volta, questa vale solo un punto.
d. Nel caso ci siano dubbi l'insegnante farà da arbitro.

GIOCO 2

Prima di parlare *Guarda i seguenti verbi e cerca sul dizionario il significato di quelli che non capisci.*

17 rimanere	28 uscire	133 mettere	199 assumere	225 fare
299 essere	1008 noleggiare	174 pulire	221 chiedere	266 abituarsi
13.300 piacere	9.900 prendere	15.750 scegliere	21.990 cercare	427 prenotare
14.000 venire	10.500 frequentare	160.000 potere	2.250.000 chiudere	28.665 avere
59.200 vedere	110 rendersi conto	17.700 affittare	23.975.000 leggere	29.000 partire
16 vincere	112 scrivere	10.185 tradurre	224.000 rompere	330.000 annoiarsi

Parliamo *La classe verrà divisa in 4 o 5 gruppi. L'insegnante farà una domanda sull'Italia. Qualsiasi membro del gruppo scelto (A,B,C...) può rispondere alla domanda. Se la risposta è giusta tocca a uno studente di quel gruppo scegliere un numero. Se lo dice correttamente avrà il diritto di usare il verbo che appare nella stessa casella in una frase al presente, al futuro e al passato prossimo, cercando di scegliere un contesto differente per ogni frase, come nell'esempio qui sotto. Viene assegnato un punto per ogni verbo usato nella forma corretta.*

Esempio: Mandare

1. **Mando** *(presente)* sempre tante cartoline ai miei parenti e amici quando vado in vacanza.
2. **Manderò** *(futuro)* alcune foto della nostra spedizione ai giornali.
3. **Ho mandato** *(passato prossimo)* dei fiori alla mia migliore amica per il suo diciottesimo compleanno.

Espressioni utili

- Normalmente ...
- Di solito ...
- Ogni tanto ...
- Ogni giorno/mattina/pomeriggio/sera ...
- Di mattina ...
- Di pomeriggio ...
- Di sera ...
- A volte... altre volte ...
- Fra poco ...
- La settimana prossima ...
- A luglio ...
- Ieri sera/mattina/pomeriggio ...
- Ieri l'altro ...
- Sabato scorso ...
- La settimana scorsa ...
- Alcuni anni fa ...

Regole del gioco

1. L'insegnante avrà l'incarico di fare le domande sull'Italia e di assegnare i punti ai vari gruppi.
2. Se per esempio il gruppo A non è in grado di rispondere, la domanda passa al gruppo B ecc.
3. Se il gruppo risponde correttamente alla domanda tocca a un solo membro del gruppo scegliere un numero. (Gli altri dovranno aspettare il loro turno). Se dice il numero correttamente deve mettere il verbo in una frase al presente, al futuro e al passato prossimo. Se sbaglia il numero perde il suo turno e l'insegnante fa una domanda al gruppo successivo.
4. Ogni frase corretta guadagna un punto. L'insegnante farà da arbitro. Se uno studente sbaglia una frase, il prossimo gruppo avrà la possibilità di guadagnarsi un punto in più.

Unità 53

BUTTIAMO VIA

Prima di parlare *Stai mettendo in ordine la tua casa/ il tuo appartamento e decidi di sbarazzarti di certe cose che non ti servono più. Fai un elenco di almeno cinque cose che butteresti via giustificando le tue decisioni, come nell'esempio.*

Esempio:

Ho sempre tenuto i miei quaderni di scuola. Ormai non li guardo da parecchi anni e sono sicuro che non mi serviranno mai più. Occupano tanto spazio nella mia camera, per cui ho deciso di buttarli via.

Parliamo 1 *A coppie confrontate il vostro elenco discutendo e giustificando le vostre decisioni. A vicenda cercate di convincere l'un l'altro a riflettere sulla decisione, suggerendo se possibile una soluzione alternativa.*

Espressioni utili

- Mi rincresce buttare via ... ma mi manca lo spazio ...
- Dopo averci pensato a lungo ho deciso di ...
- Capisco benissimo la ragione per cui vuoi buttare via ...
- Mi rendo conto che non usi ... da parecchio tempo però ...
- Forse un giorno avrai bisogno di ...
- Secondo me, dovresti ripensarci ...
- Invece di buttare via ... potresti ...
- Se io fossi in te non butterei mai via una cosa del genere ...
- Peccato gettare via ...
- Sono d'accordo con quello che dici però ...
- In teoria questa è una buon'idea ma in pratica ...
- Non sopporto più il disordine
- Occupa un sacco di spazio

Parliamo 2 *Adesso i gruppi vengono riorganizzati. Comunica le tue decisioni a un compagno di classe differente, il quale a vicenda comunicherà le sue. Il tuo compagno precedente ti ha convinto a tenere alcune cose che volevi buttare via. Quali per esempio? Spiega perché hai cambiato idea.*

Espressioni utili

- Allora alla fine ho deciso di non buttare via ...
- Il mio compagno mi ha convinto a cambiare idea perché ...
- Tutto considerato ho cambiato idea perché ...
- Il mio compagno mi ha fatto capire che ... per cui ...
- Non mi sono reso/a conto che ...
- A dire il vero non avevo pensato alla possibilità di ...

Vocabolario

l'armadio
(non) avere (più) bisogno (di)
buttare via
il cassetto
conservare
essere attaccato (a)
essere di gran valore
fare le pulizie di primavera
il disordine / in disordine
ingombrare / ingombrante
mancare
non avere il coraggio (di)
non avere rimpianti
non servire a nulla
organizzazioni benevole
per beneficenza
per motivi sentimentali
privo di valore
raccogliere polvere
regalare / il regalo
riciclare carta, indumenti, vetro
riorganizzare
risalire (a)
sbarazzarsi (di)
lo spazio
usare
utile / inutile
(non) valere la pena

ABITUDINI

Prima di parlare *Leggi le seguenti domande e indica con una crocetta quelle che corrispondono alle tue abitudini.*

1. Tendi ad imitare quello che fanno i tuoi amici?
2. Ti alzi sempre alla stessa ora?
3. Bevi sempre un tè/caffè dopo i pasti?
4. Trovi facile prendere decisioni?
5. Riservi una serata fissa ogni settimana da dedicare a qualche divertimento per esempio: andare al cinema, andare in discoteca, giocare a carte, fare aerobica, fare footing?
6. Tendi a mangiare sempre alla stessa ora – colazione, pranzo, cena?
7. Sai esattamente quello che mangerai a cena in un determinato giorno della settimana?
8. Sei riluttante ad assaggiare cibi che non conosci?
9. Fai la spesa sempre lo stesso giorno/gli stessi giorni della settimana e negli stessi negozi?
10. Arrivi sempre in anticipo per un appuntamento?
11. Decidi sempre molto in anticipo quando e dove vai in vacanza?
12. Vai a letto sempre alla stessa ora?
13. Frequenti sempre le stesse persone?

Parliamo 1 *A coppie confrontate le domande che avete indicato con una crocetta, discutendo le eventuali differenze.*

Espressioni utili

- È vero che mi alzo sempre ...
- Ormai alzarmi alla stessa ora fa parte di una routine giornaliera che ...
- Mi sono abituato/a ...
- Da parecchi anni ho l'abitudine di ...
- Ho sempre avuto difficoltà a prendere decisioni, per esempio ...
- Sono un tipo conservatore per cui non assaggio mai cibi ...
- Fare sempre le stesse cose mi farebbe impazzire
- Non sono un tipo abitudinario

Parliamo 2 *Ora confrontate le domande che non avete indicato con una crocetta, spiegando perché non corrispondono alle vostre abitudini.*

Espressioni utili

- È vero che imito ogni tanto gli altri, ma in genere ...
- Fino a un certo punto questo è vero, però ...
- Generalmente non mi alzo mai alla stessa ora ...
- L'ora in cui mangio dipende molto dai miei impegni. Se per esempio ...
- La ragione per cui mi è possibile mangiare alla stessa ora è che ...
- Direi che sono un tipo piuttosto avventuroso e quindi mi piace/mi è sempre piaciuto ...
- Devo confessare che per quanto riguarda la puntualità ...
- Quando si tratta di andare in vacanza tendo a lasciare tutto all'ultimo momento ...
- Ti faccio un esempio ...

Parliamo 3 *Ci sono abitudini di cui sei schiavo che non sono contenute nella lista in* ***Prima di parlare****? Quali? A coppie confrontatele discutendo le eventuali differenze.*

Vocabolario

l'abitudine / abitudinario
l'ansia / ansioso
l'avventura / avventuroso
cercare (di)
una cerchia di amici
contare (su)
deciso (a)
dipendere (da)
la disciplina / disciplinato
l'eccesso (di)
fare a modo proprio
fare quello che si vuole
l'impegno / impegnato
imprevedibile
inaspettato
la mancanza (di)
meticoloso
la noia / noioso
la novità
l'orario
organizzarsi / organizzato
(non) poter fare a meno (di)
predire
la puntualità / puntuale
regolare / irregolare
rimanere a letto
(non) riuscire (a)
la sorpresa

Unità 55

UN GIORNO NELLA VITA DI...

Prima di parlare *Guarda il seguente disegno e poi leggi le domande. Rifletti alcuni minuti sulle tue risposte alle domande.*

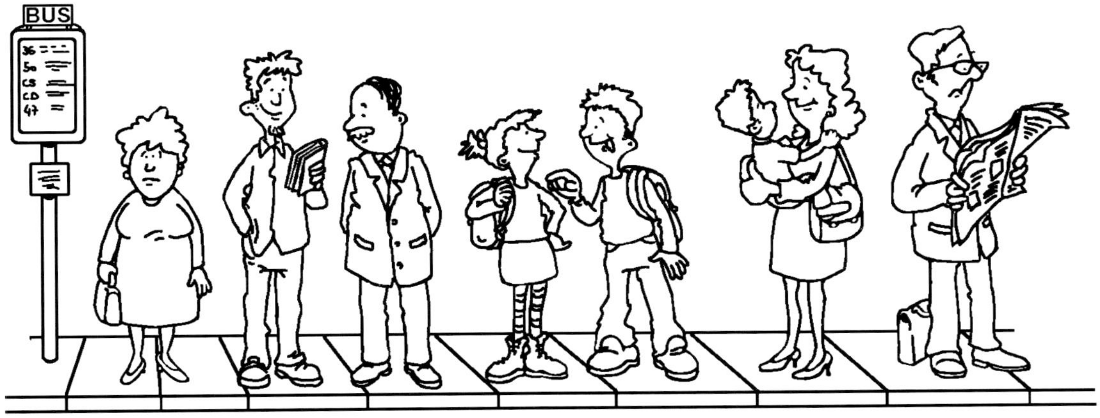

1. Dove e quando ha luogo questa scena?
2. Cosa stanno facendo queste persone?
3. Come ti sembrano – felici, tristi, pazienti …?
4. Cosa farà ogni persona quando scenderà dall'autobus?
5. Con quale persona potresti identificarti meglio?

Parliamo 1 *Adesso confronta le tue risposte con quelle di alcuni compagni, discutendo le eventuali differenze.*

Parliamo 2 *A coppie scegliete due persone che aspettano in fila e cercate di immaginare la conversazione che si svolge tra di loro.*

Parliamo 3 *A coppie. Ognuno deve immaginare di essere una persona del gruppo e descrivere una giornata tipica della persona scelta. (Per* **Parole ed espressioni utili** *vedi pagina 50)*

Parliamo 4 *A coppie. Ciascuno di voi è una persona nel gruppo. Vi ritrovate dopo molti anni e ripensate al periodo in cui è stata scattata la fotografia. Scambiatevi i ricordi di quella giornata.*

Unità 56

ALBERO GENEALOGICO

Prima di parlare *Nelle caselle qui sotto scrivi i nomi di quattro persone che conosci bene. Possono essere componenti della tua famiglia o amici.*

1	2	3	4

Parliamo 1 *Adesso il tuo compagno ti farà le domande qui sotto, alle quali devi rispondere il più dettagliatamente possibile. Attenzione! A seconda della persona non sarà forse appropriato fare tutte le domande.*

1. Qual è il cognome di questa persona?
2. Come si scrive?
3. Chi è?
4. Quanti anni ha?
5. Quando è il suo compleanno?
6. È sposato/a?
7. Ha figli? Quanti? Come si chiamano?
8. Dove abita ...?
9. Lo/la vedi spesso? Quando? Cosa fate insieme?
10. Mi puoi descrivere questa persona?
11. Quali sono i suoi passatempi preferiti?
12. Mi puoi raccontare una giornata tipica di una di queste persone?

Espressioni utili

- È un mio amico/una mia amica ...
- È una mia zia ...
- Ha compiuto 45 anni un mese fa ...
- Compirà 18 anni a giugno ...
- Non ricordo con esattezza ma penso che abbia sui 50 anni ...
- È libero/fidanzato/sposato/separato/divorziato/vedovo ...
- Abita in (piena) campagna/in città/in periferia/in una zona residenziale ...
- Lo/la vedo una volta al mese ...
- Ci vediamo raramente perché ...
- È alto/a, basso/a, / di statura media ...
- È magro/a, grasso/a, robusto/a ...
- Ha i capelli castani, grigi, ricci, lisci, ondulati, corti, lunghi ...
- Porta gli occhiali/le lenti a contatto ...
- È simpatico/a, gentile, timido/a, ambizioso/a, paziente, impulsivo/a ...
- Durante il tempo libero gli/le piace ...

Parliamo 2 *Ora è il tuo turno rivolgere le stesse domande in* ***Parliamo 1*** *al tuo compagno.*

DISEGNIAMO

Prima di parlare *Nel tuo quaderno fai uno schizzo del tuo appartamento o del pianterreno della tua casa. Sullo schizzo puoi indicare la posizione delle finestre e della porta d'ingresso. Prima di dare questo schizzo al tuo compagno devi tener presente dove si trovano esattamente le stanze e la posizione dei mobili in queste stanze. Se preferisci fa' un altro schizzo sul quale puoi disegnare le stanze e i mobili ma senza farlo vedere al tuo compagno, naturalmente.*

Parliamo 1 *Lavorate in coppia A e B. Lo studente A descrive il più dettagliatamente possibile la propria casa/appartamento. Lo studente B deve disegnarla/lo in base alle istruzioni del compagno. Poi scambiate i ruoli.*

Espressioni utili

- Il pianterreno della mia casa / il mio appartamento è composto da ... stanze ...
- Appena entri ...
- A destra / sulla destra ...
- A sinistra / sulla sinistra ...
- Questa stanza occupa ...
- Accanto a ...
- Di fronte a ...
- In fondo a ...
- In mezzo a ...
- La cucina è a forma di ...
- Il soggiorno è lungo ... metri e largo... metri ...
- Sul lato sinistro / destro della casa / dell'appartamento ...
- Questa stanza dà su / accede a ...

Parliamo 2 *Ora guardate insieme i due disegni e correggete i dettagli sbagliati.*

Espressioni utili

- Evidentemente qui c'è stato un malinteso ...
- Non ho detto che ...
- Non mi hai capito bene perché la cucina ...
- Questa stanza è un po' meno grande / larga / lunga ...

- Perché hai messo il divano qui? Io ti avevo detto che ...
- Hai sbagliato la posizione di questo tavolo. Dovrebbe essere ...
- Non riesco a capire perché ...
- Come mai hai disegnato il soggiorno a forma di... quando ho detto chiaramente che ...

Parliamo 2 *Ora disegna la casa / l'appartamento dei tuoi sogni e poi confrontala/lo con quella/quello del tuo compagno*

Vocabolario

l'abitazione
l'alloggio
l'armadio
l'ascensore
la biblioteca
la cantina
il cassettone
disegnare
l'edificio
l'ingresso
la lampada
a lato
il mobile
il piano
il pianterreno
la poltrona
il posto auto
la scala interna / esterna
lo scaffale
lo scantinato
il soggiorno
il tavolo / il tavolino
il vano
la villa
la villetta a schiera

Unità 57 B

I CASI DELLA VITA

Prima di parlare *Guarda bene la vignetta che ti verrà assegnata dall'insegnante. Devi essere in grado di spiegarla chiaramente ai tuoi compagni. Serviti del dizionario se necessario.*

Parliamo *La classe verrà divisa in gruppi di 6. Ogni gruppo formerà un cerchio. A vicenda ognuno descrive la propria vignetta e lo scopo dell'attività è quello di mettere tutte le vignette in una sequenza narrativa logica.*

Espressioni utili

- Allora chi vuole cominciare?
- Comincio io...
- Adesso tocca a te descrivere il tuo disegno
- Nel mio disegno c'è/ci sono ...
- Non capisco esattamente quello che succede ma ...
- Ecco tutto, non ho altro da dire
- Secondo me il primo disegno deve essere quello di ...
- Non ho alcun dubbio che il secondo disegno è il tuo ...
- Allora devi cambiare posto, vieni a sederti qua
- Non sono ancora convinto/a che ...
- Vuoi descrivere il tuo disegno un'altra volta?
- Secondo me, sarebbe meglio che le prime tre persone descrivessero di nuovo i loro disegni
- A mio parere, c'è qualcosa che non va bene ...
- Finalmente ci siamo. Allora ricominciamo daccapo ...

Unità 58

SONDAGGIO

Prima di parlare *Fai una lista di almeno dieci cose che hai fatto o che ti sono capitate nell'ultima settimana. (Nella tabella qui sotto c'è qualche idea.) Quando hai finito, cerca una persona che ha fatto le stesse cose oppure a cui sono capitate le stesse cose. Devi ottenere le risposte facendo domande per ogni fatto.*

Parliamo 1

Avvenimenti	Io	Nome 1	Nome 2	Nome 3
Ho comprato un paio di scarpe				
Sono andato/a al cinema				
Ho perso un oggetto				
Ho bevuto / mangiato troppo				
Sono andato/a in banca				
Sono andato/a a trovare amici				
Ho guardato un documentario alla televisione				
Mi sono innamorato/a				
Ho visitato una persona in ospedale				
Ho fatto una telefonata intercontinentale				
Ho litigato con un amico/una amica				
Sono uscito/a da casa senza chiavi / soldi / documenti				
Mi sono arrabbiato/a				
Ho preso una multa per eccesso di velocità				
Altro:				

Parliamo 2 *Quando hai trovato una o più persone che hanno dato risposte simili forma un altro gruppo e discuti ogni avvenimento dettagliatamente.*

Espressioni utili

- Quando/Dove ti è successo?
- Con chi eri?
- È la prima volta che ti succede?
- Non ti è mai successo prima?
- Che avventura!
- Che paura!
- Che coincidenza!
- Ma pensa! Anche a me è successa la stessa cosa
- È stato molto divertente/rassicurante/seccante/penoso ...
- È successo proprio mentre stavo facendo ...
- Spero non mi succeda mai più!

Chi ha la storia più interessante / divertente / originale?

Parliamo 3 *Un portavoce del tuo gruppo presenta la storia più interessante / divertente / originale agli altri gruppi.*

Unità 59

OSPITI

Prima di parlare 1 *Sei mai stato ospite a casa di amici o conoscenti? Hai mai ricevuto amici o conoscenti a casa tua per un fine settimana o una vacanza? Hai mai partecipato a uno scambio con un amico/un'amica di penna? Rifletti su una tua esperienza, positiva o negativa che sia, poi scrivi alcuni pensieri nelle caselle qui sotto o sul tuo quaderno.*

L'accoglienza

La tua stanza

Le regole della casa

Un momento imbarazzante

Il momento della partenza

I rapporti dopo la visita

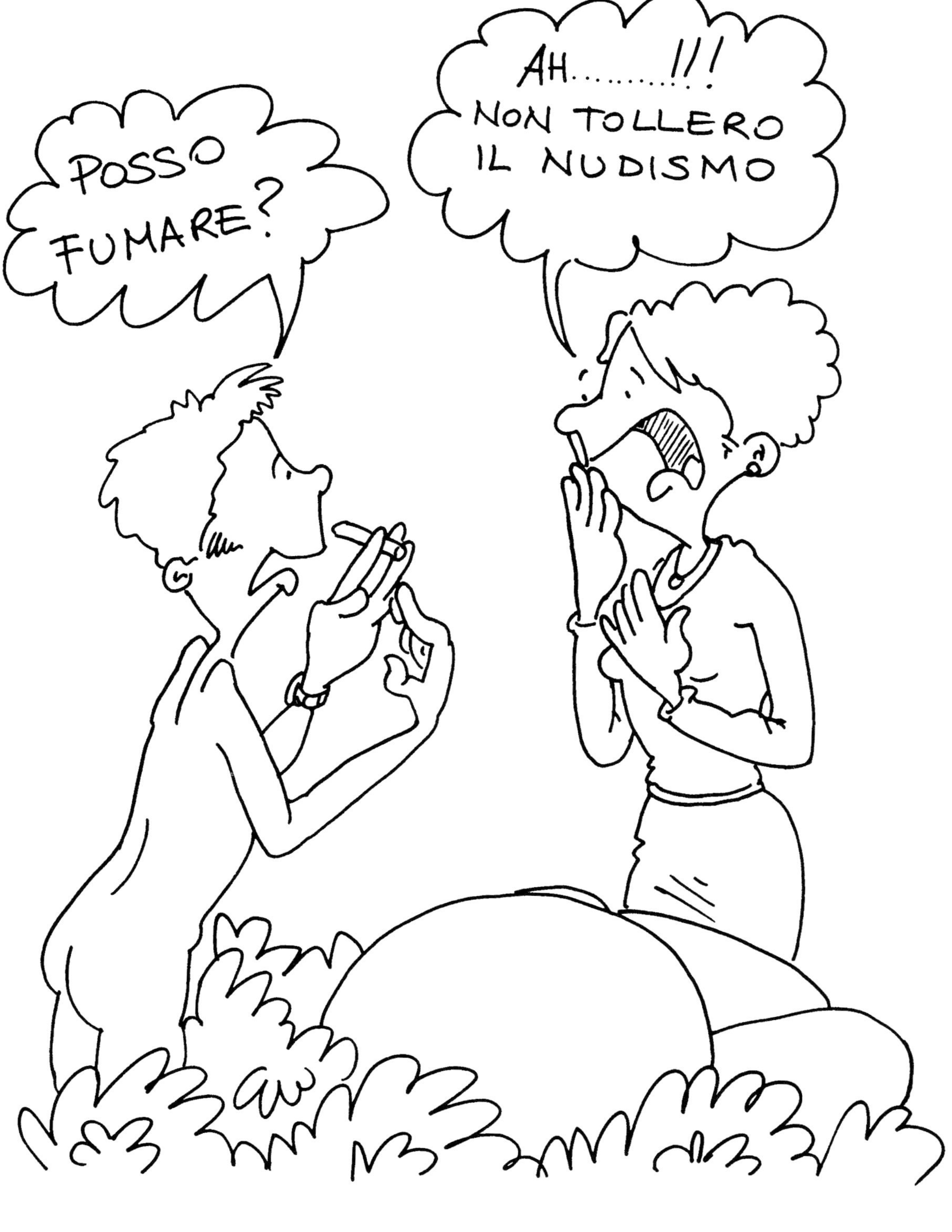
POSSO FUMARE?
AH.........!!! NON TOLLERO IL NUDISMO

Espressioni utili

- Ricordo di essere stato/a ospite da ... per una vacanza/uno scambio ...
- È stato facile/difficile ambientarmi ...
- L'atmosfera in famiglia era ...
- Sono stato/a accolto/a calorosamente .../piuttosto freddamente ...
- Purtroppo non ho previsto ...
- A tavola si parlava di ...
- Era chiaro che (non) si doveva ...
- Ho dovuto/Non potevo ...
- Non ero sicuro/a di come comportarmi ...
- Avevo aspettative differenti ...
- Mi aspettavo di ...
- È stato un momento molto (s)piacevole/imbarazzante ...
- Il comportamento della mia amica/del mio amico ...
- Da allora i rapporti si sono raffreddati ...
- Mi sono stupito/a che fosse così importante ...
- È una questione di buone maniere ...
- Per ringraziare, ho regalato ...

Parliamo 1 *A coppie o in gruppo scambia una tua esperienza con le altre persone. Chi ha avuto l'esperienza più piacevole? Chi ha avuto l'esperienza più sgradevole?*

Prima di parlare 2 *Leggi la lettera e nota come Fabrizia descrive l'esperienza e come esprime i suoi sentimenti.*

Caro Stefano,

Sì, lo so, avrei dovuto scriverti prima, ma ti assicuro che non ho avuto un attimo di tempo. Mi perdoni? Purtroppo da quando è arrivata l'amica di penna di mia figlia (sono solo due settimane ma mi sembrano due anni!) la vita familiare è diventata un inferno.
In fotografia Anna mi sembrava un angelo, bionda, delicata, molto perbene. Anche le lettere che ha mandato a Luisa promettevano bene. La realtà è ben diversa! Per cominciare si è presentata con un abbigliamento volgarissimo - minigonna vertiginosa in pelle rossa, anello all'ombelico (avresti dovuto vedere la faccia di zio Cesare ...). In effetti è abbastanza gentile e socievole con tutti in famiglia. Dovresti però vedere la sua stanza, sai quella che abbiamo ridipinto proprio per lei: tutti i vestiti buttati per terra, pezzi di panini sotto il letto, per non parlare della musica techno a volume, diciamo, un po' elevato. Non ha mai appetito al momento dei pasti (quando c'è) quindi ho deciso, per non farla morire di fame, di lasciarle qualcosa in frigo, così anche Luisa ha preso la pessima abitudine di sgranocchiare a tutte le ore. Non ha ancora alzato un dito per aiutare nelle faccende domestiche, in compenso però non ha ancora passato una serata in casa e ritorna tardissimo la sera. Dove andrà? Non oso chiedere. Luisa sta prendendo un sacco di cattive abitudini e io penso al peggio. Dove sono le mie pastiglie tranquillanti?
Telefonami presto. Sono allo stremo.

Fabrizia

Parliamo 2 *A coppie immaginate un dialogo fra Anna e Luisa / fra Luisa e la madre Fabrizia / fra Fabrizia e il fratello Stefano.*

Espressioni utili

- Ti sembra un comportamento accettabile ...?
- Io trovo incomprensibile / divertente / inaccettabile / perfettamente normale ...
- Se fossi in lei ...
- Non mi sembra consapevole ...
- Si tratta di divario generazionale ...
- Le più elementari norme di convivenza ...
- Dovresti metterti nei panni di ...
- Non te la prendere!
- Tu badi troppo alle apparenze. In realtà ...

Parliamo 3 *A gruppi. Che consigli dareste a Fabrizia? E secondo voi, come dovrebbe comportarsi l'ospite?*

Dopo aver completato questa parte presentate i vostri consigli agli altri gruppi e osservate se avete fatto gli stessi suggerimenti.

Vocabolario

accogliere
l'antipatia / antipatico
le aspettative
l'attrito
la buona educazione
i componenti della famiglia
la convivenza
dare il benvenuto
la famiglia ospitante
gradevole / sgradevole
la maleducazione
ospitare / l'ospitalità / l'ospite
partire / la partenza
presentare
presentarsi
a prima vista
il programma
il regalo
ringraziare
sdebitarsi
la simpatia / simpatico
la sorpresa
tollerare / (in)tollerante

Unità 60

IL MIO TELEFONINO

Prima di parlare 1 A che cosa mi serve il cellulare?
Se tu hai un cellulare o se conosci una persona che ne ha uno, fai una lista di occasioni in cui il telefonino è stato usato nell'ultima settimana.

Esempio: Giovedì sera stavo ritornando a casa in autobus e l'ho usato per disdire un appuntamento.

1. ....

2. ....

3. ....

4. ....

Parliamo 1 *A coppie o a gruppi di 3/4 persone. Ora confrontate le vostre liste. Chi ha fatto la telefonata più necessaria?*

Prima di parlare 2 Qual è il migliore?
Leggi l'articolo ***Mi regali un cellulare per Natale?*** *Per quale motivo scegli un cellulare? Scegli una delle possibilità – 'Per lavoro' oppure 'Per sfizio' oppure 'Per stile'. Prendi nota delle differenze fra un tipo di cellulare e l'altro offerto per ogni categoria e scegli quello che preferisci.*

shop

Mi regali un cellulare per Natale?

di Paolo Conti (conti@newmedia.it)

Il telefonino bisogna saperlo scegliere. I modelli in commercio sono tanti e le combinazioni di funzioni, tecnologie e look sono praticamente infinite. E allora, prima di recarci in negozio, dobbiamo capire come lo useremo. I prezzi, fra l'altro oscillano fra le 300.000 lire e il milione e mezzo. Quindi funzioni e caratteristiche vanno centellinate. Il telefonino del manager deluderà la cubista, e viceversa, ma il telefonino perfetto esiste: basta cercarlo.

Telefonini da lavoro, per gioco, di moda. Computer che si mettono al polso. Hi-fi tridimensionali. Guida ai doni supertecnologici

Per sfizio

Per chi ha deciso di comprare il cellulare, ma non sa bene perché (in fondo ce l'hanno tutti e senza telefonino fai la figura del dinosauro...). E allora ci vuole un modello carino, economico e senza troppe pretese, che sia solido e dia meno problemi possibili.

IN CINQUE COLORI

È facile da usare, piccolo e leggero, disponibile in cinque colori e dotato di tutte le funzioni essenziali di un Gsm dual band. In più ha il vibracall e memorizza i cinque messaggi Sms più usati. Il T10s della Ericsson si adatta a chi privilegia look e praticità alle funzioni sofisticate.
Prezzo: 520.000 lire, 268,56 euro
www.ericsson.it

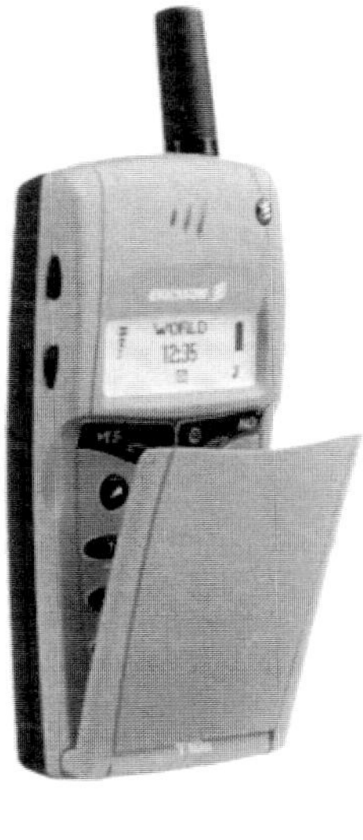

CELLULARE DA DISCOTECA

Irradia una luce colorata quando si usa al buio e garantisce fino a 4,5 ore di conversazione.
Il Gsm 509 dual band della Bosch fa moda in discoteca ed è difficile da perdere di notte.
Per il resto, le caratteristiche di questo dual band non hanno niente di straordinario, dimensioni comprese.
Prezzo: 410.000 lire, 268,56 euro
www.bosch.com

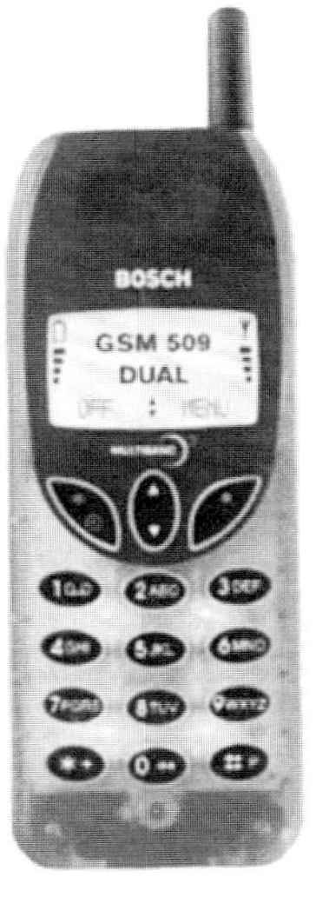

shop - shop - shop - shop - shop - shop - shop - shop

PER STILE **Un telefono cellulare dev'essere prima di tutto bello ed elegante: in fondo ce lo teniamo addosso tutti i giorni. E allora largo a dimensioni lillipuziane, a look aggressivi, ad antenne che scompaiono e a colori shocking (ma non troppo). Il telefonino può anche diventare un accessorio trendy e per distinguersi. Ma va scelto con cura.**

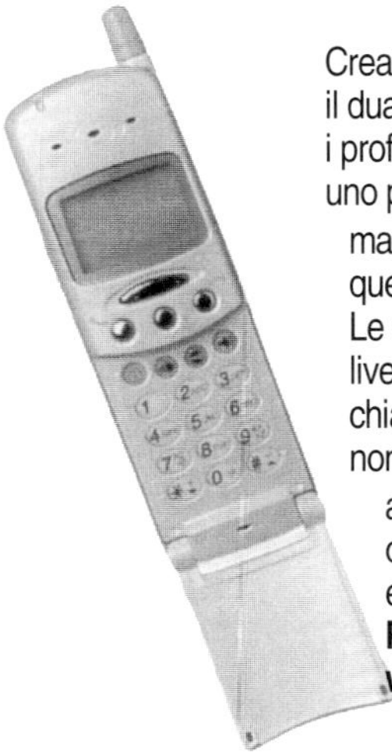

CELLULARE BISEX

Creato dalla Mitsubishi con marchio Trium, il dual band Aria è realizzato come i profumi creati da alcuni stilisti: uno per lei e uno per lui. La versione maschile ha una superficie scura, quella femminile ambrata. Le caratteristiche sono di buon livello: solo 85 grammi di peso, chiamata a vibrazione e sportellino non attivo (si può rispondere anche senza aprirlo). Garantisce oltre un'ora di conversazione e 80 ore di stand-by con la batteria slim a litio.
Prezzo: 720.000 lire, 371,85 euro
www.trium-gsm.com

SFILA CON KENZO

Ha sfilato con Kenzo a Parigi il Gsm dual band 8210 della Nokia. Sette colori diversi, 79 grammi di peso, 40 melodie diverse per la suoneria e supporto di tutte le lingue (cinese compreso) sono le caratteristiche di questo telefono; che sembra fatto apposta per essere mostrato. Inoltre, come anche altri modelli Nokia, permette di corredare con un disegno i messaggi Sms.
Prezzo: 1.300.000 lire, 671,39 euro
www.nokia.it

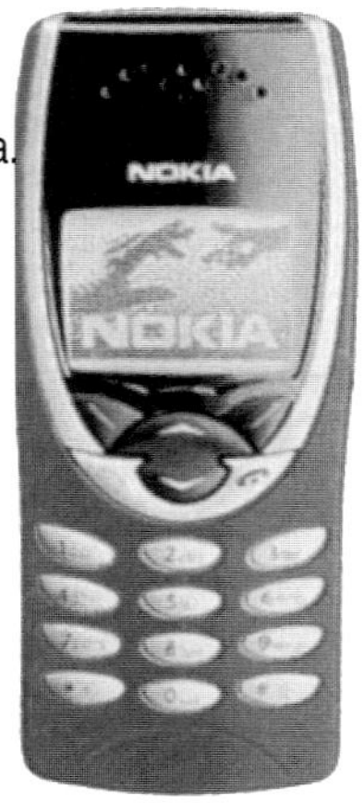

PER LAVORO **Il telefonino è prima di tutto uno strumento di lavoro. Dev'essere efficiente, durare a lungo e non deve rompersi mai. Il peso non dev'essere eccessivo, anche se si può sacrificare sull'altare della tecnologia (se serve). L'essenziale è tutto qui, anche se alcune funzioni speciali, come il modem all'infrarosso, sono sempre bene accette.**

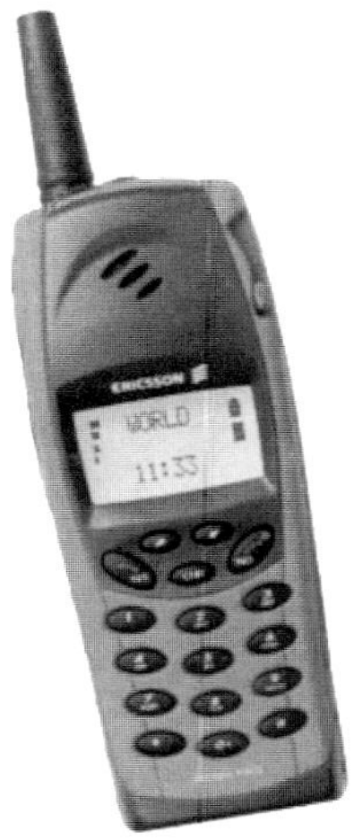

VESTITO DI GORETEX

Il R250 Pro della Ericsson è un cellulare da battaglia, superresistente. Ha la struttura in magnesio e un rivestimento in Goretex e gomma che lo protegge da acque e polvere. In più è dual band, ha un vivavoce incorporato, un tasto unico per accedere alle funzioni del telefono e un altro tasto, facile da premere, per le chiamate di emergenza.
Prezzo: circa 1.000.000 lire, 516,46 euro
www.ericsson.it

DIECI ORE DI CONVERSAZIONE

È il primo cellulare che la Acer, ex azienda di computer, vende in Italia. Il G520 non è dual band, ma con la batteria a lunga durata garantisce ben 10 ore di conversazione: un record. Essenziale nella forma e abbastanza leggero, questo Gsm è adatto a chi cerca un telefono semplice da usare.
Prezzo: a partire da 299.000 lire, 154,42 euro
www.acer.it

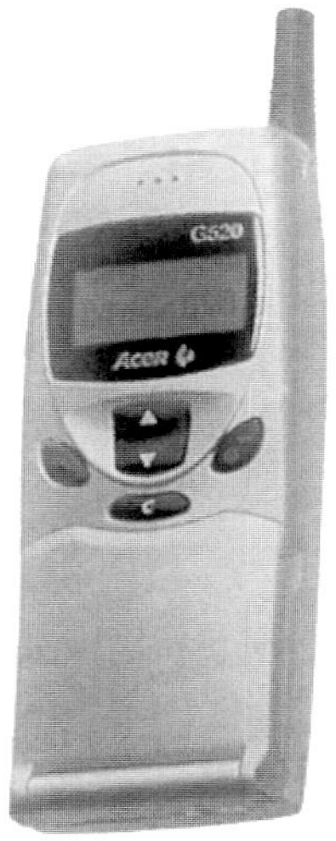

(Panorama Net, Mondadori. 9.12.1999 pp. 111-113)

Espressioni utili

- Per quale motivo hai usato ...?
- Guarda che bello!
- Hai mai visto un cellulare più carino / efficiente / sfizioso ...?
- Ha un numero incredibile di funzioni, per esempio ...
- Ma senti com'è leggero!
- Però il tuo è più pesante / costoso / meno colorato / resistente ...
- Secondo me, ha un prezzo eccessivo / eccezionale / conveniente ...
- È quanto di meglio esiste sul mercato ...
- È il più semplice / complicato da usare ...
- Ma il rapporto prezzo-qualità, dove lo metti?
- Ma come, anche il tuo ha ...?
- Hai fatto un'ottima scelta, però ...
- Sì, però il mio ha più funzioni del tuo ...
- Che bidone!

Parliamo 2 *Hai comprato il nuovo telefonino e sei felice e soddisfatto della tua scelta. Descrivilo a un amico/un'amica o a un/a collega. Anche loro però ne hanno uno, nuovo di zecca! Invidia? Gelosia? Cerca di capire se il loro è altrettanto bello come il tuo (sei sicuro/a di no!).*

Prima di parlare 3 Questionario Cellulare amore mio: qual è il migliore?

Compila il questionario segnando con una crocetta i dati che si riferiscono ai due telefonini della categoria - 'Per lavoro / Per sfizio / Per stile' - che hai scelto. Attenzione! Non tutte le funzioni nella tabella sono contenute nelle descrizioni dei telefonini.

(I nomi dei diversi cellulari sono: Ericsson = **E**, Bosch = **B**, Mitsubishi = **M**, Nokia = **N**, Acer = **A**)

FUNZIONI	E	B	M	N	A
Chiamata a vibrazione					
Calcolatore di bioritmi					
Luce colorata al buio					
Lingue straniere					
Memorizzazione messaggi					
Orologio					
Convertitore in Euro					
Vivavoce					
Suoneria					
Sportellino non attivo					
PESO					
PREZZO					

Parliamo 3 *In gruppo. È ora di fare una scelta! Consultate i vostri compagni e decidete qual è…*

Il più bello: . . . .
Il più pratico: . . . .
Il più economico:. . . . .
Il migliore per rapporto qualità-prezzo: . . . .

Vocabolario

l'abbonamento
l'accessorio
l'attrezzatura
la bellezza / bello
comunicare
la convenienza / convenienza
il costo
la funzione
indispensabile
l'invidia
la leggerezza
la necessità / necessario
la praticità / pratico
il regalo
togliersi uno sfizio

CERCO AMICI

Prima di parlare 1 Il tuo tipo

Quali sono, secondo te, le qualità essenziali nell'amicizia? E quali qualità preferiresti in una persona per stabilire un rapporto romantico? Quali caratteri o abitudini troveresti inaccettabili? Fai una lista.

	Rapporto d'amicizia	Rapporto amoroso	Rapporto fra colleghi
ideale	totale disponibilità		
accettabile	mancare qualche appuntamento		qualche pettegolezzo
inaccettabile		Calzini bianchi (specie se indossati con sandali!)	amoreggiare

Espressioni utili

- Cosa apprezzi di più in un amico/nel tuo ragazzo?
- C'è qualcosa che trovi inaccettabile?
- Che tipo di rapporto preferisci?
- Ho tanta voglia di incontrare un tipo ...
- Mi piacciono molto/Trovo insopportabili le persone che ...
- Mi dà/Mi danno parecchio fastidio ...
- Mi danno ai nervi certi atteggiamenti da ...
- In un rapporto d'amicizia vorrei idealmente ...
- Non ho ancora trovato l'anima gemella
- È importante avere interessi comuni?
- Hai pensato alle conseguenze di ... in un rapporto di lavoro?
- Una persona così mi sarebbe congeniale

PARTE A

Parliamo 1 *Ora confronta la tua lista con quella di altre due persone nel tuo gruppo. Avete qualcosa in comune? Ci sono differenze fra le risposte delle donne o di quelle degli uomini del gruppo?*

Prima di parlare 2 *Leggi gli annunci pubblicati su Campus, la rivista mensile per gli studenti universitari in Italia. C'è qualcuno che potrebbe interessarti?*

LUI & LEI

Giovane laureato milanese, 30enne, biondo, occhi azzurri, carino e simpatico, cerca ragazza molto femminile, elegante, amante del mare e della barca, scopo seria relazione. **Marco, tel. 0338/9854351**

Veronicaaaa! Sì, mi riferisco a te: 22 anni, simpatica, carina, sportiva, bionda e maggiorata, nel tuo annuncio mi hai praticamente descritto. Mi chiamo Alessio, il mio indirizzo lo hai e se vuoi potremo iniziare a scriverci. A presto! **Alessio Bagnoli, via Puccini 10 50050 Cerreto Guidi (Fi)**

Salve! Mi chiamo Antonio detto Tonio, ho 28 anni, lavoro e studio Ingegneria. Sono molto sportivo e audace, amo conoscere nuove persone, femmine o maschi che siano. Per chi cerca una forte amicizia, io sono l'ideale. **Antonio Navarino, via Borgo S. Pietro 83 - 40126 Bologna, tel. 0339/4501449**

Cerco penfriends che abbiano bisogno e voglia di confrontarsi per crescere insieme. Ho 21 anni e tanta voglia di vivere! Vi aspetto! Iaia. **Ilaria Scatassi, via delle Querce 9 61030 Tavernelle (Pesaro)**

Simpaticissimo 26enne, maturo, molto sensibile, romantico, leale, carismatico, molteplici interessi culturali, alto, carino, cerca ragazza seria, dolcissima, tenera, esclusivamente motivata al fidanzamento (no perditempo). **Telefonare le ore 20,30 allo 0347/6144854**

Cerco la ragazza dei sogni, simpatica, carina, alta tra 1,55 e 1,65, magari rossa e con tanta voglia di ridere, romantica e con una cifra di buon umore. Se esisti, rintracciami! **Michele Esposito, via 2ª traversa Coste d'Agnano 46 - 80078 Pozzuoli (Na), tel. 0338/7779499**

Ho 22 anni e sto cercando la mia indipendenza per vivere. Se anche tu cerchi la tua libertà, chiama! Solo Centro-nord, dopo ore 20,00, **tel. 0347/9065659**

Nell'era dell'immagine, capita di sentirsi soli, perché tutto è ridotto a bellezza effimera. Se credi a ciò che c'è dentro e pensi che un 24enne sia la tua possibile anima gemella, **telefonami al numero 0368/7060057**

Ragazzo scapestrato di 31 anni cerca ragazzi o ragazze per creare compagnia a Milano e limitrofi Saronno. Se avete voglia di scrivere fatelo! Vi aspetto! **Phil. Filippo Fossati, via L. da Vinci 14 - 21047 Saronno (Va); tel. 0347/2550950.**

Parliamo 2 Coraggio, buttati!

Studente A *Hai deciso! Oggi telefoni alla persona che ti sembra più congeniale. Presentati, spiega perché telefoni, parla di te e soprattutto cerca di scoprire se la persona reale veramente corrisponde alla descrizione che ha fatto di sé. Se c'è un feeling fra di voi, come mandate avanti la cosa?*

Studente B *Sei un po' depresso/a perché nessuno ha risposto al tuo annuncio su Campus. Avrai dato un'impressione sbagliata di te? Mentre pensi a come cambieresti l'annuncio per avere maggiore successo suona il telefono. La chiamata è per te!*

Parliamo 3 *Racconta al tuo migliore amico / alla tua migliore amica che hai trovato la persona dei tuoi sogni in un annuncio. Racconta la tua telefonata (***Parliamo 2***), descrivi la persona e spiega perché hai scelto proprio quella.*

Espressioni utili

- Sai che cercavo ... ebbene, questa settimana ...
- Mi sembra proprio di aver trovato .../che sia ...
- Lei dice di essere dolcissima e tenera, però mi sembra piuttosto ...
- Purtroppo cerca solo un rapporto trasgressivo ...
- È difficile giudicare il carattere da una telefonata, però mi pare che ...
- È totalmente carismatico!

(Source; Campus, ottobre 1999 p. 130)

PARTE B

Parliamo 4 *A coppie. Studiate la tabella e discutete i risultati. Immaginate lo stesso questionario nel vostro Paese: le risposte sarebbero simili? Se no, perché no? Qual è la vostra opinione sui rapporti sentimentali fra colleghi? Siete d'accordo o avete opinioni diverse a proposito?*

Nel suo posto di lavoro i rapporti sentimentali fra colleghi sono giudicati:

	nord ovest	**nord est**	**centro**	**sud e isole**
bene....................................	**17,9%**	**9,2%**	**10,9%**	**18,0%**
male....................................	**21,5%**	**14,6%**	**21,4%**	**15,5,%**
né bene né male/ ininfluenti...........................	**60,6%**	**76,2%**	**67,7%**	**66,5%**

I datori di lavoro italiani risultano sostanzialmente indifferenti in materia di amori aziendali. Prevale la sospensione del giudizio ma, fra le minoranze che si schierano, i contrari sono più numerosi.

Unità 62

SEI ORGANIZZATO?

Prima di parlare 1 *Ricordi il proverbio "Ogni cosa al suo posto, un posto per ogni cosa"? Ti riconosci? Pensi di essere una persona organizzata? Allora, cosa fa quel calzino sporco sopra il termosifone nell'ingresso? Fai una piccola prova e cerca di ricordare dove hai lasciato questi oggetti:*

?

il tuo passaporto	l'ultimo estratto conto della banca	le chiavi di casa
la bolletta del telefono	i documenti della macchina	l'ombrello
il dizionario italiano		

Espressioni utili

- Hai mai dimenticato/smarrito ...?
- Sei sicuro/a che... sia sempre al suo posto?
- Credo di essere abbastanza ordinato/a piuttosto disordinato/a ...
- Il guaio è che ...
- Normalmente posso trovare... in pochi minuti ...
- Non ricordo assolutamente dove ho messo ...
- Tengo un archivio ...
- I miei armadi/I cassetti sono strapieni ...
- Oddio, dove avrò cacciato ...?

Parliamo 1 *A coppie o a gruppi descrivete come cercate di mantenere l'organizzazione domestica, dando esempi pratici.*

Prima di parlare 2 *Compila una delle griglie (A, B o C). Studia la lista di oggetti che si trovano comunemente nelle case. Dove sono tenuti, di solito? Rispondi e poi chiedi agli altri studenti dove loro tengono questi oggetti, normalmente.*

GRIGLIA A

	A casa tua	Persona 1	Persona 2
gli appunti dei corsi	nello studio nel cassetto della scrivania		
le scarpe			
il dentifricio			
la tovaglia da tavola			
le valigie			
l'ombrello			
il computer			
l'aspirina			
il telefonino			
l'agenda personale			

GRIGLIA B

	A casa tua	Persona 1	Persona 2
i libri			
i cerotti			
i cosmetici			
la corrispondenza			
l'attrezzatura sportiva			
i vestiti			
la bicicletta			
le chiavi			
i soldi/la carta bancaria			
gli strumenti musicali			

GRIGLIA C

	A casa tua	Persona 1	Persona 2
i dizionari			
i calzini			
le lettere d'amore			
la corrispondenza			
l'attrezzatura sportiva			
i manifesti			
la bicicletta			
i soldi/la carta bancaria			
le chiavi			
i CD			

Parliamo 2 *A gruppi. Cerca di scoprire come sono organizzate le altre persone nel tuo gruppo chiedendo dove tengono gli oggetti nella lista, poi stabilite chi è la persona più ordinata fra di voi.*

Vocabolario

accumulare
l'armadio
la cartellina
il cassetto
metodico
mettere in ordine
un oggetto personale
organizzare
riporre
il ripostiglio
sbarazzarsi (di)
lo schedario
la scrivania

Unità 63

TERAPIE ALTERNATIVE

Prima di parlare *Secondo un numero crescente di persone la medicina complementare e quella alternativa stanno ottenendo un gran successo e molti preferiscono queste terapie alla medicina tradizionale. Hai esperienza diretta di questi metodi o conosci qualcuno che li abbia usati?*

Yoga	Massaggio	Agopuntura	Chiropatia
Riflessologia	Omeopatia	Ipnosi	Shiatzu
Naturopatia	Reiki	Fitoterapia	

Parliamo 1 *A coppie o a gruppi confrontate le esperienze, dirette o indirette, delle alternative di cui sopra.*

Espressioni utili

- Confesso di non avere esperienze dirette di ... ma mia sorella/un mio collega ...
- Non ho mai pensato di rivolgermi a ...
- Pratico ... da qualche mese e devo dire che ...
- All'inizio ero piuttosto scettico/a però ...
- È certo che queste terapie sono sempre più diffuse ...
- Sono convinto/a che ... mi ha aiutato(a) a ...
- Ho seri dubbi sull'efficacia di ...

Prima di parlare 2 *Leggi la pubblicità del Convegno "La risata che cura" poi preparati a lavorare in coppia.*

(Salute naturale, Riza, settembre 99)

IL CONVEGNO DI RIZA

26-27-28 novembre 1999

LA RISATA CHE CURA

Le tecniche per imparare a ridere in modo terapeutico

I moderni studi di neurofisiologia hanno dimostrato che gli effetti della risata agiscono su aree fondamentali della vita del cervello e da lì si proiettano in tutto l'organismo, in un'onda benefica. Ma hanno anche messo in luce come non tutte le risate possano essere considerate terapeutiche...

Ridere forzatamente, per compiacere gli altri, così come l'umorismo di facciata e la risata amara o nervosa non sembrano favorire nel nostro organismo la produzione di sostanze salutari. Si tratta quindi di "imparare a ridere"... Ecco lo scopo di questo convegno di Riza psicosomatica.

Intervengono Raffaele Morelli, Vittorio Caprioglio, Piero Parietti, Daniela Marafante, Liliana Tieger, Marilena Zanardi. Musiche e suoni a cura di Filippo Massara.

IL PROGRAMMA DEI WORKSHOP

Il convegno è impostato, nella tradizione di Riza, su seminari pratici (workshop)

- La risata degli organi
- Il ridere creativo
- Riattivare l'umorismo con l'esercizio delle vocali
- La risata e il tramonto dell'Io
- I giochi che fabbricano l'allegria
- Il clown interiore
- L'attivazione muscolare della risata
- La risata della comunicazione
- Buon umore al maschile e al femminile
- Ridere senza la mente

INFORMAZIONI E ISCRIZIONI

OGNI WORKSHOP DURA AL MASSIMO DUE ORE

I lavori si apriranno con una tavola rotonda, venerdì 27/11/1999. Dalle ore 13,00 inizieranno i workshop.

COSTO DI ISCRIZIONE

■ L. 350.000. Per chi si iscrive entro il 10/9/1999 il costo sarà di L. 300.000.

■ Per i possessori di Riza Card (e quindi per gli abbonati di Riza) entro il 10/9/1999 il costo è di L. 250.000.

L'iscrizione dà diritto alla partecipazione a tutti i workshop previsti.

■ Per una sola giornata il costo è di L. 200.000; 160.000 per abbonati e possessori di Riza Card.

■ Per un singolo workshop il costo è di L. 100.000; L. 80.000 per abbonati e possessori di Riza Card.

I workshop, oltre che da Raffaele Morelli, Daniela Marafante, Piero Parietti, Vittorio Caprioglio, saranno condotti dai principali specialisti del campo.

Parliamo 2 <u>*Studente A*</u> *Lei è vagamente interessato a partecipare al Convegno e vuole informarsi sul tipo di seminario, la durata, i costi di iscrizione e su chi conduce i workshop. Lei è un tipo un po' diffidente e vuole essere rassicurato dell'utilità dell'esperienza.*

<u>*Studente B*</u> *Lei è la segretaria del Convegno: dia le informazioni richieste e cerchi di piazzare la persona in uno dei workshop a seconda della disponibilità. La persona sembra un po' indecisa e Lei vorrebbe attirare ancora qualche partecipante. Cerchi di persuaderla della validità dell'esperienza!*

Espressioni utili

- Finora ho esitato a ...
- Non mi convince
- Le posso assicurare che ...
- Faccia una prova ...
- Si lasci andare ...
- Mi ha convinto!

Vocabolario

condurre una attività
entusiasmante
esitare
esperto / inesperto
insolito
l'iscrizione
osare
partecipare / la partecipazione
il / la partecipante
rassicurare
ridere / la risata
sperimentare
la tecnica
terapeutico
teso/a
la valenza

Unità 64

IN PALESTRA

Prima di parlare 1 *Frequenti una palestra? Conosci qualcuno che frequenta una palestra? Rifletti sulle tue esperienze o su quelle di altre persone che conosci e prepara brevi appunti su questi aspetti:*

Attività	
Atrrezzature	
Costi	
Orari	
Istruttori	
Ambiente	

Parliamo 1 *A coppie o in piccoli gruppi scambiate le vostre esperienze o informazioni.*

Prima di parlare 2 *Studente A Leggi il breve articolo 'Come sto andando, Computer'? e nota tutte le particolarità e i vantaggi dell'attrezzatura nella palestra Down Town.*
Studente B Leggi il breve articolo 'Gioia a raggi infrarossi' e nota tutte le particolarità e i vantaggi dell'attrezzatura presso il Cairoli Health Club.

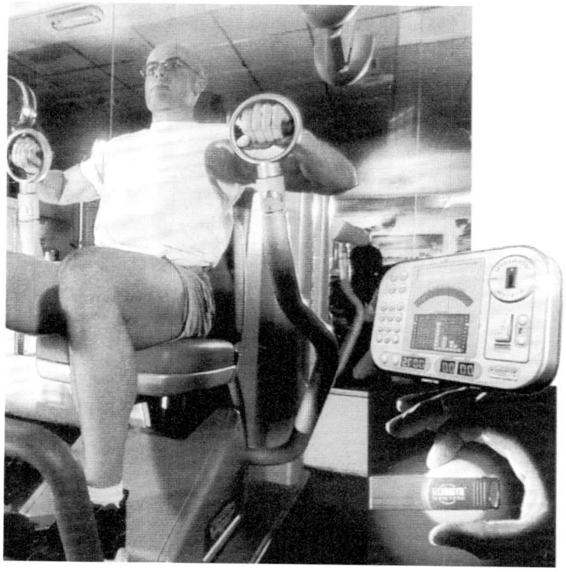

«COME STO ANDANDO, COMPUTER?»

Milano, palestra Down Town, sala Personal. Qui si trovano la Biostrength della Technogym, nove attrezzi isotonici, macchine eleganti e ultramoderne, realizzate per allenare i principali gruppi muscolari: pettorali, i due della schiena, spalle, addominali, torso, i tre delle gambe.
A sinistra, due particolari della macchina, il «power control» e la chiave Technogym System. Il primo imposta il programma di allenamenti in base alle capacità e motivazioni personali e visualizza sul display i parametri di velocità, arco di movimento, serie e ripetizioni. Il secondo è una chiave che grazie a una memoria interna raccoglie le informazioni anagrafiche, mediche e fisiologiche dell'utente e le passa alla macchina attraverso un contatto magnetico. Quindi le scarica su un server centrale dove un software riaggiorna l'intensità degli esercizi in base ai risultati raccolti per gli allenamenti successivi.

GIOIA A RAGGI INFRAROSSI

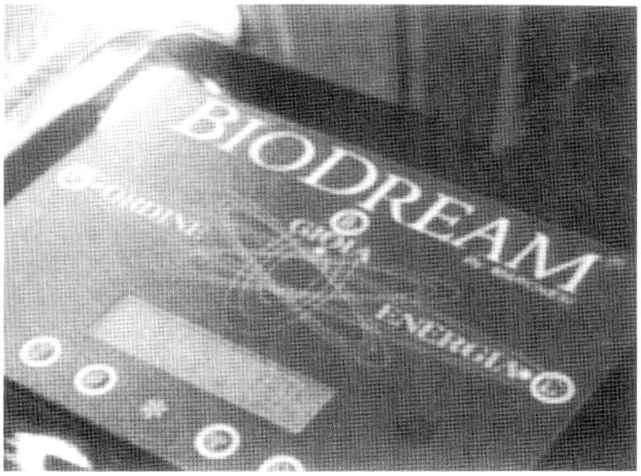

Milano, Cairoli Health Club, sala del benessere globale. Il lettino trasparente (nella foto a sinistra), dalle linee avveniristiche che è Biodream, la macchina della gioia, dell'energia e della vitalità.

Nata per far dimagrire, si è presto rivelata una macchina in grado di restituire serenità, svolgendo un'azione antidepressiva in un tempo minimo: una seduta non può essere inferiore ai 21 minuti e superiore ai 51. Le lampade a raggi infrarossi modulati e sincronizzati creano ipertemia. Ciò provoca un'abbondante sudorazione, grazie alla quale il soggetto espelle tutte le sostanze tossiche, soprattutto di origine chimica. In questo modo i muscoli e il sistema nervoso, «ripuliti», funzionano meglio. Il calore prodotto diminuisce a poco a poco aumentando la sensazione di benessere psico-fisico. Qui sopra, un particolare di Biodream: la tastiera di controllo da cui si imposta la durata di ogni seduta.

(Panorama Net 9 dicembre 1999)

Parliamo 2 *Lavorate in coppia. Ogni studente è, a turno, cliente o istruttore/istruttrice. Alla fine del primo turno scambiatevi ruoli e palestre.*

Studente A/B Cliente

Tutti i tuoi amici vanno in palestra! L'idea di frequentare una classe di aerobica non ti attira molto, ma saresti forse disposto ad andare in palestra quando ti fa comodo e usare l'attrezzatura di cui però non hai nessuna esperienza. Informati sull'attrezzatura della palestra – funzioni, parti del corpo da esercitare, programma di allenamento, intensità dell'allenamento, informazioni sulle condizioni fisiche dell'utente durante l'allenamento. Sei un po' riluttante...

Studente A/B Istruttore/Istruttrice

Il mercato delle palestre è molto competitivo. Nella vostra palestra c'è una nuova attrezzatura ed è molto importante fare iscrivere nuovi clienti. Una persona si presenta e richiede informazioni. Descrivi le funzioni degli attrezzi, il programma/intensità di allenamento, da' informazioni sulle condizioni fisiche dell'utente durante o dopo l'uso, se puoi. Insomma, sottolinea tutti i vantaggi che il cliente ne deriverebbe.

Espressioni utili

- Sto frequentando .../ Ho smesso di frequentare una palestra perché ...
- Cercavo una palestra con attrezzature modernissime
- Purtroppo non ho tempo/vado meno frequentemente ...
- Mi interesserebbe iscrivermi a una palestra ma ...
- Non saprei come usare ...
- C'è un istruttore divino che sa veramente insegnare ...
- Come funziona ...?
- Il personale ha sempre l'aria scocciata
- Che vantaggi ne avrei?
- Dovrei esercitare i muscoli .../vorrei dimagrire/rilassarmi ...
- Mi manca la motivazione
- Che tipo di informazioni mi dà questa macchina mentre la uso?
- Cosa devo fare?
- Quanto dura la seduta?
- È una macchina eccezionale ...
- Dà risultati sorprendenti ...
- Immagini che ...
- E non dimentichi gli altri vantaggi ...
- Avrà una sensazione di benessere mai provata
- Le assicuro che sono macchine ultramoderne

Unità 65

DOMENICHE A PIEDI

Prima di parlare 1 *Secondo te, a che cosa si riferisce il seguente titolo:*

Domeniche a piedi. Cosa ne pensate?

Parliamo 1 *A coppie discutete il significato di questo titolo. Secondo voi, di che cosa tratterà l'articolo?*

Espressioni utili

- L'articolo avrà senz'altro qualcosa a che fare con ...
- Hai senz'altro ragione
- A mio parere l'articolo tratterà di un'iniziativa ...
- È molto probabile che il governo italiano/le amministrazioni comunali abbia/abbiano preso dei provvedimenti per ...
- Io invece penso che l'articolo riguardi ...
- Può darsi che l'articolo tratti di ...

Prima di parlare 2 *Leggi l'articolo qui sotto. Alcune espressioni sono state tolte e scritte in ordine sparso sotto l'articolo. Reinseriscile nello spazio giusto.*

Domeniche a piedi, un progetto ..... (1) ..... ridurre nell'immediato la quantità di inquinamento atmosferico causato dalle auto nelle città e nel futuro educare i cittadini a pensare che ci si possa muovere con mezzi di trasporto alternativi, ... (2) .....

Il ministero dell'Ambiente ..... (3) ..... che coinvolge tutti i grandi centri urbani ..... (4) .... (5) ..... si chiede ai cittadini di lasciare l'auto in garage e il ministero sostiene che ..... (6) ..... condivide questa scelta. È davvero così? Quella del ministro Ronchi è ..... (7) .....? Si può fare breccia nelle abitudini degli italiani attraverso questa iniziativa? Che cosa succederebbe se il blocco delle auto avvenisse non di domenica, ma ..... (8) .....? Quanti sarebbero gli automobilisti ..... (9) ..... in bus per rispetto dell'ambiente?

a. con due obiettivi:
b. disposti a muoversi
c. durante la settimana lavorativa
d. e molte città minori
e. la maggior parte degli italiani
f. lancia un'iniziativa
g. per alcuni giorni all'anno
h. soprattutto con mezzi pubblici
i. una proposta utile

Parliamo 2 *A coppie giustificate la vostra scelta.*

Espressioni utili

- Secondo me, la tua scelta non ha senso
- Perché pensi che la frase da inserire sia ...?
- Bisogna capire il significato di quello che segue
- A seconda della frase che segue l'unica possibilità qui è ...
- Hai ragione, quello che dici è logico e completa il senso della frase
- Dal punto di vista grammaticale (non) è possibile ...
- Grammaticalmente questo è possibile, però ...
- Qui manca un verbo e quindi ...
- Bisogna tener conto della frase precedente

Prima di parlare 3 *Ora leggi l'articolo intero a pagina 237.*

Prima di parlare 4 *A coppie. Lo studente A legge il primo articolo e lo studente B il secondo. Ognuno poi deve compilare le parti relative della tabella qui sotto.*

Genere di iniziativa	
Obiettivi dell'iniziativa	
Maggiori città coinvolte	
Sostenitori dell'iniziativa	
Giorno/giorni in cui avrà luogo l'iniziativa	
Orario	
Mezzi banditi	
Mezzi non banditi	
Pene per i contravventori	
Numero di città coinvolte nell'iniziativa	
Risultati dei sondaggi	
Benefici dell'iniziativa	
Città in testa alla classifica del risparmio	

Articolo 1

Milano – Blocco totale delle auto domenica a Milano e a Como dalle 8 alle 20 a causa dell'inquinamento. Lo ha deciso oggi la Regione Lombardia con una ordinanza firmata dal presidente della giunta Roberto Formigoni. Venerdì e sabato intanto proseguirà sempre dalle 8 alle 20 il blocco parziale, riservato solo alle auto non catalitiche, già in vigore da alcuni giorni. Il provvedimento di blocco totale del traffico nelle aree omogenee di Milano e Como deciso da Formigoni, che vale anche per moto e motorini, potrebbe essere preso anche per Legnano, Busto Arsizio e Gallarate. Unica eccezione accettata le auto elettriche e i mezzi pubblici. Il provvedimento inoltre non sarà revocato neppure se l'inquinamento dovesse nei prossimi giorni rientrare entro i limiti consentiti. I contravventori non solo dovranno pagare una multa di 121.400 lire ma saranno anche costretti a lasciare sul posto il proprio veicolo. Un'analoga ordinanza dovrebbe essere emanata nelle prossime ore anche per l'area omogenea di Busto Arsizio, Gallarate e Legnano. "Il nostro obiettivo - ha spiegato Formigoni - è quello di tutelare la salute dei cittadini. Le polveri sono un fenomeno nuovo, che non conosciamo approfonditamente e che stiamo studiando. La legge non ci imporrebbe il blocco ma abbiamo deciso di attuarlo lo stesso per non far correre rischi ai cittadini".

(Giovedì, 13 Gennaio 2000, Corriere della sera - Internet)

Articolo 2

Domani ritornano le "domeniche a piedi"

Domenica si torna a respirare, domani il cielo ritroverà il suo colore azzurro (nuvole permettendo) e sarà un po' meno grigio: in 145 città italiane ripartono le "domeniche a piedi". Le auto, almeno per un giorno, restano ferme, dentro i garage o ai bordi delle strade. Si andrà in giro in bicicletta, con i pattini, qualcuno anche a cavallo o in qualche altro modo bizzarro o ingegnoso come è già successo nelle altre edizioni. Perché evitare i gas di scarico non solo fa bene in termini di inquinamento ma apre la mente, libera la testa e stimola nuove iniziative.

I sondaggi dicono che gli italiani gradiscono l'iniziativa, sono favorevoli nove su dieci e forse per la prima volta qui non ci sono divisioni tra destra e sinistra: camminare con i polmoni un po' più liberi piace a tutti. Tanto più che a trarre benefici è anche il portafoglio con un risparmio considerevole di benzina. In una sola giornata i 18 milioni di cittadini delle 145 città che aderiscono al progetto economizzano infatti più di 74 miliardi di lire in carburante.

A diffondere i dati è Legambiente che approfondisce l'analisi città per città: Roma ovviamente è in testa alla classifica del risparmio con circa 14 miliardi messi in cassaforte, poi seguono Milano, Torino, Napoli e via via sino al comune più piccolo della mappa.

Risparmio, ambiente e voglia di divertirsi sono gli ingredienti vincenti per una giornata diversa e ogni città si sta organizzando con manifestazioni collaterali per dare una cornice significativa alla "domenica a piedi".

(La Repubblica, 4 marzo 2000, Internet).

Parliamo 3 *Ora a coppie, A e B, scambiate le informazioni e completate la tabella.*

Prima di parlare 5 *Rileggi un'altra volta i due articoli.*

Parliamo 5 *A coppie o a gruppi discutete il significato e l'importanza dell'iniziativa con riferimento al vostro Paese o a quello in cui abitate. Il governo o le amministrazioni comunali hanno preso provvedimenti per ridurre il traffico? Se sì, quali? Valutate il loro successo o insuccesso. Se no, quali provvedimenti prendereste voi per ridurre i problemi provocati dal traffico?*

Contribuite già all'iniziativa sottolineata nell'articolo? Se sì, in che modo? Se no, perché no?

Unità 66

RIMPIANTI

Prima di parlare *Forse è meglio non avere rimpianti. Detto questo, è vero che tendiamo ogni tanto a rimpiangere di (non) aver fatto certe cose. Rifletti sulle tue esperienze e fai un elenco dei tuoi rimpianti come negli esempi.*

1. Ho abbandonato i miei studi all'età di 16 anni.
2. Non ho imparato a suonare la chitarra quando ero giovane.
3. Non ho comprato un cellulare / un capo firmato / una barca a vela.
4. Ho viaggiato poco prima di sposarmi.
5. Non ho mai fatto uno sport estremo (esempio: paracadutismo, immersione, roccia libera..)
6. Ho smesso di giocare a tennis quando ho cominciato a lavorare / è nato mio figlio.
7. Ho venduto la mia amatissima moto per comprare la macchina.

Parliamo 1 *A coppie confrontate i vostri rimpianti discutendo le eventuali differenze.*

Parliamo 2 *A coppie dite in che modo la vita sarebbe stata diversa se (non) aveste fatto le cose di cui avete parlato sopra.*

Esempio:

Se non avessi abbandonato gli studi all'età di 16 anni sono sicuro che sarei andato all'università e chissà, forse dopo aver conseguito una laurea, avrei trovato un lavoro più stimolante. Comunque, per quanto riguarda gli studi non è mai troppo tardi. Ho sempre la possibilità di riprenderli, iscrivendomi per esempio ad un corso serale.

Espressioni utili

- Se non avessi abbandonato i miei studi ...
- Se avessi imparato a suonare ...
- Se avessi colto l'occasione per viaggiare ...
- La mia vita sarebbe del tutto diversa se ...
- A dire la verità rimpiango di non avere/essere ...

- Per quanto riguarda ... non ho rimpianti
- Se potessi rinascere, non farei mai .../non andrei mai ...
- Quando ci penso adesso è stato un errore... avrei dovuto/potuto ...
- In quel momento mi sarebbe piaciuto ...
- Ormai, cosa ci posso fare?

Vocabolario

abbandonare
l'abilità
la capacità
deludere / la delusione / deludente
desiderare / il desiderio
l'impossibilità (di) / impossibile
l'inesperienza
la mancanza (di)
l'occasione (di)
la possibilità
rimpiangere / il rimpianto
riprendere
volere / la volontà

STUDENTI E SOLDI

Prima di parlare 1 *Siete studenti? Oppure siete amici o parenti di uno studente/una studentessa? In questo caso conoscerete i problemi di chi deve gestire le proprie risorse finanziarie al meglio. Elencate tutte le spese per cui voi siete responsabili (o, se non siete studenti voi stessi, per cui è responsabile uno studente/una studentessa che conoscete). Le spese variano ovviamente a seconda se i giovani vivono in famiglia, da soli o con altri studenti. Indicate la vostra risposta con una crocetta.*

Voci spesa	in famiglia	da soli	con altri studenti
affitto			
spese di casa: – elettricità – gas – telefono – assicurazione			
cibo			
abbigliamento			
spese di studio: – libri – tasse universitarie			
trasporti			
divertimenti			
automobile: – assicurazione – bollo – benzina – manutenzione			

Parliamo 1 *A coppie o a gruppi stabilite se le risposte date sono abbastanza simili o se ci sono molte differenze.*

Espressioni utili

- Qual è la tua situazione?
- Per quali voci di spesa sei responsabile?
- Le mie maggiori voci di spesa sono ...
- Escludendo ...
- ... è una spesa meno importante / necessaria ...
- Sono tenuto/a a pagare la mia parte di ...
- La bolletta del gas / dell'elettricità ...
- L'abbonamento al telefonino / al cellulare ...
- Pago a rate mensili / trimestrali ...
- Devo dare una caparra di .... Lire
- Per fortuna i miei genitori mi mantengono / mi aiutano ...
- Purtroppo non posso contare sull'aiuto finanziario di ...
- Anche tu devi contribuire alle spese di ...

Prima di parlare 2 *Campus, la rivista per studenti universitari italiani, ha condotto un'indagine su un campione di studenti per scoprire come i giovani gestiscono i loro soldi. Studiate i risultati dell'indagine.*

I RISULTATI DELL'INDAGINE DI CAMPUS WEB

Campus Web ha intervistato 632 studenti universitari di 12 città (Bari, Cagliari, Catania, Cremona, Firenze, Genova, L'Aquila, Milano, Napoli, Novara, Parma e Vercelli) a proposito del loro bilancio e di come lo gestiscono. I risultati espressi in percentuale, sono stati divisi tra studenti che abitano ancora con i genitori e studenti che vivono fuori casa.

STUDENTI	VIVONO IN FAMIGLIA	VIVONO FUORI CASA	MEDIA TOTALE
Il mio budget mensile è:			
fino a 500mila lire	**75,2**	**35,5**	**60,1**
da 500 a un milione	18,3	46	28,8
da un milione a un milione e 500mila lire	5,5	14,5	8,9
Totale	100,0	100,0	100,0
Il mio budget proviene:			
completamente dalla mia famiglia	53,0	46,8	50,6
in parte dalla mia famiglia e in parte dal lavoro che faccio	**38,1**	**43,5**	**40,2**
completamente dal mio lavoro	8,9	9,7	9,2
Totale	100,0	100,0	100,0
Io e i soldi:			
programmo tutte le spese con anticipo così non finisco mai in rosso	16,3	27,4	20,6
spendo tutto all'inizio del mese e poi tiro la cinghia	11,9	29,0	18,4
spendo tutto all'inizio del mese e poi batto cassa ai miei genitori	23,8	11,3	19,0
cerco sempre di risparmiare qualcosa	**48,0**	**32,3**	**42,0**
Totale	100,0	100,0	100,0

STUDENTI	VIVONO IN FAMIGLIA	VIVONO FUORI CASA	MEDIA TOTALE
La mia maggior voce di spesa (escluso affitto e spese di casa):			
libri e altre spese per l'università	22,3	38,0	28,2
divertimenti e tempo libero	**47,0**	**31,4**	**41,1**
vestiti	13,4	11,3	12,6
telefonino	6,4	10,4	8,0
dischi, videogames, Cd-rom, libri	10,9	8,9	10,1
Totale	100,0	100,0	100,0
Questo mese mi avanzano 500mila lire. Compro subito:			
Il telefonino	4,0	4,0	4,0
li uso come anticipo per il computer	4,0	9,7	6,1
parto per un week-end	24,3	29,8	26,4
non lo so, ma sicuramente li spendo	26,7	26,7	26,7
li metto da parte, non si sa mai	**41,0**	**29,8**	**36,8**
Totale	100,0	100,0	100,0

Fonte : Campus ottobre 1999

Parliamo 2 *A coppie o a gruppi. Chiarite fra di voi alcune parole o espressioni che non conoscete.*

Esempio:

– Che cosa vuol dire questa espressione: "batto cassa ai miei genitori?"
– Non l'ho mai vista, ma credo voglia dire che il giovane chiede dei soldi ai genitori.

Parliamo 3 *Lavoro di gruppo. Preparate una breve relazione su una o due delle sezioni del questionario di Campus. La relazione deve includere i commenti del gruppo sui risultati stessi (ad esempio differenze / similarità con gli studenti del vostro Paese, o altre osservazioni). Presentate la relazione agli altri gruppi. È probabile, ma non certo, che le relazioni dei vari gruppi che presenteranno la stessa relazione non siano simili!*

Espressioni utili

- Avete notato quanti studenti hanno risposto che ...?
- Mi sembra che solo gli studenti che vivono fuori casa siano .../abbiano ...
- Però, se si guarda la media totale ...
- Le statistiche parlano chiaro ...
- Fino a che punto si può credere alle statistiche?
- Vedo che il 70% (settanta per cento) dei giovani ...
- È una percentuale alta/bassa ...
- Il 2,2% (due virgola due per cento) mi sembra poco ...
- I risultati del sondaggio presentano un'immagine ...
- La maggior parte dei giovani intervistati mi sembra ...

Parliamo 4 *Cambiate gruppo. Conducete tra di voi lo stesso sondaggio, usando il questionario qui sotto. Quando avete finito, presentate i risultati al resto della classe, sottolineando le differenze con le risposte degli studenti italiani.*

STUDENTI	IO	STUDENTE 2	STUDENTE 3
Il mio budget mensile è:			
fino a € 300			
da € 300 a € 600			
Totale			
Il mio budget proviene:			
completamente dalla mia famiglia			
e in parte dal lavoro/lavori che faccio			
completamente dal mio lavoro			
Totale			
Io e i soldi:			
programmo tutte le spese con anticipo così non finisco mai in rosso			
spendo tutto all'inizio del mese e poi tiro la cinghia			
spendo tutto all'inizio del mese e poi batto cassa ai miei genitori			
cerco sempre di risparmiare qualcosa			
Totale			
La mia maggior voce di spesa (escluso affitto e spese di casa):			
libri e altre spese per l'università			
divertimenti e tempo libero			
vestiti			
telefonino			
dischi, videogames, Cd-rom, libri			
Totale			
Questo mese mi avanzano € 300. Compro subito:			
Il telefonino			
li uso come anticipo per il computer			
parto per un week-end			
non lo lo, ma sicuramente li spendo			
li metto da parte, non si sa mai			
Totale			

Fonte : Campus ottobre 1999

Unità 68

CHE AVVENTURA!

Prima di parlare 1 *Guardate attentamente la fotografia del naufrago. Poveretto! Formulate qualche ipotesi sulla sua situazione.*

Esempio:

1. Perché si trova su un'isola deserta?
2. Come ci è arrivato?
3. Da quanto tempo si trova lì?
4. Come passerà le sue giornate?
5. Com'era la sua vita prima di fare naufragio?
6. A cosa gli servirà il computer?
7. Perché cerca un casco integrale?
8. Come finirà la sua avventura?

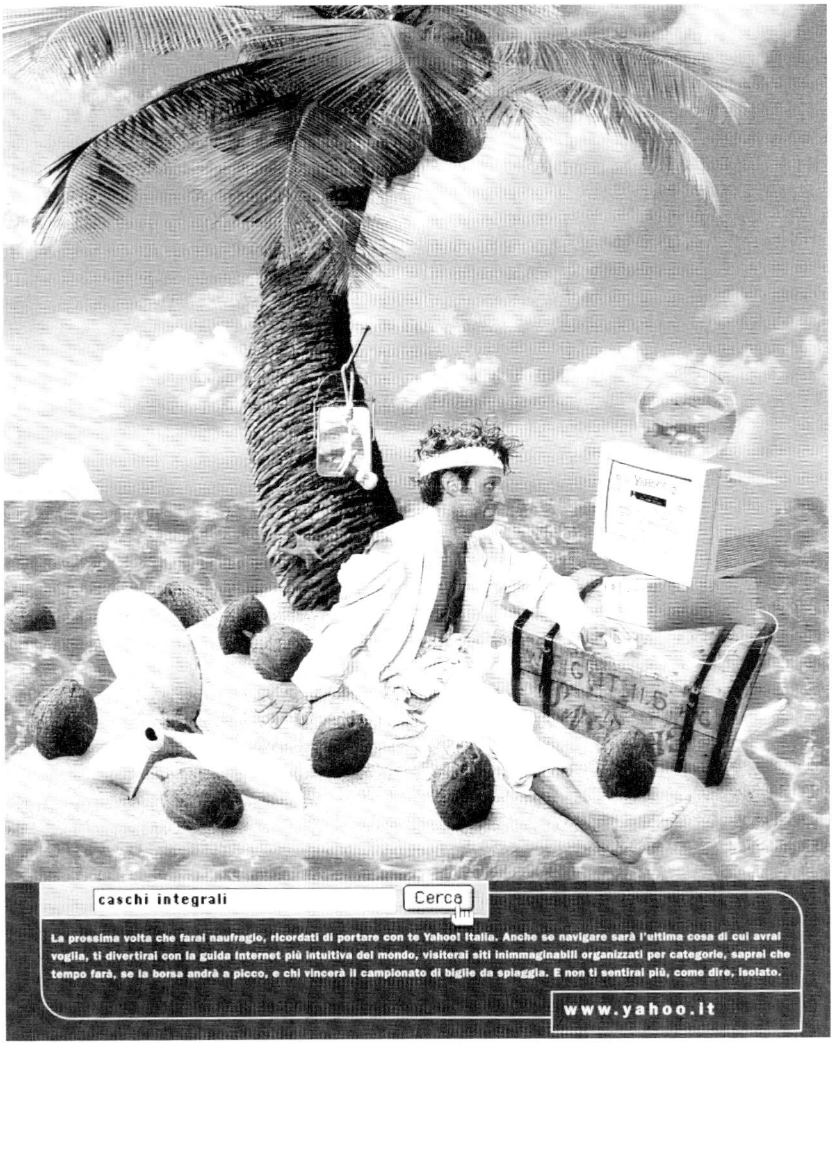

Campus

Espressioni utili

- Che situazione, poveretto!
- Chissà cosa gli sarà capitato?
- Mah, sarà naufragato dopo ...
- Sarà arrivato a nuoto
- Avrà fatto un ammaraggio d'emergenza
- Boh? E tu, cosa pensi sia successo?
- Anche voi allora avete pensato la stessa cosa
- Invece, secondo noi, si sarà buttato ...
- Non vorrei essere nei suoi panni!

Parliamo 1 *Circolando fra gli altri membri della classe, scambiate le vostre ipotesi e trovate una o più persone che abbiano formulato interpretazioni più simili alle vostre. Formate un gruppo.*

Parliamo 2 *Ogni gruppo si accorda per presentare la propria interpretazione includendo un finale della storia.*

Espressioni utili

- Secondo questo gruppo, il nostro eroe era un agente di vendita in viaggio d'affari ...
- Stava viaggiando in ... quando è scoppiato un temporale
- Coraggiosamente, non ha esitato a ...
- Ha finito per adattarsi a ...
- Non si è perso di coraggio ...
- Superando la paura di ...
- Ha deciso di ...
- Non possiamo immaginare come sia/abbia ...
- Un premio per la storia più drammatica / divertente / avvincente!

Vocabolario

l'avventura
il coraggio / coraggioso
costruire
galleggiare
l'iceberg
intraprendente
l'isola deserta / tropicale
l'isolamento
i tropici

mantenere i contatti
il mondo esterno
la noce di cocco
la palma
la pesca
il salvagente
la solitudine
sopravvivere / la sopravvivenza

Unità 69

STUDENTI MODELLO

Prima di parlare 1 *Qualunque sia la materia di studio, uno studente modello deve essere disciplinato e seguire certe regole di comportamento se desidera ottenere buoni risultati in una determinata materia. In cinque minuti di tempo scrivi tutte le regole che ritieni siano importanti, come negli esempi.*

1. È importantissimo fare i compiti.
2. Bisogna frequentare tutte le lezioni.
3. ....
4. ....
5. ....
6. ....
7. ....
8. ....

Parliamo 1 *A coppie confrontate le vostre regole aggiungendo alla vostra lista altri comportamenti importanti che avete trascurato.*

Espressioni utili

- Secondo me, la regola numero uno è ...
- Ogni studente deve senz'altro ...
- È assolutamente essenziale che si ricordi di ...
- È necessario/indispensabile fare ...
- Chi desidera superare gli esami ...
- Inoltre, è importante che faccia/sia ...
- Mi è venuta in mente un'altra regola ...

Parliamo 2 *A coppie o a gruppi discutete le regole che seguite regolarmente e quelle che avete difficoltà a seguire, spiegandone il perché, come negli esempi.*

1. Devo dire che frequento tutte le lezioni. Quest'anno sono dovuto rimanere a casa solo due giorni perché avevo la febbre e durante la notte non ho chiuso occhio. Però, in quella occasione ho telefonato a scuola per scusarmi. Penso che questo sia mio dovere e inoltre lo faccio per cortesia verso i miei insegnanti.

2. Devo confessare che non riesco a fare tutti i miei compiti. Oltre ad essere piuttosto pigro ho una buona scusa perché lavoro in un ristorante tre sere alla settimana. Quando torno a casa sono distrutto e quindi non ho voglia di studiare. Come tanti altri studenti lavoro perché ho bisogno di soldi per mantenermi. Purtroppo questo lavoretto comincia ad influire negativamente sul mio rendimento e fra poco sarò costretto a prendere una decisione difficile, quella di abbandonare i miei studi.

Espressioni utili

- Mi rendo perfettamente conto dell'importanza dei miei studi e quindi ...
- Faccio sempre del mio meglio per ...
- Per fortuna riesco (quasi) sempre a ...
- Se voglio raggiungere il mio obiettivo ...
- Voglio andare all'università, quindi ...
- L'insegnante di... mi ha avvertito che ...
- Dall'ultima valutazione/dall'ultimo esame è chiaro che ...
- Ultimamente mi è stato/a proprio impossibile ...
- I miei amici / insegnanti mi dicono sempre che ...
- Se vado avanti così ...
- Adesso basta, a partire dal trimestre prossimo ...
- Devo fare qualcosa prima che sia troppo tardi ...

Prima di parlare 2 *Ecco alcuni insegnanti che parlano dei loro alunni / studenti. Quali commenti potrebbero riferirsi a te?*

Ha sempre una scusa pronta.
Vivacissimo, non sta mai fermo nel banco.
Ha molta buona volontà e cerca di mettercela tutta.
Un po' svogliato.
È sempre disattento.
Quando è in classe partecipa alle discussioni ma non sa lavorare indipendentemente.
Secondo me, non apre mai un libro.
Ha sbalzi d'umore terribili - dev'essere in piena tempesta ormonale!
Non ha mai mancato una lezione.
Dopo qualche difficoltà iniziale, ha progredito molto rapidamente in...
È chiaro che questa materia non l'interessa affatto.
Mette molta cura in tutto quello che fa.

Parliamo 3 *A coppie o a gruppi spiegate quali commenti si potrebbero riferire a voi, citando esempi concreti. Se pensate che nessuno di questi commenti si possa minimamente riferire a voi, dite ai compagni che cosa in effetti gli insegnanti dicono o dicevano di voi!*

Espressioni utili

- Mi ricordo che quando frequentavo la scuola media ...
- Avevo l'abitudine di arrivare in ritardo e la mia scusa era ...
- Ero disattento/a in alcune lezioni ma solo perché l'insegnante ...
- Il mio professore di ... diceva .../ si lamentava sempre che io ...
- Avevo difficoltà a concentrarmi soprattutto durante la lezione di ...
- Avevo sempre paura di essere interrogato/a ...
- Gli esami per me erano una tortura ...
- Ho sempre avuto l'impressione di .../che i miei compagni fossero .../che i miei insegnanti mi dessero dei voti ...

Vocabolario

il bidello
la bocciatura
il corpo insegnante
il credito / debito didattico
dare molta / poca importanza a ...
l'esame
essere bocciato/a
essere rimandato in una materia
frequentare
il ginnasio
l'incontro con i genitori
l'incubo
l'insegnante
l'interrogazione / interrogare
la lezione privata
lamentarsi
il liceo
il metodo
l'offerta didattica
il/la preside
il programma di studi
progredire
la prova scritta
la riforma scolastica
la scuola materna / elementare / dell'obbligo
la scheda di valutazione
severo/a
studiare / lo studente / studioso
la valutazione

Unità 70

SOGGIORNO DI STUDIO

Prima di parlare 1 *Hai intenzione di partecipare a un corso d'italiano per stranieri in Italia. Quali sono le domande che vorresti porre alla scuola o all'università prima di iscriverti al corso? Quali servizi ti aspetti dall'organizzazione? Scrivine un elenco.*

Parliamo 1 *A coppie confrontate il vostro elenco discutendo le eventuali differenze. Potete aggiungere al vostro elenco aspetti importanti che avete trascurato.*

Espressioni utili

- Per me è importante sapere ...
- Innanzitutto vorrei sapere ...
- È sempre una buon'idea informarsi su ...
- A mio parere, una maggiore considerazione ...
- Il motivo per cui mi piacerebbe sapere ...
- Secondo me, un'altra domanda che bisogna porre è ...
- Inoltre, non si deve mai dimenticare di chiedere ...
- Prima di decidermi ...
- Prima di iscrivermi a un corso ...

Prima di parlare 2 *Verrà assegnata ad ogni studente una lettera, A,B,C o D. Lo studente A deve leggere le informazioni riguardanti Corso A (lo studente B Corso B ecc.) e completare quanto possibile la seguente tabella*

Periodo
Età
Livello del corso
Durata
Organizzazione del programma linguistico
Attività culturali
Visite/gite
Attività sportive/ricreative
Vitto e alloggio
Altri servizi disponibili
Certificati rilasciati alla fine del corso
Retta
Tariffe alloggio

CORSO A

Università per Stranieri di Perugia
CORSI STRAORDINARI INTENSIVI

Ammissione

Sono previsti per tutti i cinque gradi (il primo grado è per studenti senza alcuna conoscenza della lingua italiana) con durata mensile e si svolgono da luglio a settembre.

Si caratterizzano per un maggior carico orario settimanale e per le classi con un numero programmato di studenti.

Al termine di un Corso intensivo è rilasciato, a richiesta, un Attestato di frequenza a chi abbia frequentato regolarmente.

I servizi

L'Ufficio Relazioni con lo Studente. Oltre ad occuparsi della prima accoglienza dello studente e delle sue necessità informative su corsi e attività dell'Ateneo, questo ufficio attende a tutte le fasi della pre-iscrizione e fornisce indicazioni di carattere logistico e turistico-culturale sulla città e sulla regione.

Alloggi. L'Università offre agli studenti la possibilità di scegliere tra vari tipi di alloggio. Contattando Atena Service è possibile informarsi e fare prenotazioni riguardo ad appartamenti indipendenti, miniappartametni e residences, camere singole o doppie in famiglia o in albergo. In agosto è possibile alloggiare presso i collegi universitari cittadini, inviando prenotazione all'Ufficio Relazioni con lo Studente.

La Biblioteca. La Biblioteca dell'Università per Stranieri di Perugia è specializzata in letteratura, storia e storia dell'arte italiana, in etruscologia, in linguistica e nelle discipline collegate. Offre agli studenti i seguenti servizi: prestito interno ed esterno; prestito interbibliotecario nazionale e internazionale; consultazione di banche dati su cd-rom e floppy disk; consultazioni via internet; servizio fotocopie e consegna di documenti; servizio di posta elettronica per scopi accademici o di ricerca. La Biblioteca è aperta dal lunedì al venerdì, con orario continuato dalle h 9.00 alle h 17.45.

Laboratori linguistici e informatici. L'Università dispone di 5 laboratori linguistici che sono utilizzati dai docenti nell'ambito dei corsi di lingua. Sono inoltre dislocate nelle aule dell'Ateneo attrezzature audiovisive che vengono impiegate nell'ambito delle lezioni. Presso l'Università sono attivi anche 2 laboratori informatici dotati di software applicativo, con possibilità di accesso ad internet.

Ambulatorio Medico. Dal lunedì al venerdì è attivo un laboratorio medico riservato agli studenti dell'Università per Stranieri di Perugia.

Mense. Gli studenti dell'Università per Stranieri hanno accesso alle mense universitarie ad un prezzo conveniente.

Attività culturali, sportive e ricreative

Le attività del Centro Sociale Universitario. A cadenza settimanale il Centro Sociale Universitario dell'Ateneo organizza concerti, spettacoli, mostre e proiezioni di film tra i più significativi della cinematografia italiana. A tutte queste iniziative gli studenti assistono gratuitamente e, con l'assistenza del Centro Sociale, possono esibire il proprio talento artistico in concerti e spettacoli, mostre e attività teatrali.

Gite ed escursioni. Per il fine settimana l'Università organizza gite dirette alle principali città d'arte italiane e visite guidate al patrimonio monumentale, storico e artistico di Perugia e dell'Umbria.

Pratica sportiva. Gli studenti dell'Università per Stranieri possono accedere gratuitamente o con riduzioni di prezzo agli impianti del Centro Universitario Sportivo di Perugia. È possibile praticare: atletica leggera, baseball, basket, calcio, canoa, escursionismo, equitazione, ginnastica, golf, judo, karate, nuoto, pallanuoto, paracadutismo, scherma, sci, tennis, ecc.

Modalità d'iscrizione ai corsi

Almeno trenta giorni prima dell'inizio del corso, lo studente deve far pervenire all'Università:

1) i modelli A e B completi di tutti i dati richiesti;
2) attestazione di versamento della tassa relativa : a) al primo mese di corso; b) a tutto il corso; c) oppure di Lit. 50.000 (Euro 25,82) come anticipo sulla tassa stessa.

N.B. Per effettuare il pagamento è necessario un documento di identità valido.

All'arrivo all'Università gli studenti devono presentarsi all'Ufficio Relazioni con lo Studente con il documento di pre-iscrizione, dove riceveranno le informazioni necessarie per il completamento dell'iscrizione e per la frequenza ai corsi.

Borse di studio

Per la frequenza ai corsi sono concesse borse di studio dall'Università per Stranieri di Perugia, dal Ministero degli Affari Esteri italiano e da altre istituzioni, tra cui la Società Dante Alighieri.
Il Ministero degli Affari Esteri concede borse a cittadini di determinati Paesi con cui sono in vigore particolari accordi. Gli interessati devono rivolgersi alle Ambasciate, ai Consolati d'Italia o agli Istituti Italiani di Cultura, richiedendo di frequentare i Corsi dell'Università per Stranieri di Perugia.
Attraverso gli Istituti Italiani di Cultura, o direttamente, l'Università per Stranieri di Perugia concede borse di studio a cittadini stranieri e italiani residenti all'estero, con preferenza a docenti e studenti d'Italiano in Scuole e in Università estere.
Le borse sono di durata mensile e costituiscono un contributo alle spese di soggiorno e di frequenza ai Corsi. Per concorrere ad esse gli interessati devono rivolgersi all'Istituto Italiano di Cultura nel Paese di residenza.

Per l'iscrizione ai Corsi ordinari, straordinari e intensivi di Secondo, Terzo, Quarto e Quinto grado è previsto un test d'ingresso per l'assegnazione al livello opportuno di conoscenza della lingua italiana.

Calendario dei test d'ingresso: indicare con un segno le date prescelte

❑ 2001
❑ 8-9-10 gennaio ❑ 1 marzo ❑ 31 maggio ❑ 31 gennaio ❑ 2-3-4 aprile ❑ 1 giugno ❑ 1-2 febbraio
❑ 30 aprile ❑ 28 febbraio ❑ 2 maggio (Internet)

CORSO B

CORSI INTERNAZIONALI DI LINGUA E CULTURA ITALIANA

Gargnano del Garda
SOLO CORSI ESTIVI

Luglio - Agosto

Calendario dei corsi e delle lezioni

I corsi si svolgeranno in due turni di quattro settimane ciascuno: 1° turno dal 3 luglio al 28 luglio; 2° turno dal 31 luglio al 25 agosto.

Le lezioni sono così distribuite:

- al mattino (ore 9-12) lezioni di lingua italiana (distinte in tre livelli);
- al pomeriggio (ore 17,30-19,30), conferenze attinenti la cultura italiana (Letteratura, Storia, Musica, Arte, Teatro, Cinema).

Saranno inoltre organizzate attività culturali e ricreative, tra le quali una gita a Verona per assistere alla rappresentazione di un'opera lirica all'Arena.

Ammissione

Sono ammessi i cittadini stranieri particolarmente interessati all'approfondimento della conoscenza della lingua e della cultura italiane, che già siano in possesso di una buona padronanza della lingua, tale da consentire loro la regolare frequenza alle lezioni e alle conferenze, tenute in lingua italiana. Non saranno ammessi studenti principianti.
Non si accettano domande da parte di studenti che non abbiano compiuto il 21° anno di età.
A ciascun turno saranno ammessi non più di 60 studenti alle seguenti condizioni:

• 25 studenti ammessi a pagamento: retta mensile di € 400 indivisibile e comprensiva di iscrizione ai corsi e mensa (colazione e due pasti al giorno dal lunedì al venerdì). Inoltre sono a carico degli studenti le spese di pernottamento (€ 400)

• 35 studenti vincitori di borse di studio: la borsa comprende l'iscrizione ai corsi, la mensa (come sopra), assegno di € 400 (pari alle spese di pernottamento).

Le camere, generalmente in stanze doppie preso famiglie selezionate, verranno assegnate al momento dell'arrivo a Gargnano dalla Segreteria dei Corsi.

Le domande degli aspiranti dovranno pervenire alla Segreteria dei Corsi IMPROROGABILMENTE entro il 6 marzo per le iscrizioni al corso di luglio ed entro il 20 marzo per quelle di agosto, pena il decadimento della domanda.

Selezione delle domande

La selezione delle domande e l'assegnazione delle borse di studio sono demandate al giudizio inappellabile di una Commissione composta dal Direttore Scientifico del Centro e dai Direttori dei due corsi.

Le Istituzioni e i docenti che segnaleranno i nominativi dei candidati, sono tenuti a provvedere preliminarmente ad un accertamento degli interessi culturali dei singoli e della loro conoscenza della lingua italiana, e ad indicare una graduatoria di merito. Le Istituzioni stesse e i docenti dovranno inoltre garantire che non si verifichino né rinunce tardive (dopo il 30.5), né partenze anticipate. Tali evenienze pregiudicheranno le segnalazioni delle stesse Istituzioni per l'anno successivo.
Lo studente vincitore che, per giustificati motivi, intendesse rinunciare alla borsa di studio, dovrà avvertire via fax entro il 15.5. Ogni rinuncia tardiva danneggia altri possibili borsisti.
L'accettazione della borsa dovrà essere confermata dal vincitore col pagamento della caparra di € 50 (che sarà restituita a Gargnano) entro il 30.5 pena la revoca della borsa.
Anche in caso di arrivi gravemente ritardati e non giustificati all'inizio dei corsi, o di abbandoni prima del termine ufficiale, la borsa verrà revocata.
All'apertura dei corsi i candidati ammessi sosterranno in sede un colloquio con test per accertare il loro livello di conoscenza della lingua italiana.

Frequenza e Attestati

Gli studenti sono tenuti a frequentare i corsi dal giorno di inizio a quello di chiusura, senza interruzione; non sono autorizzate partenze anticipate; le lezioni e le conferenze si svolgono anche nei giorni di festività infrasettimanali. Al termine del corso, agli studenti che avranno frequentato regolarmente le lezioni e le conferenze, verrà rilasciato dall'Università un attestato di frequenza.

Gli studenti interessati potranno sostenere in sede al termine del corso dell'esame CILS (Certificazione di Italiano come Lingua Straniera) dell'Università per Stranieri di Siena (2°, 3°, 4° livello).

Documenti

Per evitare esclusioni dovute a ritardi postali si consiglia di inviare la documentazione entro il 6.3 per il corso di luglio ed entro il 20.3 per quello di agosto via fax allo 0039.258302778 o posta elettronica a gargnano@mailserver.unimi.it.

Indirizzo della Segreteria dei Corsi:

Segreteria dei Corsi Internazionali di Lingua e Cultura Italiana
c/o Università degli Studi di Milano - Dipartimento di Filologia Moderna
via Festa del Perdono 7 - 20122 MILANO
Telefono: 02/58352812 - Fax 02/58302778
E-Mail: gargnano@mailserver.unimi.it (Internet)

CORSO C

ISTITUTO ITALIANO Centro di lingua e Cultura, ROMA

L'Istituto è aperto tutto l'anno e accoglie nei suoi corsi persone adulte che desiderano iniziare o approfondire e perfezionare la loro conoscenza della lingua italiana. Ogni mese sono in funzione i sette livelli dei corsi di lingua, ciascuno con un programma specifico per quanto riguarda l'apprendimento della grammatica ed il progressivo ampliamento del lessico e delle possibilità di comunicare, dal livello principianti al corso di perfezionamento.
Il periodo minimo di frequenza è di due settimane, ma sentiamo il dover di far presente che per uno studente assolutamente principiante rischia di essere un periodo troppo breve per garantire dei risultati apprezzabili. Ricordiamo inoltre che per principianti sono previste date fisse di inizio dei corsi.

I corsi possono essere di due tipi: "intensivo" (Corso A), "vacanza" (Corso C). Nel primo caso si tratta di 4 ore e mezzo di frequenza giornaliera, nel secondo di 3 ore al giorno.

Il corso "vacanza" è stato concepito per consentire a chi studia la lingua italiana per il proprio piacere, di farlo in un modo non eccessivamente stressante ma pur sempre abbastanza intensivo da poter raggiungere i propri obiettivi.

Il corso "intensivo" propriamente detto, è stato invece studiato e programmato per tutti coloro che hanno una motivazione ben precisa, sia lavorativa che personale, per apprendere la ns. lingua, e quindi desiderano sfruttare il più possibile il loro periodo di permanenza in Italia.

Per coloro che abbiano la necessità di apprendere o approfondire la lingua italiana in tempi brevi, generalmente per motivi professionali, viene anche offerta la possibilità di seguire il corso "combinato" (Corso B), ossia il corso A (intensivo) più 5 lezioni individuali di 45 minuti alla settimana. Nel corso B (combinato) è possibile anche affrontare settori linguistici specifici (alcuni dei programmi disponibili sono per esempio: l'italiano per gli affari, per il turismo, la moda, la cucina, il settore alberghiero).

Un'intensità di studio ancora maggiore si può ottenere direttamente con il Corso Intensivo Individuale, nel quale il rapporto insegnante-singolo studente è di 2 o più, fino a 8 ore al giorno (in quest'ultimo caso è compreso anche il pranzo con l'insegnante). Trattandosi di corsi realmente "su misura" si raccomanda comunque di concordarne le modalità con la direzione.

L'istituto organizza inoltre regolarmente delle attività culturali, come lezioni di storia dell'arte, (comprese visite guidate), di letteratura, proiezioni commentate di film dei più importanti autori italiani, ecc. Il costo di Storia dell'Arte costa € 20 a settimana (12 ore in 4 settimane).

Oltre ai corsi di lingua e cultura vengono proposte settimanalmente delle attività extra-scolastiche, come corsi di cucina, degustazioni di vini italiani, cene, escursioni fuori città, visite a musei ecc., per aiutare gli studenti ad inserirsi con più facilità nel vivere italiano. Naturalmente la ns. segreteria, aperta tutta il giorno, è sempre a disposizione per qualunque informazioni che possa aiutare a rendere più agevole il soggiorno di studio.

Per quanto rirguarda l'alloggio a Roma durante il periodo del corso, l'Istituto propone diverse possibilità. Si tratta in ogni caso di soluzioni a prezzi accessibili, sperimentate, e che offrono allo studente l'occasione di trovarsi in un ambiente accogliente e amichevole. Si raccomanda comunque di esprimere le richieste nel modo più completo possibile, in modo che possiamo essere certi di fare tutto il possibile di soddisfarle.

CORSO D

LINGUAVIVA - FIRENZE

Firenze è una città unica al mondo per il suo patrimonio artistico e per la sua importanza storica e culturale. È l'ambiente ideale per un breve soggiorno di studio in cui gli studenti possono combinare delle lezioni di lingua italiana con attività di carattere artistico e culturale. La scuola si trova nel centro della città, dispone di numerose aule dotate tutte di apparecchiature audiovisive ed è caratterizzata da un efficace e moderno metodo di insegnamento.

Programma linguistico

Prevede 4 lezioni al giorno (ciascuna di 45 minuti). Gli studenti verranno raggruppati in base al loro livello di conoscenza linguistica. L'obiettivo principale del programma è di migliorare le abilità linguistiche orali con la continua pratica comunicativa, rafforzando allo stesso tempo le strutture grammaticlai e ampliando il vocabolario.

Attività

Il programma prevede varie attività pomeridiane con speciale enfasi sull'aspetto artistico. Grazie ai nostri insegnanti, gli studenti avranno la possibilità di visitare il centro storico di Firenze, musei o altri luoghi di particolare interesse. È prevista inoltre una escursione pomeridiana a scelta fra le località più rinomate della Toscana: Siena, Chianti, Pisa ecc.

Alloggio

Gli studenti potranno essere sistemati in una delle pensioni vicino alla scuola o eccezionalmente in una famiglia, compatibilmente con la disponibilità e il periodo dell'anno prescelto. L'alloggio in pensione prevede per gli studenti camere multiple con la prima colazione, se in famigllia potranno disporre di una camera doppia con il trattamento di mezza pensione.

Programma Standard - Durata: 7 giorni/6 giorni	
Periodo	tutto l'anno
Età	15-18 anni
Gruppi	minimo 18 studenti
Corso d'italiano	20 lezioni (ciascuna di 45 minuti)
Attività	- Una escursione di mezza giornata - Introduzione storico-artistica di Firenze con visita guidata al centro storico - Visita a un museo o ad un luogo di particolare interesse
Retta	€ 150 per persona. La retta include il corso delle attività previste dal programma, il certificato di frequenza, l'assistenza del personale di Linguaviva.
Tariffe alloggio	In pensione, camera multipla con prima colazione, circa € 150 per persona. In famiglia, camera doppia con mezza pensione, € 200 per persona.

Parliamo 2 *Lavorate a coppie A e B, C e D. Scambiate le informazioni sui rispettivi corsi e completate un'altra tabella.*

Parliamo 3 *Ora lo studente A lavora con lo studente C e lo studente B con D. Completate altre due tabelle con le informazioni sugli altri due corsi.*

Prima di parlare 3 *Leggi le quattro tabelle e scegli il corso a cui vorresti iscriverti.*

Parliamo 4 *Lavorate in gruppi di quattro (A,B,C e D). Ognuno deve dire agli altri quale corso ha scelto, giustificandone la scelta. Se per caso un componente del gruppo sbaglia certe informazioni sul corso, tocca a chi ha queste informazioni correggerle.*

Espressioni utili

- Dopo averci pensato molto ho deciso di scegliere ...
- Il corso ... mi attira per vari motivi. In primo luogo ...
- A parte il programma linguistico sono molto interessato/a a ...
- La ragione / il motivo per cui vorrei iscrivermi a questo corso è ...
- Anche se gli altri corsi sembrano interessanti ...
- La mia scelta è stata influenzata dal fatto che ...
- Il corso ... è proprio quello che cercavo

Parliamo 5 *A coppie discutete di un corso che state facendo attualmente o che avete fatto in passato. Potete basare il vostro discorso sui punti elencati a pagina 194.*

Titolo del corso - durata – strutturazione (numero di ore giornaliere, suddivisione in diversi livelli ecc.) - attività varie, incluse quelle extracurriculari - alloggio - mensa - altri servizi offerti.

Espressioni utili

- Il corso dura /è durato ...
- Le lezioni cominciano / cominciavano ...
- La mattina/nel pomeriggio ho/avevo ... nel pomeriggio ...
- L'anno accademico viene / veniva diviso ...
- Per quanto riguarda le attività extracurriculari ...
- Il corso si conclude / si è concluso ...
- Quanto alla sistemazine ...
- Gli studenti hanno / avevano la possibilità di ...

Vocabolario

a carico di
le abilità linguistiche
accertare il livello di conoscenza
accogliere / l'accoglienza / accogliente
un ambiente amichevole
ammettere / l'ammissione
l'ampliamento del lessico
apprendere / l'apprendimento
approfondire / l'approfondimento
assistere (a)
l'attestato di frequenza
le attività extra-scolastiche
le attrezzature
l'aula
avere accesso (a)
cogliere l'occasione (per)
la conoscenza
dotato (di)
frequentare / la frequenza
la gita
gratuito
in base a
iscriversi (a) / l'iscrizione
il livello linguistico
mensile
il metodo di insegnamento
la modalità d'iscrizione
nell'ambito di
l'obiettivo del programma
oltre a
l'orario
la padronanza della lingua
il patrimonio culturale
perfezionare
il periodo di permanenza
pomeridiano
prenotare / la prenotazione
i prezzi convenienti / accessibili
i principianti
rafforzare le strutture grammaticali
raggruppare
rendere più agevole
rilasciare
rivolgersi (a)
scegliere / la scelta
settimanale
sfruttare
il soggiorno di studio
le spese
il vitto e alloggio

Unità 71

RIFORMA SCOLASTICA

Prima di parlare 1 *Rifletti per almeno dieci minuti sulle seguenti domande e prepara le tue risposte.*

1. Quando comincia la scuola dell'obbligo nel tuo Paese?
2. Per quanti anni dura la frequenza scolastica obbligatoria?
3. Per quanti anni durano i vari cicli – scuola materna, scuola elementare, scuola secondaria?
4. Esiste l'obbligo di frequentare la scuola materna?
5. Come viene divisa la scuola secondaria? Se, ad esempio, viene divisa in due cicli, qual è la differenza fra il primo e il secondo?
6. A che età si scelgono le materie da studiare per i vari esami?
7. Ci sono legami stretti e diretti fra la scuola e il mercato del lavoro?
8. Quali sono, secondo te, i pregi del sistema scolastico nel tuo Paese? E i difetti?
9. Se avessi la possibilità di riformare la scuola nel tuo Paese, che cosa cambieresti?

Parliamo 1 *A coppie o a gruppi discutete le vostre risposte. L'obiettivo dell'attività è di avere un quadro chiaro del sistema scolastico nel vostro Paese. Per ulteriori chiarimenti potete rivolgervi all'insegnante.*

Prima di parlare 2 *Leggi il brano che ti verrà assegnato dall'insegnante e completa la parte relativa della tabella.*

Gli Stati Uniti
La Germania
L'Inghilterra
La Francia

Parliamo 2 *Ora lavorate in gruppi di 4 (A, B, C, D). Scambiate le informazioni che avete letto e completate il resto della tabella.*

Prima di parlare 3 *Lavorate in gruppi di tre.*

Studente A *Studia attentamente il grafico del sistema scolastico italiano che era in vigore nel 1997 e tieni conto dei seguenti aspetti che avrai bisogno di spiegare in seguito.*

- i nomi e la durata delle varie scuole
- l'inizio della scuola dell'obbligo
- la durata dell'istruzione obbligatoria
- i vari esami e l'età in cui si danno questi esami
- gli sbocchi per gli studenti alla fine della scuola dell'obbligo
- gli sbocchi per coloro che proseguono gli studi fino alla fine della scuola secondaria superiore
- il significato dell'anno integrativo

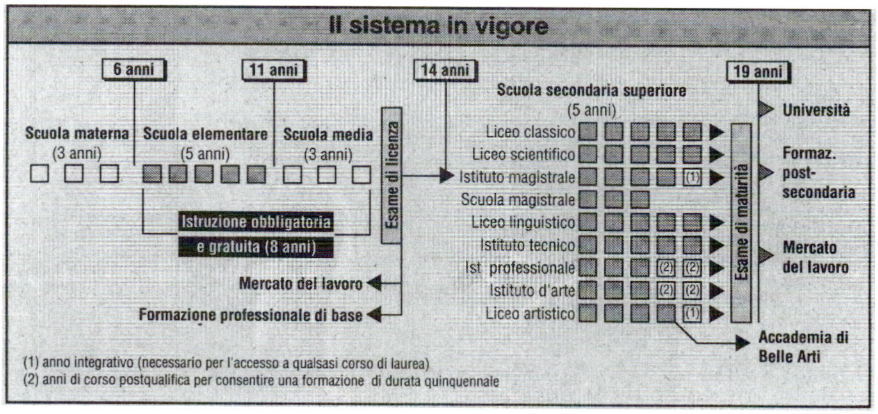

Studente B *Studia attentamente il grafico che tratta della proposta di riforme del sistema scolastico italiano e tieni conto dei seguenti aspetti che avrai bisogno di spiegare in seguito.*

- i nomi e la durata delle varie scuole
- l'inizio della scuola dell'obbligo
- la durata dell'istruzione obbligatoria
- i vari esami e l'età in cui si danno questi esami
- gli sbocchi per gli studenti alla fine della scuola dell'obbligo
- gli sbocchi per coloro che proseguono gli studi fino alla fine della scuola secondaria superiore
- il significato dell'anno preparatorio, anno di orientamento, biennio di orientamento mirato

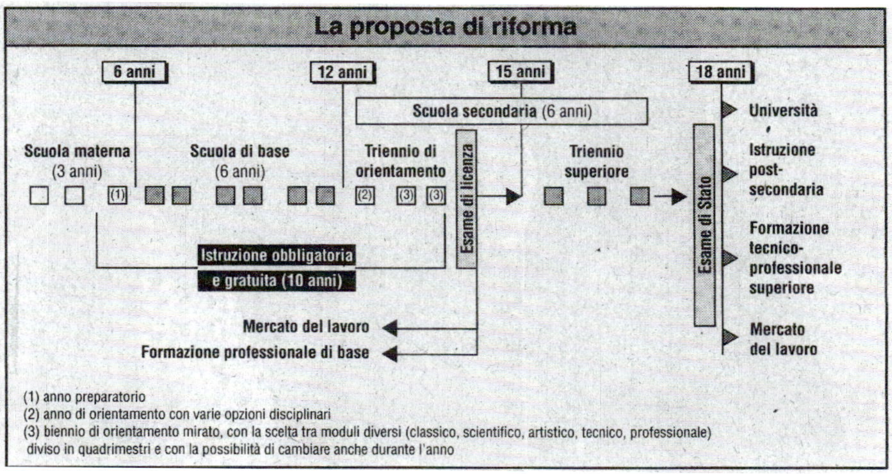

Studente C *Leggi attentamente il seguente brano tratto da un articolo di giornale sulla proposta di riforme della scuola italiana. Tu farai da segretario/a e devi aiutare studente B a spiegare e chiarire, quando necessario, il significato di queste riforme. Sarà meglio consultare il grafico dello studente B e quello dello studente A poiché serviranno per rendere più chiaro il brano che leggi. Inoltre toccherà a te comunicare ai tuoi compagni i pregi di queste nuove riforme.*

Scompare la distinzione tra scuola elementare, media e superiore. Al suo posto vengono introdotti due cicli: quello di base e il ciclo secondario, composto da una prima fase di orientamento e dalla seconda di specializzazione: Il ciclo di base ha la durata di sette anni e assorbe, oltre a quelle che oggi sono le elementari e parte delle medie, anche l'ultimo anno del triennio delle scuole materne. Quest'ultimo, ha spiegato Berlinguer (ministro della Pubblica Istruzione), non corrisponderà alla scuola vera e propria, ma avrà una funzione propedeutica, preparerà il bambino all'ingresso del mondo dell'istruzione.

Dopo il ciclo di base si passa a quello secondario. Con i tre anni di orientamento, che servono allo studente per decidere quale indirizzo di studio scegliere nel triennio successivo, si chiude la scuola dell'obbligo. La quale, pertanto, diventa di dieci anni: lo studente inizia prima (a cinque anni) e finisce il periodo dell'obbligo a 15 anni; e a 18 anni il ciclo delle secondarie. Il passaggio dal periodo di orientamento a quello di specializzazione è regolato da un esame di licenza.

In questo modo, l'Italia si avvicinerebbe ai sistemi degli altri Paesi europei, si introdurrebbe nel sistema scolastico un forte elemento di flessibilità, così da consentire agli studenti una scelta ponderata e evitare che un errore pesi sull'intera carriera scolastica, e inoltre, si creerebbe un legame più stretto e diretto tra scuola e mercato del lavoro.

(Il Sole- 24 ore, 15/1/1997)

Parliamo 3 *Lavorate in gruppi di tre (A, B e C). Prima di iniziare la conversazione studiate bene il vostro ruolo.*

Studente A

Devi spiegare il più dettagliatamente possibile il significato del tuo grafico in modo che i tuoi compagni abbiano un quadro chiaro del sistema scolastico italiano in vigore nel 1997.

Studente B

Devi spiegare il più dettagliatamente possibile il significato del tuo grafico in modo che i tuoi compagni abbiano un quadro chiaro della proposta di riforme della scuola italiana. Se non capisci il significato di certi termini sul grafico puoi chiedere chiarimenti allo studente C.

Studente C

Tu fai da segretario/a e quindi devi prendere nota di quello che dicono i tuoi compagni riguardo al sistema scolastico precedente e quello "nuovo". È possibile che lo studente B ti chieda dei chiarimenti su alcuni termini usati nel suo grafico spiegati nel brano che hai letto. Quando i tuoi compagni hanno finito di parlare, toccherà a te riassumere quello che hanno detto sui due sistemi. Inoltre puoi comunicare i pregi delle nuove riforme.

Espressioni utili

- Dunque, per quanto riguarda i nomi delle varie scuole si parla di ...
- Come vedete, c'è un ventaglio di possibilità per quanto riguarda le scuole secondarie superiori, ad esempio ...
- La scuola materna dura ...
- La scuola dell'obbligo inizia a ... e si conclude a ...
- Alla fine della scuola media/superiore ...
- Vuoi ripetere quello che hai detto riguardo a ...?
- Penso che l'anno integrativo significhi ...
- Se non sbaglio l'anno di orientamento vuol dire ...
- Mi dispiace ma non sono riuscito/a a capire il significato di ...
- Cosa si dice nel grafico che hai letto riguardo a ...?

Prima di parlare 4 *Leggi attentamente i seguenti quattro punti messi in evidenza da un giornalista in un articolo intitolato **"Obiettivi ambiziosi"**.*

1 L'esigenza di uniformare l'uscita dalla scuola secondaria a quella prevalente in Europa (18 anni) ha delle motivazioni valide. Ma un anno di scuola non rappresenta un'entità astratta, che si può togliere o raggiungere senza pagarne le conseguenze in termini di livello di preparazione. Già adesso i nostri studenti di scuola secondaria sono spesso ultimi nei confronti internazionali. Che cosa succederà togliendo un anno di scuola?

2 Un anno in meno di scuola significa anche che i giovani entreranno mediamente un anno prima nel mercato del lavoro. Questo produrrà un'offerta aggiuntiva di manodopera di oltre 500mila unità, sia pure distribuite nel tempo. Quali conseguenze produrrà questo ulteriore flusso sul nostro disastrato mercato del lavoro giovanile?

3 La proposta di rendere obbligatorio l'ultimo anno della scuola materna (peraltro oggi frequentata già da 95% degli aventi diritto) è sicuramente valida, soprattutto se si coniugherà con un rafforzamento delle capacità propedeutiche all'apprendimento formale, specialmente per i bambini socialmente e culturalmente deprivati.

4 Lascia invece perplessi la "rivoluzione" proposta per tutto il ciclo di base. Sia perché viene profondamente alterato un ordine di scuola, come quello elementare, che sostanzialmente aveva sempre espresso validi risultati; sia perché questo stesso ordine di scuola si sta appena riassestando dopo l'introduzione della riforma di struttura nel 1990; sia, infine, perché la nuova proposta di riforma introduce un ciclo primario di sei anni, che esiste solamente in Grecia e in alcune scuole primarie inglesi (ma in questo caso si comincia la prima classe della scuola elementare all'età di 5 anni, mentre in Francia e in Spagna il ciclo elementare è di 5 anni, e in Germania è di quattro. Insomma in tutta Europa l'uscita dal ciclo primario avviene a 11 anni, mentre da noi si collocherebbe a 12 anni. Sarebbe più opportuno e coerente rifarsi al modello francese, che prevede, al termine del ciclo di 5 anni della scuola elementare, una scuola media (Collège) di 4 anni, distinta in due bienni: il primo di Observation, unitario per tutti gli alunni, il secondo di Orientation, nel quale si prevede una possibilità di differenziazione del curriculum, soprattutto all'ultimo anno. Al termine (che coincide con il termine della scolarità obbligatoria) gli studenti possono iscriversi alla scuola secondaria, al cui interno i licei hanno durata triennale, per uscire dal sistema scolastico al diciottesimo anno di età.

(Il Sole 24 ore, 15/1/1997)

Parliamo 4 *A coppie o a gruppi discutete le vostre reazioni ai quattro punti messi in evidenza dal giornalista. Inoltre, cosa pensate del modello scolastico francese proposto alla conclusione dell'articolo?*

Parliamo 5 *A coppie o in piccoli gruppi confrontate il "nuovo" sistema scolastico italiano con quello attualmente in vigore nel vostro Paese. Se aveste la possibilità di scegliere fra i due sistemi, quale scegliereste? Motivate le vostre risposte.*

CINEMA, CHE PASSIONE!

Prima di parlare 1 *Ti piace il cinema? Vai al cinema regolarmente? Che tipo di film preferisci di solito? Qual è l'ultimo film che hai visto, in una sala cinematografica o in televisione? Ci sono film / attori / attrici che ti hanno lasciato un'impressione profonda? Rifletti su queste domande e preparati a parlare delle tue preferenze e abitudini.*

Parliamo 1 *Ora scambia le tue riflessioni con uno o più compagni e nota le differenze o similarità.*

Espressioni utili

- Sono appassionato/a di film d'azione/comici/western/drammatici/di spionaggio
- Preferisco le commedie sentimentali/musicali/brillanti ...
- Non andrei mai a vedere un film di fantascienza/dell'orrore ...
- Mi interesso solo di cinema d'autore/...francese ...
- Vado al cinema ma solo per far piacere a ...
- Un film che ricordo particolarmente è ...
- Trovo quell'attore/quell'attrice davvero bravo/a nel ruolo di ... perché ...
- Non dimenticherò mai l'impressione che mi ha fatto ...
- È un film indimenticabile/sorprendente/polemico/di grande successo/ poco apprezzato ma ...

Prima di parlare 2 *Studia la pagina degli spettacoli a Roma (Repubblica, 23.12.1999) e scegli un film adatto a queste persone o occasioni:*

a. un appassionato di drammi romantici, particolarmente se in costume
b. una persona che si interessa di questioni sociali ma che non ha voglia di vedere film troppo seri
c. una persona che apprezza personaggi femminili forti
d. una persona che ama ricordare il passato
e. una famiglia con bambini che adorano i cartoni animati
f. un amico stressato che ha bisogno di farsi quattro risate
g. una persona che s'interessa di questioni morali e esistenziali, ma non troppo seriamente
h. una coppia alla ricerca di una serata romantica e divertente
i. una persona che ama morire di paura!

P SCHERMO PICCOLO M SCHERMO MEDIO

TRAME

La storia di Agnes Browne
Nell'Irlanda degli anni sessanta, Agnes resta vedova con sette figli da crescere e sfamare; il compito è proibitivo, ma la donna non si arrende. La sua costanza alla fine sarà premiata. Quasi il ritratto di una moderna Madre Coraggio.
CINELAND MULTIPLEX 1 - EDEN 2 - GREENWICH 2 - MIGNON 1 - ODEON 4

La via degli angeli
Dopo Almodovar, anche Avati racconta tutto su mia madre, rievocando con nostalgia e amarezza, l'incontro fra i suoi genitori. Tutto si svolge attorno ad una balera dell'Appennino emiliano sullo sfondo dell'Italietta fascista.
FIAMMA 2

Mifune
Un apologo sul potere e la libertà e sul contrasto fra ricchezza e felicità. L'argomento non è inedito, ma la messa in scena, che risponde alle regole di Dogma, decisamente inconsueta e particolarmente divertente. Gran Premio al festival di Berlino.
GREENWICH 3 - QUATTRO FONTANE 3

Onegin
Dal romanzo di Puskin, una storia d'amore e rivalità sullo sfondo della provincia russa dell'ottocento. Il giovane dandy, Eugenio Onegin, infastidito dalla corte di Tatiana, si diverte a corteggiarne la sorella, provocando una tragedia.
SAVOY 4

Se scappi ti sposo
Sulle orme di Pretty Woman, Julia Roberts e Richard Gere in una nuova commedia romantica. Lei è una bella ragazza che, colpita da improvvisi attacchi di panico, è solita mollare i fidanzati sull'altare; lui un giornalista la dileggia pubblicamente.
ALHAMBRA 1 - ANDROMEDA 1 - BARBERINI 1 - CINELAND MULTIPLEX 11 - CINELAND MULTIPLEX 13 - DELLE MIMOSE 1 - EMBASSY - EURCINE 2 - GIULIO CESARE 2 - GIULIO CESARE 3 - JOLLY 1 - KING 1 - MAESTOSO 1 - ODEON 2 - WARNER VILLAGE 9 - WARNER VILLAGE 12 - WARNER VILLAGE MODERNO 3

Tarzan
Il celeberrimo personaggio creato da Edgar Rice Burroghs per la prima volta a cartoni animati. Avventura e ironia, sentimenti e canzoni in confenzione di gran classe. L'animazione permette a Tarzan di volare come non si era mai visto prima.
ACADEMY HALL - ALHAMBRA 3 - AMBASSADE 3 - ANTARES 2 - APOLLO - ATLANTIC 2 - BARBERINI 3 - BROADWAY 3 - CAPITOL - CAPRANICA - CIAK 2 - CINELAND MULTIPLEX 5 - DORIA 2 - EXCELSIOR 2 - GALAXY SALA VENERE - GOLDEN - LUX10 - MADISON 2 - MISSOURI 1 - ODEON 1 - ROXY ZAFFIRO - SALA TROISI - SAVOY 1 - TRIANON 3 - WARNER VILLAGE 7 - WARNER VILLAGE 11 - WARNER VILLAGE MODERNO 4

Tutti gli uomini del deficiente
L'esordio sul grande schermo della Gialappa's Band, che, fedele alle proprie tradizioni, resta solo una voce fuori campo. Un accumulo di situazioni comiche, con una miriade di personaggi impegnati in un grande concorso. Si ride molto.
ANDROMEDA 4 - CINELAND MULTIPLEX 4 - COLA DI RIENZO - DELLE MIMOSE 4 - EURCINE 3 - JOLLY 3 - LUX 1 - MAESTOSO 4 - WARNER VILLAGE 10 - WARNER VILLAGE MODERNO 1

D.M. 6/161144 del 16/9/99

Sale che aderiscono all'iniziativa Sipra "Vota lo spot, vinci il cinema": in palio ogni giorno un carnet per 10 film di prima visione e centinaia di premi spettacolari fra coloro che telefoneranno al numero 02.27764 per votare la pubblicità più bella.
In collaborazione con Alpitour, "la Repubblica" e Telecom.

GREENWICH - 4 FONTANE
LUCKY BLU (Borgo S. Spirito 75)
LUX - WARNER VILLAGE
(Parco de' Medici)

East is East

"Al Festival di Cannes 1999 **risate** e **applausi** a scena **aperta**"

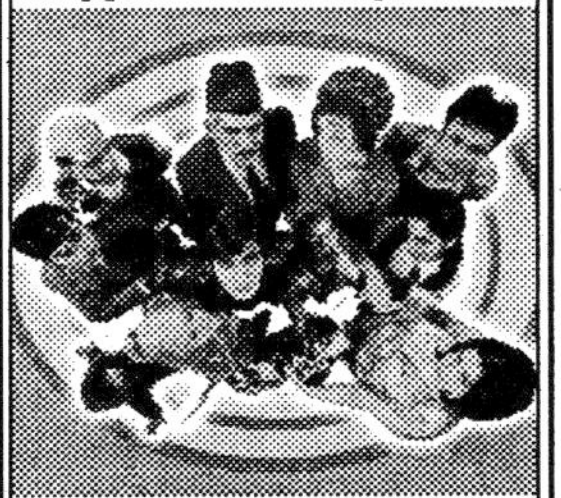

...al termine del film hanno **sbattuto i piedi** ed **applaudito** per quasi **7minuti**

IN ESCLUSIVA
AL CINEMA
LABIRINTO

Nell'estate più calda, New York vive l'incubo del suo primo serial-Killer

☆☆☆☆ (Corriere della Sera)
Da non perdere (la Repubblica)

SNCCI
SEGNALATO DALLA CRITICA CINEMATOGRAFICA ITALIANA

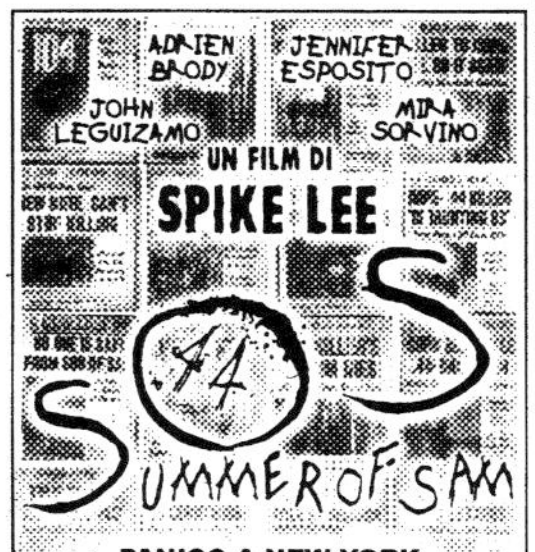

PANICO A NEW YORK

UNA DISTRIBUZIONE EAGLE PICTURES SPA

Parliamo 2 *A gruppi di tre. Lo studente A consiglierà il film più adatto allo studente B (che assumerà il ruolo di una delle persone nella lista a-i). Lo studente C, che ha già visto quel film, lo sconsiglierà, spiegando le sue ragioni. Lo studente C sceglierà quale consiglio seguire, motivando la sua scelta. Poi gli studenti potranno scambiare i ruoli.*

Espressioni utili

- Sono stufo/a dei soliti film/attori/delle solite situazioni ...
- La storia è coinvolgente ...
- Ha una trama complessa/una colonna sonora fantastica ...
- Il film è stato tratto dal libro di ...
- Ci sono scene.../c'è una sequenza in cui ...
- Poiché ti interessi di... direi che è proprio un film adatto ai tuoi gusti
- Sono sicuro/a a che ti piacerebbe/che piacerebbe ai bambini/a chi...
- Se fossi in te/voi non sprecherei tempo.../soldi...

Vocabolario

l'attore / l'attrice
avvincente
il ciak
il cinema
la cinepresa
la colonna sonora
i costumi
il/la costumista
il festival
la fotografia
il genere di fim:
- di animazione
- d'autore
- d'avventura
- d'amore / commedia sentimentale
- di fantascienza
- dell'orrore
- giallo / poliziesco
- di satira di costume
- di spionaggio
- storico

girare un film
l'interpretazione / l'interprete
premiare
la regia / il/la regista
le riprese
il ruolo
la sala cinematografica / multisala
la scena
scontato
la sequenza
lo sceneggiatore
la trama

Unità 73

AVVENTURA A LONDRA

Prima di parlare 1 *Leggi attentamente l'articolo* ***'Londra: ragazzo italiano sequestrato e liberato con un blitz'****. Che avventura per il ragazzo!*

Londra: ragazzo italiano sequestrato e liberato con un blitz

VENEZIA – Un blitz di Scotland Yard e della Squadra Mobile di Venezia ha restituito la libertà a un ventiduenne veneziano di cui non si conosce l'identità, che sarebbe stato tenuto sotto sequestro in un appartamento di Londra. Il padre del ragazzo avrebbe ricevuto la richiesta di riscatto e si sarebbe subito rivolto alla polizia italiana. Il blitz sarebbe avvenuto dopo il suo arrivo nella capitale inglese con agenti della Squadra Mobile di Venezia. Sempre secondo indiscrezioni il ragazzo e il padre dovrebbero rientrare in Italia nelle prossime ore.

(Repubblica 10.2.2000)

Parliamo 1 *A coppie. Immaginate di essere uno dei personaggi e create una scenetta seguendo i suggerimenti indicati. L'insegnante vi assegnerà il ruolo.*

a. **Ragazzo-Rapinatore** – Momento del sequestro. Il rapinatore dà istruzioni al ragazzo su come comportarsi durante il periodo del sequestro/il ragazzo chiede spiegazioni, cerca di commuovere il rapinatore e di farsi liberare.

b. **Rapinatore-Padre** – Al telefono. Il rapinatore telefona alla famiglia per chiedere il riscatto, minacciando cose gravi se le condizioni non vengono accettate. Il padre cerca di ottenere il maggior numero d'informazioni sulle condizioni del figlio e fa promesse al rapinatore.

c. **Padre-Poliziotto** – In commissariato. Il padre racconta tutto al poliziotto e chiede aiuto. Il poliziotto cerca di stabilire i fatti precisi e consiglia alla famiglia come comportarsi.

d. **Padre-madre** – A casa. I genitori si fanno coraggio l'uno con l'altro ma è chiaro che uno di loro è pessimista mentre l'altro è più ottimista.

e. **Madre-figlio** – A casa. Finalmente salvo, il ragazzo è a casa ma non vuole parlare troppo della sua avventura. La madre però lo tempesta di domande.

Espressioni utili

- Non muoverti!
- Zitto!
- Aiuto!
- Mi lasci andare, La prego ...
- ... non mi faccia male ...
- Attento, sono armato ...
- Suo figlio è stato sequestrato ...
- Lei ascolti bene e segua le mie istruzioni ...
- Soprattutto cercate di trattenerli al telefono al più lungo possibile ...
- Mantenetevi calmi ...
- Cosa dobbiamo fare?
- Caro, sono angosciata ...
- Non perdiamoci d'animo ...
- Vedrai, tutto si risolverà per il meglio ...
- Mamma, lasciami stare ...
- Non ho voglia di parlarne
- Dimmi tutto ...
- Poverino!

Prima di parlare 2

Studente A – Immagina di essere un giornalista di cronaca. L'editore del tuo giornale ti ha chiesto di preparare un articolo che sottolinei l'aspetto più umano del caso, cioè che impatto ha avuto l'episodio su questa famiglia. Prepara alcune domande per intervistare uno o più personaggi, incluso il poliziotto ma non il rapinatore che ora si trova in carcere.

Studente B – Immagina di essere il poliziotto. Il commissario ti ha chiesto di preparare il verbale sul crimine. Prepara le domande che farai alla famiglia. Ricorda che il tuo compito è quello di stabilire fatti precisi, senza soffermarti su opinioni o emozioni. Ricorda che c'è anche un giornalista che ti aspetta per farti qualche domanda.

Studenti C, D, E. – Assumete il ruolo che vi darà l'insegnante. L'editore del giornale della vostra città vi ha chiesto di concedere un'intervista. In seguito dovrete recarvi al Commissariato di quartiere per fare una dichiarazione. Preparatevi a raccontare l'episodio *dal vostro punto di vista.*

Parliamo 2 *Lavoro di gruppo*

Lo studente A intervista gli studenti C,D,E e prende nota delle risposte.
Lo studente B intervista gli studenti C,D,E e prende nota delle risposte.
Lo studente A intervista lo studente B.

Parliamo 3 *Lo studente A (il giornalista) e lo studente B (il poliziotto) riferiscono il risultato delle loro interviste a un gruppo di colleghi (la classe).*

Vocabolario

l'agente di sicurezza
la chiamata
chiedere / pagare il riscatto
il commissariato
la Mobile
il nascondiglio
la notizia
la polizia
rapire / il rapimento / il rapitore
ritrovare / il ritrovamento
salvare
scappare
sequestrare / il sequestro / il sequestratore
sopravvivere (a)
sorprendere
tendere un agguato (a)
la vittima

Unità 74

ACQUISTI IN RETE

Prima di parlare *Anche in Italia è ora possibile fare acquisti in rete, a partire dalle arance biologiche a una vacanza. Molti italiani ne sono entusiasti e i siti si prolificano a vista d'occhio. Avete esperienze, dirette o indirette, di questo tipo di acquisti? Se non ne avete ancora avuto la possibilità, che cosa sapete di questo fenomeno attraverso i giornali, la televisione o l'esperienza di colleghi, parenti, amici e conoscenti?*

Parliamo 1 *A gruppi. Scambiate le vostre esperienze dirette o indirette con i compagni del vostro gruppo.*

Espressioni utili

- Non ho ancora fatto nessun acquisto in rete
- I miei colleghi mi dicono che ...
- Sì, ho trovato parecchie offerte allettanti ...
- È stato più facile di quanto pensavo ...
- E dire che mi avevano detto che ...

Prima di parlare 2 *La classe è divisa in gruppi. Gli studenti del gruppo A leggono l'articolo* ***Decolla l'e-commerce*** *e quelli del gruppo B leggono l'articolo* ***Il regalo giusto in rete, all'ultimo clic****. Alternativamente si può dividere la classe a coppie (Studente A e Studente B).*

NEWSLINE *a cura di Paolo Conti*

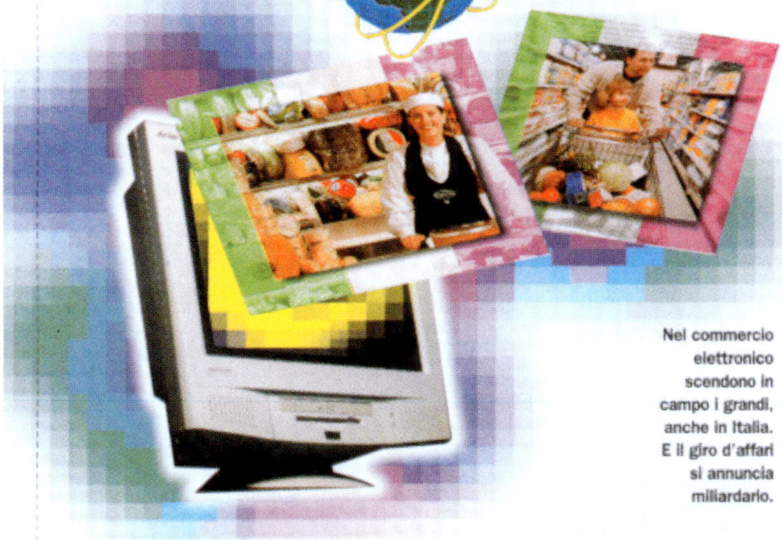

Nel commercio elettronico scendono in campo i grandi, anche in Italia. E il giro d'affari si annuncia miliardario.

Decolla l'e-commerce

I nuovi siti Internet per comprare di tutto: dai cellulari alle arance biologiche.

Gli americani il boom dello shopping natalizio in Rete l'hanno vissuto l'anno scorso, quando i negozi online d'oltre oceano hanno fatto registrare fatturati miliardari in pochi giorni. E quest'anno gli esperti prevedono un fenomeno analogo anche in Italia. Si spiega così la proliferazione di siti commerciali che ha interessato la rete nostrana nelle ultime settimane. La grande catena europea di elettronica di consumo Mediaworld ha inaugurato uno shopping center virtuale (**www.mediaworld.it**) che in pochi giorni ha registrato un notevole sovraccarico di ordini. Sul sito si possono comprare molti dei prodotti venduti nei negozi Mediaworld, oltre a una serie di offerte speciali riservate ai navigatori della rete. Più o meno nello stesso periodo ha aperto i battenti anche AlCosto.it, un sito che vende computer, telefonini e altri prodotti a prezzi da grossista (vedi box in alto a destra). Passando ai negozi on line specializzati, Alinari ha messo in vendita in Rete il proprio immenso archivio di immagini (**www.alinari.com**), mentre la piccola impresa siciliana Il Biviere ha aperto un cybernegozio (**www.arance.it**) che vende arance Doc in tutto il mondo.

Quanto ai siti già affermati, sono partite le offerte speciali natalizie. CentroHI (**www.chl.it**), per esempio, offre pacchi di prodotti «tecnologici» al 50 per cento del prezzo di listino, mentre ThinkItaly (**www.thinkitaly.com**), il negozio on line specializzato in marchi italiani di qualità, garantisce la spedizione gratuita in tutta Italia per tutto il mese di dicembre.

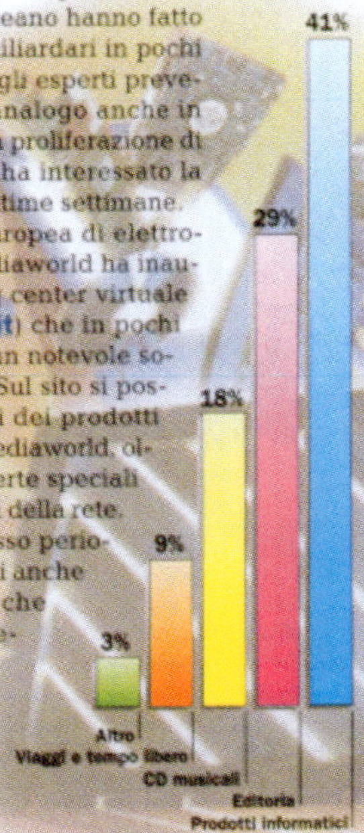

Gli italiani continuano a comprare in Rete soprattutto computer, informazioni e musica. Fonte: Anee 1999

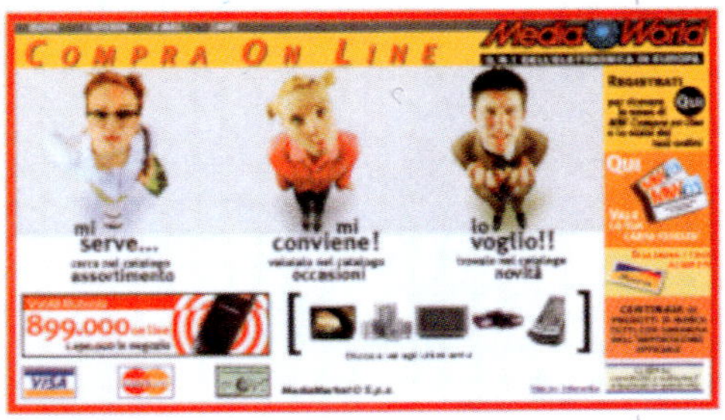

Anche la catena di elettronica di consumo Mediaworld entra nel commercio elettronico. E lo fa con un sito ben realizzato, ricco di prodotti e di offerte promozionali. www.mediaworld.it

LA FIERA DEGLI SCONTI SU ALCOSTO.IT

UN NUOVO SITO CHE VENDE IN RETE A PREZZI DA GROSSISTA

Vendere online a prezzo di fabbrica. Un'idea già diffusa negli Stati Uniti, che apre i battenti anche in Italia con il nuovo sito AlCosto.it, specializzato per ora in informatica ed elettronica di consumo. «La nostra idea è vendere on line i prodotti con il prezzo applicato dai grossisti» spiega Giancarlo Devasini, l'ideatore del progetto. «Il nostro guadagno ricade solo su una commissione di intervento fissa di 19.900 lire per ogni tipologia di prodotto». Gli acquisti su Alcosto.it sono per singoli prodotti costosi, come stampanti, computer e videoproiettori. Il sito si appoggia alla Banca Sella per la gestione sicura della transazione con carta di credito, ma permette di effettuare acquisti anche inviando solo una parte del numero di carta di credito o che verrà completata al telefono. La merce viene consegnata in tutta Italia in 24-48 ore, salvo diversa disponibilità dei grossisti.

Mark Perna

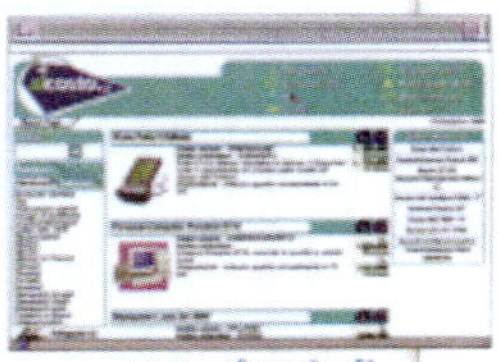

www.alcosto.it

NATALE LAST MINUTE

Web store

Il **regalo giusto**, in rete,

Meraviglie hi-tech, videogiochi per adulti, viaggi di fine secolo: gli acquisti natalizi su Internet sono ormai facili, spesso convenienti ed evitano le corse allo shopping ritardatario. Pochi accorgimenti e la rete si trasforma nella soluzione ideale per scovare il dono più adatto al prezzo più basso.

Il conto alla rovescia è cominciato. Il grande circo di Natale sta per concludersi e il rito dei regali è pronto a essere consumato. Cosa c'entra Internet con tutto questo? Facile: chi non vuole affrontare la ressa dello shopping dell'ultimo minuto può trovare in rete la soluzione. Quest'anno le chanche di trovare il regalo giusto nel cyberspazio sono davvero tante. Anche in rete i negozi si sono organizzati con offerte allettanti e idee regalo originali, con il vantaggio in più di poter comprare in pochi minuti, anche di

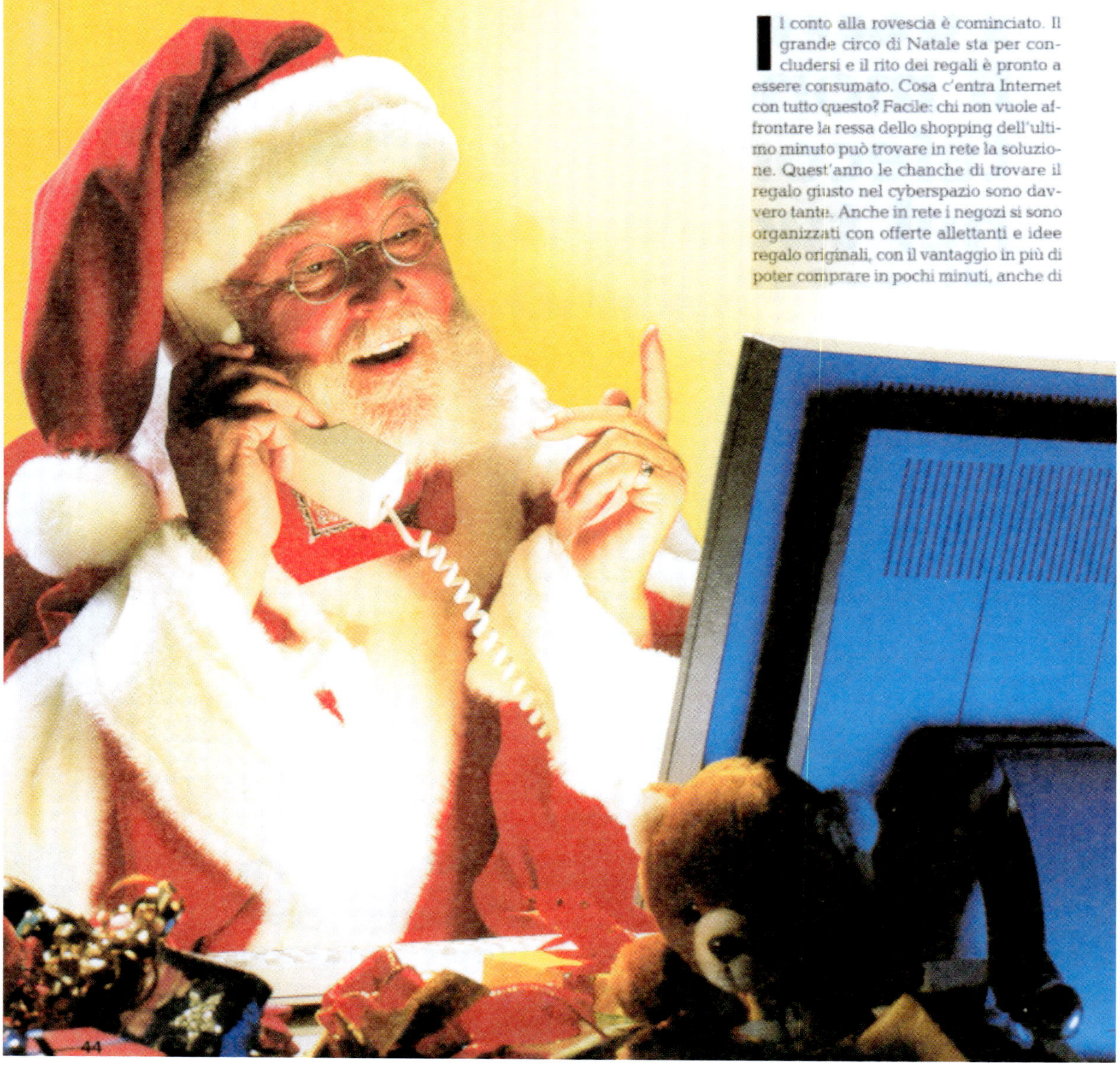

all'ultimo clic

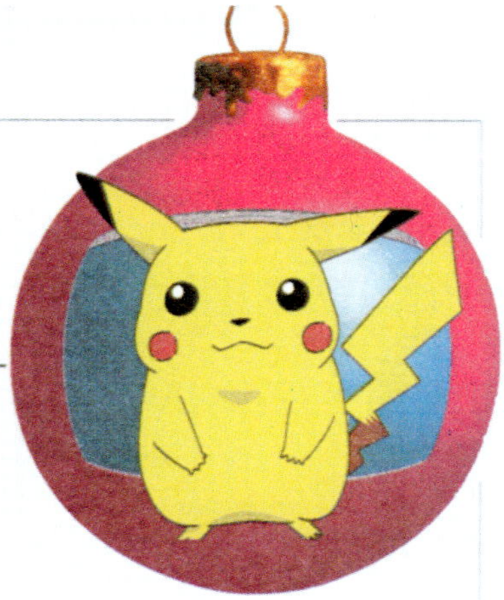

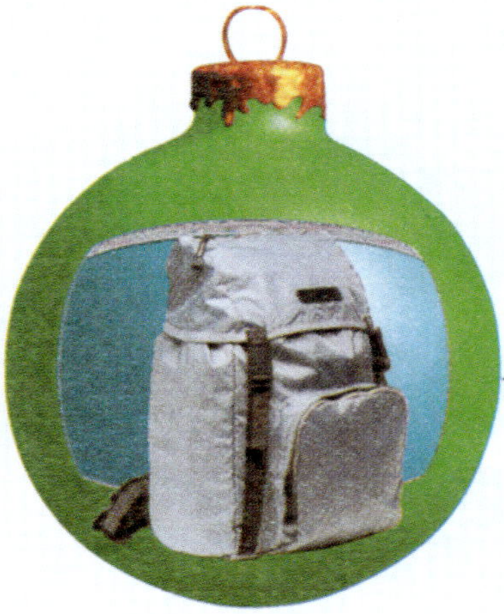

notte, senza uscire di casa.
Nei negozi online, l'high-tech la fa da padrona, fra telefonini dell'ultima generazione, computer ultrapiatti e curiosità multimediali. Ma Internet offre molto di più. Per esempio, la rete è il luogo ideale per comprare un viaggio da sogno con sconti da favola. Per non parlare dei tantissimi online shop specializzati in oggetti d'arredamento, sport, prodotti alimentari regionali, videogiochi e chi più ne ha più ne metta.
L'anno scorso lo shopping natalizio online ha spopolato negli Stati Uniti. Quest'anno sarà probabilmente il turno dell'Italia. Non per niente i principali negozi in rete italiani si aspettano fatturati da capogiro. Comprare in rete è sicuro, a patto di affidarsi a siti che gestiscono le transazioni finanziarie con il livello di sicurezza opportuno. Ma perdere altro tempo non conviene: i tempi di spedizione della merce non sono sempre ottimali e i ritardatari rischiano di regalare qualcosa che arriverà a destinazione dopo la Befana.

GIOCHI ANCHE PER ADULTI

Chi ha detto che i videogiochi li usano solo i ragazzi? Su Internet si possono comprare i migliori videogame dedicati a un pubblico adulto, dal violentissimo Carmageddon al claustrofobico KingPing, fino alle sofisticate simulazioni dell'alta finanza di Wall Street Tycoon e alle suggestioni religiose di Messiah. ***A pagina 53.***

SHOPPING FA RIMA CON GADGET HI-TECH

Se la tecnologia impazza, lo shopping risponde. Per Natale i negozi di telefonini, computer ed elettronica di consumo verranno presi d'assalto dai ritardatari del regalo. Ma su Internet si compra meglio e spesso si spende meno rispetto ai negozi tradizionali. ***A pagina 60.***

CAPODANNO IN VIAGGIO: NON È ANCORA TROPPO TARDI

Non è troppo tardi per prenotare il viaggio di Capodanno. Se nelle agenzie vi rispondono picche, niente paura: i siti che offrono viaggi scontati dell'ultimo minuto sono tanti e la vacanza che fa per voi è a pochi clic di distanza, dalle montagne italiane alle mete esotiche. ***A pagina 47.***

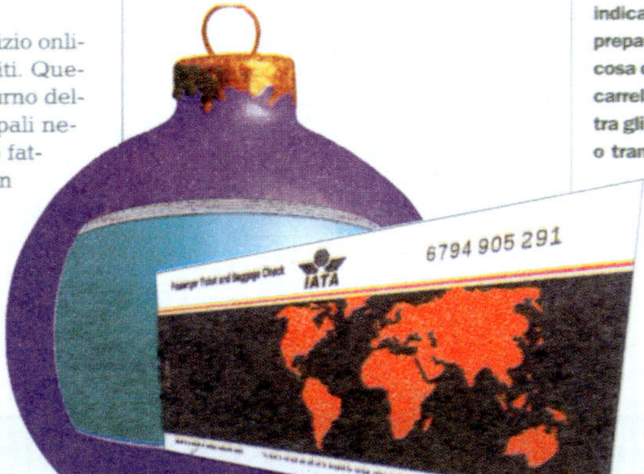

IL PUNTO DEBOLE

Comprare all'ultimo minuto via Internet si può, ma non sempre i negozi virtuali sono in grado di offrire una garanzia sui tempi di consegna. Sono molti i navigatori che hanno dovuto aspettare settimane per ricevere la merce ordinata in rete. Meglio quindi controllare i tempi di consegna con i gestori del negozio virtuale. Se volete che il regalo arrivi entro Natale, molti siti stranieri potrebbero rivelarsi inadatti.

HELP LINE

Come si fanno gli acquisti?

Nel negozio virtuale si fa la spesa riempiendo un tradizionale carrello. Di fianco a ogni prodotto appare una piccola icona o scritta che permette di «prelevare» la merce dallo scaffale e depositarla nel carrello della spesa. Alcuni siti, un po' più semplici, dispongono di un modulo da riempire seguendo le istruzioni. Alla fine della "spesa" si passa alla cassa, spesso indicata con il tasto «invia l'ordine», che prepara il conto. Se si è dimenticato qualcosa o si desidera togliere un prodotto dal carrello si fa ancora in tempo a ritornare tra gli scaffali, utilizzando l'apposito tasto o tramite il comando «indietro» di Explorer o Netscape. A questo punto i negozi più seri comunicano il costo delle spese di spedizione, chiedono l'indirizzo del destinatario e passano al pagamento. La maggioranza dei siti utilizza la carta di credito, mediante l'invio dei dati via computer. In alcuni casi, sempre più rari, è possibile pagare anche alla consegna, con un bonifico.

Espressioni utili

- Il vantaggio/Lo svantaggio più evidente è ...
- Sono d'accordo sul fatto che ...
- Non è detto che sia sempre ...
- A patto di ...
- Resta sempre il dubbio che ...
- Sarà una moda passeggera?
- Non crea forse una classe di esclusi?

Parliamo 2 *La classe è nuovamente divisa in modo che il nuovo raggruppamento includa studenti dei gruppi A e B nell'attività precedente. Il nuovo gruppo A discute tutti i vantaggi degli acquisti in rete, mentre il nuovo gruppo B riflette sugli eventuali rischi e problemi associati a questo tipo di acquisti. Alla fine il portavoce di ogni gruppo presenterà i risultati della discussione al resto della classe.*

Vocabolario

un accorgimento
cliccare
il consumatore
conveniente
il grossista
la merce
mettere in vendita in rete
a prezzo di fabbrica
la rete nostrana
rispetto a
la soluzione
il sito commerciale
specializzato
la tecnologia dell'ultima generazione
la transazione

Unità 75

AMICA MIA

Prima di parlare 1 *Pensate al vostro più caro amico / alla vostra più cara amica. Come vi siete conosciuti? Da quanto tempo vi conoscete? Siete simili o differenti l'uno dall'altro/dall'altra? Quali qualità apprezzate di più nella persona amica?*

Parliamo 1 *A coppie o in gruppi. Ora scambiate le vostre riflessioni con altri compagni.*

Espressioni utili

- Ci conosciamo da ... anni/qualche mese
- Eravamo compagni di scuola
- Ci siamo conosciuti/e durante un viaggio .../ a una festa ...
- Il mio più caro amico/la mia amica più intima si chiama ...
- Dopo ... è la persona che più influenza le mie decisioni ...
- È la persona di cui mi fido maggiormente/di più ...
- Andiamo molto d'accordo
- Non sempre siamo d'accordo su ... ma ...
- Abbiamo lo stesso atteggiamento verso .../punto di vista su ...
- Se ho un problema glielo confido .../chiedo il suo parere ...
- Lei riflessiva, io sono più impulsiva
- Lui è meno sportivo di me, però ...
- Questa mia amica è più simpatica che bella
- La qualità che più apprezzo in lei/lui è ...

Prima di Parlare 2 *Compila il sondaggio 'Chi sono i migliori amici'? stabilendo quali sono le sei qualità più importanti fra quelle elencate e mettendole in ordine prioritario. Indica la tua scelta con un numero da 1 a 6 nella casella.*

CHI SONO I MIGLIORI AMICI?

Gli amici migliori sono quelli che...

- [ ] ti accompagnano al cinema anche se hanno già visto il film
- [ ] sanno ascoltare
- [ ] non giudicano quello che fai
- [ ] raccontano gli ultimi pettegolezzi
- [ ] sono disposti a dire una bugia per te
- [ ] ti prestano soldi o altre cose
- [ ] tirano su il morale
- [ ] fanno molti complimenti
- [ ] hanno sempre qualcosa di divertente da raccontarti
- [ ] danno molti consigli
- [ ] hanno i tuoi stessi gusti
- [ ] fanno regali costosi
- [ ] sanno tenere un segreto
- [ ] aiutano in caso d'emergenza
- [ ] sono presenti nei momenti più importanti o difficili
- [ ] scoppiano a ridere se tu indossi qualcosa di ridicolo
- [ ] vogliono bene a /tollerano le persone a te care
- [ ] parlano sempre bene di te
- [ ] sono molto simili a te per carattere

Parliamo 2 *In gruppo. Ora confronta le tue risposte con quelle di altri compagni. Che differenze ci sono? Discutete e preparatevi a presentare la classifica del vostro gruppo al resto della classe, giustificando le vostre scelte.*

Espressioni utili

- In amicizia, quello che importa veramente è ...
- In amicizia, per me, la cosa più importante è ...
- Non trovi che sia meglio avere un amico che ... piuttosto di uno che ...?
- Sì, lo ammetto, però ...
- Non do nessuna importanza a ...
- Io non mi fiderei di una persona che ...
- Non sei d'accordo?
- Ecco la nostra classifica ...
- Abbiamo messo ... al primo/all'ultimo posto perché ...
- Non siamo tutti d'accordo su ...

Parliamo 3 *Un portavoce di ogni gruppo presente la classifica. (Per* ***Espressioni utili*** *vedi* ***Parliamo 2****)*

Prima di parlare 3 *Leggi attentamente l'articolo* ***Dieci cose che un'amica dovrebbe fare per te.*** *Quali sono le cose che tu non saresti disposto a fare per gli amici? Pensaci e compila una lista.*

dieci cose

CHE UN'AMICA DOVREBBE FARE PER TE

1

Ti ascolta: dovunque, comunque. Questo è sicuramente il requisito principale: un'amica deve saper ascoltare. E deve saper ascoltare quando ce n'è bisogno: non importa che sia nel mezzo di una riunione, o dopo una giornata estenuante e con due bambini che non vogliono andare a letto. Assolutamente vietato, poi, nascondersi dietro la segreteria telefonica, facendo finta di non essere a casa! Altra situazione imbarazzante da segreteria: telefoni e scatta il messaggio, richiami ed è occupato per un'ora (e se l'amica indispensabile avesse semplicemente staccato?). No: la disponibilità, in casi di emergenza, dev'essere totale. Il massimo consentito è un gentile «richiamo dopo» (ma non il giorno dopo!). L'ascolto poi dev'essere interessato, paziente (ci sono «casi gravi» in cui la stessa storia deve essere ripetuta più e più volte prima di venirne a capo), e soprattutto non giudicante. L'interlocutrice deve fare le domande giuste, annuire nei punti giusti, se necessario commuoversi o arrabbiarsi. E interrompere poco.

2

Il coraggio di essere contro. Dopo la fase dell'ascolto, arriva quella del commento, dell'analisi millimetro per millimetro di quel che è accaduto o sta per accadere, dei consigli. Con tutte le possibili opzioni: che fare, come reagire, oppure come astenersi dall'azione. Ed è qui il momento più delicato: una vera amica deve essere solidale ma non troppo accomodante, deve saper criticare senza giudicare, deve essere severa ma non rigida. Deve avere, insomma, il coraggio di pronunciarsi contro («quell'uomo non fa per te!», così come «penso che tu stia sbagliando con il tuo capo»). Ma usando il tono giusto, cercando il momento giusto, e con ferma dolcezza: un lavoro da equilibristi. E infatti, c'è chi inciampa.

3

Ti presta le chiavi di casa. O dell'automobile. Dopo la disponibilità emotiva, quella materiale: un'amica vera deve essere capace di prestare (occasionalmente) la propria casa per un incontro segreto, il computer in caso di «incidente informatico», il tailleur più elegante per un colloquio... Non solo oggetti, però: anche denaro. E questo è un grande tabù: ormai c'è più imbarazzo a parlare di soldi che di sesso. Ma una cosa è passare una serata con chi è disperata per amore, un'altra è prestarle un milione per l'affitto perché non sa come arrivare alla fine del mese. Un'amicizia vera è generosa anche in assegni, se ovviamente il conto in banca lo permette: generosità che la controparte deve essere altrettanto pronta a ricambiare. E c'è chi ricorda ancora l'aiuto inaspettato di un'amica che le «prestò» la colf nel momento in cui non aveva una lira e la sua casa un malinconico disastro.

4

Il segreto innanzitutto. Ma certo, *ça va sans dire*: ogni comunicazione davvero seria è protetta dal più totale segreto. Fanno eccezione i pettegolezzi (che si possono divulgare) e i mariti (a questi si possono rivelare alcune delle cose più scottanti, tanto in genere non ascoltano. Quindi non mettere in difficoltà una vera amica chiedendole di non raccontare nulla al consorte con cui vive in simbiosi. Tanto non saprà resistere e glielo racconterà lo stesso, in più sentendosi in colpa.

5

Complotti, macchinazioni & C. Ebbene sì, ci sono dei momenti nella vita in cui può venire richiesto di: aspettare di notte, fino alle due del mattino, sotto casa di un ex fidanzato; pedinarlo; fare un'imbarazzante telefonata in codice; fare una telefonata «di controllo»; coprire una bugia; raccontare una bugia; smascherare una bugia. I complotti sentimentali hanno sempre bisogno di detective, pedine, complici. Un'amica non può sottrarsi; anzi, a volte si può perfino divertire. A qualsiasi età.

Segue

6 Legge il libro che le hai regalato. Solo alle suocere e ai cognati è permesso accantonare i nostri regali: un'amica deve darci qualche soddisfazione in più. Gli abiti e gli oggetti quindi vanno esibiti (anche solo una volta), ma soprattutto i libri regalati con amore vanno letti: magari anche solo per dire che erano noiosissimi. Comunque vada, ricordiamoci che è un peccato veniale: lo sa l'amica del cuore che «riciclò», quella sciarpa che non le era piaciuto, e venne perdonata.

7

C'è nei momenti piccoli e in quelli grandi. Un'amica ci può aiutare a rendere più maneggevoli tanti piccoli fastidi della vita, e trasformarli in occasioni di affetto. E quindi passerà in farmacia se siamo a casa malate; ci aiuterà a preparare un esame anche se lei quell'esame l'ha già dato; ci farà da baby-sitter volante quella sera in cui non sappiamo proprio come cavarcela; o ci accompagnerà dal parrucchiere se noi odiamo andarci da sole. L'amica sincera è quella che aspetta in macchina in seconda fila quando «dobbiamo» assolutamente comprare quel paio di scarpe stupende e non possiamo proprio aspettare l'indomani. E' quella che perde una mattina per fare il «consenso» in Comune prima del nostro matrimonio, anche se non sarà lei la testimone. E poi ci offre da bere.
Non solo. E' con noi nei momenti in cui ci sembra di sprofondare nel buio. Quando il dolore è più intollerabile, quando non ci sono parole. Ma anche quando l'emozione e la gioia ci traboccano dal cuore. Nei momenti, insomma, in cui la vita segna i giorni sul calendario. E lei è lì, che sorregge e aiuta. Ci accompagna in tribunale il giorno del divorzio. Trova il tempo di accompagnarci dal notaio a firmare per una casa che non è la sua; ci tiene la mano durante la prima ecografia; ritira questi esami medici di cui abbiamo paura. E poi, capisce quando non ci può più aiutare. E allora, se è il caso, si spinge a scegliere una terapeuta. Uno psicanalista. Accompagnandoci - col pensiero - fino alla porta.

8

Passa con te un weekend anche se si è appena fidanzata. Questo è il regalo più grande che un'amica possa fare, soprattutto un'amica innamorata. Ma è anche uno dei terreni scivolosi su cui molti rapporti si spezzano. Perché improvvisamente una delle due non ha più tempo neanche per una telefonata, non va da nessuna parte senza il nuovo fidanzato, si sottrae a tutte le cene se non viene anche il marito... Addio confidenze, chiacchiere, complicità: c'è solo un senso di esclusione. A volte una serpeggiante, amare sensazione di invidia. In realtà è così semplice rendersi disponibile per delle cose *women's only:* dal cinema più chiacchiere alla vacanza-salvataggio, in cui si porta l'amica in crisi sulla spiaggia ristoratrice. Ai Tropici, se necessario.

9

Ti sa dire. questo vestito non ti sta bene. La sincerità a oltranza non è gradita, ma intendiamoci: è deleteria anche la «carineria» a tutto tondo. Se il rapporto è profondo, sincero, chiaro, allora la vera amica è quella da cui si può andare in cerca di un giudizio trasparente: per capire, finalmente, se quel vestito (quel taglio di capelli, quella casa in affitto) è un errore. Oppure no. Quanti acquisti sbagliati verrebbero evitati. Fosse così semplice per le storie d'amore...

10

Non infierisce sugli errori. «Te l'avevo detto» è la frase sdrucciolevole che una vera amica non dovrebbe mai dire. Neanche se è vero. La critica va esercitata prima del possibile errore. Con delicatezza, senza «allontanare» o ferire. Ma dopo... Be', *dopo* è tardi: e a questo punto un'amica deve semplicemente esserci, senza recriminare. Senza raccogliere la facile vittoria delle sue (magari foschissime) previsioni. Anche se non è d'accordo. Peggio: anche se non è *mai* stata d'accordo. E quindi se secondo lei quell'invito non andava accettato, quell'uomo non andava sposato, quel lavoro non andava abbandonato, quel bambino non doveva essere educato in quel modo... (a proposito: oltre al denaro, è l'educazione dei figli l'argomento più tabù tra amiche; l'avevate notato?). In ogni caso, ormai le decisioni sono state prese, gli sbagli sono stati fatti: è il tempo del sostegno. E' il tempo dell'amicizia.

Grazia, 41, 17/10/1997

Parliamo 4 *A coppie o a gruppi. Confrontate le vostre liste. Che differenze ci sono?*

Prima di parlare 4 *Purtroppo anche le più care amiche a volte dicono cose sgradevoli e indisponenti. L'articolo* ***'Non parlarmi cosi'*** *illustra chiaramente questa possibilità. Leggilo attentamente: ti riconosci? O forse riconosci una tua amica o una delle situazioni?*

Non parlarmi così!

Anche le amiche più fantastiche a volte sbagliano. E si lasciano scappare qualche frase che le rende odiose (ma più umane).

1 - Sei l'unica a saperlo. Frase da pronunciare solo se è vera: che brutto sapere di far parte di un circolo di «uniche a saperlo». Variante: «mi raccomando non dirlo a nessuno».

2 - Adesso non ho tempo. Ma il tempo, nell'amicizia, non è un optional!

3 - Mi hanno parlato male di te ma io ti ho difeso. Frase che scatena scenari negativi: meglio evitarla (oppure spiegarla nel dettaglio).

4 - Sì, sì, me l'hai già detto. Ma la ripetizione, tra amiche, è essenziale...

5 - C'è una cosa che vorrei dirti ma non posso. E allora niente allusioni! Niente di peggio dei segreti irrivelabili ma «pubblicizzati».

6 - Quando fai così assomigli a tua madre (o a tuo padre). E se fosse terribilmente vero?

7 - Lo dico per il tuo bene. Frase che prelude a qualche rivelazione sgradevole; e che, poco ma sicuro, non ci farà del bene.

8 - Tu non puoi capire. Perché non sei fidanzata/sposata/divorziata/non hai figli... Ma non si era amiche per condividere?

9 - Non mi sembra il caso di farne un dramma. Ma detto con tono gelido e scocciato.

10 - Adesso che vi siete lasciati, te lo posso dire: non mi piaceva. Tragici commenti postumi a un amore, compreso il lapidario «uno così meglio perderlo che trovarlo».

Grazia, 41, 17/10/97

Parliamo 5a *A coppie. Scegliete una delle frasi e create una scenetta fra due amiche in cui compare la fatidica frase. Usate la fantasia, nonché la vostra esperienza!*

Parliamo 5b *Studenti maschi, attenzione! L'articolo è tratto da una rivista per donne. Secondo voi, queste frasi ricorrono anche nei rapporti di amicizia fra maschi? Se voi o i vostri amici non hanno mai usato queste frasi, quali altre frasi ricorrono nei dialoghi maschili? A gruppi, fate un elenco e create una scena fra amici come nella sezione 5a.*

Vocabolario

l'affetto
affidabile
l'amicizia
arrabbiarsi
commentare
commuoversi
criticare
la disponibilità
l'empatia
fare pettegolezzi
la fede
in buona/malafede
l'interlocutore
il requisito
richiedere
rifiutarsi di fare qualcosa
sincero

VIDEOGIOCHI

Prima di parlare 1 *Sei appassionato/a di giochi elettronici? Giochi regolarmente? Quali sono i tuoi videogiochi preferiti? Con chi giochi? Oppure sei convinto/a che i videogiochi siano una perdita di tempo, esclusivamente per bambini o poveretti con vita sentimentale disastrata. Rifletti per qualche minuto su queste domande e preparati a rispondere.*

Parliamo 1 *A coppie o a gruppi. Raccogliete le informazioni/opinioni di tutte le persone del vostro gruppo e preparatevi a presentare i risultati del sondaggio al resto della classe.*

Espressioni utili

- Hai mai giocato a ...?
- Quanto tempo passi a ...?
- Cosa ne pensi di ...?
- Che cosa ti attira particolarmente ...?
- Non sono disposto/a a passare il mio tempo a ...
- Il mio primo videogioco è stato ...
- Nel nostro gruppo ci sono almeno... persone che ...
- Non c'è nessuno che ...
- Abbiamo tutti provato almeno ...

Parliamo 2 *Il portavoce di ogni gruppo comunica i risultati del sondaggio al resto della classe. (Per* ***Espressioni utili*** *vedi* ***Parliamo 1****)*

Prima di parlare 2 *Leggi l'articolo* ***'Una Fifa da fenomeno'*** *(A) oppure* ***'Videogiochi sotto l'albero'*** *(B) e prendi nota di tutti gli aspetti, possibilità e vantaggi dei giochi.*

UNA FIFA DA FENOMENO

Due stelle di Roma e Lazio avevano anticipato il derby con la Playstation. Panorama Next vi racconta com'è andata e svela i segreti del videogioco più amato dai tifosi

Sugli spalti il pubblico freme, l'arbitro sta per fischiare il calcio d'inizio, le due squadre si studiano nervosamente. All'Olimpico l'atmosfera è elettrica: sta per cominciare il primo derby della stagione. Virtuale, però. Perché il campo è uno schermo televisivo collegato alla Playstation e il campionato quello di Fifa 2000, ultimissima edizione del più amato tra i videogiochi dedicati al pallone. Di vero c'è che a sfidarsi come allo stadio ci sono Vincenzo Montella, attaccante della Roma e Sinisa Mihajlovic, difensore della Lazio. Con la stessa voglia di vincere delle partite in schedina. Scaldati i polpastrelli si parte. «Meglio il livello amichevole» azzarda Mihajlovic che rivela da subito una maggior dimestichezza con la palla di cuoio che con i pulsanti della console. Vincenzo Montella sembra cavarsela meglio. Si parte e la Roma rimane subito in 10, viene esplulso Aldair per un intervento un po' troppo duro. Ma la Lazio non fa in tempo a esultare che i giallorossi segnano: Montella esulta: «ma chi è stato?» si chiede. Zoomata sull'autore: compare la scritta e si scopre che... «Ma sono io, grande!». Passano pochi minuti, punizione per i biancocelesti. Mihajlovic si impegna calibra il pollice, controlla a video la striscia luminosa che direziona il tiro, ma la palla finsice contro la barriera. «Com'è possibile?» si stupisce il difensore. Non fa neanche in tempo a rientrare in partita che la Roma riprende il sopravvento.

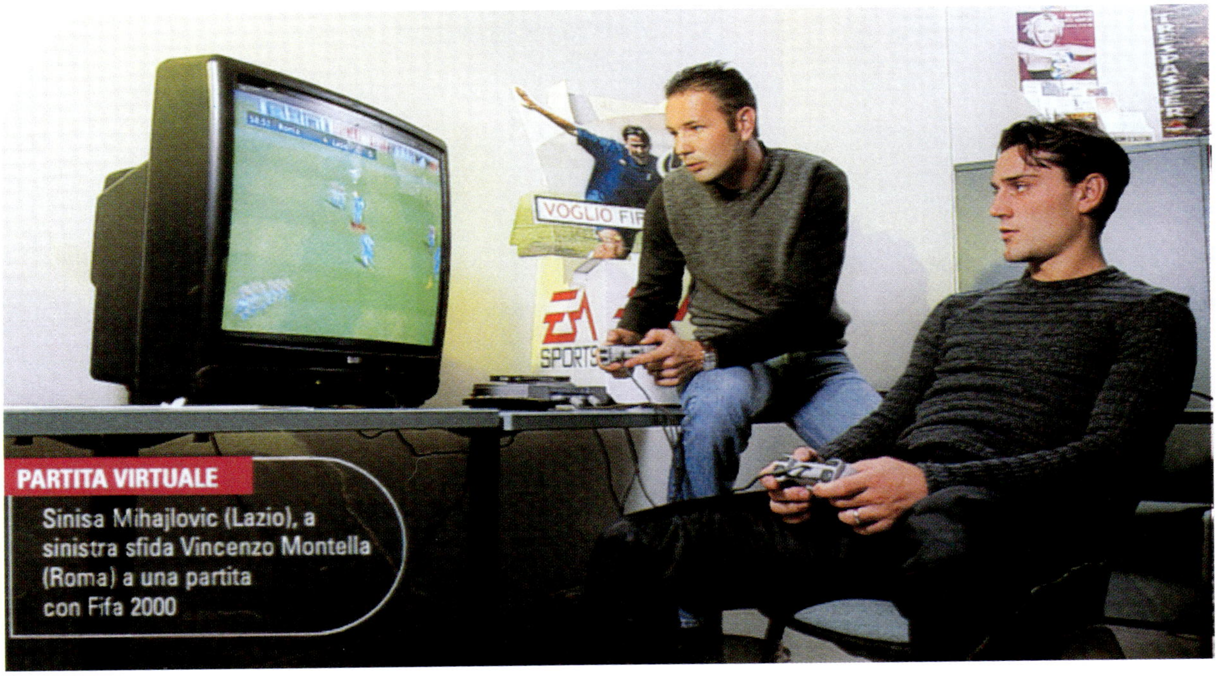

PARTITA VIRTUALE
Sinisa Mihajlovic (Lazio), a sinistra sfida Vincenzo Montella (Roma) a una partita con Fifa 2000

LOGO
Il gioco per Pc e Playstation costa 99.000 lire, 51 euro
www.fifaworld.com

UN GIOCO DA GUINNES
Nato nel 1993, presente in Italia dal 1995, Fifa ha venduto più di 16 milioni di copie nel mondo, un traguardo che ha fatto entrare il viedogioco direttamente nel Guiness dei primati. Nell'edizione del 2000 ci sono tutte le squadre di serie A e oltre 200 giocatori.

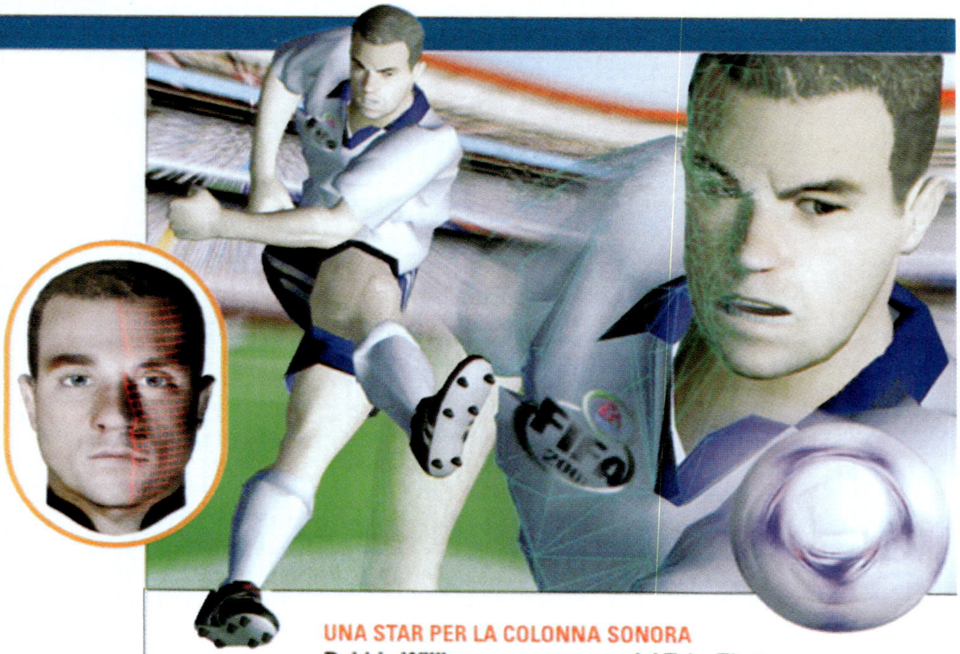

UNA STAR PER LA COLONNA SONORA
Robbie Williams, ex cantante dei Take That, ha inciso una canzone in esclusiva per Fifa 2000 e appare nella sua veste virtuale nell'introduzione filmata del gioco

Lo sapevate che?

● Oltre ai giocatori, è possibile scegliere anche la **formazione e la strategia** di ogni squadra. Proiettati in attacco o chiusi in difesa? Di quante punte deve disporre una squadra? E se il portiere giocasse in attacco? All'utente, trasformato in "mister", le importanti decisioni tattiche prepartita.

● Fifa 2000 permette all'utente di trasformarsi in **spettatore** e guardare l'incontro tra due squadre a sua scelta. Basterà assegnare al computer il compito di governare entrambi i team in gioco, scegliere i tempi della partita, da quattro a novanta minuti, e godersi la telecronaca commentata dai bravi Bulgarelli e Caputi.

● Con Fifa 2000 è possibile giocare anche **contro un amico lontano**. Non è richiesto un collegamento a Internet, è sufficiente collegare il pc a un modem cui far comporre il numero telefonico del nostro avversario e selezionare la funzione per la parttia a distanza.

Videogiochi sotto l'albero

E PER CHI DI CALCIO NE HA ABBASTANZA

Playstation

Final Fantasy VIII
Squaresoft-Sony
È l'ottavo episodio della saga fantastica più giocata nel mondo. Gli spettacolari combattimenti e la ricca trama lo rendono simile a un film d'avventura. Prezzo 156.000 lire, 80,6 euro
www.playstation.com

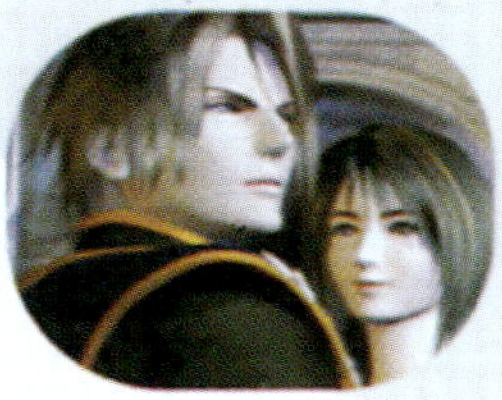

Gran Turismo 2 / Sony
È l'atteso seguito del miglior gioco di guida di tutti i tempi. Si può scegliere tra centinaia di automobili, ognuna con le sue esatte caratteristiche. E sullo schermo si può portare anche la propria.
Prezzo 115.000 lire, 59,3 euro
www.playstation.com

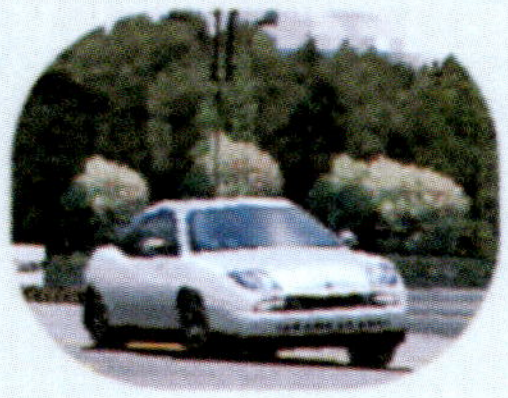

Dinocrisis / Capcom
Il giocatore, nei panni di Regina, bellissimo membro di una squadra speciale d'assalto, deve ritrovare, possibilmente vivo, uno scienziato di cui si sono perse le tracce.
Prezzo 109.000 lire, 56,2 euro
www.capcom.com

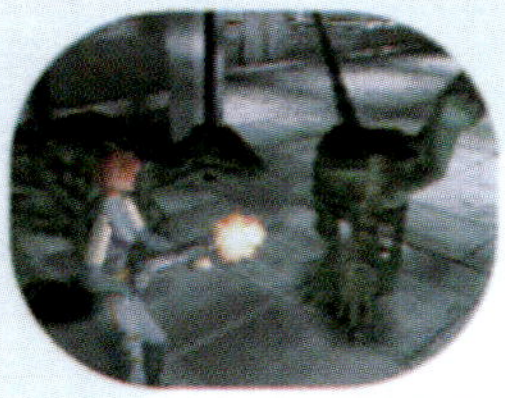

Nintendo 64

Donkey Kong 64 / Rare
Uno dei personaggi che hanno fatto la storia del videogiochi, lo scimmione Donkey Kong, torna come protagonista di una bellissima avventura ambientata nella giungla.
Prezzo circa 100.000 lire, 51,6 euro
www.nintendo.com

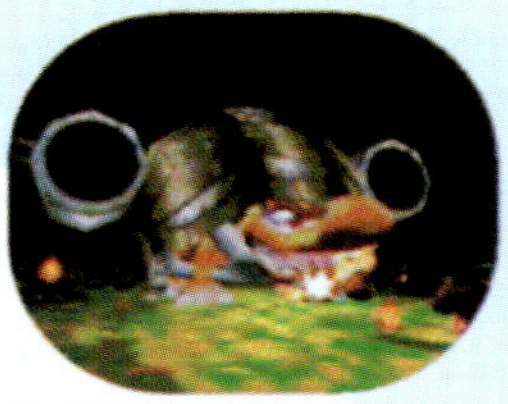

Command&Conquer
Westwood Studios
Su computer ha venduto milioni di copie inaugurando il filone dei giochi di combattimento a più partecipanti. Finalmente arriva anche su console
Prezzo circa 100.000 lire, 51,6 euro.
www.nintendo.com

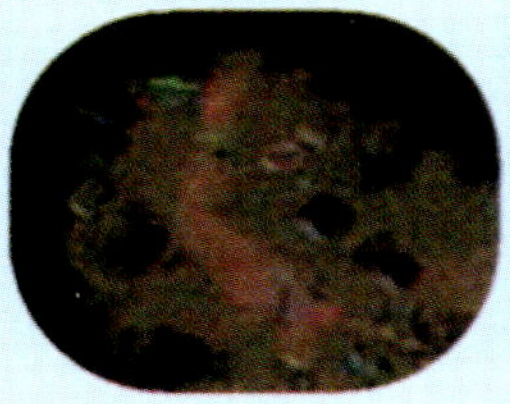

Perfect dark / Rare
Per gli amanti dei giochi d'azione fantascientifici. L'alter ego del giocatore è una donna, l'affascinante Joanna Dark che deve portare a termine una pericolosa missione.
Prezzo circa 100.000 lire, 51,6 euro
www.nintendo.com

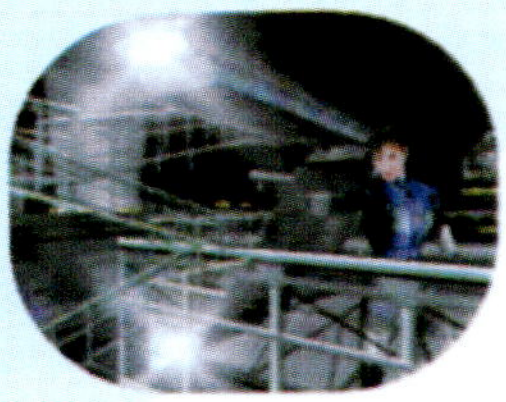

Dreamcast

Soul Calibur / Namco
È il più spettacolare gioco di combattimento per console. Ognuno dei partecipanti al torneo possiede una sua arma caratteristica e decine di mosse segrete.
Prezzo 109.000 lire, 56,3 euro
www.namco.com

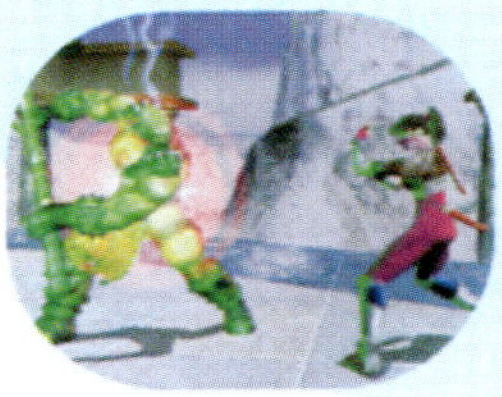

Ready to Rumble / Midway
La box è uno sport in cui ci si può fare del male ma, in versione elettronica, si rivela incredibilmente divertente, specie se giocato tra amici. Comiche le smorfie di dolore dei buffi eroi del ring.
Prezzo 109.000 lire, 56,3 euro
www.dreamcast.com

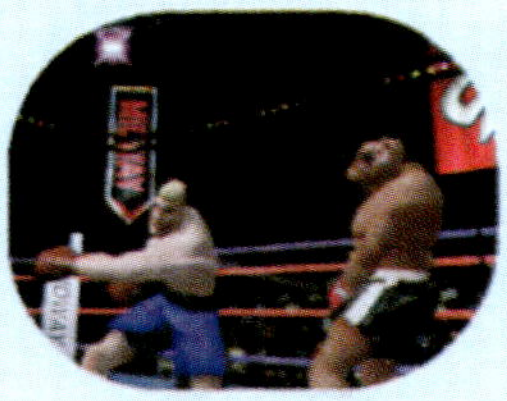

Sonic Adventure / Sega
È il primo titolo che segna il ritorno su Dreamcast del velocissimo porcospino, storica mascotte della Sega. È un gioco di piattaforme tridimensionali che ha la sua principale caratteristica nella velocità. Prezzo 109.000 lire, 56,3 euro
www.dreamcast.com

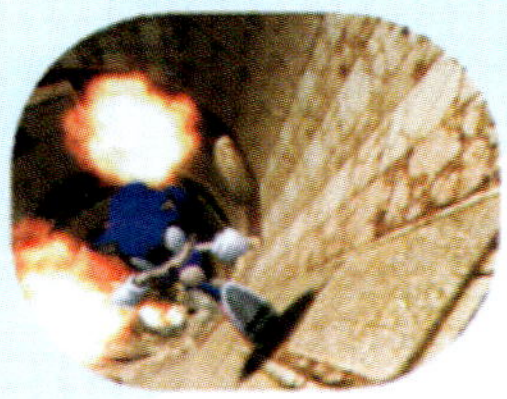

Espressioni utili

- È un gioco spettacolare!
- Cosa ti permette di fare?
- Come si gioca?
- Si può giocare a distanza?
- Come può essere simulato?
- È la saga virtuale più giocata al mondo
- Possono giocare anche i meno esperti.
- Qual è il migliore simulatore disponibile?
- Il ritmo del gioco è incalzante ...
- Non ne hai abbastanza di ...?
- È un gioco d'azione/divertente/senza grandi pretese simulative
- In versione elettronica

Parliamo 3 *A coppie.*

Studente A

Sei un grande tifoso del calcio. Per il tuo compleanno desideri ardentemente un videogioco. Ha già ottenuto parecchie informazioni sul gioco Fifa 2000. Ora si tratta di convincere tuo padre / tua madre / tuo fratello / la tua migliore amica a comprartelo! Descrivi tutte le particolarità del gioco con entusiasmo, ricordandoti che la persona che vuoi convincere non ha molta idea di come funzionino questi videogiochi.

Studente B

Si avvicina il compleanno di tuo figlio / la tua amica / tuo fratello e sai che lui/lei è appassionato/a di videogiochi. Tu non te ne intendi molto però hai letto un articolo che ne descrive alcuni. Proponi alcuni di questi giochi e allo stesso tempo approfittane per farti spiegare come funzionano.

Vocabolario

l'attaccante
i bianconeri
il calcio di punizione
coinvolgente
il combattimento
il commento
computerizzato
la console
un giocatore fuoriclasse
i partecipanti
la partita virtuale
il pulsante
sfidarsi
spettacolare
la squadra di serie A
il torneo

Unità 77

UNA VACANZA IDEALE!

Prima di parlare 1 *Preparati a parlare del tipo di vacanza che preferisci, per esempio al mare, in montagna, in campagna, in città. Giustifica la tua scelta.*

Parliamo 1 *A coppie o in piccoli gruppi. A vicenda parlate del tipo di vacanza che preferite, giustificando la vostra scelta.*

Espressioni utili

- Per quanto riguarda le vacanze, la mia meta preferita è ...
- Secondo me, i vantaggi di trascorre le vacanze ...
- Quello che mi attira più che altro è ...
- Da parecchi anni vado sempre a Firenze .../ in Portogallo ...
- La ragione per cui preferisco ...
- È consigliabile/preferibile prenotare/partire ...
- Chi sceglie questo tipo di vacanza dovrebbe andare a maggio oppure verso la fine di settembre ...
- Siccome non sopporto il caldo/i luoghi sovraffollati ...
- Quanto al prezzo, dipende molto da ...

Prima di parlare 2 *Lavorate a gruppi di tre. A ogni studente verrà assegnata una lettera, A, B o C. Leggi attentamente l'articolo che corrisponde alla tua lettera e poi completa, dove possibile, la tabella.*

Destinazione	
Durata del soggiorno	
Tipo di sistemazione	
Costo della sistemazione e quello che include	
Descrizione del luogo di villeggiatura	
Attività diurne	
Attività notturne	
Altri vantaggi specifici di questa vacanza	
Svantaggi	
Costo (globale)	
Clima	
Consigli dati nell'articolo	

Studente A

WEEKEND ROMANTICO NELLA CAMPAGNA TOSCANA

Concedersi un relax dopo un anno di lavoro, farsi almeno un week-end romantico o una settimana di riposo: un sogno a portata di mano... Per esempio, può diventare realtà in una piccola e ancora poco conosciuta struttura come La Locanda, incantevole dimora di campagna a gestione totalmente famigliare (i proprietari sono una giovane coppia "trasfuga dalla città"). Immersa tra le colline del Chianti e a 600 metri di altitudine, La Locanda nasce dal recupero di un vecchio podere fra ulivi, vigne e boschi, di fronte al borgo medievale di Volpaia. Sei camere doppie, arredate con gusto, e una suite sono nella grande casa, mentre il soggiorno, la sala da pranzo e la biblioteca-bar sono ricavati nella antica stalla. Ma si sta soprattutto all'aperto, in piscina o sulla terrazza affacciata su un magnifico panorama. L'unico pasto incluso nel prezzo è la prima colazione. È possibile però gustare uno spuntino in piscina o una cena fredda con i prodotti tipici del luogo. A due passi da Siena, Firenze, Arezzo e Lucca, La Locanda offre l'opportunità di scoprire la Toscana. Una doppia con prima colazione costa 150/175 euro; la suite 200 euro. indirizzo e telefono: Guido e Martina Bevilacqua, Radda in Chianti. Tel. e fax 0577/738833

(Grazia, n. 36 14/9/1999)

Studente B

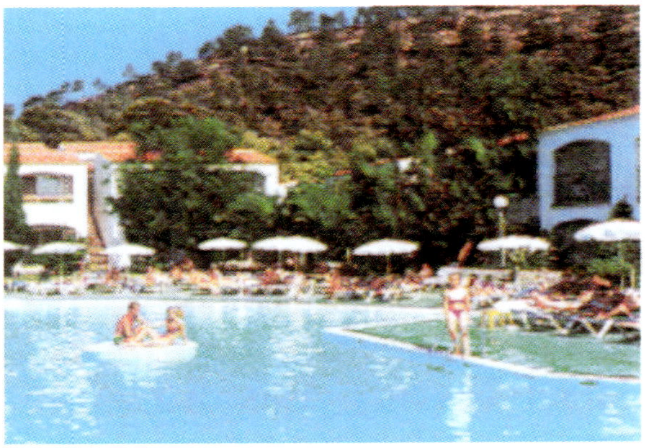

Maiorca. Una veduta della piscina dell'Hotel Club Europa sull'isola di Maiorca.

Una meta ambita da numerosi turisti da tutta Europa, situata a poche ore di aereo dall'Italia, sono le isole Baleari e, in particolare, Maiorca, la più grande. Il clima è temperato, le spiagge, con acque limpide, sono numerose, la cucina è appetitosa e la vita notturna è vivace. Comitours propone settimane di soggiorno all'Hotel Club Europa a Paguera sull'isola di Maiorca. Il complesso, immerso in una pineta, dista un chilometro dalla spiaggia alla quale è collegato da un servizio di navetta gratuito. All'interno dell'hotel ci sono tre piscine, un ristorante principale con servizio a buffet, pizzeria, discoteca, un miniclub per bambini dai 4 ai 12 anni, due campi da tennis e da squash, e una palestra. Inoltre uno staff di animatori organizza attività diurne e notturne. È una vacanza consigliata alle famiglie, agli sportivi, e tutti quelli che amano il verde. Se prenotate entro il 18 marzo, il prezzo dall'1 al 19 maggio, comprendente il viaggio aereo da Milano, Roma, o altre città su richiesta, per sette giorni con trattamento di prima colazione, cena, è di lire 656.000; dal 20 maggio al 2 giugno 761.000; dal 3 al 23 giugno di 818.000. Se prenotate dopo il 18 marzo, il prezzo è superiore del 15 per cento.

(Gente, n. 10 9/3/2000)

Studente C

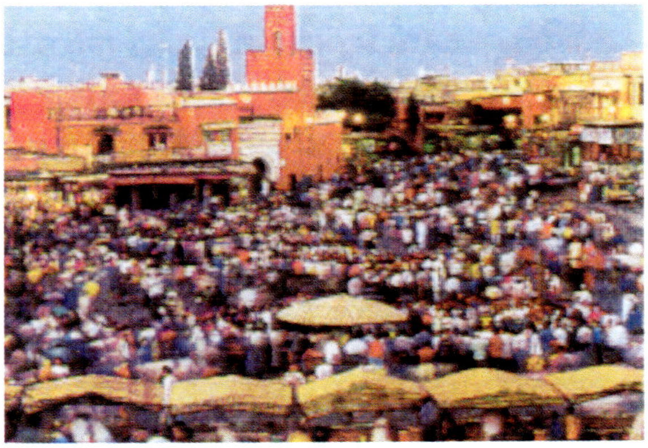

Marrakech. Il centro di Marrakech, in Marocco, con la piazza piena di bancarelle.

Club Med consiglia una settimana di soggiorno a Marrakech, una delle città principali del Marocco. Il villaggio, totalmente rinnovato e situato nel cuore della città, è immerso completamente nella cultura marocchina. Per chi ama lo sport è possibile praticare tennis, tiro con l'arco, golf, diversi tipi di ginnastica ed equitazione. Chi desidera rilassarsi può prendere il sole ai bordi di una delle due piscine, può fare il bagno turco o i massaggi, questi ultimi a pagamento. Sono accolti i bambini di tutte le età, ma non è prevista alcuna assistenza. Marrakech è una meta ottima per chi vuole fare acquisti perché si possono trovare oggetti, moderni e antichi, di artigianato, ma soprattutto è uno dei mercati delle spezie più importante di tutta l'Africa del Nord. Molto suggestiva la piazza principale, che di sera si riempie di incantatori di serpenti e giocolieri. Il prezzo che comprende il viaggio da Milano o Roma, e una settimana di soggiorno tutto compreso, varia a seconda del periodo di partenza. Se partite il 5 giugno spendete lire 1.098.000, il 12 giugno 1.088.000, il 19 giugno spendete lire 1.068.000, il 26 giugno lire 1.096.000. Il soggiorno, comunque, comincia sempre di lunedì.

(Gente, n. 10 9/3/2000)

Parliamo 2 *A vicenda, riferendovi alla vostra tabella descrivete il più dettagliatamente possibile la vacanza di cui avete letto i particolari. I compagni devono completare altre due tabelle con le informazioni che vengono comunicate. Naturalmente potete anche fare domande se desiderate dei chiarimenti.*

Parliamo 3 *Rileggete le tre tabelle e poi scegliete la vacanza che risponde meglio alle vostre esigenze e ai vostri gusti. A vicenda, parlate della vacanza che avete scelto, spiegando i motivi della vostra scelta. Può darsi che a qualcuno non piaccia nessuna delle vacanze proposte. Anche in questo caso bisogna spiegarne i motivi.*

Espressioni utili

- Siccome mi piace ... sceglierei senz'altro la vacanza ...
- Tutte le vacanze proposte hanno aspetti molto positivi ma se dovessi scegliere, preferirei ...
- La vacanza descritta da ... sembra molto attraente ma l'unico problema è che ..
- Nessuna di queste vacanze mi dice niente ...
- Per me, gli ingredienti di una vacanza ideale sono ...
- Parecchi anni fa ho fatto il tipo di vacanza proposta nell'articolo e sono rimasto/a molto deluso/a perché ...
- Non voglio che tutto sia organizzato, anzi preferisco ...

Vocabolario

affollato
in alta/bassa stagione
l'animatore / l'animazione
assaggiatore
le attività organizzate
avere tutto a portata di mano
il concetto di vacanza
diurno
divertirsi un mondo
essere tempestato di attività
fare delle passeggiate
fuori stagione
fare un bel viaggio
gustare
incluso nel pacchetto
la meta
il paesaggio
patire (da) (per)
il patrimonio culturale
pomeridiano
prendere il sole
i prezzi bassi / convenienti / concorrenziali
rilassarsi / rilassante
riposarsi / riposante
scoprire / la scoperta
selvaggio
sfogarsi
sopportare
le spese
stare all'aperto
stufarsi (di)
suggestivo
il tormentone del Ferragosto
il villaggio turistico
i villeggianti
la vita notturna

Unità 78

STUDENTI: VITA IN COMUNE

Prima di parlare 1 *Molti giovani che studiano lontani dalla famiglia optano per la vita in comune con altri studenti. Campus, il mensile degli studenti universitari italiani, ha indagato su questo fenomeno. Leggi la parte introduttiva dell'articolo*

Vita da Friends

Dividere un appartamento con amici e compagni di studio è bello e impegnativo, come dimostrano le avventure di un famoso serial americano. Ma attenzione! Quando si decide di dividere un appartamento, nella maggior parte, si fa un salto nel buio.

C'è il disordinato o il perfettino. Ma può capitare anche il rumoroso, il festaiolo o il simpaticone a oltranza. Meglio armarsi di una buona dose di pazienza, "soprattutto all'inizio, quando ancora non ci si conosce e non sai fino a che punto osare", consiglia Paola, 25 anni, di Forlì, da quattro anni alle prese con gioie e dolori della convivenza. E' vero che dovrebbe trattarsi di normali regole di buona educazione ma tante volte, per pigrizia, disattenzione o semplicemente per fretta, si dimenticano anche le norme più elementari.

Campus, Aprile 2000 - modificato

Parliamo 1 *A gruppi. Elencate almeno quattro vantaggi e quattro svantaggi di questo tipo di convivenza e commentate ogni aspetto.*

Parliamo 2 *A turno, un portavoce presenta i commenti del proprio gruppo al resto della classe. È consigliabile scrivere tutti gli aspetti citati dai vari gruppi alla lavagna (ma senza i commenti) in modo da avere alla fine tutti i contributi sotto gli occhi.*

Espressioni utili

- Mi sembra che il vantaggio più evidente sia ...
- Non dimentichiamo che la convivenza dà la possibilità di ...
- Ci sono senz'altro anche inconvenienti ...
- C'è chi (non) rispetta ...
- Il discorso è complicato ...
- La mancanza di educazione/tolleranza ...
- È una questione di educazione ...

Prima di parlare 2 *Sicuramente fra gli aspetti negativi si sarà parlato di problemi molto comuni e non gravi, ma che rendono la convivenza meno serena. Leggete attentamente l'articolo* ***'Problemi della vita in comune'****. Avete riscontrato delle similarità rispetto alla vostra situazione o a quella di vostri compagni, amici o parenti che vivono con altri studenti?*

I PROBLEMI DELLA VITA IN COMUNE...

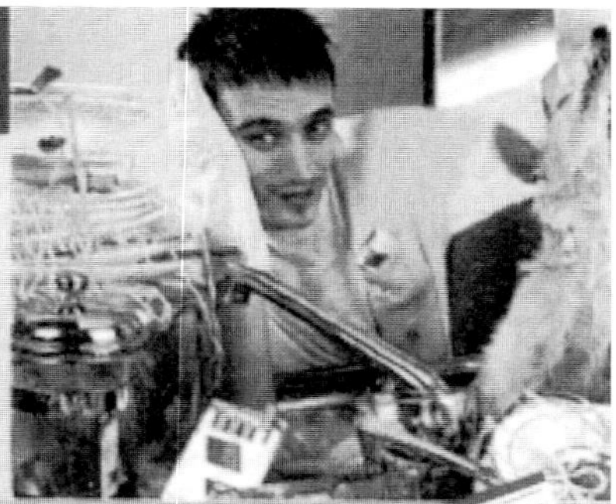

1 AHI, AHI, LE PULIZIE

C'è chi organizza feste e cenette, e poi non lava neanche una forchetta, e chi non usa mai il portacenere. I turni stabiliti per le pulizie settimanali, poi, saltano puntualmente con un sono stanco, oppure è finito il detersivo dei piatti.

2 BOLLETTE SALATE

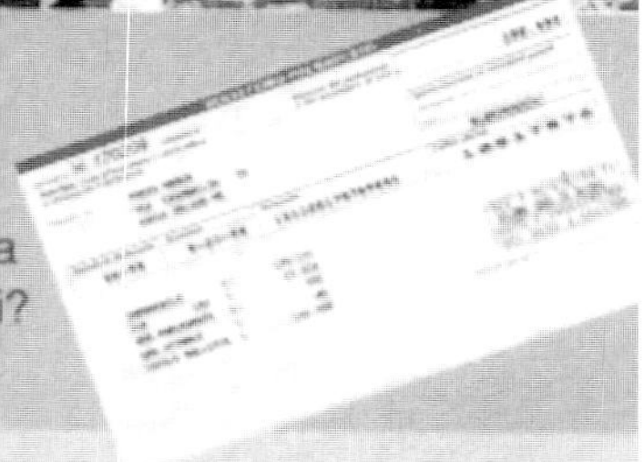

Se la bolletta della corrente è troppo alta, c'è il solito rompiscatole che accusa gli altri di lasciare sempre le luci accese e di fare troppi carichi di lavatrice. E poi: a chi tocca la fila alla posta per il pagamento dei bollettini?

3 GIÙ LE MANI DAL PROSCIUTTO

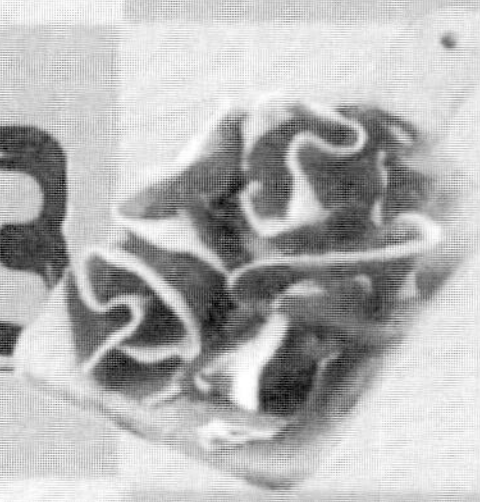

Visto che il frigo è uno solo, i «furti alimentari» sono all'ordine del giorno. Capita così di tornare a casa con l'acquolina in bocca e accorgersi che del prosciutto crudo tanto agognato a lezione, resta ormai solo la confezione.

4 MOTORINO E AUTOMOBILE: PERICOLO SCROCCONI!

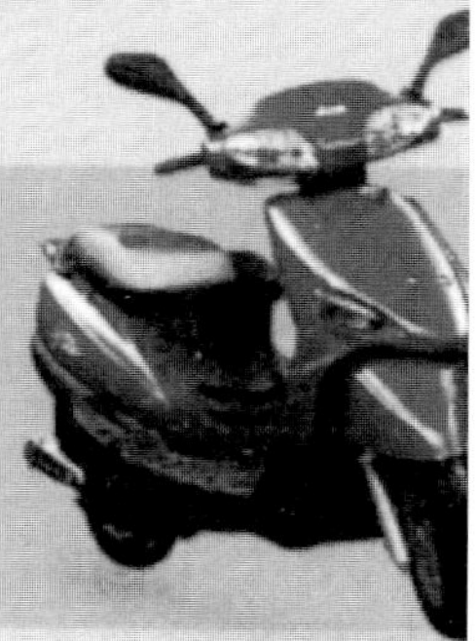

Tra gli inquilini di un appartamento ci sono i motorizzati e i pedoni: i primi prestano, i secondi sfruttano. La lancetta della benzina che va giù, la Vespa che sparisce davanti alla facoltà: chi ci rimette a volte è disposto all'omicidio...

5 OSPITI INDESIDERATI

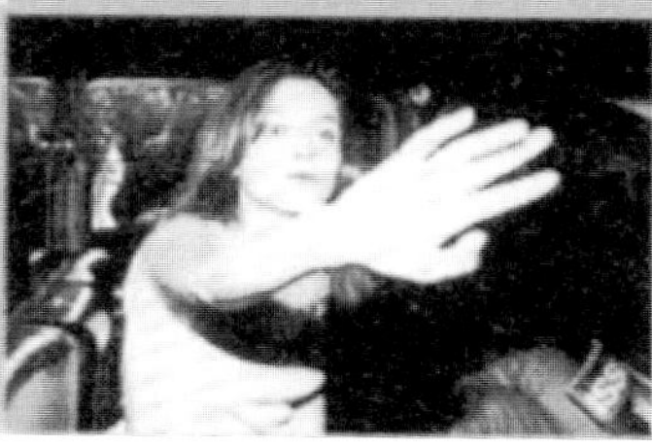

Le occasioni per invitare un po' di gente e fare baldoria non mancano mai, ma come fare ad accordarsi quando gli ospiti spaziano dal salutista/sportivo al fumatore di hashish incallito?

6

DISORDINE/ORDINE: OCCHIO AI MANIACI

Mutande lasciate sul letto degli altri, scarpe abbandonate in cucina e interi guardaroba disseminati sulle poltrone di casa, non aiutano le convivenze.

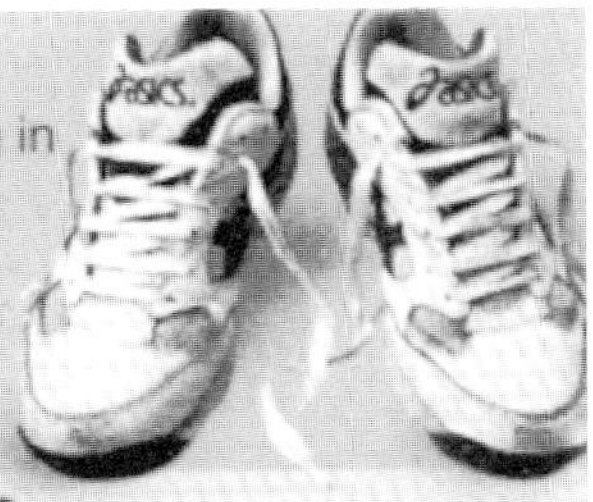

7

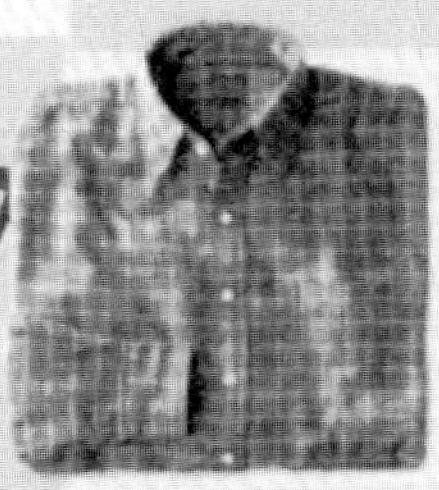

CHI MI HA RUBATO LA RALPH LAUREN?

Tra i prestiti ai coinquilini, i vestiti detengono la pole position, specie tra ragazze o vanitosi. Ma anche libri e Cd presi senza permesso e prestati a estranei, possono creare dissapori, perché di solito non tornano più all'ovile...

8

L'ULTIMA SIGARETTA, PLEASE!

Il mondo si divide in fumatori e non fumatori. E i problemi di convivenza che conseguono sono tremendi...

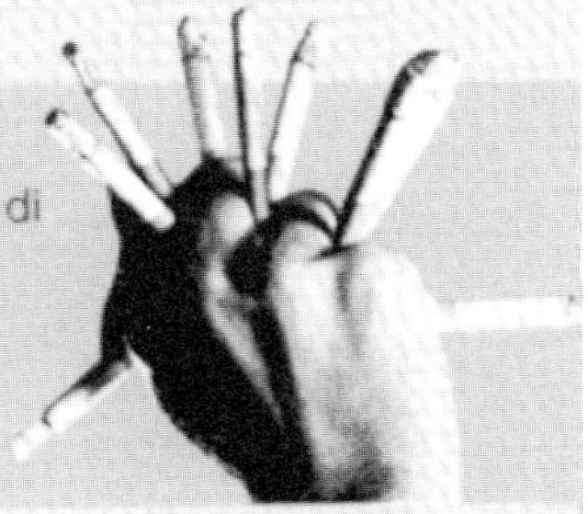

9

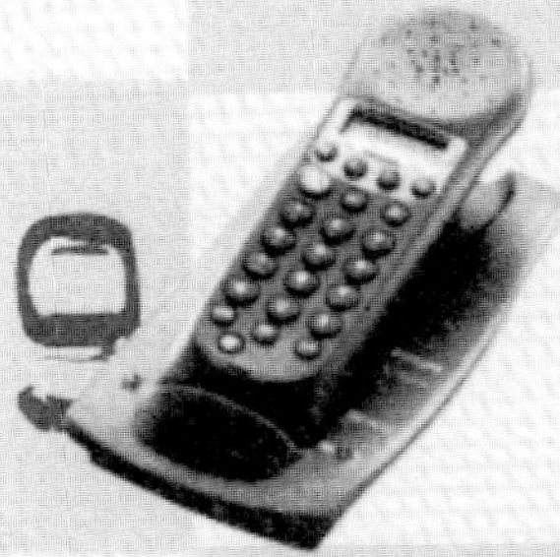

TELEFONO DELLE MIE BRAME

Anche dopo il boom dei cellulari, il telefono resta uno dei tanti pomi della discordia. C'è chi parla troppo o trascorre ore su Internet fregandosene degli altri; chi lascia il cordless dove nessuno riuscirebbe a trovarlo, chi riceve gli squilli della fidanzata gelosa alle 4 del mattino.

10

ALLARME LAVATRICE

A ogni lavaggio i calzini si scambiano, i colori delle maglie non si riconoscono, delle cinque mutande lavate ne restano tre e se poi il tubo di scarico è esterno si rischia un allagamento al giorno.

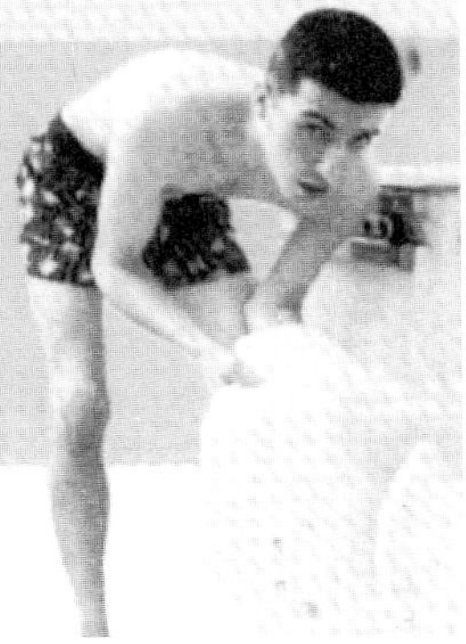

Parliamo 3 *A coppie. Lo studente A è arcistufo del comportamento delle persone con cui coabita e va a sfogarsi con lo studente B. Quest'ultimo, conoscendo il carattere un po' particolare di A, chiede schiarimenti e propone qualche strategia di condotta per sbloccare la situazione.*

Parliamo 4 *A coppie, con un interlocutore differente. Lo studente A ha veramente delle pessime abitudini! Lo studente B elenca i misfatti e chiede spiegazioni. Lo studente A si difende accanitamente. Insieme devono trovare una soluzione che sia accettabile ad entrambi.*

Espressioni utili

- Scusa sai, ma non ti rendi conto che hai .../di avere ...?
- Ho il sonno leggero e tu continui a ...
- Hai abitudini veramente strane ...
- Non sono perfezionista, però ...
- Sai benissimo che non sopporto ...
- Non sono il solo/la sola a ...
- Abbiamo tutti notato che ...
- Scusa, perché dovrei ... mentre tu ...?
- Non mi pare proprio di avere ...
- Non sono stato/a io ...
- Sei sicuro/a di avere ...?
- Credevo che tu fossi uscito/a .../ di essere solo/a ...
- Non ho fatto i conti con gli imprevisti ...
- Quando si è in tanti è difficile ...
- C'è rimedio ...
- Ecco una regola fondamentale ...
- Sei d'accordo?
- L'unica soluzione è di ...

Prima di parlare 3 *L'insegnante vi darà una copia delle soluzioni proposte dall'autore dell'articolo di Campus. Leggetele attentamente.*

Parliamo 5 *A gruppi. Decidete insieme a quali problemi (1-10) si riferiscono le soluzioni proposte (A-L). Cosa pensate delle soluzioni proposte? Sono simili alle vostre oppure no?*

Vocabolario

l'accortezza
l'autorizzazione/autorizzare (a)
la bella abitudine (di)
il brutto vizio (di)
concedere (a)
convivere / la convivenza
cronico
la discrezione
escludere / esclusivo
fare il furbo
imbronciato
incallito
l'inquilino
l'intesa
la libertà di movimento
il pagamento
i panni sporchi
permettere (a)
prestare (a) / il prestito
protestare
la quota
recidivo
rinfacciare (a) (di)
il turno

Unità 1

(a)

la Repubblica.it News

la Repubblica.it
Home Page

ore 16:08
del 12-10-99

Trova
Scrivi

News
Dossier
Fatti
Musica
Cinema
Cultura & Scienze
Tecnologie
Internet
Televisioni
Sport
Scuola
Volontariato
Sessi & Stili di vita
Giochi
Forum e Rete
Auto
Cittadino Lex
Università

Strade: super multe a chi non mette cinture e casco

ROMA - Gli indisciplinati della strada tremano. E nel mirino finiscono soprattutto i tanti automobilisti che non usano allacciare le cinture di sicurezza in città e i motociclisti che sfuggono all'obbligo del casco. Sta per partire infatti una nuova campagna di prevenzione degli incidenti stradali nelle città, organizzata dal ministero dell'Interno in collaborazione con tutta la forza di vigilanza. E' stato un dato allarmante a fare scattare la campagna: il 70 per cento degli incidenti stradali avviene in città e coinvolge in gran parte chi snobba cinture e casco.

Inizio Pagina

(b)

la Repubblica.it News

la Repubblica.it
Home Page

ore 20:19
del 12-10-99

Trova
Scrivi

News
Dossier
Fatti
Musica
Cinema
Cultura & Scienze
Tecnologie
Internet
Televisioni
Sport
Scuola
Volontariato
Sessi & Stili di vita
Giochi
Forum e Rete
Auto
Cittadino Lex
Università

Nebbia: tamponamenti a catena sulla A-13

PADOVA - Torna la nebbia e i tamponamenti a catena. Sono stati 75 i veicoli coinvolti e 25 persone lievemente ferite sull'autostrada A13 tra Padova e Boara Pisana in Polesine, dove sono rimasti a lungo chiusi i caselli autostradali su entrambe le direzioni.
Per soccorrere gli infortunati e liberare la sede stradale sono intervenute 16 pattuglie della polstrada di Padova, Rovigo e Bologna, insieme a vari mezzi dei vigili del fuoco, del pronto soccorso e del trasporto veicoli.

Inizio Pagina

(c)

la Repubblica.it News

la Repubblica.it
Home Page

ore 20:28
del 12-10-99

Aerei: il Roma-New York rientra a Fiumicino per avaria

FIUMICINO (Roma) - Il volo Alitalia Roma-New York, decollato alle 13,30 dall'aeroporto di Fiumicino con 298 passeggeri a bordo, ha fatto rientro nel pomeriggio allo scalo romano a causa di una presunta avaria a uno dei quattro motori. Boeing 747 stava sorvolando la Scozia quando il comandante ha riscontrato una perdita di potenza sul motore numero due e ha deciso di rientrare allo scalo di partenza. Tra i passeggeri anche Valeria Marini, che ha apprezzato il comportamento dell'Alitalia: "Non ho avuto paura e non avrò problemi a salire sul prossimo collegamento per New York".

Inizio Pagina

(d)

la Repubblica.it
News

la Repubblica.it
Home Page

ore 20:09
del 12-10-99

Trova
Scrivi

News
Dossier
Fatti
Musica
Cinema
Cultura & Scienze
Tecnologie
Internet
Televisioni
Sport
Scuola
Volontariato
Sessi & Stili di vita
Giochi
Forum e Rete
Auto
Cittadino Lex
Università

Treni: Roma Termini chiusa anche domani Fiumicino per avaria

FIUMICINO - Non sono finiti i disagi per i viaggiatori diretti a Roma. Sarà dimezzato anche domani e verrà deviato sulle altre stazioni della capitale il traffico ferroviario della stazione Termine, dove ieri è andato in tilt il nuovo sistema di controllo degli arrivi. A risentire dei disagi saranno soprattutto i convogli che viaggiano sulla direttrice Roma-Napoli, che verranno deviati su Roma Tiburtina, mentre saranno soppressi 136 treni locali, che verranno sostituiti da autobus sostitutivi fino alle stazioni della metropolitana di Anagnina e Laurentina.

Inizio Pagina

la Repubblica.it
News

la Repubblica.it
Home Page

Trova
Scrivi

News
Dossier
Fatti
Musica
Cinema
Cultura & Scienze
Tecnologie
Internet
Televisioni
Sport
Scuola
Volontariato
Sessi & Stili di vita
Giochi
Forum e Rete
Auto
Cittadino Lex
Università

Forum
Cani e gatti, che fare d'estate

Ho letto di questo forum solo di recente, così sono andata a leggermi diversi messaggi e voglio portare la mia esperienza di queste vacanze da poco terminate. Siamo stati in vacanza a Orosei in Sardegna e abbiamo portato con noi non uno ma tre cani. Al mattino ed alla sera correvano sulle spiagge semideserte e nuotavano contenti, di giorno se ne stavano in pineta all'ombra. Hanno potuto seguirci nelle gelaterie all'aperto e anche sotto i tavoli dell'agriturismo dove andavamo spesso a cenare. Da parte nostra abbiamo sempre cercato di far sì che i cani non disturbassero nessuno e abbiamo sempre pulito dove sporcavano.
Viva questa parte della Sardegna ancora autentica e selvaggia che ha spazi per tutti. La vacanza con tre cani è faticosa, ma chi ha nel proprio cane un compagno, sa come sanno ricompensare questo nostro sacrificio.
Entrare in polemica con chi non ama gli animali è inutile, facciamo parte di due mondi diversi, ma credo che la reciproca tolleranza e il rispetto delle esigenze altrui possono farci convivere pacificamente.

Giovanna Barberis

Inizio Pagina

OPINIONI A CONFRONTO

*Un obolo per far funzionare meglio la città più bella del mondo: è l'ultima provocazione che si respira in laguna. Il vicesindaco, **Miichele Vianello,** spiega le ragioni del ticket e il presidente della Confcommercio, l'ingegner **Massimo Albonetti**, replica con il rifiuto degli esercenti a fare da "gabellieri" per la nuova tassa.*

PAGARE PER VEDERE VENEZIA?

VIANELLO

«Non è una tassa ma un piccolo obolo per il bene di tutti»

Vicesindaco Vianello, è lei l'inventore del "serenissimo balzello" da 1.000 lire?

«Sì, confesso: l'idea è mia. Mi sono fatto carico di una proposta che suscita perplessità e reazioni, perché di fatto io sono la "vittima" designata a gestire i servizi di Venezia: dalla pulizia della città ai trasporti, dai wc pubblici alla vigilanza urbana. Per la gente sono servizi scontati e nessuno si sofferma mai a riflettere sui costi che, per una città unica al mondo qual' è Venezia, sono onerosissimi».

Allora è un problema di quadratura di bilancio delle casse comunali?

«Venezia ha poco meno di 300 mila abitanti, terraferma compresa; 300 mila persone che contribuiscono con le tasse al mantenimento della città. Sono però ben 12 milioni i turisti che arrivano ogni anno e noi non siamo più in grado di sostenere, con la fiscalità generale, una rete di servizi, per qualità e quantità, idonea a 12 milioni di presenze aggiuntive. Solo per rimuovere i rifiuti lasciati dai turisti spendiamo 18 milioni e mezzo all'anno. Non possiamo tassare di più i veneziani per fronteggiare problemi d'importazione».

Dunque 1.000 lire per tutelare i residenti?

«Sì, ma per trattare meglio anche i turisti».

Perché tanto clamore allora?

«Qualunque cosa accada a Venezia suscita sempre una vasta eco. Mille lire, da pagare su un pernottamento o in aggiunta al conto del ristorante, sono davvero un piccolo "obolo", dal quale oltre al risultato economico mi aspetto maggior senso di responsabilità e consapevolezza da ristoratori e albergatori. Una città vive non perché il Comune cattivo fa l'esattore, ma perché tutti si rimboccano le maniche e si danno da fare per trovare le risorse necessarie».

Nessun problema dal punto di vista giuridico?

«La proposta è legittima perché si tratta di un contributo al mantenimento della città e non di una tassa d'ingresso, che invece sarebbe incostituzionale».

L'idea di far pagare qualcosa in più ai turisti non crea un alone di città "respingente"?

«No. Noi diciamo solo al turista: "Amico, se tu non ci fossi noi potremmo pulire piazza San Marco una volta al giorno e invece dobbiamo farlo cinque volte. Per piacere, poiché Venezia è un bene universale, dacci un piccolo contributo per conservarla meglio"».

A. Nonnina si dà alla fuga per evitare la multa

Dev'essere un'anziana ancora piena di energie quella che a Ventimiglia (Imperia) è fuggita a piedi per non pagare una multa per divieto di parcheggio. La polizia l'ha inseguita per ben dieci minuti prima di fermarla. Ora, a 70 anni, la donna rischia una denuncia per resistenza a pubblico ufficiale e il ritiro della patente.

B. Ladro si addormenta sul bottino, catturato

Un egiziano di 34 anni residente al Cairo si era trattenuto dopo l'orario di lavoro nell'ufficio statale dove era impiegato con l'intento di rubare trecento milioni in oro. Ma, vinto dal sonno durante la rapina, è stato trovato il mattino seguente dai colleghi, ancora addormentato sulla scrivania e con il bottino in vista.

C. Cercasi modelle extra-large. Boom le risposte

Non sempre bellezza fa rima con magrezza. Un'agenzia di modelle di New York ha avviato una selezione per indossatrici di abiti extra-large. Saranno poche le candidate prescelte e i loro nomi si conosceranno in gennaio, ma sono già moltissime le ragazze di corporatura robusta che si sono presentate per il provino.

Unità 27

I bambini fino a 5 anni, in Sardegna, pagano meno di 7.000 lire al giorno.*

Vostro figlio non vi è mai costato così poco.

Club Med®

02-7735

o presso la vostra agenzia di viaggi

* Prezzo minimo per bambini, senza assistenza: 2 adulti + 2 bambini fino a 3 e 5 anni a partire da Lit. 1.198.000, solo soggiorno. Villaggio di Caprera.

PUBLICIS

Corriere della Sera, 10/6/1998

Per chiamare la Spagna c'è un numero in più.

Da oggi 4 aprile è entrata in vigore in Spagna una nuova numerazione telefonica. Per chiamare dall'Italia gli attuali numeri telefonici della **rete fissa e mobile spagnola**, è ora necessario anteporre il **9** al prefisso della città chiamata o al prefisso del radiomobile. Per esempio chi vuole chiamare Madrid (prefisso 1) deve selezionare:

prefisso internazionale	0034
prefisso città	91
numero utente	XXXXXXX

Solo per le chiamate verso la **rete fissa** di Saragozza non è necessario aggiungere il 9 in quanto già compreso nel prefisso della città. *Per qualsiasi ulteriore informazione Telecom Italia è a disposizione della clientela al numero gratuito 1723333.*

TELECOM ITALIA

Corriere della Sera, 10/4/1998

Solo fino al 6 aprile
l'Universale Economica,
i grandi tascabili **Feltrinelli,**
tutti al **25%** di sconto. **Solo in libreria.**

Leggere conviene

Corriere della Sera, 4/4/1998